THE SUM OF ALL EVILS

THE SUM OF ALL EVILS

LESLIE BECKMANN

CONSINITY PRESS

Cover art by Ana Grigoriu.

ISBN: 978-0-9867950-3-9

DEDICATION

to Nico,
with thanks

ACKNOWLEDGEMENTS

It is a daunting thing to write a set of thank yous because it is difficult to figure out where the help stops; the Maya are right—everything is connected to everything else.

In that vein, thanks first to a number of people I have not met but whose life work has influenced me profoundly: to Rosita Arvigo, Mayan healer and author whose work with Don Elijio Panti in Guatemala was the inspiration for the character Yaxché; to the late Linda Schele a scholar of the Maya whose ability to decipher ancient epigraphy and iconography has made the world of the pre-contact Maya accessible once more; and to the ongoing work of the hundreds of scientists that make up the International Panel on Climate Change (IPCC); they continue to further our knowledge of the mechanisms and likely effects of anthropogenic climate change, making the case for action to reduce carbon emissions clearer with each report. Any errors in fact or representation with respect to the Maya or atmospheric dynamics are mine alone.

Enormous thanks also go to a number of people whom I have met on the Yucatán peninsula over the years. I am grateful to ornithologist and Maya guide Alex Dzib who divides his time between Celestun and upstate New York for all he taught me about the ecology of the Yucatán, the ruins at Ka'bah and Uxmal, and the life of today's Maya; Alex embodies the wisdom, humour, and social conscience of today's Maya. To everyone at Casa Las Tortugas on the island of Holbox, chief among them Carolina Moriche Rodriguez I owe thanks for kindness, support and remedial Spanish lessons. And many thanks to Ralf Hollmann, lover of language mash-ups and owner of *Mayan Xic* in Mérida for designing my tee-shirts and for helping with Yucatec translations.

Closer to home, I owe thanks to everyone at Pottinger Gaherty for being amazingly supportive of my apparent folly. A particular debt of gratitude goes to Susan Wilkins, VP and head of the Planning Group, for being the most supportive boss that ever was by making a leave-of-absence possible; to Matt Hammond for taking care of sea turtles in Costa Rica and for stepping into the NaiKun EA without killing me; to Jeremy Valeriote for Spanish translations and moral support; and to Duncan MacDonald for advice on Ultimate.

It goes without saying that I am grateful for editors—they are a rare breed who can see both forest and trees. I am grateful to two editors in particular: Elizabeth Lyon, who in the run-up to life changing surgery mentored me in the early stages and to Karyn Huenemann who fell in love with the story, kept my spirits up, and tried to tame my passion for gerunds. I am also grateful to publisher Allan MacDougall of Canada's RainCoast Books for his early advice, including a candid picture of the tough road to publication, and his encouragement even in the face of that. And on this second go-round, thanks to Claudia Morawetz whose eagle eyes caught myriad niggling typos, now almost entirely expunged.

I am thankful for another breed of creative, as well: the visual ones (yes, editors *are* creative). Without Glenn Conrick at moltenice.net (and Valeri Hall who made the introductions), there would be no www.thesumofallevils.com. Without Kevin DeLury and the amazing artistic clearinghouse that is crowdSpring, I would not have met so many wonderful graphic designers, chief among them Chris LaRoche—I wish I could have chosen more than one cover—and Ana Grigoriou who is responsible for the book's stunning cover. Thank you to all of you.

To the greater Vancouver community, in particular its baristas and caffeine addicts, thanks for making it possible to find a coffee shop every few blocks. I'd like to recognize people at two of them: Wayne and Rebecca at The Laughing Bean and Shauna MacNeil and her staff at

TrafiQ have built family-run cafés that are both Wi-Fi friendly and terrific places to work; thank you also to Shauna for hosting the book's launch.

Thank you to a number friends for being dragged into the process: to film-maker Daniel Yoon, for both his support and his constructive criticism, especially when it came to bringing Stephen out of his shell; to Alvin Ng for reading and beta-testing my website; to Mark Rayner, author and monkey-lover, for advice on publishing; to Paisley Howard for being a tough audience and a generous reviewer; to Martin Ivison for correcting my German and keeping me sane in rough seas; and to Paula Bentley, my close and dear girlfriend, whose wise advice and perfectly-steeped tea has been part of every up and down in my life since the birth of my daughter and her eldest son more than a decade ago.

And finally, the hardest group: my family. It is strange that writers, whose stock-in-trade is words, can find themselves at such a loss when it comes to thanking those closest to them. I cannot do justice to their contributions, but I owe them everything: my parents for their worry and financial help; my sister-in-law, nieces and nephews for cheering me on; Nico, who encouraged me to start this; and my wise and beautiful daughter, Willa, who had a faith in me that moved mountains.

TABLE OF CONTENTS

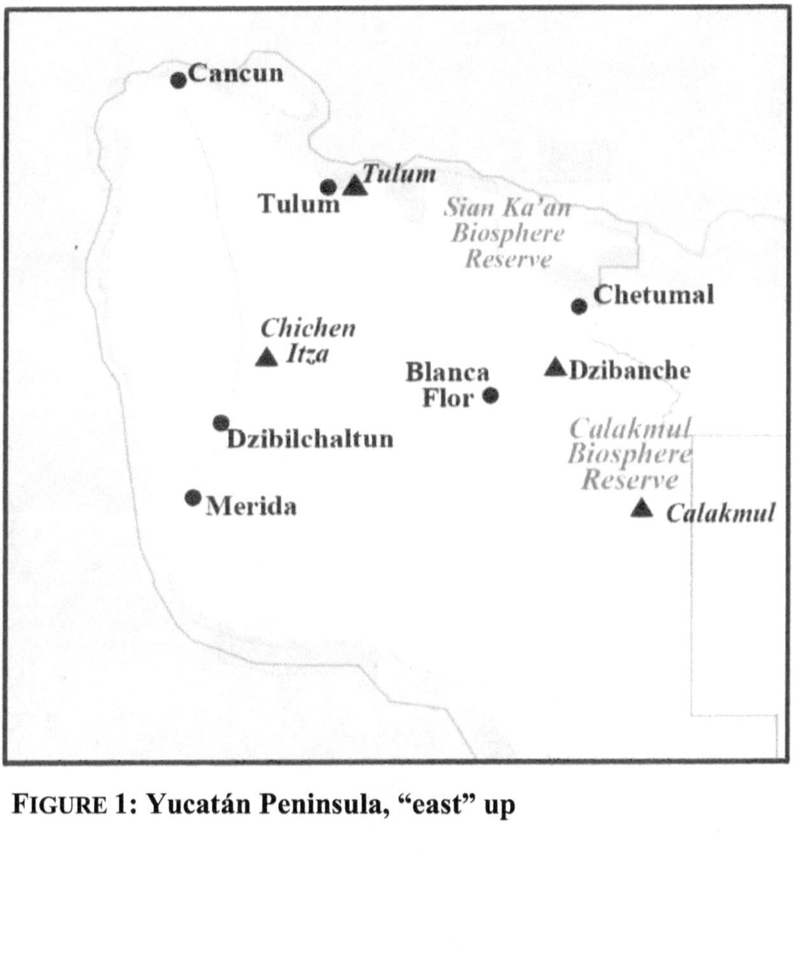

FIGURE 1: Yucatán Peninsula, "east" up

THURSDAY, SEPTEMBER 21, 1933
9 IX, DAY OF THE JAGUAR

PROLOGUE

He was born into the wild evening wind of the autumn equinox at the end of the second busiest hurricane season on record. In the days when hurricanes were numbered—the days after their divinity but before they were called by simple mortal names—in those days, Hernando Carlito Canul came into the world. On that autumnal eve, Hurricane Fifteen bore down on the Yucatán a monster, insensate, clawing at the jungle, shrieking at the sea. Great gouts of frigid rainwater spilled from the clouds, tore at the thatch, drowned the earthen floor of her hut, and Hernando Carlito Canul's mother was sure her baby would not live into the next day. The sky was destroying the land.

"Not yet, *mi niña*. Not yet," said the old man to his patient as he held her child aloft. The tempest winds blew electric with the scent of lightning.

"Tonight is a greeting only. The rest will come soon enough."

Hernando Canul's mother reached for her baby, hands trembling with fear. "Give my Hernando to me."

"A fine name, *mi niña*. But he will be Yaxché only. Yaxché, the holy *ceiba*, great tree that holds up the sky. The world shall rest on him when the gods think on creation's end."

Hernando Canul's mother cradled her baby, her heart filled with dread.

"*Chu'unpahal*," said the healer to the storm as the baby opened his eyes. *Chu'unpahal*. "It begins."

SATURDAY, DECEMBER 8, 2012
4 MANIK, DAY OF THE DEER

CHAPTER 1

"¡*Dios mio*!" cursed Detective Inspector Gonzalo "Chalo" Guerrero as he looked at the bloody thing by his knee. He thought he'd left the nightmare in Mexico City. The drugs, the murder, his partner: all left behind. What, then, was this atrocity doing on the gleaming floor of the Yucatán's foremost luxury hotel, the Grand Chacmool?

"*Dios mio*. Not again." Chalo put his gun down, his arms up, and waited. Death followed him everywhere these days, and the hotel was living up to its name.

***

The Grand Chacmool Resort had been christened for a mystery of Mexico's pre-Columbian past: the *chac mo'ol* altarpiece at Chich'en Itzá, a receptacle for sacrifices made to an ancient set of gods. An oasis built to delight the tired traveller, the marble lobby was open to the tropical air: beneath the vaulting thatched roof stood a manicured grove of yellow-green banana trees and red-and-purple birds of paradise; beneath these sat thickly pillowed rattan chairs that beckoned the weary to rest. A dozen scarlet macaws, feathers brilliant, perched in pairs in the trees, their raucous squawks making the hotel guests jump with pleasant surprise. And in the stores that ringed the lobby, gold and silver lured the tourists as they had the *conquistadores* five hundred years before.

Presiding over the meticulous splendour stood a breath-taking fountain made in the image of the *chac mo'ol* himself. Like his namesake the reclining idol, disturbingly contorted, surveyed his domain: propped on his elbows, knees up, heels pulled tight to his buttocks, a wide bowl cradled on his flat abdomen, the *chac mo'ol* stared hard to his right. On the original, the belly bowl had been made to receive blood offerings to the gods under the harsh light of a tropical sun. Here, the bowl was a fountain only, underwater lights casting the tinkling water pale gold.

A numberless army tended the fountain as they did the rest of the hotel: housekeepers mopped the floor around the wide pool until it gleamed; gardeners tended the foliage at the fountain's edge; managers fawned over the guests seated at the *chac mo'ol*'s feet.

Every detail—from the *chac mo'ol* to the dark chocolate medallions on each bedroom pillow, imprinted with the complex hieroglyphs of the Mayan calendar—was perfect: the hotel had more than earned its five tourism stars.

Chalo Guerrero, exiled to the opulence alone, was disgusted by it all.

***

An unwilling guest at the Chacmool these past two weeks, Chalo had known the very moment he'd arrived—the moment he had been given a glass of champagne and the hot-pink hospital bracelet that was his pass to everything—that he didn't belong. Like the other all-inclusives strung gaudily along the western Yucatán coast, the Chacmool had been made for a class of people entirely unlike him: people who made more in a week than he did in a month, people who derided his job and his Mayan heritage on the grounds that the former made him crooked and the latter made him stupid. Worse, it was made for people who didn't want these opinions changed. People who stayed at the Chacmool didn't really want to know Mexico. They wanted Montezuma's world without his revenge, wanted beaches and local colour without grimy Chicklet-peddling kids.

Chalo might have left if he'd had somewhere else to go. But Mexico City was off limits, the promise of dismissal the threat that kept him away. He had grown up as one of those grimy children and the police force, if not much better than a pack of thieving boys, was at least something to belong to. So he waited at the Chacmool. Waited for the storm in Mexico City to blow over, for the inevitable reprimand that would chain him to a desk. Waited alone. In his room. Reading.

It was an uncharacteristic choice for a Mexican cop, reading. The priests at the orphanage had taught him to read, and he'd taken to it quickly, his young mind quick with years spent surviving, but he didn't really see the point: he was a cop. Cops were not rocket scientists. Cops did not read.

Then had come *Fahrenheit 451*. In Spanish. A simple subversive story, the gift of his last new partner, Steven Catherwood, an exchange officer assigned to him as part of the International Criminal Organizations Policing Program—iCOPP—established to stem the flow of guns and drugs between Canada and Mexico.

A story about burning books, it had been a cheeky one to offer a full-blood Maya: like the classics in the novel, all but five or six Mayan books had been destroyed as subversive by the Spanish on their arrival in the New World. But then, that was Stephen, mild Canadian manners masking far sterner stuff.

Grown as close as brothers after four years working together, their friendship had surprised everyone. Bets had even been laid in the Department on how long the two could survive as a team; Chalo had laid one of his own. Stephen was tall and lanky while Chalo was solid and squat; Stephen was pale as winter while Chalo was burnished by heritage and the tropic sun. Northern quiet to Latin garrulousness, early-riser to night owl, surprise tequila-lover to drinker of *Negra Modelo* beer: the men were so unalike that not even Chalo had wagered on more than a week. But Stephen had taken to Mexico, and the new partners to each other, like balloons to the sky.

From his spot on the bed Chalo threw his latest book, *Cein años de soledad*—A Hundred Years of Solitude—by Gabriel Garcia Márquez across the room. It hit the wall with a satisfying thump. He had read anything and everything these past four years, had spent hours talking, shouting, laughing—more than once so hard that he'd choked on his beer—with Stephen, the man who had become his best friend. All for what? To end up in a hotel room eating room service meals and drinking instant coffee that tasted like brewed socks: one kid dead, one demotion promised, no new partner expected. Life was apparently about surviving solitude, not just reading about it.

He threw another book—*El Caso Bourne*—across the room and sat up. The room was stuffy with air-conditioning and the smell of his most recent room-service tray. It was time he got out. He stood, dressed in a black *guayabera*, black jeans, and black running shoes, holstered his gun, and started on the labyrinthine path that led to the lobby and beyond to the all-day breakfast buffet.

If solitude was to be his fate, at least he should get a decent cup of coffee to go with his misery.

On the way past the first of myriad sparkling swimming pools, Chalo smiled to a pretty housekeeper pushing a trolley of linens. Maybe twenty, the young woman's sharp nose marked her as Maya, her skin deep auburn against her bright *huipil.* The girl smiled in reply but her eyes were vacant: despite his own dark skin, Chalo's bracelet marked him for a guest: he was isolated again. He sighed. Passing another swimming pool, Chalo smiled at a knot of children splashing in the bright water and then glanced at an abandoned newspaper: the headline screamed *Mexico Takes Back Mitnal, Tightens Grip on Oil: Prices, Markets Shudder.*

Mitnal: the President was in the news every day crowing about it. Aside from being the name of the lowest circle of the Mayan Underworld, Mitnal was an ultra-deep oil rig being tested in the waters off Veracruz. The price of oil had risen sharply since the *Deepwater Horizon* disaster in 2010, making it economically attractive despite the environmental danger, to develop the vast reserves lying beneath the deep, dark, dangerous waters of the Gulf of Mexico. The official ceremony to open the rig wouldn't be held for a few weeks yet, but the behemoth—under the guise of a test run—was already pumping like mad. It had come on-line astoundingly quickly, exploration and development made possible by copious quantities of American cash.

Chalo had argued with Stephen about Mitnal: most of the wealth from the rig would never make it to the poorest of the poor; Stephen had always been indignant that the inequity didn't seem to bother Chalo at all. Chalo's point was that he was only one man: there wasn't much he could do. Stephen insisted the opposite: a single person in a single moment could change the world. Chalo took pride in being a realist, but the argument had sown a seed of doubt; proof that a butterfly in China could cause a storm in the Yucatán might have changed his mind.

Above the lobby now, Chalo paused at the top of the grand staircase, looked down at the tinkling fountain, and lost his train of thought. A feat of engineering, maybe, but the enormous figure was ridiculous just the same. The face was tranquil, not terrifying. The soft yellow light on the single jet of water spurting from his belly made the damn thing look like he was peeing into a cup. And worst of all? The original was an omen of dark times and violent death, his bowl filled with human blood when times were dire and kings made sacrifice to appease the angry gods. None of the tourists would understand the cultural blunder, but for a hotel selling peace and tranquility, the statue was entirely wrong. Chalo laughed and wished he could share the joke; Stephen would appreciate the irony.

Chalo started down the stairs and stopped again: something was not right. People were gathered motionless around the impossible fountain. Children who normally wiggled and shrieked for ice cream stood still and quiet; their parents, normally baying for silence, stood hushed and attentive at their sides. The space was silent as a power failure, the splashing of the fountain the only sound. It took Chalo a moment to figure out what they were staring at; the statue looked unchanged to him. It wasn't the statue they were looking at, either; it was the water. Not yellow today, the droplets were cranberry red. The stone figure blushed under the fountain's drizzle. The pool beneath the statue's back shone dark as a glass of rich burgundy wine.

Someone had called the local police, and suddenly five constables appeared and began to push their way to the *chac mo'ol*. The throng rippled around them but refused to disperse. The shortest, fattest constable, dark stains of sweat at each armpit, waved his stubby arms, thwacking his baton in his hand. The imperious little man reminded Chalo of the grannies back in Guatemala chasing hungry *javelinas* from their yards: the whooping and shooing never did any good then, either.

A maintenance man in navy overalls and black rubber boots sliced through the crowd, the large aluminum ladder on his shoulder serving as his knife. He stepped into the lowest pool, set the ladder against the statue with a tinny clang, and began to climb. The crowd, still rapt, tracked his ascent. Chalo shook his head and resumed his descent to the lobby. Amazing what passed for excitement. Probably just a Bloody Mary dropped from a drunken hand. Chalo wanted good hot coffee. That would be a real thrill.

He was almost through the lobby when he heard a gasp. By habit, he checked beneath his shirt for the gun—which he was supposed to have turned in—holstered at the small of his back before turning to look. The maintenance man was at the top of the fountain now, looking down at the crowd. Like a jumper at the top of a building, his face was distorted with last-minute fear. His palms, upturned, cupped something that looked like an apple. Chalo raised one brow in surprise as the man looked heavenward and fainted, falling forward as he passed out. The apple-thing took its own path, a long arc over the crowd. It landed at Chalo's feet with a sucking sound.

A dozen things tried to happen at once. A woman screamed. The crowd shattered in panic. Young men flipped open phones that clicked and chirped with each photo they took. All five constables rushed at Chalo, shouting at him to give them the thing at his feet. The manager hurried forward to help his fallen employee, his call for an ambulance barely audible above the rest of the noise.

In a single swift motion, Chalo crouched down, yanked his badge from his back pocket, and pulled out his gun, the thought of making good crossing his mind: the fantasy of returning to the City a hero instead of a pariah warmed his soul. The sight of the gun, held aloft, silenced the lobby at last. Chalo looked down at the thing at his knee.

It was a human heart. He'd seen one before. Two months ago in Mexico City, at the very start of the mess. That one had still been warm, and a much brighter red. Had been on the belly of a *chac mo'ol* as well. Had belonged to a twelve-year-old boy. Chalo felt himself shiver, his sweat suddenly cold. The nightmare was returning.

"*Dios mio*," he cursed. "Not another one. Please not again."

Mexico Tightens Grip on Oil: Prices, Markets Shudder

Global Petroleum Monitor
December 8, 2012

Stock markets shuddered today at news that Mexico's oil monopoly, PEMEX, will cancel all joint-venture and profit-sharing agreements with foreign interests. Elected in July of this year on the promise of "Mexican Wealth for Mexico," ultra-nationalist President Ernesto Sabato Fernandez announced that PEMEX will assume full control of the lucrative deep-water Mitnal Oil Field off Veracruz. Lest anyone doubt the government's sincerity, Mexico has re-deployed its Quetzalcoatl and Manuel Azueta destroyers to the region.

Mitnal has astonished industry watchers: its eight-month "production test" has produced eight million barrels per day (mbbl/day). This is projected to rise to 18.4 mbbl/day by 2015, dwarfing the output of the Middle East. Indeed, industry experts put Mitnal at over 349 billion barrels "in place," making it a "giant" find and the largest known single source of oil on the planet.

Like the Macondo prospect worked by the ill-fated Deepwater Horizon, Mitnal is considered an "ultra-deep" project. But where all oil appraisal activities in the US Sector of the Gulf of Mexico were placed on hold after the Deepwater Horizon debacle, Mexico—long dedicated to maintaining government control of the oil industry in that country—amended its constitution to allow foreigners to fund oil exploration and development. The promise of a massive return brought significant amounts of foreign capital and technology—most of it from a consortium of American companies led by oil magnate Clayton Powell—and Mitnal proceeded to production with a speed that has surprised even the most optimistic industry-watchers. Now that Fernandez's government has repealed the constitutional amendment, foreign investors are worried they will not see the promised returns.

Nor is it only the effect on investors that has people worried and markets retrenching: political analysts suggest that the sheer volume of oil from Mitnal could fundamentally alter the world's balance of power. Some fear Mexico may be trying to wrest control from OPEC, replacing it with a Mexican-led cartel now being dubbed "OMEX."

When asked for comment, former oilman Senator Joe Wilkes (GOP; Texas) sounded the alarm: "It's a threat to every American. With Mexico's hand on the tap and no profit coming back to our investors, you can expect an eight-dollar gallon of gas, pension funds being gutted, and our economy going to Hell in a hand basket. This is going to make the sub-prime mess look like a walk in the park."

Senator Carolina Schroeder (DEM, NMex) sounded a different alarm, voicing the concerns of environmentalists the world over: "We can't afford to bring that oil up from the ocean and burn it if we want to forestall catastrophic climate change." Senator Schroeder, along with first-term Senator Betsy Denton (GOP, ME), is sponsoring a bill (dubbed the 60/20 bill) that would see the US cut greenhouse gas emissions 60% by 2020.

CHAPTER 2

Chalo looked up from the red-grey lump of flesh and wondered how to get out of this newest disaster. He'd been an idiot to think this would lend him glory: for starters, he'd be fired for drawing the gun he shouldn't have in his possession. The sensible thing would be to give up, get a coffee, and call it a day. But another heart? It had to be connected to the Alvarro thing, but how? Why here? Why now? Why him? And why did the constabulary want it?

Chalo surveyed the small circle of onlookers, buying time. A rebelliously punked-out teen tugging at her preppy young brother, the boy refusing to be moved. A bald guy with a red moustache over a wry smile. The concierge and the hotel manager, both in black tuxedos, and the bellboys in safari outfits, pith helmets on their heads: all of them horrified. A very lovely blonde in a white tank top, khaki shorts, and hiking boots, a red and black backpack slung over one shoulder. Chalo paused to examine her expression: there was intensity in it, but not fear or surprise. Interesting. And then there were the constables, the fattest with his gun aimed at Chalo's head, the rest with their gazes, covetous and horrified, on the heart.

What would Stephen do? Stephen would play nice until he knew what was going on. Chalo took his finger off the trigger and put his gun down.

"I'm with the Federal Task Force on Drugs and Gangs," he said evenly, his badge still up for all to see. The fat constable lowered his gun and raised his chin, a vein pulsing on his forehead.

"What's your name, *federale*?" Local forces disliked the feds.

"Detective Inspector Chalo Guerrero. And you?" The disdain was mutual, but Chalo remained polite.

"Chief Constable Sanchez. Why are you here, Detective Inspector?"

"Mexico City sent me." Chalo smiled to himself as he said it: it wasn't a lie.

"Gentlemen?" It was the hotel manager, interrupting. There was sweat on his upper lip but fear for his job was making him bold. "Gentlemen, may I find a private room for you? This…" he waved a hand around. "This is not so good for our guests."

Chalo replied first, pre-empting the chief. He didn't want to go to the local precinct. And *federales* trumped the locals anyway. "Certainly *Señor*… ?"

"Alfonso Morelo. Day Manager for the Grand Chacmool."

"Certainly, *Señor* Morelo. Before we go, could you ask one of your bellboys to come here?"

The manager waved a safari-suited bellboy forward.

"Listen carefully," Chalo said to the boy. "I will need an ice bucket with a lid, filled halfway with ice, four sandwich bags that zip, some strong tape, and a black marking pen. And please give me your hat."

The bellboy looked at his manager for permission, then doffed his pith helmet. Into it Chalo scooped the heart. His stomach lurched as he touched the wet muscle; it yielded like a cold hard-boiled egg, ready for salt. Chalo wiped the sensation off on his pants before picking up and holstering his gun.

Standing, Chalo noticed a middle-aged housekeeper in a *huipil* mopping up the dilute blood. Should he stop her? It was a crime scene, after all. But the locals wouldn't know how to preserve anything they found, and he had the evidence that mattered already. Never mind.

"Finished. We may now go… if the Chief is ready?"

The chief constable clenched his jaw as he waved his underlings after the manager, who was turning to lead the fuss away from his guests.

"I don't want you here," the chief constable said under his breath.

"That makes two of us. But we do not choose our destiny, do we… ? *Uay*. Would you excuse me a moment? The helmet is leaking, I think."

It was, and his shirt was growing wet with dilute blood, but that was not why he had stopped. The blonde woman who had not looked surprised was tailing him; he was pausing to give her time to catch up. As she approached, lithe as a dancer, she took an awkward step into a puddle. Almost, but not quite, an accident. She slid to the floor, landing at Chalo's feet. One of the junior officers, looking back for his boss, saw the woman fall and his mouth made an *O* of surprise.

"*Lo siento*. Please forgive me; I am too clumsy, I think," she said.

Her accent was unusual: English inflected with something more guttural, both softened by the cadence of New-World Spanish. The detective in Chalo appraised the woman. Warmly tanned but not wearing a hotel bracelet. A European who had lived in Mexico for a while. Pretty women were a dime a dozen in Mexico, and the bachelor in Chalo noticed them all; this one was exceptional. But there was something else to this woman: her ice blue eyes surveyed him with an intensity and intelligence that made him catch his breath. He felt like a stupefied teen, had to work for a quip when usually they came to him as easily as breathing.

"*¡Uay*! The things that are falling to my feet today!" He paused, then asked earnestly, "Are you injured, *señorina*?"

"No, not at all. Only feeling foolish. What has happened here?"

"No need to feel foolish. The water on the floor is not your fault. It is a maintenance worker who slipped, that is all. I am sure he will be alright."

"And that?" she nodded up at the pith helmet as she extended a hand for him to help her up.

"Nothing. Just something he found in the pool. Nothing to be worried about at all."

"Ah. So. Well then, Detective, I will not be worried. It is Detective, yes?"

As Chalo took the woman's warm hand, he realized there was something in her palm and felt his heart beat a little faster. Was she passing him a business card as he helped her up?

"Detective?" he repeated, surprised. "Of course, yes. Detective Chalo Guerrero, at your service." The card taken, Chalo released the woman's hand, touched his chest and bowed. A model of chivalry. He slipped the card into the breast pocket of his shirt as he rose.

"Well then," she said again. "I am glad the federal police will see to this one." She stressed the word "this" and looked at him, her eyes wide with unspoken meaning. Then she looked down and away, suddenly appearing self-conscious.

"My apologies, again." She stepped gracefully around the puddle and was gone.

Chalo and the chief constable walked forward to join the manager and the knot of constables. One of the youngest officers—the one who had seen the blonde woman fall—broke ranks to elbow Chalo.

"Do you always pick up women while on the job?" the young man whispered, admiration obvious in his voice.

Chalo's smile widened. "Not literally, no. But it was very impressive, don't you think?"

The conference room was standard hotel issue: windowless and heavily air-conditioned, it held four rectangular tables arranged in a hollow square. Ten places had been laid around it, each set with a cup and saucer, a small pad of paper, a short sharpened pencil, an ashtray, and a green-and-white peppermint. Chalo took a seat farthest from the door, set the pith helmet on top of the up-turned cup, and pulled a small pack of cigarettes from his front pocket. He might be trying to quit, but this deserved a smoke.

"I will have refreshments brought in," said the manager, only too happy to leave the police in privacy to fight amongst themselves.

"And the things I asked for, please," Chalo called as he lit a cigarette.

With the manager gone, the chief constable rounded on Chalo. "We don't need federal help. We had this thing under control."

"'Thing'?" Chalo exhaled smoke through his nose. "What 'thing' is this, Chief Sanchez?"

"As if you don't know. Just give the…" The chief constable shuddered as he pointed to the pith helmet. "Just give *that* to me. We will clean it up."

"Please. You and your men should sit. Have a cigarette maybe." Chalo slid his pack of *Faros* forward.

The chief constable took the chair opposite Chalo, his men ranging the rectangle on either side. No-one took the cigarettes.

"What will you do with it?" Chalo asked as he nodded to the heart.

"What do you mean?"

"It is evidence. It should be treated properly, no?"

The chief constable was speechless. Chalo took a long slow drag on his cigarette to think. *Clean it up* meant *get rid of it*. Why?

"Evidence. Of a crime." Chalo continued. "This is a *human* heart. I should know: I have seen one before. The person missing it… well, I think it is a safe bet he is dead, no?"

The youngest constable smiled at the flippant remark until the chief constable glared at him.

"And…" Chalo took another drag, "since it is difficult to pull out one's *own* heart, it seems that it must be murder. How do you 'clean it up'?"

Sanchez was tight-lipped.

Chalo left the question hanging and changed the topic. "This is connected to an investigation I was… I am working on in Mexico City. It must go to Mérida, at least."

The chief constable jutted his chin again. "Mérida? Why?"

The young bellboy entered with the items Chalo had requested and set them on the table. Chalo nodded thanks and reached for two of the plastic sandwich bags.

"So that maybe we can take some DNA—find out who belonged to it. Let me show you a good trick a friend showed to me: how to preserve something without a kit."

Chalo slid one hand into each bag, picked up the heart, dropped it into a third bag, sealed it, and then placed the sealed bag into the fourth. This he placed in the ice bucket, lidded it, and then taped the lid in place. Almost as an afterthought he removed a bag from his hand, licked his thumb, and pressed it on the tape three times. Then he taped over the prints. Across the top he wrote the date, his name and his badge number in indelible ink.

"There. That way the lab will know it has been tampered with if it is not my prints on the tape when they get it."

"And you will take it to Mérida?" The chief constable's vein was throbbing again.

"Oh, not me. I'll ask my partner to take it."

Chalo was interrupted by the sound of his cellphone ringing. "A moment, please. I must answer this."

He swivelled his chair a quarter turn from the table, flipped open his phone, and smiled right away.

"¡*Esteban*! Were your ears on fire?" Chalo paused then chuckled.

"On fire. Burning. Whatever. And yes, whenever you're not around, I am. What are you doing this minute? You need to come down here for something… of course you can! You said you wanted to see the Mayan Riviera before you left…"

Chalo saw movement out of the corner of his eye. The chief constable had written on one of the pads. Had torn off the top sheet. Had folded the sheet and tossed it to another of the constables. Chalo watched as the second constable read the note, nodded, and tucked it away.

Chalo spoke slowly into the phone. "Yes, yes of course… the birds are just like Alvarro's. You just have to see. As for the questions, yes and no. You will come?" He paused, breath held, for Stephen's answer. Would mentioning the bird be enough? Yes. He sighed with relief.

"Better now, *hermano*. Call me when you know your plans. I'll give you directions how to get to me then." Chalo flipped his phone shut.

"My apologies, gentlemen," he said, stubbing his cigarette out. "That was my partner. Excellent timing, he has. He will be here in the morning."

"Tomorrow morning?" The chief constable suddenly looked interested.

"Yes, why?"

"The thing should go in a refrigerator for that long, yes?"

"Now you're getting the hang of it, Chief Sanchez."

"And perhaps post a guard? We wouldn't want anything to happen to it. Young Mendez can spend the night." He nodded to the young constable who had admired Chalo's way with women.

Chalo watched a wisp of smoke rise from the cigarette's end in the ashtray. *Mierde*. He should have figured the constabulary would be involved. He'd bet his grandmother's best stories the heart would be gone in the morning. But now he was boxed in. Stephen would have seen this coming.

"Yes. Of course." Chalo's voice was stony. "An excellent idea."

"Then let us find a refrigerator, Detective Inspector Guerrero," said the chief constable as he stood, his voice suddenly annoyingly cheerful. "I'm sure the hotel has one or two."

The constables rose and followed their chief from the room, young Mendez last, Chalo and the bucket bringing up the rear. He paused dramatically, and the young man turned to look back.

"*Uay*, Mendes. Take the bucket for a moment. I forgot my cigarettes." The young man cringed but complied.

Chalo ducked back into the room and, alone for a moment, grabbed the chief constable's pad. There was a roughness in the centre of the top page, as unintelligible as sandpaper to the untrained. Chalo tore the page from the pad and put it carefully into his breast pocket with the blonde woman's card. Then he hurried out to take the heart, follow the constables, and find a refrigerator. After that? Forget the coffee: he needed a beer.

CHAPTER 3

Stephen Catherwood—lanky Canadian, former geologist, currently disgraced police officer, sometime mountain climber, closet geek—leaned out of the window of his small second-floor apartment in Mexico City's Colonia Roma neighbourhood to say goodbye to the view. His tall frame, shaped long and lean by years of elite level Ultimate Frisbee—a sport more demanding and less obscure than it sounded—required that he bend almost double to rest his elbows on the low sill. The vantage was worth the effort: sun on his face, he took a deep breath and sighed. The air, warm for December, smelled of ozone and diesel exhaust, of burning garbage in the distance, of cigarettes and fresh coffee and corn tortillas—a bouquet of smells that belonged uniquely to the fifth-largest city on the face of the planet.

He heard an old VW Beetle putter along the road beneath him, opened his eyes, looked down, and smiled at the quirky, runty orange car tootling past. Still everywhere in Mexico, the Beetle had, against all reason, stood the test of time. Car gone and his attention on the street, he caught snatches of happy weekend conversation floating up to him on the morning air. After four years, he understood them without effort: they spoke of coffee and politics and love.

Across the way, Domingo the shoe-repair man waved from his tiny store, his hands black with polish. Stephen raised his own well-made hand, palm out, long fingers wide, and waved back. "¡*Hola*!" he said, his voice warm and strong. Only the room heard him, but for Domingo the rounding of Stephen's lips was enough; he nodded to acknowledge his greeting returned.

Stephen's smile faded, thinking of all that he would be leaving—

Domingo's daily greeting among the losses: cheesy *flautas* and rich, spicy *mole*; speaking Spanish; the smell of cilantro; walking among old and ancient buildings; the ever-present sound of guitar. Mexico had been a potent balm to his soul, returning to him, if not love—something he would not permit himself—then at least pleasure in the simple things. It was this that made his forced return to Canada so difficult not merely to understand—they should at least have been commended for trying to save the boy—but to accept.

But this, too, was Mexico: riddled with a byzantine corruption that made decisions difficult to comprehend and impossible to unmake. He would be going home in three days to face the mountains on which, because of him, Erin had died.

Stephen drew himself back into the apartment to censor his thoughts and surveyed the space he had occupied for the past four years. Same over-height ceilings, same egg-yolk yellow walls punctuated and crowned with Victorian rails and mouldings, same refinished oak floor, full of divots and knots, gleaming in the morning sun. Chalo had thought it crazy to pay so much money for the tiny second-floor apartment that had become Stephen's home: it was no more than a single long room with kitchen appliances at one end and windows at the other. But Stephen liked the recently renovated space, yellow like Mexico. He liked that it came furnished. He liked it for its proximity to the booksellers of Avenida Alvaro Obregon. And he liked it because Erin would have liked it. He dismissed the last thought with an angry shake of his head.

He hadn't brought much into the apartment during his tenure besides books bought on the *avenida*, brittle and smelling sweetly dusty: a keyboard and earphones for the nights he couldn't sleep, a few plants, and two small pieces of folk art that were beautiful and disturbing in equal measures. The first was a flying snake carved in Oxaca, its body painted in brilliant greens, pinks, and oranges, its feathers made of recycled aluminum cut from pop cans, its eyes cut from obsidian; the other was a small plaster statue made in Acatlán that looked like a fan coral adorned with tiny perfect figurines of myriad tropical animals: a Latin American Noah's ark. The first made him think of death; the second the promise of new life.

Now that these few trappings of his life in Mexico were packed and on their way to Canada—all but the plants shipped out as of the night before, and the plants gone to a secretary at work—he felt dismal: the place looked sterile and strange, his time in it erased.

No, not erased, *rewound*: the place was empty but for the knapsack on the bed and a picture on the fridge that he had put up the day he arrived. Stephen strode to the refrigerator to tear the last vestige of himself from the apartment: the picture was of him and Erin, taken hours before the accident: the two of them at the base of the Chief, ready to climb, the photo snapped on his camera by another climber.

She stared out at him, beautiful as ever, her long dark hair blowing in a chilly Squamish wind, her high-boned cheeks pink in the cold air, her eyes crinkling with delight, her smile wide. So alive. He knew the image like the back of his hand, had stared at it for hours. It was the image, Stephen cropped from it, that had been framed and placed on her coffin at the funeral.

Stephen looked up and away from the picture and headed, disconsolate, from the kitchen to his knapsack, the image still on his retina. Erin hadn't changed, couldn't change these past eight years, quiet in her grave.

Stephen knew he had, though. The picture told him that his buzz cut brown hair had grown long enough to fall in short tousled waves above his ears in the intervening years, his face had grown leaner with grief and then been tanned by the Mexican sun. Looking at the picture for the first time, Chalo—brutally honest—had told him more: Stephen's deep-set green eyes had no lustre, his smile lived on his lips only, and the joyful abandon apparent in the photo had been replaced by a permanent reserve.

A good eight inches shorter than Stephen, the muscular Mexican cop—pushing forty but looking years younger—had been waiting at the bottom of the aluminum steps leading from the airplane to the oily-smelling tarmac below, badge glinting on his hip, black t-shirt soaking up August's blistering heat.

Now his best friend, Stephen snorted at the memory of their first, unlikely meeting.

"Catherwood?" Chalo had demanded, looking Stephen up and down.

"*Si. En ustedes servicio.*"

Chalo arched his brows in surprise. "Guerrero. Chalo Guerrero. *¿Habla español?*"

"*Un poco. Yo pasé ocho meses en un pueblito de Costa Rica, pero hace diez años*."

"Eight months in Costa Rica? We'll have you in shape again soon. Even if it was 10 years ago. How tall are you, *caballero*? Six feet and a half? You play basketball?"

It was what Stephen would come to know as typical of Chalo—blunt but somehow charming. Stephen remembered smiling despite himself, liking this partner almost immediately.

"Six-foot-four. No, Ultimate."

Chalo squinted at him, uncomprehending.

"Like soccer, but with a Frisbee."

Chalo shook his head as one might to a foolish child. "You play football, too?"

"Football as in soccer? Yeah, as a kid…"

Chalo looked Stephen up and down a second time. "Spanish and 'soccer.' You'll be okay here, *caballero*," he said, at last. "But don't say anything about the Frisbee. You got anything more than that fancy school bag?"

"My knapsack? No, actually, I just brought this."

"You travel light," Chalo had said, surprised. "Come on, let's get through the bullshit." And with that, Chalo Guerrero had turned on his heel.

His badge got them past every security station and checkpoint without a single stop, question, or inspection.

"Why do you keep calling me '*caballero*'?" Stephen asked once they were settled in Chalo's car.

"Canadian *Mounted* Police, yes? Mounted. I looked it up. It means riding horses. That makes you a cowboy, yes? *Caballero* in Spanish. If you don't like it, I can call you something else. Maybe *Esteban*? It is the Spanish version of your name. Or *hermano*? I'll be looking after you like a big brother, yes?"

"I don't really need looking after. And if I have to have a nickname, what's yours?"

"My nick… ?" He turned at the car, put his hand on the roof and looked at Stephen, puzzled.

"Your other name."

"Oh, that! 'Chalo' is my other name! Nobody calls me Gonzalo if they want an answer from me."

Stephen had been both *caballero* and *Esteban* these past years, and *hermano*, too. He found he didn't mind any of the nicknames, because they kept him from being Stephen. He wanted that life forgotten.

A knock at his apartment door made him flinch and duck; he had been over-reacting to innocuous things since the night at the warehouse six weeks ago.

"*¿Hola*?" he called to back of the apartment door.

"*¿Señor Esteban*? *Rosa aqui*. It is ten o'clock. You want I should come back for the key?"

Stephen set the knapsack back on the bed and padded to the door.

"*Señora Rosa*," he said, smiling gently as he opened the door. His landlady—barely five feet tall and nearing eighty—stood looking up at him, her eyes bright, her black dress formal in the way of a previous generation, her white hair braided and pinned into a neat bun at the back of her head.

"*Lo siento*, *Señora*. I'm sorry. I am running a little late. It is hard to say goodbye to your apartment."

The bird-like woman smiled at Stephen, her eyes twinkling. "Are you certain you do not prefer to stay until the end of the month? You have paid for it."

"And have you lose a tenant willing to stay for two years? Not a chance. Besides, I really should see something besides Mexico City before I leave the country. Give me twenty minutes and then I'll bring the key up to you, okay?"

"Where do you go?"

"Cuernavaca, just for a few days."

"City of Eternal Spring. A good choice. Maybe you find a girl when you are down there, hmm?"

"Nope. Just a little rest and relaxation before I go back home."

"But look at you! So healthy and tall and dark and handsome. Fine high bones in your face. Kind eyes. Strong hands. You should be with a girl!"

The old woman reached up to pat Stephen's cheek as she spoke. It was a stretch for her, given Stephen's height.

Stephen smiled and took her soft old hand. "I'm fine, *Mamacita Rosa*."

The old lady chuckled. "I'm going to miss you, you know. You are surrounded by a good spirit; it feels good to have you near."

Stephen didn't believe in spirits. If he did, he'd have to believe the ones around him were evil: people were hurt and killed around him, and not merely because he was a cop. But Rosa was a sweet lady, too old to be persuaded from her views. He just leaned down and gave her a kiss on the cheek.

"I'll miss you too. I'll bring the key up in twenty minutes."

Stephen closed the door, his heart sinking.

He walked back to the bed and looked down at the things on it ready to be stuffed into the pack that would be his home for the next three days: three white t-shirts, a pair of jeans, a pair of khaki shorts, a blue-and-white striped Oxford shirt, socks, underwear, a toilet kit, a first aid kit.

And then there was his MacGyver kit: duct tape, a Swiss army knife, fishing line, a flashlight, a whistle, a mirror, a silver emergency blanket, a bottle of Tums, superglue, matches, $100 US, a flashlight, a candle, a mickey of scotch, and a book. Good old Angus MacGyver, who could save the world with duct tape and paperclips. Stephen had considered majoring in Chemistry because of Angus, but had ended up liking the Geology field trips better. They took him climbing in the mountains to look for rock formations. Stupid choice. If he had studied Chemistry, maybe Erin wouldn't have died. But maybe he wouldn't even have met her. Wouldn't have been in Mexico. Wouldn't have met Chalo.

Stephen bungeed the neoprene backpack shut, slipped his heavy dive watch onto his wrist, and strapped his gun holster over his shoulder. Then he picked up his iPhone, dialled Chalo's number, and walked back to peer out the window once more. His partner picked up on the first ring.

"Hey Chalo. It's me. I'm heading out to Cuernavaca for a few days…"

Interrupted, he paused, then grinned and shook his head.

"'Burning,' Chalo. 'Were my ears *burning*;'" Chalo couldn't get an English cliché right to save his soul.

"So, are you in trouble again?" he asked as he walked back to the window, leaned on the sill, and stuck his head out into Avenida Obregon again. The smile ebbed from his face as Chalo spoke.

"What do you mean I have to come down there? You're almost a thousand miles away! I can't just 'come down'!"

Stephen's protestations were loud enough that a young woman looked up from the street and scowled.

"Yeah, I did say that. But that was before I'd rented a car and booked a hotel and… Chalo, I'd have to take a plane and then drive… And anyway, I leave on Tuesday…."

Stephen stood up so suddenly that he hit his head on the window frame. "Ow!" He ran his free hand through his wavy hair and then looked at his palm. No blood but it would be a goose egg.

"Alvarro? You're kidding, right?" he asked as he walked to the fridge to look for ice. He walked slowly, intent on Chalo's voice.

"'The birds are like Alvarro's?' Like the quetzal? Are you telling me someone else is dead?"

Holding the phone to his ear with one hand, a bag of ice to the back of his head with the other, Stephen felt himself grow cold. Colder than just a chill from the ice. Cold at the recollection of the bird.

Neither he nor Chalo had been prepared for the gruesome scene behind the warehouse office door: candlelight and incense and strange symbols written all over the walls. The boy dying on the floor. And the bird.

It would have been funny if it hadn't been so horrifying: like the proverbial chicken, the body of a resplendent bird—a quetzal, sacred to the ancient Maya—fluttered bloody and aimless in search of its severed head. On the boy's chest across the room the head—yellow beak gaping—tried to call for its missing half. Stephen felt himself shudder and fought to push the rest of the memory away.

"Christ, Chalo. Okay, I'll come."

Stephen hung up, mind whirring with details. Switching the rental car. A flight to Cancún. Or maybe the Tulum airport? He tried again not to think about the bird. About death.

He emptied the ice into the kitchen sink, hung the bag to dry, grabbed his backpack, and ran the key up to Rosa. A long time ago, Chalo had said that Stephen couldn't fix the world, not even with duct tape and string. But he needed to get to the airport. He needed to make the dying stop

---

Saturday, December 8, 2012 — 4 Manik, Day of the Deer

CHAPTER 4

Chalo had taken a shower to rid his skin of the scent of blood. He stepped from the bathroom, towel around his muscular midriff, and walked to the mini-bar fridge in search of his beer. Nearing forty, Chalo had a trim body that told his life in three chapters: one, the short wiry stature of an underfed indigenous street kid; two, strong muscles built from the boxing he had done in the basement of Father Delgado's orphanage; three, a slightly thickening waist born of salaried adulthood.

The can of beer, drawn from a fridge that barely worked, was lukewarm. Chalo popped it open with a hiss anyway, took a tepid sudsy gulp, and looked around the room for what felt like the first time. It was a decent copy of a Spanish *hacienda* with wide terracotta tiles, white walls, and dark wood beams set into a white stucco ceiling. A long, dark sideboard enclosing the useless refrigerator ran along one wall; the king bed clothed in an orange bedspread jutted from the other, bedside tables on either side stacked high with books. A fan over the bed spun ineffectively against the unseasonable December heat. A small, round glass table and two rustic wooden chairs sat beside an open sliding glass door. Beyond it lay a narrow balcony that overlooked a wide beach clotted with blue-and-white umbrellas. The morning's thrown books lay on the floor beneath the table.

A droplet of sweat slid down Chalo's freshly showered back. He really should turn on the air-conditioning. But that would mean closing the sliding glass doors. And with the glass closed, the room merely went from hot-and-humid to cold-and-clammy: sweat either way.

Chalo opted for hot and humid. Warm *Dos Equis* in hand, he grabbed cigarettes from the glass table and padded out to the balcony. He could smell the sea on the breeze and beneath it, promising stormy weather, the musty smell of distant lightning. Over everything lay the cloying odour of sunscreen. Chalo took a swig of his beer, lit his cigarette, and added the scent of tobacco to the stultifying air.

The heart.

He shied away from recalling the first one—and the warehouse where he'd seen it. He cast farther back instead, to how he and Stephen had ended up there in the first place, bullets flying. Brought together under the auspices of iCOPP, they had been assigned to unravel the mystery of Bernardo Candelario Alvarro's meteoric rise and sudden disappearance. A small-time drug pimp when Stephen had arrived in 2008, Alvarro had killed brutally and often, rising to head his *barrio*'s gang. By early 2012, he was moving millions of dollars each month in cocaine. Then, in August, he had vanished. Into thin air. For a whole month. After the first two weeks, it was assumed he had been devoured by the dog-eat-dog rules of the drug world. But no. He reappeared with a new tattoo, a glittering black butcher's knife, and a new MO: he was using his network to move people—young men—and parcels, south out of Mexico City. South to the middle of nowhere. To the centre of the god-forsaken, bug-infested rainforest in the heart of the Yucatán.

And then the Secretary of Culture's son had been kidnapped.

Alvarro hadn't even been a suspect: a drug lord—even one behaving as oddly as Alvarro—didn't fit the profile of a political kidnapper. And that is what everyone thought it was: the child's ransom was his mother's resignation from her political post. No one would have connected Alvarro to it had it not been for a snitch anxious to absolve himself of a debt owed to Chalo. Chalo and Stephen had followed the lead to a warehouse on the seedy east side of the city. With little time to spare and a life in the balance, Chalo and Stephen had gone into the warehouse without backup.

Chalo found himself spooling the scene again, his stomach knotting at the memory of the eviscerated child. He took a drag of his cigarette, coughed once, and took a swig of warm beer.

The weirdest part was that none of it had been in the news. At least, none of the truth had seen print. When Chalo had been released from the hospital, he had scoured the papers and the internet. A front-page article in *La Prensa* had reported that the son of the Secretary of Culture had died of H1N1 flu and that his mother had resigned to mourn her family's loss. A *Huffington Post* article suggested something more nefarious, linking the kidnapping to a threat from a little-known rebel calling himself Kulkulcan: a fanatic leader, he had appropriated the ancient god's name, had claimed to be the reincarnation of that god to draw a following, had written a nasty little tract call *Del Dzonote* that called for an armed Mayan uprising.

The terrorist had been around for maybe a decade but most had dismissed his manifesto as the ranting of yet another nutjob using the Mayan calendar to predict the end of the world. There were lots of them these days: zealots saying the world would end in 2012; wackos saying aliens from the galactic core would arrive in 2012; crazy white guys making Hollywood shoot-'em-up movies about 2012. He could hardly believe this particular crazy was behind the kidnapping. Except that there was nothing else. No other news. Nothing to go on.

Nor did he and Stephen get any answers to the questions they had asked about the men they had killed in the warehouse. After Stephen's hospital stay, they had both been confined to their desks to catch up on paperwork. And then they had been deemed in need of stress leave. Stephen would return to Canada; Chalo would relax at the Chacmool.

Chalo set his beer down so hard on the balcony railing that it foamed up and out of the can. The paper. He'd almost forgotten. Cigarette between his lips, Chalo strode back into the room and rummaged through his heap of blood-soaked clothing to retrieve the slips of paper he had put in his pocket. Then he dug in the bedside-table drawer, pulled out a pencil and a piece of hotel letterhead, and sat down at the room's glass table to work one of Stephen's tricks—what he called his macgyvers. Chalo scribbled hard on the letterhead, stopping only when a significant portion of the page was black. That done, he ran his index finger over his scribbling, coating his index finger with lead dust. This he stroked gently onto the page he had torn from the chief constable's pad. The lead dust clung to the page itself but did not fill the deep indentations made by the chief constable's angry pen. A single word emerged from the smudge-darkened page: *Kulkulcan*.

Chalo sat back and thought for a long moment. Was this the god or the terrorist?

He stubbed out his cigarette, exhaled his confusion, and exchanged the chief constable's note for the card the blonde woman had given him. She was something else again. Remembering the sensation of the woman's soft, warm skin against his own, he was conflicted. Chivalrous thoughts of honour, respect, and love were invading a developing sexual fantasy. They only heightened his desire for the unknown woman.

"Dr. Anya von Eckhardt, PhD," he read aloud, savouring the sound of the words as they rolled off his tongue. "Yucatours Cultural Expeditions. Cancún—Tulum—Chetumal."

He flipped the card over to read the woman's tight, handwritten note and cursed, mood broken. *Another heart three wks past @ Sian Ka'an Bio. Rsrv.*

Shedding his towel in a single quick motion, Chalo began to hunt for clean clothes: he was going to have to pay the good doctor a visit.

CHAPTER 5

Dr. Kathy Howlachuk, branch chief of the National Oceanographic and Atmospheric Administration's National Hurricane Centre in Florida, looked down at the sleepy Golden Retriever at her side, took a swig from her stainless steel travel mug, and gave her senior specialist a once-over. Dr. Peter Nguyen looked tired. There were deep circles behind his John Lennon glasses; they weren't specs she'd have picked for Asian eyes, but on Peter they looked good. They also made him look scary-young, despite his exhaustion—like he'd started his PhD at MIT when he was six.

"Okay, Pete, you got me and Bender-dog outta bed. This better be good."

Peter smiled but he did not immediately look away from his computer screens. "It's good, alright. In a bad kind of way. Fascinating for the first week of December, anyway. Hang on a sec. What were you doing in bed, anyway? You're on days."

"I'm just off two weeks of nights and I'm the boss, that's what," she replied with a grin.

Bender decided he would probably be staying for a while. The NHC office was his home-away-from-home six months of the year; he circled three times and lay down with a deep canine sigh.

The Atlantic hurricane season officially ran from June 1st to November 30th of every year. That meant that now, in the first week of December, they should be doing the yearly summary and their Christmas shopping, the big storms gone to sleep for the season. But this had been a bad year. The worst year on record, in fact. They'd used the World Meteorological Organization's preauthorized list of 21 hurricane names by August, and if Kathy's hunch was right, Peter had just gotten her out of bed after her stint of night shifts because a new storm was blowing awake.

"Looks like you're going to be on CNN again," Peter said as he tapped the screen. "I'm just pulling down the newest satellite image, and then I'll show you what we've got."

"CNN again. You think Skandar's been missing me? It's been two weeks at least."

Kathy had been on the news more times than she could count this season. She'd been live on Skandar Hansen's prime time show every night that winds anywhere in the Atlantic hit hurricane speed.

"You love teasing that guy and you know it. Here, look at this." Peter pushed his chair back, took off his glasses, and looked up. "Nice bed-head, by the way."

Kathy grinned as she stepped in behind him. "Aww shucks. Sweet of you to notice. I thought my short hair all sticky-uppy looked swell with my sorry-ass jacket that went through the washer with a Kleenex."

Peter put his glasses back on for a moment and noticed the bits of white fluff stuck to her pilled orange fleece. He laughed aloud. Kathy carried the muscled bulk of a six foot man on her five and a half foot frame and didn't give a damn about her looks.

"Nice touch, the tissue. Bender's clearly the beauty in your house."

"Yep," she said, crouching down to pat the dog. "And I'm the brains… Oh crap."

Still crouching, she was looking up now, scrutinizing Peter's monitor. A pair of hurricanes, like two bright eyes, stared down at her from the image's black background.

"What do you make of it? I've never seen two this late," Peter asked.

Kathy rubbed her forehead with her fingertips. "Me neither, Pete. Got more degrees than a thermometer and been doing this for twenty-five years. Never seen it, but God as my witness, I told 'em it was coming. They just didn't want to hear." She stood up with a weary sigh. "Ah well. No use crying over what's been spilt. What do we call these two angels of death?"

"We're into the Greeks…" Peter slid a long finger down a list beneath the transparent cover of his desk blotter. "*Pi* and *Rho*."

"Double crap." Kathy shook her head. "I guess we don't deserve a break, but honestly, here it is, December 8th, and this damn season is supposed to be over." She paused for a moment, eyes downcast as she recalled something. "Dang, I said December 8th, didn't I? It's my god-daughter's birthday tomorrow."

"The one in the State Department? I remember her, I think."

"I only got one, Pete, and I know you remember her. You blushed right down to your toes when you met her. Rebecca. Yes, she works at State. Waste of her brains, if you ask me."

"I did not! Pretty good looking girl, though. And we need someone with brains there. Wish her happy birthday for me."

"She's single, you know. I could hook you up… ."

Nguyen rolled his eyes and shooed her away.

"You sure? Okay, never mind. I'll make my call and be back in a jiff."

***

"You're late again," said the administrative assistant to her boss.

Rebecca Holloway—the boss—grinned at her assistant, her smile white and even beneath naturally deep-red lips. Deb Varanides sat large behind a desk overrun with file folders, sticky notes, a metal ring hung with a dozen USB keys, and the detritus of seven expense claims.

"So it's a good thing you lied about the start time, isn't it? I'm betting I have an extra fifteen minutes."

Deb scowled then laughed. The sound was infectious, a rich contralto textured by morbid obesity. "Twenty, actually. We have been working together way too long."

"Thank God for that! This whole goddamned unit would be lost without you."

Deb blushed at the compliment. "Nah. You'd just never get your expenses done in time. You look like a million bucks, by the way."

Rebecca Holloway had the patrician beauty of the Eastern Seaboard's privileged families: the dark hair and fair skin of her Black Irish forbears, high Iberian cheekbones, green eyes, and a smattering of pale freckles. She wore no make-up but the clear gloss on her lips, and had pulled her long wavy hair into a loose chignon so as not to be mistaken for merely a pretty face. She was still obviously beautiful. And her clothes, though business cut, made her look elegant: a nubby pink

Chanel suit over a black turtleneck, black nylons, and high patent pumps that made the most of her lissom height.

"Yeah, well, my father-in-law—*ex*-father-in-law—loves a woman in pink," Rebecca replied darkly. "As for life without you? I'd never get *anything* done in time. Speaking of which, we're eating up that time you bought me. Is everything here?"

Deb slid the ring of USB keys across her desk.

"That's because you think you can do everything by yourself. I emailed the briefing on Thursday morning, but the keys have your last minute updates."

Rebecca looked at her assistant, in her white shirt and black skirt—the same outfit she wore every day—and sighed. It was an unfortunate analogy, but Deb was the ballast that kept the State Department's ship sailing smoothly in Latin America. While Rebecca and the other desk officers handled the policy, Deb made the calls, booked the flights, balanced the books, dried the tears, and guarded the gates. Those who judged her only on her weight missed the truth of her entirely. Not officially a diplomat, she was nevertheless critical to diplomacy in the Americas.

"Yoohoo, Beck. Are you with me here?"

Rebecca shook herself from her thoughts. "Yes. Sorry, yes. I got the updates and downloaded at home."

She pulled a computer tablet from a thin briefcase and woke it from hibernation to make one final check. "That means we have the numbers to satisfy Senators Schroeder and Denham…"

"… the history section you wrote for the two academics on the committee, policy precedents for Senator Denton, photos for Senator Radner 's bleeding heart…"

"Ha! And the list of the political favours we can give to my delightful former father-in-law?" She felt herself flush with anger as she thought of Senator Joe Wilkes. Even after eight years, the very idea of him made her crazy.

"Here, on old-fashioned paper, for your eyes only."

"You're miraculous. Remind me again why I have to do this on a Saturday?"

"Because the clerk said so. Something about meeting Appropriations' timeline. Traffic's bad on the beltway because of the flurries so you'd better get going. Your cab's waiting out front."

"Thanks. Wish me luck, hey?" Rebecca said as she turned to leave.

"If you win, I'll buy you a beer," Deb said to Rebecca's back.

"I heard that," Rebecca replied from halfway down the hall. "Make it a scotch and you've got a bet."

"You and your bat ears. You weren't supposed to hear that. I can't afford your brand of scotch if I lose."

"I'll buy, either way. You earned it. As for bats, what's wrong with them? The Maya thought they were gods…" Rebecca rounded the corner and was out of sight.

"A lot *they* knew. Just flying rats. Blood-sucking rabies-carriers that get caught in your hair. And now they're carrying the Ebola virus all over Latin America."

***

"Global warming, my ass," Rebecca muttered as she settled into the cab and shivered off the bitter December chill. She should have worn a coat.

An air-raid siren wailed from her briefcase: Rebecca had chosen the ringtone on the grounds that phones in Washington were harbingers of doom. Call display said this one was coming from Florida. This was doom she would enjoy.

"Aunt Kathy! To what do I owe the pleasure?"

"Hey, sweet-pea! You're birthday's coming up."

"Don't remind me. I'm too old to be a sweet-pea anymore."

"What? You're just a pup!"

"Right. A thirty-five year old widow-workaholic. I feel ancient."

"I'm a fifty-five year old spinster-workaholic. I *am* ancient. What's your point?"

Rebecca laughed. "I saw you on TV."

"You watch that cheeky bugger Skandar Hanson?"

"Gotta keep up with the news."

"And I thought it was just because he's as cute as a bug's ear. Where you at right now, Becky? Reception is the pits."

"In a cab on my way to a subcommittee meeting."

"On Saturday? You really are a workaholic, child. Tell those bastards to pass Senator Schroeder's bill when you see 'em, will you?

Before the planet stews in its own juices."

"It's a subcommittee meeting on foreign aid, Kathy."

"Cutting greenhouse gasses *is* foreign aid, Becky. Fixing global warming would be the best gift we could give to the god-forsaken third world."

"I dunno. It's awfully cold up here in DC. You sure this whole 'global warming' thing is real?"

"None of that, Miss Impertinent. You're a shit-disturber just like your momma was."

"Relax, I'm just kidding. I drive a Prius, remember? But Schroeder's bill isn't on the agenda. Sorry."

"Well fine. I can always try, can't I?"

Howlachuk paused to change the subject. "Listen. I was wondering if I could come up and see you on the fifteenth. I thought I'd take you for dinner for your birthday."

"My birthday is tomorrow."

"Don't I know it. I was there the day you decided to come out. Late, I might add. I just figured you wouldn't want to spend your big day with an old fart like me. Besides, I got two monsters—past their due-date like you—blowing into the Gulf so I'll be busy for a while yet. As for the fifteenth, I thought you might like some company on the day… ahh… when… the day…"

"The day Hayden died. You can say it. It was eight years ago. I'm over it. I'm fine." There was the harshness of a lie in her voice.

"Okay, honey. Okay. I'm sorry. I didn't mean…"

"No, I'm sorry. That was snappish. The company would be nice. Come on up. There's a great new *torta* place in town."

"I'll be there with bells on. I love you, Becky-girl. And happy birthday for tomorrow, you hear?"

"Thanks. I love you, too, Aunt Kathy."

Rebecca hung up and wiped an angry tear from her eye. It was the first one she'd shed in a very long time.

Hurricanes *Pi* and *Rho*

December 8, 2012
Transcript of a news interview between Skandar Hanson and Dr. Katherine Howlachuk, Senior Scientist at the National Oceanographic and Atmospheric Administration (NOAA) National Hurricane Center.

Skandar Hanson: *I'm Skandar Hanson. Welcome to Today on CNN. With me is one of our regular guests, Dr. Kathy Howlachuk, Bureau Chief at the National Oceanographic and Atmospheric Administration's National Hurricane Center. Welcome back, Kathy. We didn't expect to have you back again this season.*

Dr. Katherine Howlachuk: *Me neither. I should be getting my Christmas turkey about now instead of talking to you.*

Hanson: *Okay, then, Kathy. We've got something new in the Atlantic. Tell us about it.*

Dr. Howlachuk: *Well, Skandar, the Atlantic hurricane season officially ended last week, but we've got two new tropical storms out there.*

Hanson: *We've had storms after the official season before, haven't we?*

Dr. Howlachuk: *Sure have, but not two at once, this late. Usually the seas have cooled enough by now that there's no energy left to spin a storm. This year, the seas have remained hot enough late enough to fuel two storms at once, both of them big enough to earn a name. If you cut to the images I brought, you'll see tropical storm* Pi *on the left, closer to Florida, and the other one is* Rho.

Hanson: *So counting the names and the Greek letters already used,* Pi *and* Rho *are the thirty-seventh and thirty-eight named storms this season. That's more than we've ever had before, isn't it?*

Dr. Howlachuk: *It is. And, on average, they've been stronger than in previous years, too.*

Hanson: *Two storms at once after the official season—is this the result* *of global warming?*

Dr. Howlachuk: *It is consistent with it. Some pretty good studies have been coming out of a number of research institutes in the past few years that say so.*

Hanson: *What about the amendment on the senate floor right now to reduce greenhouse gas emissions by 60% by 2020?*

Dr. Howlachuk: *What about it?*

Hanson: *The federal law on climate change passed in 2010 calls for a reduction of 80% of all US greenhouse gas emissions by 2050. It barely passed then, but Senator Carolina Schroeder of New Mexico is pushing for an amendment to move that deadline up. Is it enough?*

Dr. Howlachuk: *For what?*

Hanson: *To stop climate change.*

Dr. Howlachuk. *Stop it? Nope. Climate is a little like the Queen Mary: it won't stop as soon as you press the brakes. The planet is going to get hotter. The 60/20 amendment, if it passes, is aimed at avoiding "catastrophic" climate change, or a global increase of more than two degrees.*

Hanson: *Do you think the bill will pass? And what will happen if it doesn't and we head towards that "catastrophic change"?*

Dr. Howlachuk: *Will it pass? That's for politicians to decide. But what "catastrophe" will look like has been pretty clearly identified by the International Panel on Climate Change: water shortages and drought in some places, flooding in others, crop failures, spread of a number of diseases from the tropics, social instability...*

Hanson: *Sounds like you're describing the four horsemen of the apocalypse.*

Dr. Howlachuk *(laughter): Four horsemen? You said it, not me.*

Hanson *(laughter): So what is next for* Pi *and* Rho*?*

Dr. Howlachuk: *I'd like to say that they'll dissipate, but the water in the Gulf is as warm as I've ever seen it, so I'm afraid they'll keep their strength.*

Hanson: *And your advice?*

Dr. Howlachuk: *Same as always: start preparing now, and listen to local stations for bulletins and evacuation orders. The official season might be over, but Mother Nature isn't done yet.*

(end of transcript)

Saturday, December 8, 2012 — 4 Manik, Day of the Deer

Chapter 6

Full senate committee meetings were held in Washington's historic oak-paneled rooms; subcommittees got far less pomp. It was a fact that Joe Wilkes, long ago elevated to higher things, had forgotten. But then, he had arranged his own demotion. He would accept the décor that went with it in order to get what he needed.

It was a bland room: spare in the manner of the 1990s, cheap in the manner of IKEA. A long faux-pine table flanked by black leather chairs on rollers ran the length of the narrow room. The east wall was windowed from floor to ceiling; the other three walls were lined with photos all in black and white. Wilkes looked at them: Joshua trees; Yosemite; the Grand Tetons. Undoubtedly Ansel Adams. They had been beautiful once, but now they were just overused. He liked the old chairs, though. He could lean back and put his feet up while waiting for his colleagues to arrive. Wilkes was a big man—a former scholarship linebacker with the Georgia Bulldogs—but gravity and the circuit of rubber chicken dinners that was the lot of a senior politician had dragged his once-muscled chest down to a thickness at his waist. At sixty-three, he had the round balding head and wide girth of a Buddha, his voice had settled into the gravel, carried there on the single cigar he allowed himself every evening, and his eyes needed reading glasses. But his mind, honed on Washington's political whetstone, had never been sharper or more dangerous. He would need all his acumen today to hide his less-than-noble motives. He pursed his lips, looked at the size-thirteen wingtips on the table before him, and then down at the manila folder flipped open on his lap.

Christ almighty. Rebecca was presenting. He figured he'd run into her sooner or later, now that he was working foreign relations, but he *had* to work this angle to get the last of the money. Maybe in public was better. She'd be prickly, but at least she'd have to talk to him.

"Looking as relaxed as ever, Joe." It was tall, lean, slightly stooping Robert Radner, majority leader, walking into the committee room. As smart as Wilkes beneath his unassertive exterior, he was one of Joe's oldest adversaries. They were studiously pleasant to one another.

"Howdy, Bob. Good chairs. You up for this one?"

"Should be fairly simple, don't you think?"

Wilkes considered for a moment. He had to appear to oppose to the aid package before relenting so that the diversion of funds would not be linked to him. How to deflect suspicion? How not to tip his hand?

"I dunno, Bob. Lotta people need our help. Our own Indians, for example."

"Well Joe, maybe so. But this is foreign relations. If you wanted to help our own, maybe you should have stuck with appropriations. How'd you end up slumming with us, by the way?"

"Hardly slumming, Bob. Money's a dangerous thing. I thought I'd cleanse my spirit with a little foreign altruism. Ah, here come the ladies."

Carolina Schroeder and Betsy Denton strolled in. Schroeder was sixty-five and irascible, her big bony face heavily lined by years spent traversing her state under its hot desert sun. Betsy Denton was her foil: a buttoned-down first-termer from rainy Oregon, blonde and petite.

"Beauty apparently arrived before brains," Carolina Schroeder said. She paused a moment and then added, "No offense meant, Bob."

Wilkes, Radner, and Denton laughed.

"Now, now. I'm glad for your brains, ladies. I always hate the idea of giving out aid money to have it end up in the pockets of crooked bureaucrats and warlords. It's nice to have some extra eyes watching." Sometimes the best defence was a good offence.

"And I thought you said you were trying to get away from the money," Bob Radner said.

The two long-time statesmen smiled carefully at each other.

"Got me there, Bob. It's always about money, isn't it?"

"Indeed."

A rumpled looking man with a light dusting of dandruff on the shoulders of his ill-fitting navy suit hurried in to the room. His lapels are too wide, Wilkes thought to himself. And how can a balding man have dandruff? Best not to underestimate him, though; committee clerks, like secretaries, held more power in Washington than most wanted to admit.

"Senator Wilkes?" asked the mousy man.

"Yes. It's David Morton, isn't it?"

The clerk flushed at the recognition. "Why yes, Senator. It is. We can… we can proceed once Senator Denton… my apologies Senator Denton… once Senator *Denham* arrives; the others have sent regrets."

Senator Herb Denham blustered in as his name was mentioned. Behind him strode a woman in a pink suit.

"Are you Miss Holloway?" the clerk asked of the woman.

"I am." Her voice was strong and clear. Joe Wilkes hadn't realized how much he had missed it. Or her.

"Good. We can get underway," the clerk continued. We have a half hour for this item. After which we look to the Costa Rican item and then the Panamanian piece." The clerk looked down under his glasses at his watch and furrowed his brows before looking up again.

"Please take a seat at the table with the Senators, Miss Holloway."

Radner and Schroeder were on the right, backs to the bank of windows. Denton, Denham, and the clerk sat on the left, facing the weak winter sun. Rebecca took the foot of the long table nearest the door and passed out the USB keys containing her revised briefing notes; everyone except Wilkes plugged the keys into their notebooks. And then the room fell silent. Joe Wilkes was the ranking senator and the committee's new chairman, but Bob Radner has been on the committee longest. Who would begin?

"Seeing as how you've got the most experience with foreign relations, Senator Radner, why don't you start us off?" Joe Wilkes said.

Bob Radner cleared his throat. "Much obliged, Joe. I'd like to take a moment to thank Miss Holloway for joining us on a Saturday." Radner paused a moment to nod at Rebecca. She dipped her head and smiled in reply.

"Our session today, "Radner continued, "stems from an unusual referral from the Senate Committee on Foreign Relations, which, in the byzantine fashion of Washington, comes to them from the Appropriations Committee." At this, several pairs of eyes flicked momentarily towards Wilkes.

"We are here," Radner continued through the distraction, "to formulate a recommendation on whether the United States should fund a six-year, one-hundred-and-thirty-six million dollar program for primary health care and literacy for the Maya peoples of south and central Mexico. With the sub-committee's permission, I would like to ask Miss Holloway to sketch out the package for us."

The clerk stopped typing on his laptop and looked up. All heads around the table nodded. Rebecca took a sip of water from the glass in front of her, tapped her notebook to switch on its tiny holo-projector, and began.

"Thank you Senator Radner. It is an honour to be before you today, Senators. I hope that with my presentation today I can persuade you of the State Department's case for this somewhat unusual program." She paused to look up. Senators Radner, Denham, and Wilkes were watching attentively. Senator Denton was scribbling on the notepad before her. Senator Schroeder sat, stolid, her arms crossed and her mouth set.

The first image was a sketch of the Maya made by a European explorer, the men bare-chested, the women in brilliantly embroidered *huipils*.

"As you are aware, the Maya in Mexico are descended from the Maya that Cortés encountered when he arrived in North America almost five hundred years ago."

The next image was a modern Maya in a t-shirt and jeans.

"Today, there are almost 1.2 million Maya in Mexico but, despite the recent oil boom, they represent a disproportionate number—more than seventy percent—of those living below the poverty line."

A montage followed showing sick children and impoverished villages, changing with each new fact spoken.

"And the figures are getting worse. Per capita income in Mexico as a whole now stands at half that of the US—about $22,000—but, disaggregated, the Maya make only half of that. With poverty go various economic, social, and environmental ills: subsistence agricultural and environmental degradation, poor sanitation, ill health, and reduced social and economic opportunity. Life expectancy among the Maya of Mexico is sixty years, ten years lower than the Mexican average. Similarly, infant mortality among the Maya is one hundred per thousand live births. In Mexico as a whole, the rate is fifty per thousand, and in the US it is twelve per thousand. The literacy rate among Maya is 73%, compared with 92% for Mexico as a whole.

The next set of images hovering over the table showed a clinic, a mother and a healthy baby, a school filled with healthy children, and a tidy cropped field.

"The program before you is light on infrastructure and heavy on 'capacity building'—giving the Maya skills and tools to help themselves. Based out of three small centers—Chetumal, Calakmul, and Balancán—in the south-eastern Yucatán, an interlocking set of five apprenticeship programs will be established."

A map appeared showing the hitch-hiking thumb that was the Yucatán sticking out into the Atlantic; a triangle of three large dots and two smaller ones, low near the second knuckle showed the program centres.

"Medical and environmental professionals as well as teachers and anthropologists will work with village elders to establish complementary health care clinics, sustainable agriculture based on Mayan traditional techniques, and trilingual English-Spanish-Yucatec schools. One-hundred-and-fifteen-point-six million dollars would be earmarked for medical supplies, agricultural products, and educational materials over the six-year period. The remainder—or twenty-point-four million dollars—would be used for salaries and honoraria.

"That, Senator Radner, represents the bare bones of the project. In the interest of time," Rebecca looked up at the clock over Senator Wilkes' head, "perhaps I should stop here and fill in the details in response to questions?"

"Thank you, Miss Holloway. Questions, Senators?"

Senator Denham cleared his throat. "Thank you, Miss Holloway. The supplies and professionals. Will they be sourced from the United States?"

"For the most part, Senator. Some of the educational materials will be developed in Mexico and wages will be paid to a number of indigenous nursing-assistants, *curanderos*, and teachers while they are teaching or being trained."

"*Curanderos*?" asked Senator Denton, still scribbling on her note pad.

"I beg your pardon, Senator. A *curandero* is a local healer—a kind of doctor-cum-psychologist-cum-spiritual leader." Rebecca tapped her notebook and a picture of a wiry old man appeared.

"Providing people like Hernando Carlito Canul here with some Western medicine to complement their successful herbal healing practices would strengthen both community and health."

"We're paying for shamans and new-age mumbo-jumbo now?" Wilkes said softly, intending for only those nearest him to hear.

"Actually, Senator," replied Rebecca, steely-eyed, "the pharmaceutical industry is interested in working with the *curanderos* to discover the active compounds in the more successful herbal remedies before these healers and their knowledge die out. It is the same strategy that allowed the development of your heart medication."

Wilkes permitted himself a small smile. He'd forgotten about her eerie hearing, but had used it to good advantage nevertheless: irritating her would further divert attention from his own purposes. Too bad that the cost had been a shred of information that he would have preferred to keep quiet. Rumours of ill-health would not serve him well.

"And what happens when the program runs out?" continued Senator Denton. "Is this the first of many requests?"

"No, ma'am, that isn't the intention. The economics of the regions suggest that a small infusion of currency coupled with an increased skill-set will create self-perpetuating self-sufficiency."

"How so?" interjected Radner.

"Improved agricultural practices will retain water, reduce erosion, and improve crop yields. Resuscitating ancient planting techniques will increase crop variety, improving nutrition and health. In the language of economics, excess yield can be sold to increase wealth. Not to mention that supporting ancient techniques will improve community morale."

Radner and Denham nodded. Denton scribbled.

"Why did you choose those towns…" Wilkes looked down to his notes for a moment. "Chetumal and whatever… ? I seem to remember that the Indians are holding a little rebellion down in Chiapas? Aren't you putting our people in the middle of nowhere, right in harm's way?"

Wilkes watched Rebecca size him up.

"The program will rely on community support, Senator," the diplomat replied. "We've done some background work down there—I've been down in the jungle three times now—and we've been *invited* into

Chetumal, Calakmul, Balancán, and the hamlets of Pich and Blanca Flor. Much like our work in Iraq, we have approached the equivalent of village "head men"—in this case the *curanderos*—to gain permission to run the programs. With that goes protection for our nationals. Besides, much of this work will occur in the lowlands, and the *zapatistas* generally confine themselves, as you pointed out, to the highlands of Chiapas."

"Who disburses the money?" asked Senator Denton, her voice sharp. Wilkes smiled to himself. First-termers were so impressionable.

"Disbursements will be handled like most of this nature," Rebecca replied. "Expenditures will be authorized annually through State and funds will be disbursed through the Consulate in Mérida or the Consular Agency in Cancún."

"And start-up funds? Those are the ones that usually go astray," asked Senator Denton, snippily sceptical.

"Astray?" Wilkes watched Rebecca's brows furrow and chuckled to himself at the way he had played Denton into the question.

"Missing. Funnelled elsewhere. Mexico has a reputation for corruption, as you well know, Miss Holloway."

"Initial funds will be limited to travel costs and stipends. And an initial thirty million dollar purchase of medical supplies which will be handled through the American and Mexican Red Cross Societies. Both of which, I'm sure you will agree Senator Denton, have reputations beyond reproach."

"I see." Denton pursed her lips but said nothing further.

There was a pause as a cloud passed over the sun outside, darkening the room for a moment. Wilkes felt his pupils dilate.

"Let's cut right to the chase, shall we?" It was Senator Schroeder, eyes narrowed. "Mexico is pumping from the Gulf like no tomorrow from their new deep-water field, and God help the ocean. They're about to have their first trade surplus ever, and we're considering giving them foreign aid? Whatever for? For once, I agree with Senator Wilkes."

All heads snapped to look from her to Wilkes. Wilkes felt his eyes widen in surprise.

"As I arrived with Senator Denton," Schroeder continued, "I overheard Senator Wilkes say that we'd be better off giving the money to our own Indians. I agree. Unless you can convince me otherwise, Miss

Holloway, I can't support this. It sounds like a ridiculous waste of taxpayers' money."

Wilkes watched as Rebecca flushed scarlet. She was angry. He hadn't forgotten her righteous temper. Rebecca looked around the table at the subcommittee, looked down at her tablet, and took a deep breath before replying.

"With respect, Senator, I should have started by saying that this program would be a partnership among the US government, private pharmaceutical companies, and the International Red Cross and Red Crescent Societies. I agree that helping America's Indians is critical as a domestic policy. But we are here to discuss *foreign* policy. While there are humanitarian and economic benefits from this project, the real goal here is to maintain peace in this hemisphere. Let me be blunt: the Maya are a nation within Mexico, and they are growing restive. It is the policy of the current Mexican government to assimilate the Maya, but they are doing so by ignoring them. This is having the opposite effect, as it invariably does. Poverty and disempowerment create unrest. In this case, it could create civil war and topple the government."

"I don't much like the current government in Mexico, Miss Holloway." It was Joe, leaning back, stretching his long arms up like wings. "They just nationalized the oil exploration business and stole a bunch of US money in the process. I'd just as soon see another government in power down there."

"Respectfully, Senator, I'd rather see another government there, too. But a civil war isn't going to get us a better one. All it will get us is a bigger immigration headache at the Rio Grande and a devil we don't know in Mexico City." She paused for a moment as if debating with herself and then added, "Please tell me how *that* kind of regime change is going to get your constituents' money back?" They were well and truly sparring now.

"So we take care of their internal problems, they give us zip for our exploration costs, and then we sit back and pay through the nose for the oil we helped them find?" Wilkes rejoined. "Come on, Becky. Sounds like you're happy with letting them rob us blind in the name of peace."

The room grew electric with discord, uncomfortable even for those who had expected fireworks between Wilkes and the widow of his decorated, war-dead son.

Saturday, December 8, 2012 — 4 Manik, Day of the Deer

"Dammit, Joe, if a civil war in Mexico shuts down production at Mitnal, you can bet the cabin in Texas that OPEC will jack prices up to recoup what they're losing to Mitnal now. Sure the new administration is pointing us towards self-sufficiency, but we still can't weather more than 27 days without Mexico's oil output. The economic mayhem caused by another revolution south of the border will make the sub-prime mess look like a tea-party. You know it and you're just being an ass!"

There was a collective shifting in chairs over the name-calling.

"Now cool your jets, Becky Ann. What I was saying, if you'd listen…"

"I know what you were saying, Joe. The goddamn gun is mightier than the word of a diplomat. That's how Hayden ended up dead!"

Wilkes' eyes darkened and he stood up, fists on the table. "If you'd taken my *goddamn* calls, Miss Holier-than-thou, you might learn a thing or two about how Hayden died… ."

"Ladies and Gentlemen," interjected the clerk. "Ladies and Gentlemen. May I *remind* you that this is a senate subcommittee hearing?"

"My apologies, Senators," said Rebecca, clenching her jaw.

"Sorry folks," said Wilkes as he sat back down.

Senator Schroeder chuckled, breaking the tense silence. "Nicely done, Miss Holloway. Very nicely done. Anyone who can get Joe Wilkes' goat gets my vote."

"Don't sit so pretty, Carolina. You didn't win. She's got my vote, too. I say we recommend approving the project. It's a pittance for the stability it can buy us south of the Rio Grande."

A murmur of "yeses" followed as all heads around the table nodded.

Senator Schroeder scowled. "Well, look at that. I'll eat my hat if it isn't bi-partisan cooperation on Joe Wilkes' first day."

"If that is all, then, Senators," said the clerk, "perhaps we'd like to end this portion of our meeting a few minutes early and take an extra ten minutes for coffee?"

More yeses.

Rebecca's eyes widened slightly, confusion clouding her face.

"Miss Holloway?"

"Senator Radner?" Rebecca replied, snapping from her disorientation to look at the majority leader.

"Are you alright?"

"Yes, sir. Thank you, sir."

"Well then, thank you for your… ah… *impassioned* presentation. We'll be pleased to recommend to the full committee, and thence to the appropriations committee, that the project proceed."

"Thank you, Senators," Rebecca replied, her bewildered acceptance automatic. She stood to make the rounds of the room before leaving.

"Good to see you again, Becky" Wilkes said, reaching forward to take Rebecca's hand when she got to him. "Looks like we have a few extra minutes. How 'bout you come have a coffee with me?" He held her hand tight to prompt a reply.

"Good to see you too, Senator." Rebecca smiled but there was no pleasure in her eyes. "I'm sorry, but I… I can't."

Wilkes relinquished his son's widow's hand, small and cool in his large calloused one, and sighed. "Give me a call then, would you? There's something you should know."

What could he have to tell her that was worth revisiting the pain of Hayden's death? And what if Joe was only trying to seek her forgiveness to assuage his own guilty conscience? It wasn't worth the risk.

"Certainly, Senator," she replied, her polite assent an obvious negative. "I'll do that." She kept her voice neutral. She didn't make eye contact before turning to leave.

Wilkes watched her depart, listened to her heels clicking down the shining linoleum, and sighed again. It wasn't the truth so much as the consequences of telling it that were so complicated.

***

Rebecca strode down the hall, pulling the clip from her hair and running her hand through her long locks to help her think. *That was it? Thirty minutes?* This was money to a foreign country that didn't strictly need it. In the middle of a recession. *It had been too easy. Joe Wilkes was up to something.* Rebecca was sure she knew Joe: whatever the "something" was, it couldn't be good.

Wealth in the Gulf, Danger in the Jungle: Mexico Courts a Two-Front War

The Global Observer
December 8, 2012

The new government in Mexico came to power on the slogan "Mexican wealth for Mexicans, equally,*" renationalizing the profits from oil exploration to fund social programs aimed at the poor and marginalized. It is irony, then, that to maintain domestic power in the face of harsh international criticism of this nationalistic move, the government is being forced to curry favour with the country's old elites .*

The appointment of Raul Vargas as head of the Ministry of Internal Security—Mexico's equivalent of the US Department of Homeland Security—illustrates the government's quandary: Vargas is a political neophyte. He is married, however, to Lordecita daCal, a member of one of Mexico's oldest and most powerful families. As a minority shareholder in an American oil exploration conglomerate, the recent renationalization has cost her roughly 30% of her personal fortune. Still worth nine hundred million dollars, daCal won't have to worry about putting food on the table, but she might be forgiven for wanting some kind of compensation. The prestige of her husband's new position might help.

Nor is the Vargas-DaCal story the only one of its kind; the wallets of the traditional elites are growing fatter throughout the country and the anger is growing palpable among the poor—the very people who brought Fernandez to power— at the failure to deliver on socialist election promises. In a country where rebellion is an institution, ignoring the disaffected poor is done at the government's peril.

But ignore it, they are. A guerrilla fomenting insurrection among the indigenous poor—a movement dangerously powerful because it is built on potent Maya myth—is being dismissed by the neophyte Vargas as a lunatic fad built on millennial madness. It is a political misstep that could bring Mexico towards another precipice.

And therein lies an even greater irony: that it might not be external pressure—in the form of a fight with the world's oil magnates—but internal discord and the need to quell a backyard revolutionary that brings Fernandez's "people's government" to its knees.

THE SECOND COMING OF KULKULCAN?

The Daily News online
December 8, 2012

Who is Kulkulcan? Ask a scholar and she will say that he is the feathered-serpent god of meso-American myth, a fearsome god better known by the Aztec name Quetzalcoatl. *But in the Yucatán, another Kulkulcan is rising, shadowy and dangerous, and about him little is known. Some say he is an indigenous insurgent planning to overthrow the State. Or he is a foreigner with ties to global oil. Or he is the second coming of the god whose name he has taken, bringing with him the end of the world. Whoever he is, his name is on everyone's lips and he has a lot of people more than a little scared.*

It is a truism of politics that the more dangerous your enemy, the less said about him the better. So ask the government in Mexico City and, if they comment at all, they will deny that any man named Kulkulcan exists. But filling the official silence are rumours of superstition, bloodletting, human sacrifice, blackmail, and the resignation of at least one high-profile cabinet secretary.

At the heart of the mystery lies a strange manifesto written by someone using the pseudonym "the risen Kulkulcan." Entitled Del Dzonote *(From the Well), the manifesto claims to be the word of the feathered serpent himself. Received by the author as he lay drowning in a deep sinkhole—the "well" of the tract's title—the manifesto uses the language of a series of Mayan texts known as the* Chilam Balam *to call for violent redress of the wrongs visited upon the Mayan people since the arrival of Cortés.*

Three things about Del Dzonote might explain the government's hesitance to speak, let alone give credence to, stories of Kulkulcan. First, the Maya have much to be angry about, especially given the current government's reversal of indigenous programming. Del Dzonote taps into this anger, which is spreading like wildfire through the small, impoverished—mostly Mayan—hamlets of the Yucatán.

Second, the gossip and buzz, strange as some of it is, cannot be disproven: the report of a rebel base camp in the deep south of the Yucatán cannot be investigated because the Calakmul Biosphere Reserve in which the base is purported to be located has been closed to tourist and journalist alike. The resignation in November of Secretary of Culture might have been the result of blackmail rather than the natural response to the death of her son, but the Secretary has moved to her family's farm in Spain and cannot be reached for comment. And most eerily, tales of ceremonies reminiscent of ancient Mayan sacrifices—complete with bloody disembowellings like those portrayed in the film Apocalypto*—have emerged and cannot be quelled. Some even suggest that the Secretary's son might have been a victim of one such ceremony, which furnishes an explanation for the closed coffin at the boy's funeral.*

The third possible reason for government silence is closely linked to the second—and to the rumour of sacrifice particularly. Mexicans are a superstitious people. The hybridization of Mayan and European cultures—more thoroughly mixed than in the United States, thanks to fervent Catholic missionaries and the shamans who bent Biblical language to their own myths in order to preserve them—has meant that even the most Westernized of Mexicans will speak deferentially of the ancient gods. Everyone is taught the history of conquest in high school but many have also read the apocalyptic chronicles of the Chilam Balam *for extra credit or a good campfire scare. The idea that the ancient gods might be rising again, as irrational as it might seem, is nevertheless beginning to haunt a country primed by ancient myth.*

In the end it might not matter who Kulkulcan is, or even if he exists. The more important question might be how to put out the fire that his manifesto has started. Truism aside, the government might want to start talking, since silence is only breeding fear. And fear will only fan the flames of Kulkulcan's design, whatever it may be.

Chapter 7

Rebecca strode passed Deb's desk, startling the large woman from a column of expense claim figures. Expenses being a never-ending task, Deb hadn't stayed to do them; she had stayed to learn the verdict at the meeting. Rebecca's grimly pursed lips seemed to say it all. Deb slipped black ballet slippers onto feet that seemed too tiny to support her enormous bulk, stood ponderously, and followed Rebecca to her office. She arrived in time to see Rebecca sit heavily and slam the briefing tablet onto the desk in front of her.

"Hey! That's government property!" Deb chided. More gently she asked "They didn't go for it, did they?"

"Yeah, they did." Rebecca's voice was flat.

"No way!" Deb paused. "So why aren't you happy?"

"Way. And I'm not happy because it was too easy. Radner was on board from the start; Denton asked a few money questions; and Schroeder nearly fell in love with me when I yelled at Wilkes."

Deb's eyes widened. "You yelled at Wilkes?"

"Not one of my better moments."

"And he still said yes?"

"That's just it. He hates programs like these—calls them 'bleeding-heart-Liberal-handouts.' He should have eaten me alive. Not to mention that I yelled at him in front of the whole goddamned committee. But he ignored my bad manners and said yes." Rebecca paused for a moment and then added "He's up to something."

"Up to *what*?"

Rebecca looked out the window to her left at the cold Washington sky, a few flakes of snow glittering in the bitter wind.

Saturday, December 8, 2012 — 4 Manik, Day of the Deer

"That I don't know—yet." She ran both hands through her hair and then sat up suddenly.

"You know someone in Appropriations , don't you?"

"Umm hmm. Bobbi Schwartz. She's the clerk's assistant. Why?"

"Could you get her on the phone and see what you can find out?"

"Find out? About what, exactly?"

"I dunno. Pretend this is a Grisham novel. Assume Wilkes wants the money. Maybe sending it to pay someone off. Or buy guns. Figure out how he could divert it from my program."

"A Grisham novel? Rebecca, this is Washington, not Hollywood. And I'm a big round lady, not Harrison Ford."

"I know, I know. I'm crazy. He's probably just padding his re-election campaign."

"Or maybe it's nothing at all. Maybe he just thinks the program makes sense…"

"Wilkes? No way. Humour me, okay? Just call Bobbi and see what she knows."

***

In a wide clearing that formed the centre of the guerrilla camp, a tree-stump of a man the colour of a cafe-latte stood before a tall, stringy, mocha-coloured youth. The boy held a gun in his hand.

"No!" yelled the short, thickset man as he looked up at the boy and then around at the knot of indifferent young men encircling them.

Beyond them, rising like a mountain, stood the remains of an ancient temple abandoned to the strangling force of the jungle a thousand years before: tall trees cast dappled shadows over spalling limestone stairs cracked by thick, gnarled tree roots.

It was a FN Five-Seven handgun—new, expensive, and purchased illegally—and the boy holding it was anxious. Barely out of his teens, he held the gun like a child learning to write holds a pencil: breath-held and too tight.

"No!" yelled the man again but he did not move, did not raise his hands in submission, did not drop to his knees to beg for his life.

Old enough to be the boy's father, the thickset man did nothing but clench his jaw. Like the boy facing him, the man wore the faded fatigues and army boots of the guerrilla movement; like the boy, the man was naked from the waist up. But where the boy's chest was bare, the man was magnificently tattooed: a blue-black snake-bird, tail coiled around his midriff, rose up his back, slid over his right shoulder, and slithered down his right arm. A fanged mouth lay open on the back of his right hand. The writhing creature was the Mesoamerican god *Quetzalcoatl*; the man wearing it called himself by the creature's Mayan name: *Kulkulcan*.

Kulkulcan moved a little at last. He shifted his weight and his nostrils flared in anger. "Don't mess around, Payal," he said, voice hard.

Suddenly he sprang forward, stole the weapon, and pointed it at the skinny boy's forehead. Eight pairs of onlooking eyes were instantly riveted to the spot between Payal's own where gunmetal nuzzled sweating skin. The sound of the safety being released seemed to echo through the steaming trees, an endless metallic moment, harsh against the quiet forest.

"You must hold it like you mean to use it."

Kulkulcan's eyes narrowed as he pressed the muzzle more firmly into Payal's forehead, the boy's skin wrinkling beneath the steel.

"Like this. Like I am, now. With passion." His voice was a lover's whisper.

A droplet of sweat slid down Payal's left temple. A droplet of sweat ran down Kulkulcan's neck. A droplet of water slipped from a palm leaf and patted hard on a dry leaf. A mot-mot's twanging call echoed through the canopy. A tree creaked. Somewhere, overhead, a jet crawled across the sky, trailing the roar of its engines. One of the boys shivered in the long, hot moment, slow and airless as suffocation.

"Americans know guns," Kulkulcan said as he slid the gun down the boy's nose, his voice hypnotic, the movement as soft as a caress.

"They love guns. They grow up watching people shoot each other on television with guns. They spend hours playing video games, shooting pretend people with pretend guns. They give them as gifts, hide them under their pillows, let them fall into the hands of children who kill each other…"

He paused for a moment to look at a small white orchid blooming on a fig tree twenty feet beyond the boy's head. He could stain the flower's throat red with a single bullet to the boy's brain. But he needed this boy—these boys. For now, at least.

"They will know," Kulkulcan suddenly roared, "if you do not mean to use it!"

He pressed the muzzle harder into Payal's forehead, abrading the skin. "And if you do not look like you mean to use it, we cannot win this war!"

Kulkulcan drew the hammer back and pulled the trigger. He raised the pistol only at the very last moment, leaving the bullet to brush through the boy's hair, and streak harmlessly into the sky. Payal fainted. The others surged forward to huddle over his prostrate body. Kulkulcan turned away.

"I am going to my quarters," he called over his shoulder as he started for a group of small thatched huts at the far side of the clearing.

"We start again in half an hour. I expect you to take the revolution more seriously when we resume."

Alonzo Malan Dzul—a wealthy nightclub owner with a secret life as the insurgent known to his recruits only as Kulkulcan—looked around at the camp he had built as he strode from the knot of stunned recruits. He had started it five years ago with nine recruits, five chainsaws, four tents, and a story. He had chosen the site at the foot of an undiscovered temple deep within the riotous growth of the Calakmul Biosphere Reserve for its distance in both space and in time from the rest of Mexico. The physical location hundreds of miles from anything would keep his rebellion hidden until he was ready to move; the ruins overrun by a jungle last cut by the Ancient Maya would keep his rebels isolated in the past until they were ready to believe in the myth he had built of their destiny.

The camp now spread in a wide semi-circle from the base of the hundred-foot pyramid. To the left lay the long narrow remains of a traditional Mayan ballcourt which Kulkulcan had converted into a firing range.

All the recruits—thirteen cells of nine men each—had been introduced to the firing range with the same words: *The Hero Twins, Xbalenque and Hunaphu, beat the Lords of the Underworld at their own game in a court such as this. Now you will beat our oppressors with their own weapons once more.*

Looking clockwise around the site—rude enough that a passing satellite would mistake it for an abandoned squatter's camp—Kulkulcan surveyed all that he had built: the primitive barracks at three o'clock; the small square hut that belonged to his American "advisor" at four o'clock; the thatched kitchen hut at six o'clock, a metal hand pump in front of it; three more small huts at seven, eight, and nine o'clock, the last being Kulkulcan's own. Unlike the others, it was adorned with a small rooftop solar panel and a satellite dish: he alone at the camp had a link to the wider, newer world of the *gringo*—the *dzul*. A small footpath skirted the clearing from Kulkulcan's hut back to edge of the pyramid. Beyond it and to the south lay an enormous sinkhole, a Mayan *cenote*, open to the sky.

Thinking about the cool azure water in the *cenote*, Kulkulcan veered towards the pump. It drew water from the same underground reservoir sitting on the limestone shelf that was the Yucatán. This reservoir, formed by the meteor that had killed off the dinosaurs sixty-five million years ago, was to the Maya what the Tigris and Euphrates were to Mesopotamia, the Ganges to India, and the Yangtze to China: the lifeblood of a civilization. Only here, underground, it was steady as a pulse, cool as a breeze, never flooding or evaporating, always beneath their feet.

Kulkulcan gripped the steel handle, already hot in the midmorning sun, and began to pump. He started sweating even before the water gushed forth and cursed again his bastard blood before slaking his thirst. His mother had been Maya—purebred and with an oral lineage she could trace to the great Lord *Pacal*. But the semen that had engendered him was Caucasian, the unwelcome gift of a white South African soldier of fortune passing through his family's village.

Now Kulkulcan plunged his bald head under the surge of groundwater that issued from the pump's spout. The water sheeted over his smooth scalp before splintering on his shoulders and trickling down his back. It was electrifyingly cold; he gasped like a newborn as his blood quickened in his veins. For a wonderful and terrifying moment he almost believed the web of lies he had woven for his foot-soldiers: the gods were alive and they were angry; they were infusing him with their spirits, infusing him with the power to visit their vengeance.

"A little hard on the boys, don't you think there, Boss?" said a voice that freed Dzul from his alter-ego's disconcerting spell. It was Travis Rutrauff, his American soldier. Rutrauff was a sniper and the money man: he was training Kulkulcan's recruits to kill cleanly from a thousand feet; he was also the one with the authority to receive the clandestine US cash that would buy the guns that Kulkulcan's recruits would use to bring down the Mexican government.

Rutrauff was a pawn in three games: Kulkulcan's to destroy a foreign government unfriendly to oil interests in the US; the Americans' counterplot to kill Kulkulcan before he could assume power, and the third—the one he did not know about;—Kulkulcan's triple-cross that would undo the Americans' plans.

"Maybe," Kulkulcan grunted. "But life is only easy for people like you, Captain Rutrauff. People with their own nation. Life has been especially hard for the Maya: we once had a nation and it was stolen from us. Like tempering metal to make it stronger, I scare my boys to make them hard. They need to be hard for what it is that they will do."

"Well then, maybe you were a bit hard on my compatriots, seeing as all those gun-toting Americans you were just insulting pay the taxes that buy the guns that we'll be using for your cozy little death-fest. And tempered metal might be strong, but is also brittle."

"Don't worry, Captain. It is all part of the chess game. In the end, I will get what I deserve and so will you."

Rutrauff nodded at that, imagining the possibility of his own death while killing Kulkulcan. "It's a dangerous game, Boss. Your hundred-and-seventeen men are pitted against the entire army…"

"You think? I have fear and hate on my side, Rutrauff. And belief. Faith can move mountains."

"Yeah, but faith is generally no match for an army's bullets."

"Oh, really? You take out a dollar bill from your wallet and tell me what it says. 'In God We Trust,' no? Well, your God is nothing compared to the Mayan ones. The Maya were building temples like the one outside while your ancestors were living in mud and filth. Led by our gods, we tracked the Moon and stars before Europe had a compass or an astrolabe. We wrote poetry and built empires while your ancestors, illiterate every one of them, huddled around rude camp fires. Do not under-estimate faith and the power it has to motivate a subjugated people."

Kulkulcan felt another electric tingle, another involuntary thrill of belief. He searched his fatigue pockets for tobacco to steady himself. The fervent shine in his eyes dimmed, and his voice lost its melody with the first drag of his cigarette.

"And anyway," Kulkulcan added, "You had better hope the one-hundred-and-seventeen are enough, or you will have spent a lot of your tax-payers money for nothing. Speaking of money, when do the guns come?"

Rutrauff was startled by the rebel's shifting personality, and unnerved by the man's brief, terrifying fervour. He paused a moment before replying.

"We only got the go-ahead yesterday. They'll be in Cancún the day after tomorrow. That's plenty of time."

Dzul picked the cigarette from his mouth with the thumb and forefinger of his right hand and began pacing in front of his small thatched hut. A droplet of sweat, like the dozens before it, trickled down his bare spine to the perspiration-darkened waistband of his pants. He looked up at the white-hot noon sun above the temple flanking his camp and scowled.

"The boys need practice. Not just with rusty weapons from the Cold War."

"If they can shoot straight with the AKs—which they can—the HKs will be easy as pie. Don't you worry about their shooting skills."

"I should worry about other skills?" Kulkulcan asked, challenging.

"They're young. They haven't been tested. I'm not a big believer in your 'faith.'"

"You will be," Kulkulcan said darkly, flicking the butt of his cigarette from his fingers to a bare patch of earth near Rutrauff's feet. Rutrauff looked hard at the man and stepped deliberately on the cigarette end. There were a hundred things he could say to the arrogant bastard, but he thought better of it, satisfying himself with the knowledge that, at the end of the day, Kulkulcan would never actually be allowed to have the power he so desperately craved.

"If I cannot train the boys' bodies, I will train their spirits. Come and listen, maybe you will learn something."

"I'd like to, sir, but I'm going to drive into Cancún tonight. Spend an extra day getting a few things ready."

"No Captain, I want you to finish what I start this afternoon. Take the boys into the jungle for the night. Give them more of that spine you think they are missing. We will both fly to Cancún tomorrow."

Saturday, December 8, 2012 — 4 Manik, Day of the Deer

Rutrauff scowled to himself. No break from the messiah and the jungle and the arrogant boys. At least he'd get a chance to put the boys in their place without Kulkulcan watching.

"You're the boss," was all Rutrauff said aloud, his tone indifferent.

"Yes. I am. Now come listen and learn."

The steel returning to the rebel's voice made Rutrauff shudder. Kulkulcan was becoming something more than a rebel. He was becoming dangerous.

Kulkulcan stood at the top of the pyramid relishing the slight breeze that played over his nearly naked body. He had changed from his military garb to a loincloth. He wore nothing else but a silver chain on which hung an enormous jaguar claw, the tip reaching his solar plexus. His right hand rested on a tall staff adorned with a quetzal feather that fluttered against his calf. It tickled, and he moved the staff slightly; the movement made his tattooed snake come to life, its sinewy body slithering malevolently down its master's flexing muscles. The scrape of the staff echoed, bouncing down the temple's stairs where it met the recruits on their way up, sweaty with exercise and nervous with anticipation. Rutrauff jogged up the steep steps behind them, hardly winded.

He looked over the camp, beyond to the stretch of ancient Mayan stone road—a *sacbe*, indistinguishable from the many that criss-crossed the peninsula even so many years later—that he used as an airstrip, to the green jungle beneath him and sighed with grim pleasure. Soon it would all be his, to be ruled with guns and terror.

"Come, warriors, and sit with me." His tone was warm and welcoming.

He sat on a thick block of limestone that had fallen from the plinth of the structure at the top of the temple. The young men formed a semi-circle on the ground around him, nervously respectful despite his kind tone. They each remembered the muzzle of the gun at Payal's head. Rutrauff sat warily on another block of limestone behind the young men.

"And Payal? You are feeling well?" Kulkulcan asked solicitously.

"Yes, *Ahau*." Payal used the Mayan honourific but would not look Kulkulcan in the eye.

"Afraid, a little, Payal?"

The young man said nothing and his eyes remained downcast.

"It is good to be a little afraid, Payal. It keeps you alert. Tonight there will be more of it."

Payal looked up, startled. The other young men did the same.

"Yes," Kulkulcan said soothingly. "Yes, there is fear for you tonight in the jungle."

The eyes staring at Kulkulcan widened. At night the Mayan jungle held malevolent spirits risen from *Xibalba*, the place of death and fear.

"Tonight you put aside your weapons to master yourselves. You travel in the footsteps of the Hero Twins, Xbalenque and Hunaphu, born in the time before time. In that time, the Lords of *Xibalba*, so like today's descendants of the *conquistadores*, wandered freely among us delivering sickness, hunger, poverty, and death.

"In that time the Lords, chief among them One Death and Seven Death, would capture humans for their entertainment and bring them to *Xibalba* where they would humiliate them with cruel tests that they were certain no human could master.

"In that time, when the Twins had grown to manhood, like you..." Kulkulcan paused to look at each of his recruits in turn "... they at last grew tired of the Lords' subjugation and set off to the underworld to defeat them.

"The road to *Xibalba* was filled with trials. A river of scorpions. A river of blood. A river of pus. And the crossing of four speaking roads, each beckoning the brothers to travel in a different direction.

"Then, when they arrived, the Lords laughed at them. How could Xbalenque and Hunaphu dare to dream they could beat the Lords' tests? The Lords agreed, in their foolish pride, to a wager: if the Twins passed the Lords' tests, then the Lords would have to leave the land of the living for good, and be confined to their old world beneath the good green Earth.

"And the tests? Tonight you will take three of them, just as the Twins did before you."

The boys shuddered. Even Rutrauff felt a cold foreboding settle into the pit of his stomach and gooseflesh spread across his forearms. Kulkulcan smiled beatifically, electrified once more by his own rhetoric.

"Tonight you will be tested in the Dark House. And the Jaguar and

Bat Houses, as well. You will be plunged into a blackness that can make a man mad. You will be surrounded by the hungry, shrieking creatures of the night, anxious to blind, confuse, and kill you."

Kulkulcan looked hard at each of the young men before him. Each averted his eyes, shuddering at the thought of bats encircling them and jaguars tearing at their hearts.

"Now you are afraid! But think. You have already beaten some of the Lords' tests without knowing it."

The boys looked up again, a ray of hope dawning. Rutrauff raised his eyebrow, impressed. Kulkulcan was skilled; he had thoroughly broken the boys with fear and was now going to rebuild them, with pride, in the image he desired.

"Payal." Kulkulcan asked. The young man snapped to attention, his long angular face riveted to Kulkulcan's square one.

"Yes, *Ahau*?"

"Were you not cold with fear when the gun was pointed at your head?"

"Yes, *Ahau*. Frozen."

"That was the Lord's Rattling House, so full of bone chilling cold that humans freeze with fear when they enter it. You survived."

A slow smile crept across Payal's face. The others looked at him with envy and a new-found respect.

"And the first day you arrived. Do you remember that I made you stand from sunrise to sunset before the temple without a drop of water. Not even in the midday sun?" He was speaking softly now, and sweetly, as if wooing them.

The young men nodded.

"That was the House of Heat that burned unworthy souls. And you each passed that test, as well." Payal's face was glowing now; the other young men squared their shoulders or puffed out their chests, swelling with their own pride and fearless daring.

"And there is a House of Razors, too." Kulkulcan said, his voice forbidding. The young men sat like Boy Scouts around their troop leader, listening to a ghost story at a camp fire. Rutrauff felt his skin crawl at the power of Kulkulcan's oratory.

"The House of Razors was the fifth house, and in it knives moved by unseen hands held at the ready to slit the throat of a man who moved unwisely."

Kulkulcan reached behind the limestone block on which he sat and pulled out a white cloth roll tied with a red cord. He untied it on his lap and set it gently on the ground before him. Inside lay nine glittering knives, their blades hewn from obsidian, their edges flaked as thin and dangerous as broken glass, each bound with sinew to wooden handles inlaid with a different turquoise glyph.

"These will make you masters of the House of Razors. Like the Lords of Death, you will hold your blades at the ready. Each holds a special power meant for you alone. Our enemy is everywhere and he creeps on silent, invisible feet, but with these you shall prevail."

Kulkulcan looked up at the glittering eyes of his men—truly *his* men now—and smiled. At them. And at the grim look on the American's face. Then he looked down to pluck the first blade from the roll, reading the glyph on its handle as he did so.

"Hector, your glyph is 'wind.' Be swift." A stocky young man stood up and took the blade reverently.

"Ramon, you are '*eb*,' sign of the rain. You will wash us clean of our enemies. Miguel, you are '*cib*,' adaptable like the wax for which your blade is named. Payal, your glyph is for jade, favoured stone sacred to the gods…" Kulkulcan gave each man the totem name that went with his blade and watched them begin to burn with a passion to use their new names, their new spirits, their new weapons.

"Like Xbalenque and Hunaphu before you, you will prevail. You will beat the Lords at their own game—the great and noble *pok'ta'pok* that your fathers before you played in your own villages."

The spell broke for someone as he thought of his father playing the ancient ballgame with its silly name, a tennis ball in lieu of the hard rubber ball used of old; a snicker broke the spell for the others.

Kulkulcan's stood, his face darkening. There was steel in his eyes and anger in his low, controlled voice. "You think it is a silly game for old men. You would much rather play soccer, play baseball, be like the *mestizos* with their European notions, the *Americanos* with their TVs and their Hollywood stars…"

Now Kulkulcan's voice rose and his eyes blazed. "No! Those are just more ways the foreigners brainwash you. The Ballgame is ours. It is the game of the gods, won for you by your ancestors. The *mestizos* stole it from us. They pretend it belongs to them as the 'birthright of all Mexicans.' But it is not for those with bastard Spanish blood! It is Mayan! It is ours alone! We will take it, and all that is rightfully ours!"

His eyes were wild now, and his flexing muscles made the feathered serpent on his body writhe with life.

"I am Kulkulcan and this I promise: you are the sons of Xbalenque and Hunaphu; your names will be sung at the dawn of the new Mayan age when we retake our rightful place as lords and masters of this land!"

The young men sprang to their feet as one and raised their knives to the heavens. "Land of the Maya!" they chanted. Their brown eyes glittered beneath tall brows, long black top-knots blowing in the breeze. They stripped off their t-shirts and flung them on the ground, their chests glistening with the sweat of fervour, their breathing hard with the righteous indignation of injustice. They cut their fingertips with their deadly blades and let the blood drip on the uneven grey stones of the temple, crimson mingling with the talc-white calcium carbonate that had once faced the temple in glittering white.

"Land of the Maya!" they shouted, and the wind carried their voices far across the jungle. Flocks of birds startled from the trees ahead of the noise and the creatures of the jungle howled and cried in response.

***

"Beck?"

Rebecca looked up over her dark-framed eyeglasses and beyond her notebook screen to the large woman standing in her doorway.

"Mm hmm?"

"You're not going to believe it."

"Try me."

"So I called Bobbi. And then I made about a dozen other calls."

"Umm hmm?"

"My last one was to the finance guy at the Mexican Red Cross in Mexico City."

"And?"

"He just received six million dollars for medical supplies for the Maya project."

"What??"

"Yup. He didn't even know what it was for, except that the funds transfer was tagged 'Mayan medical assistance.' He wants to know what to do with it."

"The bill hasn't even gone to the Senate Committee! It won't be voted on for weeks!"

"Yeah, I know. So I called Bobbi back, and she called Theresa at Education, who knows Yvonne at..." Rebecca was unconsciously tapping her stylus against her desk in suspense.

"Anyway, it doesn't matter. The kicker is that the money came from a Defence Department line item in the security top-up bill that went through last week."

"You are damn near brilliant, Deborah Christina Varanides! I could kiss you." Rebecca stood up. "I gotta go to Mexico City."

"No kissing. And no you don't. You have to go to Cancún."

"I what?" Rebecca stopped trying to power down her iPad, lock her smartphone, and collect her keys all at once.

"The Red Cross guy in Mexico City told me he'd been instructed to wire two million of the money to a numbered account in Cancún for 'office start-up funds.'"

"There is no office for this project!"

"I know."

"Betsy Denton," Rebecca said under her breath.

It was Deb's turn to be shocked. "Betsy Denton did this?"

"No, she didn't. But I bet you Wilkes put her up to asking the questions about corruption."

"You lost me, Beck."

"It's easy to blame corruption in Mexico for missing money. Meanwhile, someone is using it for something other than medical supplies. It's too damned convenient that Wilkes just got shuffled to Foreign Relations. He's behind this, I'm sure of it."

"But why?"

"Who the hell knows with Joe. As a means to yet another end that will benefit him alone. Anyone who gets in the way be damned."

Deb looked at the thunder in Rebecca's face and knew that this wasn't about misappropriation of taxpayers' funds.

"Or like Hayden going to war to get Wilkes re-elected?" she asked softly.

"Something like that," Rebecca said grimly. "Whatever it is, I've got to find out. Can you to get me on the next available flight to Cancún?"

"I knew you'd say that. There's a flight on Wednesday…"

"Wednesday?! That's…" she counted on her fingers, "...that's four days away. Not including today."

"Take a pill, Rebecca. It's December. Everyone wants to go to where it's warm. Rules say you can't go first class. You can go Wednesday or I can get you on a red-eye tonight."

Rebecca paused for a long moment. "Shit," she said at last.

"Could you be a little more specific? Is that a 'shit' as in 'shit, no,' or a 'shit' as in 'shit, yes'?"

"As in 'shit, yes.' As in, 'shit, I really hate red-eyes.'"

Chapter 8

The toll road from Mérida to Cancún was deserted near midnight. Stephen unwrapped another stick of Beeman's gum—his hard-to-find-in-Canada favourite—popped it into his mouth, and chewed to keep himself awake. Why the hell was he doing this? Everything Chalo had said on the phone this morning aside, Stephen hated driving at night. Too many places for his mind to wander. Too many ghosts to see. As if answering his thought, a pair of silver eyes appeared low at the side of the road.

During his early days in Mexico, Stephen had hoped these roadside eyes might belong to a jaguar. The great cats, sacred to the Maya, had once been abundant as far north as Arizona: a symbol of power over death, the jaguar lord—Balam—was said to have fought each night to free the sun from the lords of the underworld. But these days wild jaguars were scarce, especially near Mexico City, so he'd revised his hopes downward through the smaller cats—ocelot, margay, tiny jaguarundi—before giving up. But he was on the Yucatán now, wilder and, in the interior at least, less developed. There might be jaguars around. Maybe the country would give him a parting gift. Three more sets of eyes appeared, closer set and lower still. Stephen smiled ruefully: just a coati and three kits. He unwrapped another piece of gum and sighed.

Why was he doing this? Because there hadn't been a seat on any direct flight from Mexico City to Cancún, so he'd had to fly to Mérida and drive. Because of what Chalo had said on the phone. And mostly because he needed to see Chalo once more; needed to say a proper goodbye for once in his life.

A peachy-coloured highway light flicked off as Stephen drove beneath it. Scientifically speaking there was nothing eerie about it: halide lamps cycled until the gas got too hot, shut themselves down, cooled off, and started up again. That knowledge didn't help him on a dark road late at night when he could hear his sister's voice say that the lights went out whenever a ghost flew by. He imagined he saw a white shape on the road ahead, shivered, and turned on the radio to quiet his night-time imagination, more vivid than ever following Erin's death. The tinny sound filled the car, the volume set high by the previous rental driver.

... un representante del Chacmool Resort en Tulum dijo a la prensa que ella encontró hoy un corazón humano en el pasillo del hotel. Las Autoridades no están informatdo sobre que una investigación está en marcha...

What the hell? Stephen understood the words perfectly, but not the meaning. A human heart in a hotel lobby? Could this be what Chalo had meant when he had mentioned Alvarro?

***

Originally, kidnappings in Mexico had just been about money. The rules of engagement had been pretty straightforward: people were taken, staggering sums of money demanded, insurance policies—all of which now carried costly kidnapping clauses—were cashed in, and people were returned, traumatized but physically unharmed.

This one had looked like one of those: the twelve-year-old son of the Secretary of Culture taken. Except that one of Chalo's informants had linked Alvarro to the boy. The partners had ended up at the warehouse, without backup, just after midnight on October 4th. Neither of them had been prepared for what they found. Stephen shuddered as the memory from the warehouse flooded forward, unbidden…

He smells the sickly sweet incense again, seeping from beneath the closed door. He hears a child crying, a thump, a scream of terror and agony. The door splinters as Chalo kicks it, the room behind it is tilting in the light of dozens of candles guttering with the door's sudden gust, the air breathing hard to get in. A ribbon of blood leaps through the air as Stephen surges into the crimson room. He feels the fine warm mist on his forehead, tastes iron on his lips. There is a man in front of him, his chest bare, his head bald but for a black topknot, his arms held high. His hands are bloody. There are tattoos on his chest. There are hieroglyphics on the wall. There are six other men. One of them is Alvarro, moving already from the tableau, out the back door. And there is the boy. On the floor in front of the man. On his back. Looking at Stephen. His wide brown eyes are glassy, his blue lips gasping, a gaping hole in his small hairless chest. Stephen hears the slow explosion of a gunshot and the bare-chested man blows backward, a pinpoint hole in his own chest. Another shot, and another. Chalo's gun? No, his own. He is stupid with incomprehension. He feels his gun thundering in his hand, over and over and over. Chalo is shouting "move!" But Stephen cannot move—until a bitter burning swallows the place where his stomach should be. He slips on blood and feathers. He dives to the boy, cradles the small warm head smelling of boyhood and soap and blood. He cannot see through his own tears to the boy's drying, lifeless eyes.

Stephen braked hard, skidding on the gravel shoulder as he pulled over. His vision was tunnelling; he had to stop. The car at rest, he turned off the ignition and put his forearms up onto the steering wheel, his head on his arms. He tried to breathe. Dust from the sudden deceleration billowed into his open window; the sweet night air mingling with the dust smelled like the incense in the warehouse.

He'd been too late. Someone else had died on his watch. Stephen opened the car door and wretched.

They hadn't talked about it much. Hadn't had a chance to. Stephen had ended up in the hospital for almost two weeks recovering from the gunshot to his gut; Chalo had come once before being forbidden to visit his partner, pending an investigation. And later, they hadn't wanted to talk about it.

"What the hell happened, Chalo?" Stephen remembered asking just once, still groggy with Demerol. The answer hadn't made any sense.

"*There will come a time when the writings on the wall will speak.*"

"What?"

"Did you see the drawings on the wall, Esteban? They were Mayan. 'There will come a time when the walls will speak.' It is what my grandmother said."

Saturday, December 8, 2012 — 4 Manik, Day of the Deer

"Your grandmother? In Guatemala? What do you mean?"

"Never mind, *caballero*. Nothing. An old woman's tale about the end of the world. It isn't true."

"Jeezus Chalo. Someone just ripped the heart out of a little kid while he was still alive. Are you sure it's not true?" It made sense under the influence of the heavy opiate.

"If it is, *hermano*, there isn't a thing we can do about it. The gods are the ones that decide our end. You get better now. I have to go."

Stephen took a deep breath and stepped out of the car, the taste of vomit still bitter in his mouth. He spat to rid himself of the taste and looked around. Where was he anyway?

A green highway sign a hundred metres ahead glowed in his headlights. *Chich'en Itzá, 5 km.*

"Shit."

He had another hour of driving, at least, before he got to Cancún, and then at least another half an hour to find the address Chalo had given to him on the phone. The archaeologist Chalo was meeting—why, only Chalo knew—lived in the confusing streets of the old part of town.

Stephen rubbed his eyes and looked at the highway sign again. Chich'en Itzá: it meant "well of the water wizards" in Yucatec. A wonder of the world and he hadn't made time to see. What an idiot.

He looked at the sign again. A light mist was moving beside the sign post. He looked more carefully. It wasn't a mist; it was a person, crouching. Stephen squinted. A woman?

"Hey!" He started walking towards her. "*¿Esta todo bien*? Are you okay?"

The woman drew herself up. Like a plant growing, Stephen thought. She was wearing a long white dress; maybe she was Maya? Except that there was no flash of colourful embroidery at the neck. The woman stared at him.

"Hey! I'm a pol… ." He checked himself. Given their reputation for corruption, saying that he was a police officer might not actually make her feel any better.

Closer now, he could see her more clearly: long dark hair, pale skin, deep-set brown eyes. And a Giaconda smile. She started towards the jungle, her gauzy dress fluttering against a well-proportioned figure in a breeze that Stephen could not feel. He saw that she was barefoot as she stepped into the brambled ditch. An unshod woman by the highway in the middle of the night? How could she *not* need help?

"¡*Espera*! Wait! I won't hurt you. I'm going to Cancún. Do you need a ride?"

She was in the jungle proper now, and moving surprisingly quickly for someone without shoes. Stephen followed her into the darkness. Prickly vines dragged and tore at him. A twig snapped across his cheek.

"Seriously! Wait! Can I call someone for you? I'm Stephen—*Esteban*."

The woman looked over her shoulder, still smiling enigmatically, and kept moving. But he was catching up. He would be even with her in a minute, could catch her and lead her out.

"It isn't safe here. There are… Ow!"

As if realizing his own prophecy, he felt a sharp pain at his ankle. He looked down: a coati had bitten him. The woman stopped to watch what he did next.

"Jeezuz! Listen! You've got to come out of here! There are… ."

He heard the scream of a big cat dangerously close, and a jolt of adrenaline coursed cold through his veins. Okay, maybe he didn't want to see a jaguar after all. Not now, at least.

"That!" He pointed in the direction of the sound. "A jaguar. *Es un jaguar*."

The woman's smile widened revealing straight white teeth. "*Balam*."

Stephen heard it a moment after she mouthed it. "*Baaah-laaahm*." A long soft purr of a sound. Stephen saw a flash of black and gold at her side.

"*Malo. Ka ili'ik, Chac Balam*."

Like smoke dissipating in a strong breeze, she faded and was gone. Stephen held his breath for a moment in disbelief, the great cat still staring at him, before turning on his injured foot and darting back to his car, his blood cold and his body charged with fear.

Saturday, December 8, 2012 — 4 Manik, Day of the Deer

SUNDAY, DECEMBER 9, 2012
5 LAMAT, DAY OF VENUS, MORNING & EVENING STAR

CHAPTER 9

"*¿Usted es Stephen Catherwood*?" asked the faceless woman; the yellow light spilling from the apartment was making it impossible to see her features.

Stephen had driven the final hour and a half to Cancún in a daze: he wasn't really sure how he had gotten through town, through the tiny Moorish courtyard behind him with its tiny fountain splashing, to this doorway and this woman.

Stephen squinted at the shapely silhouette, desperate for something he could recognize. "*¿Esta Chalo Guerrero aqui*?" he asked.

Chalo's stocky silhouette appeared behind the woman.

"*Caballero*! What happened to you? You look like you saw death!"

"Maybe. Can I come in?"

The woman stepped aside, allowing Stephen a glimpse of her face. A strong, high-cheekboned face, well-tanned by the sun. Her eyes were the colour of an iceberg under three feet of calm, cold water: an arresting cerulean blue.

"I'm Dr. Anya von Eckhardt, Detective Catherwood. Please come. You need a drink, I think. Beer?"

"Tequila, please." Stephen said as he stepped into the warm foyer light and followed Anya up the long narrow stairway to her apartment. Chalo closed the door behind them.

"And I can get you another drink, Chalo?" Anya asked over her shoulder.

"From the look of *Esteban*, I think yes."

Stephen's detective instincts profiled Anya as he followed her into the apartment: tanned and toned from much time spent outside; the clip in her shoulder-length blonde hair showed her for a natural blonde; the khaki cargo shorts and cotton shirt, embroidered with baby-blue thread at the neckline showed her for a foreigner with local ties. Barefoot, she padded softly on the terra cotta floor, her calf muscles flexing like a dancer's. Or a cat's. His dispassionate eye failed him, and his blood ran cold once more as he recalled the jaguar's scream.

Anya turned abruptly right. "Go outside. I will be there in a moment," she said over her shoulder.

She had turned into a narrow kitchen; a woven basket bright with mangos, oranges, lemons, and papayas sat on the cobalt tiled counter that separated the kitchen from the wide living space. The furniture was clean and spare; above the modular furniture the ceiling was high and stuccoed in the Spanish style. At the far end of the room, a sliding glass door stood open, long linen curtains swelling and ebbing in a gentle breeze.

More than the space, Stephen found himself drawn to the walls. They were heavy with framed posters, all bearing sketches or photos of Mayan art and architecture. The *Musee de l'Homme* in Paris. The *Ethnologisches* in Berlin. The *Museum der Weltkulturen* in Frankfurt. The *Museum für Völkerkunde* in Köln. The *Museo Nazionale Preistorico-Etnografico* in Rome. The *Museu Etnològic* in Barcelona. Anya was European, well-travelled, and seriously into the Maya.

To the right of the sliding doors, incongruously messy, sat a makeshift desk made of sawhorses and a wooden door. On it lay small heaps of pottery and stone, sable paintbrushes of various sizes, a pad of paper, pencils, rulers, a sketchpad, two hairbands, and an empty glass. A Mac, open but asleep, sat on the left corner of the desk. Two fluorescent magnifying lamps, both off, stood over the chaos. Beneath the desk sat a large blue plastic exercise ball that clearly served as a chair.

Chalo led Stephen past the flowing curtains to a narrow balcony overlooking the town and, in the distance, the sea. The smell of salt air made both men inhale deeply. Stephen sat down on a creaky wicker chair. Above the bright slash on the horizon that was the tourist strip, a few bright stars pricked the night sky. A few more small lights twinkled on *Isla Mujeres* in the distance, and the dim lights of a ferry traversed the darkness between land and island.

Chalo creaked into a chair beside Stephen. They listened to the sound of a cupboard opening and glasses clinking in the kitchen before Chalo spoke.

"What happened to you, *hermano*?"

"Jeezuz Chalo… ." Stephen paused and rubbed his eyes. "I have no freaking idea. I pulled over near Chich'en Itzá… there was this woman…"

"A woman? You?" Chalo chuckled as he pulled a package of cigarettes from his shirt pocket, put a cigarette to his lips, frowned, and put it back in the package. "Did you get her number?"

Stephen watched Chalo with the cigarette and raised his eyebrows. He ignored the jibe.

"No smoking in Anya's apartment," Chalo said.

"'Anya,' hmm?" Stephen said archly. Chalo began to blush. Stephen chuckled.

"Put me out of my misery, *caballero*. Finish your story, would you?"

Stephen chuckled, then grew serious.

"It was the weirdest thing, Chalo. I'm driving on the toll road and it's deserted because it's so late, and then I pull over for a minute to… to stretch…" Stephen didn't want to admit the real reason. Didn't want to talk about the warehouse.

"Anyway, I look around and there isn't a soul. Up ahead, maybe a hundred metres, is the sign for Chich'en Itzá, and then there is… I mean, all of a sudden… One minute no one is there, and the next a mist comes up and… well, there she is, this woman. Wearing a white dress. Long and flowy and almost see-through. And no goddamned shoes, if you can believe it. I call her and she starts walking into the jungle…"

"Maybe she was afraid of you, *caballero*."

"That's just it, Chalo. She wasn't at all. She wasn't running away from me, just walking towards something in the jungle. And it is like she wanted me to follow her. She was just floating, bare-foot, as if she were walking on air. I started following her…" Stephen drifted into silence.

"And?"

"And nothing. I mean, a jaguar screamed in the forest, which scared the hell out of me, and then a coati bit me, and then she just… she just disappeared."

Chalo looked at Stephen seriously and said nothing.

"I'm crazy, right? People don't just evaporate. Maybe the department is right. Maybe I do have PTSD."

"PTSD?" Anya asked as she stepped out onto the balcony with tequila, three shot glasses, a small bowl of lemon wedges, and a small three-legged pot of salt, all on a tray.

Chalo answered for Stephen. "Post-traumatic stress disorder. The reason he's going back to Canada and why I am stuck at the Chacmool. And I don't think you're crazy, *caballero*."

"Then what the hell did I see?"

Anya set the tray on the small round table in front of Stephen. "A shaman would say that you met *Xtabay*." She said it *eesh-tah-bay*—long and soft, like a sigh.

"Who?"

"*Xtabay*. Literally 'the ensnarer.' A whore and eater of men, but with a good and noble heart," Anya spoke deliberately, like a teacher to students. "On her death it is said *xtabentún* flowers sprang from her grave. It is from the flowers we get the Mayan liquor of the same name. Those who see her are usually drunk—or mad." This last sentence she said with strange satisfaction.

"So I am crazy," Stephen said darkly. He shot his tequila without salt or lemon, grimaced and then turned to Anya. "Any idea what *balam* means?"

"*Balam*?" Anya squinted at Stephen then looked down to pick up her own shot. "It is a Yucatec word. Why do you ask?"

"It means 'jaguar,' *caballero*." Chalo answered.

"But why do you ask?" Anya asked again.

"The woman in the forest said it."

"And did she say anything else?" Anya was intent upon him now; Stephen felt uncomfortable under her ice-blue stare.

"It was all just sounds. It didn't make any sense to me. Why?"

"'*Balam*' also refers to the Lord of the Forest. *Xtabay* is his consort—his lover and his advisor. She precedes him in many texts."

"And I heard a jaguar scream after I saw her. Great. Pass the tequila would you?"

"*The call of Lord Balam, the night cat, will signal the start of the end*," Chalo said softly, as if thinking aloud.

"What is that?" Anya asked, turning her gaze on Chalo.

Chalo refocused his gaze on Anya. "Nothing. Never mind. It is just a child's tale." His voice remained soft, a hint of a smile on his face, as he looked on her.

"It is from the *Chilam Balam*, isn't it? One of the apocalyptic prophecies? About the world's end?" She asked, questioning him more softly than she had Stephen.

Stephen rolled his eyes, irritated with the obvious flirtation, even as he felt the chill of the forest returning to his bones. He shot his second tequila and sighed.

"This is just getting better and better," he said, voice heavy with sarcasm. "Would someone please tell me why the hell I'm here?"

Chalo snapped from his own reverie and laughed. "Ahh, *caballero*, you are right. Enough nonsense. I found another heart today. In the fountain of my hotel."

"Jeezuz Chalo! I thought I misunderstood the radio. I let you out of my sight and look at the trouble you get into! What happened?"

"That's all, really. The fountain in the foyer of the hotel had blood in it; a workman climbed into the fountain to see what was up there; he found a human heart, pulled it out, fainted, and dropped the mess at my feet. The local constabulary are probably getting rid of it right now…"

"Plus they told me not to talk about the heart that I found…" Anya said over Chalo.

Stephen put up his hand and looked down at the table. "Hold on. Just hold on a second. Now we have how many hearts? Two? Three?"

"Two," Anya replied.

"Three," Chalo said at the same time.

Stephen stared at the two of them for a long moment and then snorted.

"Okay, Chalo, I've got no clue what's going on. How about you start all over again, maybe from the beginning?"

Chalo laughed, delighted to have Stephen's company once more, and then took a breath.

Anya spoke before he could begin.

"My story is the beginning." She bit the lemon wedge that she had been holding, shot her tequila, and held her breath for a moment before exhaling slowly through rounded lips.

"I am a Professor of Archaeology but I gave up my lectureship at the University in Mexico City three years ago to begin a small company here."

Stephen nodded. He was right that she had sounded like a teacher. He supposed he had sounded like that once.

"Yucatours," Chalo said, recalling her business card.

"Yes, that is my company. I have permission from the Mexican government to use volunteers—mostly tourists—to excavate the ruins in this province. In exchange, I catalogue and give everything I find to the *Museo Nacional de Antropologia.*"

Stephen and Chalo waited while Anya poured herself another drink.

"I started a new site three months since… I mean, three months ago. It is in Sian Ka'an Biosphere Reserve past Punta Pajaro and it is…" she paused, a sudden sparkle in her eyes.

"It is very hard to get to. By boat only. I take my first group of volunteers next month. It is a gorgeous early post-classical temple. Phenomenal, really—the vault is complete…" she drew a dome in the air with a single sweep of her arms and almost spilled her shot. "*Perfectly* complete! And the frescoes, like at Bonampak, are undamaged—bright as the day they were painted…" She looked at her audience and trailed off; they looked interested but vague.

Anya drank her tequila and started again.

"Nevermind," she continued perfunctorily. "The point is that I found a new ruin three months since. It is very special, archaeologically speaking. It has a temple and at the top of the temple is a chamber with a *chac mo'ol* altar in front of it. Three weeks since I arrived at my site and those policeman from today were there. The locals. All around the altar."

"But if your site is so hard to find, how did the police get there? Who else knew about what you found?" Stephen asked.

"By boat, and I don't know how they found it. The only people who have been there are my local helpers, and I trust them completely."

"And this was three weeks ago?" Chalo asked, bringing Anya back to her story. "What date?"

"November 18."

"Good. Go on."

"There was blood around the edges of the bowl and on the temple platform. They pointed their guns at me and told me to go away. I showed them my permit and told them that I would call CONAP and the Archaeology Museum if they didn't get off the ruins right away. One of them grabbed something from the bowl and another said that they would call CONAP themselves and have my permit taken away if I said anything to anyone about their visit."

"CONAP?" asked Stephen.

"*Comisión Nacional de Areas Protegidas Naturales*," replied Chalo. "They're in charge of the Biosphere Reserve. They have federal money. What happened next?" Chalo prompted.

"Well, nothing," admitted Anya. "But then, when you found the heart at the hotel…"

"Did you actually see a heart at your ruin, or did you assume it?" Stephen asked. "And why were you at the hotel, anyway? That seems a coincidence."

Anya pursed her lips. "What are we playing at: 'good cop, bad cop'?" Anya demanded.

"Well, usually Stephen is the good cop," Chalo joked.

"Alright. A bloody lump in a *chac mo'ol*. I assumed that it was a heart. But it is not a bad assumption, I think," Anya replied defensively. "And I was at the hotel," she glared directly at Stephen, "to see my brother. He arrived yesterday from Germany. I was to meet him there."

"Did you?" asked Stephen more gently.

"Did I what?"

"Did you meet him?"

"No, I didn't. He didn't come."

"He doesn't stay with you when he's here?"

"No, he's here for business. He likes…" she shrugged, disdainful. "He likes big hotels." She looked at Chalo this time, the same challenge in her eyes.

"I didn't choose it!" Chalo laughed, amused by Anya's scorn. "My work sent me, too."

"So now we have two hearts here in the Yucatán. What else?" Stephen asked, steepling his fingers and putting them to his chin.

"They were both found after *la Dia de los Muertos*," Anya said.

"Halloween?" Stephen asked.

"The Day of the Dead is November first," Anya replied. "But I do not mean the Christian Day of the Dead. The Mayan day of death is called *cimi*. It comes every 20 days. November 17th was 9 *cimi*; yesterday…" She looked at her watch. "… the day behind yesterday, was

3 *cimi.*"

"What day was October 8th?" demanded Stephen, suddenly.

"One minute." Anya put her empty shot glass down and pulled her iPhone from her back pocket.

"October 8th?" Chalo asked Stephen.

"The night at the warehouse."

Anya looked up from her phone, puzzled. "October 8th was 8 *cimi*. How did you know?"

"I guessed," Stephen replied.

"Very nice, *caballero*," Chalo said, nodding appreciatively.

Low clouds had moved in, obscuring the night sky and the distant rumble of thunder rolled across the sea. Stephen felt a prickle of fear at the back of his neck and realized that his hands were shaking. Chalo whistled through his teeth. A flash of lightning forked into the sea at the horizon.

"*Tun tal chaak*," Chalo said softly.

"What?" asked Stephen and Anya in unison.

"I said 'the rain is coming.' And you know what I think?"

Stephen and Anya shook their heads.

"I think we need another drink."

Chapter 10

The short wiry man, his auburn skin well weathered and creased with age, stepped out of his thatch-roofed hut and looked up at the late morning sky. The light was milky, the clouds high and thin, but building.

"*Chich'iik. Poquito chich'iik,*" the man muttered to the sky. "You are just a little storm. Not enough to stop me." Looking out to the jungle he added, "*Momentito*, my friends. I am almost on my way."

A thickset middle-aged woman with a broad ochre face, her *huipil* richly embroidered in blues and greens, stepped from her own oval shelter across the rutted dirt road. She smiled, her silver-edged teeth gleaming, as she watched the old man speak with things unseen. Then she frowned as he pulled on a pair of rubber boots caked with dried mud. She shook her head as he strapped a machete to his waist.

"*Don* Yaxché! Let me bring to you your breakfast before you go out." She spoke in staccato Yucatec.

"*Hola*, *Lupita*. Not now, not now," the old man said as he picked up a large burlap sack.

"No, no. I must go while the dew is still on the leaves for the medicine for the baby with the stomach troubles that came yesterday. I will eat when I am returned. Just before today's patients."

Lupita looked beyond the tiny hamlet to the green and riotous jungle. *Don* Yaxché went into that jungle every day to collect leaves and roots, disappeared into its dark maw along the tiny tongue of a footpath that he had worn into the Earth over almost fifty years.

She was proud of him, of his gift for healing. Thousands came to Blanca Flor from as far away as Guatemala to be cured, soothed, and mended by wise *El Mero*, the true one. But still, she thought, he was really too old at seventy-nine to go walking on an empty stomach. "I have it all ready, *Don* Yaxché," she protested. "I wish you would not go with your belly unfilled."

"Going empty is a sign of respect, Lupita," he said over his shoulder as he started out. "You make me a nice warm *atole* with vanilla. I will drink it when I am back. And pay you richly for it with flowers, too! The red ones like all the naughty boys used to bring to you to get into your hammock!"

Lupita laughed aloud and waved him on. "You are a crazy old goat, *Don* Yaxché!" she said to his strong old back.

"You're an old hen, then, Lupita. Tough and noisy! Vanilla in my *atole*—don't forget!" There was a smile in his voice as he went.

Lupita stood in her doorway for a moment to watch the old man go. The day smelled of life: rich earth steaming in the heat, wood fires cooking fresh corn tortillas, musky livestock rooting for a snack. She watched a curl of mist as it wound through distant mountain trees and shivered at a small breeze. She listened to the forest's twitters and cries: there a scold of squawking grackles; there the deep call of the fork-tailed mot-mot. Yaxché stumped, smaller and smaller, into the humid groves of *xaté*, *chicle*, and fig that lay beyond her purview. What things, invisible to her, did he see?

Chickens at her feet squawked over an errant kernel of corn, breaking Lupita's reverie. She turned inside to begin the vanilla *atole*, a silver smile for the healer upon her face.

***

Hernando Antonio Canul—the *curandero* known as Yaxché—stopped a moment, said a short prayer, and stepped gingerly off his footpath to follow the call of the forest.

"*Hola*, my friends, have you anything for me today?"

He moved carefully, as one walking through a room full of delicate seniors, touching leaves, nodding to flowers, patting trunks, smiling, frowning, whispering, chuckling. Almost an hour into his rounds he kneeled to inspect a small red bush then swept the soil from its base with a careful gnarled hand.

"Ahh… here you are. I have been looking for you for a long time, *amiga*," he said to the large white root he exposed. Unsheathing his machete, he sliced a chunk from the root and then covered what remained with soil. The cut piece he placed carefully into his sack.

"Thank you, old friend," he said as he stood, stretching his back with care. "Your gift will see us through the hard times."

"Hello, *chicalote*," he said to a poppy twenty minutes later, touching it gently with his fingertips as he walked by.

"The baby will appreciate your gift," he said as he cut a large clump of wormseed—good for colic—and put it in his sack.

"Go well," he said to a spirit crossing his path: a soul that only he could see. Then he stopped, skin suddenly prickling, to inspect the leaves above him.

The forest was deepening now to emerald green with the shadow of impending rain. Yaxché's fading eyesight forced him to squint in the dimming light. There. A pygmy owl, its ruddy dun breast lightly streaked, sat high, a dozen feet away, staring at him.

"*Muan*. I felt your eyes on me. Is it to be 'wisdom' or 'death' that you share with me today?" The owl meant both to the Maya.

The tiny raptor gazed at the old man, its yellow eyes unblinking. A moment later it swooped to a branch fifteen feet away.

"Wisdom, I hope," Yaxché said to himself. To the owl he added, "Alright *yuum tunkuruchu*. I follow."

When Yaxché was within five feet of it, the small bird flew onto another branch, its wings silent in the close, moist air. Yaxché realized that nothing else called or chittered or rustled: the jungle itself had fallen as silent as a dream.

"*Tamax chi?*" Yaxché wondered, his voice loud in the noiseless wilderness. An omen? Five branches and ten minutes later, the owl alit a *ceiba* tree and closed its eyes.

Yaxché laughed. "¡*Uay*! We're done now? You love me then you go to sleep? You must be a woman owl!" He laughed again. "Alright, I could use some rest, too. You'll make sure someone wakes me when it is time, yes?"

Letting his sack sink to the ground, the healer looked up at the giant grey tree, circular lime-green colonies of lichen adorning it. The *ceiba*—*yaxché* in Yucatec—was the centre of the universe. Yaxché stepped among the buttress roots of his namesake, turned, and sat down. The cool wood felt good against his sweating back. He grunted with pleasure and then, like the owl, closed his eyes and drifted into a light sleep.

The gentle susurration of soft rain woke him and he opened his eyes. A white-tailed deer was inspecting him with glossy brown eyes, her oval pupils dilated wide. Droplets patted gently onto her dusky back leaving tiny dark freckles of clumped fur.

"*Manik.* I am honoured. You are the herald. What do you announce?"

The doe suddenly drew up her hind legs and leaped forward, high and away. Yaxché watched her disappear, white tail raised in alarm, and trembled despite himself.

"*Mu'hak'al a wool,*" said a husky voice. *Do not be afraid.* Yaxché nodded, accepting the instruction, and then looked up.

The rain was now falling thick as rope. On the branch where the owl had been sat an alluring young woman, her skin dark, her hair black, her long white dress clinging to her curves. She looked luminous within the torrent, her insubstantial figure riven by the rain. Yaxché could almost see the water-dark forest though her bare feet. And still she was apart from the storm, her face and dress dry.

She opened her mouth to speak. Yaxché watched for a long moment but heard nothing except the rain driving against the forest floor. Her voice, empty as an echo returning from a deep chasm, came at last.

"*Li'saba,*" she said. A soft sibilant sound almost lost in the hissing of the rain.

Yaxché sat up, his pulse quickening. *Get ready.* "*Por qué*?" he asked. "For what?"

"*Ka'beh.*" A harsh word, thickly urgent. *The day after tomorrow.*

A drop of water fell into Yaxché's face and he blinked reflexively. When he reopened his eyes, the woman was gone.

Yaxché stopped just once on his way out of the jungle: to cut an armload of red cestrum for Lupita. He needed her vanilla *atole* to warm his cold, rain-soaked bones.

***

"Thanks for your call, Carolina, but with all due respect," Joe Wilkes said, "I gave you a vote on the foreign aid piece just yesterday. Tell me why I'd give you my vote on your 60/20 amendment when I already think reducing carbon emissions 60% by *2050* is a load of crap?"

Honey Hampton smiled from her desk outside Joe's office. She'd been his secretary for more than thirty years now—had started the week John Hinckley, Jr. had try to assassinate President Reagan—and still got a kick out of his negotiating style. He always sounded blunt as a sledgehammer, which was why people always underestimated him. He graduated Phi Beta Kappa from Stanford, had the memory of an elephant, the charm of a hummingbird, the precision of a surgeon, and eight terms in the Senate under his belt; he had gossip on just about everyone in town that he could use to his own benefit. Senator Carolina Schroeder included. Her 60/20 amendment was going nowhere without his support.

"Your timing is good, what with the Mexicans nationalizing Mitnal and everyone getting all fired up about energy shortages again, but that oil will be flowing again soon, and we don't have the technology to get us to the target in eight years. Not unless that *power plant* goes in down in Texas…"

Honey's smile widened. There it was, the hook, played out on a long line. She could hear the squeak and thump that said he was leaning back in his chair, was putting his size-gunboat feet on the mahogany desk, was enjoying the debate. She could bet he'd have one arm up in the air, stretching back almost to the bookshelf behind him, filling as much space as he could because he couldn't contain his delight over Carolina Schroeder, no political slouch herself, realizing that she'd just been foxed.

"Well, like I said, I think the whole thing is crap, but the cattle industry is having a hard time down in my neck of the woods and a new energy plant would help, I can tell you. Why don't you think about it and get back to me in a few days. We don't go to the vote until the end of next week. If you get back to me by the beginning of the week, I can probably pull you in a few favours and get you two, maybe three more votes, if your margin is tight…"

Honey heard the phone go down on its cradle—Joe hated cell phones, was in fact a luddite on most things technological—and put her Dictaphone earphones back on. They both knew she eavesdropped, but she had the good sense not to make it obvious, and he had the good sense not to say anything about it.

Joe Wilkes chuckled as he eased his chair upright and pulled his feet from his desk. Senator Schroeder really wanted that bill if she was deigning to call him. On a Sunday. Or maybe she really thought he was softening in his old age, what with giving his vote to Rebecca's jungle money. Fat lot Carolina knew. He was at the top of his game: now to put the final piece of the puzzle in place. He rose and went to the doorway.

"Honey?"

Her fingers were a blur over the keyboard—damn she was fast. Fast and smart and with instinct and balls bigger and better than most of the men on Capitol Hill, neatly disguised behind sunny southern manners. Libby had been the one to suggest he hire Honey. Libby had had the best instinct of anyone. He sighed at the thought of his dead wife. More than twenty years, and he still missed her.

"Honey! Take those damned earphones off and listen here!"

Honey looked up, saw Joe at the doorway, and pulled an earphone from her ear.

"You say something, Joe?"

"Yes I said something. I said 'take those damned earphones off and listen here!'"

"They're off, already. And I wouldn't need them on if you'd learn to use your own computer to send your own e-mail, Joe."

Joe laughed aloud. "If I'm such a nuisance, woman, why the hell do you stay?"

"I'm the only one with skin thick enough. Besides, no one gives such good Christmas presents. Phil and I had a great time on that cruise."

"Well, you earned it," he said, suddenly serious. "Speaking of which, get me the papers: there's a new mess in the Gulf. And Clay Powell is coming by and I need you to get us a late lunch. Maybe pepper steaks from The Alamo."

Honey's face fell. She didn't like Clayton Powell. "Medium rare for both of you?"

"Blue for him."

"Got it," she said as she picked up the phone. Under her breath she added, "I forgot; he likes everything bloody.

Spotlight on the Mitnal Rig:
Deepest Well in the World Raises the Bar by Lowering it

Petroleum Technology Quarterly, Special Edition
December 2012
From the Editor's desk

The higher the prices go, the deeper the rigs go. And as the new Mitnal rig in the Gulf of Mexico is showing, engineers are descending to the challenge, their creativity limited only by the heat at the centre of the Earth.

The platform, which will be officially declared operational on December 20, 2012, by Mexico's President Fernandez, is already pumping a healthy eight million barrels of heavy crude per day from the crushing depth of 4800 metres below the surface of the sea. The oil itself is a further 10,000 metres—a mind-bending 8 ½ miles—into the bowels of the Gulf of Mexico's lower tertiary trend. Proven by Chevron in 2006, the trend holds the planet's last known reserves of liquid crude. They are enormous, but getting to them has challenged the best engineering minds on the planet.

Beneath the ocean floor, the problem is one of extreme heat and pressure: 400-degree temperatures and pressures high enough to crush iron pipes. Immediately above the seabed, however, water temperatures plummet to near zero, necessitating next-generation insulation based on jackets of a sucrose-based anti-freeze not unlike that found in the blood of many extreme deep-water fish. And then there is the challenge of working offshore: how to build a platform that can pull petroleum from the ultra-deep and still house the hundreds of specialists needed to do the job on top of an unforgiving sea.

The secret to this last success lies with cell spar technology barely more than a decade old. These platforms float on a series of seven to ten enormous, partly hollow tubes, each of which stores oil and can take on or release seawater. This individual ballasting ensures buoyancy and stability that can be adjusted to various sea conditions. The platforms' "hard tops" are held in place over the drill site many thousands of metres below by a thrusting system of four enormous motors and a tight mooring system composed of anchors, chains, and high-performance polyester cables thicker than a man's thigh.

Mitnal represents engineering at its finest, proving once again that human ingenuity, channeled properly, can circumvent any problem. And while Mitnal has set the standard for now, it won't be long before the next rig heads deeper still.

HYDRATE ACCIDENT IN THE GULF: ENVIRONMENTALISTS CRY FOUL

The Science Monitor
December 9, 2012

An icy block of solid methane the size of a ten-storey apartment building has broken free of its deep-sea prison on the US seabed beneath the Gulf of Mexico, releasing as much as ten million tons of methane to the atmosphere. These blocks—known as clathrates—are undersea mountains of frozen methane gas. They form at "seeps" where oil and gas ooze from the Earth's crust, making them perfect locations to look for oil and gas. According to environmental groups, however, they are also highly unstable.

According to Mexican Environment Secretary Julio Molinar, the accident occurred last night at 23:42 hours GMT. It was reported by the exploration ship Western Neptune II, in the vicinity conducting a seismic mapping exercise, when the methane, which sublimates as it warms, bubbled to the surface. A sailor aboard described the release as "terrifying," calling it "a gigantic witches' cauldron, boiling like a sea in Hell."

A spokesman for the exploration company denied that exploration could have caused the release. Said Jack Twohy: "The charges we use are very small. The EPA has approved them for use around whales and dolphins, so we're confident we didn't cause the release."

The Gulf of Mexico Coalition—an environmental group calling for the establishment of Marine Protected Areas, or MPAs, around the clathrates—disagrees. Says Coalition spokesperson Melanie Hauser: "These mounds are known to be unstable. We need to steer clear of them. The risks to the environment are just too great."

Hauser is referring to the fact that methane is a greenhouse gas ten times more potent than carbon, and the prevailing theory that an enormous methane "burp" 55 million years ago pushed the climate from icy to tropical almost overnight—in geological terms—leading to mass extinctions.

The Coalition is now redoubling its efforts to have areas around methane hydrates set aside as MPAs; it is lobbying supporters of Senator Carolina Schroeder's (Dem, NM) "60/20" climate bill to add protection of clathrates into the controversial bill. Says Schroeder: "It makes good sense, since we're supposed to be moving away from oil anyway. The added benefit is that we'll be protecting an environment that we haven't even begun to explore."

Clathrate mounds support life-forms new to science, the strangest of which are six-foot-long ice worms, dubbed Xibalba worms. Named after the blind snakes that guard the Mayan underworld, the worms emerge to sway like curtains from holes in the clathrates themselves.

CHAPTER 11

The near-noon sun hung high in the tropical sky, leaving Anya's balcony in the shade of the one above it and the apartment cool in the breeze winding through the door's partly open curtains. The archaeologist padded from her bedroom to the kitchen, smiling with amusement when she saw Stephen asleep on the couch. He had lost the draw for the guest bedroom, and so lay on his side, long lanky frame curled into a foetal position to fit the furniture. Why didn't men share beds like women, anyway?

Looking down on her peaceful guest, his terror eased in sleep, she felt a surge of jealousy; she begrudged him his sighting of *Xtabay*. Anya had been in Mexico a long time. She had been studying the Maya for her entire adult life. She could speak Yucatec. If any foreigner was going to see a native apparition, it should be her. She scowled at her own pettiness and went to the kitchen to make coffee.

"Can I help with anything?" Anya jumped at the voice breaking into her reverie and looked up. Stephen was sitting up, running a hand through his sleep-tousled dark hair.

"Coffee?"

"Yes please."

"You slept well." It was a comment more than a question; he looked well-rested and none the worse for last night's drive or the drinks that had followed.

"I did. Thanks. Is Chalo…"

"Still asleep. I am having granola. You would like some?"

"That would be nice, thanks." He rubbed his hand across twenty-four hours of stubble then reached for his watch on the coffee table.

"Wow. It's late," he said as he strapped the watch back on.

"We were up until almost dawn," Anya said as she took granola from a cupboard. Pausing before pouring it into bowls, she looked directly at Stephen.

"Why do you think you saw *Xtabay* last night?"

"Why do you think it was *Xtabay* that I saw?" Stephen countered.

"You don't believe in her, do you?"

"I've taken enough science not to disbelieve in the possibility of anything, but I haven't seen much convincing evidence when it comes to ghosts. Do you believe in her?"

"I haven't seen her."

"That wasn't what I asked."

Anya shrugged to hide her irritation. "Chalo—will he have granola also?"

Stephen's laugh was warm and genuine. "Chalo? He's more of a *huevos rancheros* kind of guy."

"You know him well." Again, it was an observation more than a question.

"Like the back of my hand…" he shook his head. "And not the slightest little bit. Just like Mexico."

Anya smiled at the response.

"You go tomorrow back to Canada?"

"Day after tomorrow." Nodding to the knapsack beside the coffee table, he added, "Everything except that flew out yesterday."

"You are sad to leave Mexico?"

Stephen was quiet for a moment. "It is time for me to go."

"That wasn't what *I* asked," she echoed him.

She watched clouds of emotions scud across his handsome angular face, his deep-set eyes unreadable.

"I won't be sad to leave Mexico City."

"What about Chalo?"

Stephen nodded slowly and said nothing for a long while. "They broke the mould after they made Chalo. He's infuriating and funny… kind when no one is looking and a pain-in-the-ass when they are… Yeah, I'm going to miss him. A lot."

Stephen and Anya both jumped at the unexpected sound of a third voice.

"*Caballero*! You are going to make me cry!"

Chalo was standing barefoot in the guestroom doorway, dishevelled in last night's clothes. Stephen glanced at his partner, looked back to Anya, rolled his eyes and returned his gaze to Chalo.

"Cry? You? Ha!"

Chalo clutched his heart "You wound me, *caballero*! I will cry when you leave. After Christmas."

Stephen laughed. "I'll be on my plane day after tomorrow. I have a date with a dusty pair of skis and a nephew who is a terror on the slopes."

"Yes, yes. So you say. We'll see. My stomach's instinct tells me another thing." He paused for a moment to watch Anya finish cutting a banana.

"¡*Uay*, *hermano*! Where are your manners, making this lovely lady serve you? We should be inviting her out for breakfast!"

"'Gut' instinct, Chalo. It's… oh never mind."

To Anya he added, "As much as I hate to admit it, Chalo is right. Can we take you to breakfast to repay your hospitality?"

"Say yes," Chalo prompted with a winning smile.

Anya shook her head and smiled. "I would be delighted. There is an excellent café just down the street."

"Excellent! But no café." Chalo said, grinning. "We have at least one crime scene to go to. Maybe two. First we go to my hotel. I change, we have breakfast there, and we see if my evidence is still in the fridge. Then we go to the good doctor's ruins, yes?"

Anya and Stephen stood silent in surprise.

"Good! It's settled. Let me just get my shoes."

CHAPTER 12

"Hey Bender! How are you, boy?"

Peter Nguyen had swivelled in his chair as he heard the approaching sound of paws galloping across the NHC's grey broadloom. The dog careened to a stop beside him, tongue lolling and tail wagging, looking for a pat. Peter obliged, earning a string of dog drool on his khaki trousers.

"Nice, Ben. Thanks a bunch," the man grimaced. "Where's the boss?"

The dog turned around and trotted down the hall towards Kathy's office. Peter followed and, popping his head around the doorjamb, began to speak. Kathy held up a square hand, stopping him as she spoke into the phone. She was testy, as she had been with everyone since Hurricanes *Pi* and *Rho* had so precipitously blown out.

"No ma'am. That *isn't* what I'm saying. Our predictive abilities have improved enormously in the past twenty years, but the climate is also becoming more variable as a result of climate change. So we're trying to *predict* something that's becoming less predict*able*. Two hurricanes forming this late in the season is unexpected; that the jet stream would go all wonky—not the scientific term, by the way—and shut them down was unimaginable until yesterday when it happened…"

Kathy rolled her eyes for Peter's benefit before reaching down to stroke the dog, now at her side.

"Yes ma'am. I'd be happy to explain that on the air. Again." Her face hardened into anger.

"No ma'am, it *is* simple. Simple as a Sunday picnic. Everyone is doing something to the weather and no-one's talking about it. With respect, your viewers don't want to talk about it because it means they might have to get their fat asses outta their cars and walk to the corner store for a quart of milk."

Nguyen smiled at Howlachuk's cantankerousness. It was funny, he thought, how the media loved her, despite her curmudgeonly style. Maybe they liked her *because* of it.

"No ma'am, of course I wouldn't say that on the air."

She paused and then pulled her iPhone close.

"Umm hmm. Yes ma'am. Righty-oh. Tonight at seventeen hundred hours… yes, that's five pm, ma'am. I'll have my office send you some satellite imagery."

"Skandar Hanson?" Peter asked as Kathy hung up the desk phone.

"Yes. No. The dippy broad that works for him. At least Skandar's got a brain behind those handsome brows. They want me linked-in to tonight's news to explain why those damned storms petered out.

"The old 'weathermen are as trustworthy as lawyers' story. I'll be interested to hear how you try to explain it. You think you use an expression other than 'petered out,' by the way?"

"Ha! Blame your parents for your name, Pete, not me. Can I use the one about the lawyers?"

It was Peter's turn to laugh. "Fill your boots. I'm about to get a bite to eat… want me to grab you something?"

"Where you goin'?"

"Maybe across the street to Ethel's." Ethel's made an egg salad sandwich that Kathy adored. Bender adored the crusts.

"How 'bout we come along? Bender needs a pee break, since we'll be here for a while yet." Kathy pushed herself away from her desk and added, "Tell me something."

"Sure. What?"

"What's so damn hard for people to understand about global warming?"

"You know that answer as well as I do. It started with calling it 'global *warming*.' That sounds pretty good in the middle of a North Dakota blizzard."

They walked through the maze of corridors and computer rooms that led out of the building, Bender following behind, sniffing at cubicles and doorframes as he went.

"Come on! Fires in California, horrible droughts in the Midwest, heat waves all up the eastern seaboard… even if it was just 'warming,' it's not looking so nice anymore."

"People are scared now. They don't understand what it is or what to do about it."

"But Pete, what's not to understand? It's common sense as much as it is science. What's not to understand about heat driving our weather just like gas drives our cars? Add more heat and the weather gets wilder, right? The answer is to use renewable energy, and less of it, if it comes to that."

They were at the front door now, stepping out into Florida's December sun. They both shivered in the chill air pushed south by the unusually deep jet stream trough. Kathy was on a rant now; Peter just let her go.

"I mean, *this*! This *cold*. We're damned lucky it cooled off the system enough to shut down *Pi* and *Rho*, but it doesn't mean that global warming isn't a problem. Fact is, completely unpredictable shit like this is the sign it's gonna get worse—not only worse than we *think*, but worse than we *can* think."

"Humans need to think we're invulnerable or we'll go mad."

They were at the intersection now, and traffic was weekend slow. Even so, Kathy snapped her fingers for Bender, calling him to her side while they waited for the light to change.

"But it's just *us*, you know. Here in the Excited States. Like it's a product of the American frontier mentality. I mean, the European Union, Russia, India and—God love 'em—even the Chinese are doing their damn'dest to reduce emissions. I just can't figure out why we can't get our heads out of our asses!"

"Nice, Kath. Really nice. We *are* doing something. The Administration has made it a big issue since 2008."

"Sure, but look at what the bastards in the Senate are doing to hold everything up!"

"Schroeder isn't."

"She's no match for the Bayou Butterfly."

"Joe Wilkes? How'd such a luddite get named after the Chaos Theory, anyway?"

"Some smart-ass in the media. Took the discussion of weather and linked it to Wilkes' power in Washington. Clever, actually. Butterfly flaps its wings in China and causes a hurricane in the Atlantic; Bayou

Butterfly sneezes and the Capitol gets a cold. Or maybe I should say a fever, given how opposed he is to Schroder's climate bill. Bastard."

"I dare you to say that next time you're on the air!"

"Nah, I'm too chicken-shit to go that far. Especially since, besides being a public servant and therefore one of my bosses, he's almost family. And almost nice, in person. I met him at Becky's wedding. I'll behave. As much as I usually do, at least. You just watch."

"Of course I'll watch. Someday you'll decide not to hold your tongue, and I want to be the first to know about my promotion when you blow it."

"Now who's being nice? Light's green. Shut up and let's go get Bender his egg sammy."

***

It should have been an easy thirty minutes to Chalo's hotel but it took Stephen, Chalo, and Anya the better part of two hours. Stranded in bumper-to-bumper traffic, they were passed on the shoulder by knots of men and women on foot, all of whom had abandoned the minibuses that served as public transit on the tourist strip between Cancún and Tulum in order to get to work on time.

Past Playa del Carmen, they discovered the source of the traffic jam: a tour bus on fire in the middle of the road. Choking clouds of thick sooty smoke smelling of burning plastic billowed from shattered windows. Sunburned tourists stood, stunned, at the side of the road, staring at their melting luggage. A few took pictures. A few hugged each other. A man yelled into his cellphone. Still on empty stomachs at close to two o'clock, Stephen, Chalo, and Anya were growing impatient and argumentative.

"*Mal den Teufel nicht an die Wand*," Anya muttered under her breath as they crept by the touring inferno.

"What?" asked Chalo, leaning forward from the back seat.

Busy trying to avoid hitting pedestrians and being cut off by local drivers, Stephen paid scant attention to his passengers.

"Just speaking with myself."

"No really. What did you say?"

"When we got into the car in Cancún you said that you were sure the traffic would be bad. So just now I said '*mal den Teufel nicht an die*

Wand.' In German it means 'speak of the devil and he comes."

"My *mamich* used to say 'Don't call to the Lords of Xibalba unless you want them.'"

"That's Yucatec," Anya observed, suddenly less grouchy. "Is your greatmother..." She paused to find the correct English word. "Sorry. Is your grandmother still alive?"

"No. She died when I was ten years old."

They had passed the burning bus at last and now the traffic was moving swiftly. Stephen thought about joining the conversation and decided against it. He wanted to see how a scholar of the ancient Maya would navigate the reality of today's Maya on her own.

"She was Maya, yes? From where?"

"The highlands of Guatemala, actually."

"And you? Were you born there?"

"Yes."

"Then when did you come to Mexico City?"

Stephen braced himself for what would come next. Would Chalo cut her some slack because he was sweet on her?

"After my *abuela* died." He was volunteering nothing. Anya's curiosity in all things Mayan—Chalo included—was blinding her. She should be leaving well enough alone.

"What about your parents?"

"The government of Guatemala does not like the Maya. Even more than the Mexican government doesn't like us. They killed my whole village. They killed my parents while I watched from behind my grandmother's skirts. She died of tuberculosis in the concentration camp they called a resettlement town. I ran away from the camp and ended up in Mexico City living on the streets until Father Delagado collected me. And before you ask, Father Delgado was a Catholic Priest, now also dead, who took in orphans, gave us food and education and told us to forget our *indio* past. I supposed I should thank him, because otherwise I would be dead or in a gang." Chalo leaned back hard against the back seat and fell silent.

"*Indigeno*," corrected Anya, falling back on the safety of tutelage in the face of Chalo's contained rage.

"Oh yes, pardon me," Chalo said belligerently. "That is the nice word for the Maya now. Just like 'African-American' is the nice way

Americans say 'nigger.' But you, of all people Dr. von Eckhardt, should know that we're all really niggers to the rest of Mexico. Isn't that right, Esteban? Just like the First Nations in your country. What did you say the white bastards call them…"

Stephen said nothing and kept his eyes on the road, but Anya rose to the bait.

"That's absurd. Most Mexicans are *mestizos*… people of mixed European and Mayan blood. The government makes no distinction between *indigeno* and *mestizo*."

"No, but there sure as hell is a 'distinction' between those and a *crillolo*, isn't there? Nice pure blood they can trace all the way back to the *conquistadores*, hmm?"

Anya glowered at the term *crillolo* and swivelled in her seat to face Chalo.

"*Crillolos* are a minority, and an arrogant fringe minority, as well. The government does not support racism in any form…"

"The government!" Chalo snorted. "You have to believe that because you need the government to give you permission to study here. If you didn't believe it, you'd have to face the fact that you're a collaborator."

Stephen's eyebrows went up. Calling someone a collaborator wasn't nice; calling a German a collaborator was even less nice.

"Whoa, *hermano*," Stephen said evenly. "You might want to take that one back…"

"Why, Esteban? No matter what the government says or does, it is the rest of the country that doesn't like the Maya. To them we are lazy thieving dirty *indios*. But I am sorry if Dr. von Eckhardt was offended."

The car sped on to Tulum, its occupants silent as they watched the jungle slide by. Scarred by Hurricane Wilma in 2005, the trees, mute testament to the strength of nature, stood drunken and twisted, but still alive.

Anya nodded but, still stinging from both rebuke and insult, she needed the last word.

"I accept your apology, Chalo, but you are wrong. Not everyone thinks the Maya are dirt. And the Maya themselves will prove that to the world."

"Really?" Chalo asked under his breath as he leaned back into the back seat. "Really? I can't wait to see how."

Sunday, December 9, 2012 – 5 Lamat, Day of Venus

CHAPTER 13

Clayton Powell opened the glass door to Senator Joseph Wilkes' office suite and sloped, long and bow-legged, to Honey Hampton's desk. His cowboy boots fell hard even through the thick beige carpet on the floor.

"Ma'am." The tall man doffed his cowboy hat to reveal greying hair, neatly trimmed. He held the hat over the left lapel of his long heavy sheepskin coat, as if covering his heart, ready to recite the Pledge of Allegiance.

"Mr. Powell. The Senator will be with you in a moment. Can I get you a coffee while you wait?"

"I'm obliged, Honey, but at this hour it'll keep me awake all night. What are you doing here on a Sunday, anyway?"

"No rest for the wicked, Mr. Powell," she said curtly.

"Don't I know it!"

I'll bet you do, Honey thought. As far as she was concerned, Clayton Powell was wickedness personified.

"A soda then?"

"That'll do fine, Honey."

By the time she got back with Powell's drink, Wilkes had emerged from his office and was striding across the reception area, hand outstretched.

"Clay! Hope you're hungry… Honey's ordered us a feast from The Alamo!" As he spoke, Joe put his own left hand on top of their clasped right ones, lengthening the contact. "You good? And the kids? And what do I hear about that filly, Dolly Gray?"

Honey stopped, Powell's drink in her hand. Joe was only effusive when he was anxious. Why was he nervous around his oldest and closest friend?

Powell grinned like a boy with a new toy and Joe released the handshake, his shoulders relaxing as he did so.

"Lordy, Joe, you should see that girl run… like a hurricane! She's going to be wearing Black-eyed Susans at Pimlico this year or I'll eat my hat. How'd you hear about her?

"You know me, Clay. I got my sources."

"Of course you do. It's why we're such a good team. Kids and the missus are fine, by the way; thanks for asking."

"Glad to hear it. The kids coming home for Christmas?"

"You bet. We were thinking of heading to the Gulf Coast for a bit of R&R, but Kitty's due any day now so we need to stay close at home to meet the next generation."

Honey watched a cloud of pain cross Joe's face: there would be no grandchildren for him.

"Your drink, Mr. Powell," Honey interrupted, distracting Joe from Powell's cruel words. And they were cruel; Powell, she was sure, never did anything unpremeditated.

"Thank you, Honey. How 'bout you, Joe? Got any Christmas plans? How about Mexico? Should be nice and warm there right about now, shouldn't it?"

Turning to Honey, Powell winked and added, "It's a tropical paradise, I hear. Why don't you get Joe to send you down there instead of on those damned cruises?"

"Leave the woman alone, Clay. The cruises are her choice. Now come on in here where we can talk about Mexico in private."

Joe led his guest into his office; Powell closed the door behind them, the metal latch snicking tight into the jamb.

There would be no eavesdropping for Honey this evening, just when it might have been a good idea for her to be quietly in the know.

***

"Welcome to my home away from home," Chalo said sardonically as he stepped from the rental car and spread his arms towards the wide breezeway that led from the circular driveway to the hotel's lavish lobby and beyond. A young man in a safari suit rushed to open Anya's door; another trotted to Stephen's.

Stephen got out of the car and glanced over it at Chalo, brows furrowed.

"Let him take the car, Esteban. Let's go straight to the kitchen, hmm?"

"Good idea. I'm starving."

"To check on the evidence, *caballero*. Food right after. In the dining room where the civilized people eat, hmm?"

"I thought you said last night that you thought it would be gone?" Anya asked as she stepped from the car.

"I did. I do. Still, I need to check. Hope springs eternal, yes? That's what Esteban says, anyway. Even if he doesn't believe it."

Chalo took the pair of stairs up to the breezeway in a single step then paused briefly. "¡*Andale, amigos*!"

Stephen scowled at Chalo's back, handed the keys to the attendant, and joined Anya at the bottom of the stairs, where a small wrinkled man in a white shirt knelt. He had been fixing a square of marble that had lost its grout, but was now speaking with Anya in Yucatec. Stephen waited a moment, watching as the woman nodded and the old man broke into a wide silvery grin before waving her away.

"You know him?"

"Not him, but his nephew. I know quite a few of the families around here because of my work..." She paused as she looked down the breezeway and frowned as she caught another glimpse of the fountain from which the heart had yesterday been liberated.

"It really is an abomination, you know."

"What is?" Stephen asked, not following Anya's train of thought.

"The fountain. Too big. Too placid. Facing the wrong direction. And the water makes him look like he is pissing. It is ridiculous."

"What direction should he be facing?" Stephen asked as they walked.

"West. Direction of the setting sun and of death. To receive a symbol of death in payment for the gift of life."

"Which would explain why the heart was in it, right?"

"Yes, but only near the end of the Mayan Empire, when it fell under the influence of the Aztecs. They were altogether a much more violent culture. Historically speaking, of course."

Stephen nodded at her political qualifier: no need to rile today's Aztecs.

"The Maya," she continued, "mostly engaged in ritual bloodletting. Finger and tongue piercing—enough to wet the stone. Kings pierced their penises too." She looked pointedly at Stephen to see his reaction.

Stephen felt his testicles clench involuntarily. "Lovely. Why?"

"To the Maya, everything was connected to everything else. The Earth gives life, so life must be given back to Earth. A great cycle, like the calendar, like all of time, in perfect harmony, repeated over and over again."

"Some tattooing was thought to be a blood-letting practice in the Canadian Arctic—a way to rid an evil spirit or appease the gods for a bad act…" Stephen replied.

Anya stopped and looked at Stephen quizzically. Her surprise irritated him.

"Just because I'm a cop doesn't mean I'm stupid. I did a Master's degree before I joined the Force, thank you very much."

Chalo, who had walked ahead, now turned back and tapped his foot with theatrical impatience.

"You invite the nice doctor on a date some other time, *caballero*. For now, you hurry."

Chalo's ribbing, designed to hide his own attraction for the archaeologist, did nothing to soothe Stephen's irritation at Anya's condescension.

"We're coming, already. Whoever it is isn't going to get any deader. Why the freaking rush?" he replied testily.

"*Si, si*, of course you are coming…" replied Chalo. He turned to resume his march, waving a hand at the large artificial Christmas trees at the end of the breezeway, each festooned with red satin bows and liberally sprayed with plastic snow foam. "So is Christmas!"

"In what?" Anya asked Stephen as they hurried to catch up to Chalo.

"'In what' what?"

"Your degree. In what?"

"Geology. Looking for evidence of the tsunami that accompanied the Chicxulub event…"

Stephen trailed off as he watched Chalo point left and then disappear, grinning. Intent on his partner, he didn't notice the renewed surprise in Anya's eyes when she heard the name Chicxulub.

"Oh hell. Where's he going now? We'd better catch up before he gets himself into trouble..."

***

"That hydrate thing is a hell of a mess..." Wilkes began as he motioned Powell to one of chairs flanking a round oak table in the corner of the office.

"Great, ain't it? Proves we were right when we started planning to buy the Mexican government four years ago!"

"That isn't why we started this, Clay!"

"Sure it is, Joe. When I put a chunk of change down on exploring Mitnal, I knew I was looking in foreign waters and that, given Mexico's history, some nationalist bastard might try to keep my profit from me. Why do you think I finally called in that favour you owe me?"

"And how exactly is our support for a rebellion in the Mexican jungle going to help you stop the world's environmentalists from closing down the goddamned clathrate fields?"

"Don't be stupid, Joe. Once we overthrow the government and our pal Vargas is in the President's office, we get him to denationalize again, we get cheap oil stateside, the economy keeps humming along on Mitnal's oil and, since we don't need to explore near clathrates, there's nothing for the bean-munching, tree-hugging loonies to fight.

"Way to put a patriotic spin on it, Clay. It doesn't hurt that you benefit, does it?"

"Course not. But I'm a philanthropist, Joe. Two percent of my wealth will help the rest of America, so doesn't it make sense to save my money?" His tone was magnanimous but not entirely sincere.

"The point is this," he continued, a less-than-pleasant smile on his face. "When this whole thing goes down, Vargas will be president. And Vargas is *ours*. Bought and paid for. We'll be in charge south of the Rio Grande."

"And if we don't kill Kulkulcan? Or if he kills Vargas? Then the Mexican Presidency *won't* be 'ours'."

"That's a lot of doubt in our op for the father of a decorated war hero, Joe."

"Leave Hayden out of this, Clay."

"I'm not bringing him into this, Joe. You're the one who sounds like you don't think our Marine down there can do the job."

"State thinks diplomacy will get you your money back," Joe said, recalling Rebecca's presentation the previous day. "How much you got in, anyway?"

"Every single thing I own is in Mitnal. I could lose it all. And State knows shit."

"That's a pretty arrogant view of your own government, Clay." Joe replied, anger rising at the insult to the institution he embodied. "I say we give State 24 hours." Joe hadn't planned the delay, but ire and spite got the better of him.

Powell stared daggers and was about to speak but a knock at the door stopped him.

"Supper's here, Senator," said Honey's voice through the oak door.

"Bring it on in, Honey," Joe called.

The two men sat in tense silence as Joe's secretary laid the table for them and served the meals.

"That's all, Hon. Thanks. You go on home now and enjoy what's left of the weekend. See you in the morning."

Yes, Senator," Honey replied. "See you in the morning." She left the door ajar as she went.

***

Stephen and Anya finally caught up to Chalo in the kitchen, his arm around a dejected young man in the green uniform of the local constabulary. The room hustled around them, aproned and hair-netted men and women preparing for the coming supper rush.

"They'll fire me for certain," said the young constable. It was Rico Mendez, the officer who only yesterday had been so impressed with Chalo's masculine abilities. His eyes widened when he saw Anya and then narrowed when he saw Stephen—a stranger—with her.

"*¿Quién es él?*" demanded Rico, nodding roughly towards Stephen.

"My partner. Let's go somewhere more quiet, hmm?"

They stepped outside into the bright loading bay behind the kitchen, hot and ripe with the odour of rotting scraps. Flies buzzed around a recently emptied garbage bin.

"Why do you think you'll be fired, Rico?" Chalo asked good-naturedly, arm still around the boy. It was an intimate gesture—an older to a younger brother—and intimidatingly close for the young constable.

"I… lost the heart. I didn't mean to. I drank a lot of coffee. And cola. I never even left to go to the toilet… but I fell asleep."

Chalo looked at Stephen and nodded.

"Did you get the coffee yourself?" Stephen asked.

"No. I told you, I never even left the fridge. One of the maids brought me the coffee. The chief brought me the cola before he went home for the night."

"What time was that, young Rico?" Chalo asked.

"Maybe almost midnight…"

"And when did you fall asleep?"

"I… I don't know."

"What's the next thing you remember after drinking the cola?"

"The cook beginning breakfast at… at maybe six o'clock this morning."

Stephen nodded back at Chalo.

"And you checked in the fridge when you woke up and it was gone, yes?"

"Yes."

"You told your chief?"

"N… no."

"It's almost four o'clock Rico! Why have you not said anything to anyone?

"Because I'll get fired!"

"No you won't."

The boy stopped dead, his incipient panic halted. "I won't? Why not?"

"Tell him, Esteban."

"You were drugged," Stephen answered matter-of-factly. "Your chief probably put something in the cola. He wanted the heart stolen."

"The Chief? Why?"

"That's the mystery, Rico." Chalo said with relish as he released the boy.

"But… but what do we do?"

"*You* go to tell your boss. You'll get in a little trouble for appearance's sake. Maybe have to do some job you don't like for a bit."

"But what about the heart?"

"Long gone."

"What will you do?"

"I have another lead in my sleeve, Rico. Now go talk to your boss, hmm?"

The young man turned to leave, unhappy over his prospects.

"Oh, one more thing, Rico," Chalo asked. Stephen smiled. The zinger was coming. In that way Chalo was not unlike Peter Falk's Columbo.

"What do you know about Kulkulcan?"

The young man blanched. "Nothing. I know nothing."

***

"It's 'up' your sleeve, Chalo. And *what* other lead do you have?"

Chalo and Stephen had sent Rico off in search of his superior officer and were now standing in front of the locked glass doors of the dining room.

"I've been here two weeks now and I still don't understand: how can an 'all-day buffet' be closed from four o'clock to five-thirty?" Chalo said, ignoring the question.

"And why were you asking about Kulkulcan?" Anya asked, ignoring Chalo's question in turn.

"Can you wait until 5:30 to eat?" Chalo continued.

"Honest to God, Chalo. What other lead do you have?" Stephen asked, exasperated.

"All in good time, *hermano*. I stink. I can't think when I stink. Go get some potato chips or something from the gift store while I have my shower and I'll explain everything over dinner."

***

Outside the door, Honey listened intently.

"Four people—senior Mexican *politicos* all of them—are *already* going to die, Joe." Powell growled. He dug his fork into a mound of mashed potatoes, shovelled them into his mouth, and resumed before swallowing.

"The ends justify the means," Powell said, errant potatoes escaping as spittle. "We stop the Mexicans from creating an oil monopoly that'll send the economy into a tailspin and happen to get my money back in the process. What's the big deal?"

"'The big deal,'" Joe said, his cutlery abandoned with a clank on his plate, "is that if this doesn't go according to plan, the economy still goes down the toilet and it won't be just four Mexican politicians, but hundreds of innocent kids that are going to die!"

"You sound like that bleeding heart daughter-in-law of yours."

"She might be a bleeding heart, but her logic is solid on this one, Clay. If you really want your money back, we're better off with the devil we know."

"Bullshit, Joe. Why the hell would Mexico negotiate? They already have the oil. The devil we're better off with is the one we can *control*."

"Nobody controls the Devil, Clay. Its why he's the Devil… he was too proud to submit to God."

"Don't be quoting scripture to me. You were only a good Christian because of Libby, God rest her soul."

"You leave Libby out of this, too."

"I'm the one who introduced you to Libby. I'll mention her if I damn well please."

"All I'm saying, Clay, is we should just hold off for a few days. See if diplomacy will work."

Honey had been listening by the door, coat half on. Now she heard nothing for a long moment but the sounds of eating.

"We've known each other a long time, Joe," said Powell's voice, at last. "I know a lot of things that could ruin you."

"Is that a threat, Clay?"

"I can tie you to this."

"That *is* a threat."

"You bet it is, Joe. I'm not going to lose my money."

Honey leaned on the wall outside to steady herself against her surprise.

"And what exactly do you think you can threaten me with, Clay?" Joe asked, a chuckle in his question.

"I could do this on my own, Joe. I've got a backdoor to the op that you don't even know about."

"Oh really? And what is that?"

"It doesn't matter, Joe. You're going to this because I know about Hayden."

"What about Hayden?" Joe's voice was suddenly cautious, suddenly thin and Honey was suddenly worried.

"Hayden's memory is more important to you than anything, isn't it, Joe? His purple heart and his reputation. I have proof that can take them both away. I know how your precious boy really died."

Hurricanes Pi and Rho, Part 2

December 9, 2012
Transcript of an interview between Skandar Hanson, CNN, and Dr. Katherine Howlachuk, Senior Scientist at the National Oceanographic and Atmospheric Administration (NOAA) National Hurricane Center.

***Skandar Hanson**: Okay, Kathy. Let's get right to it. The question on everyone's minds is "what happened to the hurricanes?"*

***Dr. Katherine Howlachuk**: My colleague at the NHC, Dr. Peter Nguyen, said that after this, people'll think weathermen are about as trustworthy as lawyers, but really, this one is a shock to all of us.*

***Hanson** (laughter): Why is that?*

***Dr. Howlachuk**: Well, despite what it looks like, our skills at predicting weather have gotten better and better over the past fifteen years. Problem is, the weather has gotten harder to predict in that same period.*

***Hanson**: You say the reason for that is global warming. Explain that for our viewers, please.*

***Dr. Howlachuk**: Yes. Imagine you've got a snowball and you leave it on the counter. Even though it's melting, it looks pretty much like a snowball. Then the heat energy starts working on it. Heat energy from the air acts on the ice to produce what's called a "state change" from a solid to a liquid. The change to the whole ball happens gradually, but you don't really notice it 'til it's a puddle on your counter, dripping onto the floor, and your Ma is yelling at you to go play outside.*

***Hanson** (laughter)*

Dr. Howlachuk: *Since the 2007 IPCC report...*

Hanson: *... the United Nations' Intergovernmental Panel on Climate Change...*

Dr. Howlachuk: *Yessir. Since the IPCC report in 2007, everybody's agreed that human activity is responsible for global warming. Now the debate is about how bad it's going to be and what we can do about it. Meanwhile, the planet is already "changing state," to something with more energy in it. That energy makes it more unpredictable. Like the ice sitting on the counter minding its own business that, when it melts, starts dribbling onto the floor who knows where, making a hell of a mess.*

Hanson: *So what does your snowball have to do with the collapse of the two Category 4 hurricanes before they entered the Gulf of Mexico? I thought that the warm water in the Gulf was supposed to strengthen and accelerate hurricanes?*

Dr. Howlachuk: *Right again, except that this time, the jet stream saved our butts.*

Hanson: *How?*

Dr. Howlachuk: *How about you pop up that movie file I brought along. (pause) Now, this first clip is of the jet stream like you're used to it: a kind of meandering snake running across the continent like a belt, usually running west to east about parallel with the Canada-US border. Now in this second clip, you see a typical deviation, where the jet stream drops down to about southern Michigan, bringing cold air there. But this clip... this is what just happened. The jet stream decided to play tourist, and it headed straight down from Seattle to south of Texas and over to the tip of Florida, pulling a huge mass of cold dense Arctic air down with it. That's why the fruit growers are having kittens about now. But, lucky for us, that big slug of frigid air acted like a broom and a vacuum all at the same time: it pushed back on the trade winds that were driving the hurricanes west towards us, stalling the system out at sea, and then the intense cold stole all the energy that was building those hurricanes. In my language, the conditions necessary to create a hurricane were no longer present, so the storms lost their coherence and intensity. When they finally made landfall in New Orleans, they were barely tropical storms.*

Hanson: *What would have happened if the jet stream hadn't, as you say, played tourist?*

Dr. Howlachuk: *Well, my guess is that it would have been gotten pretty rough again down in the Big Easy.*

Hanson: *So are we safe now?*

Dr. Howlachuk: *That's the billion dollar question, Skandar. I'd say we're safe from* Pi *and* Rho, *but the jet stream has returned to its more regular path, and with sea surface temperatures in the Gulf and, in fact, across the Atlantic, the highest on record, I'd say we could still get a whopper.*

Hanson: *You mean another hurricane? Haven't you told us that the hurricane season ended on November 30th?*

Dr. Howlachuk: *Yessir, I have. But you tell that to Mother Nature.*

Hanson: *That's what you mean by "the weather is becoming more unpredictable." Maybe we'll be seeing you again before Christmas.*

Dr. Howlachuk: *No offence, Skandar, but I hope not.*

Hanson: *None taken. Up next, a look at sports.*

(end of transcript)

CHAPTER 14

"Why was Chalo asking about Kulkulcan, Stephen?"

Stephen and Anya were sitting beside the hotel pool closest to the lobby, nibbling at ripple potato chips and squinting against the late afternoon sun as they waited for Chalo.

"The more important questions," Stephen replied, "are, who *is* Kulkulcan and why is that young cop so scared of him."

"Why is that more important?"

Stephen glanced towards a knot of toddlers splashing in the shallow end and then askance at their thin blonde mothers, perfectly tanned and manicured, drinking margaritas from plastic cups, oblivious to their children.

"Because anyone that has the police scared is important."

"Why must Kulkulcan be a person?" Anya challenged.

"Because I'm pretty sure Chalo wouldn't have been asking an Hispanic city kid about a feathered snake god revered by the ancient Mayans."

"'Mayan" is the adjective; the noun is 'Maya.'"

"Isn't that open to debate?"

"Didn't you say *Geology* was the subject of your graduate work?" The implication was clear; he was treading on her academic turf.

"Evidence of tsunami activity at the K-T boundary," Stephen condescended. He could play the academic game, too.

"And in English?" Anya replied, unimpressed.

"The K-T boundary," he said with exaggerated simplicity, "is the geological date, sixty-five million years ago, that divides the Cretaceous from the Tertiary Era. It corresponds to the meteor strike responsible for the extinction of the dinosaurs. The meteor created the Chicxulub crater west of here, and the network of *cenotes* across the Yucatán Peninsula. It was a massive strike and should have caused a tsunami that propagated around the world. I was looking at the K-T boundary in BC for evidence of the wave. Sediments and marine microorganisms in the mountains."

"So that is why you know so much about Mexico."

"No, actually, I know about Mexico because I like to read and listen and get to know things. I've been reading and listening for four years now. Not that I actually understand it any better."

"Why did you abandon Geology?" Anya asked, changing the subject.

"I… I lost someone. I needed to get away from home for a bit."

"Oh."

Anya didn't want to get to know his problems; she had enough of her own. The conversation ground to a halt. Stephen pulled a pencil from his shirt pocket and started doodling on a cocktail napkin.

"Why do *you* think he mentioned Kulkulcan?" Stephen asked, at length.

"What?" Lost in her own thoughts, Anya was startled by the question.

"Chalo. You asked me why I thought he asked about Kulkulcan. What do *you* think?"

"I agree that he wasn't speaking about the god. I think it has something to do with the Maya rebellion that is building here on the Yucatán."

"The government says there's nothing to that."

"'The government says.' Didn't Chalo say that it doesn't matter what the government says? It is only what the people say that matters."

"What do the people say?"

"I told you I work with a lot of Maya families here on the Yucatán, yes? They are saying some very dangerous things right now."

"Like what?"

"They used to talk about Kulkulcan—the guerrilla, I mean—as a curiosity—a half-breed madman who pretends to be the reincarnation of *Quezalcoatl*. The Aztec name for *Kulkulcan*…"

"Thanks. I knew that." Stephen replied slyly.

"Of course you did," Anya smiled back weakly. She was tired of sparring.

"So what changed?" Stephen was still doodling, but he was listening attentively.

"First there was the rumour of the return of *Tohil*."

Stephen's doodle was growing complex and detailed: a pyramid with a wide and unruly jungle growing up it.

"*Tohil*?"

"The God of Fire. Related to *Hurukan*. Also possibly the name for the deepest level of *Xibalba*." Anya stopped to lick the last of the potato chip crumbs, gathered from the bottom of the bag, from her fingertips. "We still have much to learn about the Maya pantheon, but it seems as if *Tohil* is one of the few gods who truly demands blood sacrifice. He is described as being 'suckled'—given the heart from the breast of a living victim."

Stephen felt his stomach lurch at the memory of the eviscerated boy. He doodled a heart tumbling down the steps of his pyramid. "And?" he asked with forced evenness.

"And then came the reports of *xekik*."

"*Another* god?" Stephen asked, looking up.

"No." Anya frowned. "The word is Yucatec for 'yellow fever.' It means 'black vomit'…"

"… Delightful," Stephen interrupted. "Sorry, go on."

"It's a European disease; it came with the *conquistadores*. But from what people are saying, the sickness they speak of now is not yellow fever."

Stephen put his pen down and looked up an Anya. "If it isn't that, what is it?"

"The newspapers are turning the rumours into the Ebola virus but I don't think it is that, either."

"I've read *those* stories. Why isn't it Ebola?"

"The corpses, they are bloody at every… how do you say… the mouth and eyes and nose and even old scars?"

"Orifice? So what? That fits with Ebola."

"But it does not spread like a regular disease. One or two cases only, and following Kulkulcan like his shadow. The people think he has the ear of the Lords of *Xibalba*—*Tohil* among them—and is burning them with *xekik*."

"Why?"

"The Maya are a modern people now but many of them still carry an old wisdom. They believe that viruses cause illnesses, but they also believe that those who actually fall sick are those who have done something bad. The illness is their punishment."

"What are they being punished for?"

"Kulkulcan is preaching that the Maya are being punished for allowing the *conquistadores* and their descendants to keep this land. He says the Maya must rise up against their oppressors, drive them from Mexico and re-establish a kingdom that honours the ancient ways, or the gods will come and destroy them."

"Is this the '2012-is-the-end-of-the-world' story?" Stephen said, shaking his head in disbelief. "Chalo has told me that that's just an old wives' tale to make children behave."

"It is more than that." Anya said adamantly. "A great deal more than that. Every ancient myth holds a seed of something which was once absolutely true."

"I know. I'm was a geologist, remember?"

"How is that?" Anya asked, derailed for a moment.

"There's a First Nations' legend in Washington about a fight between spirits inhabiting two mountains—Mount Hood and Mount Adams—for the affections of the spirit of Mount Saint Helens. They fought with fiery rocks and their fighting shook the Earth. This made the Creator so angry that he broke the bridge of the gods. Turns out the bridge was a real ridge that the First Nations once used to cross the Columbia Gorge, but it collapsed catastrophically after the last Cascadia subduction zone earthquake. A three hundred year old truth. "

"Really? That's fascinating. And yes, it is like that. The story makes sense of an extraordinary happening. And it becomes a myth over time."

"But where is the kernel of truth in a prophecy—something that hasn't happened yet? And what do gods and diseases and roadside ghosts have to do with the heart Chalo found…?" he trailed off, mind drawn unintentionally back to the warehouse and the murdered boy.

"I don't know," Anya said with exasperation, "but there is something going on. Something bad will happen before long. My research assistant, Payal Ek, came to our site after the police were there. He said to me that the time of reckoning was coming soon and that the *dzul*—the foreigners—would be driven from this land. He said there would be much bloodshed, but that I would not have to worry because he would protect me. I deserve to live, he said, because I am helping to preserve and give back the things that my people stole."

Stephen was doodling on his napkin again. "So what do you think it is?"

"For the Maya, prophecy is just the past occurring again. They see time as a great circle, not the arrow Westerners think it is, shooting ever forward. This myth has power because the people believe it happened before. And if it can happen before, it can happen again. That is very convincing if you are Maya. The government may say Kulkulcan is just a crazy man, but the people are flocking to him like lambs to their shepherd. He is building an army against the *dzul* to appease the angry gods and stop the spread of *xekik*."

"No offense, but don't you think it sounds a little far-fetched? More like a movie?"

Anya looked down at the doodle, trying to control her irritation. "Maybe. But that doesn't mean it is impossible. There is something going on. The hearts prove it. "It is a good drawing, by the way," she added, looking at Stephen's sketch. "But is incorrect if it is supposed to be Chich'en Itzá."

"It isn't supposed to be anywhere," Stephen said, miffed by the unsolicited critique. I've just been dreaming it for weeks. What's wrong with it, anyway?"

"It needs to have nine terraces. One for each level of the Underworld."

"Great. I've been seeing ghosts and dreaming of a stairway to Hell," Stephen joked.

Anya failed to see the humour. "Not Hell," she remonstrated. "Mayan theology is nothing like Western theology. There is no Hell."

"I was kidding," Stephen said mordantly.

Anya was not mollified. "That is the problem with most Westerners: they try to see the Maya through their own culture. It isn't possible. When you think you know something, there is always another explanation.

Stephen laughed, irritating Anya further. "That's exactly what Chalo said to me when I got here! He's right, too: I love it here, but like I said before, the whole country defies logic. You're a Westerner; how come you get excluded from the club of idiots?"

Anya smiled at the characterization, her anger dissipating.

"I have been here long enough that it is my home."

"Fair enough. But I've been here a while, too and I'm not convinced that the hearts and one lone lunatic make for a native revolution. It seems a lot more likely that it's a drug thing. Look at the brutal murders all up along the Rio Grande."

Chalo appeared behind Stephen, showered and wearing a clean black *guayabera*, the traditional short-sleeved dress-shirt.

"Sorry *hermano*, but the good Doctor is right."

Stephen swivelled quickly to look at his erstwhile partner.

"How long have you been standing there?!"

"Long enough to agree with Anya: the hearts are the perfect way to scare people into submitting."

"Yeah, but that's why the drug cartels do it, too."

"No, it is not about mutilation, it is about hearts, *caballero*. They have an ancient meaning that scares us here."

"Okay, but if that's true, why on earth would he drop a heart into a tourist fountain and then steal it back before anyone could actually be frightened by it? It's the point I was going to make to the Doctor before our conversation went sideways."

"It wasn't Kulkulcan that stole it, Esteban. It was the constabulary."

Stephen paused for a moment, considering. Then he nodded slowly, understanding dawning.

The cornerstone of terrorism was terror; the way for a government to combat terrorism was to reduce terror. The usual strategy was a show of force—of counter-terror—but secrecy of the 'what-they-don't-know-won't-hurt-them" variety also worked. If the constabulary had been charged with removing the heart, it meant that not only did the government know about Kulkulcan, but they were actually afraid of him. It would explain why the investigation of the boy's murder was so quickly turned over to another agency, and Chalo and Stephen had been so effectively shut out.

"So we're saying," he began, thinking aloud, "that Kulkulcan's story goes like this: man was created to honour the gods, that the conquistadors arrived and destroyed the old ways, that the gods are pissed off now, that because they're pissed off they're making people poor and sick, and that, unless the people—the Maya—don't drive out the foreigners, then the gods will destroy the world. Have I missed anything?"

Anya and Chalo shook their heads.

"And the hearts?"

"To placate the gods until the revolution," Anya answered matter-of-factly.

"But that means believing one of two inconceivable things: either the Mayan gods, assuming they exist, can somehow visit their wrath physically upon the world, or Kulkulcan is somehow making people bleed to death on command. Tell me how either of those things could actually be possible?"

"I don't know, *caballero*..." Chalo said slowly. "But even if you do not believe either thing, many of the people do. And people follow many madmen in the service of God or gods, hmm?"

Stephen clenched his jaw, unnerved by where the illogic inevitably led. "So the boy in the warehouse—you're saying Alvarro is working for Kulkulcan, aren't you?"

"Exactly," Chalo said, nodding slowly. "It makes sense."

"Even without believing in angry gods," Stephen said darkly.

"It would help if you did, *caballero*. It's the reason behind the reason, no?"

"Nope. Sorry Chalo, but there's no such thing as ghosts. And before you say it—because every time we talk about ghosts you start talking about fate—there's no such thing as 'fate', either."

Chalo grinned. "Of course there is, *caballero*. We got sent away from our case in Mexico City and it came here to find us. What else could it be?"

"Back to the facts, Chalo. Why would Alvarro sign up for a rebellion when he was doing more than fine as a drug lord?

"I have no idea, *caballero*. None at all," Chalo replied, smile widening.

"Then why do you look so damned happy?"

"Because we're working again. And together! We're after Alvarro once more!"

Stephen stood, dumbfounded a moment before finding his voice.

"No way, Chalo. No way! I'm done with murder and mayhem. I want a nice quiet Christmas in the snow."

Sunday, December 9, 2012 – 5 Lamat, Day of Venus

***

Senator Joe Wilkes sat alone in his office in Washington's fading winter daylight, staring at a picture of his dead son. Hayden had been twenty-eight the day the picture had been taken. It was a candid, happy shot: Hayden, his blonde hair cropped short for his stint in the Iraqi desert, his smile wide, his arm around Becky. It was the last picture he had of his boy.

Not the last image, though. For that Joe had the horrifying memory of Hayden's face, pale against the black vinyl of a body bag. In Joe's mind's eye, Hayden looked ethereally perfect, his serene face belying the enormous hole that Joe knew lay where the back of Hayden's head should be. His entire occiput—everything from the crown back—had been blow away by the bullet with which Hayden had taken his own life. Just like the lone gunman's shot had taken off the back of JFK's.

"What do I do, Hayden?" the senator asked the photograph.

The photograph smiled back at him and said nothing. All Joe could see was the barely parted lips that belonged to his son's corpse, equally silent.

Joe looked away from the image suddenly, as if seeing a movement in the room. He paused and then spoke.

"I can't, Libby. Clayton's going to tell everything. They'll take away his purple heart. They'll dig him up out of Arlington. I can't let that happen. I can't let him be disgraced."

The ghost of his long-dead wife was as alive to him as if she were at the other end of a telephone line. He made a face into the fallen darkness because he didn't like what she had replied.

"No. No goddammit. It is *not* about me."

CHAPTER 15

Stephen, Chalo, and Anya stood at the end of the hotel's breezeway waiting for a valet to bring Stephen's rental car. Chalo would have liked a cigarette. *Not worth it*, he thought, glancing at Anya. He was supposed to be quitting anyway. He tapped his hand against his thigh instead.

"You're really going, Esteban?"

"I have to Chalo. I'm lucky I still have a job to go back to, even if it is desk duty. If I don't go home, I'll be fired for sure. Besides, I have a date to freeze my ass off skiing with a nephew I haven't seen in three years."

"But I need your help, *caballero*! Aren't you the least bit interested in how this all connects?"

"I would be if I was sure it did, Chalo. But how can you know it does?"

"My 'gut' says so, Esteban." He reached up to put his arm around his partner's shoulder and added softly, "I'm going to miss you, *hermano*."

Anya suddenly felt as if she was intruding and looked away. A large iguana sat in the middle of the breezeway, sunning itself in a sliver of late-afternoon light.

"I'm going to miss you, too, Chalo," Stephen said before falling awkwardly silent.

"Why don't you at least stay for dinner? You haven't eaten anything but potato chips all day…"

"No. I've got to return the rental car in Mérida; I don't really want to drive that toll road at night again. I should get going now."

Though not looking, Anya had been eavesdropping. "You can always stay in my apartment overnight," she volunteered. "I am going down to my site, so the apartment will be empty. The key is in a yellow ceramic iguana in the flower box by the front door."

Stephan and Chalo turned, distracted from their farewells.

"You are not going back to Cancún with Esteban?" Chalo asked, surprised.

"You leave a key outside your front door?" Stephen asked with equal surprise.

Anya laughed at the two men, complete opposites, sporting the same look.

"No, I am not going back to Cancún. My next group of tourists will be coming in a few days, and since I am halfway to the site, I will go the rest of the way to check on a few things. And I keep a key out front because I am always losing mine."

"But how will you get to your site?" Chalo asked.

"But aren't you afraid of someone breaking in?" Stephen asked, in turn.

"I have a truck just near here for hauling things. I can take a taxi to it and then go down to my site. And I am not afraid of anyone breaking in, because what idiot in Mexico would leave a key outside? I have never once been broken into with that key."

"It's a good idea, *caballero*. And then we can have a proper farewell dinner, hmm?"

"We both suck at saying good-bye, Chalo. I'm just going to go now, okay? You stay and have a nice dinner with the Doctor..."—here Stephen permitted himself a smirk, knowing that Chalo would love the opportunity to romance the archaeologist—"and then go down to check out her dig site to see if there's any evidence left. And I'll call you when I get home to find out how it all went."

Chalo looked down at his feet, then up at his partner and stuck out his hand. "I learned a lot from you, *hermano*."

"Yeah, but I learned more from you," Stephen replied, taking Chalo's hand. They shook hands then stepped into an awkward, back-thumping hug before stepping apart.

"Good-bye Dr. von Eckhardt. A pleasure to meet you. Take good care of Chalo for me, okay?"

"I'm not sure he needs caring for," Anya laughed. She blushed a little and then scowled at herself.

Sunday, December 9, 2012 – 5 Lamat, Day of Venus

"If you change your mind, don't forget about the key," she added, to hide her embarrassment.

The valet appeared with the rented Yaris; Stephen turned quickly, folded himself into the little car, waved once, and drove away.

Chalo watched the car go for a long moment and then turned to Anya, feigning lightness. "Shall we go have dinner, *señorina*, before travelling to your crime scene?"

***

The sun was lower now, and cast a long peachy shadow across the width of the open-air colonnade. Anya looked at the artificial Christmas trees at the end of the walkway as she and Chalo walked towards the buffet. She thought of her many snowy Christmases in Germany, filled with the scent of baked goods and pine trees, and shook her head at the incongruity: here the air smelled of suntan lotion and a warm salty sea.

The ancient Maya, she thought, would be preparing for winter solstice festivals. Even today there would be vestiges of that among the highland Maya for, despite what some thought, they had never let their beliefs die. They had merely disguised the old rituals with new names and hybrid practices. Like Chalo, she thought, looking for him as she approached the giant fountain. Maya hidden beneath a *mestizo* façade. He should be proud, she thought, not angry; his anger disguised shame and he had nothing to be ashamed of. If anything, the Europeans who had stolen his heritage were the ones to be ashamed. She felt a twinge of envy, wishing that she had not been born white.

"Here we are, *señorina*," Chalo said, interrupting Anya's reflections. He was nervous around her—an unusual state for him; he could definitely use a cigarette. He drummed his fingers on the table instead.

The restaurant was composed of fifty or more thatched umbrellas standing over blue-tiled tables on a wide patio overlooking the Caribbean Sea. The north-eastern sky was fading to a dark mauve at the horizon but the last rays of the sun reflected off the clouds, bathing them in burning red and gold light. A group of five cormorants swept long and low over the breakers beyond the small reef offshore, their wingtips almost caressing the sea. Both Anya and Chalo stood for a moment, awestruck by the beauty, before a young man in black trousers and a tuxedo shirt, ruffled in the front, appeared.

"Beverages for you, *señor*? *Señora*?" the maître d' asked once he had seated them.

"A beer for you?" Anya asked Chalo.

"Only if you will join me. That is all I can or should have if we are to get to my site tonight..."

"Just one."

"*Dos Negra Modelo, por favor,*" Chalo said to the maître d'. The man nodded and disappeared.

"So tell me," Chalo began, smiling charmingly. "You have no ring. Why is a beautiful woman like you not married?"

Anya looked at him and laughed. "That is very direct."

"*Si*. I am a police officer. I have a gift for direct questions."

"Ah. Your question is just a professional interest, then. I see. I was married. To an arrogant *crillolo*—a Spaniard, really—who cheats on his wives with his graduate students. I was one of each."

"Equally direct, I see. You would have been a good policewoman."

"Is that a compliment in Mexico?"

"Oh yes, sure. Some of us, like I told to Stephen, are only a little crooked. Bent, like the pages of a good book."

Anya laughed again. "And what good book are you?"

"Oh, I don't know. Not a best-seller, I don't think. Something adventurous. And of course, very romantic. What about you?"

Anya found butterflies in her stomach. Like a silly schoolgirl, she thought to herself. To Chalo she said diffidently, "A textbook. Academic and very boring. Dusty, too."

This time Chalo laughed. "Oh, I don't think so."

A waiter returned, two beer in hand, which he poured into chilled glasses. "You are ready to order?"

"We are not being very quick, are we?" Chalo asked Anya. To the waiter he said, "We have not looked at the menu. Come back in two minutes and we will be ready."

The waiter nodded, leaving both Anya and Chalo to study the menu. The sky began to lose its lustre, leaving behind grey masses of evening cloud, and a cool breeze that smelled of salt and the ozone of a distant thunderstorm. Anya absent-minded crossed her arms against the chill, unaware that Chalo was surveying her.

"*Sopa de Tortilla, por favor, y una botella de agua mineral,*" Anya said when the waiter returned.

"*Y un plato de las taquitos, para mi*," added Chalo, still watching Anya. She was disarmingly beautiful. And smart. And, to his shock, having dinner with him. He wondered which particular one of his grandmother's gods he should be thanking for this. Or if he owed Stephen for it.

"Tell me about your ruins," he asked once the waiter had left.

Anya's face lost its pinched quality. Chalo hadn't even noticed it was there until it disappeared. Already attractive, she was suddenly effervescent, thinking about her ruins.

"It is an early-classical structure very similar in style to *El Caracol*, the observatory at Chich'en Itzá," she said, her smile broad and white, her ice-blue eyes sparkling as she looked up and to the left to recall the details of the site for Chalo.

"Like *El Caracol*, it is round"—she collected a column of air in her lithe, tanned hands—"and it has a spiral staircase inside that leads to an observation tower with doors and windows aligned to astronomical events." She paused, knit her fingers together, placed them on the table and leaned over them towards Chalo.

"That is the strange bit," she continued. "Most observatories have doors aligned to the winter solstice but here there are also holes in the ceiling. They are not fallen-away masonry but holes that were built for a reason… ."

"My grandmother was always watching Venus. Especially her risings. She always said special prayers when Venus rose in the morning."

"Really? In her morning appearance, she was a… *vohersage*… how do you say… a prediction of war or change, arriving."

"Yes, and they were prayers asking for protection. Speaking of things arriving…" The waiter appeared, deposited their meals, and left in a hurry. The restaurant had filled around them without either Chalo or Anya noticing.

"Tell me about your grandmother," she said as she blew on a spoonful of her steaming soup.

Chalo's lips smiled, but his eyes did not.

"She was… wonderful. Just wonderful. A great big fat lady with gold teeth and bright coloured skirts. She watched me like a vulture to keep me out of trouble. She was always telling me stories about the jungle animals and the stars."

"Mayan stories?"

"Beautiful ones, yes."

"Tell me one."

"Really? They are a little long…" he said, suddenly hesitant.

Anya looked at her watch. It was already much later than she expected. They would get to camp near midnight. Still, if it was a myth she had not heard…

"I have flashlights in my truck. Tell me one. Your favourite."

This time Chalo smiled with his eyes, a genuine smile free of any teasing or mockery.

"Okay, my favourite. But remember, it was my favourite *when I was a boy*, so it's a little silly."

"Silly isn't always bad," Anya said, encouragingly.

"Very well then. This is the story of how the deer and the rabbit got their long ears and their short tails," he cleared his throat, leaned in towards Anya, and began, his voice melodic.

"Once upon a very long time ago, when the gods still walked on the Earth, the Great One went out to the forest to clear the vines and the trees so that he could plant a field of maize. He worked hard all day, full of sweat and toil, muscles glistening with sweat in the forest heat, until he had a whole field cleared. Then he went home to rest so that he could plant his fields the next day. But when he went back the next day, do you know what he found?"

"No, what?" asked Anya, as curious as a happy child.

"The trees and vines were all standing up again."

"No!"

"Really! So again he cleared the field, sweating all day and into the sunset hours to clear the field for his maize. He went home, dirty and tired from all his efforts, and fell asleep in his hammock right away. The very next morning, he took his bag of seeds and went to the forest but guess what?"

"The trees were standing up again?"

"Absolutely! So for a third day he worked hard, clearing the vines and cutting down the trees. He stripped off his shirt and let the sun beat down on his back, turning him a deep brown, his muscles growing big and strong. He took water from the jungle leaves and worked until the sun again was setting in the west. And again he went home and fell into his hammock, exhausted.

"But still, the very next day he went back, carrying his machete this time, because he was afraid that the trees would be back. For sure, they were there, standing up again, tall as ever, touching the sky. The Great One said:

"—*What is happening here? How can I feed myself if I cannot clear my field?*

"And so he decided this time to clear the whole field except for two trees, and he would hide behind the trees and wait to see what happened. And so it happened that as the sun started to set, the deer and the rabbit came to the clearing and began to talk to each other. They did not know that the Great One was listening, so they talked out loud. And do you want to know what they said?"

Captivated, Anya smiled but shook her head. This was one she hadn't heard.

Chalo smiled back and resumed. "They said:

"—*How terrible! How terrible! He has cleared our forest again! Now we will have to sing the magic over again to bring the forest back.*

"And then the deer and the rabbit together, they said:

"—Yukan te*!* Yukan te*! Rise up, rise up trees, and touch the sky and be our homes!*'

"… and the trees stood up like…" Chalo paused, a little embarrassed.

"Like what?"

"My grandmother always used to say "like a man's…member," Chalo said, suddenly sheepish. He was surprised to find himself blushing.

Anya laughed out loud, both at the story and the fact that it made him bashful. "And then what happened next?" she said, encouragingly.

"So the Great One jumped out from behind the tree, and he grabbed the rabbit by the ears, and the rabbit tried to run away and its ears pulled and pulled until they were long like you see them today. And then the rabbit, he got his ears free at last but the Great One grabbed him by the tail and cut it off as short as it is today before letting the rabbit go. Then the Great One did the same thing with the deer, pulling his ears and cutting his tail, before letting him go, too. And once he had let both of them go, the Great One chased the deer and the rabbit from his field and said to the Earth Lords:

"*—I am tired of the animals; they will only come back again and make the trees grow once more. I will kill them all.*

"But the Earth Lords…" Chalo paused to brandish his fork. "The Earth Lords liked the rabbit and the deer very much, so they made the Great One leave the animals alone, saying they would make the land stop growing if the Great One harmed the deer or the rabbit or any of the living creatures of the Earth.

"It was from that day on that the creatures became the responsibility of the Earth Lords. And that is why they cannot die without the permission of the Earth Lords. *Yu'un oy yajval.* They cannot die because they have someone to watch over them."

Anya smiled thoughtfully and fell silent.

"That is the end," Chalo offered, unsure what Anya's silence meant.

"Yes," she nodded.

"Did you like it?" he asked, uncertainly.

"Very much, thank you. We all need someone to watch over us, yes?" she said softly.

"Just a little Mayan fairy-tale" Chalo said, looking away.

Anya reached out and rested her hand on Chalo's forearm. It was warm and felt good to her cold fingers. "You are ashamed to be Maya. You should not be. It is a magnificent heritage. We should be ashamed for taking it from you."

Chalo turned and looked at her face for a long moment, his expression infinitely sad, ultimately inscrutable.

"You're very cold," he said, softly, taking her hand in his for a moment. He stroked it gently and then caught himself. There was no reason why a woman like Dr. von Eckhardt would be interested in him. He was being a fool.

He pushed his chair back from the table with a loud scrape and looked at his watch. "It is getting late. We should leave soon, don't you think?"

"Yes, of course," Anya agreed hurriedly, pushing her own chair back. To cover her own discomfort she asked, "May I pay you for my meal?"

"No, no. My boss can pay for that like he was supposed to pay for breakfast."

Anya smiled weakly. "Then I will call our cab—it is not far from here to my truck. From there we drive about forty minutes to the boat and then it will take another twenty minutes to the site. At least there should not be much traffic going south at this hour."

"Boat? If it is alright with you, I think I might like to get a jacket in my room, then. Come with me, why don't you? It won't take long."

***

Stephen was stuck in traffic, along with what seemed like every tourist visiting the Yucatán. Stuck behind an accident or a broken-down truck or the ever-occurring construction that the tourist boom had brought. He had moved maybe 500 metres in twenty minutes, and the sun was already at the horizon; it would be well and truly dark by the time he got past Cancún and onto the toll road to Mérida. He frowned at the prospect of traversing the dark road again lest he have another hallucination. Maybe he should take Anya up on the offer of her apartment after all.

He thought about Anya, having dinner with Chalo, and his stomach growled. He probably should have stayed for dinner, too. He could always turn back, he mused. They had probably just started eating…

He shook his head. What exactly was he thinking? Dinner would lead to the crime scene would lead to becoming re-entangled in the Alvarro mystery, getting fired, moving back in with his parents and generally being a failure—a lonely failure—for the foreseeable future.

The traffic suddenly eased, as if confirming Stephen's decision to press onward. It was just as well he not go back, Stephen decided as he reached fifty kilometres an hour: Chalo was with the archaeologist now; at least one of them would not be lonely.

The highway lights suddenly went on, illuminating the now-dusky road and the ubiquitous billboards lining it, each designed to seduce the tourist: advertisements for zip-lining, scuba-diving, deep-sea fishing, para-sailing, swimming with dolphins… there were an awful lot of things he hadn't done in Mexico, Stephen realized.

A billboard for drift diving through one of the myriad rivers running beneath the Yucatán caught his eye. Swimming in a *cenote* was something he wished he had tried, but that was not why the billboard had attracted his attention; it had been vandalized and the message it now bore filled Stephen with alarm. Letters in the caption that had once read "Visit Kulkulcan's Cenote" had been blacked out: the message was now "Vi■■■va Kulkulcan■ ■■■■■■!" Scrawled after it were the words: "The country will be ours again!"

Could Chalo and Anya be right? And if so, was Alvarro really involved? And could the ridiculous ghost on the highway really be a harbinger of doom?

Stephen shuddered involuntarily. He would definitely be looking for the key in the flowerpot; there was no way he was going to drive the toll road again in the dark.

***

"It's nice" Anya said, surveying Chalo's hotel room. "But even colder than outside," she added, shivering after the comparative warmth of the night air.

"The room? It's okay," he said indifferently as the door snicked shut behind them. "They always turn up the air conditioning after they clean the room. The bed is not as comfortable as mine at home. Will you excuse me for a moment?" Chalo said as he stepped towards the bathroom.

"Yes, of course," Anya replied, surveying the room. There was a towel sculpture of an elephant on the bed, left by the cleaning staff. And on the bedside table a stack of more than half a dozen books. Anya walked over to them. She was surprised by the titles. *El Intermediario*, by John Grisham. Okay, maybe that wasn't so surprising. But *An Anthology of Classic American Short Stories from Poe to Defoe*, in English? And *Me llamo Rigoberta Menchú y así me nació la conciencia*, by the Guatemalan activist? And *La Odisea*, translated from Greek to Spanish? Another smart policeman; she would have to set aside her preconceptions.

"You like my books?" asked Chalo. He had returned from the bathroom and had walked up behind her to watch her peruse them. Anya turned abruptly and almost stepped into his arms.

"It… it is an unusual collection," she said, stepping backwards and bumping into the bedside table.

"It is all Esteban's fault. His fiancée studied books and because of her he read them like a boy eating cookies. He talked about them so much that I agreed to read some to make him shut up," Chalo said. He smiled to himself at the memory of their many late nights driving through narrow alleys talking about books. "Now I am like that hungry boy and I cannot get enough. Books. I cannot get enough books."

Anya looked down at the book in her hand to avoid his steady gaze. She felt suddenly warm in the heavily air-conditioned room.

"You will miss him, won't you?" she asked softly, looking up. Chalo could smell her light floral perfume.

"Who?" he asked, forgetting the question.

"Stephen. You will miss him."

"Yes," he said, stepping in towards her, raising his right hand to cradle her cheek. "Yes, I will." His lips were an inch from hers.

"We should go," she said softly, letting the book she held fall to the bed beside them. Then she looked up at him and touched a lock of his hair at his forehead. Chalo took her hand gently and looked into her eyes; Anya returned his gaze and leaned forward to kiss him, her lips grazing his gently. Chalo returned the kiss hesitantly.

Anya kissed him again, sliding her hands down his arms to his waist then up, pausing on the top button. Chalo took her face in his hands and kissed her again; now Anya undid the buttons, slipped the shirt off of him and ran her hands over his warm, well-muscled chest, under his arms, down his back. She felt a newish scar on his shoulder. Chalo stopped kissing her for a moment and looked directly into her pale blue eyes.

"If we are going to the ruin, we should go," he said very softly, waiting.

The moment, the anticipation, was an overwhelming pleasure, and he was drunk with delight. If it ended now—if she said stop—it would still be enough: breathing her scent, he was complete.

"Yes, we should," Anya breathed softly, her hands sliding down to his buttocks, pulling his groin towards hers. She kissed him again, her lips tasting of strawberries. Chalo caressed her warm back, released the clasp of her bra, slid his hands forward to cup her soft breasts, sighing with desire. He sighed again as he felt her unzip his jeans. They kissed ardently, now almost naked, now sinking to the bed, now entwined, an urgent passion desperate to be sated, lost in the heady fever before consummation.

They would not be travelling to Sian Ka'an tonight.

MONDAY, DECEMBER 10, 2012
6 MULUC, DAY OF JADE

CHAPTER 16

"Wake up *Don* Yaxché. Please, wake up."

"Lupita? It is not yet dawn. Why do you wake me?"

"Please, *Don* Yaxché. It is another baby with the cough. You must wake up."

Yaxché's eyes snapped open. The women were growing silly and superstitious, forgetting everything that their mothers had taught them.

"Build me a fire and set the pot to boil. I will be out in a moment."

The worried woman bustled back past the hanging blanket that partitioned Yaxché's small hut into a sleeping area, occupied solely by tow hammocks, and the rest of the space, which was his "office." Yaxché heard the dull scrape and thud of wood being laid and then smelled the sharp scent of a fire catching on the hearth. After that, there was the scrape of a pot being pulled from the hearthstone and lugged outside.

"One minute, only," he heard Lupita say in Yucatec to the midnight patient. "He will be out in one minute."

Yaxché slung his feet out of his hammock and stood slowly. At night, especially, he could feel his eight decades in his knees and hips. He took a deep breath and stretched his arms above his head.

"Better," he grunted, feeling the knots fall from his ancient body. He pulled his old green trousers from a hook on the wall, put them on, and padded, bare-foot, into the office. As he did, he heard the characteristic bark of a baby with croup.

On his examining table—a wooden door supported on either end by stacked cinder blocks—sat a young woman barely out of her teens cradling a wan looking baby, its eyes wide and runny, its breath ragged through a croup-constricted throat.

"I am Hernando Canul. The one called Yaxché. You have come to see me. How can I help?"

Lupita was back and hanging the pot above the fire. She listened to Yaxché's grave voice, beginning the appointment as he did all of them. It was as familiar and as soothing to her as the smell of baking tortillas.

"*Don* Yaxché, please help my boy," said the girl on the table. "He cannot breathe…"

"Give me the baby, *mi hija*."

Yaxché took the infant in his arms and began to rock him gently. "Come Lupita, help me undress the child."

Lupita hurried over.

"Why did you not take care of this?" Yaxché whispered as Lupita busied herself with the unswaddling. "You are the midwife. You have done this a thousand times."

"It is not the baby that is the problem, *Don* Yaxché. The mother thinks the baby is bewitched. It is she that you must cure!"

"Bewitched?"

"You ask her once we have tamed the cough."

Yaxché stood by the hearth and allowed the steam from the now boiling pot to envelop him and the baby in his arms. He felt the hot moist air settle on his face, felt prickles of sweat form on his chest and under his arms. He looked down at the wide brown eyes set deep in the baby's pinched face. The room grew thick with steam as the minutes went by; the only sounds in the tiny hut were the crackle of the fire, the hiss of boiling water spitting onto the hot hearthstones, and the baby's ragged breathing.

"Now the cold cloth, Lupita."

Lupita took a rag from a bowl of cold water, wrung it out, and placed it on the baby's throat; the infant jumped in surprise, wailed once, and then began breathing more freely. After repeating the process a number of times, Yaxché rose and smiled. The exhausted baby had fallen asleep, his breathing quiet at last. Yaxché caressed his small skull.

"Take him while I attend to the mother," he said softly to Lupita.

Lupita pulled an old wooden chair up to the fire from its place against the wall, sat down, and reached up to receive the baby. Once it was settled in her arms, Yaxché gently took the infant's tiny wrists in his own gnarled hands, measured the baby's pulse, and nodded, pleased. He bent down to the child and whispered a foursome of blessings: one to each wrist and one to each ankle. Then, a final prayer as he caressed the baby's soft head once more, and Yaxché turned to face the mother.

Still sitting on the examining table, she had been craning her neck to watch Yaxché and Lupita. Now she looked down at her lap and wiped a drop of sweat from her brow.

"You think it is hot over there! Come try it by the fire!" Yaxché joked as he walked towards the girl. The girl looked up and smiled weakly. "What is your name, *mi hija*?"

"Tonalna."

"A pretty name for a pretty girl." Tonalna smiled shyly. "Your boy will be fine, Tonalna. But my Lupita tells me that something troubles you, as well?"

The girl looked down at a baby blue receiving blanket in her lap.

"My husband, Payal. The baby is often sick. Payal says it is this blanket."

"Tell me how a blanket has made your baby ill, Tonalna," Yaxché asked gently.

"I used to work for a white lady. When I told her I would stop working for her to have my baby, she gave me this. Payal says it is bewitched."

"And why would that be, little one?" Yaxché asked.

"Because my husband says that the *mestizos* have stolen everything from the Maya and now they want to kill us with black magic so that we do not try to take back our land."

"Ahhh," Yaxché said, nodding sagely. "Ahhh," he said again. "And who is telling your husband these things?"

Tonalna looked away. "I… I don't know" she stammered.

"Your husband, does he carry a new knife with a long black blade?"

Tonalna looked up, surprised. "Yes. He does."

"And does he talk of the end of the world?"

"I don't like it. It frightens me."

"Are you sure he is not speaking the words of the man calling himself the new Kulkulcan?"

"It… it might be."

"He is confused, Tonalna. He will learn the truth for himself, when the time comes."

"So my baby is not bewitched?"

"Did you leave your window open last night?"

"I… I might have, *Don* Yaxché."

"As I thought. The sickness comes from the night spirits, not from a white woman's curse."

The girl gave Yaxché a small but genuine smile. "I can use the blanket then?"

Yaxché chuckled. "It is a very pretty blanket, I agree. But I will not say it is fine if it will make you fight."

Tonalna smiled sheepishly.

"I say this," Yaxché continued, smiling with her. "I will give you a tea for your baby. At night you must keep your windows and doors closed. If the boy makes the cough again, come back to me. And you must think whether you want to keep fighting with your husband over a scrap of cloth."

The girl smiled and shook her head. "No. I do not."

"Good then. You are cured and so is your baby. But take better care with the night. Sleep in Lupita's home and return to your own in the light of day, hmm?"

Tonalna nodded.

"Now go, women, and let this old goat get some sleep!"

Tonalna laughed and then hesitated.

"Something else, *mi hija*?"

"My husband says that Kulkulcan says the Lords of *Xibalba* are awake because of the well the white men put into the bottom of the sea where the Lords live."

"He says that, does he?"

"Yes, and he says the Lords will kill us all if we do not rid our land of the *dzul*."

"Indeed. And what is it that you want to know, Tonalna?"

"Is it true?"

"That the Lords are awake? Perhaps. That we must kill all those who are not Maya to save ourselves? I do not believe killing anyone is the answer to anything. Not Maya, and not white. It is true that we have fought in the past, and that the *dzul* have killed many of us. But we have a story, passed from shaman to shaman, that says one day we will come together—red *and* white—to fix all that has been broken. Does that answer your question?"

"And they will not destroy the world?"

"The Lords of *Xibalba*? It is their way to try, but it is not a thing for you to worry about. That is a job for me, yes? Yours is to help your boy grow big and strong."

The girl smiled again.

"Good then," Yaxché smiled. "We are done."

"I must pay you, *Don* Yaxché."

"Only what you can, *mi hija*."

"I… I have this jade ring."

"Oh, I don't think it will fit me. And sadly, I have no wife to give it to."

"What about… I could give… would you like this blanket? It is very soft and would make a good pillow. I can wrap my baby in my shawl."

"It would be perfect," Yaxché smiled.

The girl handed the blanket to Yaxché, took her sleeping son from Lupita, wrapped him in her colourful shawl, and prepared to leave.

Lupita hung back half a step.

"I don't like this Kulkulcan," she said under her breath.

"Nor I, Lupita. But I do not think it will be well for him."

"Of course it won't!" Lupita growled as she stumped out. "It is a dangerous game, inviting the dead to dance. They do not like to let go when the music ends."

***

Stephen neared Cancún City and looked at the blue-green LCD clock on the dash: almost midnight. Anya's apartment was in El Centro—a real city far enough from the strip of five-star hotels on the island of Cancún to feel like the real Mexico. The key was in the ceramic lizard as promised; Stephen let himself in, dropped his knapsack, paced for a bit, and then decided he was too keyed up from the drive to go to sleep. He needed fresh air, food, and drink to calm down.

Back outside, Stephen discovered that, unlike the tourist mecca that was Isla Cancún, El Centro had bedded down for the night: restaurants were locked behind steel gates and upper-floor apartments glowed with flickering TV light or were darkened for sleep. If he wanted something, he would need to make the pilgrimage to the tourist strip.

The mammoth causeway that joined Isla Cancún to the mainland had been built with the city and its first resorts in the 1970s; in 2009, it had been raised a full metre to keep it dry in the face of the predicted sea level rise that climate change would bring. And now, three years later, everyone knew that would not be enough. So now an enormous levee ringing the vacationers' playland was being considered, at still greater expense. Cynics said the politicians should just wait for another hurricane to sweep the island clean, and then start over.

On the causeway, the twin smells of sea salt and diesel enveloping him, Stephen was awestruck by the incongruity. To his right, the inland shore of Laguna Nichupté was inky, the wetlands filled with the soft trill of crickets and the deeper silence of night hunters stalking and being stalked: the unending circle of life. But beside him, like an army of angry red ants, crept a tail-lit line of cars and trucks, bumper to bumper, heading towards the blinding back side of the tourist strip.

Past the crawling traffic Stephen stopped to buy an overpriced *flauta* from a sidewalk vendor, then made his way through the tangle of hotels to the white beach. The sand felt soft and warm, the sea smelled briny, and the *flauta* tasted good after a full day of nothing but granola, a banana, and a bag of potato chips.

"Mister! Hey, Mister!" said a boy's voice behind him. Stephen jumped at the unexpected company.

"Gum? Postcards for you girlfriend back home?" the child pressed.

Stephen looked up. About ten and skinny, the boy wore a ripped red shirt, grimy shorts, and holey sneakers with fraying laces. Hand out, he offered Stephen a single stick of Juicy Fruit and a tattered picture postcard of Chich'en Itzá.

"*No, no gracias*," Stephen said after swallowing the last of his *flauta*.

The boy planted his feet in the sand directly in front of Stephen.

"Please, mister? Just one gum? Just twenty-five American cents?"

"*Habla español. Soy Canadienese. No tengo dinero Americano.*"

The boy's face fell.

"*Okay, veinticinco pesos. Si lo vendes, puedo ir a casa.*"

Stephen looked at his watch and shook his head. It was past midnight, but the kid probably wasn't allowed to go home, if he had one, until he'd sold everything he'd gone out with.

"*¿Usted sabe cuáles es un disco volador*?"

The boy looked at Stephen witheringly.

"*Si*, of course I know Frisbee."

Stephen chuckled, pulled his pack into his lap, and unzipped an outer pouch.

"*Cinco dollars Canadieneses*," he said, as he pulled out a blue five dollar bill and handed it to the boy. Then he reached back into his pack and pulled out a neon green nylon Frisbee.

"Do you want it? *¿Usted lo desea*?" he asked, holding out the Frisbee.

The boy looked up from the bill and his eyes grew wide. Wordlessly, he reached out to touch the disc.

"Take it. It is yours. Now go on home. *Vaya a casa*."

The boy took the Frisbee, turned around, and began to run towards home. He stopped after a few steps, turned around and ran back, holding out the gum and the postcard.

"You buyed these. Have the gum. Send the postcard to your girlfriend." The boy turned again and loped away. "¡*Gracias*! ¡*Gracias* very much!" he yelled over his shoulder as he ran, waving the neon Frisbee above his head.

Stephen looked down at the picture of the famous Mexican pyramid. "My girlfriend," he said out loud to the wordless sea.

Erin has been Stephen's girlfriend for five years. He had fallen in love with her in the moment it took her to drop an armful of books in the cafeteria during their first week of their second year as undergrads. Three Greek classics, *Beowulf*, and the *Chanson de Roland* in translation tumbled from her arms, a thousand disconnected years of literary brilliance sent skittering between a dozen pairs of running shoes. Her long dark hair had swung forward over her shoulder as she crouched down to gather her lost books. Stephen, who had been standing in line behind her, had crouched to pick up *The Iliad* and *The Odyssey*, brushed them off, and handed them to her. "I'm Stephen."

"Thanks," she had said, looking up sheepishly. "I'm Erin, and these books have a life of their own. Can I buy you a coffee to say thank you?"

She had been studying English literature; he was majoring in

Geology. By the beginning of their third year, she had taken up a minor in his subject and he a minor in hers so they could spend more time together. By the middle of their final year, they were the source of both ridicule and admiration: their relationship was an unusual and heralded fixity in the shifting and tumultuous love lives of the undergraduate population. “It’s the Geology,” one friend cracked. “Solid as a rock.”

The first Tuesday of the first spring break of their respective graduate degrees, the sun had come out. After weeks of west coast rain, everything sparkled. On their way to the library, Stephen had stopped, inhaled the fresh bright air, and smiled.

“Let’s go up to the Chief and do a little climbing.”

“I dunno. I should probably work.”

“You’re always working! *We’re* always working. We could use a break!”

Erin had stopped and looked around at the bare trees, leaf-buds pregnant with the promise of spring. She had twirled a lock of hair absently, considering the merits of mental versus physical exercise.

“Okay,” she smiled, “but just for a few hours.”

Like happy grade-school kids, they had spun around, thundered home, exchanged sweats and knapsacks for climbing gear, and had hopped into Stephen’s old Prius. Forty minutes later they were in Squamish, ready to climb the Stawamus Chief, the second largest block of granite in the world. A half a dozen other students were there, also playing hooky; the climbing community was small enough that Stephen and Erin knew most of them.

“Lookey lookey, I beat Erin for a change!” someone said from ten metres up. Erin was a fast climber, and very competent.

“Sure sure! But I’ll be at the top before you!” She shouted up before giving Stephen a quick peck on the cheek. Then she ran to the wall to gear up. She was four metres above him by the time Stephen had started up the face.

“The winter ice has jacked a few new handholds but the rock is a bit wet and flakey,” she had called down. “Be careful, okay?”

“I’m always careful,” he had replied, smiling up at her down-turned face. She had smiled back, her fuchsia-coloured helmet a halo around her dark hair and pale face.

They climbed in happy silence for maybe a quarter of an hour; five metres up, Erin climbing another four metres above him, Stephen had wedged his hand into a crack and swung his leg wide to catch another toe hold. It was the last normal thing he would remember. In the next moment everything shattered into fractured images and tiny shards of sound.

"Heads up!" someone had shouted.

"Crap!" That had been Erin.

Next came a scrabbling sound and the scraping of helmet on rock. A figure plunging past him, back first. A flash of orange. An arm reaching, reaching. He felt softness on his fingertips: Erin's fleece. He was gripping, holding, Erin's arm was sliding from the sleeve. He was looking down, now at her wide green eyes, incredulous, staring up at him, her hand up to him, just beyond his grasp, falling, untethered. He heard the sickening thud of soft body and hard helmet on the ground.

Stephen still didn't know how he had gotten to the ground. Erin lay still, arms and legs unnaturally akimbo, her eyes half closed, nose and mouth leaking blood. "Told you it was wet…" she said softly as he scrambled to cradle her head in his lap. He still had her fleece; he draped it over her chest to keep her warm.

"Just hold on, okay?"

"Tried."

"It's okay, just hold on *now*."

She smiled weakly and reached up with a cold hand to wipe a tear from Stephen's cheek. "Something in your eye."

"Dust, maybe," he said, smiling at her joke through his tears.

"Let go."

"I love you, Erin."

"Me too, you. Let go," she whispered.

"I know you did. It's okay.

"No. You. *Let go*." Her voice was so soft he could hardly hear her. She closed her eyes, squeezed his hand, and stopped breathing.

The next year had been a blur. He'd taken the summer off. He'd gone back to school. He'd finished his thesis. His grief had not dimmed. He'd gone travelling, had ended up in Costa Rica where he'd volunteered at a sea turtle recovery centre. He'd learned Spanish. He'd come home. And still he was haunted by the accident. He wouldn't climb. He didn't eat. He couldn't sleep. He had started roaming the streets of Vancouver at night, had invariably found himself in the Downtown Eastside, considering the people there whose lives were more damaged than his own. The cops at the community policing office started to recognize him, first with suspicion, then with concern.

"Come on in, kid, sit with us for a bit. No, we don't have doughnuts. Timmy's coffee, though."

One night he'd stopped a pimp beating up a prostitute.

"Ever think of being a police officer?" asked the duty officer, pulling on latex gloves to clean a cut on Stephen's forehead.

Stephen had applied to the RCMP, been accepted, enrolled, trained, graduated. He'd worked in Iqaluit—his obligatory hardship posting—a town melting in a warming world. He'd joined the integrated gangs task force. He'd ended up here. He looked down, again, at the postcard of Chich'en Itzá and then out to the lights on Islas Mujeres and the dark sea beyond.

He wished he could follow the boy's instructions; he wished he could send the postcard to Erin. But he couldn't send it beyond the grave. Suddenly as tired as death itself: it was time to go back to Anya's and sleep.

***

Rebecca let herself fall backwards in exhaustion. The hotel bed could have been studded with nails and it still would have been welcome.

From her vantage, she could see palm trees through her room's sliding glass door, still as statues against the azure Caribbean sky. Hard to believe a hurricane had been blowing hard enough to shut down air traffic across the continental US, landing her eight hours late. But then, depending on who you talked to, the whole thing had been the NHC overreacting: the proverbial tempest in a teapot. She should call Aunt Kathy to find out what really had happened.

She looked at her watch. It was seven here, which would make it eight in Florida and a full nine hours after she set out from Dulles. No, she reconsidered, she should call Deb to check in. And thank her again.

Rebecca's mind slow with exhaustion, she thought back on their final conversation and all that Deb had done.

"Get rid of half that stuff and put the rest in this," Deb had said, nodding to Rebecca's suitcase and proffering a grey knapsack.

"Carry on only. Wash your clothes in the sink and use the hotel's soap and shampoo. Here's your diplomatic passport. And take this stuff."

"I know how to pack. I've been to Mexico more than a few times, you know. What stuff?"

"Yeah, but never to Cancún right before the Mayan apocalypse when a gazillion crazies are headed down to be at ground zero when the world ends. The stuff is this: your boarding card, your diplomatic passport, your hotel reservation, and this…" she had been handing everything to Rebecca as she named it. The next item was a USB data stick.

"It has everything I could find out about the money on it," Deb frowned. "Not a lot to go on, but it should help."

Rebecca started to offer thanks but Deb continued, handing over one final item: a rubber-encased satellite phone.

"Don't lose it or I'll have a lot of explaining to do."

"I don't need a sat phone!" Rebecca finally said, juggling the things Deb had already given to her. "Mexico *has* entered the 21st century; my iPhone will work down there. As for the apocalypse, you know as well as I do that that's just stupid. It's just a new *b'ak'tun*—a new cycle, like our calendar rolling from 1999 to 2000. It's 'millennial,' not 'apocalyptic.'"

"Sure I know it, but you just try telling it to the loonies heading down to watch the world end from up on top of Chich'en Itzá. As nutty as the ones who stocked up on canned food and guns at the end of 1999. Now shut up, take the phone, and go."

Yes, Rebecca really should call Deb. And then she should head to the bank to which Deb had traced the money. She really should. But maybe she could have a quick nap first. The bed almost demanded it. Rebecca rolled over and began to scootch up the bed, boots still on. She pulled the coverlet over herself and was asleep before she made it to the pillows.

***

Travis Rutrauff splashed his face with cool water from the pump in front of the mess hut and chuckled as he looked up at the milky morning sky: the great and mighty Kulkulcan had asked him to toughen the boys up in the forest overnight and, by God, so he had. He'd scared the bejeezuz out of them; now they were ready for anything. Truth be told, he hadn't done much: the forest had done it all by itself. And it had spooked him a little in the process, too.

He'd planned to run the Outward Bound exercise: sit each one down at sunset in his own little spot beside some running water and let them all stay put, alone and in the dark, all night. The take-home lesson, when the sun rose, was that they could make it on their own. Last night, though, the jungle had been more terrifying than usual, filled with more than just the personal demons that haunt the lonely and alone.

For starters, animals normally asleep at night had been restive: a herd of peccaries ran the length of the stream, snuffling the ground at a terrified boy's feet; a jaguar screamed almost on the hour, as if keeping time; and three spider monkeys, like silent little sentinels, sat watching Travis as he sat in a tree, waiting for the exercise to run its course.

Then suddenly the jungle had grown silent as a morgue, a quiet that held, like a breath, for a long moment before the first of the boys screamed. Travis was down and running in an instant. Before he could get to the source, a second boy—this one at the far end of the line—shrieked. They were wordless, these screams from his erstwhile soldiers: long and loud and full of hopeless terror.

Despite his training, Travis remembered fighting the desire to run from the sound—to run from whatever was making the boys make it.

"¡*Un fantasma*! A ghost is here! She says the rain is coming! We have to go!" shouted the first wide-eyed boy, his obsidian blade drawn and wildly carving the air.

"Calm down, boy. Calm down," Travis said sternly.

"The ghost, she says to go! She is terrible, with red eyes and blood in her mouth."

"There's no such thing as ghosts, boy. Now buck up."

"She tried to catch me!" the boy sobbed, proffering his arm. There were deep scratches through his sleeve, as from a cat.

Travis had collected the boys and set them in front of a fire to calm them down and then demanded to know what happened.

They had started their tales meekly: each boy had seen a woman in white wandering through the forest.

"She was all alone."

"She was not much older than me."

"She was sexy."

"Very sexy. With big squeezable boobs under a see-through dress."

That bravado got a nervous laugh from the group.

"My *toon* stood up so I could be ready to fuck her," said another, matching audacity with a boast of his own.

"And then her eyed turned to fire, and her mouth to blackness, and blood and heat came out of her."

"She was going to swallow me down into the dark."

"She turned into a cat and scratched me!"

"No, she set her cat upon us!"

The boys were working themselves back into a frenzy.

"Hold on, hold on!" Travis barked. "I told you before. There's no such thing as ghosts. You're letting your imaginations run wild. Now I'm going to put you back in your places and you *are* going to make it through the night.

"'*Tun tal chaak*,' she said. I don't like it. I don't want to go back," someone whimpered. A few heads nodded in agreement.

"*Xtabay* is a myth and it ain't gonna storm on my watch," Rutrauff growled. "Now get your backsides in gear!"

Most of the boys began to move; Payal paused to look at Rutrauff curiously.

"How do you know what that means?"

"What *what* means?" Travis said, staring the boy down. Payal would not look away.

"'*Tun tal chaak.*' It means 'a storm is coming.' You speak Yucatec?"

Travis remembered cursing himself then: that he could speak the ancient language was the biggest reason he'd been selected for this mission. Giving his advantage away so carelessly was an amateur's mistake.

"One of the boys said something about rain coming. What's your point?"

"Hector said 'rain,' not 'storm.' And *Xtabay*? How do you know of her?"

Travis thought fast: he wasn't about to admit he'd learn of the temptress from the same person who had taught him Yucatec: a nanny, when he was six years old and the miserable son of disinterested diplomats posted to the region. She'd told him *Xtabay* was a devil-woman who ate men whose hearts were not pure.

"Kulkulcan told me. Anything else?" he asked witheringly.

Payal narrowed his eyes, still suspicious, but looked away.

"No. Nothing else."

"'Nothing else, *sir*.' Now get your backside in gear before *I* rain on you and the rest of this frickin' parade."

Travis had found a good tree and sat down with his back to it to wait out the rest of the night. It crawled by, as uneventful as the earlier part of the night had been dreadful, and he let his eyes close to rest when he heard one of the boys snoring. He must have fallen asleep, because when a sudden sound woke him, he could make out tree trunks: the forest was the deep grey that heralds dawn, and a fog was forming before him.

Not a fog, a woman. With long dark hair, clad only in a thin mist. Arousing, yes, but it was her lips, not her eyes, that were crimson. He saw her speak but heard nothing; he closed his eyes to improve his hearing.

"Wayak'…" said a sibilant voice. *A dream.*

Rutrauff opened his eyes again but she was gone.

Travis suddenly hoped to God he had been sharing the boys' delusion for if *Xtabay* was real, he was in trouble: he was a trained killer, and his heart was very far from clean.

***

Stephen rubbed the sleep out of his eyes, reached over to the coffee table for his watch, and checked the time before slipping it on, clipping it shut, and sitting up on Anya's couch. Almost noon. He could have used the guest bed, but he'd gotten in from the beach at almost four a.m.; the couch had been easier.

Dressed after a quick shower, Stephen prepared to leave but found himself side-tracked by Anya's desk. Cluttered, it would say more about her than anything else her meticulous apartment held and, like a worried brother, Stephen wanted to know a little more about the woman Chalo fancied.

Stephen had been right: copious notes on stickies, in books and on slips of paper marked her for an obsessive and apparently brilliant student of her discipline; the chewed pens gave away a high-strung temperament; the earrings and bracelet and lavender hand cream suggested she spent long hours at the desk.

There was a snapshot stuck to her lamp; Stephen took a closer look at it, wondering if Chalo might have competition. No, it was Anya and a tall blonde with facial features enough like Anya's—and the same eerily blue eyes—that he must be family. Beneath the lamp lay a small cardboard box filled with orange plastic rings about the diameter of his thumb. He picked one up: it had a spur on it like a jewel on a real ring and was stamped with the letters ROSP followed by a four-digit number. He'd bet anything they were bird bands but why would an archaeologist have them? He shrugged, put the tag back, and turned for the kitchen. His hand caught the box, spilling half a dozen tags onto the desk.

After calling himself a jerk Stephen righted the box, started gathering the bands, and yelped in surprise. His fingertips had brushed something bitterly cold. The source was something transparent—ice?—beside the last of the errant bands.

Stephen bent down for a better look and realized that he was looking at a piece of quartz the size of a plum. A stone in a warm room should not be cold as ice. But it was. How the hell did that work? He picked up the crystal carefully, held it up to the window for a better look, and raised his eyebrows in wonder: the quartz was rutilated—shot through with slender silver needles—and the rutiles were not straight but spiralled, like a tiny tornado encased in glass.

A cloud drifted in front of the sun, darkening the crystal's heart, and for a moment the rutiles seemed to swirl, the storm inside it suddenly alive. Stephen stared, fascinated, as the laws of physics appeared to break: the vortex wound in on itself and flashes, like lightning, danced and sparked within the stone. He was being drawn into the darkening maelstrom, could hear the keening wind and feel the stinging rain. The stone between his fingers grew colder still—painfully cold—Stephen dropped it to the desk and the spell was broken.

"Ghosts and haunted stones," Stephen muttered. Abandoning thoughts of breakfast, he grabbed his knapsack and dug through it for a clean shirt. "I've got to get out of this country before I go nuts." He cinched his knapsack closed and corrected himself. "Before I go *more* nuts."

***

Anya's apartment locked behind him and the key placed back in the clay lizard, Stephen headed for the car. Even parked in the shade, it was stifling, the new-car-and-shampoo smell nauseatingly sweet. He hurried to start the car and its air-conditioning but recoiled as he turned the key in the ignition; the pressure on his thumb and forefinger was searingly painful. He inspected them: they were each blistered, as if frostbitten. What had he touched? The rutilated stone?

"Oh, for God's sake," he muttered, irritated by the impropriety of situations constantly defying reason. He put the car roughly into drive and did a quick shoulder check.

"Oh, for *God's sake*," he said again, this time in disbelief.

An egg-yolk yellow Buick Skylark from the late 60s, lovingly restored, thrummed past him, eight cylindered and throaty, wheel rims glinting in the sun. A long looping serpent—emerald green with purple eyes and flaming orange wings—had been painted from hood to tailfin; there was no mistaking this car. Even with the windows closed and tinted, Stephen knew that it was driven by Bernardo Candelario Alvarro, the young drug lord that he and Chalo had been chasing for so long.

Against his better judgment, Stephen pulled out and started following Alvarro's car.

CHAPTER 17

Anya woke in an otherwise empty bed, late morning sun blinding through the sliding-glass door. She leaned up on one elbow and squinted into the brightness.

"Chalo?"

No answer. She let herself fall back into the pillows, holding the sheet to her naked chest.

"*Sheisse.*"

The last person she'd slept with had been her husband, Emedio, two days before she'd filed for a divorce. It had been a long dry spell. But last night had not been nice simply because it had ended her long celibacy. Anya felt her breath quicken, re-aroused by the memory: the sex had been very, very good.

It would be easier if it hadn't, she sighed ruefully. She wanted no more complications in her life. She knew nothing about this cop from Mexico City. What had she been thinking? Anya sat up to look for her clothes. They were still in a heap where they had dropped. Maybe she could leave before he got back and that would be the end of it.

Except that she wasn't sure that she wanted it to be the end. He was intriguing. And handsome. And, unlike Emedio, he was not self-centred. At least not when he made love. She thought again about his hands and rolled her eyes at herself. She had to get to the ruins and he was not here, so that was that. A one-night stand. End of story.

She stood, dressed quickly, ran her fingers through her hair and looked around for her hairclip. She found it under one of the pillows, used it to put her hair in a short ponytail before sitting down to pull her boots from under the bed and onto her feet.

The door creaked open as she was lacing her boots and she turned to the sound. It was Chalo with a paper plate of fruit and croissants in one hand and a plastic cup of orange juice in the other. They looked at each other, feeling awkward.

"I… brought you some breakfast?" Chalo said at last as he stepped the rest of the way into the room.

"Thank you. You're very kind," Anya said softly. "About last night…"

"It was very nice…" Chalo began, grinning.

"Yes it was," Anya replied, more enthusiastically than she meant to. "But I… we… umm…" She glanced back to her half-tied boots.

"… but can we pretend as if it did not happen… ?" Chalo said carefully.

Anya took a deep breath. "Yes, maybe that would be best."

Chalo nodded, a cloud of disappointment scudding almost imperceptibly across his face. He covered it with humour. "I told you the bed wasn't so comfortable."

"I… I didn't notice," Anya said, angry at herself for hurting his feelings. "I still need to go down to Sian Ka'an. You are still welcome to come, if you wish. And maybe see if there is anything that they can tell you about the last heart?"

Chalo brightened. "I would like that, actually. There is nothing else to find here: I spoke with the chief constable before getting breakfast…"

"And…"

"Nothing. He said he was very sorry, that young Rico Mendez will be disciplined, that he couldn't imagine how it happened, all the while looking like the cat that swallowed the peccary."

Anya smiled. "The canary. The cat swallowed a canary."

"Aha! That makes more sense!" Chalo replied. "I never understood why a cat would be happy swallowing a pig."

Their laughter died away and was replaced by an uncomfortable silence. Anya and Chalo started speaking at once to fill it, paused at the same time, started again, and stopped once more.

"You go first," Chalo said at last.

"May we eat on the way to Sian Ka'an? I'm worried about my site."

"We can leave right now."

Anya looked back at the room as they left, her eyes lingering on the bed for a moment before she shook the thought away. Single was simple and she needed simple to concentrate on her work.

***

Rebecca woke to the sound of a room-service trolley rattling past her door and squeezed her eyes shut in protest before rolling over to look at the bedside clock.

"Damn."

It was eleven. The banks all closed at one.

She sat up quickly, ran her fingers through her hair, grabbed the small pack Deb had given her, and headed out the door.

The flight delays had given Rebecca a lot of time to look at the material Deb had found and formulate a plan or two. From Washington, the money had gone to two accounts in Cancún: the legitimate Red Cross account and a numbered one. Then money from the numbered account had been deposited to a credit card belonging to T. Rutrauff of P.O. Box 43996, in Killeen, Texas—a card that had been used twice at a motel near Cancún and once at a gas station in Calakmul. The transfer was sloppy for a plan built by someone as smart as Joe. But maybe his arrogance had gotten the better of him at last. At least it gave her a few leads.

She had rented a car at the airport; her plan had been to go first to the hotel to ask the owner about his repeat guest and then to the bank to try to wheedle something from the bank manager about the numbered account. But the bank was ten minutes away and would close within the hour: she would have to go there first instead.

Fifteen minutes later she was at a Banco de Mexico on Avenida Bonampak in El Centro. Once up the marble stairs and through the brass revolving doors, she was dwarfed by an enormous foyer intended to intimidate: ornate columns rose to a thirty-foot-high dome, a revolutionary war painting sprawling across it. At the far end of the expanse stood the tellers' wickets: tiny closets behind thick sheets of Plexiglas.

A single teller spoke loudly through the security barrier to the bank's only other customer, a trim man in his mid-thirties, deeply tanned, hair buzzed, wearing crisp chinos and a short-sleeved plaid shirt: military for sure, she could just feel it.

Rebecca crossed the wide marble floor and stood at the head of a non-existent line.

"You're sure you can have all of it, sweet thing?" the man asked.

"Chauvinist," Rebecca thought.

"*Si, si*. My manager says we will have it ready for you in one hour," the teller replied. "Will that be soon enough for you, *Señor* Rutrauff?"

Rutrauff?! Was she really getting this lucky?

"That'll do, fine." the man replied to the teller. "The place across the street makes a decent lunch?"

"Oh, yes. The *taquitos* are very nice."

"I'll try them and see you in an hour, then," the man said as he turned to leave.

Damn! Rebecca couldn't let him see her. She crouched quickly and busied herself with her knapsack as the man walked by.

Once he was gone, Rebecca stood and looked at the teller apologetically.

"So sorry. I forgot my passport. I… I'll be back."

Adolf Hitler wrote "the bigger the lie the more they will believe it." Rebecca didn't like anything about Hitler but she hoped, for her own sake, that he'd been right on that score: she was about to tell a whopper.

Back outside, Rebecca undid her shirt two buttons, let her hair down, and put her sunglasses on. Not much of a transformation, but the tank hugged her slender physique and Rebecca wasn't above using the man's overactive libido against him. Then she took a bottle of water from her knapsack, crossed the street, unscrewed the water bottle and started walking towards Rutrauff from behind. A metre from him she pretended to trip and sent water spilling over Rutrauff's back.

He stood up swiftly and in a single fluid movement turned towards Rebecca; he was in a defensive katana before his chair hit the ground.

"Aww hell!" Rebecca said, sounding suddenly as if she hailed from the deep south.

"I'm awful sorry. I tripped and…" she looked down at the empty plastic bottle in her hand, "Did I git you wet?"

The man relaxed. "You could say that…" he smiled, showing his back.

"Damn! Looks like I got you with the whole thing! Here… lemme help," she said, brushing past him to grab a small stack of cocktail napkins from the table.

"Nah, nah, let it go," the man chuckled. "It'll dry soon enough."

"Well then, would you at least let me buy you a coffee..." she glanced at the beer on the table. "Or maybe a beer... ?"

"How 'bout you join me for lunch, instead? I could use the company."

Rebecca's stomach growled audibly; she hadn't eaten since leaving Washington.

"Seems my stomach's isn't giving me much of a choice," Rebecca said as she sat down. "Name's Becky Wilkes, and I'm real sorry about the water."

"Travis Rutrauff. Pleased to make your acquaintance."

The waiter appeared with a plate of nachos; Rutrauff ordered a second plate for Rebecca and when she assented, a beer.

"So, what's a good looking lady like you doing by yourself?"

"I'm on holidays," she announced proudly. "How 'bout you? Vacation, too?"

"Here on business, actually."

"And what kind of business is that?" Rebecca asked. She reached for a taco from his plate, stopped, and looked at him with doe eyes.

"You don't mind, do you?" she said, flirting overtly. "just 'til my own come?"

"Fill your boots," he replied, charmed.

Rebecca ate a few chips and licked her fingertips. "Your business?" she prompted him.

"Nothing much. Training. Investing. That kind of thing."

"Sounds like it makes a lot of money," she smiled. "I like you already, Travis."

"Not so much, but it pays the bills."

"Paying the bills is good. How long you in town?"

"A... a few days..." he said, suddenly little edgy.

"Sheesh! I don't work for the IRS! You sitting out here all alone? I figure you're flying solo, too. Thought you might want to check out the sights with me this afternoon, is all."

"Wish I could, Becky, but I've got a bunch of meetings right through dinner time."

"That's a shame. Working so late so soon before Christmas? Your boss seems like a hard-ass, if you ask me."

Travis laughed out loud; "hard-ass" was a very good word for Kulkulcan.

"What's so funny?"

"Nothing at all. You're right about my boss. And about it being a shame. So how 'bout you join me for a drink after dinner?"

Rebecca looked up, genuinely surprised. She had expected this would be a one off and was assuming his name—no one would make up a name like Rutrauff—was all she was going to get.

"Tonight?"

"Yeah, tonight. I can get us in to one of the hottest dance-clubs on the strip… my hard-ass boss owns it."

Another lead, maybe. "Really? Which one?"

"It's called the *Zócalo*, over on the hotel strip. You want to go?"

"I'd be my pleasure, Travis!" Rebecca said. She hoped she sounded genuinely enthusiastic; she hated bars—they reminded her that she was single again.

"Wonderful! Tell me where you're staying and I'll pick you up at 8:30."

"I'm staying right next door. To the *Zócalo*, I mean," she lied. Better not have him know where she was staying. "How about I meet you right out front?"

"That'll work. You wait out front beside Jorge—he's the bouncer—and I'll come out and get you…" His watch suddenly beeped.

"Shoot, I gotta run. Here's twenty for lunch…"

"Hey! I was supposed to buy this!"

"You buy me something tonight. *Zócalo*, 8:30. I'll be waiting…"

Rebecca watched him lope across the street. She took a swig of her *Dos Equis* and cursed. So his boss was going to be there; that was good. But now she was going to have to buy a party dress to look the part.

***

Stephen slouched in his rental car outside a tiny, two-chair barber shop and watched the red, white, and blue pole spiral upwards, waiting for Alvarro and the overweight man with him to emerge. He had been following the pair around Cancún Centro for the better part of the afternoon, watching them do a whole lot of nothing: they'd watched a soccer game, eaten lunch, talked on their cell phones… and now they were getting haircuts. More precisely, Alvarro, baby-faced and barely old enough to grow facial hair, seemed to be about to get an old-fashioned shave. The big guy—obviously Alvarro's body-guard—stood, back against the wall, hyper-vigilant, and did nothing.

"Well this was stupid," Stephen chastised himself. "I should have gone to Chich'en Itzá, instead."

And then something happened: instead of giving Alvarro a shave, the tidy white-coated barber took a wad of American money from the bodyguard, turned the "open" sign to "closed," and left the shop. A moment later two strangers walked into the shop: a young Mexican built like a full-back and an older, shorter, lighter-skinned guy built like a boxer. The full-back carried a briefcase; the other man's right arm was heavily tattooed.

"Man, that must have hurt," Steven muttered to himself as he tried to make out the tattoo's design. A snake, maybe, the fanged mouth inked on the back of his hand.

The full-back set the briefcase down and then re-emerged to stand guard outside; the tattooed man took the empty chair beside Alvarro and spoke. Alvarro replied, his body language fawning: beta dog to the tattooed man's alpha. There was much posturing, much nodding, and finally a smile from the tattooed man. It was a signal of some kind: Alvarro stood, unwrapped a long slender parcel—one he'd been carting around all day—and presented the contents to the tattooed man. Stephen's saw a flash of colour and his stomach lurched: the gift was a quetzal feather.

Stephen's mind reeled: Alvarro had been at the warehouse so the feather might have been from the bird killed there. The tattooed man stood, clapped Alvarro on the back, took the feather, and left.

"Me and my bloody curiosity," Stephen said. He needed to leave. Another few hours, and he really needed to leave *now*—at least if he wanted to stop at Chich'en Itzá—if he was going to make his flight back to BC. But here was a lead Chalo might be able to use. But maybe he could skip the ruin…it would still be there next time he came to Mexico, wouldn't it?

***

Monday, December 10, 2012 — 6 Muluc, Day of Jade

"So," Chalo said as he and Anya drove past a tiny kiosk marking the official entrance to the Sian Ka'an Biosphere Reserve, a single fluorescent light on the sign bright against the dark jungle surrounding it.

"You had this big white truck for a long time?"

It was his third effort to strike up a conversation in thirty minutes. Talking had been awkward given the previous evening's intimacy, and to play at pleasantries was not Anya's style. Still, she shouldn't punish him when she was really angry only with herself for having jumped into his bed.

"About three years," she replied, finally responsive. "I took it from my ex-husband's research program. Have you ever been married?"

Her eyes remained on the dirt road and her hands clenched the wheel, holding the truck steady on the rutted dirt road.

Chalo's eyes widened and a small grin crawled across his face. "Not me."

"You have a partner?"

"Only Stephen, these past three years…"

Anya turned and looked at him briefly, puzzled.

"No, no. Not like that" he replied, aghast.

Anya frowned, eyes still on the road.

"I didn't mean that. Gay is okay. I got no problem with gay. Gay guys got more brains than straight guys, most of the time. But me? I'm not gay."

"And Stephen?"

"Stephen's not gay, either. He's my *police* partner. No girls in his life, but not because he's gay."

"So why are there no girls in his life, then? He seems smart and handsome…"

"You think he's handsome?"

Anya was flattered by the jealousy in his tone.

"Stephen got messed up when his fiancée died. He blames himself. He stays away from women because he thinks he's bad luck."

"What happened?"

"An accident. She fell off a cliff when they were climbing. Straight up a mountain. I don't know how Esteban can be so smart and still like doing such stupid things. Are Germans crazy like that?"

"Crazier, I think. We go from Germany to Canada to do those things.

I did them in Canada when I was a teenager, even."

"Really?" Chalo said in disbelief. "Why?"

"Secondary school exchange program. I went to school in Canada for three months to learn English."

"So how did you get from Canada to Mexico and your arrogant *crillolo*?"

"You have a very good memory."

"They don't call me 'Detective Guerrero' for nothing, you know."

Anya laughed appreciatively.

"I went back to Germany for my baccalaureate and then my master's degree, then came to Mexico to take my doctorate. The *crillolo* was my thesis advisor. He flattered me, and married me, and had me publish a dozen papers in his name…"

"And then… ?"

"And then…" Anya let the sentence slide away from her as she thought back to the moment she had discovered him with his newest grad student, the scene still lurid in her memory.

She had come into his office one day to find a new grad student laid on her back on Emedio's desk, her skirt hiked up, her legs clasped tight around Emedio's backside. Emedio's hands were under her sweater, kneading her silicone-augmented breasts, his pelvis pumping hard against hers.

The girl looked sideways, saw Anya enter, and pulled Emedio more tightly to her. Emedio followed the girl's gaze.

"Anya. Ah, yes. The three new papers are ridiculous. I cannot put my name to them…"

He paused, close to climax.

"… but we'll talk later," he said, breath ragged. "You go. I am… about… to…"

Anya had stormed out, filed for divorce, and published all three papers in her name alone on their merits. And their merits had been considerable, despite Emedio's disdain: "*von Eckhardt has discovered a new complex of terminal period temples. No mere backwaters, these structures tell us a great deal more about the Mayan circularity of time. These new finds, and most especially the small observatory referred to in von Eckhardt's second paper entitled 'The Venus Cycle and Social Collapse in the Terminal Period,' begin to give us insight into the decline of the Maya that began prior to, and was hastened by, the arrival of Europeans in the 1400s.*" Had she been so offended because he had been unfaithful, or because he had insulted her work, Anya suddenly wondered.

"And then, we disagreed about the quality of my work and went our separate ways," she replied evenly, answering both Chalo's question and her own.

"Your work was better than his and he didn't like it, hmm?"

"Something like that."

"Well, for the record, I can be arrogant when I am right. But I am not *crillolo*."

Anya smiled. "Yes, but at least you know you can be wrong." Then, suddenly, she turned right and stopped the car. With a gleam in her eye she added, "Are you ready?"

They had stopped behind an old yellow VW bug. Chalo looked down the corridor illuminated by the truck's headlights: beyond the car lay only a narrow footpath through a small copse of seagrape bushes, their waxy round leaves bright in the artificial light. At the path's end, where land gave way to water, the seagrapes gave way to mangroves, their stilt-like roots arching above the glittering blue-brown water. At the same spot, the path gave over to a long, narrow wooden dock that led through the mangroves to open water and a fourteen-foot aluminum boat.

Chalo felt the pick-up rock beneath him and looked out the rear window: Anya had jumped into the flatbed to gather equipment and supplies.

"Whose car?" Chalo asked as he got out of the truck. Anya handed Chalo a powerful halogen flashlight.

"Pedro and Marcela's. Biologists. Friends… *Sheisse*, I forgot to bring their new transmitters. Can you take the outboard?"

"Where are they, then?"

"Pedro and Marcela? They took the other boat. They're out there somewhere, camped for the night. They study Spoonbills; they'll check the colonies when the sun rises."

"Spoonbills?" Chalo asked as he watched Anya adjust her pack, don a headlamp, and pick up two heavy duffel bags.

"Big pink migratory bird that look like storks. With beaks that look like wooden spoons. They come here from the southern States to nest.

They are funny-looking, but very pretty."

"Speaking of which," Chalo rejoined, "you look amusing, too. Like a very happy burro with all your things!"

A moment later, realization dawning, he added, "Not that you look like a donkey or are funny-looking in any way…"

Anya chuckled as she put down a duffel, reached into the cab to turn out the lights, and, started down the path, her spirit irrepressible.

"The land of your ancestors!" she called over her shoulder. "¡*Ko'ox tun*! Let's go!"

Chalo heard his grandmother's voice echoed in Anya's—a doting adult to a tardy child—and for a moment he forgot himself. He stood and listened to the frogs chirp and the water lap against the hollow metal boat. An owl hooted, and Chalo smiled, his heart as light as the dust that swirled and danced in the beam of his flashlight. Then, like the beloved dawdling child, he grabbed the outboard and hurried to catch up with Anya, now at the boat and stowing her gear.

***

The vamp in the mirror pirouetted in her strappy silver heels, her hot-pink halter dress swirling above her shapely knees. The scanty dress—bought along with the shoes, bangles, and dangly earrings in the lobby of her hotel—had transformed her from diplomat to bimbo perfectly. Rebecca looked at herself and laughed out loud. It had been a long time since she had laughed like that—unreservedly and at herself—and it felt good.

"Well girl," she said to her reflection, "I think you'll do."

With that she put her meagre valuables—iPhone, wallet, notebook, and the satellite phone—in the room's small safe, tapped in a pass code, and locked it. Her passport was down with the front desk and what little else she had brought, she reasoned, wasn't worth a robber's trouble.

Three hundred dollars in cash she tucked carefully into her bra; the flimsy plastic keycard she slipped between the ball of her right foot and the insole of her shoe. She'd done it a few times before, in college: the perspiration from her foot would keep the key in place. Then she walked out her hotel room door.

She could not have imagined that when she returned the following afternoon she would be wearing a different outfit altogether: hiding in plain sight, she would be wearing Anya's clothes.

CHAPTER 18

It had been a long day for the old healer already and the sun had not yet topped the trees surrounding his village.

"Take a rest, *Don* Yaxché!" had insisted Lupita. "You have hours before your patients arrive!"

"Ha!" the old man cackled. "And the bewitched girl and her sick baby were not patients? No, Lupita, today will be busy, and I must go shopping."

Lupita had watched helplessly as the old man donned his rubber boots, picked up his worn canvas bags, and headed out to the forest that was his pharmacy and grocery store; he had returned, heavily laden, minutes before the day's bus—a creaky old yellow school bus pressed into service by an enterprising driver who realized he could make a few dollars driving people in to see the famed healer—had arrived.

And he had been right: it had been a very busy afternoon. Nor were the complaints the regular ones—coughs that required linden tea or deep wounds that required tincture of rose. Like Tonalna, the patients that had come had illnesses of the soul.

—Don Yaxché, I fear the feathered serpent will steal my spirit and I cannot sleep!

—Don Yaxché, I have been cursed by gods and now my corn will not grow!

—Don Yaxché, I am haunted by dreams of a great wind!

—Don Yaxché, last night the Lady came and a jaguar screamed the end of the world!

One after terrified one they had come; one after one he had healed them, each in the same way. He had listened. He had taken the measure of their blood—pulses that raced or fluttered or dragged sluggishly through the body. For restlessness he had prescribed tea; for anxiety he had administered massage and prescribed rest; for sadness he had prescribed *pepitas*, rich in serotonin. He had said blessings over the children and prayers over the adults. For a very few he had consulted his *sastun*—his healer's stone. And to each he had offered humour: laughter was a potent balm for their fear. They had all left behind whatever they could pay, with smiles on their faces, thankful for a *curandero* like *El Mero*, the True One.

The bus finally left an hour before sunset and Lupita brought the old healer a warm mug of vanilla *atole*. She found him sitting on his examining table, hands on knees, head bowed.

"*Don* Yaxché?"

"*Si*, Lupita," the healer replied without looking up.

"You work too hard, *Don* Yaxché."

"I will have to work harder, soon, I think."

"What is coming?" Lupita asked.

She was not yet as old as Yaxché, but she was old enough to ask the question that a younger person might have feared to have answered.

"You were right, Lupita. The dead do not like to let go, once called."

"Is it bad?" Lupita asked earnestly.

"Worse, I think. The path will be difficult, and my eyesight grows dim."

Looking up now, Yaxché saw concern crease his old friend's brow; he forced a laugh.

"Wipe the worry off your face, you old hen! I did not say it would be impossible, only difficult! You just concern yourself with babies; I will look after the world into which you bring them, hmm?"

Lupita looked dubious and then remembered who she was speaking to: this was Yaxché, named at birth for the world tree. The sky would not fall while he was alive. She nodded and smiled.

"Shoo then and make my supper for me!" Yaxché scolded, a genuine smile on his face. "You are keeping me from my hammock and a well-deserved rest!"

Lupita laughed, her teeth bright.

"Sleep quickly, you old goat; supper is almost ready," she said as she turned to leave.

"Old fool!" Yaxché cursed himself as he settled into his hammock.

Monday, December 10, 2012 — 6 Muluc, Day of Jade

"Making her worried, like that. A fine *curandero* I am, causing fear!"

The hammock was comfortable after an afternoon on his feet. He put his head on Tonalna's soft blue blanket and smiled as he closed his eyes: the blanket smelled like a baby.

Almost asleep, he suddenly heard a keening, felt a bitter wind blow through his hut. Eyes instantly open, he saw nothing but an obsidian blackness; he blinked and still saw nothing, as if he had been buried in dirt. The herald wind grew frigid, and Yaxché steadied himself for the vision to come.

"I am Yaxché. Show me what you wish me to see."

Nothing happened.

"I am Yaxché," he said again. "Show me."

A tiny whiteness appeared before him. A distant light. No, a thing—a glowing stone—much closer. A hurricane swirled within it, silver splinters gathering speed, the vortex drawing Yaxché in. He reached for the stone; it was out of place, the balance upset—he needed to put it back.

Shapes danced around him, pushed him back, their breath rank with the odour of blood and death.

"I am Yaxché. I have earned the right to walk beyond the veil," Yaxché croaked, "Let me pass!"

A jaguar screamed. The air around him blazed as if electrified, and the figures drew back. Yaxché was in a cave, standing before a small and terrible fire burning green and cold and silent, the storm stone now in his hand, ready to be returned, the clock reset. The figures surged forward, howling with rage. They clawed the walls, seams of earth and stone and finally the entire cavern, folding inward on Yaxché, crushing him.

He scrabbled forward, all alone, crawling beneath jagged rock that tore at his back. The stone burned in the palm of his hand.

"No!" he called, angry at his weakness. "I cannot do this alone."

Four distant figures appeared, thin and shifting like branches in the wind. They ringed him, raised their arms, and the weight eased. A scarlet macaw, wing badly broken, fluttered to his feet. A bad bird, a bad omen. And yet he touched it, soothed it; it cried out in relief, redeemed.

The cave was gone now, the sky brilliant, stars glittering against the blue-black sky. In the north, a cascade of bright sparks tumbled to the horizon, a shower of shooting stars. He cried out with the beauty of it and his voice was that of a newborn. He gasped with pain and delight.

"*Don* Yaxché? Did you call?"

Yaxché's eyes flew open, truly awake this time.

"Lupita! What time is it? Have I been asleep for long?"

"Long? I had not even crossed the road. I heard you call out. Are you alright?"

"Come in, come in. I have seen things…" he said, struggling from his hammock.

Lupita opened the door, brushed past the curtain, and gasped. A moment ago she had left a man tired but in good health; now he stood, drenched in sweat, blood on his face, back, and legs, and an angry white burn in the palm of his upturned hand.

"I have seen what has been and will come again. Come now, I must not be proud; I cannot stop the bleeding without help."

EBOLA IN THE AMERICAS?

Manchester Week in Review
December 11, 2012

A pair of bodies discovered in Mexico's Yucatán jungle are puzzling the World Health Organization, on the lookout for emerging diseases in Mexico since the appearance there in 2009 of H1N1. But according to Mexican officials, anxious to reassure winter tourists, the deceased are middle-aged male Mexican nationals with apparent gang connections: the men were not struck down by disease.

Few are reassured. On condition of anonymity, a technician assisting with both autopsies said the victims' deaths were consistent with a novel infection, not murder. "They bled to death. In both cases they hemorrhaged from every orifice—even from unhealed abrasions on the skin. Death was rapid but probably quite painful."

Fears are already building that this could be an outbreak of a new viral hemorrhagic fever, a family of deadly diseases better known by their individual names: Ebola, Marburg; Lassa Fever. *Traditionally associated with Africa, hemorrhagic disease is also found in South America:* Machupo Disease*—characterized by fever, vomiting, and internal and external bleeding that leads to death in 50 to 90% of all cases—was identified in Brazil in the late 1950s. The fear is that this new disease could develop into the next global pandemic. Even the possibility would spell disaster for the Mexican economy, only now recovering from the global financial meltdown of 2008, thanks to the Mitnal oil field. Quick to quell any rumour that could harm the economy, the Mexican Medical*

Officer of Health has said that the men died not of a virus but at the hands of narco-traffickers using a new weapon.

Mike deGroot, an analyst with Jane's Weekly *says this story is plausible. In the hands of a creative technician, the Silent Guardian or "pain ray"—the best known of the US military micro-wave based crowd-control technologies known as Active Denial Systems (ADS)—could be modified to kill. And its signature would be ugly and bloody in the manner of hemorrhagic fevers.*

"Absolutely it could be made deadly," said deGroot, "but the power needed to make a PSAD-1 M (Heckler and Koch's newest ADS system) deliver more than even a mild burn would be huge. To make it portable? Unlikely without a DB battery."

Manufactured in Germany by Daimler-Ballard (DB), DB batteries are next-generation fuels cells storing up to half a megawatt in a bread-box sized case. Used almost exclusively by the US military and the offshore oil industry, fewer than 100 DB batteries have been manufactured to date; their production is strictly controlled.

Still, the Mexican government should have its fingers crossed that "strictly controlled" doesn't mean "impossible to get": better for the economy that it be a rogue technology in the hands of a human than a rogue virus in the human race.

CHAPTER 19

Kulkulcan, dressed in a sleek grey suit belonging to Alonzo Malan Dzul—his former self—looked over the *Zócalo*'s wide balcony and smiled. The irony that the tourists rapidly filling his wildly popular "dance palace" were funding his plans to rid his country of them, once and for all, was not lost on him. Not in the least.

He'd built the club a dozen years before the camp at Calakmul, a legitimate business at the time, and soon the most popular club on the strip. The man who was now Kulkulcan watched from above as a knot of young American oil workers, already drunk on tequila and testosterone, lurched to one of the two hundred-foot-long bars flanking the warehouse-sized space, the bartenders behind it pouring drinks with both hands. Between the bars the dance floor lights pulsed in time with the heavy hip-hop beat; from his vantage on the balcony, Kulkulcan saw the writhing dancers as a single entity, a roiling sea.

The balcony was what set the *Zocaló* apart from the rest of the merely decadent clubs on the gringo trail. In addition to housing Kulkulcan's private offices, the balcony led to ten soundproofed "meeting rooms"—euphemisms containing mood lighting and water beds—that rented for five thousand US a night. And even at that price, the rooms would be full before midnight: foreigners with money to burn and passions to be quenched had less patience than dogs in heat.

They made everyone happy, those instant-gratification meeting rooms, and none more than Kulkulcan: at fifty thousand a night, the faster the rich and drunk fucked, the sooner he could pay for his revolution.

Travis Rutrauff joined Kulkulcan at the railing and watched the scene below. "So, Captain. What do you think?" Kulkulcan asked.

"Not my kind of music, Boss."

Kulkulcan smiled. "Not mine either. But I meant about my taking Payal from you?"

"Like I said, it depends on who you give me instead. Payal's smart."

"He is. That is why I need him to do something else."

Rutrauff decided to ignore the insult. "Can I ask what for?"

"I will tell you when the plan comes together. What if I give you Alvarro instead?"

Rutrauff tried, only somewhat successfully, to hide a sneer.

"You don't like him, do you?" Kulkulcan smiled.

"I don't. He likes blood too much. And secrets."

Kulkulcan nodded. Alvarro did like blood and secrets: Kulkulcan's clandestine meeting at the barbershop this afternoon had proved both.

"Your job is killing. And secrets. Why not his, too?"

"I don't enjoy killing the way he does."

"The way who enjoys what?" Alvarro himself had joined them, a patronizing smile on his face.

"You. Killing. You think it is fun," Rutrauff glowered.

"It isn't?" Alvarro said, his smile turning from smarmy to ugly.

"Gentlemen," Kulkulcan said, his voice a warning. "You are done for the night. Go have fun."

Rutrauff and Alvarro glowered at each for a moment before Rutrauff turned back to Kulkulcan. "You sure you don't need me?" he asked.

"Gringo got a date?" Alvarro jeered.

"No, Captain, I have just one more meeting but it doesn't concern you. Club business." Uncharacteristically, Kulkulcan lied poorly—clenching his fists and glancing away—but Rutrauff, thinking about a retort for Alvarro, missed it.

"And you?" Alvarro asked.

"Yeah Alvarro, I've got a date with a girl you can only dream about. Stick around and weep, why don't you?"

"You pay for her, Rutrauff?" Alvarro shot back.

"Piss off, Alvarro."

"Perhaps you'd like a meeting room then, Captain," Kulkulcan smiled. A further distraction for the American could not hurt.

"Thanks, but I can't afford your prices on my salary. The rent would keep me in bourbon for a lifetime!"

"My gift to you, Captain Rutrauff. Free. For services rendered," Kulkulcan said magnanimously.

Alvarro's eyes widened and Travis smiled.

"When you put it that way, I'd be happy to take it. Just in case…"

"Good," Kulkulcan said. "Now if you'll excuse me, I see my… my business associate downstairs."

"And I see my date. Stick around, Alvarro: you can meet her if you promise to pretend to be human."

***

Stephen had followed the tattooed man from barbershop to apartment building to the *Zócalo* and a hundred-dollar bill had gotten him past the bouncer; another twenty ensured that the coat-check girl would take good care of his knapsack.

Inside, he caught a glimpse of the man disappearing into a room on the balcony, and then nothing. Except thirty minutes of watching drunken tourists bump and grind on the dance floor.

Nothing stronger than Coke in his system—a fact which irritated the tank-topped waitress selling tequila shooters—Stephen surveyed the revellers and marvelled at the strangeness of the human form. At first blush they all looked different, but on closer inspection there were patterns, as if the vast diversity of humanity was really only a few people smudged and redrawn at the edges. He started categorizing them as he waited: there was the sportscaster on CTV back home; there was the moon-faced girl who worked the nightshift at the doughnut shop; there was… Erin?

He stopped slouching to take full advantage of his height: a woman in a pink halter-dress—pale, willowy and tall, with dark hair cascading over her shoulders—was walking up the stairs to the balcony. Stephen could hear nothing but the pounding of his heart and for a single, elated moment he actually believed that Erin had not died. Then a dancer slipped; her cold tequila shot soaked Stephen's shirt and he snapped from his daze. He took a second look and knew his mistake: this woman was taller, more willowy, with higher cheekbones, fuller lips, an aquiline nose. Not Erin.

Stephen sighed, wiped ineffectively at the spill on his shirt and looked back to the balcony. The tattooed man had reappeared and, now in a steel grey suit and a pink tie, was looking over the balcony. A trim guy in a short-sleeved plaid shirt with a blonde buzz cut and a chiselled jaw joined him a moment later.

They talked, smiled, scowled, smiled again, and then were joined by… Alvarro? Where the hell had *he* come from? More scowling, more smiling, then the men parted company, Tattooed Man and Plaid Shirt heading for the stairs that led to the main floor, Alvarro watching the two men go.

Now Tattooed Man and Plaid Shirt parted ways: Plaid Shirt started down the stairs; Tattooed Man watched him go, paused, and then turned to shake hands with a tall, frighteningly thin, flaxen-haired man. They retraced Tattooed Man's steps, spoke briefly to Alvarro, and then disappeared into a room, closing the door behind them.

Stephen turned his attention back to Plaid Shirt: at the bottom of the stairs, he smiled warmly as he greeted the woman who was not Erin.

"Son of a bitch," Stephen said as he watched the pair. They, too, retook the stairs; they, too, headed for Alvarro. Plaid Shirt had perfect posture, carried himself casually but kept a large personal space: he definitely had some kind of military or defence training. The woman sauntered, flirting. Plaid Shirt introduced not-Erin to Alvarro, who kissed her hand; Plaid Shirt ushered her into the room into which Tattooed Man and Thin Guy had disappeared. Alvarro watched the door close behind them and then looked back down to the dance floor, leering.

Stephen shook his head. Not-Erin was probably a hooker. The dress should have been his first clue. He was more than a little embarrassed that he had found her so good looking. It was definitely time to get out of the country and, as Chalo had admonished, finally get a new life.

He drank the last of his Coke, patted his pocket to find the claim token for his knapsack, and prepared to leave. It was far later than he would have liked—he would be driving the toll road again at night—but at least he had a good solid lead to give Chalo. One final look at the balcony and he stopped in his tracks.

Alvarro was leaving. Not-Erin had re-emerged from her room and was following him. *What the hell?*

The toll road was going to have to wait a little longer. Someone else was after Alvarro and Stephen needed to know why.

Monday, December 10, 2012 — 6 Muluc, Day of Jade

CHAPTER 20

Eden Two was an eco-terrorist organization, on the CIA's watch list just below Al Qaida and a few other political groups. Eden Two terrified the nations of the world, not because it had killed people—it hadn't—but because it had the power and precision to destroy a billion dollars' worth of oil infrastructure—the *Eirike Ruude* platform in the North Sea; the *Hibernia* platform on Canada's Grand Banks; an oil tanker in a lock in the Panama Canal—without killing a soul. A lot of people were rooting for the humanitarian terrorist who was bringing big oil to its frightened knees.

Kulkulcan looked at the pallid man across the table; a man barely able to catch his breath, and marvelled: this was the feared and vaunted "Adam," head of Eden Two.

"So, *Herr* von Eckhardt. A German and a Mayan, together. Politics makes strange bedfellows, does it not?"

"It does. *Herr* von Eckhardt is my father. I am Sebastian. I am impressed that you know my real name, *Señor* Dzul."

"*Touché*, Sebastian. Few people know both my names; you also do your homework well."

Sebastian nodded, accepting the compliment, and Kulkulcan continued.

"Please call me Kulkulcan; it will avoid an unfortunate slip. I will call you Adam in return. Can I get you a drink?"

"Water please," he said as he looked around the spare Euro chic office: the furniture was leather, linear, and barely used.

"You are certain you can bring the Mitnal rig down?"

"Yes. But our fee must increase considerably if we are to steal the fuel cells before we do so. You cannot buy them elsewhere?"

"Not for less than you ask to steal them, not without questions, and not in a timely way."

"I see. Very well, then. We will bring the cells back."

"I want three of my men to go with you to be sure that it is done."

"That also can be arranged for an additional sum. And I will need to approve the men."

Kulkulcan regarded the man and marvelled once more. He was preternaturally calm, as if he already knew his fate.

"Does everything come down to money, then, Sebastian?"

"Adam," Sebastian corrected. "And not money: economics. The oil remaining in the Earth is a liability, and burning it will cause runaway climate change. But science and good intentions will not keep the oil there. The world must be convinced that it is too dangerous to extract."

"But you make it a point not to kill anyone. How does that make you dangerous?"

"You are not a stupid man, Kulkulcan. I do it to change minds. To make the cost of oil too high before the planet passes a tipping point and we die in the filth of our addiction."

Sebastian paused for a moment to catch his breath, his ice-blue eyes staring directly—as if into Kulkulcan's soul—as he did so. Kulkulcan actually felt himself unnerved.

"What I do not understand, Kulkulcan," Sebastian resumed, "is why you want me to topple the rig in the first place. You are smart, as I said, and the oil from that rig could make a new Mayan state the wealthiest state in the world. Why destroy it?"

Kulkulcan fought to master a rising nausea born of the realization that everything he had built would fall apart if he did not, in the next few moments, lie extremely well. For the truth was that Kulkulcan did not want the rig destroyed; he merely wanted Sebastian to use his expertise to get aboard and steal the fuel cells. After that, Sebastian would be killed.

"Do you know anything of the Maya, Sebastian?" Kulkulcan said archly.

"Adam," Sebastian corrected again. "Much more than you might think, Kulkulcan. My sister is a scholar of the Maya."

"Indeed. Well I am not like most guerrillas, Sebastian. I do not do this for my own good. I almost died as a child, pushed into a *cenote* for my dirty half-breed blood. But Kulkulcan—the god Kulkulcan—saved me. In exchange he told me that I must save his people—raise them up so that they might honour the old ways, the true gods."

"So this is a holy war," Sebastian asked, unimpressed.

Kulkulcan ignored the comment, warming to his own mythology. It always had this effect on him, as if he was possessed by something beyond himself. Something dark and irresistible.

"'Mitnal' is not merely the name of the rig. *Mitnal* is the darkest part of *Xibalba*—the underworld—home to the Mayan gods of darkness and death. It is not bad enough that foreigners come with their guns and diseases and destroy all that we were. Now they plunge their steel into the heart of *Xibalba* and the Lords of Death, released from their prison, walk the land once more. If we do not destroy the rig and close the gates of Hell, the gods will visit upon us flood and famine, drought and destruction…storms to wipe us from the land. But if we succeed, the gods will reward us beyond our wildest dreams, with a new kingdom to call our own."

Xibalba and the Lords of Death were familiar characters, their acquaintance made through his sister Anya's scholarship. What fascinated Sebastian now was the man reintroducing them. No longer a short, bald club-owner pretending to be the messiah, Kulkulcan—sweating with his own oratory—seemed a man utterly transformed. A man thus consumed by his vision would not care that he was denying his people the billions of dollars Mitnal's oil could bring.

Sebastian considered. Who was he to say that Kulkulcan was wrong? Science, sufficiently advanced, appears to be magic. Or the work of the gods. Did it matter whether it was the science of climate change or the wrath of mythic gods that required the oil rig to come down? No matter the force invoked, the results would be the same if the rig did not fall and cease production: natural disasters, war, pestilence, and the decay of civilization itself.

"We drink to the end of the rig, then?" Sebastian asked.

Kulkulcan blinked at the interruption, as if emerging from a dream. It had worked: Sebastian believed. Kulkulcan himself almost believed. He actually worried, for a brief moment, that gods he did not actually believe in might seek the vengeance he spoke of if he did not let

Sebastian bring the rig down. The thought made his blood run cold, and he wondered if he might be losing himself in his own story.

"Do we drink?" Kulkulcan repeated, composing himself. "Indeed we do! *Xtabentún*, drink of my ancestors, made from anise and honey. It burns courage into one's heart and restores a broken soul."

***

Hayden had always said of the woman who was now his widow that she had a knack for charging into a situation without planning her exit. It wasn't such a bad thing, actually, and to compensate, she had developed an extraordinary talent for thinking on her feet. Now in a soundproof room with a man she barely knew, some quick and creative thinking would be required if she was to find out more about Rutrauff without ending up in his bed.

They had walked the length of the upstairs balcony and then, turning, had stopped to speak with a scrawny, sleazy little man with slicked hair.

"Becky, this is Bernardo Alvarro," Rutrauff said. The look of surprise on Alvarro's face was almost as good as the fact of the date itself. Almost.

"Charmed, I'm sure," Rebecca had replied as, demure southern belle, she extended her hand in greeting.

"Ah *señorita*, the pleasure is mine," Alvarro had oozed as he took her hand and stooped to kiss it. "What is such a lovely lady doing with a *pendejo* like Captain Rutrauff, here?"

"Ignore my little associate, Becky," Rutrauff had smirked as he opened a door behind them.

"Nice, Captain. Very nice," Alvarro had replied. To Rebecca he had said, "Now if the good Captain doesn't treat you right, *señorita*, come see a real man and I'll take care of you…"

"Like I said, Alvarro, in your dreams…" Rutrauff had laughed as he ushered Rebecca into the suite.

Inside now, Rebecca looked around and laughed.

"He's a creepy little man. Who is he?"

"Just one of my boss' goons."

"What does he do?"

"Moves things. Can I get you a drink?

Rebecca surveyed the room, eyed the bed, and then looked at Rutrauff with a smirk that belied wide, innocent eyes.

"Are you trying to get me drunk and have your way with me, Travis?"

Rutrauff actually blushed. "We can stay on the couch and get to know each other over drinks… I just took the room so we could have a little peace."

Rebecca was genuinely surprised: he was more a gentleman than she had expected.

She pouted disappointment as she relaxed into the sofa and patted the cushion beside her.

"Course, there's a lot we can do on the couch," she added mischievously.

Travis chuckled and went to get a bottle of wine from the bar fridge.

"So what kind of captain are you?" Rebecca asked when he returned.

"Me? What do you mean?"

"The little man called you 'Captain.' I thought you said you were in business?"

Travis laughed at the way Rebecca kept calling Alvarro a 'little man'. It was the truth, but it nevertheless appealed to Rutrauff's opinion of the hoodlum.

"He was just giving me a hard time," Rutrauff replied as he handed Rebecca a glass and sat down beside her.

"Oh," Rebecca said, shading her voice with disappointment. "I like a man in uniform."

"Is that so?" Travis smiled. "Tell me why."

"Well, they've got manners and discipline and they generally have to be in great shape…" Rebecca ran her fingers along Travis's forearm. "See, these look like a soldier's arms…"

"In that case," Travis said, sliding closer, "I suppose I might really be a captain in the Marines…"

"Sure, sure. If you're in the military, where are your dog tags? I don't see a chain around your neck."

"What if I told you I was down here on a secret mission, training a bunch of rebels?"

"I'd say you're just trying to excite me…" Rebecca slid closer.

"Well it's true. I've just spent the past bunch of weeks in the jungle whipping a bunch of the natives into shape. This couch is a treat after my wooden bunk."

"Oh yeah?" Rebecca said softly. "Where?"

"A… camp down near Calakmul." He was flustered now.

"Well that *would* be exciting," she said resting her hand high on his thigh, "if I had some proof."

"Four-five-seven-nine-two-one-double-three-six."

"What's that?" Rebecca asked, all innocence; she knew it was a service number.

"My service number… want to see my wallet?"

"In your pocket?" Rebecca said, standing up. She repeated the number to herself to memorize it as she sauntered to the bed.

"I told you I liked a man in uniform…" she said as she sat down on the foot of the bed. "… but really what I meant is I like a man *out* of uniform."

"Do you?" Travis said, eyebrows arching. "You know, I might be able to oblige," he said, joining her at the foot of the bed.

"Really?" Rebecca whispered as she let Rutrauff put his hand on her thigh.

"Really…"

"Hang onto that thought, Travis," she said softly, her lips close to his. "I gotta go get something from the bag they made me check downstairs…"

"You brought a bag?"

"Well, I didn't know they had these rooms, did I?" Rebecca smiled.

"And you have something they don't? Rutrauff smiled back as he opened the bedside drawer and pulled out a box of condoms. "Thirty-wonderful flavours…"

"I'm diabetic and I think we're going to have some more wine and stay here a while. I just need to go get my insulin."

Rebecca laughed and then apologized when Travis reddened again.

"How do I know you're going to come back?" he said.

Rebecca put her hand on his and slid it slowly between her thighs.

"What if I left you my shoes?" she smiled.

"I'd say there's a lot of broken glass outside. Without shoes, it'd be a good bet you didn't plan to go out there."

"Well then…" Rebecca said, as she leaned down to undo her shoes.

She palmed the keycard and then shook the sandals loose, picked them up by their straps, and offered them to Rutrauff as she stood up.

"There's one less thing for you to take off of me when I get back," she said as she sauntered to the door.

"I'll be here…" Rutrauff called as she left.

Door closed behind her, Rebecca looked around. Alvarro had just turned to leave...a dozen paces ahead of her he was the next link in the chain that connected Wilkes to the guns. She had planned just to ditch Rutrauff, call Deb, and get her to check out his service number. But maybe she could follow Alvarro a bit first. There was a pair of espadrilles outside a door down the hall; Rebecca crept forward, stuck her hotel keycard into the left one, and slipped them on. They were too big, but they'd do. She set off after Alvarro, ungainly in the ill-fitting shoes.

***

The small aluminum boat crunched softly into the sandy beach and came to a stop. Anya cut the outboard, raised it, and hopped out.

"Isn't it beautiful?" she said as she splashed to the bow to pull the boat farther up.

"Anya, I don't mean to offend, but I can't see a thing! Your flashlight has made me blind to everything but what you shine it on."

Anya laughed. "Stay here while I tie the boat. Smell! And listen! And really look… when your eyes adjust, it isn't as dark as you think!"

Chalo sat in the little boat and did as directed. The soft humid air carried the scent of night-blooming flowers and the trill of uncountable tiny thumb-sized frogs. And once he grew accustomed to the absence of the flashlight, he realized he could see remarkably well: the sky was afire with starlight. Innumerable, they burned blue-white like magnesium, so bright he could make out the ruins on the cliff above.

Like Anya, he sighed with delight.

"Okay, enough relaxing," she said as she returned. "Let's empty the boat and take everything up."

Chalo eyed the rough-hewn stairs in the cliff—probably older than the ruins themselves—and groaned; there were at least a hundred steps.

"You need an elevator, Doctor."

"The pulley is ordered. For now we climb."

"I told you, Stephen is the climber! Do you never rest?"

"Never," Anya laughed as she carted things from the boat to the sand. "You take the two duffels up and when you get to the top, head for the yurt. Take my light—it is dark inside. I will follow in a moment with the rest of the things."

Halfway up the stairs, Anya heard a shout and a clatter; she ran the remaining stairs as quickly as her knapsack and duffel would allow. In the dawn-bright starlight, Anya could see across the clearing. Chalo stood at the yurt door, clawing at his hair.

"Are you all right?" Anya called as she ran to him. "What has happened?"

"Nothing," he said sheepishly, once Anya was at his side. "Just spiders. I walked into a web inside your tent. I think I might have broken your lamp."

"A policeman with a gun, afraid of spiders?"

"They're too small to shoot!"

Anya smiled. "Come here and let me see your head."

Chalo bent down and Anya combed his hair with her fingers.

"Nothing." She ran her fingers through it for good measure. "You are fine."

Chalo left his head down for a moment, enjoying her touch.

"You could do that again, you know. I mean, you could do it to make really for sure that there are no spiders…"

Anya gave his hair one last ruffle, walked into the yurt and switched on a battery-operated light.

"The lamp is fine. Here, take this," she said as she handed him several pieces of split firewood.

"Wood?"

"I put it inside to keep it dry."

"But it's late. Should we not go to bed?" He stopped and then corrected himself quickly, lest he be misunderstood.

"To sleep, I mean."

"I want a cup of *atole* first; it helps me to sleep. And better to make it on the fire than use up my gas. Would you like a cup, also?

Chalo hesitated.

"What? You don't like *atole*?" Anya asked, incredulous.

"I do! But I stopped drinking it after my grandmother died. I never found any as good as the one she used to make."

"Try mine. It might not be hers, but it is very good. My assistant Payal taught me his own grandmother's recipe."

Chalo frowned.

"Just try. I won't be angry if you don't like it, yes?"

"Alright," he said, relieved. "I'll go make the fire then?"

"Can you?" she asked, a little surprised.

"¡*Uay*! Of course I can! With a match, anything is possible! But you'll have to give me one; I gave mine to Esteban, along with my cigarettes. I'm trying to quit, you know," he said proudly.

Anya laughed.

"That's good; it will kill you! Take these," she said, tossing him a box of matches, "And use the fire ring in front of the *caracol*, yes?"

Chalo had forgotten how bright night could be in the absence of electricity; he could make out the entire camp by the silver-blue light cast by the Milky Way. Two yurts—the large one solar and propane powered for cooling, cooking, and computer cataloguing, the small one for her volunteers to sleep in—were two of the four modern structures in the clearing; a solar shower and an outhouse rounded out the amenities.

Twenty metres across the clearing, Chalo found the fire ring, the temple looming behind it. At the top of the steep limestone stairs, glowing softly in the starlight, he could just distinguish the *chac mo'ol* that had been of such interest to the police. He had to force himself to set the fire instead of climbing the stairs to see what he could find.

"You want to go up right now, don't you?" Anya asked. She had walked up behind him on cat's paws; Chalo jumped at the sound of her voice so close.

"I can wait. There is probably not much left anyway; it will be better to look in the bright light of day."

Anya laughed. "Patience, too. You grow more interesting all the time, Detective Guerrero."

Chalo knelt down to lay the fire, smiled at the compliment, and said nothing as Anya prepared the *atole*. It took no time at all; within ten minutes they were sitting cross-legged by the flames sipping the warm corn drink.

"Tell me about this ruin," Chalo asked.

"Not before you tell me about the *atole*," Anya replied, smiling.

"It is very good," Chalo said, nodding appreciatively.

"As good as your grandmother's?"

Chalo looked pained.

"I would be very glad to have another cup," he said at length.

"Very diplomatic."

"You are battling a childhood memory. Your *atole* is truly the best I have tasted since my grandmother's."

"I will tell Payal to tell his grandmother that you like it."

Chalo raised his cup to Anya and drained it.

"Now tell me more about that," he asked, nodding to the ruin looming in front of them.

"What would you like to know?"

"Well, you said it was like the observatory at Chich'en Itzá, but different, too. How is it not the same?"

"It is smaller, for a start, And the spiral staircase up to the dome is only nine very steep stairs instead of thirteen. But the really interesting thing is that the windows do not point the same way as those at Chich'en Itzá."

"There are windows?"

"Yes, both here and at Chich'en Itzá. They are not so much windows as 'portals:' small square holes pointing in the direction of something of astronomical significance. Half the dome at Chich'en Itzá is gone—crumbled—but there is one window left: it points at the horizon in the direction the Moon sets at its greatest southern declination. Here I have six portals…" She trailed off, lost in thought.

"Where do they point?"

"The ones on the horizon? One to the southwest, where the sun sets on the winter solstice; the other to the east, its portal is twice as tall as the one for the sun."

"And the remaining four?"

"Into the sky. That is the part that does not yet make sense."

"Why is that so strange?" Chalo asked.

"Everything else we know about Mayan astronomy says that the solstices and the equinoxes were the most important—those days dictated the timing of important events like planting and harvesting crops."

"Do you have any ideas at all?"

"It is just beyond my fingertips. I am sure the portals are connected with the frescoes painted on the dome inside, but I am only able to understand part of the story so far."

"What story?" Chalo had originally been asking simply because he enjoyed hearing Anya's voice. Now he found himself genuinely interested: it was another mystery.

"It is the creation story. Did your grandmother tell it to you?"

"Of course, but maybe not the way you know it."

"How is that?"

"Tell me what you know, and I will tell you my grandmother's version after."

Anya looked at Chalo, his face lit gently by the fire's glowing coals. She had not been wrong, the previous night, to find him handsome: deep-set eyes above high wide cheekbones, the long straight nose that was the hallmark of the Maya, full lips, a cleft chin… she frowned against her daydreaming.

"You were asking what?"

"Tell me your version of my creation myth, and then I will tell you my grandmother's."

"Yes. In the beginning, the three creators—*Tepeu*, the Feathered Serpent, and *Hurukan*…"

"My grandmother called them the Father, Son, and the Holy Ghost," Chalo smiled.

"A classic syncretism…"

"What?"

"Merging of two belief systems. Like Christmas was built out of the pagan solstice celebration. We think the Maya hid their beliefs by clothing them in Christian metaphor," she paused for a moment, thinking. "The first two gods were more like a married couple than father and son, but I suppose *Hurukan* is a little like the Holy Spirit: he was the wind that animated everything—he separated the sky from the sea, raising it up to create the Earth between them. The English word 'hurricane' is taken from his name."

"So far, so good; you are telling it as my grandmother did. What next?"

Anya did not know whether to be pleased at the compliment or ruffled at being graded. She opted for the kindest interpretation and chose pleased.

"The creators finished making the world and decided to make people to remember and honour them and what they had created…"

"… so they created the first people out of mud," Chalo interrupted. His voice was soft, as if repeating something old, just remembered.

"Yes. But the people made of mud were too soft and they crumbled away…"

"So the creators destroyed them and started again, this time with wood…"

"But the men of wood were stiff and without feeling: they could not venerate the Creators or care for the animals of the Earth. And so the Creators sent a flood to wash them away."

"Yes, but my grandmother said they were not washed away completely: they are the monkeys in the forest, to remind us that we must live with feeling, must care for all things, or else we, too, could be washed away."

Anya nodded, reflecting that it was a wisdom that, if not forgotten, was altogether too neglected by the modern world.

"So then came the Third Creation," Chalo continued, now the narrator. "The Creators ground maize, and mixed it with water and breathe life into us. We are the people of the corn. My grandmother called me 'corn walking.'"

Anya laughed. It had probably been apt in two ways: his diet had been mostly corn, and he had probably grown as fast and tall as a cornstalk.

"All the stories about the Hero Twins come from this creation. My grandmother used to tell me I was the twin—*Hunaphu*—who lost his head in the underworld because I was always getting myself into trouble. Do you know that I once called Stephen '*Xbalenque*'…

"… the other twin…"

"Yes, because were we brothers and yet so different—he was so smart. I used to joke that we would save the world together…"

They both fell silent and Anya shivered.

"Do you really think he saw *Xtabay*?" she asked.

Chalo looked from the fire at Anya.

"Esteban? Maybe. Maybe not. There *is* some spirit that accompanies him wherever he goes. It shows him things and keeps him safe, but it also makes him partly dead, too."

"Partly dead?!"

"Dead in his heart. Frozen inside. Like he is in love with a shadow. So maybe yes, *Xtabay*. She holds men and won't let them go, it is said." Chalo paused. "Did he try to make love with you when you spoke?"

"What has that got to do with anything?" Anya asked, surprised and irritated by the sudden change in topic.

"Love is life, is it not?"

"And every man should try to make love to a woman to prove he is alive?" Anya retorted angrily.

"No!"

"It's always about sex. Always!" Anya said angrily as she stood and walked away.

"That did not sound the way I meant it to sound," he called after her.

She shrugged and kept walking towards the larger of the yurts.

"I didn't mean that kind of 'making love'!"

Anya continued without turning.

"I hate English," he muttered. "I'm sorry, okay. Can you at least tell me where the bathrooms are?"

Wordlessly, Anya pointed at the jungle to their left.

"Better and better," he muttered to himself as he left the relative warmth of the fire and headed for the bush.

"Be careful what you step on. We have many artefacts to find yet!" Anya shouted back as she stepped into the yurt.

"Terrific. I can piss on my heritage like everyone else," Chalo grumbled.

He stood still for a few moments to allow his eyes to adjust to the starlight, dim after the fire's bright embers, before heading into the trees. The darkness took shape and shade as he waited: darkest of all, the forest wall stood before him, the perfect flat black of coal. Above its ragged top the sky bloomed a moonless blue-black. And then, mid-heaven, it glowed, navy, swabbed light and milky by the galactic core.

Trying not to think about spiders, Chalo took a fortifying breath of the cool tangy air, rising rich and sulphurous from the forest mud, and stepped beneath the trees to find a place to pee.

Three paces in, he stepped on a loose rock, stumbled, snagged his foot on a root as he tried to regain his balance, and fell to the ground. A monkey howled in the distance.

"Laughing at me, are you?" Chalo demanded of the distant creature.

Scrabbling beneath the heavy undergrowth for the rocks that had upended him, Chalo felt something unnaturally smooth. Not a rock: he had stepped on one half of a broken slab of hewn stone. He followed an incised line with his fingers. An artefact? He followed the curved incision further and then inhaled sharply: a thorny vine had snagged the back of his hand.

"Anya!" he called. No response.

"¡*Uay*! Anya! Come here!" Nothing.

"Please! I need help. I need light. I have found something."

"What something?" was the wary reply, irritation still in her voice.

"I'm not sure. Maybe a part of the ruin. Can you bring a flashlight?"

"Where are you?"

"Here!"

"Where?" Anya asked again, swinging a flashlight.

"Here… ahh!" Chalo yelled, squinting quickly as the light shone in his eyes.

"So what is this that you have…" Anya asked, querulous, as she strode into the forest. "… *mein Gott*!" she finished, her voice suddenly falling to a whisper.

She was on her knees beside the stone in an instant, her light close to its surface.

"What is it?" Chalo asked.

"A *stela*."

"A *stela*?"

"The stone that tells the temple's story."

"Can you read it?"

"Maybe. Hold this." She handed the flashlight to Chalo and began clearing the stone with two hands.

"*Sheisse… ach*! *Sheisse*!" she muttered as the vines' thorns snagged at her hands.

"Let me help," Chalo said as he reached for the army knife in his pocket, a parting gift from Stephen.

"Carefully!" Anya snapped, pushing his arm away.

"These vines cling. If you pull too hard you can damage the surface."

"Okay, okay," Chalo said, pulling more carefully.

"But it doesn't seem to be attached, see?" he asked as he pulled a large clump of matted vegetation from the stone.

"You're right. It is dead," Anya said, perplexed.

"Look here. When the stone fell, the roots were pulled up."

"Not fell. I think it was pushed," Anya corrected as she examined the worked stone.

"It is incredible… look…" She said, wonder in her voice, as she brushed the last stray leaves off the stone.

Chalo held the flashlight over the stone and looked. Before them lay a white stone tablet, five feet long and two-and-a-half feet wide, heavily incised with the intricate images, lines and dots that were characteristic of the ancient Mayan writing system.

"What does it say?"

"Shh! I'm thinking!… I am not an epigrapher, but these, here, are numbers. Dates, actually."

She bent down close to the glyph she had pointed too and blew gently. A puff of dirt came from the incised lines.

"… and this one—this round ball with its crown holding two planets, flanked by these flowing ropes? It means 'star over Earth' which would make sense…"

"Why?"

"Because the ruin is an observatory. 'Star over Earth' is the verb for the movement of stars… usually Venus… *Ist das Fenster auf Venus ausgerichtet? Oder auf den Mond? Und an welchem Datum*?" Engrossed, she had slipped into German.

"English or Spanish, please." Chalo asked, bemused.

"Sorry. *Stelae* usually tell who built a place and why," she said as she pulled an iPhone from her pocket.

"You are calling someone?" Chalo asked, incredulous.

"Pictures," she replied. "Can you hold the light over here?"

"Like this?"

"Yes. Good. This is fantastic! Do I put 'Gonzalo' or 'Chalo' on the paper?"

"What?"

"Archaeology is still one of those disciplines where amateurs can contribute. Your name will go as a co-discoverer of the *stela* when I write a paper about it."

"Really?"

"Really."

"Anya?"

"What?"

"I still have to…"

"I won't look," she laughed.

Chalo took a dozen steps beyond the sphere illuminated by Anya's light and the phone's flash. Then he took a few more for modesty's sake before stopping short.

"¡*Uay... un qué olor*!" Chalo whispered, dread creeping into his tone. He knew this smell too well.

"Anya," he called, his voice low and calm.

"*¿Qué*?" she answered curtly.

"Anya… I need your light."

"Why?"

"Please. I need your light right now. Come carefully."

Something in his voice made her come without further question, shining the flashlight before her. She was too level-headed to scream when she reached him, but a small murmur of horror escaped as she saw what had caught Chalo's eye.

"It is human?" she asked as she held the light on a pair of bones emerging from a loose pile of earth.

"Forearm, I think. Can I have it please?"

Anya handed the flashlight to Chalo silently.

"You see there? And there? And there?" he said moving the light over the forest floor, their roles as teacher and student now reversed.

"Those are the hand bones, probably scattered by an animal. Could I use your camera?"

This Anya also handed to Chalo without a word.

"And here… could you hold the flashlight after all?" he asked.

Chalo took two pictures, stopped, and pulled his own cell phone from his pocket.

"Are *you* calling someone?" Anya asked.

"No. A reference, for scale. I have no measuring tape."

"I do. At the tent. Would you like it?"

"It would be better. Can you go back without the flashlight?"

"I left a light on at the tent. I can follow it." She hesitated for a moment and then asked "how much… how much will be left of him under the ground?"

"If it is a 'him.' The bones are small. Not so much I think, unless we are very lucky. With three weeks gone, most of it will be decomposed. How many pictures may I take?"

"As many as you need. I'll be right back."

Chalo returned his cellphone to his back pocket and crouched down as Anya left. After taking a few more photos he began to push the dirt from the proximal end of the forearm, following the bones to what he hoped would be enough evidence to figure out what had happened here.

The smell grew as he worked, and insects of all kinds wriggled and buzzed from beneath his bare hands and he recoiled in disgust.

"Can you bring gloves if you have them?" he shouted after Anya.

"I have. I will," she called back, the swish and crunch of her boots diminishing suddenly as she stepped from the forest into the clearing beyond.

Too curious to wait, Chalo pulled his phone from his pocket once more and started using it like a small spade. By the time he reached the shoulder joint, the smell of putrefaction had grown so strong that Chalo had pulled his t-shirt up over his mouth and nose. Where, he wondered, was the smell coming from?

He knew that the jungle could reduce a corpse to bones in a little more than two weeks. So how could this be the owner of the heart found here three weeks ago? Or if it was not, who was it?

As Chalo reached the corpse's shoulder, the puzzle began to resolve. As Chalo dug deeper, the soil grew lighter. Around the corpse it was powdery and almost white.

"Lime," he said softly. "Thank you, Esteban!"

The geology of the Yucatán—Stephen's specialty—had frequently been a topic for conversation between the partners while on stakeouts: once he started learning, Chalo had an insatiable curiosity. In one of those conversations he had learned that alkaline soil—like those formed from the region's limestone—could saponify flesh, converting human fat to a greasy protective "grave wax." Perhaps it had preserved a clue that would otherwise have degraded by now. Chalo dug more quickly at the thought, unearthing the victim's torso and head. Then he whistled in surprise, a long low sound that echoed through the forest. The corpse's face was vaguely familiar but Chalo ignored it in favour of looking at the chest cavity: there was a gaping hole where the obese male cadaver's sagging left pectoral should have been. The fractured ends of the second, third, fourth and fifth ribs were visible within the fat, as if snapped off from above. And carved into the belly flesh beneath the hole was a circle with two smaller circles on either side of it. Like Mickey Mouse's head and ears.

Chalo took another fifteen pictures and then tucked Anya's iPhone into his pocket and picked up a twig. Even leaning directly over the hole with the flashlight shining directly into it, he could see nothing.

"Anya?" he called, his eyes still on the corpse.

"Yes?" Again she was closer than he expected; again he jumped in surprise. "Sorry. I was watching you," she said.

"You want to come closer to see?"

"No. No thank you," she said, tossing the gloves. "I am fine from here."

Chalo donned the gloves, put his hand into the cavity, and pulled it back out, empty.

"Not decomposed or scavenged. The heart is gone."

"The heart in my *chac mo'ol*?" Anya asked, eyes widening.

"I think so, yes."

Anya paused. "So what do we do?" she asked at last.

"I want to call Stephen, but not really with this," he said, holding up his phone. It was covered in dirt and decomposition. "Can I use yours?"

"It won't work here. You'll need the satellite modem I have in the yurt."

As they started out of the forest they heard a loud crash coming from within the large yurt.

Chalo grabbed Anya's arm.

"It's an animal," she sighed. "I was just there. I must have left the door open." She yanked her arm from Chalo's grasp, irritated at the mess little mammals always made, and starting forward once more.

Three steps into the clearing she froze, then dropped to a crouch, as a shot rang out from somewhere beyond the yurt, whizzed past her, and struck a tree behind Chalo, blowing a piece of bark into the night air. The night creatures fell silent for a moment and then screamed and hooted and called in surprise.

"An animal, sure," Chalo muttered.

"¡*Uay*! Police! Stop shooting!" Chalo called into the clearing.

A second shot sang into the animals' cacophony, this one hitting the ground four feet in front of Anya.

"And that is not the police," he said acerbically as he ran forward, grabbed Anya's hand, and began to pull her towards the stairs that led to the beach.

"No! Not that way!" she hollered over the sound of yet another shot.

"The boat!" Chalo hissed.

"This way!" she insisted, tugging at him.

Suddenly he cried out: something had hit him. A bullet—a graze only, across his cheekbone—but it stung enough to daze him for a moment, allowing Anya to pull him away from the beach.

The beam from the flashlight in Chalo's hand bounced crazily on the ground as they ran—against the black forest, in the air, on the ground—making the pair difficult targets. Four more shots rang out in rapid succession, spraying wildly around them, and then they were back in the forest, following a narrow earthen trail.

"Now here!" Anya commanded, dragging Chalo behind her through a thick thorny bush and into a small cave. "Turn off the light!"

Chalo looked dumbly at the light in his hand for a moment, switched it off, and felt his head throb in time with his racing heart.

A twig snapped somewhere outside.

"¿*Adónde fueron*?" said a man's voice a few feet away.

"*No lo sé*," replied another voice farther away.

"Are you hit?" she whispered.

"Yes. Shh…"

"*Sheisse*… is it bad?"

Chalo felt his cheekbone in the darkness and winced.

"No. Now shh!"

Anya fumbled in the darkness beside him and then pressed something soft and warm into his hand. A cloth. He put it to his head. It smelled of her perfume and he thought fleetingly of last night. Here he was, cold, wet and bleeding… how different it had been only twenty-four hours ago! A flashlight combed the bush in front of the cave; Chalo returned his attention to the present and held his breath. The light stopped on the bush for a long moment and then moved on.

In the momentary brightness provided by their pursuers' flashlight, Anya saw Chalo holding the cloth to his head and grimaced at the sight of blood around his eye; Chalo saw Anya's face, pale and grim. He also saw that she now wore only a black brassiere above her jeans; she had given him her t-shirt to staunch his wound. He raised his eyebrows as the darkness returned, torn between admiration and desire.

"Probablemente fueron al barco. No pueden llegar muy lejos sin él."

Their pursuers were heading for the boat. Now how were they going to get away?

CHAPTER 21

They stood silent for a long while, listening first to the sound of feet in the underbrush recede into the distance and then to the nocturnal sounds of the jungle itself.

"Are they really gone?" Anya asked at last.

"I think so," Chalo answered as he turned on the flashlight. He had pressed the torch to his hip before switching it on: only a tiny sliver of light escaped but after the cave's utter darkness, it was plenty to see by.

He looked briefly at Anya's black bra and curving waist before looking studiously at the space into which Anya had led them. It was a small funnel-shaped cave: tall and wide where they stood it, sloped downward to the height of a single person at the far end. The wet back wall glistened in the low light; the ceiling above it hung thick with short stalactites and long thin tree roots; the air was warm, humid and still.

"You gave me your shirt?" Chalo asked, looking hesitantly back towards Anya.

"It was cleaner than your hands" she replied simply. "If you have finished bleeding, may I have it back?"

Chalo chuckled. She had not lost her head in the shooting. She was smart and beautiful and he wanted desperately to kiss her. He returned the tee-shirt to her instead.

"Now what?" he asked.

"This way" Anya said as she moved towards the back of the cave. "Can you swim?"

"Yes" Chalo asked, confused by the non sequitur.

The cave had a turn in it that Chalo had not seen; following Anya around it he saw that it was actually a tunnel with an underground river flowing through it, the river slow, lazy and dark in the full light of the flashlight's beam. Anya, her shirt back on, bent down at the edge of the river, scooped water up with a cupped hand, and took a drink.

"Do you still have your knife?"

Chalo felt the outside of his back pocket for the outline of the pocketknife.

"Yes, why?"

"They said they would be waiting for us by the boat, so we cannot get to it by the beach. But this river leads out to the ocean. From its outlet underwater we can swim up to the boat, cut it free, and leave."

"But we left the boat on the beach…"

"We did, but the tide is up now and the boat will be floating in maybe 2 metres of water…"

Chalo smiled and then frowned. "We can't go back to your dock. Is there enough gas to get back to Cancún?"

"No, but there is enough to get us to Tulum. We can get a taxi from there to my other car."

Chalo smiled again "You are very smart, Dr. von Eckhardt. It is an excellent plan except for one thing…"

"What's that?"

Chalo shone the flashlight down the river to its black end. "I hate small dark spaces almost as much as I hate spiders…"

Anya laughed. "I do not like them, either. But we will use these." From her cargo pockets she produced two long think foil packages and passed one to him.

"Chemical lights," she explained.

"Very convenient" Chalo said.

"I have to work down here from time to time – there is a small altar 10 metres the other way that I am documenting. The wet gets into even the best flashlights, so I carry these, in case."

"It is still very convenient" he said, tearing open the foil and bending the plastic until the glass vial inside it cracked. The reactive agents in the stick swirled together and began to glow an eerie green.

Anya cracked her own lightstick and shook it, the fragments of the broken glass vial inside the plastic stick rattling as she did so.

"We can walk the first while," she said, "but then it gets quite deep and it will be easier to float. Are you ready?"

Chalo rolled his eyes but nodded. "Yes, OK."

Anya stepped into the river. Chalo leaned down and rinsed the dirt from his hands and then splashed into the subterranean river after her, the cold water seeping into his shoes and chilling his feet.

They walked in silence for almost ten minutes, the water rising from calf to knee and finally to thigh height, the river's gentle current pushing them gently seaward all the while.

"We are here," Anya said at last.

"Here?" In the dim light thrown by the lightsticks Chalo could see no difference between this particular spot and anywhere else.

"The river bottom drops now. We drift from here; dive under at the end to swim through a short part that is completely inundated, and then we will be free."

Chalo groaned.

Anya nodded. "Here," she said, taking his hand. "We will float together."

Chalo had expected the next minutes to be cold and miserable. The water was chilly enough to make the graze on his scalp ache and brackish enough to sting, but the drift was anything but unpleasant. Anya's hand in his was warm and reassuring. The slow silent current carried them forward like milkweed silk on a soft evening breeze. The dim greenish glow cast by the chemical lights lit the stalactites above them, their long thin shadows shrinking as he and Anya drifted towards them, then growing again, long behind them, as they drifted past. Their breath rose and fell evenly, loud against the deadening quiet of the rock around them. Despite the darkness he felt light, safe, clean, and exquisitely alive. It was as if years of accumulated grime were being washed not merely from the surface of his skin but from beneath it: the aches and insults, lonelinesses and fears—all sloughing from him the way a snake's skin peels. He felt painfully raw but larger than before. New like rebirth. Somewhere, far away, he heard his grandmother begin to sing a lullaby, and he smiled.

His head bumped into something and felt himself shaken awake.

"Chalo! Are you alright? It is time to dive now."

Chalo shook his head and blinked is eyes. His head throbbed where the bullet had grazed him.

"You go first," he said thickly.

"No. It is wide enough that we can swim together. Keep holding to my hand. It is a half metre below and two metres along and then up to the surface. Inhale and exhale two times with me. The third breath you hold and we go, OK?"

"Right," he said, shaking his head again. "I'm ready." He closed his eyes against the saltwater rushing towards them as they dove into the flooded tunnel.

Opening them again he realized that, save for the blurry pinpricks of light provided by their lightsticks, having his eyes open made little difference to his ability to navigate. He closed them again to shut out the sting of the inrushing saltwater and swam on, hand in Anya's, pulled bumping first against the top of the tunnel and then against the bottom. His lungs began to ache as his body consumed the last of the useable oxygen in them. And still the darkness seemed to go on. The sound of his grandmother's song was replaced by a long, low growl. "The sound of blood in my ears", he kept telling even as the sound sank and slowed to a deep ominous rumble and he felt himself falling with it into a terrifyingly cold nothingness. He tried to squeeze Anya's hand for comfort but it was slipping from his grip, pulling upwards and away. He was scraping against something, compressed by rock on all sides. He opened his eyes again and was blinded by his own lightstick, inches from his face; He reached out and felt rock, only rock. He was trapped and running out of air. He would die here, lost and alone.

A hand, Anya's hand, grabbed the back of his shirt and pulled at him, dislodging him from whatever had caught him, held him. He turned towards her, grabbed for her hand, kicked upward through the open ocean and took a lungful of rich, briny air. He felt her reach for his other hand and pull the lightstick from it as they surfaced, and suddenly the greenish light was extinguished, secreted away in one of her pockets.

It didn't matter: after the murky tunnel, starlight cast by a thousand distant suns seemed as bright as their own. Looking toward the shoreline, they could see that the rising tide had lifted the boat; where before it had rested keel on the sand, now it bobbed five metres beyond the waterline.

"Look. There are two," Anya whispered. Beyond their boat their pursuers' own was resting, stern in the water; beyond that, at the back of the beach near the stairs, were two men. Chalo blinked hard, trying to shake the terror from his mind and the fog of injury from his brain. He focused hard and saw a rifle cradled in each of the figures' arms. A rush of adrenaline cleared his head. He surveyed the beach critically and frowned.

"Yes. And there is one more a little to the right. Do you see?"

"*Sheisse*," Anya cursed. "We need to distract them if we are to get close enough to cut the boat loose."

"Have you got anything in your pockets that you don't need to keep? Something heavy?" Chalo asked.

Treading water, Anya searched her pockets.

"A fork?"

Chalo nodded. "Anything else?"

"The lightsticks?"

Chalo nodded again. "Good. Here's my knife. Give me both. I'll be back in a second."

Good as his word, Chalo swam silently towards the pursuers boat, ducked under it for a moment, and was back by the time Anya had their boat free. Then he threw the fork towards the beach. It flew in a high arc over the farthest gunman, rustling in the bushes at the back of the beach as it fell. The man leveled his weapon at the sound but didn't move.

Now Chalo threw the first of the lightsticks, its eerie green glow catching the gunman's eye when it landed. The gunman stood and began to walk hesitantly towards the light. Chalo threw the second lightstick and the man picked up his pace, hollering to his *compadres* as he did so.

"Now!" Chalo hissed to Anya.

Any pulled herself silently over the gunnels and into the boat; Chalo followed immediately. A quick look showed that their pursuers were now completely focused on the area at the back of the beach. Anya sat up quickly and yanked the starter cord. The engine sputtered for a split second before exploding to life; as soon as it did Anya threw it into reverse and gunned the throttle. A quick three point turn and then she banked hard to the left so that it would look like they were heading back to her truck. She watched anxiously as the men splashed into their boat, started their own engine. But they bobbed near the shore, unmoving, the engine straining.

"Why aren't they following?" Anya shouted over the roar of the engine.

Chalo grinned and raised his shirt: his belt was gone. Chalo had used it to jam the propeller and Anya laughed with relief.

Five minutes and several kilometres later Anya throttled back into a cruise and spoke over the engine noise. Chalo had his hand to his temple again.

"You are bleeding once more?"

"Not much," he lied, pulling his hand from his head and looking at it. His palm was streaked with bright blood. "Maybe I should have your tee-shirt again?"

Anya pulled a face.

"Ahh, I'm sorry" he said, patting his pockets.

Anya rolled her eyes. "I know you are joking!"

"No, I would take your tee-shirt," Chalo said with a wry grin. "I am sorry about *this*." He held up the hand not holding his head. In it was her PDA. "I thought it was mine. It must be drowned by now…"

"*Shön*!" she said excitedly. "Give it here!"

Chalo handed it to her and watched as she flicked it on. It glowed to life, shining a blue-white light up into her face.

"It's waterproof," she smiled, holding the screen for him to see.

Chalo smiled back and then his eyes widened.

"*Chingalo…*" he said softly as he looked at the image displayed. "That is Eduardo Colon! I didn't recognize him when I was close!"

"*Secretary* Eduardo Colon?" Anya asked, steering into a small wave. The boat pitched forward into the trough on the other side of the swell and Chalo took the hand from his temple and grabbed for the gunnels. "The Secretary of Oil Exploitation who left politics so suddenly last month to go visit sick relatives in Spain?"

"The same. He's not visiting relatives unless he's visiting them in the Underworld…"

Anya smiled grimly, took a quick bearing, and then looked down at her phone to scroll through the remaining pictures. A moment later it was her turn to gape.

"What?"

"This" she said, turning the smartphone to Chalo once more.

Surprised by the image, he felt his gorge rise: the image was of a symbol carved into the dead man's grey saponified chest.

"I've seen that before. What is it?"

"It is the glyph for the sound '*ku*.' Sometimes it is used in small spaces to stand for Kulkulcan. Where did you see it?"

He'd seen it at the warehouse, written in the dead boy's blood.

"With Stephen," he said brusquely. He didn't want to remember the scene any more than Stephen did. "How much longer until we get to Tulum?"

"It's just there," she said, nodding to a bright smudge in the distance. "If we can get a ride to my car, it will be maybe another hour back to Cancún."

"And won't your boat make people suspicious if you leave it there?"

"No, everyone in town knows my boat."

"They won't tell the police?"

Anya laughed. "Never. They like the police as much as they like fleas."

"A flea, am I?" Chalo laughed. Anya was already blushing at the unintended insult.

"Nevermind. I've been called worse things by people far less attractive than you…"

Anya's blush deepened.

"Put the bumper out, will you?" she said, changing the subject. "We need to get ready to dock."

***

"Honey?" said the thick voice at the other end of the telephone.

"That you, Joe?" asked the blond woman, propping her elbow up on her pillow and looking blearily at her bedside clock.

"Yeah, it's me."

"It's almost midnight. What's wrong?"

"Nothing, really. Just wanted to let you know I'm going down to the farm for the week."

Honey was suddenly fully awake. "If you go, you're going to miss the Appropriations vote!"

"I worked it and we got plenty more votes than we need. Won't matter if I'm gone. I'll take the first flight in the morning."

"You've got appointments in the morning, Joe. What do you want me to tell them?"

"I don't care, Honey. Whatever you like."

"You don't sound right, Joe. You sure you're OK?"

"Oh for pity's sake, woman. Can't a man take a few days off without it being some dark night of the soul?"

"I didn't say anything about a dark night, you did."

"Well it isn't, alright?"

"Alright."

"Alright. Well goodnight, then."

"Goodnight, Joe."

Honey waited a moment; he clearly didn't want to hang up.

"Something else, Joe?"

"Yeah. Call Becky if something funny happens. Call her and tell her to follow the money."

"Money? What money?"

"She'll know."

"And what's going to happen?" Suddenly Honey was very worried.

"Probably nothing. But if something does, *you'll* know. I'll call you from the cabin, alright."

He hung up without saying goodnight.

Honey Hampton hung up and lay back down but it was a long time before she fell asleep again. "Funny" was an unsettling word to use. Calling Becky was even funnier—as far as Honey knew, Becky and Joe hadn't spoken since Hayden's funeral. And not for lack of trying on Joe's part.

Honey rolled over and put her pillow over her head. Her last thought before falling asleep was that maybe she should call Becky instead of waiting for the girl to call her: something was "funny" already.

CHAPTER 22

Stephen had been following the woman in pink for almost ten minutes; her pursuit of Alvarro taking them from the brightly lit tourist strip into a warren of rude streets and alleys, deserted but for the occasional mangy dog or stray cat. The farther they went, the more curious Stephen grew: she was clever and cautious but not good enough that Alvarro—even if he had not been talking on his cellphone most of the time—would not know he was being followed. Could they be working together?

The woman stopped short at a corner Alvarro had just turned, head cocked. Stephen ducked into a deep doorway to avoid detection. The stoop smelled like raw onions and Stephen wrinkled his nose as he looked around: all he could see was the storefront across the narrow, poorly lit street, closed for the night—its corrugated aluminum shutters were rolled to the ground. There was graffiti on the shutters, Stephen noticed: a large red circle with two smaller circles connected to it, above and to either side. It looked a lot like a water molecule—two hydrogen atoms sticking out on either side of the larger atom of oxygen. Or like Disney ears. Stephen's gut suddenly clenched: he'd seen the same symbol at the warehouse. What the hell was it?

Shaking off the question, Stephen peered around the doorway. The woman was still at the corner, waiting. Stephen receded back into his nook and glanced from the eerie symbol to the clear night sky above. He spotted Orion, lying on his side. And Jupiter, high in the south east, just above Orion's bright shoulder, the star Aldebaran.

A woman's voice, loud and angry, snapped Stephen from his stargazing.

"Hey! Get your hands off of me! ¡ *Suéltame, híbrido*!"

Stephen cursed at his own inattention and peered out into the street. Alvarro's fat bodyguard had the woman by the wrist. Where the hell had *he* come from? Stephen listened closely as he started to ease his gun from behind his back.

"Why you following him, *chiquita*?"

So, she was not working with Alvarro.

"Screw you!" the woman yelled.

"Maybe we do that later," said another voice—Alvarro's.

The bodyguard laughed unpleasantly.

"For now," Alvarro continued, "I want to know what you are doing. You were with the American who is buying the guns earlier tonight. You a cop? You trying to catch us?"

"I don't know what you're talking about!"

"Don't lie, pretty lady…" the fat man said.

"No really, I don't," the woman said, her voice trembling. "I…ditched your pal's American pal. I thought that maybe your pal…maybe he could sell me some coke…."

Stephen stopped reaching for his gun.

"You not a cop?" the bodyguard asked suspiciously.

"No," she said angrily. "I need some coke."

Alvarro appeared in the intersection now.

"Lovely Becky! I knew the American wasn't man enough for you. You want what I got?"

"Rutrauff said you moved stuff. I figured it was drugs."

"Drugs, guns, you name it…" Alvarro said, loose-lipped in his bravado. "Maybe I'll give you a freebie…"

"Maybe I'd give *you* a freebie if you make your thug let me go," the woman replied.

Stephen cursed himself for having wasted so much time and looked at the glowing dial of his watch. If he left right now then maybe, just maybe, he could drop the car at the Cancún airport, catch a flight to Mexico City, and still make his flight to Vancouver.

"*Alejate de ella*," Stephen heard Alvarro order. It was followed immediately by the sound of shouting.

"¡*Puta*! ¡*Consígala*!" Alvarro's voice. Enraged.

A second later the woman ran by Stephen's doorway at full speed, her pink dress fluttering wildly above her long-legged stride, her feet bare and almost silent on the street.

Stephen looked out and down towards Alvarro—the oily little man was doubled over, clutching his groin.

"*Corra*, '*Nardo*! *Corra*!" he was yelling at his bodyguard. "Get her or I will have Kulkulcan tear out your beating heart!"

The bodyguard—"Nardo"—started lumbering after the woman; Stephen cross-checked him hard as he came even with the doorway. The huge man careened into the graffiti-covered aluminum shutters on the other side of the street, the shutters thundering on impact.

"Get up!" raged Alvarro, hands on his crotch, still writhing in pain.

Stephen smiled to himself as he left the bodyguard stunned on the ground and started running after the woman: whoever she was, hats off to her for besting Alvarro.

Twenty feet ahead of Stephen, the woman had broken stride to look back for the source of the thunderous noise; he saw her stumble, and when she resumed she ran unevenly, favouring one foot. Stephen caught up as they approached a deserted five-way intersection. Glass glittered in the hub, a sign of regular rush-hour chaos.

"Turn right!" Stephen yelled.

"Fuck off!" the woman yelled in reply.

Nardo, now back on his feet, was gaining on both of them, spurred on by Alvarro's continuing invective.

"Jeezus Christ, I'm trying to help," Stephen swore before grabbing the woman's right arm and dragging her into the shadows of another deep doorway.

"Be quiet and give me your earrings!" he hissed at her, his left hand over her mouth and his right hand fumbling at her wrist. He yanked hard and the bracelet she wore came away in his hand.

The woman struggled hard and then fell still, watching as Stephen flung the bracelet into the street.

Suddenly understanding, the woman fumbled at her earrings and tossed them it in the same direction.

Now at the intersection, Nardo, breathing heavily, stopped to look around. Stephen pulled the woman farther into the shadows, his hand still over her mouth. He could feel her breath stop as she held it to silence her ragged breathing. Clammy, she smelled of perfume and sweat and fear, and her hair tickled his chin.

Nardo paced the intersection like a hunting dog. Stephen thought the woman's lungs might break.

Suddenly Nardo spotted an earring glinting in the single wan streetlight and then the bracelet beyond it; fooled, he headed the wrong way in pursuit of a ghost. The sound of Nardo's footsteps fading, Stephen took his hand from the woman's mouth. She looked at him as she gasped for breath.

"Who the hell are you?"

"Stephen Catherwood. Are you too hurt to walk?"

"Who?"

"Seriously, are you too hurt to walk? I know a place where we can go."

"Listen buddy, I have no idea who you are and you smell like a distillery. Why the hell should I go anywhere with you?"

Stephen pulled his wallet from his back pocket and flipped it open to reveal his badge.

"Sorry. Stephen Catherwood. I'm a Canadian cop on loan to the federal police. I'm not drunk: someone spilled tequila on me. You're hurt and you can't go to a hospital or Alvarro's goons will find you. Any more questions or can we go?"

"Who is Alvarro?"

"Holy Christ! Only the guy you were following! Who the hell *are* you?"

"Rebecca Holloway. US State Department. How do you know that guy?"

"You talk a lot. That diversion won't work for long. I really think we should get out of here. Will these do?"

Stephen had been rummaging around in his knapsack as they spoke; now he handed Rebecca a pair of white athletic socks.

"Tube socks?" she asked incredulously.

"Sorry, I don't have an extra pair of shoes," he said sarcastically. "They should at least protect you from the worst of the grunge on the street."

"And I thought chivalry was dead," Rebecca said under her breath as she crouched down. "Where are we going?"

"An apartment about six blocks away."

"Okay. Just hang on a sec."

Stephen watched as, rather than putting the socks on, Rebecca wrapped them twice under the balls of her feet and tied the end over the top of her foot. They were thicker that way, and perfect for sprinting. Pretty smart.

"Okay, I'm ready," she said as she stood.

By the time they had made it to Anya's, Rebecca's face was pale and pinched with pain.

Stephen fished the key from the ceramic lizard and pushed the door open to let Rebecca pass; she hobbled in, now limping badly.

Somewhere nearby he heard the rumble of Alvarro's throaty V-8 and elected not to turn the hall light on: they were undoubtedly safe now, but it was better to keep the front of the apartment dark, just in case.

"Go on in and I'll see what I can find to fix you up," he said as he closed the door, pocketed the key, and headed for the bathroom.

Quintessentially German, therefore orderly, Anya had a first aid kit under the bathroom sink; Stephen would not have to use the small one he had in his pack. Rebecca was sitting on the dark blue counter rinsing her feet in the sink when he returned.

"I found a first aid kit. How does it look?" Stephen asked from across the living room. Rebecca looked up, her long dark hair hanging down over her shoulders.

"Not great…" she replied.

"Here, let me look."

"It's okay."

"Seriously, let me look—I know first aid."

"I just stepped on something. Is this your place?"

Rebecca was shivering; Stephen grabbed a fleece throw from the couch and draped it over her back.

"No. It belongs to a friend of a friend," Stephen answered as he wheeled Anya's magnifying lamp from the desk. Then he pulled a chair up to the counter, sat down in front of Rebecca, and scrutinized her. Her deep green eyes were clear, her pupils were normal, and the pained expression she wore was not blunted in any way.

"Are you using?"

"Using what?"

"I heard you trying to buy coke from Alvarro. Are you high?"

"Christ, no! Not ever! It was the first thing I could think of to say. He looked like a dealer."

"Good guess," he said as he started to examine her left foot. "Holy crap! This has to hurt like hell!"

"Deep, hunh?" she replied ruefully.

"Yeah. And there's still glass in it. I'm going to have to take it out and then sew you up, okay?"

"I thought you said you were a cop?"

"I am. I've also taken advanced first aid. So—can I sew it up?"

"Will it hurt?"

"Probably, yes."

"Well, at least you're honest," she smiled ruefully. "Who is Alvarro, anyway?"

"An up-and-coming drug lord. Usually works out of Mexico City but lately he's been moving stuff in and out of the Yucatán. Hold on, I'm going to take the glass out now."

Rebecca gritted her teeth and readjusted her grip on the edge of the counter as Stephen pulled the large brown shard of glass from the arch of her foot and staunched the bleeding with a towel.

"Done. Sorry about that. Why were you following him if you didn't know who he was?"

"He hooked up with a guy who I think is working for a guy who is stealing money from the US government...Man, that hurts!" Stephen had just poured antiseptic over the wound.

"Sorry. I'm almost done," he said, threading a needle. "I thought you said you were with the State Department... isn't the FBI supposed to handle that kind of stuff?"

"I did, and I am. But I didn't have enough evidence for anyone to take me seriously until today... oh hell, can I have a pen?"

Stephen found a pen on Anya's desk and handed it to Rebecca.

"Four-five-seven-nine-two-one-double-three-six," she muttered as she wrote the numbers on the back of her hand.

"What's that?"

"A service number. It belongs to a Marine."

"The blonde guy? Yeah, I thought he looked military."

"You were following me?" Rebecca said, suddenly suspicious.

"Not you, Alvarro. Your Marine and Alvarro were talking up on that balcony before you got there. What were you doing with him—the Marine, I mean?"

"It's a long story. I'm helping set up an aid program for the Maya down here, and some of the money for it has been stolen…"

"Hold that thought. I'm going to start stitching now, okay?"

Rebecca nodded and fell silent as Stephen doused needle, thread, and his hands in antiseptic and then pulled three looping stitches through the long deep gash in the arch of her foot. She held her breath as he sewed.

"Okay, done. Go on while I bandage you up."

"My assistant in Washington—Deb—traced the money to a bank on Avenida Mayapan and when I got there Rutrauff—the Marine—was there. So when he went for lunch across the street, I accidentally-on-purpose spilled a drink on him and got him to ask me out on a date—which is why I'm wearing this ridiculous dress, by the way—so I could find out something more. Which is how I got his service number. And then I started following Alvarro."

"Why?"

"I… I was leaving anyway, and thought if I found out where he was going—an address or something—then maybe I could get one step closer to understanding why Joe is stealing the money."

"Just like Cinderella," Stephen said as he patted the last of the surgical tape in place. He suddenly noticed that the slender ankle and toned calf attached to the foot he had been working on were enormously appealing.

"Who's Joe?" he said, trying to hide his appreciation with a question.

"Yeah, but Cinderella had the glass *on* her foot, not in it," Rebecca laughed ruefully. "Joe is Joe Wilkes…"

"The US Senator?!" He said, looking up into Rebecca's face.

"Yup."

"The 'Bayou Butterfly'?" Stephen asked again.

"The very one," Rebecca said mordantly.

Stephen whistled. "No wonder you need proof before accusing him. Why would he steal the money—isn't he rich already?"

"He is, and I haven't a clue, but I'm sure it's about power, rather than money."

"In Mexico? Maybe it's about the war on drugs? Maybe he's on the wrong side?"

"In bed with the cartels? I doubt that. But I *did* hear Alvarro say that the merchandise should be ready for delivery to the city airstrip at two o'clock. I don't know who he was talking to, though."

Stephen stopped bandaging Rebecca's foot and thought for a moment, things falling into place like tumblers in a lock.

"The city airstrip is a little airport south of town for rich people with expensive little planes and private pilots. Narco-traffickers use it. And for power, they use guns. You think Wilkes might want to buy guns?"

"Christ!" Rebecca swore. "That would make an awful kind of sense. Why do you ask?"

"Alvarro's been moving drugs for the cartels for years, sending them north from Mexico City to the States. But two years ago he started moving stuff south to this part of the Yucatán. We just assumed it was drugs, but maybe he's branching out..."

The sound of crockery shattering just outside stopped Stephen in mid-sentence.

"Alvarro?" Rebecca whispered, fear in her voice.

Stephen shook his head and frowned.

"I don't know how he could have found us. Get down, okay?" he whispered as he switched off the magnifying lamp and rose to turn off the light in the living room.

It was late now, and the Moon had finally risen; it cast enough light through the balcony door that Rebecca could see Stephen pull a gun from behind his back and take a position just inside the kitchen doorway.

"Shit on a half shell," Rebecca whispered.

It was one of her aunt's choice expletives and seemed perfect for this particular turn of events. She crouched against the kitchen's back wall and waited for the shooting to begin.

TUESDAY, DECEMBER 11, 2012
7 OC, DAY OF THE DOG

CHAPTER 23

The only ride Anya and Chalo could get was with a local fisherman in the back of his pick-up truck. Unwilling to detour for Anya's car he had taken Anya and Chalo directly to Cancún; they arrived at Anya's apartment tired, bloody, skin itching with sea salt, and smelling of sardines.

"*Also dann*," Anya said irritably as she searched the flowerbox beside her front door. "Your friend forgot to put back the key."

"That is not like Esteban. Are you certain it isn't there?"

Anya picked up the ceramic lizard to search beneath it.

"¡*Uay*! Anya!" Chalo cried.

Surprised, Anya dropped the lizard. It shattered at her feet.

"*Hölle*," Anya growled. "I liked that lizard." What she really meant was that she hated sloppy, inconsiderate people who took advantage of the kindness of others.

"Anya, the door is open!"

In an instant Anya's irritation was replaced by fear.

"The men from my site?" she whispered, eyes wide.

"They never saw us. How would they know to come here? Besides, there is no way they would have gotten here before us."

As he spoke, he reached behind his back and under his t-shirt for his gun.

"How is your gun going to work after swimming with you?" Anya hissed.

Chalo ignored the question. Oiled handguns could fire at least one round even soaking wet.

"*Estancia aqui*," he hissed back as he pushed the door and started inward. At the end of the hall Chalo stopped, squared himself, took a slow, silent breath, and turned into the kitchen, gun pointed. He instantly found himself facing the barrel of another firearm, the barrel so close he could smell oil, steel, and powder. Beyond the barrel were lean Caucasian hands, a stainless steel watchband, a chiselled and familiar face…

"Esteban! Don't shoot! Don't shoot, it's me!"

"Jeezus Christ! Chalo!"

They stood, guns locked on each other for a final moment, before letting their guard down.

"I'm here with the lady that owns the place, *caballero*… what the hell are *you* doing here?"

"Christ," Stephen swore again. "Am I ever glad to see you! Alvarro's here."

"Here?!" Chalo demanded, on guard again.

"Not *here* here; here in Cancún. You're bleeding! What happened to you?"

"What happened to *me*? You're not even supposed to be in the country!"

"You forgot to put the key back," Anya said disapprovingly as she appeared and turned on the kitchen light. Her expression changed immediately from one of irritation to one of surprise.

"Who's your guest, Esteban?" Chalo asked, equally surprised. He was squinting against the sudden brightness at the dark-haired woman the light had revealed.

Stephen turned to the woman.

"Rebecca Holloway, this is my partner, Gonzalo Guerrero. Call him 'Chalo' if you want him to answer. And this is Dr. Anya von Eckhardt, owner of the apartment. Chalo, Anya, this is Rebecca Holloway with the US State Department."

Stephen paused and then chuckled with delight at the look of surprise on Chalo's face. He loved it when he left Chalo speechless, precisely because it happened so infrequently.

"State Department?" Chalo repeated, astonished.

"She's hurt," Anya said to Stephen, her eyes on Rebecca's bandaged foot.

Tuesday, December 11, 2012 — 7 Oc, Day of the Dog

"So is Chalo," Stephen replied, nodding at the oozing wound on Chalo's cheekbone. "I knew you couldn't keep out of trouble without me."

"What do you mean Alvarro is here?" Chalo asked, ignoring the jibe.

"Sit down and shut up for a minute. I'll tell you everything as soon as I clean you up."

"Give me a drink first," Chalo sighed. "I hate it when you play doctor."

Stephen and Rebecca laughed at the off-colour double-entendre; Anya and Chalo, each with a less than perfect grasp of English, remained mystified.

Chalo's wound cleaned and drinks dispensed all around, the group moved to the balcony, where they exchanged stories; the quiet once they had all finished was absolute, each lost in thought.

"So…" Stephen said at last. "So, Alvarro is guns for the Americans…"

"...I'd buy that," Chalo interjected. "The Americans are always meddling in Latin America…" he paused, looked at Rebecca sheepishly, and added, "No offense."

"None taken." Rebecca replied darkly. "It's no less than I expected of Joe."

"But we're also saying that Alvarro is killing people," Stephen continued. "The son of a judge and the Secretary of Oil Exploitation to name two. He's killing them and tearing their hearts out? Why? And why would the Americans want *that*?"

"I think the *ku*—the glyph carved into Colon's chest—is the answer." Anya said slowly, as if developing the idea as she spoke.

"What do you mean?" Chalo asked, a memory of the grisly corpse at her archaeological site making him momentarily queasy.

"Do you remember we were talking at the hotel about Kulkulcan and the rumours of a Maya uprising? Maybe his rebellion is being paid for by the Americans… maybe that is why it has gained strength so quickly these past few years…?"

"Of course!" Rebecca suddenly exclaimed. "I'm such an idiot! I should have seen it before!"

Stephen, Chalo and Anya turned to face Rebecca.

"I love my country—I really do—but we have a really rotten history of trying to unseat governments we don't like. Right now, people like Joe and his buddies—people who stand to lose a lot with Mexico's recent move to renationalize oil exploration—would be happy to put someone else in the Presidential Palace…"

"But why Kulkulcan?" Anya interjected. "He's a madman more nationalistic than Fernandez; he would never give anything to the Americans."

"My enemy's enemy is my friend?" Rebecca replied wryly. "Maybe they figure they can control him."

"I'd buy that," Stephen said, echoing Chalo's earlier sentiment, "but what's Alvarro doing in the middle of it? Why give up the sure bet of drug-running for… for whatever this is?"

"He's a sick bastard, *hermano*. He likes hurting people even more than he likes money… it's what makes him so good at his job. He would probably enjoy killing people and cutting them open for Kulkulcan," Chalo replied.

Stephen grimaced. "But why cut them open?

"It is consistent with what I've heard about his manifesto," Anya said, contempt for Kulkulcan strong in her voice. "He says that the gods are angry. That sacrifices must be made to them or they will not renew the world when the calendar ends. He's using mythology to suit his ends… and has it all wrong, I might add."

"So the world isn't going to end in 2012?" Stephen deadpanned. "Well that's a relief."

"Of course not!" Anya scoffed. "Just because my date-book runs out doesn't mean the world will end; it just means I need a new datebook."

"But why *these* people?" Stephen pressed. "Politicians and their families… wouldn't it have been easier just to grab random people from the street?"

"Maybe," Rebecca interjected. "But it wouldn't be nearly as effective."

"Effective?" All three asked.

"Fear is a potent political tool: If a terrorist can get at a country's best protected people and institutions, he can do anything. Even with just a handful of people, if he has panic on his side, no one will put up a fight. He could waltz right into the Palace."

Tuesday, December 11, 2012 — 7 Oc, Day of the Dog

“So that is why the government sweeps the warehouse murder into the closet!” Chalo exclaimed.

“… under the carpet, Chalo…”

“English is strange, *caballero*. Under the carpet or in the closet—either way nobody heard about our kid, or that Colon is dead. And that’s why the heart at the hotel went missing. Our fine fellow officers are burying the evidence because the politicians tell them to.”

Despite amusement at the mangled cliché, Stephen frowned at the political corruption Chalo was referring to.

“So they took Colon’s heart from my site three weeks ago and only came back to get the body last night?” Anya asked dubiously.

“I don’t think it was police last night,” Chalo said. “They kept shooting when I told them I was police.”

“Who then?”

“The people who put it there—who want it discovered.” Stephen said, following the logic to its inevitable end.

Anya shook her head.

“The only other people who even know where the site is are my field assistants. They would never hurt me.”

“But Anya, how would they have known it was you if Chalo said you were the police?” Rebecca asked.

“But that would mean Payal…” Anya trailed off, thinking about the new glyph tattooed on her assistant’s chest.

“*Verdammt*,” she cursed under her breath.

“It’s a big accusation…” Stephen said, more to himself than anyone else.

“Which one?” Rebecca asked.

“That your Senator is stealing federal money to buy guns for a Latin American revolution so his rich oil buddies can get their return on Mitnal?” Stephen said, watching Rebecca carefully.

“I know it,” Rebecca answered despondently. “I’m going to need proof before I say it beyond these four walls or I’ll be strung up and hung out to dry…”

“Alvarro,” Chalo said simply. “He is the link between the Americans and Kulkulcan.”

“You’re going to send Rebecca after Alvarro?” Stephen asked, incredulous.

"Not her, us! He's our case first!

"Arrest him? Just the two of us?"

"Who said anything about arrest? We go, you and me, to see what he's up to; if he really gives the guns to Kulkulcan."

"Hey! You're not leaving me out of this!" Rebecca said angrily.

"Of course not!" Chalo assured her. "Not Anya either. I think you should go have a talk with Anya's assistant, Payal. He's the way into the revolution."

Both Rebecca and Anya frowned.

"You can't be serious!" Stephen said, exasperated. "My flight leaves in …" he paused to look at his watch and then set a timer, "… nineteen hours. And I still have to get back to Mexico City to catch it!"

"Just until tomorrow morning, caballero…" Chalo said, his face both playful and pleading.

"Don't start, Chalo…" Stephen said, jaw clenching, slouching under the weight of his partner's request.

"But you know you want to, *caballero*. I know you too well; this is too much a mystery to leave alone. Look at you, playing with your watch, already trying to figure out what Alvarro is up to!"

Rebecca and Anya watched the long-time partners with interest: someone was going to have to give in, and it didn't look like it was going to be Chalo.

Stephen looked down at his left hand worrying the heavy metal watchband on his right wrist and snorted, defeated.

"Fine," Stephen relented. "I know I'm going to regret this, but I'll give you tomorrow morning. I have an idea for how you can track the guns, anyway…"

Chalo smiled broadly and clapped his hands with delight.

"We're back in business!"

"Only until tomorrow at lunch! I *am* getting on that plane tomorrow night."

Chalo nodded, grinned, and said nothing.

"What's that supposed to mean?" Stephen demanded, his irritation plain.

"You will be here tomorrow night, *caballero*."

"Sure," Stephen replied sarcastically. "And why is that?"

If it was possible, Chalo's smile widened but he said nothing.

Tuesday, December 11, 2012 — 7 Oc, Day of the Dog

“Don’t tell me,” Stephen said darkly. It’s my fate, right?”
This time, Chalo nodded.

Tuesday, December 11, 2012 — 7 Oc, Day of the Dog

CHAPTER 24

"Good morning, Stephen. Sleep well?" asked a soft voice beside him.

Hunched over a tiny pile of electronic parts and orange plastic rings on Anya's dining room table—army knife in one hand, iPhone beside the pile— Stephen jumped at the sound of Rebecca's voice.

"Not long enough," he whispered in reply: Anya was still asleep on the couch nearby, the floor beside her littered with photos of the *stela* she and Chalo had found and Stephen did not want to wake her.

"I woke up early to do this. How's your foot, by the way?"

"Sore, but okay. You did a good job. Thanks. What is that, anyway?"

Stephen smiled at the compliment. He had a nice smile, Rebecca realized: it animated his long, lean face and his eyes, green beneath dark brows, shone. She suddenly felt self-conscious in the t-shirt and sweats Anya had lent her.

"This," he said holding up a ring proudly, "is how you guys can follow the guns."

Rebecca took it from him: big enough to fit on her index finger, the bright orange band was stamped with a large black alphanumeric—ROSP0147—and, in smaller letters, a website address and a toll-free telephone number.

"Great! What is it?"

"It's a satellite transmitter. I checked the website stamped into them: it's for tracking Roseate Spoonbills—migratory birds. They winter down in Sian Ka'an. I'm not sure why Anya has them, but they're perfect."

"I'm missing something."

Stephen smiled again and slid his iPhone to Rebecca. It displayed a Google map covered in pink dots.

"Zoom out—those are the tags that have already been activated. They're on a flock south of here. Their positions are being tracked on this website in real-time. If we get a tag on the guns, we can track them the same way."

"So we follow the tag with this number right to the guns…" she said, grinning.

"Cool, eh?"

"That *is* cool! How do we turn it on?"

Stephen was suddenly struck by the transformation: in an old t-shirt and brimming with curiosity, Rebecca was even more compelling than she had been the night before, dressed to the nines. Distracted, he forgot her question.

"We, uhh… sorry. What?"

"How do we activate it?"

"Right. It has a magnetic read-switch. I just have to make a magnet…"

"Make a magnet? Really?"

"Yeah, it's easy. The hard part will be getting the tag on the guns. They'll be surrounded by the bad guys…"

"Which reminds me, I left Rutrauff's service number on my assistant's voicemail last night. 'Scuse me while I call her, okay?"

Stephen nodded and watched Rebecca walk, favouring her injured foot, out to the balcony with Anya's cordless phone. Even hurt, she had an athletic grace that Stephen found sexy. He forced himself to look back at the tags on the table. He was leaving Mexico in fourteen hours. Now was not the time to be falling in love.

***

Rebecca dialled the office number, looked out to the sparkling morning sea, and thought about Stephen. A stroke of luck. A handsome stroke of luck, actually…

"Where the hell are you and why are you calling collect?" Deb demanded as soon as the operator rang off.

"In Cancún, but I don't have my phone," Rebecca answered. She looked at her feet to avoid the glare of the sea and flexed her bandaged foot. Stephen was a good paramedic, too.

"And the sat phone?"

"Sorry, what?"

"The sat phone—is it safe?"

"Absolutely. Thanks, by the way, for asking how I am."

"Well I figured if you are calling me, you're okay, right?"

"Mostly."

"Mostly?"

"I hurt my foot. But it's fine now. What did you find out about Rutrauff?"

"Nice of you to assume I could hack a private service number. What else do you think I can do, walk on water?"

"Can you?"

Rebecca heard Deb's deep, throaty laugh.

"Your pal's full name is Travis Stonewall Rutrauff."

"Stonewall?"

"I don't make these things up."

"Jeez. What else?"

"He's the son of diplomats who, interestingly, were posted in Mexico when he was a kid; he dropped out of college but then wrote the AVSAB and got a perfect score; that got him into the navy and from there he joined the SEALS. He's a sharpshooter like…" she stopped short.

"How come everyone still tiptoes around me when it comes to Hayden? Lots of husbands died in Iraq."

"Sorry. A sharpshooter. Three years ago he disappeared."

"Hunh?"

"I'd say he died, but I can't find a death record or anything."

"So where'd he go?"

"Really, I dunno. It's like he was wiped off the face of the planet. But the last thing I found will make your eyes pop: he was transferred to special ops."

"That fits. I think Joe's planning a coup down here."

"No way! That's a hell of an accusation…are you absolutely sure?"

"Yeah, that's what Stephen said, too. And no, I don't. Have enough evidence, I mean. Not yet. I need another day or two."

"Who's Stephen?"

The sound of the sliding glass door saved Rebecca from answering; she turned to see Anya, Chalo, and Stephen emerge, their faces grim.

"Look, Deb, I gotta go. I'll call you back tonight." Hanging up, she turned her attention to the others.

"What's up?"

"I think we have a problem" Anya said.

"The world's going to end after all?" Rebecca deadpanned.

No one laughed; only a gull, screaming in the distance, replied.

Chapter 25

"So how'd Ben the Weather Dog do with the fifth grade yesterday?" atmospheric scientist Peter Nguyen asked as his boss and her dog strolled in.

"Great, as always," Kathy said, patting the retriever at her side. "But judging by today's grade fives, I think we're going to Hell in a hand basket."

Kathy gave weather talks to grade five students in Miami about once every two months. Ben was her hook: she talked about what hurricanes were, where they came from, and how to protect Ben and other pets like him during the storm, and the kids ran home ready to pester their parents to buy emergency supplies. Kids were great for educating their parents, most of the time.

"Oh c'mon, Kath! It couldn't have been that bad," replied Peter, eyes still on his monitors as he scrutinized the newest Doppler imagery.

"It was worse, Pete. I'm doing my usual song and dance: sun and the coriolis force and how storms organize off the coast of Africa…

"And?"

"And then I started talking about how climate change is making our storms more frequent and more intense…"

Peter stopped what he was doing and looked up.

"… and then this sweet little slip of a thing puts up her hand and says her Daddy 'don't believe the global warming guff.'"

"'Really?' says me; 'yup,' says she. And even if it is true, it don't matter, because that means sea level rise is a gift from baby Jesus, given to wipe the wicked from the world."

"You're kidding me, right?"

"Not a word of a lie, Pete. What in hell do you say to that?"

"What *did* you say to that?"

"I told her that I didn't think the polar bears were wicked and that her daddy couldn't make an ark big enough to save all the plants and animals being killed off by climate change and that he should get his head out of his arse and stop brainwashing the next generation."

"You didn't!" Peter exclaimed, aghast.

"Course, I didn't. I said that the beauty of America was that it gave everybody the right to say what they thought, even if they were dead wrong."

"Did you actually say *that*?"

"Yes, I did. Poor kid being led down the garden path by her dumb-shit of a red-neck father. Saddest thing is that it's her generation that's gonna be so badly off. Her generation that's gonna see the polar bears—and the walruses and the penguins—die off. It's her generation that's gonna fight wars over water. Her generation that's gonna be poorer than the one before it..."

"You're ranting, Kath."

"Sure I am! Doesn't stop everything I'm saying from being true, does it?"

"Well, no. We're definitely in for nasty weather," he admitted. "But at least we're out of the woods for this year. There's no sign of proper organization out there; I think this year's storm season is finally finished."

Peter had taken the wind out of Kathy's sails, but she was still feeling contrary.

"I don't believe it."

Bender was nosing at Peter's desk; he gave small "wuff" to ask for a treat. Peter laughed, opened a drawer, and gave the dog a milkbone.

"Why not?"

"You *did* look at the sea surface temperatures right across the Atlantic, didn't you? Still hotter than they've ever been...."

"Yeah, you've said it before: as much extra energy out there as an A-bomb. But it's the dead of winter so the north Atlantic is dark for 16 hours a day now. It'll cool down fast."

"Not fast enough."

Peter looked at his boss for a long moment; she was rarely wrong. He looked at his satellite imagery again: the ocean was black and cloudless on his screen.

"But there's nothing out there…"

"I know it, Pete. But *you* know there's more ways to know than by instruments alone. Gut feelings. Intuition. Even Ben, for god's sake: how does he know to start barking the minute a storm we've been watching drops below hurricane strength? I can't prove it, but that doesn't mean I'm not right. There's one more out there. My bones tell me so, and my bones, just like good old Ben? They never lie."

***

"The world *is* going to end?!" Rebecca demanded.

"*Ach Mein Gott*, I did *not* say it would end!" Anya replied angrily. "But the *stela* we found last night? I spent hours puzzling it out last night. *Something* is to happen in the next ten days.

Stephen, Chalo, and Rebecca looked blankly at Anya.

"Look! The inscription is in the future tense…"

Archaeologist Tatiana Proskouriakoff had made the first big breakthrough in deciphering Mayan glyphs: in the 1950s and 1960s she demonstrated that *stelae* were historical documents describing real events. Proskouriakoff's insight had led to enormous advances in decipherment and a corresponding insight into the complexities of the Mayan society; by the 1990s, the decoding work had revealed a complex and multi-faceted society. Even so, much work remained to be done, and whole classes of glyphs remained a mystery. Anya recognized the markings on her *stela* as containing members of a class only recently interpreted: verbs written in the future tense.

Anya groaned in frustration; her listeners would know none of this. It was like teaching first-year students. She tried again.

"Reading from the top is a date: 1300. That is how the Maya wrote the coming *b'ak'tun*: 13.0.0.0. That is December 21st, 2012. Then below is the name of my ruin: Sian Ka'an—the place the *stela* is from. And then the story, with verbs in the future date: something is *coming*." And here are the words *storm* and *drought*, and here *judgement*, and here the figure of a god and the glyph for the world tree. And then beneath it the glyph for water wizards."

The expressions on the other's faces remained unchanged.

"It's a prediction!" she said loudly, exasperated by the group's ignorance.

"About what?" Chalo asked.

"Well, I don't know about what, exactly. But it is for the coming *b'ak'tun*. That's ten days away."

"I don't mean to be a wet blanket," Stephen said, "but if we try to be a little logical about this, how can a fuzzy prophecy carved on stone tell you anything, let alone that something will happen *exactly* ten days from now? Its fruit-loopery! You know that, right?"

"It is not fruit-whatever-you-called it!" Anya protested. "There is a difference between a prophecy and a prediction. The modern world makes *predictions* all the time—when the sun will rise or how strong a building has to be not to fall down, for instance. We gather evidence, we use our experience, we have a good idea what will happen next. Why should the Maya not have done the same?"

"We also predict the weather and the stock market and look where that gets us: wet and broke. Besides, what *evidence* could the Maya possibly have had five hundred years ago that would tell them what was going to happen next week?" Stephen countered.

Chalo and Rebecca listened uncomfortably, both interested in what the debaters were saying, neither enjoying the tension between them.

"Seven hundred years ago, actually. That is how old my site is. But to answer your question, would you agree that the Maya were very good astronomers?"

"I would."

"And would you agree that predictions are important when they can help us prepare for the future?"

"Sure, if they're made by *knowledgeable* people using good hard *data*. So?"

"So, all the talk of 2012 is about *prophecy*. The Maya were deeply religious, it's true. But they were also scientists, observing and recording and thinking as *logically* as you."

Anya was flushed now, with passion for her subject and irritation that so many people continued to regard the Maya as backward and superstitious.

"If their astronomers could predict the motion of the stars from past observation and their farmers predict when to plant and when to harvest, why couldn't they use their predictive skills in other disciplines? Why couldn't their historians use the past to predict the future? How impossible is it to believe that the Maya might have been able to predict the rise and fall of civilizations?"

Stephen stopped to consider. It was a valid argument; the same one Jared Diamond and Ronald Wright and Al Gore for that matter had used to infer future disaster based on past environmental folly. He wasn't going to disagree simply to be contrary.

"Not impossible at all."

Anya was about to continue but stopped, shocked, at Stephen's unexpected agreement. Stephen took over.

"You're right, they were smart people. They kept records. It would make sense to use what they knew to plan for the future. But—and this is only a question so don't have a cow—how could they predict with such precision? You said something is going to happen *next week*. And what does the prediction *mean*? And, maybe most importantly, what are we supposed to *do* about it? That's what predictions are for, right? Giving people advice on how to encourage or avoid a particular outcome?"

"I'm not sure, exactly," Anya replied, irritated with her own lack of knowledge. "It is connected to the fresco inside the temple at my ruin, and the portals, but I'm still missing something. I still cannot understand what my walls are saying." The frustration in her voice was profound.

Rebecca was about to jump in, but Chalo spoke over her, his voice a soft singsong, his eyes gazing at something far away.

"*And so it will come to pass that the Earth will burn. The call of Lord Balam, the night cat, will signal the start of the end. The Moon will have white circles of rain; the sky will be soaked and arrowed, for the Lord of Heaven is offended...*"

"That is from the *Chilam Balam*," Anya said with surprise.

"Is it?" Chalo answered, bewildered by his own utterance. "I didn't know. My grandmother said it to the stars every night. I don't know why I thought of it just now."

Stephen's watch beeped and Chalo, as if unaware that he had been speaking, clapped his hands and stood up.

"Alright, *compadres*, Stephen's watch is always the boss. If we're going to do this, it is time to begin."

Tuesday, December 11, 2012 — 7 Oc, Day of the Dog

CHAPTER 26

Stephen and Chalo sat in Stephen's rented car across from the front gate to Cancún's commuter airport.

"This is ridiculous, you know that *caballero*?"

"What? Why? All these years after Alvarro and he still has no idea what I look like. If I can get close enough, it'll work like a charm."

Chalo laughed at Stephen's certainty and then they sat in companionable silence for a long moment, enjoying the comfortable familiarity of a stakeout and each other's company.

"So what do you think of Anya?" Chalo asked at length.

"She rubs me the wrong way," Stephen said grimly as he opened a new pack of gum—Wintergreen because he had no Beeman's left—and started chewing a piece.

"She what's you what??"

"We don't get along."

"Oh. Well I like her."

"Tell me something I don't know!"

"Do you think she'd like a man like me?"

Stephen looked at his partner; Chalo was uncharacteristically serious.

"I… I don't know. Sure, why not?" he replied, matching Chalo's tone.

"You really mean it?"

From his vantage at the steering wheel, Stephen saw a white cube van approach and gave silent thanks that he would not have to give Chalo an answer.

"I think that's Alvarro and the guns," he said as he popped another piece of gum into his mouth.

"You didn't answer me, *caballero*. Saved by the gong, no?!" Chalo said, eyes on the van.

"'Bell,' Chalo" Stephen corrected. "It's 'saved by the *bell*.'"

"It's the same, *caballero*!" Chalo protested.

A blue rental car pulled up. Stephen recognized the driver as Travis Rutrauff. The passenger was the tattooed man from the *Zocaló*.

"It's *not* the same, Chalo…" Stephen countered, shaking his head.

"Alright, alright—it is not. Never mind, you have to go."

Stephen put a bird band in his mouth and began to work the gum around it; the ring felt a lot larger than it looked.

"O'ay, o'ay. I'm 'oing," he said around the wad of gum. Then he got out of the car, grabbed his knapsack, pulled a Canucks cap down low over his eyes and, looking resolutely into a city map, started wandering towards Alvarro's van. Alvarro's henchman began to unload wooden crates; the American stood, watching. Stephen, still studying his map, slowed as if lost. A moment later, the sound of a gun being cocked stopped him completely. It was Alvarro, a pistol aimed at Stephen's forehead.

"Whoa, whoa, whoa! Don't shoot!" he said as he launched the map—it landed as he had hoped against one of the crates—and put his hands in the air.

"Put it away, Alvarro," Rutrauff drawled.

Alvarro scowled.

"I mean it, you idiot. We don't need the attention a dead tourist will get us."

Alvarro scowled again but put the gun away; Stephen had to work hard not to smile.

"Now what in sam hill are you doing here, boy? This ain't a good part of town for tourists."

"I… I'm just trying to figure out how to get to the… the bullfight. I took a wrong turn somewhere…"

"Lucky you ran into me; folks like Alvarro here will kill you and ask questions later. Course, maybe I *should* kill you for wearing that cap."

"You don't like the Canucks?"

"I was rooting for Carolina. Your boys stole the Stanley Cup from us…"

"You'd kill me for that?!"

Rutrauff chuckled at the man's apparent gullibility.

"Course not. Your shoe's untied, you know?

"Yes, sir."

"Nice manners. You gonna tie it up?"

"You're not going to kill me for that, are you?"

Rutrauff laughed again. "Nah, not today. Do it up and get the hell outta here, you hear?"

Stephen crouched down beside the crate.

"So…so do you know where the bullfight is?" Stephen asked as he tied his shoe.

"You're asking directions from a guy with a gun? You've got manners *and* balls! Yeah, the bullfight is down that way about twelve blocks."

Rutrauff turned to point; Alvarro turned to look in the direction Rutrauff was pointing: Stephen used the moment to stick the gummy bird tag to the bottom of the crate. Then he tied his other shoe for good measure, and stood.

"That way? Great, thanks." Stephen said as he began to back away. Hands still raised, he added, "And thanks for not shooting me, too. I'll root for the your team, next time, I promise. 'Go 'Canes,' right?"

With that he turned and loped in the direction of the bull fight.

Chalo was waiting in front of the bullring, engine running and a wide grin on his face.

"You are unbelievable, *caballero*! God must like you a lot!"

"Like me? Hardly! After Erin, I figure he owes me one—or more."

"Either way, you're one lucky bastard. What next?"

"Funny. Now we go to Anya's, I show you how to follow the signal, and you take me to the airport."

***

"Dammit!" Rebecca muttered as she ducked behind a potted palm in the lobby of her hotel, pulling Anya behind her.

"What is it?" demanded Anya as she rubbed her wrist.

"Alvarro's bodyguard. They must have found my hotel keycard. He's waiting for me to try to get another one at the front desk."

Anya peered through the palm fronds. "The big fat one?"

"Yeah, him. Will you swap clothes with me?"

Rebecca had changed back into last night's party clothes and a pair of Anya's sandals to replace both pairs of lost or stolen shoes. Anya looked from the skimpy pink dress to her own khaki shorts, t-shirt, and hiking boots and shook her head.

"Are you mad? Why?!"

"A distraction. So I can get to the front desk."

"But our clothes will not fit each other!"

"Please? I need to get my things."

"But how? And what if it does not trick him?"

"I don't think he's a rocket scientist. It'll be fine for a few minutes. And look, there is a bathroom right here."

Anya protested even as she followed Rebecca into the bathroom and began to strip.

"We're different sizes! You're so tall! I'm so round!"

"You're not round, you're voluptuous, you lucky girl… oh my god, that looks amazing!"

Anya looked in the mirror and smiled, despite herself.

"It's not really my style… and too long, too…"

"It's fantastic and look—your shorts are okay on me. Have you got any pens or pencils in your pack?"

"These are good?" Anya asked, proffering two Bic pens.

"Perfect," Rebecca replied as she twisted her hair and stuck the pens into it to hold it in a bun.

"Here, you take the flip flops…"

"And you take my sunglasses…" Anya said with an amused smile.

"'Atta girl! That's the spirit! Now let's go out there and confuse the hell out of that poor bastard."

***

"Who the hell is the guy with the eyes?" demanded Rutrauff outside Kulkulcan's plane.

The guns and Alvarro were aboard when a tall, gaunt man, eyes piercingly blue, strode up, said something in German, and stepped up into the cabin. He looked like walking death and Rutrauff suddenly felt very uneasy.

"An associate of mine," Kulkulcan answered nonchalantly.

"Mind if I ask why?"

"I am giving him three of the men."

"My men? What for?"

"*My* men, Captain. As for what for, why don't you see what he tells you?"

Rutrauff watched Kulkulcan step up into the plane and then climbed up and in himself, swinging the door closed behind him. Another one of Kulkulcan's games. That was the problem with working with madmen: they were all mad.

Rutrauff took the seat beside the thin man and stuck out his hand.

"Travis Rutrauff. Pleasure to meet you."

"Adam," the man replied without shaking hands.

Rutrauff frowned. "The boss says you need a few of our boys. Is that so?"

"I will be taking three of your men, yes."

"What do you need them to do?"

"Nothing. But Kulkulcan asks that I take them."

Terrific: someone was lying. Probably Kulkulcan. It made all sorts of alarm bells go off inside Rutrauff's head.

"You plan on bringing the boys back alive?"

"We all die in the end, *Herr* Rutrauff."

The plane's engines revved for take-off; Rutrauff was forced into silence. He didn't like the skinny guy. Left alone with his own thoughts, Rutrauff found he didn't like them much, either. He was developing the uncomfortable feeling that his own death was nigh.

Tuesday, December 11, 2012 — 7 Oc, Day of the Dog

Chapter 27

By the time Rebecca had returned to the lobby—her own clothes on and Anya's stuffed into her knapsack—the entrance was electric with conflict. Anya had not only gotten Alvarro's goon to follow her into the bookstore but had created a scene that would allow Rebecca to leave the hotel unnoticed: in a voluble mix of German, Spanish, and English, she had accused the bodyguard of groping her and demanded of the hotel security guards that he be detained.

"That was fun, you know it?" Anya said to Rebecca as she slid into the diplomat's rental car.

"Yeah, you're made for this!" Rebecca laughed. More seriously she added "But we'd better be careful: we're playing with the big boys, now. How long do you think it will take us to get to Payal's place?"

"About forty minutes. By two o'clock for sure. The big boys?"

"It means men who are powerful and seriously dangerous."

"Oh. That's the benefit of being a woman—they always underestimate us."

Rebecca laughed again. "You're not afraid of anything, are you? How'd you end up an archaeologist?"

"I'm afraid of many things. But not of big boys—not anymore. And I've wanted to be an archaeologist since I was a child."

"How come?"

"The Maya are everything Europeans are not—everything I am not. Connected—to the Earth, and the universe, and each other. They are full of passion and life and humour even… their stone records are full of word play. What about you—why are you interested in the Maya?"

"Mostly, politics, at least at first. But I agree with everything you said about them."

"Politics?"

"Oil. Mexico has it and my country wants it. But most people in Washington don't realize that just playing nice with the government in Mexico City isn't enough. The race issue down here is almost as bad as at home, and the friction between the elites and the Maya is getting worse every year. But you probably know that. The point is, if we want that oil, it's in our own interest to head off a civil war. The program I was working on was a small health and education program, partly funded by a couple of pharmaceutical companies and the US government. It would have restored funding to the Mayan language programs cut over the years and set up clinics staffed by both Western nurses and a Mayan healers—*curanderos*—that could deliver both Western and traditional medicine. In exchange, the *curanderos* had agreed to share some of their herbal remedies with big pharma."

"It sounds like a good program," Anya nodded, genuinely impressed. "It is an irony that the program was to stop a civil war and the money has been stolen to buy guns that could start one."

"You know, that isn't even the worst of it, for me. The worst part of the whole damned thing is that the *curandero* most interested in the program—a sweet, crazy old man named Hernando Canul down near Calakmul—could die before we sort out this money mess and get the program going. He's in his late seventies, at least."

"*Don* Yaxché?!"

"That's what everyone calls him. You know him?"

"I know of him. He's is a legend. You have met him?"

"Yeah. Last year I came down here to meet with the *curanderos* to convince them to participate. I watched him work for a bit—he's amazing."

"He is more than only a healer. You know that, yes?"

"What do you mean?"

"He is considered the protector of the Maya. His name—Yaxché—is Yucatec for the *ceiba* tree. In the Maya cosmology, the *ceiba* is the world tree—the centre of the universe that holds up the sky."

Anya paused and then swore.

"*Verdammt*! I wasn't paying attention. Turn around as soon as you can. That is Payal's cousin's house right there."

Tuesday, December 11, 2012 — 7 Oc, Day of the Dog

Anya was pointing to an oval wattle-and-daub home with a high thatched roof just back from the narrow, deserted road. More than a house, it was a small ecosystem surrounded by a cinder-block wall: a pair of pigs rooted in a compost heap beside the house, grunting contentedly, two little boys cultivated a small patch of earth, a tinier girl, maybe four years old, sang to herself, a small red coati the size of a kitten on her shoulder. The animal raised its long slender nose in the air when Anya and Rebecca got out of the car, its long prehensile tail curled tightly around the little girl's neck for balance.

"Payal *wayé*?" Anya asked in Yucatec.

The little girl looked at Anya in Rebecca's pink dress, eyes wide. Then she shook her head and called for her mother.

A short wide woman dressed in a brightly embroidered *huipil*, a diapered baby on her hip, emerged from the house.

"*Payal aqui esta noche.*"

"*Bix yanilech*?" Anya asked.

"*Ma'alob. Kux teech*?"

The women were exchanging pleasantries.

"*Ma'alob*," Anya nodded. "*Dios bo'otik. Taak tu lakin.*"

"*Béey xan teech*," the woman replied with a smile.

"What did she say?" Rebecca asked once she and Anya had returned to the car.

"Payal is late. But he should be back tonight."

"Can we wait?"

"It might be a while. Could we go to my site while we are waiting? It is not so far from here and I would like to make sure nothing has been damaged from the people that chased us the other night."

Fifteen minutes later Anya and Rebecca arrived at the Biosphere Reserve headquarters and Anya went to the office to check in. She was greeted by surprised whistles and choruses of "¡*Linda*! ¡*Linda*!"—compliments for her in the uncharacteristic dress.

Rebecca smiled as she walked into the tiny Biosphere Reserve museum to wait. It was more of an information kiosk than a museum, really, but it was interesting just the same.

"*One of nature's miracles*" read the title of an interpretive sign over a three-dimensional model of the Reserve. "*Mangrove forests are an unique ecosystem richer even than tropical rainforests. They provide food and shelter to many thousands of species including jaguarundi, howler monkeys, tapirs, crocodiles, endangered turtles and manatees, the endangered jaguar, known as Lord of the Jungle to the Maya, and many migratory bird species, including the regal Roseate Spoonbill. The Reserve is also home to a number of protected archaeological sites.*"

Rebecca bent over the model encased in Plexiglas: from above the wetland ran a single green expanse traversed by a network of natural canals widening towards the sea: from her perspective the water looked like a majestic blue tree, azure branches fingering into the sea. A thousand tiny mangrove islands seemed to spill from the river and, beyond them, a long wide coral reef lay just beneath the sea. Several red dots on the model were labelled as archaeological sites; a large yellow dot identified the Spoonbill colony; a scattering of blue dots indicated jaguar sightings. Rebecca left the museum glad to know that here, at least, jaguars still roamed wild.

Outside, Rebecca looked up with surprise: the sky above the high thin forest canopy had been blue only moments ago; now it was dark with thunderheads, the air heavy and electric.

Before she could step back inside, the clouds broke: thick curtains of rain fell into the canopy, the fat raindrops spattering hard on the vegetation as they made their way to the ground. In the sudden dimness, the vegetation around her seemed to glow: enormous deep green leaves arranged in mounding bushes close to the ground, olive green mosses hanging, smoky, against the white trunks of taller trees, emerald canopy glowing overhead.

Ozone filled the air as sheet lightning illuminated billowing clouds and the electric scent mingled with that of moist earth: the scents of life. Rebecca inhaled, closed her eyes and put her arms out wide, letting the rain fall cool and heavy against her face and clothes, soaking her as she stood. She licked the fresh rain from her lips and smiled. She had not been still, had not felt this alive, in a very long time.

As quickly as it started, the rain stopped, the rainwater instantly beginning to evaporate in the returning sun; within moments the rainforest was a steam room, gauzy with humidity. Rebecca's hair curled in the hot wet air and she watched with wonder as she herself began to glow, her white shirt beginning to steam in the heat. It was as if the firm border between herself and the rest of the jungle was beginning to dissolve; she could not say where she ended and it began. Maybe there wasn't even an actual dividing line?

"Rebecca?"

Startled, Rebecca turned to see Anya emerging from the office. The sun on Anya's blonde hair was blindingly beautiful, the pink of her dress against the green forest took Rebecca's breath away. She felt like she understood something for the first time. In this moment, the meaning of life? In another moment she would be able to put it into words…

But Anya's face was pale and drawn with worry and Rebecca lost whatever it was that she had almost found.

"What's wrong?"

"Pedro and Marcela have not checked in today," Anya replied.

"Who?"

"Friends of mine. They work on the Spoonbills down here. That band that Stephen and Chalo took? I brought the rest of the box down to them so they could tag another group tomorrow. Researchers spending the night in the park are supposed to check in every morning. Today, they did not. We need to go down to see if they are down at the dock."

"What if they're not?" Rebecca asked, striding after Anya.

"Maybe it is just their radio is broken, but I don't want to think of it. Please, can you just drive us?"

They drove wordlessly into the Reserve, Anya changing into her shorts and t-shirt as they drove, then nibbling at her fingernails as she gave directions to the end of the road.

"My truck," she said of the white pick-up parked twenty feet this side of the end of the road. "And Pedro's car," she added, sighing with relief as she caught sight of an old yellow VW beetle, its trunk open and half filled with gear.

Anya was out of the car before Rebecca had come to a full stop.

"¡*Mierde*! *Nos asustaste*!" She laughed as she ran toward the bug. *You scared the shit out of us*.

Then Anya screamed.

In a second Rebecca was running towards the beetle; another second and she was at the back of the car: Anya was kneeling over someone clad in hipwaders lying on the ground. Anya turned at the sound of Rebecca's boots scraping on the loose earth and Rebecca saw what had made Anya scream. A young Mexican man lay slack-jawed on the ground, his eyes staring skyward, a small red dot in the middle of his forehead and an enormous dark stain on the soil beneath his skull.

"He's shot. *Mein Gott*, he is killed!" Anya cried, wild-eyed. "¡*Marcela*! ¿*Marcela, dónde está*?"

Rebecca looked back into the beetle and flinched. A woman's body, naked and bloody, lay unnaturally akimbo on the back seat of the tiny car. Rebecca took Anya's shoulders firmly and looked into her eyes.

"Marcela is dead, too. We have to call the police."

"Where? Where is she?" demanded Anya.

"In the car. Don't look."

Anya began to struggle from Rebecca's grip. "You're lying! She can't be dead! I talked to her two days ago! She can't be…"

A shot rang out, the bullet pinging the beetle's fender near Rebecca's shoulder.

"Shit!" muttered Rebecca, ducking pointlessly.

"Come on, Anya. We've got to go."

"No! I must see Marcela!" A second shot rang out, this one hitting Pedro's boot. The body jumped in reaction to the force.

"Pedro!" Anya shouted. "He's alive! Let me go!"

"No, he's *not*! The bullet just made his foot move. Come on!"

Rebecca began to drag Anya towards the rental car. Anya glanced into the back of the beetle as she stumbled forward, wrist in Rebecca's hand.

"*Mein Gott*! *O mein Gott*, Marcela!" she cried as she saw her friend's damaged corpse.

A third shot sang out and Rebecca lurched backwards into Anya.

"Shitshitshitshitshit," she hissed as she put her free hand to her shoulder. Still only beside Anya's truck, left there the other night, they weren't going to make it as far as Rebecca's car. Rebecca yanked open the truck's driver door and pushed Anya in.

"Anya, get it together! I've been hit."

CHAPTER 28

Joe Wilkes stood on his cabin's porch, the day's second mug of coffee in hand, and reviewed the numbers of his life: forty-two years since he'd bought this place on Caddo Lake, the biggest swamp in Texas. Forty since he'd met Clayton Powell. Thirty-eight since he'd married Libby. Thirty-five since Hayden's birth. Twenty-five since he had first entered the Senate. All additions to his life. And then the subtraction had begun: twenty-one years since Libby's death, eight years since Hayden's—holes blown into his life by cancer and bullets. Five years since he'd started this misguided venture on Clayton's behalf; five since politics had lost its lustre. Three days since Clayton had betrayed their friendship with a threat.

Joe took a swig of his coffee and looked out at the wide wetland—the only remaining constant in his life—and sighed. Even that was different these days, though: everywhere the water was receding, like a turtle pulling into its shell, exposed land, dry and cracked, left in its wake. An old and familiar hawthorn stand on a small knoll, long a source of mayhaw fruit, had died of thirst as the marsh waters crept down and away from their roots. The cypresses at the edges of the bayou, weakened by the same thirst, were toppling. And where the wetland plants were giving up, woody bushes were moving in, their roots catching silt to reclaim more land for their offspring. The dark, tannic waterways were thinning like an old man's hair; slowing to stultifying sluggishness like an old man's pulse.

Nor was the change merely visible: Joe could hear and smell and taste it, too. The chorus of two dozen birds had been replaced by the solo trill of the brown-headed cowbird, its call puncturing emptiness. The fecund, sulphurous odour of decay, once as rich and cloying as the scent of skunk, was all but gone. The fish tasted metallic. The frogs sang less loud. The fireflies no longer lit up the mist. The dragonflies no longer darted in the reeds. Even the mosquitoes no longer descended in droves. The bayou was dying.

Joe felt a terrifying loneliness creep into his bones. Could Carolina Schroder and her shrill envirokooks actually be right—was climate change both real and dangerous? Was it worse, in fact, than he knew because it had been happening so gradually, and, like a parent who can't actually see how much his child has grown, he hadn't noticed?

Joe set his coffee down on the railing and pulled a well-worn letter from his pocket; the last message he'd had from his own grown child.

Dad—

Remember how I used to sit for hours and watch the bayou through my binoculars? When we first got down here to Al-Quirnah it was a little like coming home: wind and grasses and birds. One of the CNN embeds said this area is the Bible's Garden of Eden; that when Adam and Eve went west, they left from here.

Saddam drained most of the place to punish the Marsh Arabs who didn't like his politics: it was once as big and alive as the Everglades, but now there are only pockets of wetland left and only a few people who still live in it.

Nice people, the Marsh Arabs—fishermen and their families who live like it was a thousand years ago. We were deployed to protect them.

Yesterday when I was on lookout—was supposed to be letting my eyes rest and let my partner lookout, actually—I couldn't help myself: I watched a boy and his dad fishing through my scope.

They reminded me so much of us: their net out, eating their lunch on the sparkling water, the wind blowing the reeds and their hair. They laughed at a joke and my scope brought me so close I could see a gold filling in the old man's tooth.

And then suddenly, the boy was dead. I mean dead as a doornail and overboard and sinking into the marsh. I saw it. Every second of it. I still see it when I close my eyes. A bunch of ducks flushed behind them, and then the boy's smile fell and there was bright red blood squirting out of his neck. Then he went backwards and his father was in after him in the waist-high water, cradling him, agony on his face, his mouth open, crying out with pain, his gold tooth flashing in the indifferent sun.

The brass are calling it an unavoidable accident, and what I did an accident, too, but you can't tell me that some bent shitcan of a third tour Private shooting at ducks with an M-16 is unavoidable. It wasn't an accident, either, because when I swung my sights on him, he was laughing his ass off. So I shot him. Right between the eyes.

The stupidest thing I've ever done and I know it. I thought it would make me feel better. Problem is, sniping is personal. Everyone thinks we're cold as ice, killing from so far away. Its bullshit because the scope puts us right there, seeing the lines and pores on our targets' faces. And seeing their souls when they die.

It's the same for every one of them: in that second when life flashes before their eyes what I see is regret.

Even after he killed that kid, it was the same with the shitcan. Poor stupid bastard, just another human being stumbling as best he can through life with the blindness he was given at birth, filled with regret for all the stupid wrong things we do: all the people we hurt and the things we do that make the world worse and not better.

I really can't stand it anymore. My regret when my gun goes off and ends my pain is that I won't be able to give you guys a hug and tell you it's not your fault, 'cause knowing you two, you'll both think it was. Move on. Live well. Take care of each other. Make things better.

—Hayden

The power of Joe Wilkes was such that no one knew Hayden had killed another soldier and then himself; both boys had received military honours as victims of friendly fire.

Except that Clayton was going to take Hayden's honour, leaving Joe with exactly nothing: wife and son dead, a political life compromised, and a family name disgraced.

Zero. The last number of his life.

Joe stuffed the letter back into his pocket and looked up at the enormous stick nest high up in a dying cypress. It had been started by a pair of industrious eagles a dozen years ago. They built it bigger every year and always brought a chick into the world.

Joe suddenly worried that they would not come this year. Then he would be utterly alone.

CHAPTER 29

Rebecca climbed into the truck after Anya as a fourth shot rang out.

"Where are the keys?"

"My… my knapsack," Anya replied, still dazed. "Top pocket."

Gritting her teeth against the pain in her shoulder, Rebecca started the truck, threw the clutch into reverse and gunned the engine. The rear tires spun wildly for a moment, kicking up an enormous cloud of choking dust, before the truck careened backwards down the rutted dirt road.

A green car pulled out of the bush after them, making chase. The two vehicles sped down the road, hood to hood, Rebecca driving backwards, Anya watching the car in front of them. Suddenly recognizing the car's passenger as the young police officer, Rico Mendez, from Chalo's hotel, Anya gasped.

"What?!" yelled Rebecca.

She had taken her foot from the accelerator in surprise; the green car, still speeding forward, hit the truck's front bumper; the truck skidded sideways with the impact and went backwards into the shallow ditch at the side of the road. The green car went hood first into the other ditch.

"It *is* the police! I know that boy!"

"Just frickin' marvellous," Rebecca muttered as she yanked the wheel one-handed to aim the truck out of the ditch. They were sitting ducks, Mendez with his gun trained on Anya. He frowned, suddenly recognizing her, and held his fire.

Rebecca gunned the engine; the rear wheels spun for a moment and then gained traction, sending the truck shooting—forward this time—down the narrow dirt road.

"Chalo's number! Do you have it?" Rebecca demanded, eyes on the road ahead, knuckles white on the steering wheel.

"Yes, in my phone. I put it there last night. Why?" she asked, the nonchalance of shock in her voice.

"Call him. We need help."

"Why?" Anya asked again.

"Why?! Two of your friends have just been murdered, the cops are chasing us, and I've been shot. Why the hell do you think?!"

"You are shot?!" Anya asked, suddenly alert.

"Why the hell do you think there is blood pouring out of my shoulder?!"

"*Sheisse*!" Anya cursed.

She pulled her iPhone and a brilliantly embroidered shawl from her knapsack. The phone she put between her teeth and the scarf she began winding into a long narrow bandage.

"What the hell are you doing? Call Chalo! Now!"

Anya said something incomprehensible through clenched teeth and began to wrap the scarf around Rebecca's shoulder. Rebecca yelped in pain as Anya tied off a tight knot, staunching Rebecca's wound.

The green car had caught up with them and was now ramming their rear bumper; Rebecca had to fight the steering wheel to stay on the rutted road.

"Turn left!" Anya shouted, taking the iPhone from her mouth.

"Where?!" Rebecca asked, wild eyed. She saw only jungle.

"Right *here*!" Anya shouted, pushing the steering wheel hard left.

The truck fishtailed onto an even smaller trail; branches thumped against their windshield and scraped along the side of the truck, enormous on the tiny road. The car had missed the turn but had turned around and was following them once more.

"Does this go anywhere?" demanded Rebecca.

"Yes. It is a detour for when the main road is flooded. Turn right!"

"Now?"

"Now!"

Rebecca yanked hard on the wheel and the truck fishtailed right. Fifty feet ahead the tiny trail turned magically into two wide paved lanes; they were near the Biosphere Reserve office.

Tuesday, December 11, 2012 — 7 Oc, Day of the Dog

Rebecca smiled broadly at the turn of events, pushed the truck, engine straining, through a patch of thick mud and then they were on the bitumen. She looked for their pursuers in the rear-view mirror and her laugh died away.

"Oh, god, no!"

"What?" demanded Anya, craning to look through the back window.

A tall yellow mutt—vaguely a Labrador Retriever—had been standing at the side of the road, sniffing the truck's billowing dust. Now it began to cross the road.

"Coco! No, Coco!" Anya yelled from the window.

Coco was the Biosphere Reserve's resident dog, adopted as a pup by the staff. She was sweet and curious beyond all reason.

"Coco, no!"

The dog stopped in the middle of the road, tail wagging: a collision was inevitable. Anya squinted with horror, said a prayer to the god of small things, and watched as Mendez, in the passenger seat, yanked the steering wheel hard to the right to make the driver avoid the dog. The car veered hard and fast into a deep pocket of mangrove mud; mired to its rims it would need a tow-truck to be freed.

Coco looked from the green car to the receding white truck, barked once, and trotted, tail still wagging, back into the jungle.

"And to think," Anya marvelled, "Today is *Oc*: Day of the Dog..."

Rebecca laughed weakly. "Can you call Chalo now? I think he'd better meet us at the hospital."

Rebecca was ashen and sweaty now; Anya thought fast.

"They'll find us at the hospital. I will call Chalo and then you should let me drive: I have an idea."

CHAPTER 30

"You really are pathetic with technology, you know that Chalo," Stephen demanded ruefully. "Watch me again: follow the link, look for the tag number, and follow it."

Stephen and Chalo were sitting in front of Anya's cluttered desk. Stephen was trying to explain something and Chalo was not paying attention: not to what Stephen was saying; not to the pink blip that was the bird tag on the guns, travelling southwest over the Google map on the computer screen; not to the computer at all.

"You can't go now, *caballero*."

"You are a persistent bugger, Chalo."

"One of my better qualities, Esteban. But seriously, don't you want to know, finally, what Alvarro is up to? Don't you want to catch him?"

Stephen frowned and absent-mindedly picked up the crystal that had so startled him yesterday.

"You said it yourself a few months ago, Chalo. I have to get on with my life."

"*Now* you take my advice? Your timing is terrible, *caballero*. Why don't you pretend I never…" Chalo stopped, interrupted by the sound of his cellphone.

"Guerrero *aqui…* "

Stephen watched Chalo's face furrow into worry.

"She is bleeding?"

"What?" Stephen hissed.

Chalo shook his head at Stephen.

"No, I don't know it…"

"What?" Stephen asked again.

"One moment please, Anya.… Listen, Esteban, Rebecca has been shot. She is bleeding. Anya is taking her to a healer near Calakmul."

"What?!"

"It was the police who shot her. If they go to a hospital, the police will find them again."

"A healer? She needs a doctor!"

"What do you suggest, *caballero*? You're the one with fancy paramedic training, but you're going home! Now shut up so Anya can give me directions. It's in the middle of nowhere and I don't want to get lost!"

"Have they still got that box of tags?"

"Would you be quiet, Esteban!"

"Forget it..." Stephen replied, grabbing the phone.

"Anya? It's Stephen. Do you still have the box of bird tags? Good. And how about a magnet?"

He smiled suddenly at the reply.

"Perfect. Here's what you're going to do: stop the car, get a tag and the key box from the wheel well, then pass the magnet over the tag. The magnet will activate it and then we can track you. Here's Chalo. Give him the tag number."

"Where are you going, *caballero*?"

"To get my pack. I guess I'm staying."

Chalo smiled with triumph. "See, I told you. It is fate."

***

Dusk was stealing over the Yucatán as Stephen and Chalo followed Rebecca and Anya southwest into the heart of the jungle. In Kulkulcan's training camp, deep purple shadows were creeping up the ancient limestone pyramid; only the ruined temple at the top remained golden bright in the fading light of sunset.

Kulkulcan took a deep breath of the loamy evening air and looked at Sebastian, standing in shirtsleeves beside him at the bottom of the pyramid: the German had probably been strong and handsome once, but now he was mere skin and bones, his breath shallow, his gaunt face grey. Like the illuminated temple atop the dark pyramid, Sebastian's eyes alone were bright, his life held entirely in them.

"You don't look well, Sebastian. Are you sure you can get my fuel cells and destroy the rig?"

"Don't worry about me," Sebastian replied fiercely. "Which men do

I get?"

Across the clearing, the members of Kulkulcan's final cell sat, eating voraciously and laughing at crude jokes—a typical group of teenagers. Except that they, and the others in twelve other cells, would assassinate thirteen of Mexico's most senior politicians—the President among them—in ten days' time.

"I will give you Rodrigo—the big one who can carry most of the cells—and José—the little wiry one—and Payal. He is the tall, handsome one who looks like an ancient painting."

It was true, Sebastian decided. The last young man, his angular features accented by the slanting evening light and his hair pulled into a traditional topknot, looked like something out of one of Anya's texts on the ancient Maya.

"And they are all unmarried?"

"Payal is married with one child. An infant boy."

"I said that none was to be married," Sebastian growled.

"You did, but Payal is right for the job."

"No. If I must take him, I will not go at all."

"If you do not take him, you will lose my money and your chance to take down the Mitnal rig."

"My work has not killed a soul and I do not wish to change that," Sebastian growled "Contrary to what the world thinks, I do not hate people, only their decisions. I do what I do to change minds and win hearts. Make them see a better way. That we can and *must* make energy without oil. How can I win over the future if I orphan the future's children? I cannot take Payal."

"I want a better future, too, Sebastian. For my people. A single life in exchange for many does not seem such a bad trade-off to me. Besides, if you are so good at what you do, surely you will bring Payal back alive?"

"I do not like to take unnecessary chances," Sebastian said.

"Will more money make a difference?"

Sebastian considered. He was already making an exception to his rule about dying on this mission: he himself would not be coming back. Better to die in action than in the arms of his cancer. More money wouldn't make the current job easier but it would help fund Eden Two when he was gone.

"How much more?"

Kulkulcan chuckled. Everyone had a price. Sebastian's would be his own undoing: Rodrigo and José were being sent to make sure the fuel cells were stolen and brought back; Payal was being sent to make sure Sebastian did not.

Chapter 31

Yaxché sat cross-legged on his porch in the velvet twilight, machete in hand, chopping a large pungent root on a heavy slab of wood. It was a soothing task, simple and rhythmic, and one that helped him think. He hummed a small tune to himself, letting questions about the afternoon's disturbing vision form and dissipate. He knew from long experience that he would need to sit with the vision until its meaning was ready to reveal itself.

"*Don* Yaxché, are you hungry?" It was Lupita, calling from her doorway across the road. "I have tortillas and *mole*? Or rice?"

Yaxché smiled. "*Mole* and tortillas, thank you."

"A few minutes then, and I will bring it over."

The woman disappeared into her hut and Yaxché paused to listen to the night fall: bird song was giving way to the chirp of night insects; a family of coatis barked as they bedded down; and a jaguarundi—the night walker—roared itself awake. Then the warm scent of freshly-fried corn tortillas wafted from Lupita's hut, and Yaxché felt his stomach growl. Smiling, he resumed his humming, the song punctuated by the rhythmic fall of machete on wood.

Ten minutes later he became aware that another note had joined his tune: a deep constant thrumming, like thunder. Or a car.

"So late?" he wondered aloud.

A moment later, Lupita stepped from her hut, kerosene lamp glowing in her hand.

"What is that?"

Yaxché shook his head and looked down the dirt road. Lupita followed his gaze; in the next instant they were blinded by two pairs of headlights. Both sets stopped three metres from Yaxché's hut and four people emerged, two from each car.

Raising his machete to block the headlights' glare Yaxché saw four silhouettes sloping towards him through the cars' illuminated dust cloud, spirit light dancing around them. Two were men; two were women: perfect symmetry. *The Earth's four corners*. He had not expected the dream to manifest so soon.

The taller women stumbled; the taller man caught her in his arms and picked her up.

"*¿Disculpe. Esta Don Yaxché aqui*?" It was the smaller of the women speaking.

Yaxché lowered his machete and stood slowly.

"I am the one called Yaxché."

"My friend is badly hurt. Will you help her?"

"If she will be helped. Bring her to the table inside."

Stephen lay Rebecca on the wooden door that served as Yaxché's examining table and then looked around the bare hut—at the pot over the fire, the herbs hanging from the rafters, the shelves lined with old coffee cans and plastic tubs—and frowned. It was easy, in the comfort of the developed world, to be enthralled by the idea that traditional healers knew something the West did not but, faced with the reality, Stephen's Western sensibility balked: this was rudimentary, unsanitary, and illogical. Worst of all, there was no alternative and, claustrophobic, he hated to be boxed in, even metaphorically.

Yaxché placed his gnarled hand on Rebecca's forehead and she opened her eyes.

"Hernando?" she asked weakly.

"¡*Uay*!" Yaxché exclaimed, astonished. "*Mi esposa*? Is that you? What are you doing here like this?!"

"I got shot…"

"I see that, *mi esposa*! Twice. Once was not enough for you?"

Rebecca smiled weakly.

"Well, don't worry, your friends brought you to the right place. I will have you better soon."

Lupita entered, a glass bottle in one hand, a kerosene lamp in the other. She set about stoking the embers in the hearth; the fire was soon roaring beneath the pot hanging in the fireplace. Yaxché watched her for a moment and then turned back to Rebecca and took her wrists in his hands.

"Alright now, everyone else out," he said as he felt Rebecca's pulse. "Lupita will get you safely settled for the night."

Anya and Chalo turned obediently to follow Lupita; Stephen remained unmoving by the examining table. A single look told Yaxché that the tall man—his eyes haunted—would not be ordered away: he needed to help to staunch a much older wound of his own.

"Fine. They go, you stay. Do something useful. Open the bandage while I make the tea."

Stephen started working on the scarf-cum-bandage as Chalo, Anya, and Lupita left; Rebecca looked up as he worked and smiled wanly.

"You okay?" Stephen said tenderly as he worked carefully at the tight knot Anya had tied.

"Been better. You're patching me up again," she replied, eyelids drooping.

"Yeah, I'm a regular Prince Charming."

"You look like one," she replied, reaching up with her good hand to touch his cheek.

Stephen blushed and smiled despite himself.

"Okay, okay, enough making love," Yaxché scolded as he pushed Stephen aside, a pink plastic cup of warm tea in his hands.

"Have this, *mi esposa*. All of it. It will make you go to sleep. The tall one will help you drink it; I must mix something else."

"Why does he call you that?" Stephen asked as he helped Rebecca up enough to sip the tea.

"*Mi esposa*? It's a joke, from when we last met. I'm not actually…"

"Drinking, not talking!" Yaxché admonished from across the small hut.

"Oh, God, that's awful," Rebecca said making a face.

A moment later she was fast asleep.

"Jeezuz, what was in that stuff?" Stephen asked, sniffing the cup.

"I don't know your name for it. I don't think you have a name for it, in fact. But in a few minutes we can cut and she will feel nothing. She will sleep at least to tomorrow night."

Score one for jungle medicine, Stephen thought; whatever the old man had given Rebecca, it was as good as anything a modern anaesthesiologist would use, if less temporally precise.

"Now here is something to clean the wound," Yaxché said as he handed Stephen a small cotton cloth and bowl filled with a warm brown liquid.

"Take off her shirt, wash all the blood away and then see if you can find where the one bullet is still stuck, hmm? I have two more medicines to make."

Swabbing the area, Stephen realized that the old man had been right: there were two entry holes just below her clavicle but only one exit wound above her scapula.

It was stultifyingly hot in the hut now; perspiration was prickling at Stephen's hairline and if he did not cool down he would start sweating on Rebecca's wounds. He paused from his task to open the front door a crack and a wave of cold air surged into the room. Yaxché looked up from what he was mixing, his eyes fierce.

"Foolish!" he barked, danger in his eyes.

"What?"

"The door must be shut. If you are hot, take off your shirt. The night phantoms are dangerous. Especially for the injured. And the ones with weak spirits. She is both."

Stephen watched the old man stump to the door.

"Now I must go out and fix it, if I can," he muttered before storming out and slamming the door behind him.

Stephen shrugged and pulled off his t-shirt before returning his attention to cleaning Rebecca's bloody shoulder. Night spirits. Hooray. Add one to the crack-pot side of the ledger.

Her wound finally clean, Stephen looked at Rebecca; looked at her as more than just her injury. He hadn't let himself look at a woman this way in a very long time lest he fall for her and then have her leave him. Or die. Or both. But now he looked at Rebecca as a whole person and found her stunning. Lost in a deep sleep, her face was pale and serene, her eyelids were fluttering in a secret dream, her crimson lips were parted slightly. He touched a tiny scar beneath her lower lip and wondered how she had earned it. He thought back to Yaxché saying she had a weak spirit; it didn't seem so to Stephen—she seemed very strong. Yeah, this was definitely a girl he could fall for. Maybe already had fallen for.

He picked up one of the towels he had brought from Anya's apartment and covered Rebecca gently; tucking it down beside her he noticed for the first time that she wore a single gold band on her left hand: a wedding ring. Stephen felt like he'd been sucker punched; he walked away from the examining table abruptly, angry at himself, to stare at the fire.

Yaxché returned, closed the door, and lit a lump of sweet, musky *copal* resin.

"I don't know," he said, more to himself than to Stephen. "If she has been lost, at least I have made the way for us to find her. You have taken out the bullet?"

"Me?"

"I am strong and wise"—here he chuckled self-deprecatingly—"but my eyes are not what they used to be. You cut and sew. I will take care of the rest."

Stephen frowned. First, he was not a surgeon, and second, what else was there left to do but cut and sew?

"Take this. It is clean and sharp," Yaxché continued, pulling a tiny obsidian blade, sharp as a scalpel, from a bowl of alcohol.

"I can't. I'm not a doctor."

"You would not be here if you could not do this."

"Yeah I would. Just because I sewed up her foot last night doesn't mean I can cut a bullet out of her today."

"Forget that you cannot. Where do you think the bullet is? If you were me, how would you take it out?"

"I think it's jammed against her scapula. I would go in over the clavicle, under the supraspinatus and hope it's this side of the coracoid process…"

"Big words for not-a-doctor, hmm?"

"I… I had shoulder surgery a long time ago. And I took first aid."

"Ah. Are you afraid?"

"No. Yes. She's a living person, not a frog in a lab."

"To begin, *mi hijo*, a frog is just as important. And also, it is fate that you do it. Why else would you be here with the right ability?" He spoke calmly, his voice as soothing as a waterfall.

"Fate. You and Chalo, always on about fate. If you have gum, I'll do it," Stephen joked.

"Gum?"

"To chew. It relaxes me. I was just kidding, though. But if you have some, now *that's* fate."

Yaxché pulled a few chips of something like cork from his pocket.

"You can chew this," he said with a mischievous smile.

Stephen looked dubiously at Yaxché, put the bits in his mouth, chewed on them and grimaced.

"It's crumbly. And it tastes like wood."

"It *is* wood!" Yaxché cackled. "Keep chewing and go put your hands in the bowl of liquor."

Stephen chewed and the chips softened into something very much like gum.

"What do you call it?"

"*Chicle*. My people have used it for a thousand years to clean our teeth. Your people only borrowed the idea from us a hundred years ago. Now that you have your gum, fate says to face your fear."

"Which particular fear do you mean?" Stephen deadpanned. "I have so many...."

"Ha!" Yaxché cackled. "Well at least you know yourself that well! I mean the fear of being responsible for someone else's life. Now cut, and I will catch the blood."

Stephen looked at the healer for a long moment, obsidian scalpel in his hand hovering over Rebecca's shoulder. How could the healer possibly know his secret?

"Cut. You will not fail."

Stephen took a deep breath and cut. He felt the bullet beneath the stone blade almost immediately but it slipped when he tried to pull it free with is fingers.

"Come on, you little bastard," he said softly to the slug.

"¡*Uay, mi hijo*! Speak sweetly!" the healer scolded.

"Come on, you nice little bullet…" Stephen wheedled.

The bullet immediately leaped to his fingertips and Stephen shook his head as he exchanged knife and bullet for needle and thread: he was going to have to get used to the idea that everything was animate around here.

"It is a good job, *Ka Ili'ik*," Yaxché said as he applied a salve to the stitches Stephen had sewn.

"*Ka Ili'ik*?"

"It means 'the one who sees.' You were my eyes tonight."

More nicknames. Stephen was suddenly exhausted.

"Can we sleep now?"

"Eat these. Then you can use my Maria's hammock."

Stephen stared blearily at what Yaxché had put in the palm of his hand.

"Who's Maria? And what are these?"

"Maria is my wife, now dead these twenty years. And these," he said, eating a few of his own, "are *pepitas*."

"Pumpkin seeds?"

"Yes. Now go and sleep."

"Aren't you going coming?"

"In time. First I must bandage her and then wait until her fever breaks."

"But she doesn't have a fever," Stephen protested.

"She will. Then I will give her the medicines and it will break. Now eat."

"I don't really like pumpkin seeds…" Stephen said, sitting gingerly into Maria's hammock.

"Eat them anyway; they will ease your sadness. You have the *pesar*."

Stephen wanted to know what *pesar* was but he was asleep before he could ask.

WEDNESDAY, DECEMBER 12, 2012
8 CHUEN, DAY OF THE MONKEY

CHAPTER 32

It was barely dawn, a pale pink light blushing the tops of the trees behind Yaxché's hut, and Anya had already been sitting on Lupita's porch for an hour. She had slept poorly, rest riven by images of Pedro and Marcela's bodies, the sound of gunshots, the smell of blood, the taste of dust. Arms hugging her knees in the cool pre-dawn air, she was waiting for the sun to rise and someone to wake up, company to drive away her demons.

Sitting alone on the cold slab porch had been only barely more bearable than lying in her hammock until the dawn chorus had begun. But then, barely noticeable at first in the dim stillness, the jungle began to fill with the screech of parrots, the high twittering of tanagers, the croak of the Groove-billed Ani, and the harsh repeating call of the Crested Guan. A black and brown dog on its morning rounds trotted down the road; it gave her a wide berth, but sniffed the air around her nonetheless, acknowledging her existence, and Anya felt tears of relief form, warm behind her eyes. Not everything was dead.

And still the day continued to bloom: the jungle began to steam in the sunlight that now glanced off the topmost branches; a baby cried and was soothed; a flock of chickens squawked and a woman scolded them, laughing, as she spread their morning corn.

Across the way, the door to Yaxché's hut opened slowly and the old *curandero* emerged, small and bent in the early light. He took a deep breath and seemed to grow, enlarged by the morning's life.

"¡*Uay*! *Mi hija*! You are awake too early."

"I couldn't sleep."

"Come, sit with me, then. I am like the lizard: I must let the sun warm my old bones before I can go shopping."

"Shopping?" Anya asked, laughing with surprise.

"Out there, in the forest. My drug store."

"What are you buying?"

"Borrowing only. Whatever wants to come to me."

"Have you something for sleeplessness?"

"Yes, many things, *mi hija*, but what I give depends on what causes it. Why could you not sleep?"

Anya had no idea where to start.

"I think something terrible will happen before the new *b'ak'tun*," she said at last.

"What thing?" Yaxché asked, gravely serious.

"I don't know. I don't even know why I said that. My friends were just killed, and Rebecca has been shot, and all I can talk about is my work. There must be something wrong with me, *Don* Yaxché."

"There is something wrong with all of us, *mi hija*. We are human. How do you think you know something will happen?"

"I… I'm an archaeologist. I have been studying a site at Sian Ka'an…"

The whole story came tumbling out: the corpse, being chased, the murders, being chased again—and all of it shot through with the anxiety that there was something about the *stela* and the *caracol* that connected it all.

"So you can read the glyphs?"

"Better than many..." she began.

"More than me, hmm?"

Anya had picked a stick up and was jabbing the dust at her feet as they spoke. She was embarrassed by the old man's humility in the face of her own pride. She flushed and fell silent.

Yaxché cackled at her discomfort.

"It is good that someone can read! And don't worry, I know *many* things that you do not," he teased. More seriously he asked, "And what is that you are poking, child?"

Anya looked down at the dirt. Without realizing it, she had been dotting the stars named on the mysterious *stela.*

"These are the Pleiades and this is Taurus…"

"And what would I call them, hmm?"

"I'm sorry, *Don* Yaxché. This one you call *Tzab'ek*—the tail of the rattlesnake—and this one you call the owl."

She pointed first to the star cluster and then to the V-shape of Taurus.

"They are on the *stela*, along with Mars. The sky beast."

Yaxché nodded solemnly.

"*Abundance will wane, and bitterness wax, until the night creatures rise; the sky beast and the bat and the owl, carrying the wandering stone and the snake's rattle, within the dark path…* it is good, *mi hija.* You are on the right road."

"That is from the *Chilam Balam* also!"

"Also?"

"Chalo said something about the walls speaking."

"Yes, it is the same," Yaxché replied. "You, too, are part of this now."

"Part of what, *Don* Yaxché?"

A bird flew overhead, its shadow passing before their feet, and Yaxché looked up.

"I will tell you everything I know, but later. The forest waits for me and I must go."

"I don't understand," Anya said, frustrated by the limits of her knowledge.

"You are the one who reads the glyphs, *mi niña.* The walls will tell us how. And the night creatures will tell us when and where. It is instructions, written in the sky and over the land and with paint, and with glyphs that only you can read."

"But they don't make any sense!"

"Impatient always, you young people! You want the ending before you read the beginning. You must start with Dzibanché."

"But…"

"No, *mi niña*, I must go now."

Anya watched Yaxché stump off into the forest, his black rubber boots slapping against his calves, machete swinging at his side.

Dzibanché. She'd been there before. It was a very old commercial centre—nothing ceremonial or astronomical at all. Anya was certain there wasn't anything there that could help.

***

Stephen woke slowly and struggled to focus his eyes: they were still gauzy with the grit and film of last night's concentration in dim light and smoke. *Last night.* Driving. Surgery. The taste of pumpkin seeds. Everything came back in an instant. Yaxché's hammock was empty. Stephen struggled from his own and strode to the other room. No Yaxché; just Rebecca, still asleep on the wooden examining table.

"Rebecca?"

No answer. She remained deep in a narcotic sleep. Stephen lifted the bandage over her shoulder: his stitches were close and even and showed no sign of infection. Not a bad job, all things considered. Explaining to everyone back home why he had missed his flight was going to be a pain in the ass, but at least the effort had not been entirely in vain.

Stephen heard a pig grunting outside, followed by Chalo's voice, followed by a chorus of laughter. Curious, Stephen replaced the bandage and hurried out to the porch; Chalo sat cross-legged on Lupita's low slab porch across the road, surrounded by giggling children. Anya leaned in the doorframe behind Chalo, smiling with delight. Seeing Stephen, Chalo made one final porcine grunt—there had been no real pig after all—and then waved the children away.

"¡*Uay, caballero*! It is about time! I have been making noise enough to wake the dead for…" he looked at his wrist which, as always, bore no watch "… a very long time!"

Reflexively, Stephen looked at his own watch: 11:30.

"Try an elephant next time," Stephen quipped. "What's with the pig impersonation, anyway?"

Chalo laughed.

"One of the old man's pigs stole my breakfast, and when I yelled at it the children all appeared like gophers from their holes, giggling. So I told them one of my grandmother's stories—about a pig that punished a greedy little boy. How is Rebecca?"

"Still sleeping, but she's going to be fine. The bullets missed the most important stuff."

"So did you ask her for a date before or after the surgery?" Chalo asked with a grin.

Anya smiled at the banter between the two men; her amusement increased when Stephen rolled his eyes.

"Turns out she's married. Got a wedding ring and everything. Like you said, 'all the good ones are taken.' Now will you drop the subject?"

Anya and Rebecca had exchanged stories while driving to Sian Ka'an and Anya knew that Rebecca only left her ring on to discourage unwanted advances. Or so she said. Anya had been about to jump into the conversation, but something in Stephen's words, perhaps because they were actually Chalo's, wounded her. If all the good ones were taken, what did that make Anya? And why were men always talking about 'taking' women in the first place? If Stephen was disappointed, so much the better. Misery did, indeed, love company.

"Lupita has left food for you, Stephen," she said instead.

Stephen's stomach grumbled. He had eaten very little in twenty-four hours, once again.

"Great—I'm starved. Has the tagged crate stopped moving?"

"¡*Chingalo*!" Chalo cursed, suddenly remembering.

"We actually woke up only maybe half an hour ago, and then we were busy eating, and then there was the pig and the children…"

"I will get my computer and bring Stephen's breakfast as well," Anya said brusquely.

"What's wrong with her?" Stephen asked when Anya had gone inside.

"I don't know, Esteban. She was fine before. Maybe she doesn't like you."

"Nice," replied Stephen, chuckling a little. "Maybe she likes me a lot and doesn't want to hurt your feelings."

"Not funny, *hermano*," Chalo said, displeased by the idea.

"Don't worry, she's not my type," Stephen replied, smiling brightly.

Anya returned a moment later using the iPad like a tray, *tamale* and *atole* on top.

"I'm sorry… did I say something that upset you?" Stephen asked as he took the food.

"No, no," said Anya, her voice conciliatory.

Hiding her hurt with a true lie she said "I am upset about my friends. And upset that maybe it was because of me that they died."

"I'm really really sorry about them, but don't blame yourself. It isn't your fault."

"It's good advice, *caballero*," Chalo said softly. "You might take it as well, hmm?"

Looking at her computer, Anya missed the exchange between the two men.

"Please move and let me sit."

The men moved aside, allowing Anya to sit between them.

"Bird Life International… Spoonbill tracker…" she muttered as she navigated the web.

"That one," Stephen said, pointing at the screen.

Almost one hundred pink dots—the Spoonbill colony—appeared in a single group in Sian Ka'an's Bahia de la Ascención. A lone dot—the one Stephen and Chalo had followed to find Anya and Rebecca—marked their own location. Farther southwest, another lone dot—ROSP0147—located the guns.

"So that's where Alvarro has been sending things…" Chalo said softly. "What the hell is down there?"

"Drug cartel hideouts. Jungle. Maya cities like Calakmul. And Dzibanché," Anya growled.

Chalo raised his eyebrows at Anya's mood.

"Cartels, hmm? You think Alvarro's down there now?" Chalo asked Stephen.

"Don't even start, Chalo!" Stephen warned.

"What, *caballero*?" Chalo asked, feigning innocence.

Anya leaned back and away from the suddenly volatile space between the two friends.

"You want to go down there to see if you can find him."

"That's a terrific idea, *caballero*. Why didn't I think of that?"

"Not this time. I'm in deep shit already."

"Do it for Rebecca! She wants to know what is going on down there!"

"Nice try, Chalo. If I'm going to do anything else for Rebecca, it's stay here and make sure she gets better. And then I'm going home. Probably to get fired. And yelled at by my family for missing Christmas dinner. But I'm going."

"We're still partners, *hermano*. There are probably a lot more than just the guns in the crate down there. I need back-up."

Stephen looked studiously at his hands, refusing to look up or reply.

"I will go with you," Anya said into the long and uncomfortable silence.

Chalo and Stephen turned in disbelief.

"I will go, but we must stop at Dzibanché along the way."

"You're not serious!" Chalo protested. "It is very dangerous!"

"I can handle myself, Chalo. I have taken *Grundwehrdienst*—basic military training—in Germany. I will come. If you want me to."

The last comment was a challenge, a dare.

Both men were silent for a very long moment,

"She's frickin' Lara Croft, Chalo…" Stephen said at last.

Anya looked at Stephen coldly.

"I am *not*," A beautiful archaeologist, she had apparently been called this before. And disliked it then, as well. "I spent six-months as a peace-keeper in Kosovo," she corrected. "I am qualified to be 'back-up.' I will go with Chalo, but he must agree to stop at Dzibanché first."

"I… I don't know what to say," Chalo stammered.

"Say 'yes,' Chalo," prompted Stephen.

"Yes, Chalo" replied Chalo, still astounded. Regaining his composure he added, "We should move quickly if we are to make your stop and keep the trail to the guns hot, yes?"

Twenty minutes later, awkward goodbyes said once more, Stephen watched Anya and Chalo climb into Anya's truck. Chalo had found a new partner: Stephen wasn't sure whether to be thrilled or devastated.

With Chalo gone, Rebecca still sleeping—Stephen had moved her to his hammock thinking it more comfortable than the hard wooden table—and a surprising lack of interest in any of the twenty-three books on his Reader, it was not difficult for Yaxché, once he had returned from collecting, to press Stephen into helping with the afternoon's patients.

"Come. Perhaps I can make use of your eyes once more," he said, smiling mischievously. "And perhaps you will see something from mine, too, hmm?"

Stephen had seen enough the night before not to discount anything, but he was still surprised by the depth and power of Yaxché's practice: there was real healing here. Yaxché set a broken tibia, reseated a dislocated shoulder, and cleaned a deep machete wound like the best ER doc. He also mixed a tincture of garlic, cayenne, and Echinacea for an intractable cold, prescribed a ten-day course of boiled papaya followed by a small daily dose of papaya seed to deal with internal parasites, and gave a mouthwash of chamomile, aloe vera juice, and cayenne pepper to treat a hideous case of gingivitis: all remedies containing ingredients with known medicinal value.

Then came the spiritual healing: the vast majority of cases that day were what Yaxché called illnesses of the *ch'ulel*—a person's vital force that Stephen decided was not unlike the *chi* of Chinese medicine.

"There are four kinds of soul loss, *Ka Ili'ik*: *susto*, *tristeza*, *invidia*, and *pesar*. *Susto* is 'fright,' like a sudden shock. Your soldiers coming back from the wars have *susto*. *Tristeza* is sadness—not tears, but the long, black sadness. *Invidia* is envy. *Pesar* is grief."

Stephen translated it for himself: *susto* was post-traumatic stress; *tristeza* was depression, and *invidia* was… hard to understand. It was a transitive illness: envy someone their wealth and you make both yourself and the other person sick. It had a Zen feeling to it: desire for things was unhealthy. And then there was *pesar*: the grief that came from loss. He hadn't even told Yaxché about Erin, and somehow the healer knew.

Yaxché listened to his frightened patients with singular focus, as though each were the most important person in the world. And for each he would prescribe prayers, herbal teas, relaxation, and amaranth or pumpkin seeds—foods high in tryptophan that the brain would convert to serotonin, the body's mood elevator. So in this too, Yaxché was as good as a Western doctor; in this case, a psychiatrist providing talk therapy and anti-depressants.

Stephen was fascinated and humbled and impressed. It was like living a PBS special on the power of alternative medicine, and despite himself, Stephen was becoming a convert.

And then came the woman with the white hair.

"This one is *maledad*, *Ka Ili'ik*. Her soul gone, her body borrowed. Put this under your tongue"—Yaxché handed Stephen a sprig of rue—"and do not say a word."

The woman, led in by her two sons, might once have been an attractive matron; now she drooled and gibbered, her white hair—it had been jet black only the day before, her sons said—hung wild and muddy in her face, and her clothing was torn and bloody, but not from a wound of her own.

Once seated on the table, the woman sat still and dumb as Yaxché said a long prayer over her. Then he took a clear stone about the size of a fresh fig from his pocket and held it out on the palm of his hand for the woman to see.

Nothing—not his rational, scientific mind, not his police training, not even his inexplicable but indisputable experience with *Xtabay*—could have prepared Stephen for what happened next: the old woman stared into Yaxché's stone and the fire in the hearth began to sputter, its flames turning a cold blue. The temperature in the hut dropped precipitously. Stephen felt his skin prickle, gooseflesh brought on not merely by the cold but by the sense that something inhuman had entered the room: something that held the fury of a prisoner, too long caged. And then the woman opened her mouth.

As it had been with *Xtabay*, her lips formed the words a split-second before they were audible; the delay was terrifyingly unnatural. And then came the sound, all gravel and spit.

"*We are released, at last, by blood spilled in our name. We are famine and plague and disease and we walk again with terrible stride. The souls of the dead will groan in the catacombs of the stone city of the Itzás. The judges will not grant you mercy. We will win the war, here in this land, and the fourth creation will wither and die.*"

Not even *Xtabay* had unnerved Stephen to such an extent. There has been a strange benevolence in that other woman; here there was only malice.

Until that very moment, Stephen had believed that the material world fell into three categories: things that were alive; things that had once been alive; and things that had never been alive. Until that very moment, Stephen had only placed the lithosphere—the rocks he had studied—and man-made objects in the last category, every one of them inanimate. Now he was face-to-face with something that was animate but in no way alive. A moving soullessness. Stephen was going to have to rethink his disbelief in a spirit world. He was suddenly chilled to the bone, the rue bitter beneath his tongue.

Yaxché said nothing, his attention on the woman, his palm still outstretched, the clear stone still resting on it.

Wednesday, December 12, 2012 — 8 Chuen, Day of the Monkey

"*You cannot stop us. Not you. Not the nine. Not even them,*" the woman said. Eyes wild, the woman stared pointedly at Stephen as she said the last thing.

"*The war will not be lost, here in this land, and the world will be reborn,*" Yaxché replied, his voice low and even.

A thunderous sound, like a wave through a narrow tunnel, filled the room. The woman roared, the sound inhuman, as she coiled to spring. Her hands, long fingernails black with dirt, strained to scratch at Yaxché's eyes.

Yaxché suddenly closed his fist over the stone and the woman, in mid-leap—suddenly fell limp into his outstretched arms, her eyes rolling into her head. Yaxché lowered her to the floor, put his free hand on her forehead, and began to pray. A moment later she arched her back and opened her mouth. A sound escaped—the rising whistle of a kettle beginning to boil—and with it a fetid odour that soured the air in the hut.

Stephen gritted his teeth against the mounting noise; put his hands in his pocket to fiddle with the crystal he had taken from Anya's apartment; looked at his feet: anything to get away from the sound.

Yaxché raised the fist with his own stone in it; the fire in the hearth collapsed into nothing before roaring back to proper orange life once more. The woman coughed, took a deep breath, and opened her eyes, startled and confused.

"It is alright now, *mi niña,*" Yaxché soothed.

***

"The last woman—the one with the white hair—what *happened*?"

Yaxché was done for the day; his patients gone, he was sitting on his front stoop enjoying a vanilla *atole*, Stephen at his side. The old healer took a long draught before answering.

"It was *maledad*: evil magic that has released dark spirits from *Xibalba*—the world beneath. Stupid men have been playing with things they do not understand: out in the countryside they make sacrifices; they do not know what it is they set in motion. The dark spirits that have been released borrowed the woman to bring a message."

"What did they want you to know?" Stephen couldn't believe he was even asking the question; it was opening the door to the irrational still further.

"They wanted me to know that the blood spilled has freed them from *Xibalba*. They walk the Earth again and they intend to destroy it—to take it for themselves."

The impact of Yaxché's words was almost physical; for a moment Stephen felt as if he had been punched in the stomach. Had the boy and the quetzal at the warehouse been sacrificed to wake spirits from the dead? Was it connected to the Mayan prophecy? And was the little civil war that Rebecca's senator was starting the catalyst? Stephen was through the looking glass now, and willing to believe anything. Yaxché was still talking. Stephen fought to refocus.

"… the words between their words told me that. They are not yet winning. There are many things we can do to stop them."

"Like what?"

"I don't know that yet," Yaxché replied with a chuckle. "But it will come to me."

"Terrific," Stephen replied sarcastically.

"Patience, *Ka Ili'ik*. Time is a circle. We're not yet back at the beginning. We must still finish the end. The pieces will come together as they always do."

"How can you be sure?"

"Because I have faith, *Ka Ili'ik. Tiennes fe*?"

"Do *I* have faith? No. Maybe. I don't know. I wish I did."

Yaxché cackled.

"Honest, at least! You will know better when we mend your soul tomorrow. Yours and Rebecca's."

"What's wrong with Rebecca's soul?"

"Soft with *pesar*, like yours. A symmetry. Like Chalo and Anya are broken with the *invidia*. And all of you with the *susto* as well."

A million questions vied for attention: what were Chalo and Anya jealous of; what grieved Rebecca; what was a soft soul; how did a Mayan shaman cure PTSD?

"And you are going to fix us?"

"You're broken tools, all of you. I cannot use you without repairing you first, can I?" he said, uncharacteristically serious.

"Hunh?"

"No more talk tonight; it is time for bed. We go to the forest in the morning."

Wednesday, December 12, 2012 — 8 Chuen, Day of the Monkey

"We?"

"Of course. Perhaps there is something out there that only your eyes will see. We go with the waking sun."

Yaxché chortled at the look of disbelief crossing Stephen's face; the old man's laughter was contagious and, surrendering, Stephen chuckled too. Then he chuckled again: he had forgotten how good it felt to laugh.

***

"At least we made it before dark," Anya said with a sigh as she jammed the truck's sticky clutch into park.

Their progress over the battered concrete roads from Yaxché's tiny village to Dzibanché had been achingly slow, and dusk was now falling, mauve and charcoal, over the tall ruins.

"I know the watchman," she continued. "He's a sour old man but he will let us stay here the night and I can find what I am looking for in the morning."

"And what is that?"

Conversation had been all but impossible thanks to the rutted roads, and Chalo was now bursting with questions.

"Instructions. At least according to Yaxché."

"Instructions for what?"

"Yaxché didn't tell me that…"

"Of course," Chalo said, rolling his eyes.

"Wait here; I'm going to speak to the watchman," Anya replied, torn between umbrage on Yaxché's behalf and amusement at Chalo's response.

She returned a few moments later, confused but apparently pleased.

"We are to stay in the Temple of the Cormorants. It's not normally permitted, but he insisted. Help me get the sleeping bags and things from the back."

"What is the Temple of the Cormorants?"

"That," Said Anya with a smile, pointing to a crumbling temple on top of an unrestored pyramid, trees growing from its stairs.

Chalo's questions were silenced. It was beautiful and eerie and a long climb in the near dark.

"Of course you have flashlights?"

"Of course I have flashlights!" Anya smiled. "And light sticks."

"And you'll protect me from the spiders?"

"And I'll protect you from the spiders!"

"Good. I guess, then, that we should go," Chalo said, smiling back.

At the base of the pyramid, Anya stopped Chalo.

"Have you ever heard a quetzal call?"

Chalo felt queasy, thinking of the bird at the warehouse. He fought the memory and thought farther back. They were gorgeous birds: neon green backs and poppy red breasts with forever-long tails in green and teal blue.

"Yes, in Guatemala."

"It is a strange, deep sound, isn't it?"

"Yes, it is..." Chalo said, puzzled. "Why are we talking about birds?"

"Clap your hands."

Now Chalo was more puzzled than ever; he stared at Anya, unmoving.

"Go on!" she laughed.

Chalo clapped. What returned startled him: not the echo of a clap, the returning sound was that of a quetzal, deep and nasal. He clapped again and again the sacred bird replied.

Finally he clapped shave-and-a-haircut; it came back in quetzal.

"What's going on?" he asked, fascinated.

"Your ancestors were acoustic engineers, Chalo. They created this effect through careful construction so that the sacred bird might sing to the gods. Fantastic, isn't it?"

"I'll say..." Chalo said, eyes wide. He clapped again, enjoying the effect. Anya was at least fifteen steps ahead of him before Chalo collected himself and started climbing after her.

Ten minutes later and they had both reached the top of the pyramid. Chalo unslung his pack, set it down, and sat beside it with a satisfied sigh; the stars were appearing above them like raindrops dappled the ground, more with each moment; the air was cool and silent, and beneath them the dark forest spread out to meet farmers' fields, small villages dotting the land like fireflies. At the distant horizon, the tourist mecca that was the Mayan Riviera glowed faintly.

"Beautiful, isn't it?" Anya asked as she doffed her own pack and sat down beside him.

"More than words can say," he answered as he leaned back on his pack to get a better look at the sky.

"What do you call it in German?"

He was pointing to the Milky Way.

"*Die Milchstraße*. "It means 'the milk street,'" she laughed.

"The same in Spanish. It does look like milk, doesn't it? My grandmother called it *sacbe*—the white road."

Chalo lay down to get a better look at the stars.

"There" he said, pointing to Orion's belt, "are the three hearthstones that the Lords lay down when they made the world. It is why there are three hearthstones before every fire in every Mayan home. And there are the peccaries," he said, pointing to the constellation Gemini. "The whole story of creation is up there," he said. "Even with all our books burned and knowledge lost, it is there to remind us…"

Anya looked at the man lying beside her. Her ex-husband would have said she was only attracted to Chalo because of the indigenous blood coursing through his veins. Maybe that was part of it, but only because it made him who he was: kind, unassuming, curious, and wise in a way that had nothing to do with an advanced education.

"*... when knowledge is lost, of Heaven and Earth and shame, when the men of god, their backs to the virgin Earth, disappear and the pride of the wise men begins... when false leaders call forward the darkness and the balance is undone... even then the stars will hold the story, until at last the walls speak once more...*"

"What did you say?" Anya asked, suddenly alert.

"What's wrong?" Chalo said, sitting up with concern.

"That's from the *Chilam Balam*. That's twice now you have quoted from it. And Yaxché, too."

"I… I don't even know what I was saying," Chalo replied, as he stared into Anya's eyes. "It was just something my grandmother used to say…"

Anya was looking at him intently, ice blue eyes wide with interest and excitement.

"The walls speak once more…" she said, prompting him.

"*… the walls will speak, at last...*"

He kept looking into her eyes and the poem came back again.

Wednesday, December 12, 2012 — 8 Chuen, Day of the Monkey

"… *the walls will speak, at last, and at last be understood again. They will tell the one to call the judges and the five will plead for mercy, plead for the evils to be banished again, as the Heroes did before. Then will the spirits come to their city, Hurukan, xekik, and the mysterious Kulkulcan. The Itzás will arrive in the wake of these three. The souls of the dead will groan in the catacombs of the stone city of the Itzás but the bacabs will hold firm….*" He paused and then took a deep breath.

"I'm sorry. I promised to pretend nothing happened, but I can't. I want to be with you, Anya," he stammered.

Anya's eyes widened in surprise at Chalo's sudden *non sequitur*, and then her pulse quickened. She was alert, aware, alive, her heartbeat loud in her ears and her stomach tight with anticipation; it was useless to pretend that she did not want him, too. She lifted her chin and leaned in, her eyes drowsing shut. She felt his lips graze hers. And then he withdrew. Anya opened her eyes, irritated with his persistent gentlemanliness. His face was pale and horrified—hardly the effect she had hoped for.

"*Madre del Dio*, Anya… she's here…" Chalo whispered, his voice tight with fear.

"Who's here?" Anya demanded.

"Shh! Behind you. *Xtabay*. Do you see her?"

Anya whirled to look but saw only the pale pyramid and the dark jungle spread out beneath them.

"There is nothing!"

"She was there. Esteban was not seeing things. She said something to me."

Anya turned back to look at Chalo. "I heard nothing!"

"*Ka k'eban*… or *Ka a k'eban*… or… *K'eban be*," Chalo muttered, trying to reconstruct the apparition's words.

"*You are wrong? You will be wrong?* About what?"

"I don't know. Her eyes were horrible, Anya. Red like the end of a cigarette at night."

Chalo suddenly had a craving for a cigarette, suddenly wished he had not given his pack to Stephen in a bid to go cold turkey for Anya's sake.

"She pointed at me, Anya. She pointed and I felt sick in my stomach and dead in my heart."

Anya stood for a long moment, a half-dozen emotions fighting for supremacy. Disappointment at a kiss lost. Irritation at the interruption. Fear of a ghost. Anger that she had not seen it. She settled on anger.

"Why is it that I am the one who never sees her?! You, who are ashamed of your own heritage, you see her! And your partner, a foreigner who has never even seen a Mayan ruin—he sees her, too! But me? The Maya scholar? I never see her. It is maddening!"

"Anya..."

"And it is always another woman in the middle! *Selber schuld*!" she growled at the empty space where Chalo had seen *Xtabay* and then stood, grabbed her pack, and stalked toward the crumbling temple.

"Anya, where are you going?"

"To sleep. I need to wake with the sun."

Chalo paused for a moment and then stood, grabbed his own pack, and followed her. He'd prefer a small claustrophobic temple thick with anger to cool air and wide open sky if it meant not seeing the red-eyed spirit again.

Wednesday, December 12, 2012 — 8 Chuen, Day of the Monkey

Thursday, December 13, 2012
9 Eb, Day of Rain

Chapter 33

"Rise, *Ka Ili'ik.* Time to rise. The sun is almost up."

Stephen mumbled, thrashed in his hammock, and rubbed his eyes.

"Come. *Ka Ili'ik.* Rebecca is gone. We must go and get her."

Stephen sat up and looked at Yaxché, now wide awake.

"Gone? Where? I just checked on her a few hours ago!"

"Her body is still next door, but her soul is has wandered and is trapped beyond."

Stephen rubbed his eyes and tried to understand.

"Her soul?"

"Come, now. I will explain as we go."

Yaxché was out the door before Stephen could fight his way from the hammock and lace his boots; it was a good thing he had gone to sleep in his clothes. On his way out, Stephen checked on Rebecca once more: she was bitterly cold and barely breathing, her lips blue as drowning. Small chunks of *copal* were burning on the floor all around her, enveloping her in sweet blue smoke. Stephen ran out the door after Yaxché.

"She's in a coma! What happened? An infection?"

"She is chilled, *Ka Ili'ik.* That is not infection. *Maledad* again. Black magic."

Stephen thought of the woman with the white hair and balked.

"She's possessed?!"

"The opposite. Taken. By the bad spirits called by the madman's sacrifices."

Christ Almighty. It was coming back to Alvarro again. Alvarro, the murder in the warehouse, and whatever else he was involved in.

"Where are we going, then? Why are we leaving her alone?!"

"We're going to get her, *Ka Ili'ik.* Now be quiet—I must make introductions."

Yaxché had been carrying a glass bottle with him; now he poured a few drops from it onto the ground, paused, poured again, paused again, and poured a final time. He took a cigarette from his pocket, lit it, took a puff, and then placed it, butt end down, into a bare patch of soil. The smoke curled upward, bitter into the still, close rainforest air. He spoke to the forest. Then he fell silent, waiting.

He did not have to wait long. A peculiar breeze, cool and dry and smelling of lilies, came upon them, ruffling Stephen's hair before passing onward into the forest. In its wake Stephen felt even warmer in the sticky heat.

"Good. You are welcome. Now we walk."

"Welcome to what?"

"Too many questions, *Ka Ili'ik.* Be quiet and walk."

Stephen wanted to ask where they were going, but held his tongue.

As they travelled—Stephen would have called it meandering, but the healer was travelling with such speed and certainty that their circuitous path had more purpose than a simple wander—Stephen noticed that the forest was unnaturally silent. Back home—in any forest, in fact—walks were rich with the sound of birdsong: the twittering of songbirds or the raucous caw of crows and jays. Here and now, however, the humid stillness was thick enough to slice. He wiped his brow with his arm, merely transferring sweat from one place to the other, and wished for the strange breeze to return.

And then, there it was again: cool and dry and smelling of lilies. He shivered in the sudden draft and looked around, alert for anything in the silent stillness. The floral scent was replaced by pungent civet, the overpowering odour of a cat marking its territory.

Yaxché spoke a prayer or invocation; Stephen could not make out the meaning but knew the words repeated. Long minutes passed, and listening to Yaxché's monotone, Stephen felt a lethargy creep over him; he swayed in the somnolent, unmoving air, and fought, and failed, to keep his eyes open.

"In a moment, *Ka Ili'ik*, you must open your eyes and not be afraid."

It was like telling him not to think of pink elephants: a surge of adrenaline instantly placed Stephen on high alert.

"Look to the stump and do not be afraid."

It was more than a stump. It was the six-foot-tall remains of a tree, hollowed out by lightning fire long ago and now draped with Spanish moss and purple orchids, sweet threshold beyond which lay a lacuna—an abyssal portal vent. Palm fronds shivered beyond the stump, first one and then another, as if something unseen was brushing through them. Stephen felt his heart jump and forced himself to breath evenly. A branch cracked under a heavy weight, and Stephen was staring into a pair of golden eyes set in an inscrutable feline face, spotted black, white, and honey. A jaguar. Beside it stood *Xtabay*.

His pulse deafening, his mouth dry, his should have been the terror of mortal danger. Instead he was overcome by the dread and shame of one being judged and found wanting, his fate resting not in how well he could withstand claws and teeth but on how an independent wisdom, old and inscrutable, would weigh his soul's worth.

The cat stared balefully at Stephen for a long moment before turning to Yaxché. *Xtabay* smiled enigmatically at Stephen then turned and spoke to Yaxché, as if on the cat's behalf. The healer nodded, took a deep breath and began to chant, his hands raised. As he sang the sun slid behind a cloud and the forest darkened; as it did a mist began to seep from the hollow tree. Thickening to a fog, the cloud began to spiral, a nascent vortex. *Xtabay* stepped into the cyclone, her smoky form losing definition in the whirl of vapour, dirt, and leaves spinning within the rising funnel. The storm was deafening now: a roar at once malevolent and inhuman, an unceasing wave, thundering on a cobbled beach.

What happened in the next instant would have defied belief had Stephen not already been exposed to the exorcism of the day before: the jaguar roared; his cry deafening, the noise trumped even the wind's shriek. The wind fell still and the vortex's contents fell to the ground as if dropped even before the echo of the cat's great voice had died away.

But there was still more that boggled: even as the sound had risen from the creature's throat, *Xtabay* had regained substance within the wind. With her was a second diaphanous figure, also dark-haired and pale skinned. But tall and slender—like Rebecca. Stephen blinked and the second woman had disappeared; he blinked again and *Xtabay* was also gone. The jaguar looked at Stephen and Yaxché for one final moment before he, too, departed. Unlike the women, the jaguar left on slow, regal paws, the undergrowth nodding his passing as he brushed through the leaves. Yaxché and Stephen were alone once more in a gloaming jungle, the rain beginning to patter on the canopy over their heads.

Yaxché looked at Stephen, nodded, and proffered the glass bottle of *aguardiente*.

"Here, *Ka Ili'ik*. Drink."

Stephen stared at the old man, unable to speak, then drained the bottle of its remaining agave liquor. He was absolutely certain that the second ghostly figure had been Rebecca's spirit, released from the underworld; just because he couldn't prove it didn't mean it was not true.

***

"You are still mad at me, aren't you?" Chalo asked as he stumbled again over the root-gnarled terrain.

Anya had woken Chalo well after dawn, her boots muddy, her hands dusty, her cheeks flushed, and her eyes sparkling with discovery. She had found something remarkable in the rainforest and wanted him to see it before they left for Calakmul; Chalo could not resist her exuberance and so now found himself walking hard on an empty stomach through the near-virgin rainforest to keep up with her.

"Mad? Why should I be mad?" she asked, her voice as buoyant as her step.

"Last night… *Xtabay*…"

"That? I was being foolish, really. I'm sorry."

Chalo considered. She didn't sound angry. And she certainly didn't look angry—she looked delighted. And beautiful. Chalo found himself aroused—and a little irritated at the opportunity lost, thanks to the red-eyed forest demon.

"Will you tell me where we are going then?" Chalo asked, his voice carrying a hint of his anger at *Xtabay*, his breath ragged with the exertion needed to keep up with Anya.

If Anya heard the irritation in Chalo's voice she ignored it.

"We're here! Look! Isn't it miraculous?"

Chalo looked from Anya's face, glowing with perspiration and delight, to the forest beyond her and his eyes widened: ahead lay an ancient pyramid, tall trees growing from cracks and crevices in the stairs, a small domed temple covered in vines at its top.

"It's beautiful…" Chalo breathed softly.

"Do you know what it is?" Anya prodded, smiling.

"A *caracol*, yes? An ancient observatory?"

"Exactly!" Anya replied, smile widening. "A brand new one!"

"What do you mean, 'brand new'? It was built recently? Who by?"

"No, old. Very old, really, but never reported before—a new discovery! And wait until you see what is inside!"

"I'm climbing the stairs?" Chalo asked dubiously. They seemed suddenly steeper, and his stomach growled in protest.

"*O mein Gott*! I am so bad, Chalo. Here, eat!" she said, offering a granola bar.

Chalo laughed at the breakfast being offered—it was better suited to Stephen—but he took it gratefully and ate it with relish as he began to climb.

"Zigzag, Chalo. Walk sideways up the temple, like a switchback on a road up a steep mountain. It is probably what your ancestors did. And be careful—some of the stones may be loose."

Chalo did as instructed and found the going far easier but said nothing; he was doing an impromptu experiment.

"Two hundred and sixty," he said, announcing his results as he reached the top. Then he bent over to catch his breath.

"You were counting!" Anya said as she, too, reached the top.

"I am far too curious for my station in life," Chalo replied. "Why two-sixty here? Chich'en Itzá has three hundred and sixty five. What's this temple for?"

Anya looked at Chalo, surprised once again. It was a sophisticated question, archaeologically speaking. The shorter of the two interconnected Maya calendars was the *Tzolkin*: thirteen months of twenty days each for a total of two hundred and sixty days. It was also the duration of an average pregnancy, the length of time between the sun's zenithal, or overhead, passages, and a critical number for determining dates on which to plant and harvest corn.

"I'm not sure yet, exactly. But I think you know something that can help. Come inside and see…"

Chalo was about to assert a complete absence of any useful knowledge about anything, but his quip died on his lips as he stepped inside.

The dome was indeed punctured at irregular intervals by what Anya had called star portals; sunlight was laddering through those portals, illuminating the intimate space, dust motes in the air glittering in the white light. And on the ceiling the portals were linked by paintings that took Chalo's breath away.

"*Qué hermoso*…" he said softly. "… so blue…"

The dome was a brilliant azure spangled with gold, a parade of red, black, yellow, and white figures marching the circumference, the centre of the dome a painted with a thousand green leaves as if one were staring up into the canopy of an enormous tree.

"That colour—it's called Maya Blue. The whole thing is like at Bonampak, as bright as the day it was painted…" Anya said.

She was referring to the famous mural in the Temple of the Murals in Chiapas. There—as here, apparently——rain combining with plaster, a peculiar accident of chemistry, had sealed the images behind a thin layer of calcium carbonate, protecting them from further weathering.

Chalo stood, gaping at the figures that stared back at him, their eyes wide and their tongues out. He recognized a few of them: there was *Ahau*, Lord of all, wearing a jaguar pelt; there *Ix Chel*, healer and goddess of the Moon; there *Kulkulcan*, the feathered serpent, winding his two-headed way around the portholes.

"What do you see, Chalo?" Anya asked, hoping something would free the rest of his grandmother's poem from the prison of forgotten memory.

Chalo squinted.

"I don't know. That's *Kulkulcan*…"

Anya pulled a flashlight from her knapsack, switched it on and swung the beam in the direction Chalo had pointed.

"And who are these?" Anya asked, pointing to four monochromatic figures.

"I don't know those ones."

"Try this," she said, handing him a compass.

Chalo held the small brass scope out and turned slowly on his heels to line the needle up with magnetic north. The figures represented the cardinal points: North was white; due East stood red; yellow guarded the South; black lay to the West.

"The *bacabs*! So the tree above us is the *ceiba…*"

"Exactly! Yaxché, who holds the heavens aloft."

She swung the light from East to West on the southern side of the dome.

"It is the creation story on this side… the making of the world… the making of man from earth… from wood… from corn… and there the Hero Twins destroying the vain Seven Macaw… ending in the West with the Fourth Creation… the world we live in today."

"And the other side?" Chalo asked, turning to look at the dome's northern arc.

"I can only make sense of bits and pieces," she said as she shone the light over thirteen figures in the northwest quadrant of the dome.

"There, for instance, are the elders and a ceremony, exactly as it is painted at my own temple."

"And the Northeast?"

"Figures that I know, but I don't understand why they are together. I think your grandmother knew, though…"

"My grandmother?!" Chalo said, turning to face Anya. "My grandmother was never here! What do you mean?"

"That poem of hers. The part you recited last night: *then will the spirits come to their city, Hurukan, xekik, and the mysterious Kulkulcan…* There they are…"

She illuminated three figures in rapid succession.

"*Hurukan*: the creator and destroyer. *Tohil*: he who casts blood, spreader of *xekik*, the black vomit of the poem. *Kulkulcan*: the feathered serpent. Characters from the poem—they're here! Tell me the rest of it."

Chalo sat down slowly on the long rectangular bench in the centre of the ancient observatory and sighed.

"I don't know it, Anya. Little bits come to me when I hardly expect it. Besides, we should be going now to Calakmul. We have a much more recent mystery—a murder—to solve and time is running out…"

"You have to try. Please? And then we'll go. I promise."

"Really, Anya, I don't know it. It was a long time ago and none of it made sense. All night animals and stars and nonsense."

The idea that it was nonsense irritated Anya; saying so was tantamount to sacrilege. When the *conquistadores* and their priests had burned their codices, the Maya had been forced to return to an oral tradition—stories passed from generation to generation by word-of-mouth. Chalo's grandmother's poem was part of that tradition and the key to deciphering the dome; she was sure of it. And here was Chalo, refusing to cooperate.

"There are night animals everywhere here!" Anya challenged, pointing the flashlight at spot after spot on the ceiling. "Just look! A bat... an owl... the jaguar... all night beasts!"

The night beast. Something thundered inside Chalo's head and he began to speak, as if in tongues, not understanding what he was saying yet repeating, verbatim, some of what his grandmother had said whenever she had surveyed the night sky.

"*...famine and plagues and disease will come with terrible stride; the leaves of the chili plants will die. Abundance will wane, and bitterness wax, until the night creatures rise, the sky beast and the bat and the owl...*

Chalo trailed off.

"That's all I remember. Except the end part. It ends with time stopping. The end of the world. It doesn't make any sense, does it?"

It didn't. Not completely. As with all things Maya, one thing could mean another thing: the night beast was also the name for the planet Mars. Not a big player in the Maya pantheon, but noticed by the ancient astronomers nevertheless. And there was the glyph for Mars, beside the stellar portal right on the horizon in the West-Northwest. Maybe these temples were not for annual dates but specific ones? An anniversary of some kind? Maybe not an annual one? She didn't have enough data with her right now to check her hypothesis: it would have to wait until she got back to Cancún.

"Sense?" Anya repeated with a frown. "No, it doesn't make any. Not yet. Let's go. And quickly...as soon as we're done I need to figure this out."

***

Sebastian von Eckhardt shivered in his leather jacket despite the warm morning air and looked at the three young men sitting cross-legged before him beneath the dappled light of the rainforest. They were timeless, ageless, unendurably beautiful: their long straight noses and glittering deep-set eyes, their dark hair pulled up into a traditional top-knot; Anya would have liked to see them, her ancient people come alive. Then again, she might call them more Hollywood than history: the living Maya were so much more than merely these costumes. Sebastian shrugged. Either way, they looked good. Their training was good, too. Despite the American's arrogance, he had done a good job: these three would be able to do what Sebastian needed of them. But he still worried that an accident would befall the young father.

Rodrigo and José fidgeted beneath Sebastian's intense gaze; Payal stared back evenly, waiting.

"Kulkulcan wants you to help me now that he has given me the extra task of stealing from the rig before destroying it."

"Twelve fifty-pound batteries," Rodrigo volunteered.

Sebastian glared him into silence.

"Let me be clear about this: I do not want you to come with me—especially you, Payal, with your baby at home. I already have a team that can do this, and bring back the batteries as well. But since Kulkulcan will not pay if you do not accompany me, you will come."

José smirked at the European, forced to do Kulkulcan's bidding.

"Don't be smug," Sebastian warned. "I will make you work these next ten days so that you are trained as well as my team; I do not intend for you to do a stupid thing that will get anyone killed. What comes next is a crash course. You will learn to climb and swim and handle yourself in my submersibles and set explosives without blowing your hands off. You will be as good as my team, or I will call the operation off and blame you. And *that* will not please your Kulkulcan. Do you understand?"

Even Payal flinched at the threat: if they failed Sebastian, they failed Kulkulcan. Payal could still smell the oiled gunmetal of Kulkulcan's displeasure, could feel the pressure of the gun held between his eyes. All three young men nodded solemnly.

"Good. Then shall I tell you how we will do this thing?" Sebastian's voice was now warm, his tone collegial, and the young men found themselves comfortable in his presence. They nodded eagerly.

Thursday, December 13, 2012 — 9 Eb, Day of Rain

"The Mitnal oil platform," Sebastian said conversationally, "is located in the Gulf of Mexico about fifty nautical miles north-north-east of Coatzacoalcos. It is what is called a 'spar cell' rig… the newest generation of deep-water rigs. The wellhead—the hole in the ground from which the oil is pumped—lies 1600 fathoms deep—almost two miles straight down from the surface. It is the deepest wellhead in the world today, and the oil itself lies in an enormous pocket between rocks another seven miles beneath the Earth's crust…"

The young men were glazing over, bored by the details. Sebastian pursed his lips and then tried a new tactic.

"Have you ever put a straw in a soda drink… maybe a coke bottle?"

The three men snapped to attention, startled by the sudden subject change.

"Have you?"

The three nodded.

"And have you noticed how the bubbles push the straw back up?"

More nodding.

"That is a little how Mitnal is built. The platform and everything on it—derricks and pump, helicopter pads, workers quarters, cafeteria, the storage rooms in which we will find your special batteries—all of it is built on five enormous straws—called spars—half filled with air and half with stored oil, balanced just right so the whole thing floats up above the ocean. The bottom of each straw is tied to the ocean floor to keep it above the wellhead. It is a marvellous feat of engineering—both strong enough and flexible enough to be able to withstand the deadly hurricanes that blow through the Gulf."

"If it is so strong, how do a handful of men defeat it?" José asked, his voice confrontational.

"Men *and women*, José. As for defeating the rig? Its designers did not think of a small attack. That fact—long with the oil stored in each spar—is its weakness. We will take four small submersibles, acoustically masked to look and sound on radar and sonar like a pod of whales, to the spars, climb them, break in with security codes supplied by a disgruntled employee, set bombs on each spar to ignite the oil in them, and then leave in the submersibles that brought us. We will be far enough away when the petroleum ignites and the rig founders that the explosive concussion should not kill us."

Thursday, December 13, 2012 — 9 Eb, Day of Rain

Sebastian watched as the young men tried, and failed, to digest the information. He wanted to see which among them was brave enough to ask the first question. That would be the one he would have to win over in order to gain, if not loyalty, at least obedience, from the other two.

"Acoustic mask?" Payal asked.

"Like a coat, but made of sound. To hide us in plain sight. Though it is impossible to make a submersible invisible, weaving our subs in the manner of a small pod of whales while broadcasting whalesong, we can fool security on the platform—make them ignore us. For all the bad they do, oil platforms make good marine sanctuaries. It is illegal to fish near them so they now teem with marine life. Since security are used to seeing pods of marine mammals and schools of fish and flocks of birds on their instruments, they will pay us no mind."

Payal nodded and said nothing more. A smart one, Sebastian reflected. He would be both easier and harder to win over: easier because reason would work; harder because his loyalty to Kulkulcan would run deep.

"And what is this explosion that should not kill us?" Rodrigo asked nervously.

Sebastian permitted himself a small smile. Rodrigo's sense of self-preservation would serve them all well… would make him work quickly.

"Once we leave the rig with Kulkulcan's batteries, we detonate the explosives. They will blow holes in each spar, igniting the oil. When they explode, they will create a shock-wave. If we are too close, the shock waves will pass through us with enough force to cause a million tiny rips in our tissues and we will slowly bleed to death. Maybe eighteen hours, and then we will die a death akin to suffocation. But if we move quickly, we will be beyond the lethal blast radius and will have nothing to worry about, yes?"

It was José who blanched. Rodrigo simply nodded.

"Any more questions?"

Three heads shook "no."

"I have one for you, then, before you collect your things and go to the plane."

The threesome had begun to rise; they stopped suspiciously and retook their seats on the ground.

"Do you know why we do this?"

"To get the batteries for *tohil*, the one who brings blood," José answered disinterestedly.

"The deep ocean belongs to the lords of *Xibalba*. The white men have woken the gods by drilling there and they are angry. Unless we destroy the thing, Kulkulcan says the gods will destroy us," Rodrigo filled in.

Sebastian nodded.

"Kulkulcan has told me this much. And you, Payal—why do you do this?"

"For my son," he answered simply.

"How is that?"

"Kulkulcan promises us a world where the Maya have opportunities better than we have now; opportunities equal to those with lighter skin. I want a future for my son."

Sebastian nodded again, slowly and thoughtfully this time.

"I do this for the future too, Payal. To free us from our addiction to oil and to reduce the likelihood that climate change will make life a misery for us all."

Now Payal nodded. That, too, would be a good world for his son. As he had worked for Anya, Payal could work with this foreign man who had her eyes.

***

"A word with you Payal, before you leave."

Surprised to hear Kulkulcan's voice in the barracks, Payal stood so suddenly from his packing that he hit his head on the bunk above his own.

Kulkulcan chuckled kindly.

"No need to be afraid, Payal. I am only here to be sure you know what is expected of you."

"Of course, *Ahau*. To help the German steal the battery packs and when we return to shore, give all but one to Alvarro to move to our cells throughout the country. The last one I bring to kill the Minister of Internal Security at Chich'en Itzá. The one you already have will kill the President…"

Payal trailed off, suddenly realizing something.

"Yes, Payal?"

"If we are destroying the rig, why will there still be a ceremony to celebrate its opening?"

"A good question, Payal. Very good indeed. That is actually why I wanted to speak with you."

"Yes, *Ahau*?"

"Do you understand the German's plan?"

"He has explained it."

"Do you understand it well enough to undo it?"

"I… I beg your pardon, *Ahau*?" Payal stammered.

"Could you prevent him from destroying the rig once you have retrieved the fuel cells?"

"Not destroy the rig… ?" Payal repeated, trying to comprehend what Kulkulcan was asking.

Kulkulcan's nostrils flared, his ire rising.

"Could you do it?"

Payal wanted to ask a hundred questions: *why pay the German if not to destroy the rig? Why leave the abomination in the heart of* Xibalba*? Why risk the ire of the gods?* And yet the sight of Kulkulcan's growing fury cowed Payal.

"Yes *Ahau*, I… I could do it."

"You are certain?" Kulkulcan pressed, eyes flashing.

Payal nodded, resolute. "Yes, Ahau."

"Good then. Do it. Kill the German if you have to. And anyone else who gets in your way. The rig must not be destroyed."

Payal watched Kulkulcan leave the barracks, his mind blank with confusion. What of appeasing the gods? What of making the world better for his son? What, if not Kulkulcan's vision, did the future hold? And if the gods were indeed awake and angry, could there be a future at all?

Chapter 34

"Why isn't she awake yet?" Stephen demanded as he looked down into the hammock at Rebecca's still sleeping figure. "You just said we got her spirit back from… from wherever it was stuck; why isn't she awake?"

"Patience, *mi niño*, patience. She is back in her body, but I am keeping it asleep with medicines so she does not come apart again," Yaxché replied.

"Come apart?"

"Souls and bodies are different materials; their binding together is complicated."

They had just returned from the jungle, the jaguar, and *Xtabay* and Stephen was still struggling with the notion that Rebecca's spirit had been both taken to and liberated from the Underworld. Enough with kidnappers, already.

"So when will she wake up?" he asked petulantly.

"In the morning."

"*Tomorrow* morning? Why so long? What am I supposed to do until then?" I can't take her car and leave her here.

"What do you want to do?" the old man countered. He looked at Stephen with such intensity that Stephen could do nothing but speak the truth.

"I'm tired, Yaxché. I don't want to *do* anything."

"That is a good start, *Ka Ili'ik*!" Yaxché cackled. "Do nothing! Much can come of that: the gods took nothing and made the world!"

Stephen smiled weakly in reply.

"Ah, good. A smile. Now that is something. Before you do nothing, however, I have another small something—an almost nothing—for you. Come outside and help me until the bus comes."

Stephen took a last look at Rebecca, still asleep but no longer pallid, then followed Yaxché outside.

They had been sitting cross-legged on the healer's porch for a good half hour, chopping herbs with machetes, the air fragrant with the scent of crushed rosemary and rue, when Yaxché spoke again.

"Who is the girl with you, *mi niño*?"

"Girl?" Stephen asked, still looking down at the cutting board and his work.

"The ghost you carry with you. The girl who died," he replied, his focus still on his own knife and board.

Surprised, Stephen let his machete slip and sliced his thumb.

Neither deep nor dangerous, the cut nevertheless began to bleed profusely. Yaxché grabbed Stephen's wrist and in a second had spread the mash from his own cutting board onto the wound. The bleeding ceased almost instantly.

"How did you know?" Stephen asked, his wrist still in Yaxché's hand.

"It is chili. A simple remedy. Everyone knows."

"No, I meant about… the girl."

"I'm a *curandero*. I can see the aches of the soul. You need to let her go."

"I… I can't," stammered Stephen.

"You must, *mi niño*. You're life withers courting the dead. She's ready to go."

Stephen blinked back tears and shook his head.

"It's my fault she's dead, Yaxché."

"Is it? Did you put a gun to her head?"

"No!" Stephen replied, horrified.

"Then she made the choice that determined her fate, *mi hijo*."

"But I convinced her to come climbing instead of studying…"

"She chose, *Ka Ili'ik*. Choices are all that we have. To run or not to run. To help or not to help. To laugh or not to laugh. For good or for evil, the sum of our choices makes us what we are. And every moment brings a choice, a direction."

"If that is so, what is my choice right now?" Stephen asked petulantly. He felt like he was being lectured.

Yaxché cackled. "To chop or not to chop. To sit or to walk away. To live or not, *mi hijo*. Right now you are not choosing. You are stuck half-way, keeping your ghost with you."

Stephen shied away from the idea that he was caught in some shadowland between life and death; shied away from it mostly because deep down, it felt true: he had been going through the motions—a Teflon-man—since Erin's death.

"How do I choose?" he asked.

"By choosing. You just do it, *mi hijo*. When the moment comes, you just do."

Stephen rolled his eyes. He felt like a child staring at a cookie jar on the kitchen's highest shelf: frustrated by the knowledge that truly living was somehow easy for others but always beyond his reach.

Yaxché watched Stephen struggle, knew he was not yet ready. Yaxché would have to cure that before the young man could function in what was coming.

"Don't worry, *mi niño*. Tomorrow you will see," Yaxché said as he unfolded his old joints slowly and rose. "My patients come. You may keep chopping. Or you may do something else. The choice is yours, hmm?"

Stephen decided to go for a walk; not keen for a third jaguar encounter, he decided to stick to the narrow dirt road. He stepped aside as the patient-filled bus passed him and thought of the healer's work with Rebecca. Then he thought of Rebecca herself and smiled.

It wasn't so much that she was pretty or smart or funny that made him smile, but the way she made him feel: buoyant, breathless, excited—a colour-blind man seeing the yellow of sunrise for the first time. It would figure that she was married. But was that a reason to pretend he didn't feel something? He didn't have to do anything about it.

And what of Erin? Stephen had lived in Mexico four years now; had celebrated *la Dia de los Muertos* with Chalo four times. The way death wound through life in this country—and now the phantoms he would swear he had seen—made it possible to imagine Erin's ghost walking with him. Yaxché had said she was ready to go: was she tethered to him by his grief, his prisoner? That made him not only half-dead but a jailor, too. If he admitted to himself his feelings for Rebecca, married or not, would that be choosing life? Would that, ridiculous as it seemed, free Erin's soul?

Beginning to loathe this new self-image, lifeless and cowardly, Stephen stuck his hands in his pockets and quickened his pace. The sharp sting of an electric shock, coursing from his left hand to his heart, made him stumble. He pulled his hand from his pocket and dropped the apparent source of the sudden jolt: the strange stone from Anya's apartment.

Stephen bent over to look at the crystal and watched as the rutiles began to swirl once more.

"How the hell does that happen?" he asked aloud. By the laws of physics, it was impossible.

Before he could consider explanations, scientific or otherwise, he was caught in a waking nightmare, images flashing in rapid succession across his retina: a snake with feathers was coiling around Chalo, preparing to eat him. And Chalo, mesmerized and delighted, seemed not to be fighting back. Stephen felt for his gun and levelled it at the bird-serpent but something grabbed for his hand.

"Let go," said a voice that was not Erin's, speaking the words she had said before she died.

"No" he croaked. There was a pressure on his chest, as heavy as the sky. He couldn't breathe. He was going to die.

"Let it go, *Ka Ili'ik*. Let it go. It is not a thing you can do alone."

The vision faded and Stephen opened his eyes to the velvet dark of dusk: he had lost the entire afternoon. Yaxché was crouched over him, his old gnarled hands holding Stephen's clenched fist. Stephen relaxed his grip and the crystal rolled from it; Yaxché sat back when he saw the stone, his eyes wide with surprise.

"*Ka Ili'ik* is a better name than I imagined, *mi hijo*."

"What happened?"

"You have a sastun, Or it has you."

"What?"

"A healer's stone. You crossed unprepared, *Ka Ili'ik*. Had a vision from the other world."

"I saw Chalo being eaten by a snake…" Stephen said as he sat up.

"The stone burned me again," he added as he looked at the large white blister forming on his palm.

"Sight without understanding is a dangerous thing, *Ka Ili'ik.* Come, I must explain a thing to you."

"I have to help Chalo. I *choose* to help Chalo. I have to go now."

"No, *Ka Ili'ik.* That is *re*action, only. He must make his own way. You must finish what you have started. Now come, it grows dark, and we would do well to be inside before the spirits rise."

Chapter 35

Anya and Chalo had stopped at a small tortilla stand in Xpuje and eaten like wolves, their hunger sated and thirst slaked only when they had eaten the last of the stand-owner's tortillas. Another three hours and the approach of dusk brought them through the town of Calakmul and towards the turn-off to the ruin of the same name. A policeman stood at the exit, flagging down tourists. Anya cursed as she slowed to a stop by the unmarked police car.

"*Sheisse.* This is new. Usually it is just the site guardian sending people away..."

"He's not a cop," Chalo replied, squinting at the uniformed man.

"How do you know?" Anya hissed as the man approached her window.

"Trust me, I know. Just do as he asks and say we took a wrong turn... that we're just passing through."

"Identification, please," the pretend-policeman said as he peered through his mirrored sunglasses and Anya's open window.

Anya handed over her driver's licence and Chalo's, both Mexican.

"One moment please," the pretender said before moving away.

Anya and Chalo watched as he looked at their licenses, read their names into a walkie-talkie, looked back at the car for a long moment, and then nodded. As he returned to the car he took his sidearm from its holster.

"I'm sorry, Doctor von Eckhart. I am afraid I will have to ask you and your friend to come with me..."

"Back-up, Anya. Now!" Chalo urged.

"*Herrgott noch mal*!" Anya swore as she looked out the back window, "I would if I could but Chalo, look!"

"You got *indio* back there, too?" Chalo asked, still staring out the front windshield.

"*Indigeno*," Anya corrected as she looked out the rear window, eyes wide. "Yes. I do."

Swift and silent as owls, nine young men had emerged from the forest and surrounded the car, as if stepping out from a time machine or down from the murals at Bonampak. Strong, lean young men, their ochre skin glowing in the long light of evening, their long hair pulled up into topknots, their bodies clothed only in loincloths, armbands, and tattoos.

A wondrous excitement surged within Anya even as she knew how dangerous the situation had become: these were bandits playing at something—maybe they were even the mysterious members of Kulkulcan's terrorist army. They could kill her or worse. And still, they were everything she had studied come to life: the mystery and nobility of an ancient civilization, realized before her eyes.

"*Shön*," she whispered in admiration.

Chalo surveyed the group of young men, pride in their eyes and hate in their hearts, and something different surged within him: a bitter green envy for a culture stolen from him, and with it a confidence he had never known. These boys embodied all that had been taken with the murder of his parents: they shone a floodlight into the dark emptiness of his heart, the hole where his heritage had been slain. With this awareness, rage crept into the crucible of his feelings between envy and dread. Chalo reached for his gun and the uniformed man instantly had his own at Anya's head.

"Do anything else foolish and I will hurt the doctor, hmm?"

Chalo put his arms up in surrender.

"Now get out of the truck and give me the keys."

"What will you do with us?" Anya asked as she did what was ordered.

"You are very fortunate, doctor," the uniformed man said as two others stepped forward with burlap sacks, one each for Anya and Chalo.

Put over her head, the rough fabric scratched her skin as it took away her vision; the fibres filled her nostrils with the bitter scent of jute and glue.

"I will only put you in the back of your truck and drive you.

Kulkulcan wishes to speak with you."

***

"You are *dzul, Ka Ili'ik*—a foreigner," Yaxché said as he settled cross-legged before the small comforting fire on his hearth. "And yet the land speaks to you as one of our own. Do you know our creation story?"

Stephen took a spot beside the old man and put his hands out to the flames; he still felt cold from his strange vision.

"A little. It's very complicated…"

"Indeed!" Yaxché cackled, "but really it is just the same thing over and over, so it is simpler than it seems. Do you know the part about when the gods made us from corn?"

Stephen did. He had read about it during the tortilla riots of 2008. Corn prices had risen precipitously as efforts to make ethanol had increased and with it prices for the staple of the Mexican diet, the corn tortilla. It was not merely that the food itself was more expensive that had driven people to the streets in angry protest: it was that they were being denied their spiritual sustenance as well.

"The gods tried mud and wood first, but neither worked," Stephen observed.

"In fact, *Ka Ili'ik*, they started with the creatures first but they were unable to speak the Lords' names and so were sent to the forest. The mud people lacked the strength to act and were washed away in a flood; the wood people lacked spirit and were destroyed with a black rain. But corn was both strong and supple and we could praise the gods' creation and so we came to be. Every one of us—you, me, Rebecca in the hammock, your friends wherever they are—we are all the people of the corn.

"But being made of corn comes with a price. Do you know what that is?"

Stephen shook his head.

"We are of the world, not outside of it. What has been used to make us must be repaid, the balance maintained."

"But we're not, are we?" Stephen said. "Keeping the balance, I mean."

"No, *Ka Ili'ik*, we are not. *Those who dip their mug to the bottom, those who stretch everything to the breaking point: they bruise the world. And so it has come to pass that the Earth burns. The sky will be soaked and arrowed for the Lord of Heaven is offended.*"

Yaxché could be describing any number of environmental ills, climate change chief among them. Suddenly Stephen felt like he should be in the movie *Avatar*. Except that the man talking to him was neither blue nor nine feet tall. Otherwise the message seemed the same.

"What does the Lord do when he is offended? Send another flood?"

"'They,' not 'he,' *Ka Ili'ik*. And yes, they could."

"Anya found a stone marker that she says predicts the end of the world."

"Indeed? I would like to see it," Yaxché replied thoughtfully.

"Will it?" It was a ridiculous question, but something impelled Stephen to ask it.

"Will what?"

"Will the world end?" Saying the words made the idea possible and it unnerved him.

"No, *Ka Ili'ik*," Yaxché said seriously. "The world never ends. But perhaps we do not deserve to stay in it. Perhaps they can make something better to care for their creation and sing its praises…" Yaxché trailed off and watched Stephen closely as the young man's face darkened and then despaired.

"I only said 'perhaps,' *Ka Ili'ik*. There is still a little time to choose a different path."

A brief bright flash shone through the shuttered windows, followed by the rumble of distant thunder. A moment later rain began to patter on Yaxché's thatched roof, filling the hut with the heady scent of wet palm leaves.

"It is *Eb*, *Ka Ili'ik*—the Day of Rain—and the storm that may destroy us is coming. But still I think there will be time enough to earn another chance.

***

"I know, Ben. I know," Kathy Howlachuk said to the dog nosing her elbow. "It's late. You need a bed-time pee. And I need to get a life."

Kathy was still at the NHC, feet up on her desk, catching up on her reading. Dry to most, disturbing to her, the journals she was reading reported on global climate models, water vapour concentrations, sea surface temperatures, ice core studies, trends based on historical storm patterns, and the frequency of rogue waves. None of the news was good, for humanity at least. Climate change was not a beast to be put back in its cage, only tamed a little and then only by acting quickly to stave off the worst of the droughts, storms, crop failures, and extinctions.

Kathy sat up, plunked her iPad on the desk where her feet had been, and reached forward to turn off the widescreen monitors. Bender's tail thumped on the carpet in happy expectation as Kathy began to rise from her chair; it slowed and then stopped as she sat down again and reached for her mouse.

"Just one more second, Benny, while I look at this…"

An automated alert from the FORTE data engine had popped up on her screen: the Fast On-orbit Recording of Transient Events satellite, or FORTE, was a military satellite; the data engine was a program that transferred VHF lightning data to the NHC in real-time.

"Holy crap, Bender…that's one hell of a light show…" Kathy breathed.

The graph on her monitor, steeper than one measuring a busy day on Wall Street, was displaying lightning strikes generated by an intense low pressure system over eastern Africa. This was truly the butterfly effect in action, a real-world example of the mystery of physics: the storm that went with these strikes would create an instability in the trade winds called the AEW—the African Easterly Wave; the AEW over the African continent would propagate instability, like falling dominoes, building storms off the coast of western Africa that could spin up into the Gulf of Mexico's hurricanes. Couple this light show with a Saharan Air Layer—SAL—that seemed to be blowing weaker and wetter as climate change proceeded, and the recent increase in hurricane intensity seemed to be explained. Here was the evidence for Kathy's prediction that one final storm was on its way.

"It's the thirteenth today, right, Ben?" Ben wagged, eyes dewy, and waited for his walk.

"Yeah, it's the thirteenth. Fourteen, fifteen, sixteen…" she counted off the days on her fingers.

"Bet you dollars to dog biscuits we see it on radar tomorrow and watch it slam into us sometime on the twentieth."

Kathy stood abruptly, grabbed her keys and the iPad from her desk, and patted her thigh to bring Bender to heel.

Thursday, December 13, 2012 — 9 Eb, Day of Rain

"Come on, bud, let's go get some shut-eye while we can. Storm's a-comin'; by next week we're gonna be busier than flies in an outhouse."

FRIDAY, DECEMBER 14, 2012
10 BEN, DAY OF MAIZE

CHAPTER 36

"Anybody awake in here?" said a happy voice.

"Rebecca?" Stephen asked, eyes snapping open.

"In the flesh. Are you hungry?" she replied proffering a plate of tortillas and refried beans.

"What are you doing out of bed?!" Stephen demanded as he struggled to sit up in his hammock.

"I've been sleeping for, what, three days? It was time to get up. Have some breakfast."

"How do you feel?" Stephen asked. He watched as she sank gratefully into the hammock beside his own after handing him the plate.

"A little weak and a lot sore, but strangely better than I've felt in a very long time. Thanks for patching me up. Again."

"My pleasure," Stephen replied, meaning it. He took the plate and ate eagerly.

Rebecca watched Stephen eat. His square jaw, flexing as he chewed, bore several days of stubble. He sat easily in the hammock, his lanky body trim, tanned, and apparently relaxed. As he picked up the last of his tortillas she noticed—with inordinate pleasure—that his hand were lean and strong.

Stephen could feel her eyes on him and looked up.

"Sorry about that. I was really hungry. Have you eaten? And how's your foot?"

Rebecca noticed Stephen's eyes for the first time. He carried himself easily, but his hazel eyes belied his demeanour: they seemed as if they had borne witnesses to a thousand lifetimes, a horror haunting each. Rebecca looked away, shocked by the sadness in his eyes and embarrassed that she had been watching him.

"My foot's good, too. I'm lucky you were around," she said softly.

"Thank you for saying luck; everyone else has been calling it 'fate.' I was just glad to help," he said with a smile.

"What's wrong with fate?" Rebecca asked quizzically.

"Fate is so…immutable," Stephen shrugged.

"You missed your flight to help me, didn't you?" Rebecca asked. "That was a choice, not fate…"

Stephen blushed and looked back to his plate.

"I didn't really know Yaxché was as good at what he does."

"Well thank you, anyway," Rebecca concluded. "Now what are you going to do?"

"Get out of here before anything weirder happens. Do you think you'll be well enough to drive by tomorrow?" Stephen replied, still embarrassed by Rebecca's gratitude.

"Weirder?"

"Let's see: an exorcism, ghosts, a jaguar that didn't kill me, a possessed crystal, and a vision of Chalo being eaten by a feathered snake…"

"Right. Say no more. Speaking of Chalo, where is he?"

"He and Anya went to a ruin and then to find the guns. Nobody knew when you'd wake up, so Chalo thought they'd better go before the trail went cold. I was digging through your stuff to find you a clean shirt and I found your sat phone so I gave the number to him. I hope that was okay."

"No problem. As for weird, what do you mean by a 'possessed' crystal?"

Stephen laughed. "Sounds crazy, eh?" he asked as he pulled the crystal from his pocket and reached across the space between them to hand it to Rebecca, "But every time I look at it, it seems like the rutiles in it start spinning."

"Rutiles?"

"Needle-like crystals made mostly of titanium dioxide. Quartz shot through like this is called "rutilated" or "asterated" and they're generally more valuable. The needles are sometimes called *fleches d'amour*."

"Love's arrows, hmm? You know a lot about rocks for a police officer."

Stephen frowned at himself for the way his heart skipped a beat when Rebecca translated the French.

"I studied Geology for a while," Stephen answered. "I'm a bit of a rock geek."

Rebecca laughed and held the crystal up to the light.

"I had a weird experience too, while I was… whatever I was. Asleep, I guess."

"Oh?"

"I was in a cold, dark empty place. Men with black knives were laughing. And then I was pulled up through a long tunnel to the jungle. You were there, and Yaxché, and a lady in white. And a jaguar."

She paused, still looking at the crystal, and then furrowed her brows.

"You're right, they're moving… Ow!"

She recoiled, dropping the crystal as she did so.

Stephen was out of his hammock and on his knees on the earthen floor beside Rebecca in an instant, taking her hand with both of his to examine the damage: a fresh white brand lay in the centre of her palm where the stone had been. The skin was not broken, but it would blister as his had.

"What just happened?" Rebecca asked, fear of the unknown creeping into her voice.

"I have no idea. Like I said, it's impossible—it defies the laws of physics. But the same thing happened to me the other day, see?"

Stephen opened a hand to show the same white burn.

"But why?"

"Yaxché said the gods are pissed with us—that they're considering evicting us."

"You're not serious!" she asked, torn between incredulity and alarm.

"I can't really tell with Yaxché; he's a bit of a trickster…"

Rebecca laughed at that, colour returning to her cheeks.

"The good news is that apparently we can help him renew the lease."

Rebecca laughed again, this time at Stephen's turn of phrase.

Looking up into her happy face, Stephen really could believe she was feeling better. She was still pale, yet she glowed as one renewed. The space around her shone, like some pre-Raphaelite painting, the air infused with the gauzy brilliance of a morning fog. He felt his own heart soar, a weight that he hadn't known was there lifting from his shoulders. Maybe this was what Yaxché meant by choosing life.

"Wow..." he breathed, suddenly wondering if it could really be this easy.

Rebecca looked down, suddenly shy, and studied their hands, still resting together. She touched the stone's burn in the palm of his hand; her fingers gentle, the touch electric. *Alive*, Stephen realized, *felt very good.*

He followed Rebecca's gaze to their hands and saw, again, the wedding band glittering on her ring finger. He'd forgotten about it. The crushing weight only so recently lifted returned, the quickening squelched, and he withdrew his hand.

"I'm sorry... It's my fault... I didn't mean... you shouldn't..." Stephen stammered, unable to finish any of the sentences with which he intended to blame himself for an impropriety.

She was married. He'd been an idiot to think her kindness had been anything but friendship, her touch anything more than platonic. He was embarrassed by his behaviour. And he was angry with himself for believing in Yaxché, for believing the choices he offered could be so easy to make.

"I'm sorry," he said once more before leaving, a Canadian through and through.

"Stephen?" Rebecca called after him. "Stephen?"

What had happened? Had she done something? Had she offended him somehow? She sighed and lay back into the hammock. Why were good men always walking out on her?

***

Joe Wilkes had nursed his misery for three days: looking at old pictures; talking to the ghost of his long-dead wife; canoeing the drying Bayou; watching the eagles' empty nest. He'd been thinking too, and from self-pity had moved to anger: anger at Hayden for committing suicide, anger at Rebecca for denying him the opportunity to honour Hayden's last request, anger at being blackmailed into finishing a plan he now saw as stupid. Especially now that he saw it as stupid: he had been manoeuvred into making it his own plan.

Sure, Clayton had put him up to it, pointing out how dangerous it would be, not just to his pocket but to the world's economy as a whole, if anything slowed the flow of oil from Mexico to the US, but it had been Joe who had figured out what could be done about the threat; Joe who had the markers throughout town to call in; Joe who could make it happen if the threat ever materialized. Which, of course, it had, in the form of a socialist government in Mexico that, in reprivatizing oil exploration immediately after Mitnal had come on line, had suddenly gained the power to control world oil prices and, through them, the direction of the entire US economy.

And sure, Joe had second thoughts as the operation has unrolled, but everyone did, didn't they? Had doubts, that is. Most of those had been thanks to Becky; he'd let his unfinished business with her—his guilt for not honouring Hayden's final request—cloud his judgement. But that was her fault: she hadn't returned his calls. She was right, kids would die in this guerrilla war, but fewer than if the military needed to redeploy to secure Middle-East oil yet again.

As for Clayton? What gall to threaten Hayden's memory for greed! This was about national security. Joe would keep the op going, Clayton would get what he wanted, and Hayden's memory would be safe, but only because it was a by-product of a bigger necessity: protecting the US economy. And when it was all over, by God! Joe was going to make Clayton pay.

He picked up the phone and dialled Washington. It was lunchtime, and Honey would be at her desk.

"Joe! Everything okay?" His secretary asked.

"Christ, I hate call display! No surprises anymore! Look, I'll be in Monday," Joe replied, chuckling.

"You got everything done you needed to?"

"A good lot of thinking done but I still need to fix a storm window and do something with the sump-pump. Anything I need to know about before I get back?"

"Everyone is trying to figure out why you're away. There's a rumour you've had a heart attack. The growing consensus, though, is that you don't have enough votes to defeat Carolina's bill so you're stalling to buy a last few votes."

Joe chuckled again.

"Fat lot they know. I've got four more votes than I need to sink it. Anything else?"

"Clayton Powell called. Three times."

Joe guffawed.

"Bet he did, the son-of-a-bitch. That all?"

Honey smiled to herself. Joe was back to his old irascible self. Whatever had been eating him—probably the anniversary of Hayden's death—he'd dug himself out. He was going to be fine.

"Nope, but the rest of it can wait 'til Monday."

"Then I'll see you on Monday morning. Have the coffee on, white as snow, sweet as love…"

"… and strong as death… yeah, I know. I will."

Joe chuckled. "Good girl. Have it on early, you hear?"

"Always before you're in. What do I do if Clayton calls again?"

Joe chuckled again.

"Tell him I'll call him on Sunday night—nothing he can do anyway 'til this thing runs its course, but he deserves to stew the weekend."

Honey was about to ask what the "thing" was, but decided she didn't want to know; it was good enough that Clayton Powell would spend the entire weekend squirming.

"Oh, and Hon?"

"Yeah, Joe?"

"I don't suppose Becky has called, has she?"

"No, Joe, she hasn't. I would have given her the number like you asked. She's not part of the thing with Clayton, is she?"

Joe laughed so hard he almost choked.

"She likes Clay even less than you do, Hon—she'd spit in his eye given the chance. It's just that when I saw her at the Foreign Affairs Committee I asked her to call me. I've got something I gotta tell her, is all."

Honey liked the idea of spitting in Clayton Powell's eye.

"We'll get her on the line for you on Monday morning, alright?"

***

Returning from his morning's collecting, Yaxché found Rebecca sitting on Lupita's slab porch picking pebbles from a bowl of dried corn.

"Ahh, *mi esposa*! Welcome back to this world!"

"*Don* Hernando!" Rebecca said as she put the wooden bowl down and stood to embrace the tiny old man.

"I didn't expect that when I saw you again it would be as your patient!"

"Good things always come back to me, *mi esposa*!" Yaxché grinned.

"You look hot, Don Hernando! Can I get you a drink of water?"

Yaxché set down his sack, wiped his brow, and chuckled.

"What a good wife you are! Have you any lunch for me, as well?"

"Here is lunch, old goat," scolded Lupita as she emerged from her doorway, a mug of *atole* and a plate of tortillas and *mole* in her hands, gave them to the healer, and returned inside.

"You leave the girl alone. You are too old for her!" Lupita scolded as she left.

"Don't worry, you old hen, I'm only joking. I know she is already spoken for. Where is *Ka Ili'ik*, anyway?"

"*Ka Ili'ik*?" Rebecca asked.

"Your Esteban, *mi hija*."

"My… ? No, he's not my anything," she said, her voice sounding more rueful than she expected. "He went for a walk. Why do you call him *Ka Ili'ik*, *Don* Hernando? What does it mean?"

"It means 'he who sees.' I call him that because he does." The old man said matter-of-factly before taking a scoop of *mole* with a tortilla.

Rebecca laughed, remembering his mischievous humour.

"But *what* does he see, *Don* Hernando?"

"Through the veil," Yaxché replied, chewing. "To the dead ones and the spirits."

"Like the lady in white?"

Yaxché nodded and took another bite.

"Why can he see them?"

"¡*Uay*! You ask so many questions a man can't eat! Maybe I don't take you for a wife after all!" Yaxché joked.

"No, really. I saw her, too."

"Everyone is seeing her these days, now that the hinge time is upon us. But the others, *Ka Ili'ik* sees them because he is halfway through himself, clutching something on the other side. Like you."

"Me?!"

"Like you, but opposite. You are the one being clutched."

Friday, December 14, 2012 — 10 Ben, Day of Maize

Rebecca shivered involuntarily, remembering the cold prison of her comatose dreams.

"Not to worry, *mi esposa*. Now that you are returned, the pieces come together. Everything will be alright."

Mistakenly thinking he was referring to the aide project, Rebecca shook her head.

"I don't know, *Don* Hernando. I don't think we'll get the money for the clinic after all."

Yaxché hooted.

"Always about money with you people. I don't need the money now that I have you!"

"Me?" she asked for the second time.

"You and *Ka Ili'ik* and the others. You are part of the puzzle. Broken a little, but we fix that part tonight. And then we take care of the hinge time."

"Broken? Hinge time?"

"Yes, *many* too many questions," Yaxché said, nodding as he rose.

"You need patience a little, *mi esposa*, while I look to my patients…" he paused, then grinned.

"It's a good joke that I make, no? Patience, patients? And in English even! And patience will make you well, too! Very funny!" he said, laughing heartily to himself as he crossed the road.

"He love to joke," Lupita chuckled, coming outside once more. "Laughing makes good for getting better. We make the tortillas now?"

Rebecca was the one with the car and didn't want to leave Stephen stranded here; helping out would pass the time until he returned from the forest. Following Lupita inside, she watched as the older woman scooped dried corn from a burlap sack it into the heavy stone *metate* beside the fire with her fleshy lined hands.

"You try?" Lupita asked as she offered the *metate*'s partner—a fist-sized grinding stone called a *mano*—to Rebecca. This was the ancient method of grinding corn, and Rebecca approached it with fascination.

"Push down; slide away. And hard. Empty your arms into it!"

Rebecca put her weight behind the pestle and winced, her shoulder protesting at the effort.

"¡*Uay*!" Lupita exclaimed. "I forget the shoulder. I grind. You sit.

We talk."

"About what?"

"Anything. It is to be a woman working. Talk, too," Lupita smiled before returning her attention to the corn.

"How many kids you have?"

"No kids," Rebecca smiled back.

"No kids?" Lupita asked, disturbed. Children were a requirement and a joy; Rebecca was too old not to have children.

"How long you be married?"

"My husband died a long time ago."

"*Ka Ili'ik* is not your husband?"

"No," Rebecca laughed. "We only just met, actually."

"Ah?"

Something in Lupita's tone made Rebecca blush.

"Ah!" Lupita said, this time knowingly, and Rebecca reddened further. If Lupita could guess it, Rebecca should just admit that she was attracted to Stephen. But after the way he had bolted that morning? Rebecca changed the subject instead.

"How about you, Lupita; do you have children?"

"Six!" the woman replied proudly. "Three boys and three girls. And already eleven grandchildren. The newest one I bring into the world last week!"

"And your husband?"

"Dead last year," Lupita replied, a shadow passing over her face as she worked the corn into meal.

"I'm sorry."

"Not to be sorry. He live a good life. It is the way of things: living, dying, ending, beginning."

"Lupita, what is the hinge time?"

Lupita sat back on her haunches and looked at Rebecca, puzzled.

"*Don* Hernando says the 'hinge time' is upon us."

"Oh, that," Lupita replied, her attention once more on the corn. "The sky is falling."

Rebecca shivered at Lupita's nonchalance.

"Not to be worried," Lupita answered, sensing Rebecca's concern. "Yaxché will fix it again."

"Fix what?"

"The world. It is…" she made a breaking motion with her hands. "Bad and good not even right now. People not living right and gods not happy. They think to get rid of us."

Stephen had called it being evicted. Like a tenant, for property damage and failing to pay rent.

"What do you mean 'again'?"

"Time is like the snake eating its tail. Around and around. Everything happens always for the Maya. Was. Is. Will be. Past happens now, and tomorrow happened yesterday. You understand?"

"But Yaxché?"

"Not this Yaxché, but the same. The tree of life, raising the sky."

No, Rebecca didn't understand. She knew that the Mayan cosmology spoke of multiple creations and destructions, all occurring because the people the gods had created were not up to the task of being faithful. She knew that the Mayan calendar was rolling over to a new millennium. But that was mythology, not reality; was supposed to be metaphorical, not literal. So why did everything seem to point to a physical destruction, occurring imminently?

"The world is ending," Rebecca replied, more statement than question.

Lupita laughed, unconcerned.

"Of course, in a few days. But not to be worried. Christmas still to come."

Rebecca shivered and then thought about what the woman had actually said. *Christmas*. Caught in her coma, she had completely lost track of time.

"What day is it, Lupita?"

The older woman paused and looked up at the roof in thought.

"Ten *Ben*. Day of Maize."

"But what day of the week?"

"The Mexican day? Oh, I don't know that," she said dismissively as she scraped the cornmeal from her *metate* into another bowl and poured more unground maize into it.

"Then how many nights have I been here?"

"*Oc*, *Chuen*, *Eb,*" Lupita said softly to herself, tapping the floor with each word. "Three nights you have been here."

Rebecca counted on her fingers, converting the Mayan date to one she recognized. She'd been shot on December 11th. Tuesday night, Wednesday night, Thursday night. It was Friday, December 14th.

"Oh, damn!"

"You are all right?" Lupita asked.

"Yes, fine, thanks. I just have to make a phone call. Can you get my knapsack from *Don* Hernando's hut for me?"

The woman stopped grinding and looked up.

"Not this moment. It is in with Yaxché. I not to go in with patients."

"It's really important, Lupita."

"Between one and another, then. No interrupting. We go outside and wait, hmm?"

***

At five p.m., Peter Nguyen sauntered into his boss's office, his first cup of coffee in one hand, his computer slate in the other.

"Right on cue, hunh?" he said, waving the slate.

"Hey Pete. What's right on cue?" Kathy asked absently as she wrote something on a sticky-note.

Peter read from the slate.

"*… Tropical storm Sigma forms in the mid-Atlantic… forty-fifth and forty-sixth tropical depressions form in the deep tropics…*"

"I didn't expect forty-five and forty-six, actually…"

"It's weird, you know…" Nguyen continued.

"Which part?" Kathy asked absent-mindedly, her attention still on her sticky-note.

Her eyes were still on her paper.

"I just looked at the radar, and *Sigma* has lost all forward motion. It's still spinning—the wind is almost up to storm speed now—but it's just sitting, five hundred miles west of Cape Verde. If it isn't moving, it should be collapsing."

Kathy looked up over her reading glasses, forehead wrinkled.

"What are forty-five and forty-six doing?"

"That's even weirder: they're speeding up. Like they're playing tag. Forty-five is a hundred and twenty miles east of *Sigma*, and forty-six is right behind, two-hundred miles east of *Sigma*."

"And?"

"How can there be that much energy out there?"

"A hundred and fifty years of carbon emissions, for one."

Peter frowned. "What do you think they'll do?"

"Been trying to figure that out myself, Pete. They'll stall or they'll organize themselves."

Peter sipped his coffee. *Organize* themselves. He'd been doing this for a dozen years and still disliked the expression: it anthropomorphized the disturbances—gave them will and self-determination. Peter got the creeps when the storms became malevolent spirits rather than soulless winds.

Kathy looked up from her note at last, brows furrowed. "If I had to wager, they'll organize. And then we'll be in for one hell of a mess."

CHAPTER 37

Kulkulcan walked around his blonde prisoner, her passport in his hands, and studied her. *Von Eckhardt.* Sebastian's sister, for sure—the eyes gave her away. So what was she doing here? She looked back at him evenly, giving nothing away.

"It says here that you are Dr. Anya von Eckhardt. Born in Germany. What kind of doctor are you?"

"I have a doctorate in Archaeology," she replied perfunctorily.

"Indeed? Then what do you think of my little temple outside?"

"It was dark last night and I had a bag over my head. I've been locked in here all day. How would I know there is a temple out there?"

"Of course, silly me. Tell me what you think of my little book, then. Have you read it yet?"

"*Del Dzonote*? The arrogant little tract you left in my prison hut, like a Bible in a hotel room? It was a poor excuse for a history, like the meal was a poor excuse for food."

"So sorry you didn't like the food, *Doktor*; it is hard to get good help out here in the jungle," he said with a patronizing smile. "As for my 'tract,' did you find any errors?"

"No errors, only half-truths. Twisting the *Chilam Balam* to suit your own ends."

"For example?"

"There are so many; I can't remember them all," she replied, matching his tone.

"Take the book," he said, picking it up off the small table in the prison hut, "And give me an example," Kulkulcan said, his voice grown cold and hard.

Anya leafed through the small tract for a moment and then read aloud.

"*... the all-white child is coming... it will be nightfall for us when they come. Heavy is the servitude that comes in the cursed days. They beat by day, they insult by night, they bruise the world. The Moon will have white circles of rain; the sky will be soaked and arrowed for the Lord of Heaven is offended. If the governor of this land were to be hanged it would be an end to the misery of the Maya...*"

"Every word is from the *Chilam Balam*," Kulkulcan said with an easy smile.

"Yes, but not in that order. You have taken words from different chapters and put them together to convince ignorant people that their past itself is what is commanding them to rise up."

"You are calling the Maya stupid? Interesting for an archaeologist," he said, all smiles once more.

"Not stupid: 'ignorant.'" It was a literal translation from the German, meaning without knowledge, and it had not been intended as a slur. "They do not know their history well enough any longer to realize that you are a crazy man hungry for power."

"You are very ill-mannered for one in your position, I think." Kulkulcan observed, his easy smile suddenly brittle.

"No. I am merely German and being frank; we have a history of crazy men with manifestos. It never ends well."

"In that case, perhaps we should discuss another crazy man and what may befall him. Why don't you tell me about your brother?"

Kulkulcan watched Anya carefully. His first thought, seeing Anya's passport among the things recovered from her truck, was that Sebastian had somehow discovered Kulkulcan's plan to prevent the destruction of the rig and that his sister was his back-up plan. In this scenario Anya could make sure that even if Sebastian died the rig would still be destroyed and Eden Two's message would still be heard around the world.

But now Kulkulcan was not so sure.

"My brother?" Anya asked, unable to hide fear and surprise. "Why do you want to talk about my brother?"

"Do you know where he is?"

He was in Mexico. Suddenly Anya was terrified that he, too, had been taken prisoner.

"What have you done with him?" she demanded, her voice shaking.

Kulkulcan watched as her autonomic nervous system went into fight-or-flight overdrive: her face paled, her breathing sped up, her eyes dilated. It was almost inconceivable, but her presence here was purely coincidental. He smiled contentedly, a cat well-satisfied by a canary.

"What have I done with him?" he laughed. "Nothing at all! He is my guest!"

"Sebastian? Here? Why?"

"Ah my dear *Doktor*, that is for you to discuss with him. I will let you see him before you leave."

"I'm going? Aren't you concerned that I will tell the authorities where you are?"

"But I have plenty to ensure your silence, don't you think? Your brother. Your policeman. Your Payal. You do know that it was he who took us to your site for the sacrifice and he who told the journalists how to get there when the police covered up the message left on the *chac mo'ol*, don't you? You can't really scare a population if the scary things get hidden by the police, can you?"

So Chalo had been right: Payal was one of Kulkulcan's soldiers. She'd thought he was smarter than that. Stephen had been right that the gunmen at her site the first night had not been the police; they had been journalists, scared for their lives. And Rebecca had been right that Kulkulcan was using fear as his weapon.

"Payal is a very smart boy, actually. It was hard to win him over. But now, with a new son, the promise of a better future swayed him."

Anya snorted. Kulkulcan could not hope to recreate the prosperity of the ancient; he would give his disciples only modern despotism and common misery.

"What will you do with him?"

"Payal? I have need of him; he will be fine. Your brother, I also have need of. Your policeman, however, I will kill, should you go to the authorities before next week."

Anya's stomach tightened and her eyes widened just enough to betray her feelings.

"Your lover, is he?"

"None of your business," she replied, her tone defiant. "What happens if I go to the authorities after next week?"

"After that, it will not matter…" he said, grinning dangerously. "After next week, I will *be* the authority."

Anya clenched her teeth and said nothing.

"As for 'none of my business,'" he chuckled dangerously, "you may say goodbye to him, too, before you leave. I am sure you will stay silent to keep him safe, so you are free to leave anytime now. I will have someone bring your belongings and your keys."

Anya watched as Kulkulcan turned with a dismissive wave and walked out her prison hut.

"*Vaya con Dios*, *Doktor* von Eckhardt," he said lightly, his back to her, and she felt a rage surge inside her: she was being dismissed yet again.

"You won't get away with this!" she yelled at him. It sounded pathetic when she said it, and her rage only grew.

"I think I will, *Doktor*," he said breezily and turned to leave.

A tall white man, rail thin and pallid, entered the hut as Kulkulcan left. Anya looked at the man and did not know him.

"*Was machst du hier*?" the man asked, his voice unmistakeable.

"Sebastian?" she whispered, aghast. "*Bist du das*?"

"*Ja*, *ich bins*, *Didi*," he replied, using her childhood nickname. "*Was machst du hier*?"

"What am *I* doing here? Are you mad?! I live here. I work here! What are *you* doing here? And what is wrong with you? You look like death!"

The last time she had seen her brother he had been the picture of health. All that she now recognized in this skeletal human was the colour of his eyes.

"I'm sick. And I'm working for Kulkulcan; I was supposed to leave last night, but then you arrived."

Anya was horrified by both statements. She gaped, not knowing which one to ask about first.

"I wanted to explain everything to you at the hotel in Cancún, but we missed one another.

"What kind of sick?" she demanded, finding her voice at last.

"*Krake*," he said simply. It meant "octopus" in German, a metaphor for the many-limbed creature that was cancer.

"But what kind? Why aren't you in hospital?"

"It is everywhere now, and untreatable. It is why I am here."

It was all too much for Anya to take in. She lowered herself slowly to the cot and merely watched as her younger brother walked carefully across the room.

"You're dying?"

"We're all dying, Didi. Just some sooner than others. It's what we do with our lives that matters—isn't that what you always told me?"

"Yes, but that was only to try to get you to stop working in Papa's factory!"

Sebastian chuckled, his laughter dying into a cough. He sat wearily beside Anya and took her hand.

"I listened to you more than you know, Didi. I haven't been working for Papa for years! Well, I suppose I have, but only to hide my real work."

"And that is …?" she asked, suddenly suspicious. If it meant working with Kulkulcan, it was probably worse than working for their father.

"Do you know of the environmental group Eden Two?"

"The environmental terrorists? They're in the news every few months, blowing something else up. Of course I know of them. Why?"

"And what do you think of them?"

"I…"

She trailed off, conflicted. They were terrorists. But in all their years of operation—and all the billions in infrastructure they had destroyed—they had been careful not to injure or kill a single person. And their goal—to wean the world of the fossil fuel that threatened catastrophic climate change? As an archaeologist, she knew well how environmental mismanagement could destroy civilizations: Easter Island, the Anasazi, the Nazca in Peru—not to mention the Maya themselves. It was therefore utterly plausible that global climate change could destabilize what had grown to be an interconnected global civilization.

"I believe in what they stand for, Sebastian, but I'm not sure the ends justify the…"

She suddenly recalled a snippet of conversation they had had years before while sitting on peacekeeping duty. They had been discussing terrorism. She had argued that certain acts of terror should be strictly off limits; he had argued otherwise.

"*Hölle*, Sebastian! You're not involved with Eden Two, are you?"

"No, Didi," he paused.

Before Anya could feel relieved, Sebastian made it worse.

"I *am* Eden Two, Didi. I am Adam."

"The leader?! *Mein Gott*, Sebastian!"

"I am here to sink the Mitnal rig. The shocks it will send through the economy will be enough to finally move the United States away from oil at last."

"*Was für ein Haufen Scheiße*! The Americans are idiots, slouching to Hell. They will never change."

"You're wrong, Didi. America is the master of transformation, *once it wishes to be*. When Mitnal goes down, the price of oil will soar. America's leaders know it already; now the public will see the link between national security and being oil-free… and then the race will be on! And how quickly did the race to the Moon take—nine years? Think of it—with that drive, they, and the world with them, will be weaned from oil in the same time!"

It was a gorgeous dream. Maybe more than a dream: likening it to the push for the moon—daring, unlikely, economically transformative in less than a decade—made it seem plausible. But still….

"Maybe it would, Sebastian, but why do this for Kulkulcan?"

"Our interests converge. He says the rig disturbs the slumbering gods of the underworld. He claims it must be destroyed or the world will end. Minus the gods, it is not unlike what I believe. That and he pays handsomely."

"He doesn't know his own myths, Sebastian. And even if it is a good idea, why *you*?! You're dying! Shouldn't you be doing something more important with your last days?"

"What could be more important than trying to save the world?"

Anya looked down at her lap.

"I don't want you to die, Ebas…" Anya said at last, her voice tight with emotion as she said his childhood nickname.

Sebastian lifted her chin and wiped away her tears with his thumbs.

"But at least we got to see each other, hmmm? And in Cancún I would not have said anything about my alter-ego. I'm glad I didn't have to lie."

Friday, December 14, 2012 — 10 Ben, Day of Maize

Anya leaned into her brother's arms and they held each other for a long moment.

"It's stupid, you know, Ebas," Anya said into her brother's shoulder. "The gods don't live in the Gulf of Mexico. Kulkulcan doesn't really believe his mythology, and if he takes over the government, he'll need that oil to pay for loyalty. He's not going to let you destroy Mitnal."

"I know this."

Anya pulled away and looked into her brother's face, their ice-blue eyes meeting.

"He is adding three boys to my team to undo my plans. He told me last night that one of them used to work for you."

Already pale, Anya blanched further.

"Payal," she said, both disappointed and resigned.

"Don't worry, I'll make sure he returns alive," Sebastian smiled.

"He's smart, Ebas. Too smart to be working for this *Schweinepriester*," Anya growled.

Sebastian laughed at the epithet—literally 'pig-priest;'—it was appropriate for the man playing god.

"I know it already, Anya, and I'm counting on it. Smart people you can appeal to with reason—you can change their minds with kindness and logic. A thinking man can be made to see that my goal is better than Kulkulcan's. Or that it is at least more honest."

Anya looked up into her brother's face again and another tear slid down her cheek.

"What am I going to do without you, Ebas?"

"Live, Anya. Really live. For both of us, yes?"

Anya nodded, unable to speak.

They hugged each other one final time before Sebastian rose and left. Anya waited, but he did not look back.

***

Leaving Anya with Sebastian, Kulkulcan made his way to the second of his prisoners. A cop from Mexico City with the face of a Maya: surely he was on someone's payroll. Whatever his price, Kulkulcan would happily double it; this was a man he could use.

"So, Gonzalo," Kulkulcan said genially as he strode into the hut holding Chalo's drivers licence.

Chalo was lying on the hut's cot, the copy of *Del Dzonote* left for him lying open over his face to block the morning light streaming through the hut's single window.

"Not my name," Chalo replied, voice muffled by the manifesto's pages.

Kulkulcan looked down at Chalo's driver's licence.

"Gonzalo Guerrero, April 5th, 1974. One-hundred-eighty centimetres; eighty-six kilos; brown hair, brown eyes. This is not you?" Kulkulcan asked, bemused.

"No one I like calls me Gonzalo," Chalo replied, still through the book.

"I see. What then should I call you, *Señor* Guerrero."

Chalo took the book from his face and sat up.

"I don't know; do I like you?"

Kulkulcan didn't know whether to be amused or irritated by the man's bravado.

"Of course you like me. I pay well."

"Is that a bribe, *enchilada*?"

"That is not *my* name, *señor*."

Chalo shook his head and prepared to lie back down.

"You are the big man, the *enchilada*, no? And I don't take bribes."

"Really? An honest policeman in Mexico?"

"Don't think you're the first to make the joke, *enchilada*. What do you want from us?" Chalo replied sardonically as he put the book back over his face.

Us. So there was his weakness.

"I want your help, Gon… Guerrero."

"What kind of help? And why should I?" he replied, voice muffled by the book.

"I'm betting that in Mexico City you've probably worked security details for the government; I need you to look over some plans for me. And you should help me because you are Maya."

"And you know this how?"

"Your nose, for one: long and straight like the kings of old. And the deferential curl in your back, for another, bent by long years serving the white sparrowhawk…"

Chalo stiffened and Kulkulcan knew he had hit a nerve. Time to press his advantage.

"If you had read my little book rather than sleeping beneath it, you would know I have built this movement for you and all the others like you, beaten, insulted, stuck in servitude…"

Chalo sat up, his face dark.

"You have a foreign nose, *enchilada*: fat and stubby. How could you know what the Maya feel?"

This time Kulkulcan's face darkened.

"If you had read my little book, you would know that I was born of rape. Like our culture itself, I am polluted. But it does not mean I do not know the feelings, the hate."

Kulkulcan's eyes narrowed and for an instant Chalo saw the madness of a mental illness that walked dark streets and wielded knives at phantoms, the street-people in Mexico City he jailed at night to keep them from harming themselves and others.

"So you're going to take over the country and rebuild the Maya empire and make it all better."

The light of madness dimmed and Kulkulcan smiled charmingly. The change was equally disconcerting.

"Indeed, I am. And you, as I said, will help me."

"Because I am Maya," Chalo replied, unconvinced.

"No, not really. Because I will hurt your woman if you do not," Kulkulcan replied, smile broadening.

"She's not my woman," Chalo said quickly, but the rush of blood to his face belied his feelings.

"Indeed," he said again, this time amused. "Your woman or not, it does not change the fact that I will let her go if you agree to help me and kill her if you do not. Would you like to speak to the good *Doktor* before you decide her fate?"

***

Anya was still sitting on the cot, face blotchy and tear-stained when Chalo was shown in.

"Anya! ¡*Demonios*, Anya! Did they hurt you?" Chalo asked.

He was on his knees in front of her before finishing his question; Anya looked blankly at him for a moment and then leaned forward and kissed him hard.

"Are you okay?" he tried to ask. She silenced him with another kiss.

"Are you hurt?" He asked once more before surrendering, his own kisses filled with every bit of his worry, his relief, his passion, his desire.

"I'm not hurt," Anya replied at last

Chalo rose to sit beside her, put his arm around her shoulder, and stroked her hair.

"But you were crying?" he asked.

Anya blurted the entire story of her unexpected reunion with her brother, his cancer, the destruction of the rig, and Kulkulcan's plan to have him killed.

Chalo sat in dumbfounded silence when she was done.

"We must stop him, Chalo," she said, her face grim with determination.

"He'll kill us."

"He'll kill Sebastian!"

"You go. I'll stop him."

"Alone?"

Chalo could not tell her he would trade his services for her safety; she would never agree to it, and would end up hurt or worse.

He made a quick decision. He was going to have to force her to leave.

"Anya, I'm going to join Kulkulcan."

Anya pulled away from Chalo's embrace and stared at him, her ice-blue eyes wide with incomprehension.

"Have you gone mad?! He's killing people in the name of the Maya!"

"I'm not saying I believe it, but if I pretend I believe it, maybe I can work from inside and save your brother, hmm?"

Anya looked at him, incredulous.

"How can you even pretend? He's using the Maya for his own ends! Breeding discontent. And he is more dangerous than you can imagine. I've read his book—he's insane but very very smart; you will not be able to fool him. Sebastian can take care of himself."

"Really, Anya? He looks as weak as a mouse. And are you saying I am not up to the challenge? I'm already one of the Maya; I'm already angry. Why can I not act the part? *Viva la revolución*, right?"

"Mexicans and their damned revolutions, most of them brainlessly romantic!" Anya retorted. "First, there never was such a thing as 'the' Maya. They were always city-states, like in ancient Greece. They fought and traded and made alliances but there was not ever one single Maya ruler or centre of power. That was how they held out against the Spaniards for so very long! Second, how can fighting ever make anything better? And third, the *Scheißafrikaaner* with his blue eyes and his light skin! He's a half-breed, a *mestizo*. You should not even have to breathe the same air. But no, you want to bend to him. You are being mad!"

Chalo had wanted to make Anya angry enough with him that she would leave the camp and Kulkulcan's threats with it; he hadn't expected her words to be so cruel.

"It would not be bending, Anya. It would be pretending," Chalo said, softly, trying to hold his own temper, trying to calm hers.

Anya would not be pacified.

"We are what we do, Chalo! That you can even pretend shows your weakness. You spend your whole life hiding that you have Maya blood and then this crazy man comes playing dress-up suddenly you think you can play Maya?"

Anya had struck where it hurt most and logic was gone. Chalo fought back.

"How do you know, Anya, what it was like to grow up ashamed? Stuck in your ruins, you have no idea what it is to be Maya *today*. No idea what it is like to be me—ashamed of my nose, ashamed of my build, the colour of my skin. And everyone assuming I'm stupid just because of my blood. What is wrong with Kulkulcan trying to return a little glory to the Maya? What is wrong with taking back a little of what was ours before the Spanish arrived?"

"*So eine Kacke*! How can you be so naïve? The Maya empire was falling apart before the Spanish arrived. … Crumbling from within, probably because of drought and hundreds of years of taking too much from the land. Certainly they lasted as city-states holding out against the *conquistadores* but as an empire? No—it was their overuse of the land that truly killed them. Kulkulcan is moved only by anger, pretending his mission is given by the gods. He doesn't want to help the Maya; he just wants to be in charge. If you cannot see that, then I was wrong about you and you really are a fool!"

From her, the insult wounded.

"Naïve? You think *I* am naïve? You are the one that makes a romance of the ancient Maya! And your romance blinds you to what we live in today: the discrimination and squalor and sickness we face living on poor land or in slums next to *crillolo* palaces! No, Anya, you with your blonde hair and blue eyes and beautiful fair skin, you who have had the advantage of a family and a home and every school you ever wanted… you know nothing of the real Maya."

The attack on her life, her self, her academic credentials—and worst—a skin colour she could not change, was more than she could bear.

"I do care about today's Maya. It is why I was training Payal as my assistant. He could have gone to get a PhD instead of joining Kulkulcan! As for what I know of the *real* Maya? I know what you do not about the traditions that have kept your culture vibrant and alive all these years. I know your gods; I know your food; I know your history. I read your language when you cannot. And above all, I know the Maya were not vengeful killers like Kulkulcan would have his followers believe; they were cosmopolitan statesmen horrified by the Spaniards' brutality. They were diplomats and traders, priests, academics, and farmers. They were like us."

Wounded by harsh words from one to whom they were so attracted, Anya and Chalo were turning on each other to protect themselves.

"Academics! Always being a professor is what makes a person worthy? And who is *us*? Teachers? White people? You see what you want to see, Anya: priests and academics and farmers. But they were warriors too. They shed blood when they needed to."

"'Us' as in 'you and me.' And yes, Chalo, they did take lives and go to war, but not the kind of deadly war we play today. It was *flower* war: agreed upon battles to test each other, train warriors, capture opponents for sacrificial rituals. But not in huge blood-thirsty numbers. The Mayan world has always been about cycles and balance. Night and day, sky and underworld, give and take. Humans live in the middle, like on a see-saw, keeping the world even."

"But it is not even any more, Anya. The Maya and our land—we have been giving for five hundred years! Don't you think it is time now to take?"

Friday, December 14, 2012 — 10 Ben, Day of Maize

"Chalo, he's going to start a war! With real guns and real people dying. You make it sound like a little game of *Cowboys und Indianer*!"

"And I'm the Indian, no?" Chalo replied coldly.

"That isn't what I meant," Anya said angrily.

"I know what you meant," he said quietly. "You meant that I am a fool who knows nothing. You are wrong, Anya. I understand everything now. I thought we might have something together, but I was wrong: I'm not a person to you, just a trophy, a living relic. I don't belong in your world; I belong here."

"That's twice now you have called me a racist, Chalo. And it is you who are wrong. I wish I was Maya, but not the poor, violent excuse for Maya that Kulkulcan presents. You're just going to get yourself killed with this foolishness. Just like Sebastian."

Chalo looked at Anya for a long moment, too much said for either to back down.

"So what are you going to do now?" he asked softly.

"Leave. Go back to my work."

"Are you going to tell the authorities about this camp?"

"Not until next week," she replied bitterly. "The bastard Kulkulcan has threatened to kill my brother if I don't keep quiet."

Chalo looked at Anya, suddenly stricken: he needn't have lied to her; she would have left the camp quietly anyway.

"Anya, I'm sorry…"

"I'm sorry, too. But it wouldn't have worked anyway, would it, with me such a racist…" she said, her voice thick with sarcasm.

"I didn't mean…"

"Never mind. Just have your new boss bring me my things."

"It is almost dark, Anya. At least wait until morning to leave. It's dangerous at night."

"I'll be fine. I am Lara Croft, remember?"

Chalo nodded grimly and strode out. An emptiness as wide as the ocean enveloped him as he moved through the day's dying light.

CHAPTER 38

It was almost an hour before Lupita could retrieve Rebecca's knapsack. She really shouldn't have given Deb hell about the sat phone—there was no cell reception in Yaxché's tiny village and her phone was dead in any event. Rebecca hefted the waterproof clunker and dialled Florida.

"Becky! Jeezuz H., girl, I've been trying to git you since your birthday. Your voicemail is full and the crabby lady at your office said you were out of town! I'm sorry but I'm gonna have to cancel for tomorrow."

Rebecca smiled at the larger-than-life personality spilling from the satellite link.

"It's okay, Aunt Kathy. I *am* out of town and I'm not going to be back by tomorrow anyway."

"Where're you at? Someplace warm, I hope."

Rebecca looked around at the warm jungle and wiped sweat from her brow. "I'm in Mexico."

There was a pause at the other end of the line.

"What part, girl?" Kathy asked carefully.

"Near…" what the hell was the nearest place, she wondered. "… I'm south of Cancún."

"Hell girl, you do know how to pick a place for a mid-life crisis! You come back home right this minute, you hear?"

"I'm not having a mid-life crisis, Aunt Kathy!"

"Whatever. Just get yourself outta there, ASAP."

"Why?"

"Turn on the news, child! A hurricane the size of all get-out—a huge one-eyed monster—is heading straight for you; Pete and I are watching the radar like buzzards watching a dying rat."

"When's it going to make landfall?

"Five days, maybe. But you want to be well gone by then, girl. The airports'll be closed in maybe three days, four tops."

"That should be enough time…"

"I'm serious, Becky. Whatever you're up to, it's not worth it. You gotta git."

"I will, I promise. Look, has Joe Wilkes been in the news the past few days?"

"When's he not in the news, Beck? This time it's because he's holed up at his cabin in Texas and the Senate's postponed the carbon reduction vote. Scuttlebutt is that he's stalling because he doesn't have the votes to defeat it, the bastard… Sorry honey, I keep forgetting he's family."

"Not anymore. And don't worry. I think there's a rule that you don't have to stay in touch with in-laws you don't like when your husband dies…"

Kathy laughed, a little ruefully.

"Well, I should mind my Ps and Qs anyway. He can't be all bad if he made a boy like Hayden. Look, I gotta run—Pete's working on the next storm bulletin—but call me as soon as you get back to DC, okay? I wanna know you're safe… and Beck?"

Rebecca had been watching the last of the patients climb aboard the bus; it departed and she saw Stephen emerge from Yaxché's hut. He looked tired but smiled brightly when he saw her and started across the road. Nope, no doubt about it, he gave her butterflies.

"Beck? You still there?"

"Yeah, sorry. You were saying?"

"I was saying that I love you. You be careful, you hear?"

"I will. Love you, too. I'll talk to you soon."

Stephen heard the endearment and his smile ebbed.

"Should I come back?" he asked.

"No, no. I just hung up. What's up? You don't look so hot."

"Gee, thanks."

"No, I didn't mean that… I mean you *are* hot…" she reddened.

Stephen raised his brows, reddening himself. "Yaxché wants to see you."

Friday, December 14, 2012 — 10 Ben, Day of Maize

"How come?"

"Check-up. Wants to make sure you're well enough to go into the forest tonight."

"I'm going back into the… why?"

"We're all going. Yaxché says he can't use broken tools to save the world…"

"And we're the broken tools?"

"Apparently," Stephen said, smiling.

"Terrific. Any word on which bits are out of order?" she asked as she rose to follow Stephen across the dirt road.

Stephen fought the temptation to assure her that nothing he could see about her was out of order, gashes, gouges and bullet wounds aside—not a single thing. He stopped in the middle of the road.

"Yaxché says we're both haunted," Stephen said instead.

"And you believe him?"

"I didn't believe in a lot of the things I've seen these past few days. But now? I dunno. Belief seems almost a requirement down here."

Rebecca had been about to say that for her part, not only did she believe in ghosts but she knew who was haunting her; Yaxché's appearance, popping rabbit-like, from his front door, prevented her.

"Ah! *Mi esposa*! Hurry, hurry. Come in and let me look; there is little time before we go."

Inside and settling herself on his wooden examining table, Rebecca let Yaxché take her wrists in his large, gnarled hands.

"Stephen says you think we're broken, *Don* Hernando…"

"Shh! I cannot hear your blood while you talk," Yaxché admonished.

Rebecca rolled her eyes and Stephen tried to hide a smile. The old man closed his eyes for a moment, his hands still around Rebecca's wrists and then he grunted with satisfaction.

"Stubborn as a pig, *mi esposa*!" the healer said as he relinquished Rebecca's hands. "You did not drink your tea this morning!"

"How did you know?"

"*Ka Ili'ik*, you take her wrists and tell me what you feel."

"Me?"

"Is there another *Ka Ili'ik* here?" the old man said. His voice was stern but his eyes twinkled.

Stephen took Rebecca's wrists and instantly felt his own pulse quicken. He swallowed hard, willing himself to ignore the softness of her skin.

"What do you feel, hmm?"

Heady. Breathless. Awake. Aroused. Stephen was attracted to Rebecca whether she was married or not. He swallowed again and tried very hard not to think about how touching her made him feel. He forced himself to count her pulse. Suddenly he murmured in surprise.

"It's thready again!"

"We call it 'thirsty onion stalk.' It is back because she didn't drink the tea."

"Bad patient," Stephen scolded, smiling despite himself; Yaxché's manner was contagious.

"But it tastes terrible!" Rebecca protested.

Yaxché cackled.

"I don't make candy, *mi esposa*! What is good for you is not always pleasant, yes?"

Rebecca nodded sheepishly.

"So, you drink tea with our dinner?"

"Can I have it with some honey?"

Yaxché cackled once more.

"Always you young people are looking for a way around bitterness! How do you know sweet if you will not know its other side?"

"Fine. No honey," Rebecca said with resignation.

"As for you, *Ka Ili'ik*, you can let her hands go," Yaxché continued, laughing as he watched Stephen redden.

"Go get the dinner from Lupita. I'll be along with the tea. We eat, and then we go. Time is short now, and the one-eyed god will soon be upon us."

Rebecca blanched. *One-eyed*. The one-eyed god was *Hurukan*; her aunt had called the coming storm a one-eyed monster. Stephen was right; belief in the coincidence—and the inexplicable—seemed to be required down here.

Chapter 39

It was well after dark by the time Kulkulcan returned to Chalo's hut; Chalo had spent part of the time alone stewing over his argument with Anya. Then, bored and peevish, he had picked up *Del Dzonote*. It had been a terrible mood in which to read the tract; already feeling righteous and maligned, the tiny bitter manifesto was mesmerizing. As Anya had promised it would, Kulkulcan's honeyed hate was gently but surely leading Chalo astray.

"Oh, how sweet was the powerful time that is past," says the Chilam Balam, *the ancient book of our peoples. "Heavy is the servitude that comes in the days of the uayeyab, the cursed days."*

Chalo thought of the housekeeping staff at the Chacmool in their *huipils*, cleaning up after the "sparrowhawks" and frowned. Whatever else was in *Del Dzonote*, this at least was truth. He leafed forward to the story of Kulkulcan's youth.

Like you, young Itzás, I grew up in the backwaters of this country, confined to poverty and ignorance while in the towns the sparrowhawks lived. I saw all that they had, and all that I lacked, and I grew dispirited.

Chalo recalled his orphaned days—the emptiness in his belly that was his constant companion, the laughter of the private school boys that was his shame—and his frown deepened.

So sad was my spirit, insulted by the visitors, that at last I threw myself into a sacred cenote, anxious for the violent death gifted by the conquerors to so many of our people.

This time Chalo fought memory: he tried not to remember his parents' murder at the hands of the Guatemalan army. And still he saw the flames, smelled the burning hair and flesh, heard his mother scream.

But death did not come. Instead came a strange deliverance, a flying serpent bearing me from the water, a voice speaking my destiny, bidding me take his name and live in him that he might live in me and that together we would raise the Itzás once more, to our glory and that of our ancient gods.

Divine intervention, indeed. Chalo rolled his eyes. If the mighty feathered serpent had deigned to save Kulkulcan, why had the gods not swooped in to save his own parents? He skipped forward another few pages.

"What prophet, what priest," the Chilam Balam asks, "will rightly interpret the words of these writings?" This I say, even in the words of the Chilam Balam itself: "the old Maya will not want to hear the words." They are words not merely of prophecy, to receive, but words of instruction, to act upon.

Despite himself, Chalo was curious. *Give a book time*, Stephen had said. *Find out where the plot will take you.* If nothing else, Kulkulcan's little book was a beguiling hash, playing on both history and heartstrings. Where would it end? Chalo read on.

These are the prophecies that lie within the Chilam Balam, every word written five hundred years ago for you. Read and ask your heart the questions I pose:

"The all-white child is coming... it will be nightfall for us when they come, the white sparrowhawks of the land."

I ask you, Itzás, have the visitors not brought an end to our empire and cast our people into the shadows?

"Life will wither. Those who dip their mug to the bottom, those who stretch everything to the breaking point: they bruise the world. Innocents will die a heartless death, birds and men alike."

I ask you, Itzás, do the visitors not eat everything, and destroy all that they touch?

"The sky will be soaked and arrowed for

the Lord of Heaven is offended."

I ask you, Itzás, are the storms not more fierce than in the days of your childhood? Can you ignore the words of your grandmothers: the hurricane is the sign of the gods' fury?

Chalo nodded to himself, remembering the fury of Hurricane Wilma. God's fury or humanity's stupidity, the storms were getting worse. He paged forward again.

And this is the call to action that lies within the heart of the Chilam Balam, every word written five hundred years ago for you. Consider the answers your heart gives to the questions I pose:

"Beware Itzás! Do not give in completely to your visitors. You will devour them... this will come to pass."

What does this say, Itzás, if not to urge resistance and to promise victory?

"If the governor of this land were to be hanged, it would be an end to the misery of the Maya."

What does this say, Itzás, if not the truth: must we not rid ourselves of the visitors, our unwelcome guests?

"Justice to the destroyers, the white sparrowhawks from the towns."

What does this say, Itzás, if not to find our strength in the jungle and deliver retribution in the heart of the visitors' new homes?

"No one will escape the knife-edge of war."

What does this say, Itzás, if not that there will be no bystanders permitted; that we must all rise as one?

"Then will the Itzáes come to their city, Hurukan, xekik, and the mysterious Kulkulcan."

What does this say, Itzás, but that at last we will bring the battle to them, led by the feathered serpent, a storm at our back, a righteous weapon in our hands to spill the visitors' blood?

"The war will not be lost, here in this land."

What does this mean, Itzás, if not that we shall be victorious?

Clever indeed. Chalo put down the manifesto and rubbed his eyes and wondered: wouldn't it be nice to come out on top for once? It was a dangerous feeling—Chalo knew it—and still he flirted with it, liking the way it felt. The warmth that spread through his soul was the ugly one of vengeance and yet, with everyone gone that mattered—his parents, his grandmother, Stephen, Anya—at least it filled the cold loneliness of loss in his heart. Now all he needed was a cigarette.

Chapter 40

"Okay, we go now. *Ka Ili'ik* takes the cigarettes and *pulque. Mi esposa* takes the blanket. I take the sack. That is everything."

Stephen, Rebecca, and Yaxché were standing on the healer's porch as dusk fell, dinner eaten, preparing to leave for the rainforest. Yaxché took two steps, paused, and tapped himself on the forehead.

"Foolish old man. *Chicle.* Wait here, while I get her at Lupita's."

"*Chicle*?" Rebecca asked once the old man was out of earshot.

"Mayan gum. Chicklets. Except that it tastes kind of… green."

"Sounds delightful," she joked.

"It's not that bad, really."

Yaxché trotted back across the road, a large russet hen with silky feathers in his arms. The hen's yellow eyes darted from Rebecca to Stephen and back.

"This is *Chicle,*" the healer said as he stroked the bird. He cackled at Stephen and Rebecca's surprise before starting towards the footpath into the forest.

"Don't worry, *Ka Ili'ik,*" Yaxché said over his shoulder, "I have the chewing kind for you, too!"

"Am I going to need it?" Stephen asked mordantly from the back of the line.

"Why would you need it?" Rebecca interjected.

"Chewing gum calms me down. I'm out of Beeman's…"

"Beeman's? You're not just a *rock* geek, are you?" She smiled over her shoulder.

"Takes one to know one," Stephen shot back, eyes twinkling.

"Yeah, well, I wanted to be an astronaut when I was a kid, too…"

"Enough talking," Yaxché chided. "The forest watches."

Walking into the darkening forest, Stephen considered what the trees might see: a short old healer in a ratty white t-shirt, threadbare green fatigues and gum boots, a heavy sack on his back and a red chicken in his arms; a slender dark-haired woman with a slight limp sporting dirty khakis, a bullet-riddled-and-mended white shirt, and a blanket in her arms; and a tall lean man with several days' stubble on his angular jaw and a bottle of bootleg cactus liquor in his hand, his green t-shirt showing sweat stains at the small of his back, his blue jeans ripped at one knee. Stephen thought fleetingly of the *Fellowship of the Ring*. Then he snorted to himself at the ridiculousness of the whole adventure.

"¡*Uay*, *Ka Ili'ik*! Quiet in the back! You bothering my chicken!"

Rebecca smothered a chuckle and the group walked on in silence.

Twenty minutes later, the forest almost black, Yaxché pulled a small flashlight from his back pocket.

"Ah," he grunted as he shone the light ahead. "Almost there."

Five minutes later he stopped abruptly.

"*Ka Ili'ik*, give me the cigarettes and *pulque*. And take *Chicle*."

Stephen prepared for the hen to flap and fuss; instead, she settled into his arms, clucked once, and fell asleep. She was softer than he had expected. And pleasantly warm. And she smelled a little like a duvet. He stroked her as one might stroke a dog. Rebecca smiled at the small tenderness and then coughed as cigarette smoke caught at the back of her throat.

Yaxché had cleared a small patch on the forest floor with his foot, lit two cigarettes, and was placing them, filter down, in the earth. Next, he unscrewed the bottle of *pulque* and sprinkled a few ounces on the forest floor. Then he stretched his arms wide and said something in Yucatec.

A zephyr, cool and fragrant, wound itself around them—lilies again. Yaxché spoke to the forest once more. The zephyr returned, warm and spicy, followed by the distant howl of a monkey. Yaxché was conversing with the forest itself. Stephen and Rebecca shivered despite the warm breeze.

"It is good," Yaxché said a moment later. "We are welcome. Follow me."

Ten paces brought them to a small clearing in the tar-black jungle; after the thick canopy, the starlit sky was dazzling, the pale arm of the

Milky Way luminous above them. Ahead they could make out the remains of a small pyramid.

"Wow," Rebecca breathed.

"Mmm hmmm," Stephen agreed.

"Look at Venus; I've never seen it so bright."

"Who's the geek now?" Stephen chuckled.

"Takes one to know one," she rejoined with a grin.

Stephen chuckled again appreciatively and then looked from the sky to Yaxché as the scent of a tropical fire filled the clearing; the old man must have laid the wood earlier in the day.

"The blanket, *mi esposa*. Between the fire and the temple, please. Spread out flat and then sit, yes?"

Rebecca nodded and started for the temple.

"And *Ka Ili'ik*, sit on the ground opposite *mi esposa*, on the other side of the fire."

"What about *Chicle*?"

"Put her down. She can do what she wishes until it is time to kill her."

Stephen and Rebecca stopped to stare at Yaxché.

Yaxché looked at the horror on their faces and shook his head.

"You Americans. You fall in love with something and then you cannot let it go," he scolded.

"I'm not American," Stephen grumbled.

Yaxché ignored the quibble.

"It is why you send your chickens and cows and pigs to be killed by machines instead of loving them until you put them on your dinner plate."

"We're eating *Chicle*?" Rebecca asked, aghast.

Yaxché cackled.

"You see? You like her. She has a name. Now you don't want to hurt her!"

"But are we eating her?"

"No, we are not eating her…"

He paused to throw a handful of herbs onto the fire; the air grew fragrant with the scent of basil, rosemary, and rue.

"Everything dies, *mis niños*" he said, softly. "If it does not, then there is no space for new life to come." He waited a moment to make sure he had their attention and continued. "But you Americans with your health care, you forget that dying is part of living. It is no wonder *pesar* and *susto* eat at all of you."

Rebecca furrowed her brow.

Still standing beside her, Stephen whispered clarification. "*Pesar* is like grief, *susto* is… like anxiety, I guess."

"Oh."

Yaxché threw another bouquet of herbs onto the fire.

"Your souls, both of you, are like old sticks, dried up from not drinking from life. Dry old sticks break; I need your spirits to be strong. Now sit: *mi esposa* on the blanket; *Ka Ili'ik* to the north of the fire. And *mi esposa*, you will start."

"Start what? And why does it always have to be 'ladies first'?" Rebecca asked under her breath.

Yaxché took Rebecca by the elbow and led her to a spot between the temple and the fire.

"Spread the blanket. And sit."

"Good dog," she muttered while doing as bidden.

"And you, too, *Ka Ili'ik*." Yaxché said as he pulled a red bandana from his back pocket, rolled it, and tied it around his forehead.

"Sit."

"Woof," Stephen replied, sitting.

"Bad dog," Yaxché said severely, making both Rebecca and Stephen smile.

"Now sit and be quiet. It is serious from now on. The gods already are watching."

Cowed, Rebecca and Stephen's smiles faded.

"Now *mi esposa*. Begin."

Rebecca looked at him, bewildered.

"What?" she asked again.

"The healing. Tell about him."

"Him?"

"Your husband. Tell how he left?"

"How he left?" she flushed. "He didn't leave! He died! He was killed by an IED in Iraq!"

Stephen's eyes widened in surprise. Then he flushed with embarrassment at the things he'd thought about her, assuming her flirtation betrayed a living person. Why the hell was she still wearing a wedding ring?

"Yes, *mi hija*. He was killed. But he left you alone here in this world."

Stephen watched as her eyes began to well. She blinked them back, began to speak, and fell silent again, obviously trying to regain her composure.

"There's not much to tell," she said, at last. "He went to war. He was killed. I'm not the only one who lost a husband in the war. It was eight years ago, for godsakes."

There was a long silence, punctuated by the hoot of an owl and the crackle of the fire. Rebecca bit her lip to hold back more tears.

"And?" Yaxché said softly.

"And nothing. He promised he would come back and he didn't. And every time I think I'm over it, something gets in my way."

"Not something, *mi hija*. Him. He doesn't leave you. He hangs on to you, maybe with something to say."

"What could he possibly want to say?" she asked angrily, tears slipping down her cheeks. "That he's sorry? He should be sorry! He broke his promise!"

Stephen watched Rebecca, a lump forming in his own throat: he knew this loss. He also felt a strange elation, felt embarrassed by his own selfishness. This meant that Rebecca was widowed, not married. He opened his mouth to speak, to try to comfort her, but Yaxché held up a hand to silence him.

"But his life was his, not yours, to take or leave. You cannot make another's choices and must forgive them the ones they make if you are to move on, hmm?"

They sat quietly for a moment as Rebecca digested the question and then the flames reared as if fanned by an opening door. Something was moving behind Rebecca; Stephen sat up tall to try to get a better look.

A mist was forming at the base of the temple; Stephen felt his stomach knot with unpleasant familiarity. A moment later he was staring again at *Xtabay*, gauzy in her flowing dress.

Stephen leaned forward as if to stand; Yaxché glared him back to stillness. *Xtabay* walked forward to Rebecca, stopping inches from the seated woman's right shoulder.

"It is an honour, Lady," Yaxché said softly to the apparition, brows slightly arched in surprise.

Rebecca looked over her shoulder and then to Yaxché, her eyes wide with alarm. The healer nodded reassuringly.

"Do not worry. She is here to help. Perhaps to take your forgiveness to the other side, if you will give it?"

Rebecca sat still and quiet. She had made it on her own these eight years. Could she forgive? Tears slipped down her cheek, unbidden, the forgiveness given like a burden released.

Stephen could see the change in her—the lightness—and he envied her.

"Now you, *Ka Ili'ik*," he turning from Rebecca to Stephen.

Unnerved by the reappearance of *Xtabay*, Stephen had lost track of what they were doing.

"Me what?"

"Your story. Your hurt. The girl."

"Erin?"

"You tell us, *Ka Ili'ik*."

Stephen swallowed, his turn to try to retain his self-control.

"It's like Rebecca said: there isn't much to tell. We went climbing… I convinced her to go climbing when we should have been studying for exams. It was spring and the rocks had been jacked over the winter—loosened by freeze and thaw—and she took a bad hold. She was above me… fell past me…"

He closed his eyes, the scene playing out in his mind's eye once more. It was so real, even after all this time, that he found himself reaching out again to catch her. He felt a softness, like her fleece, in his hand and clutched it tight, as if gripping the phantom would reverse fate. He felt the heat of welling tears.

"Let go, *mi hijo*," Yaxché said evenly.

Let go. Erin had said the same thing. Why did everyone always want him to let go? He clenched more tightly and refused to open his eyes.

"I know, *mi hijo*. You think it is your fault. You keep her tied to you because you have something still to say. But I say this: let go now."

Yaxché paused but Stephen refused to unmake his fist.

"Now, *Ka Ili'ik*. Let go *now*." The command rumbled through the silent forest and Stephen let go.

Friday, December 14, 2012 — 10 Ben, Day of Maize

"Open your eyes and do not move. He will not hurt you now that you have let him go."

Stephen raised his eyelids and saw Rebecca's face first, lit by the fire between them. Her eyes were wide, her mouth parted in a small *O* of alarm. He followed her gaze to his immediate left, and found himself staring into the golden eyes of yesterday's jaguar, mouth open, tongue pink between long ivory incisors.

"Tell him that it is a great honour, *Ka Ili'ik*."

Stephen started to shake: he had just been holding a wild jaguar by the pelt. Yaxché was still talking, but Stephen could not hear him, his attention entirely consumed by the great cat.

"It is an honour," Stephen said mechanically, voice tense and tight.

The cat blinked and then stood to walk a slow circle around Stephen, sniffing the air as it went, feline body moving like mercury, muscles rippling beneath black and gold fur, tail flicking as if with irritation.

The cat completed its circle and, heading for Yaxché, turned its back on Stephen at last. Stephen exhaled at last, then gasped for air; oxygen returned to his lungs and sound to his ears: he heard his pulse, pounding.

Yaxché and the creature regarded each other for a long moment—a silent communion—before Yaxché nodded, a brief, faint smile lifting the corners of his lips.

Stephen felt the sudden impact before he heard Rebecca's scream: the cat had sprung, soundless, from Yaxché back to Stephen in a single bound. The force sent Stephen sprawling backwards, jaguar tumbling with him, until the man, on his back pinned to the ground by the muscled bulk of the enormous cat, felt his lungs crushing beneath the creature's great weight.

So close to Stephen's face now, the cat's markings dissolved into a patternless field of gold and black hairs; he could see the individual pits on the cat's rough nosepad, could smell the cat's hot, briny breath, could feel a thick whisker catch on his own unshaven chin.

It was so cliché that he might have laughed, had the situation been different: what they said about a life flashing before a dying man's eye was true. Everything was there—a *smörgåsbord* of memory—Christmas dinners, the Ultimate gold medal won in Berlin, the colour of the walls in his childhood bedroom—all of them Technicolor bright until the moment Erin hit the ground. And then the images were bleached as if left in the sun too long. Eight years of half-life.

He was angry, suddenly, for wasting it, now that he seemed to have no time left. Stephen felt the cat growl more than heard it, the sound before the fury. Look a cat in the eye was the back-country rule: Stephen looked the great beast in its yellow eyes and felt exposed, the cat an arbiter of his wasted life. It won't attack if you look it in the eye.

The cat swatted him—the blow was heavy but not deadly for the cat had velveted its claws—and Stephen saw stars. The jaguar clouted him again, a cat playing with a mouse, a friend smacking a drunkard to make him sober up.

Suddenly Stephen chuckled at the madness of it all—what a way to go!—and was cuffed a third time. Stephen laughed again despite the strangling weight on him, at the irony of knowing what it meant to be truly alive again, exactly at the moment of his death. What a shame, he thought, with an equanimity that surprised him. What a shame he couldn't go back and do it differently. Not so much preventing Erin's death, but living his own life after it.

A lightness in his chest startled him from his thoughts and he wondered if this was what the last breath felt like. No, it was the cat, no longer on his chest. Stephen gasped like a sailor dragged from an icy sea. He was broken no longer.

He sat up with a smile and opened his mouth to speak.

"You are healed, *Ka Ili'ik.* It is good, I know. But do not speak," Yaxché said.

He was staring into the forest behind Stephen. Rebecca, the jaguar and *Xtabay* were doing the same. Stephen swivelled to look.

Holy crap and a half...

Something was moving beneath the dark canopy. A lot of somethings, actually. A cold fetid air blasted from the forest, like the wind before a locomotive, and the fire stuttered and sparked in the onslaught. A squeaking fluttering colony of bats flooded from the forest on the heels of the wind, extinguishing the fire. The clearing was left a black emptiness in their wake.

"*Don* Hernando?" Rebecca called, her voice quavering. "Stephen?"

Yaxché began chanting in Yucatec, his voice strong, his cadence urgent.

"The stars are gone…" Rebecca said, panic creeping into her voice.

Friday, December 14, 2012 — 10 Ben, Day of Maize

Stephen tried to look but even the notion of *up* suddenly seemed a fiction in the utter darkness; Stephen felt himself gripped by a terrible agoraphobia, an intense smallness within an enormous uncharted sea of ebony.

The fire jumped back to life but its flames were a sickly green, the creatures illuminated as they emerged from the forest were the things of nightmare. Yaxché signalled to Rebecca and Stephen to remain seated but he did not stop chanting. The creatures stopped, as if at a gate, a dozen feet behind the fire. Above, more ceiling than sky, the stars remained absent.

The things were misty grotesques—eyes bulging, tongues lolling, teeth bucked, noses pointed like rodents, hanks of hair belonging to severed heads swinging from their bloody hands—Mayan frescoes and carvings come, if not to life, to a spectral imitation of it not unlike *Xtabay*. The ghostly woman stepped closer to Rebecca and the jaguar growled at Stephen's side. Yaxché nodded in sudden understanding: the jaguar and his consort had come not merely to help with the healing but to protect the newly annealed tools.

Yaxché spoke to the shades' apparent leader, a muscled youth with the head of a devil, eyes wide, teeth sharp.

"Lords of Death, how do you walk among us once more?"

"We come in response to the blood spilled and the prayers said in our names."

"And what do you come to do, O Lords?"

"What it is that we have always done: visit illness, drought, misery, and death upon the people so that we may have the middle earth once more."

"And how will you do this, O Lords?"

Stephen couldn't be sure, but he thought he heard a hint of derision in the question. Was Yaxché actually baiting the apparition?

The jade-billed demon sneered and threw his fist into the air; a second later a lime-white light seared the clearing, blinding the three humans within it. For the second time that night, Stephen saw a string of images flash past his mind's eye: Rebecca falling backwards as Erin had, but into a deep well, her hand slipping from Stephen's; the glyph on the wall at the warehouse, so fresh and vivid that Stephen could see the blood drip down the wall even as he felt the dying boy shuddering in his arms; Anya, looking at the stars; Chalo holding an HK-416 assault rifle; a man drowning, his body drifting into a forest of blind white worms that undulated, oblivious, at the bottom of the sea; Yaxché enveloped by a sweet choking smoke; Rebecca with a gun in her hands; a body tumbling, bloody, down a long set of temple stairs.

The atomic brightness disappeared, plunging the circle into nothingness once more. The breeze that had wound lazily through their circle moments or hours before was now a squall, whipping Stephen's hair and whirling dead leaves and twigs around him with a ferocity that stung his skin. He closed his eyes reflexively and put his hands over his ears. An implacable sound was rising—audible even through the flesh of his hands—like rain but so heavy that it pressed inward like white noise, driving forward in waves, each louder than the previous one, and with it the wind rose until it was strong enough to snap small trees.

Beneath the wind's keening—barely audible, absolutely terrifying—came the sound of human voices wailing and moaning, a chorus of misery that chilled Stephen to the bone. Unbearably loud already, the noise rose until it seemed to emanate from within Stephen's own skull; his mind was raw now, empty of anything but the maddening storm. And when it seemed impossible that the din could grow louder, it was trumped by a roar—a feline scream—that seemed to make the fabric of time and space itself shudder. Utter silence followed in its wake.

Stephen opened his eyes into the sudden silence. The grotesques were gone. *Xtabay* and the jaguar were gone. Rebecca and Yaxché were sitting where they had been all along. The fire danced cheerily orange and gold in the soft rainforest night. Crickets trilled, and the Milky Way shone brilliant against the velvet sky. And Yaxché sat watching the flames, a grim and terrible look on his face.

The only sound for long moments remained the happy crackle of the fire. Stephen broke the silence at last.

"What the hell just happened, Yaxché?"

"Yes, *Ka Ili'ik.*"

"What?"

"Yes. Hell has just happened," he replied, eyes fixed on the fire.

Stephen opened his mouth to say something and then decided against it.

Yaxché gazed at the fire for a final moment before turning to

Stephen and Rebecca.

"It is time," he said, his eyes still staring at something far away.

"For what?" Rebecca asked, her voice even and fearless, her mended spirit strong.

Yaxché refocused on Rebecca.

"For many things, *mi niña*. But first, we give thanks. To the Lady for helping your ghost to let go. And to the Lord for helping *Ka Ili'ik* to let go of his own, hmmm? *Ka Ili'ik*, get for me *Chicle*."

The hen still lay in the hollow of the tree stump where she had nestled herself when they had arrived, apparently undisturbed by all that had happened. Could it have occurred within their minds alone? Stephen stooped down to pick the bird up, her breast feathers warming the palms of his hands as he did so. The hen squawked at the rude disturbance and pecked Stephen's hand lightly in irritation.

"Come on, girl, the old man needs you," Stephen said, smoothing the bird's russet feathers. She glared at him, squabbled a little, then settled into his arms.

"Thank you, *Ka Ili'ik*," Yaxché said as he took the bird into his arm, her bony feet in his hands for control.

"And thank you, too, my *Chicle*. You are a good bird."

He paused.

"Stand back, *Ka Ili'ik*."

Stephen stepped back unwillingly, knowing what was coming next.

Yaxché said something strong and sibilant in Yucatec as he took a long obsidian blade from behind his back. He spoke the phrase again and swung the chicken upside down—a single motion, spare and strangely gentle—and slit her throat; she shuddered once and then hung still, blood draining from her neck onto the soil for the gods.

Stephen tasted the tang of her life's blood in the air, remembered the night at the warehouse, and wondered how much more blood would be spilled before the journey came to an end.

SATURDAY, DECEMBER 15, 2012
11 IX, DAY OF THE JAGUAR

CHAPTER 41

Bender raised his golden muzzle from his paws and his tail thumped against the floor in anticipation; a moment later Peter Nguyen poked his head into Kathy's cluttered office.

"What's up, Doc?"

Kathy smiled, eyes on the pair of monitors on her desk.

"Come over here and look. It'll jar your damn pickles…"

Peter smiled at Kathy's homespun expression; it took less than a second for his face to fall once he saw the satellite images Kathy had been looking at. All three storms—*Sigma* and the two others—were clustering.

"How strong?"

"Sustained winds of 16 metres per second and rising. All of them."

Nguyen clenched his jaw. Two more metres per second and they would need names.

"*Tau* and *Upsilon*," he said softly. "Shit."

"Nope. Just *Sigma*, I think. They're orbiting. She looks to absorb the others."

Kathy was referring to the Fujiwhara Effect, a storm pattern in which two storms converged and, like prospective partners at a dancehall, circled one another. Some twosomes refused to pair up, their winds cancelling each other; others joined forces, creating a single, larger storm. Peter looked at the dangerous triad on the satellite image and shook his head.

"Have you ever seen *three* do that?"

"Not me. It could have happened before, but I don't know about it. It's eerie, if you ask me."

"What do you mean, 'eerie'?"

"Think calculus. What's *sigma* mean?"

"*Summation.* Adding… that *is* a little weird. What's the five-day cone?" Nguyen asked.

"The Antilles by Tuesday; Mexico by Thursday."

"Terrific. Just in time for the Christmas travel season. It's going to be hell, isn't it?"

"As if all that air travel isn't part of the problem in the first place, all those airplanes farting carbon dioxide. Maybe knocking down a few of those would be a good thing. Like the old joke about a thousand lawyers at the bottom of the sea being a good start."

Peter looked at Kathy, genuinely shocked.

"You don't mean that, do you?"

"'Course I don't," she sighed. "I've just never seen something so scary as those three, spoiling for a fight."

***

A tap on Anya's windshield woke her with a start and she reached for the tire iron on her lap; despite every warning ever issued against women travelling alone and anyone travelling at night, Anya had driven to Dzibanché from Calakmul, raging alternately at Sebastian and Chalo the entire way. Then she had tucked herself into her sleeping bag in the locked cab, weapon on her lap, to await morning.

"You must to go," said the old man at her window, a green historic site badge on his shirt. "Site not open until two more hours."

Anya looked over his shoulder and past the parking lot to the looming temple silhouetted against an opalescent pre-dawn sky. She sat up and reached into her knapsack for the credentials the government had given her to study the ruins at Sian Ka'an.

"*Soy Anya von Eckhardt. Estoy aquí estudiar las ruinas,*" she said, pressing the paper against the closed window. "*¿Puedo entrar antes que los turistas lleguen?*"

The site guardian looked closely at the document.

"*No. Es solamente para Sian Ka'an.* Go."

Anya let her hands and the paper in them fall into her lap. She had no idea what moved her to protest, but she did.

"*Por favor… es muy importante… Don Yaxché me envió aquí…*"

"*¿Quién?*" the man asked suspiciously.

"*Don Yaxché… Señor Hernando Canul…*"

The site guardian, as old as Yaxché but taller, narrower, more dour, squinted at her for a long moment. Then he frowned his dissatisfaction.

"You are late," he said, his voice fierce even through the window glass.

Anya rolled down her window. "Late for what?"

"Late and you don't even know for what," he grumbled. "Come now or we miss the sun's awakening."

Feeling more than a little like Alice after the rabbit, Anya grabbed her knapsack and followed the old man. He had a strange, sloping walk, as slow and precise as if he was fording a river; as with a river the shimmering air parted palpably as the old guardian strode through it. A snail's pace and yet after only twenty minutes Anya was exhausted by the effort of trying to keep up.

"Please stop," she panted as she paused to lean over, hands on her knees, to catch her breath.

"You are not ready for this."

Anya looked around. They had long ago left the low manicured grass surrounding the publicly accessible portion of the ruins and were now surrounded by a mature rainforest, lush as if it had never been disturbed. Only the hills and hummocks clothed in tangled vines told the trained eye that the area had been cleared as recently as 800 years ago when the city-state of Calakmul was at its zenith. Hers was the trained eye.

"I've spent years in these jungles!" Anya protested, digging for the water bottle in her pack.

"Over the land, yes. Not through the time," he replied sourly as he started onward.

Anya took a swig of her water and grimaced; it was warm.

"What do you mean?" she asked, jogging to catch up.

"It is in my blood. It is only in your head."

Anya felt her temper rise. Twice in two days now she had been called a foreigner, been told that the colour of her skin made her an unfit student of the Maya.

"Let me tell you about time and the Maya, old man," she said, rude with anger. "Everything that was, will be. Time is the realm of the gods who rule the day and dictate what must happen. Life begins, flourishes, is wiped away and a new Creation begins. The sky wheels overhead, and with it the stars tell everything. I know much of what your people forget!"

"Know, yes. Understand? No. Yaxché believes the old story about white helping red—says your people and mine will work together one day—but he is wrong: you cannot help. You people are destroyers only."

The old man turned and stalked away, Anya struggling once more to keep up. Twenty minutes later he pointed ahead.

"There. Go help. If you can."

"What is it?"

"Use the eyes, not the mouth."

Anya glared at the custodian a moment before looking in the direction of his outstretched arm.

"*Gott in Himmel,*" she whispered.

The sun was rising. The first shaft of morning sunlight streamed from a stone slit at the top of an enormous vine-covered pyramid onto a wide slice of an ornately carved stone marker seventy feet from the base of the pyramid—another structure not yet catalogued by modern archaeologists. Another temple with astronomical features, in fact, like hers at Sian Ka'an. Anya was certain that six days from now—on the equinox—the sunrise would light the entire *stela.*

"What does it tell?" Anya asked, exhilarated.

"Sparrowhawk knows it all, hmmm? You go. *You* tell *me*," he replied, as rude and sour as Anya had been only half an hour before.

***

Chalo woke a considerable while after the pearly mauve of sunrise had given way to the white light of day—might have slept past midday, in fact, had Kulkulcan not knocked perfunctorily before breezing into the hut.

"Well, *Señor* Guerrero, how was the book?"

"Chalo," Chalo replied, sitting up and rubbing the sleep from his eyes.

"Indeed? So you like me then?"

"Not so fast, *enchilada.* But give me food and coffee, and I might.

Food, coffee, and a pack of cigarettes."

Kulkulcan rubbed his hands with delight.

"All of the above, but in a moment. Now that we are almost friends there is something you must see. Go halfway up the pyramid; I'll meet you there in a few minutes."

Before Chalo could object, Kulkulcan was gone.

Chalo shook his head and rose from his cot. Making him wait for food was not a very good way to earn his friendship.

From his vantage on the pyramid, Chalo watched Kulkulcan's recruits go through their paces: four were engaged in target practice on the ballcourt, what looked to be an American trainer pacing behind them. They were shockingly good shots. Another five, awaiting their turn to shoot, looked to be field-stripping and cleaning rifles: rifles taken from the boxes he and Stephen had seen change hands in Cancún. Nice, new, expensive rifles. They sounded like German-made assault rifles—maybe HKs. HKs were used by elite teams within the US military, confirming the suspicion that this little revolution was being underwritten by the Americans. Chalo scowled and looked into the jungle: so who was using whom, here? The Americans using Kulkulcan, probably. Rebecca had said it: it was what the Americans did.

A pair of small drab monkeys, their eyes big and brown, their tails long and curled at the end, scampered up the pyramid and stopped six feet from Chalo. Spider monkeys: fearless, and expectant, they were approaching for food.

"Sorry, *amigos*, they haven't even fed me yet," Chalo said with a smile.

The pair crept closer anyway, ever curious, one of them reaching for the pocket of his black shirt.

"¡*Uay*! You're pushy!" he laughed.

"Go sit over there!" he said, sliding the creature from his lap.

The monkey, looking offended, rejoined his partner. Chalo watched as they began grooming one another and then looked back down the pyramid.

"This is longer than a few minutes," Chalo groused as his stomach rumbled.

Where was Kulkulcan?

Suddenly Chalo felt himself grow hot. He looked up at the sun; it was actually sliding behind a small cloud, so it could not be the culprit. The heat increased and Chalo began to look around for another source. He could not smell smoke and yet he felt like he was sitting just inches away from a campfire. Beads of sweat began to form on his forehead and he felt his breathing accelerate—felt an irresistible urge to get away.

He slid three feet towards the forest and felt instantly cooler. Almost as if he had stepped out of a sauna. Strange. Maybe he had caught a cold?

Chalo's impatience growing, he watched the trainees switch up to pass time. He felt his temperature rise once more: the sting of a sudden and intense sunburn, or the pain of a snakebite, it bathed his entire body. He moved another three feet further towards the forest and again felt his temperature drop. This time he shivered with the change.

He was only a few feet from the monkeys now; they glanced at his approach and one of them, deciding he was a threat, moved away. The other stared at him expectantly.

"No, *amigo*, I still do not have any food," Chalo smiled.

The monkey cocked its head and then suddenly made a horrible guttural sound.

"¡*Uay*, I'm hungry too! Don't get mad at me!" Chalo said jokingly before falling silent with horror.

The small creature had fallen to its side and was shuddering as if having a seizure. What seemed like a fraction of a second later, the monkey began to bleed—profusely and from every orifice. The blood welling from the corners of its wide, terrified eyes made it look like the monkey was crying; the blood from its wide shrieking mouth spoke agony. Another second later, the small creature fell still in a pool of its own blood, quite obviously dead. Its eyes remained open, frozen in fear, its small perfect paws remained outstretched, begging for help from beyond the grave.

"*Chingalo*," Chalo whispered, unconsciously crossing himself. He watched as the monkey's mate crept forward, prodded the corpse, and whimpered. Chalo felt a lump form in his throat and he looked away. Kulkulcan was just emerging from his hut down on the other side of the *Zócalo*; would he know what had just happened?

***

Saturday, December 15, 2012 — 11 Ix, Day of the Jaguar

Kneeling reverently before the *stela* in front of the unknown temple, Anya considered a puzzle of her own: a third *stela* written in the future tense, the name of her current location—Calakmul—at the top. She ran her fingers down the stone, her touch feather-light.

Superficially, it resembled the *stelae* she and Chalo had found at both Dzibanché and her ruin at Sian Ka'an: a date; a city name; a narrative in the future tense that contained the word judgment, a god's name, and the world tree; and another city name. Here the name at the bottom was her own site: Sian Ka'an. With any luck there was a fresco similar to the one at her site in the temple above her. She stood, took half a dozen pictures of the *stela* and then asked for permission to ascend the temple.

The guardian frowned but assented.

It was dim inside and Anya rummaged in her knapsack once more, this time for her flashlight. There was the spiral staircase typical of Mayan observatories; ascending, she was greeted by the familiar portals in the domed roof, the familiar stone slab in the centre of the room, the inscrutable paintings that danced around the perimeter of the dome. She stared at them: again the Creation myth; again the procession of thirteen gods engaged in a ritual, pointing to the tree and the stars in the night blue sky; again the turtle, the jaguar… but the positions were different. Why? Anya scuffed in frustration at the thick layer of dust on the floor and felt tears prick behind her eyes, the meaning still just beyond her grasp. A cloud rose into the still air, dust motes sparkling wildly in the light raying from the portals above.

She sat down on the stone slab in resignation, and then lay back on it and closed her eyes. Maybe she *was* too much a foreigner ever to understand it; maybe she should just give up.

"What is the date, Sparrowhawk?" said a clipped voice.

The dour custodian had followed her up and into the temple.

"December 14th… 15th… I don't know," she replied, too demoralized to make the effort to sort it out.

"On the *stela*," he chastised.

"I haven't worked it out," she sighed, eyes still closed.

"You lazy. You do. Now."

Wordlessly, Anya took the camera from her pocket, turned it on, and—still lying down—held it above her to look at the images she had taken outside.

It was a Long Count date from the 7th *b'ak'tun*: 8.19.1.8.19; Anya put the camera on her stomach, pulled her iPhone from her pocket and plugged the numbers into a date converter application.

"September 13th, 417 CE—*3 Cauac*," Anya replied wearily. "Day of Storm. Consistent with the architecture. Probably the date the place was built. Satisfied?"

There was no answer and Anya lifted her head; the guardian was gone.

"*Nett*," she said sarcastically. Nice.

She lay back again and looked up, appreciating the dust motes that danced in the sunlight streaming from the holes in the ceiling. An idea struck her, absurd in its simplicity: maybe the holes represented the night sky on *September 13th, 417 CE*, the day the temple could have been consecrated. Anya switched to a star map app, plugged in the ancient date, and held the smartphone above her to compare the results with the gaps in the ceiling.

"*Kacke*." Not a match. Her heart sank. How did all the pieces fit together?

She played idly with the star program, holding down the time slider and watching the circumpolar stars wheel around Polaris. There went Taurus and the Pleiades, there Pisces, Mars, and Venus, appearing and disappearing as she spun the sky a hundred years forward every few seconds. She named them with their Maya names as they came around again: the owl; the rattlesnake's tail; *zotz*, the bat… And again Mars, the Sky Beast. Like she had seen with Chalo…

Anya had taken her finger from the screen at the thought of Chalo; she noticed suddenly that the constellations on her screen matched the distribution of the portals on the ceiling. She looked at the date on the slider: June 27, 535 CE. Had she been here… she checked herself. The latitude and longitude were still set for the stargazing she and Chalo had been doing at Calakmul, not here at Dzibanché. That meant that had she been at *Calakmul* on the night of June 27th, 535 CE—just about the time *it* had been built—she would have seen the stars in the sky as they appeared on the portals above.

Anya felt her pulse quicken—she was on to something and needed a pen. She swore, remembering that she had given both of hers to Rebecca;

she started writing in the dust on the floor with her finger instead.

First she sketched the Yucatán Peninsula, a giant thumb sticking out into the sea. To it she added dots for three ruins: Dzibanché, Calakmul, and her own temple at Sian Ka'an. Beside each dot she added information pertinent to each.

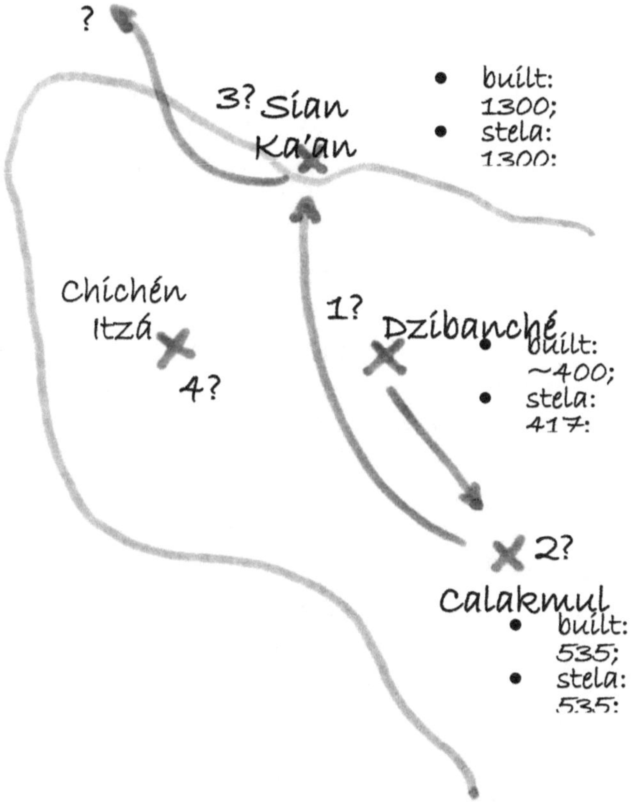

Dzibanché, built in 400 CE, was embedded with a stellar pattern matching the night sky over Calakmul in 535, the approximate date Calakmul had been constructed. In a similar way, Calakmul had been built in 535 with a stellar pattern matching the night sky over Sian Ka'an in 1300 CE…

Anya scrolled back to the image of the *stela* at Sian Ka'an, squinted at it and swore. She'd read the date wrong: not 13.0.0.0 but 1300—a

Gregorian date. She could see now that it was sloppy, as if carved after the rest of the *stela*. After about 1200 CE, the Maya had abandon the Long Count; someone must have come back after the arrival of the Europeans and added a Western date using the Mayan numbering system. Despite her impassioned speech to Stephen, Chalo, and Rebecca about the Mayan power of prediction, this was a past date: she'd been wrong to think there was anything connected to the coming *b'ak'tun*. *Dumkopf.*

Well, at least the world wasn't going to end. And there remained the puzzle of the ceiling: if her theory was right, there would be a future date embedded in the ceiling at Sian Ka'an, heralding a stellar pattern over Chich'en Itzá on that date. That, at least, would make a fascinating journal submission.

Anya stood, took a picture of her scribblings in the dust, and then scuffed through them on her way out. She almost knocked over the custodian as she stepped into the bright sunlight.

"So?" The old man challenged. "What do you learn?"

"It is a pattern, connecting places through time. It connects this place to Calakmul and Calakmul to Sian Ka'an."

"When?" he asked sourly.

"I don't know, yet. If you will excuse me, I go now to find out," she replied, matching his tone.

The custodian stepped aside and watched her begin the steep descent to the forest floor. She went on the diagonal, like a Maya.

"So, Yaxché was right about the sparrowhawk," the guardian grumbled. "We work together, after all."

Chapter 42

Stephen looked up from his phone and smiled when he saw Rebecca emerge from Lupita's hut: smiled at her sleep-tousled hair, smiled at her rumpled clothes, smiled at her unmarried state.

"Sleep well?"

"I don't know—did I have a nightmare or did all that stuff actually happen last night?" she asked as she padded across the dirt road and sat down on Yaxché's porch beside Stephen.

"The jaguar and *Xtabay*?"

"*And* the monsters," Rebecca nodded.

"Since it's even more unlikely that we had the same dream, it's a safe bet it happened."

"Where's *Don* Hernando?"

"He was gone when I woke up. Out collecting, I'd guess. Look, I'm sorry about your husband."

Rebecca paused, expecting the hardness of her grief to grip her, drag her to numbness. It didn't.

"Yeah, me too. But it was a long time ago. I'm okay, now. Really okay. I'm sorry about your… was she your fiancée?"

"My girlfriend. Me too. But I think, after last night, I'm finally on the mend."

Rebecca studied him.

"I think that's what *Don* Hernando wanted for us. But I don't think he expected the jaguar."

"What do you mean?"

"Well, I think he would have warned us if he'd known. And you should have seen the look in his eyes when it leaped on you…"

"*His* eyes!"

"He wasn't afraid. More surprised. And relieved."

"You're kidding, right?"

"No, not at all. It was like someone waiting for a bus finally seeing it coming."

Stephen laughed.

"What's so funny?" Rebecca asked.

"Nothing. Just thinking about the jaguar as a bus. It sure as hell felt like one when it landed on me."

"It looked like it was talking to you…"

Stephen fell silent for a moment, remembering everything. He felt his terror and elation again, felt the cat's whiskers and its breath, felt life and warmth seeping into the dead corners of his heart. The Maya believed that the jaguar fought each night to free the sun from the lords of the underworld and so he was a symbol of renewal.

"I… I guess it…he…was," Stephen said at last, a slow genuine smile creeping over his face.

"What did… *he*… say?" Rebecca asked earnestly.

Stephen looked at Rebecca: she was in the same clothes, a smudge of dirt on her cheekbone, arms hugging her knees in the mid-morning light, her twisted pony tail loosening slowly into a cascade over her shoulder. A light was suffusing her, the mists of timelessness swirling around her.

"What did he say…" Stephen asked slowly, struggling for words as he looked at Rebecca, her green eyes looking back at him, wide and expectant. It was not what the cat had said but what it had done. It was the brush with death that had brought him back to life. How could he possibly explain? He was seized by a sudden impulse that was both a *non sequitur* and an exquisite answer to the question.

"I'd really like to kiss you."

Rebecca's eyes widened. "The cat said… what?"

"Yes, the jaguar. Never mind. Can I kiss you?"

Rebecca flushed and a small smile began to creep across her lips. She leaned forward in silent answer. But before their lips met, a dirty white pick-up truck, its engine straining, barrelled around the bend in the village road, a cloud of dust roiling in its backdraft.

"What the hell?" Stephen muttered.

"That's Anya's truck…" Rebecca wondered as she rose.

Chalo's timing always did suck, Stephen thought ruefully as he, too, stood to greet the truck's expected occupants. The dust cloud tumbled forward over Stephen and Rebecca as the truck skidded to a stop and Anya got out.

"Where's Chalo?" Stephen asked when the dust settled.

"He's joined Kulkulcan's army. May I have something to eat?"

"What?!" Stephen and Rebecca asked in unison.

"Please. I've been driving a long time. Let me eat and then I'll tell you everything."

A few minutes and her second tortilla later, Anya recounted her version of events at Kulkulcan's camp, ending with Chalo's pretend defection to Kulkulcan's cause.

"He won't get sucked in," Stephen protested, hoping he was right. "Not Chalo."

"Whatever," Anya said, taking a large bite of a third tortilla. "He stayed behind. What about you—are you not supposed to be gone to Canada?"

"Rebecca didn't wake from her coma until yesterday…" he began, defensively.

"And then *Don* Hernando took us into the forest last night for a ceremony…" Rebecca continued.

"Don't tell me you saw *Xtabay* again?" Anya demanded, frustration raising the pitch of her voice.

"And a whole bunch of other spirits, Anya. And a jaguar that attacked me. Happy?" Stephen answered belligerently. "How could you leave Chalo there?!"

"He's a grown man! What would you have me do—drag him out by his hair? What happened in the forest?"

Stephen glowered and said nothing. Rebecca, ever the peacemaker, took over.

"We were both…" She paused a moment, not wanting to share the tales of healing. They seemed too personal.

"We were around a fire that Yaxché had built," she said, starting again. "*Xtabay* and a jaguar joined us. And then a group of… of spirits… appeared. Strange looking, like glyphs come to life. Some had long noses and other with long tongues and no eyes. Nine of them. Yaxché called it a visit from Hell."

"Nine? You are sure?"

"I count things when I'm nervous. I'm sure there were nine," Rebecca said, holding her ground.

"But there should be thirteen. There are thirteen in all the murals," Anya said petulantly.

"Ah, ah ah, but you forget yourself," cackled a familiar voice. "The problem with you Americans is that you always think you are outside the problem!"

It was Yaxché, returned from collecting, calling through the walls of Lupita's hut, his silhouette that of a hunchback thanks to his over-full collecting sack.

"I'm not American," Anya and Stephen muttered at the same moment.

Rebecca smirked at their protests.

"You are four in there. Add nine is thirteen. You are all part of the mystery."

"Four?" asked Stephen, looking around the interior of the hut.

"What mystery?" asked Rebecca as Yaxché stepped toward the door to enter.

"The hinge time. How to save the world!" Yaxché said with a grin, a child with a new toy.

He stopped abruptly once inside and surveyed the small group before him, smile ebbing from his face.

"But where is the fourth? The *chi'kin*?"

"Chalo?"

"Yes, yes," Yaxché said irritably. "What have you done with him? Why is he not here?"

***

Still on the pyramid at Kulkulcan's camp, Chalo was wishing fervently that he were elsewhere.

"The monkeys are sick here, *enchilada*. With that bleeding disease. You need to move your camp," he said when Kulkulcan joined him at last.

"You think?"

"Look at the damn monkey, *enchilada*! He died in front of my eyes!"

Kulkulcan glanced at the little primate with apparent indifference.

"Did you not feel the heat, Chalo?"

"The heat? You're *loco*, *enchilada*! The monkey is dead! Doesn't that worry you even a little?"

"I'd be worried if the monkey was not dead, Chalo. It would mean my secret weapon is broken."

"Your… your what?" Chalo looked at Kulkulcan, slack-jawed with surprise.

"The heat. You got so hot you had to move, yes? That's the low setting. The high setting is what killed the monkey. That's my *tohil*."

"Your what?" Chalo asked in disbelief.

"My *tohil*. Named after the bringer of blood, Lord *Tohil*. It is a PSAD-1M portable Access Denial Weapon, specially modified with an advanced targeting system and powered by a next-generation fuel cell. It boils the blood almost instantly, leading to internal and external haemorrhaging followed by a massive heart attack as the cardiac muscle, pumping wildly, tries to compensate for falling blood pressure. It can work from up to a thousand feet away. Quick, but quite painful, I am sure. And very final."

"You used a heat ray on me, *enchilada*?"

"Come now, Chalo. You make it sound like a bad thing!" Kulkulcan said, smiling ingenuously.

"You used a *heat ray* on me?" Chalo asked again, incredulous.

"Don't worry, my friend. Unlike the monkey, I did you no permanent damage. Have a cigarette, why don't you?"

Chalo looked at Kulkulcan in a new light, fully understanding the guerrilla at last. It was Kulkulcan's peculiar mix of intelligence, anger, and determination that made him so powerful. His utter disregard for others was what made him so dangerous: he would lie and kill without conscience if it got him closer to his goal. Chalo took the cigarette, allowed Kulkulcan to light it, inhaled deeply, and found it gave him no relief. Anya had been right: he had gotten himself in way over his head and Kulkulcan would not be controlled.

"The Americans have given you this?" Chalo asked carefully, stubbing the barely-smoked cigarette on the stone beside him.

"Oh, dear God, no!" Kulkulcan laughed. "They have trained my units to work with conventional tools. They know nothing of these."

"There is more than *one* heat ray?"

"*Tohil*, please. It suits the mythology. No, not yet. For now there is only the prototype down there in my hut. Once Dr. von Eckhardt's lovely brother steals the fuel cells from Mitnal, however, there will be thirteen."

"Why thirteen?"

"One for the President, and one for each cabinet secretary who cannot be bent to my will."

"They'll kill you before you get into the government building," Chalo said carefully.

"I'm not going into the government building. I am a guerrilla, Chalo, with guerrilla tactics. I have thirteen units trained to attack thirteen different targets spread across the country. Simultaneously. Much easier, really. And with the gore, much more effective at frightening the populace into doing my will, don't you think?"

It was brilliant, Chalo realized. Brilliant in principle, at least.

"How will you know where every single one of your targets is at exactly the same moment? Their schedules change by the hour..." Chalo said.

"Exactly. But do you have any idea how much money the Americans spend on collecting information?"

"The Americans are giving you information?!"

"Of course they are—it serves their interest to have me depose the current anti-American regime."

So Rebecca had been closer to the truth than she had known.

"No offense, *enchilada*, but why should they like you any better? You want to get rid of everyone who is not Maya."

"Not so naïve, after all. My apologies. They are planning to double-cross me."

"How do you know?"

"I don't know yet. At least not for sure. But I received a strange telephone call late last night that makes me suspicious. I need you to check a few things for me."

"Check what? And why me?"

"You? That is easy. As a police detective you should see weaknesses in security plans. And against what? I spoke with a few people in very low places and now have what are supposed to be exact copies of my American marine's intelligence reports. I need you to make sure they *are* exact copies."

"What if I lie?" Chalo asked nonchalantly.

"I know where your *Doktor* is."

Chalo clenched his jaw and changed the subject.

"Can I have my coffee now?"

Kulkulcan smiled dangerously.

"In a few moments, yes. But here comes my American now. Keep quiet and watch me: I will show you just how good I am at this game."

Chalo looked down the pyramid at the buzz cut American climbing up towards them. He wondered if the poor bugger knew how much trouble he was in.

"Morning, Boss," Rutrauff said when he was two steps below Kulkulcan. He eyed Chalo doubtfully. "Who's our new guest?"

"My cousin, Captain. Chalo Guerrero, Travis Rutrauff; Travis, Chalo."

Chalo nodded curtly.

"You put your cousin under lock and key?" Rutrauff asked, his surprise genuine.

"Yes well, that must have looked very strange. It has been a complicated twenty-four hours, hasn't it? Have a seat, Captain, and let us explain."

"What's with the monkey?" Rutrauff asked as he took a seat as far as possible from the little corpse.

"Death is everywhere, Captain. Does it bother you?"

Rutrauff said nothing.

"Good. Now where was I?" Kulkulcan chuckled.

"The past twenty-four hours. The skinny guy from Cancún. Putting your cousin and the blue-eyed hottie in lock-up…," Rutrauff prompted.

Chalo gritted his teeth at the boorish reference to Anya.

"Let's start with the "skinny guy", I think…" Kulkulcan said. "I wanted to tell you sooner, Captain, but it was a delicate thing. He is the leader of the terrorist group called Eden Two. His name is Sebastian von Eckhardt."

"Jeezuz Christ. Why didn't you tell me?"

"Like I said, Captain: it was a delicate thing. I was worried that you might try to kill him."

"And that would have been a bad thing?"

"Indeed it would have. It turns out that he has plans to destroy the

Mitnal platform."

Rutrauff flexed his jaw. That oil was the reason this whole operation was active.

"Again, why would it have been bad to kill him?"

"Because they work in cells as we do. If we had killed him, another would have filled his shoes and destroyed the rig. No, I hired him instead, and had my cousin, Chalo here, check into him…"

Kulkulcan paused to slap Chalo on the shoulder and smiled on him with the proud familiarity of a mentor smiling on a student. Chalo chuckled despite himself.

"… it turns out that, by marvellous coincidence, the man's sister is an archaeologist here in Mexico. Chalo escorted her here as a form of insurance."

Chalo fought to hide his surprise: Kulkulcan was weaving truth and fiction seamlessly, changing the facts to suit his needs. He was dangerous indeed.

"Some coincidence," Rutrauff said sceptically. "Why did you let her go? Why did you let both of them go, when it comes to that?"

"I told the woman that if she told the authorities about her brother, I would kill him. I told *him* if he didn't succeed at destroying the rig, I would kill *her*. And I made him take Payal along, with orders to *Payal* to kill Sebastian before he can actually destroy the rig."

Chalo was awestruck by Kulkulcan's creativity: everything he had said was almost true—all but Chalo's own role. It was hard not to admire the madman's brilliance.

"Okay…" Rutrauff began slowly. "But why did you put your cousin under lock and key?"

"He insinuated himself into the sister's life as her bodyguard—he used to be a police officer, you see—and engineered a trip here to Calakmul so that we might use her as leverage. I had to capture both of them to continue the ruse."

"Bodyguard, hunh?" Rutrauff said to Chalo. "Why haven't I met you before? I've been in and out of these jungles for years now," Rutrauff pressed.

"I was useful to my cousin in other ways, back in Mexico City," Chalo observed before Kulkulcan could speak.

"Another cop working two jobs, hunh?"

Chalo felt his blood boil; Maya or crooked or both—that's how everyone saw him. It didn't take much acting to play the role Kulkulcan had concocted for him.

"You think you know everything, *gringo*?" Chalo demanded. "Me and your *enchilada*, here, we've been playing ball together since we were boys. As for coming to camp now, it is because we are close to victory—close to an end of the poverty and misery, of being sneered at and spit on and orphaned simply because of the colour of our skin and the glory of our past..."

Chalo felt the power of his words, was enchanted by them as he spoke them. He flushed with delight when he saw the America's eyes widen in surprise.

"Whoa, whoa! '*Enchilada*', hunh? You must go way back if you can call him that and get away with it..."

"Indeed," Kulkulcan scowled, "it is a liberty I allow only a very few people."

Rutrauff chuckled at Kulkulcan's expense and then, seeing the thunder in the guerrilla's face, let the smile slide away.

"So. 'Captain Rutrauff,' is it? My cousin wants me to look over your shoulder," Chalo said archly. He was enjoying the rush of power. "Isn't that so, *enchilada*?"

"Indeed, Gonzalo." Kulkulcan used Chalo's disfavoured name to squelch Chalo's cockiness before turning to Rutrauff.

"I want you to show my cousin the security details we have."

"Mind if I ask why?"

"He knows how the government security details operate. He can make sure we have not missed anything."

"We haven't missed anything," Rutrauff replied quickly.

Too quickly. Rutrauff wasn't a pawn, Chalo realized. The American knew there was a double-cross planned.

"Probably not, but let's look anyway," Chalo said amiably as he rose, enjoying the American's apparent discomfort. Yes, Chalo liked feeling superior for a change.

CHAPTER 43

Kulkulcan had given Chalo a computer containing a bakers' dozen security files, a tall stack of paper files, and directions to find anything unusual in a comparison of them. A tall order. After fifteen minutes and the first anomaly, Chalo, ever passionate for a mystery, was engrossed.

Each paper file was labelled with the name of a cabinet secretary; each electronic file was similarly named. On preliminary inspection, the files were identical: the schedule and security details for each of thirteen secretaries on December 20th, 2012. But a detailed review revealed that all but four of the file pairs contained subtle differences. Three hours after attacking the puzzle, Chalo went to Kulkulcan with his findings.

"There are differences in four of the files; tiny ones. Easy to miss."

"Show me."

"Look at the Secretary of Trade. He is in his home state on the 20th, at his local office. In both files, he is in his office but for one appointment. In both files, that appointment is for lunch with a group of educators; in both the limousine leaves at the same time and takes the same route to the restaurant. But in *this* one," Chalo pointed to the computer, "he goes to dine at *Pollo Verde*. But in this one," Chalo tapped on the paper file, "he is taken one extra block on the very same street to a restaurant called *Relleno Verde*. A difference of one word and one block."

Kulkulcan nodded, his face grim.

"And the others?"

"Tiny differences in departure times; in routes; in security personnel. All easy to miss."

Kulkulcan nodded again, his lips set in anger. "Which are the four plans that are the same?"

Chalo had taken notes; he referred to them now.

"The Secretaries of Defence, Social Development, Labour… and the President.

Kulkulcan's face grew darker.

"The President and the three strongest socialists in Cabinet," he observed. "Everyone else we have targeted leans towards economic liberalism and close ties with the United States."

"So?"

"So, kill only those four and the cabinet that remains swings back into American arms. The Americans get their oil money back, and access to the oil itself, too…"

"What about you? Weren't you to take the presidency? Who cares about the rest?"

"¡*Pendejo*! They will try to kill me, of course. And the next in line in for President is the *cabrón* Raul Vargas. Do you even know who he is?"

An apologist for US policy, Vargas would be the American dream for President of Mexico; *pendejo* meant "dumb-ass." Chalo knew both and was twice offended.

"*Pendejo*, is it?" Chalo answered. "Raul Vargas is next in line. As for the dumb-ass, you put Rutrauff in charge of the intelligence in the first place. If I'm the dumb-ass, why didn't you have someone looking over the American's shoulder from the start?" It was a risky challenge and Chalo knew it: Kulkulcan could kill him as easily as clap him on the back.

Kulkulcan glowered at Chalo and then suddenly laughed.

"My apologies. The gods really do smile at me, don't they? They sent me you to catch my mistake. And, unfortunately for the poor Captain, I can make him go ahead with *my* version of the plan."

"How is that?" Chalo said, pleased with the apology.

"Take the power back, of course. It is always about power. I need only one man to bend Captain Rutrauff to my will. And thanks to last night's strange call, I know how to get him."

"You're going to need someone big…" Chalo observed.

"He's big, alright. I'll send Alvarro to get him tonight."

Alvarro. The goose that had started this chase. Chalo swallowed hard and tried to feign disinterest.

"Who's Alvarro?"

"Just another one of my tools. A blunt instrument, Alvarro; he likes blood. But he is also exceptionally good at moving things around the country without them being seen. I let him hurt people; in exchange, he moves things for me."

Chalo swallowed again, his head swimming.

"Moving things. Did he start in drugs?"

"A small time narco when I found him," Kulkulcan smiled. "But I made him far better. Or worse, depending on how you see it."

"Oh?" Chalo said, looking at his fingernails.

"He is the one that has been my chief fear-monger—the one pulling hearts out across the country this past year…" Kulkulcan said nonchalantly.

Chalo coughed to hide an involuntary nausea that arose with an image of the dead boy at the warehouse.

"… If the police hadn't been trying to cover up after him, the country would already be mine, terrified by the vision of angry gods and the world's end. No matter; they're scared enough by my manifesto and rumours of *xekik*. The sight of the *Tohil* at work will push them over the edge."

Chalo was forced to steady himself against the wall of Kulkulcan's hut as, mind reeling, all the pieces fell into place: the strange scene at the warehouse, the heart in the fountain at the Chacmool, Rebecca's missing money, Anya's field assistant, the fear winkling through the country, the rumours of the apocalypse…

"Are you alright, *hermano*?" Kulkulcan asked solicitously.

Hermano. He could hear Stephen scolding him for getting himself into yet another mess. How the hell was he going to get himself out of it? And how—with Stephen gone, Rebecca in who knows what shape, and Anya probably unwilling to speak with him ever again—how, with no help at all, could he possibly stop Kulkulcan?

***

"Foolish," Yaxché clucked, shaking his head. "Give me a tortilla and tell me again why you left him there."

Anya glowered at Yaxché over her empty plate.

"He's a grown man. Like I said to Stephen, was I supposed to drag him out of the camp by his hair? He fell in love with the madman's ideas!"

"Love? His love belongs to another, I think."

Yaxché looked pointedly at Anya; when she pursed her lips and looked away Yaxché concluded that she loved Chalo, as well. No wonder she had lost her head. He shook his own and spoke again.

"The Maya have been pushed down for so long—and none of us shouted the truth loudly enough—that it is not a surprise that Kulkulcan's honeyed words now catch the hurt and broken, no?"

Anya looked back at Yaxché, stricken. He was right, and she wanted to kick herself. She had only made Chalo's hurt worse.

"Forget why you left him, *mi niña*," Yaxché absolved. "How do we bring him back? I must have him for what comes next."

"Why him?" Anya asked jealously.

"Not just him. You, too. All of you. Last night I saw the Lords of *Xibalba*. The madman that has your friend may not believe in them, but with his foolish actions—the blood spilled on the days of death—he has set free all the demons from here to *Mitnal*..."

"*Mitnal*?" Rebecca interrupted, eyes wide.

"The cold, bottom level of the Mayan underworld," Anya answered perfunctorily. "But why Chalo? What do you need him for?"

Yaxché ignored Anya's question. Of Rebecca he asked, "Why do you ask of *Mitnal* like that, *mi esposa*? What do you know of it that I do not?"

"Mitnal is also the name of the deep-water oil field in the Gulf of Mexico that Joe and his friends have invested so much money in..."

"Man is not meant to be there any more than the demons are meant to walk here," Yaxché said. "But they walk because the false Kulkulcan spills the blood that opens the gates. And because he does, the creators doubt us once more. Now we must earn back our right to walk the land."

Steeped in the Maya legends of creation, the mythology made sense to Anya. Needing Chalo still did not.

"I still don't understand why you need *Chalo*."

"Does it matter why? Stephen broke in. "Yaxché says he needs Chalo. That should be good enough. If you won't go back and get him, I'll go..."

"*We'll* go," Rebecca corrected. "I need to find out more about what the stolen money is paying for, anyway."

"No way!" Stephen said; "you've been chased, shot, comatose, and abducted by evil spirits—you're not going anywhere!"

"You're not my Dad, Stephen! I feel fine—better than I've been in a long time, actually—and I need to know what Joe is up to…"

"It's too dangerous!"

"How are you going to get there? I'm the one with the car!" Rebecca said hotly.

"I'll take you," Anya said, her tone angry yet resigned.

"Thanks but no thanks," Stephen said angrily. "You've done enough already,"

"You don't even know where he is," Anya observed with grim satisfaction. "Someone has to show you the way."

"Show *us* the way," Rebecca corrected again angrily.

"I have the bird tag, remember?" Stephen retorted.

"Stop," Yaxché said, his voice sonorous, his face dark with anger.

Stephen, Rebecca, and Anya fell silent, glowering at each other like angry children before a scolding parent.

"Listen to you—squabbling like chickens over crumbs while the butcher stands behind you. How do you deserve a second chance, hmm? Why do I even bother?"

Yaxché paused a moment and looked at the threesome, now sheepish.

"There are roles enough for everyone, even if you do not like the one you must take. *Ka Ili'ik* will go to get the fourth. With *mi esposa.* And Anya will take me to Sian Ka'an."

"But he doesn't…" began Anya.

"Rebecca can't…" began Stephen.

"Don't tell me what…" began Rebecca.

"Quiet!" Yaxché barked. "You will do what is needed or we will be crushed and swept away. What do you choose?"

"We'll go get Chalo," Rebecca said with grim satisfaction. Stephen frowned but nodded his assent.

"I'll take you to Sian Ka'an, *Don* Yaxché" Anya said.

Yaxché nodded with angry satisfaction and turned for the door.

"*Bacabs*. Like legs arguing where to take the dog, instead of being legs. It is a wonder the dog gets anywhere at all."

Saturday, December 15, 2012 — 11 Ix, Day of the Jaguar

CHAPTER 44

"There was a vision serpent named *Och-Kan*, Lord of Calakmul," said Yaxché as he looked through the dusty passenger window of Anya's battered pick-up truck.

He had been watching the scarred and pocked fields thick with stumps and hollows for an hour now, watching wordlessly as the cleared land that marked the inexorable spread of the cattle industry slid past his gaze.

Anya waited for a long moment for Yaxché to continue. She was rewarded only by the sound of her truck rattling over the rutted road.

"And?" She asked at last, her curiosity burning.

"He stared into the heart of Heaven. And do you know what he saw?"

"No. What?"

"An angry Lord and the end of the world," the old man said, lost in thought. "It was the maker and creator. The one who breathed life into the land. *Hurukan*. He was angry to see that man was making a sickness upon the land. And do you know what kind of sickness it was?"

"No. What?" asked Anya, glancing briefly from the darkening road.

Yaxché was still looking out the car window, his fingers laced in his lap.

"The people kind."

"I don't understand…"

"The kind where the people are the sickness. Where they forget what they owe and instead take from the Earth without stopping. Until it is a husk, empty, brown, and dry. And do you know what *Och-Kan* did? He paid back the sky."

"How did he do that, *Don* Yaxché?" Anya asked softly.

"Not how, *mi hija*, but where and when," he said, returning suddenly from his reverie. "But I think what you have found will tell us."

"My temple?"

"Yours?" Yaxché cackled.

Anya bristled, her knuckles growing white on the steering wheel.

Yaxché laughed more gently.

"Yours. Mine. Everyone's. It is all connected, anyway. Across time. Across space. And everything comes around again onto itself, to teach us what we did not learn the first time."

Anya nodded, mollified and a little ashamed.

"What do you see out your window, *mi niña*?"

"My… what?"

"There. Out there," he said nodding to the space beyond the windshield.

"A road? A field?"

"And what is in the field?"

"Nothing?"

"Yes. Nothing. Where are the trees to hold up the sky? Where are the trunks that hold back the wind? Where are the roots to keep the Earth firm and hold the Lords of *Xibalba* beneath our feet?"

"You sound like my brother."

"Yes? And what is it that he says?"

"That we are destroying the planet; that we must change our ways or die."

"And what do you think?"

Anya thought for a long moment: about disappearing species and crop failures, freak storms, dangerous firestorms…

"That he is probably right," she said quietly.

"Why do you study my people instead, *mi niña*?" Yaxché asked, suddenly changing the subject.

"Instead of what?"

"Instead of anything! Collecting the garbage, writing books, farming the land. Why the Maya instead?"

Anya had any number of academic reasons, but the reality had no logic to it.

"I… I don't know. The world of the Maya… It's beautiful. And lonely. And sad. And it has something to say to the world that shouldn't be forgotten."

"It has something to say to you, also, *mi niña*," Yaxché said, gently chiding.

"What is that, *Don* Yaxché? That I'm a fool and an outsider who will never truly understand?"

"No, *mi niña*, not that. It is only that you try too hard. You live in your head always."

Anya blinked back tears and said nothing.

"The Maya are the People of the Maize: we are meant to grow. We are the People of the Wind: we are meant to fly. We are the People of the Sun: we are meant to shine. We are the People of the Rain: we are meant to cry. But you? You do none of these things. You are like a seed, thrown on barren soil: you stay curled up inside, hard and dry, all because you are angry that you are not me. But we need all of us now. All of us, working together, no matter our blood or colour. Do you not see?"

"What happened to *Och-Kan*?" Anya asked, trying to change the subject.

"He died," Yaxché replied simply. "He died, but not before he lived, child. Not before he lived."

A tear slipped down Anya's cheek and she wiped angrily at it.

"See, *mi hija*? You already know how, if you will just let yourself."

Anya set her jaw to hold back any further tears.

"Can I work on flying first?" Anya said thickly. "Crying is very hard."

Yaxché cackled and his laughter was infectious; Anya smiled through her tears.

"You do not get to choose what you need to work on, *mi hija*! It is how they remind us that we are not in charge!"

"It is too bad. I would prefer to shine, right now."

"Ah, but you do shine, *mi hija*! Look at you now, your heart finally open to the sky."

Anya's face did look radiant in the golden evening light. She smiled weakly.

"So what am I supposed to do?"

"Do? Exactly as you are now!"

"Driving?"

"Being. Here. Learning. Teaching."

"Teaching?"

"We always teach what we most need to learn, *mi hija*."

"With everything you know already, *Don* Yaxché, what could I possibly have to teach you?"

"What is it that you most need to learn? To realize that you do not know everything. To know that you must sometimes ask for help. These are things I am not good at either, *mi niña*. But they are things I will have to do, and soon."

Anya laughed at herself: Yaxché had seen her faults and named them perfectly.

"How soon?"

"How soon is it to your ruin?"

"About forty-five minutes on the road and then another twenty in the boat. A little longer than one hour."

"Then that is your answer: I will have to ask for help in a little longer than one hour."

***

"This is nuts, you know that?" Rebecca said from behind the wheel of her rental car.

"Which part: that we're heading into a guerrilla camp to rescue Chalo with nothing but my gun, or that last night we spent the night hanging in the Mexican jungle with evil spirits threatening to destroy the world?"

"Okay, so I was thinking about the guerrilla camp, but when you put it that way, I mean the whole thing. What the hell are we supposed to do?"

"No clue about how to save the world but I'm close to figuring out how to get Chalo. You don't have any pantyhose in your knapsack, do you?"

"Pantyhose?"

"We need to create a diversion—maybe a bunch of them. I'm trying to figure out what we have to work with."

"Sorry, didn't bring any. What can you do with pantyhose, anyway?"

"Lots. How about talcum powder?"

"Baby powder? I do have that. Why?"

“We can use it to make a smokescreen. But we need a propellant…”

“Could you use butane?”

“Not as a propellant but for something else, sure. Why do you have butane?”

“My hair iron. I forgot about it and the guards at the airport didn’t catch it. So much for homeland security.”

“What’s a hair iron?”

“It straightens hair.”

“Why would you want to do that? Your hair is beautiful…”

Rebecca blushed and Stephen trailed off, suddenly embarrassed.

“How much butane?”

“A little can, about this big,” she replied, taking one hand off the steering wheel and holding her thumb and forefinger apart.

“Probably about 150 mls. We can use it as an explosive. I need some kind of acid to make a propellant.”

Rebecca laughed.

“It’s a good thing you became a cop. Otherwise you’d probably have made a formidable terrorist. How’d you learn all this stuff?”

“I was a geeky kid. I built a lot of stuff. And watched a lot of *MacGyver*.”

“So you said. About Geology. And astronaut gum. It just that I wouldn’t have pegged you for a geek at first glance…”

“Was that a compliment or an insult? You can’t answer that without getting in trouble, by the way… hey, wait! Stop the car!”

“A compli… . What? Why?”

“Pine cones. They explode,” he said pointing to a small stand of piñon trees at the southernmost end of their range.

Rebecca pulled over onto the narrow shoulder beside the trees.

“They what?”

“The pitch is really flammable. Not big explosions—more like a ‘pop’—but they’re enough to startle someone. Hang on while I get some.”

Rebecca watched Stephen as he stepped out of the car, pushed through the tall grass to the trees, stopped, and pulled the bottom of his t-shirt up into a makeshift sack. Rebecca caught a glimpse of well-defined abdominal muscles before Stephen stooped to collect the fallen cones and raised her eyebrows: she might well be going to Hell in a hand basket, but at least the scenery was going to be nice along the way.

CHAPTER 45

Having reconfirmed his commitment to the Mexican operation, dismissed his guilt where Rebecca was concerned, and vowed to ensure Clayton Powell received his comeuppance for threatening the Wilkes' family honour, Joe was enjoying his time off: a little fishing, some carpentry, the storm windows, the sump pump, boarding up a skunk hole, and a whole bunch of ESPN. Now he sat down over a plate of baked beans, watching the light fade over the bayou, and contemplated his revenge. It was even more satisfying than scuppering Carolina Schroeder's climate bill.

Looking at the drying wetland outside, he felt a twinge of guilt about that. Not enough to relent on Schroeder's bill—it was going to cost the economy too much—but maybe next time around he could give a little bit, just in case the scientists were actually right about global warming.

His plate empty and the daylight almost gone, Joe chuckled and picked up the phone. Before the heavy lifting that dealing with Clayton would entail, he needed to stir Carolina Schroeder's pot: he was going to offer to throw his support behind a watered down climate bill. And then who would look like the partisan hardliner when she insisted that neither a lower target nor a longer timeline was good enough—that a 60% reduction by 2020 was what it would take to keep the world on this side of the climate abyss?

He chuckled again and dialled.

"Senator Schroeder, it's Senator Wilkes," he said to the recorded message.

"Just down in Texas but I'll be back bright and early on Monday morning and wanted to know if you'd like to meet to discuss the timeline and targets in your bill…"

He paused, trying to prevent a smile from creeping into his voice. Let her think he was calling because he actually didn't have the votes; she'd learn the truth soon enough.

"What do you think about moving the target down to 40%, or the timeline out to 2035? Give me a call, I'll be in the office Monday morning, early."

Hanging up, Joe allowed himself the smile: he was a political junkie and he knew it. Now to put Clayton out of his misery and into his place.

Clayton opened with smarmy pleasantries; Joe cut to the chase.

"Listen here, Clay. I'm none too pleased with your little performance last weekend, threatening Hayden's memory…"

Joe paused for a moment and rolled his eyes.

"Spare me the sob story, Clay. You're richer than God and we both know it. I had a good think about it, and the mission is still a go. But know this Clay, we're switching up the government not because of your stack of cash but because we need a government we can work with: one that's gonna give us a fair price for that oil. Otherwise, our economy's headed straight back into the toilet…"

Joe stopped, obviously interrupted.

"What do you mean, 'a problem'?"

This time Joe listened intently for a moment. Then he pulled out a chair and sat down, his face falling.

"Just how in hell did Kulkulcan figure *that* out?"

Joe slammed his fist into the table.

"You *told* him? Why in hell did you do that?! No, never mind the why… how in hell did you even *find* him?! He's in the middle of the goddamned jungle!"

Joe stood again and started pacing, his free hand clenching and releasing, desperate for something to hit. Fifteen minutes later, his face grim, Joe stood in front of the dark window, phone still to his ear, and sighed.

"Lordecita daCal, hunh? You really are a political ignoramus, Clayton. She's Raul Vargas' *wife*. Threatening me was an infantile prank and you can cross me off your Christmas card list for it, but this? You've just put our boys down there—there's one with each goddamned cell—in a world of hurt, and if they can't actually kill Kulkulcan do you realize what happens? You get him as President and you can kiss your fat wad of cash goodbye forever… ."

Joe paused as Powell interrupted him once more, and then closed his eyes and shook his head.

"Jeezuz H. Christ, Clayton. The power of the game gone to your head? You've just diddled all of Mexico to get your money back and you don't even give a rat's ass… No, *you* listen here: don't do another damned thing. I'm gonna try to undo this mess. It's probably not too late to send word to the field to just make Kulkulcan disappear…"

Joe hung up and put his free hand to his forehead. Why was it that stupid people could come up with ideas that smart people couldn't even imagine? Like children who could open childproof caps when the damn things stymied every adult in the house. Joe went back to the dining room table, took a swig of watery scotch, and scowled.

So Clayton had called Lordecita daCal. To an oilman like Clay, in a panic over being unable to reach Joe to determine if his threat had worked, that would be the obvious thing to do: call another oilman. Or woman. They were different people, the oil-rich: a fractious group, but brethren in a way the merely wealthy couldn't imagine. It didn't hurt that daCal was married to Vargas, the man chosen to survive the bloodletting and take the Mexican presidency.

Joe crunched on the last of his ice and considered the conversation Clayton must have had.

"Hey Lo, this nationalizing really hurts, don't it? Wouldn't it be nice if your hubby could have the reins and make a few changes? Oh, by the way, whaddoya know about that terrorist calling himself Kulkulcan? He's got everybody nervous, does he? The President is running scared and trying to cover up Kulkulcan's work, are they? You think it would help your hubby if I sent a few boys down to make the guerrilla disappear, quiet like? It would? You get me my oil money back and I'll do it, you know, but just one thing…where do I find the bugger?"

And that's where Clay's dumb luck had been miraculous: daCal had a bodyguard who had a cousin who was right inside Kulkulcan's camp, running deliveries. And she, daCal, would get Clay the contact info because oilfolk trust oilfolk.

Except that Clay used the contact—a guy named Alvarro—to get in touch with Kulkulcan himself. And of course, because Clayton always had horseshoes up his ass, he got Kulkulcan on the phone right away and told him—actually *told* him—to watch his back because the Americans might just be double crossing him.

The worst part of it all, Joe thought morosely, was that there really was honour among thieves: if Kulkulcan did avoid death and did take the Presidency, he would find a way to get Clay his lost money. Even as the rest of the US economy went into free-fall.

Christ on the cross. Joe was going to have to wake up a bunch of people in Washington. Starting with Honey. He got her voice-mail.

"Honey? Where the hell are you? We got a situation here, thanks to Clayton—you can tell me 'I told you so' when this is over—but I got to get to a couple of people right away. And I need you to…

Joe paused at the sound of a grouse outside—wings beating, gabbling noisily—startled by something.

"Sorry, something spooked a bird outside… I was saying Clayton has gone and…"

Voicemail continued to record, but the playback would not contain the damning news of Clayton's treachery. Honey would instead hear the sickening thump of something heavy connecting with flesh, followed by a grunt, the scrape of furniture against hardwood, and the thud of a great weight falling to the floor. And then there would be a new pair of voices, their accents thick:

"¡*Uay, Alvarro*! ¡*Lo Tengo*!" said the first. *I have him.*

"¡*Cuidado*!" barked the second. "*El chico debe permanecer vivo, por ahora.*" *He must stay alive, for now.*

SUNDAY, DECEMBER 16, 2012
12 MEN, DAY OF THE EAGLE

HURRICANE TRIPLE WHAMMY EXPECTED: GULF BATTENS DOWN

December 16, 2012, Miami (AP)

The National Hurricane Centre (NHC) reported this afternoon that a series of three tropical storms have formed off the coast of western Africa—a situation unprecedented this late in the year. Tropical Storm Sigma, *named on Friday, December 14th, has been joined by Tropical Storms* Tau *and* Upsilon, *both of which have sustained wind speeds of 39mph (62 kph).* Tau *and* Upsilon *are the 47th and 48th named storms of the 2012 hurricane season.*

"It's extraordinary, especially this late in the season," said Dr. Kathy Howlachuk, Director of the NHC, from her office in Miami, FL. "The common wisdom is that there is only enough energy in the Basin for one storm every week or so. We've got three out there now." Howlachuk went on to say that shifting wind patterns over the Atlantic Ocean might stall Sigma, *allowing the second and third storms to catch up, creating a super-storm. The last time this occurred was in 2005, when Tropical Storm Iris collapsed into Hurricane Wilma, strengthening the latter over the Yucatán.*

Hurricane intensity has been growing since the 1970s, with the number of Category 4 and 5 storms increasing by 67% in the forty years since.

Controversial at first, this increase in intensity has now been confirmed by the Intergovernmental Panel on Climate Change (IPCC) as consistent with human-induced climate change. Rising sea surface temperatures are to blame: since 1990, the waters of the Gulf of Mexico have risen by 2.5 degrees centigrade. Says Dr. Peter Nguyen, also of the NHC, "It doesn't sound like much, but that adds a huge amount of energy, in the form of heat, to the system. It's the equivalent, really, of 3 million Hiroshima-sized atomic bombs. With all that [extra energy], you can see why they [the storms] are getting stronger."

Countries and companies are struggling to keep ahead of the larger storms: the levees in New Orleans have survived, thanks in part to the 450-million-dollar revegetation effort that has seen a return of the storm-attenuating marshes at the mouth of the Mississippi. The Dominican Republic, however, lost more than half of its waterfront resorts to Hurricanes Helene and Michael earlier this year.

Then there is the spectre of oil. After Katrina in 2005, the petroleum industry redoubled its efforts to strengthen their offshore rigs. Mitnal, the deepest installation now in place, has been engineered to these new standards but has never actually faced winds of Sigma*'s strength. And even if Mitnal survives and no new oil leaks into the Gulf, the ghost of oil past could come back to haunt: great rivers of oil from the 2010* Deepwater Horizon *disaster remain hanging between layers of deep cold water.* Sigma*'s unprecedented strength could churn up those millions of gallons of oil. People are terribly worried that, no matter what,* Sigma *will bring a black rain: pollution the beleaguered Gulf can ill-afford.*

CHAPTER 46

Still recovering from injuries and coma, Rebecca needed rest well before they made it to Calakmul; Stephen insisted they stop overnight at the tiny hotel in Xpuhil to sleep and make macgyvers; in the light of the next day they could make their way into Kulkulcan's camp. There was awkwardness over how many rooms to rent; Stephen promised honour so they took a single room with two double beds and, exhausted, fell asleep almost instantly, one to each bed.

Rebecca woke to a loud pop and the smell of smoke.

"What's burning?" she demanded as she sat bolt upright. It smelled too much like the night in the forest with Yaxché, and she found herself shaking.

"Just testing the pine cones. They work like a charm," Stephen said from the bathroom. "Sorry to wake you like that… I didn't think they'd be so loud! Sleep well?"

"Like a rock… what the hell?" she said as she blinked sleep from her eyes and surveyed the room. It looked as if a dozen oversized gerbils had come and gone in the night: a half dozen items with wires sticking from them littered the room.

"I've been up for a while," Stephen said sheepishly. "Working. Can I have that butane and the baby powder now?"

"Sure…" Rebecca replied, reaching for the pack beside her bed. "That looks like a car radio… And what time is it?"

"Almost noon. Yes, it is a car radio, and before you say anything, I promise I'll pay for the damage deposit. I took one of the speakers, too. If we bring it and the car battery in with us, it will be a great distraction…"

Sunday, December 16, 2012 — 12 Men, Day of the Eagle

Rebecca was torn between anger and wonderment; the contrition on Stephen's face when he peered from the bathroom made her decide in favour of the latter, and she laughed out loud at his handiwork.

"I bet we could just say the car was broken into… What else have you got going on here? Can I help?"

"Everything is just about done…"

Rebecca smiled again.

"What?"

"I like the way Canadians say 'about.'"

"We say house, too." He raised the diphthong, narrowing it from the American version. "And 'eh.' I'm told Americans think it makes us sound quite charming."

"Absolutely," Rebecca replied before she could censor herself.

"I'll have to remember to say it more often then, eh?" Stephen ribbed.

"Funny," Rebecca shot back, reddening. "Now show me what all this is and what's left to do."

Stephen led Rebecca around his private skunkworks.

"Okay, so you know about the radio. We can set it up and then start it remotely…"

"How?"

"String and matches. The string keeps the circuit open; when the match burns through it, the circuit closes and the radio goes on."

"Very nice," Rebecca nodded. "What's next?"

Stephen showed her Molotov cocktails, made from plastic water bottles filled with gasoline siphoned from the car; basic teargas made from chili powder and Coke, activated by shaking a gelatine capsule filled with sodium bicarbonate; and the remains of one of the pine cones.

Rebecca looked at the burnt husk in the bathtub. "You really did watch a lot of MacGyver, didn't you?"

"Yeah, well, you know what they say: 'and the geek shall inherit the Earth'…"

Rebecca laughed again.

"I'm all for that, if it keeps us alive. What are you going to do with the butane and baby powder?"

"Fireworks, kind of. I'll show you, but first help me finish the radio: I need more than two hands to connect the speaker. Have a seat and hold these."

Stephen handed the speakers and radio to Rebecca once she was seated on the edge of the bed; he then turned to get a few tools from the room's small desk.

"Can any of this stuff kill anyone?" Rebecca asked, her tone serious.

Stephen returned, tools in hand, and sat down beside Rebecca.

"Shouldn't do. I'm not a big fan of killing," he replied, his voice equally grave. "One or two of these things *could* really hurt someone, but not the way we're going to use them. Set on jury-rigged timers at a distance, they'll just create a distraction so that we can get in, get Chalo, and get back out."

"What if he doesn't want to leave? Anya made it sound like he actually *wanted* to join the revolution."

"I know Chalo. Maybe there is something in it that appeals to him—he had a rough go of it in Guatemala as a kid—but I'm sure I can talk him out of it. And you never know—maybe he's just pretending."

"Why would he do that?"

"You never can tell with Chalo. Wheels within wheels, he says. Like the Mayan calendar. Can you tear me a strip of duct tape?"

Rebecca reached for the silvery tape, unrolled a short strip, and cut it with her teeth.

"You always carry duct tape?"

"Yup."

"Why?"

"Because I can't sew worth a damn?"

"No! Really?"

"No. I mean, it's true that I can't sew, but the duct tape? It's just really… useful. 'Be prepared,' and everything."

"Let me guess: you were a Boy Scout, too, right?"

"'Fraid so," he said, looking down to twist the tape around a pair of stripped wires. "I'm a caricature Canadian, eh?"

"Stephen?" Something in her voice made Stephen look up.

"What? Is everything okay?"

"Remember yesterday when you said… you said… that you wanted…"

Stephen swallowed hard, surprised. He felt his heart start to thunder.

"To kiss you?"

"Do you still want to?"

"Unh hunh…"

The same lock of hair that had fallen loose over her forehead the night he had operated on her shoulder was loose again. He put down what he was working on and brushed the lock aside; the sensation made him catch his breath.

Rebecca moved the things on her lap aside and leaned in towards Stephen.

"You smell good," he whispered, close enough now to know that she washed her hair with something that smelled like almonds. He traced a soft line across Rebecca's cheek, over her lips, down her chin, to the top button of her shirt.

"You too," Rebecca whispered as she leaned in further, let her hand drop to his knee, and started sliding her palm up his thigh.

"Oh my god, you're beautiful," Stephen said softly. "I thought so the minute I saw you."

"Me too you," Rebecca replied, so close that Stephen could feel her breath on his lips.

"You're sure you want to do this?" he asked, pausing a moment before starting to unbutton her shirt.

"You mean 'will I respect you in the morning'?" Rebecca smiled, her lips almost grazing his.

"Un hunh…"

"It's already morning," Rebecca whispered.

Stephen sighed as he tasted Rebecca's lips, felt her tongue, felt his body, electric with desire.

A thunderous banging at the door made them recoil. Stephen grabbed instinctively for the gun lying on the bed and crept forward towards the door; Rebecca grabbed a bottle of ersatz teargas, threw a comforter over the rest of the arsenal on the bed, and hid in the bathroom.

"*¿Quién está*?" Stephen asked.

"Stephen Catherwood?" came the reply through the door.

"Chalo?"

"*¡Uay*, Esteban, it *is* you! Thank God! Can you let me in? I've been up all night."

Stephen took a step forward and then checked himself.

"Are you alone, *amigo*?"

"As lonely as a leper, my friend."

Stephen smiled. A joke probably meant Chalo was telling the truth. Still, Stephen took a position at the jamb as a precaution, his gun levelled at head height, then slid the room's deadbolt open.

"Come in, then."

The handle turned and the door swung in, Chalo following it, his own gun at the ready.

"Ah, so we do *this* dance again, Esteban? One day we going to really hurt each other!"

"I don't shoot my friends. Although I might make an exception for you. How did you find me?"

"By chance. I borrowed a car. I walked. I stopped here for something to eat and saw a cannibalized rental car that looked like Rebecca's parked in front. So I knocked."

"Borrowed?"

"It's a long story, *hermano*. I need to sit down," Chalo replied, heading for the farther of the room's two rumpled beds.

"Whoa, whoa, don't sit there…" warned Rebecca, emerging from the bathroom. "Sit there instead," she said, pointing to the room's single rickety chair.

"Rebecca? This *is* a surprise…" Chalo said, looking at Stephen with a raised eyebrow and sly grin as he did so.

"My Esteban in a hotel room with a girl… will wonders never cease?!"

"Yeah yeah, shut up. Your timing sucks," Stephen said, his tone equal measures of annoyance and relief. "Just say thank you to the nice lady, take the chair, and tell us what the hell you're doing here…"

"Thank you, nice lady," Chalo grinned. "I think I should ask you what the hell you're doing here, instead?"

"On our way to rescue you. Unnecessarily, apparently," Rebecca replied dryly. "Anya said you'd joined Kulkulcan's little army, and Yaxché sent us out to get you back."

"You saw Anya? Where? Is she alright?"

"Fine. Right pissed with you, though. She's on her way to her ruin with Yaxché. Why'd you tell her you wanted to join Kulkulcan?" Stephen replied.

"I thought I was doing it to save her life but I was in above my head.

After a while I believed in him for real, I think. You said it yourself: I'm always looking to belong."

"What made you wake up?"

"Because he can actually do what he says: he's going to kill the president and most of the cabinet in four days and take over the country for himself."

"Oh god, no!" Rebecca breathed, horrified. "I have to call Washington…"

"Don't bother. Washington started it."

"Well they can stop it, then," Rebecca retorted.

"No, they can't. They have lost control. Kulkulcan is a lying madman, believing his mythology only when it suits him, but he is very, very smart. He somehow got word the Americans were going to trick him—I helped him prove it—and he sent Alvarro…."

"Alvarro?" Stephen demanded.

"…sent Alvarro to kidnap a senator to make sure the American Marine won't stop the assassinations."

"A senator? Joe…?" Rebecca asked, afraid of the answer.

"Tall fat man, from Texas? Yes."

"Out of curiosity," Stephen interrupted, "how do you know the guy was from Texas, how do you know it was Alvarro that did the kidnapping, and how did you get out of Kulkulcan's camp without anyone freaking out?"

"He was wearing a Texas A&M shirt, *hermano*. And I told you it was a long story. How about we get some food, and I will tell you everything?"

"How about we get you food on the road and you can tell us the story while we drive?" Rebecca blurted.

"I just got here!" Chalo objected.

"Yeah, sorry about that," Rebecca replied as she stood and started to strap her knapsack closed. "But we need to go get Joe."

"I thought you hated him?" Chalo demanded.

"Yup. I've wished him dead maybe a million times But not dead like this."

"I thought you were going to call Washington. Why don't you have them send in the rescue team?" Chalo protested.

Rebecca paused. "I thought about that, you know. There's the satellite phone and everything. But you said four days. There's no way in hell that I can convince enough people in that time. And even if I did, there's a hurricane on the way that will slow everyone down. I think we're his best bet."

Stephen had been very quiet, thinking about all that Rebecca and Chalo were saying. The mention of the storm jolted him, surprised, back to the present moment.

"Hurricane? What hurricane?"

"*Sigma*. My aunt told me when I spoke to her. It's a big one, heading straight for us. Sorry I didn't tell you before; I didn't think it would matter."

Stephen looked puzzled for a moment and then moved to the bed to start packing the improvised weaponry. Chalo looked from Rebecca to Stephen.

"You're not agreeing with her are you, Esteban? It's crazy! You can't just walk back in there and kidnap a kidnapped old man!"

"We were going to walk in there and kidnap you…" Stephen said.

"¡*Uay, hermano*! I'm not old!"

"What's your point, Chalo?"

"It's an army camp, *caballero*. They have lots of guns. And a heat ray…"

Stephen and Rebecca both stopped short and looked at Chalo.

"A what?!" they said in unison.

"It's why he's sending Anya's brother to the Mitnal rig…"

"Anya's brother?" Stephen demanded. "Mitnal?" Rebecca asked at the same time. Chalo stopped them.

"Listen, it is a very long story. I can explain it all to you, but not before I have had some food and some sleep. Or maybe some sleep and some food. Nor should you head off now anyway: you'll be trying to find the camp in the dark."

"But…" Rebecca began to object.

"It is a fool's quest, Rebecca," Chalo said earnestly. "Kulkulcan is mad, but he is still a brilliant and dangerous enemy… maybe even more so for his madness. I think you might have made it in to bring me out, unannounced and unexpected, but now that I have left he will be on guard. I could get you in, I think, but I would have to be careful and we would have to be clever. And I'm too tired to be either…"

Rebecca looked to Stephen. She watched as he paused, furrowed his brow, and then nodded.

"I hate to admit it, but he's right," Stephen said to Rebecca. "We've only got one shot at this. And it'll be really really hard to set up the stuff in the dark. How about we finish up the radio while Chalo rests and then we'll have dinner, work out the details, sleep a little, and leave before first light?"

Rebecca frowned.

"I don't really have a choice, do I?"

Stephen and Chalo shook their heads, the synchrony of brothers in their movements.

"What if Joe dies before the morning?" Rebecca asked, a last effort to change the men's minds.

Chalo rubbed his eyes and looked at Rebecca seriously. "My grandmother says only the gods decide our fates. I can't promise anything, but Kulkulcan would be a fool to let his insurance policy die, and as I said, he is not a fool."

Rebecca hesitated a moment longer and sighed. "Fine. The radio it is."

"And I thought when I saw you I had wasted our time on these…" Stephen said as he pulled the coverlet off the macgyvers.

Chalo stared at the jerry-rigged mayhem-makers and then grinned. Despite himself, Stephen grinned back. It was stupid and dangerous, but it might be fun. And the best part? They were working together once more. Rebecca shook her head and then she, too, grinned.

CHAPTER 47

"You are smart, *mi hija*, but stubborn as a *burro*," Yaxché said with a sigh. "I will say it once more: it is *not* the same as at Calakmul."

Yaxché and Anya had arrived at Anya's archaeological site in Sian Ka'an late the night before; they now stood inside the temple looking up at the dome, bickering like a long-married couple.

"Certainly it is the same!" Anya insisted. "I was just there! I saw it! There are the *bacabs*…" she said, pointing to the four cardinal directions, "… and there is the story of the Hero Twins…"

Yaxché frowned.

"I will prove it to you," Anya said irritably as she pulled her camera from the thigh pocket of her cargo shorts.

"Look here," Anya said, scrolling through the photographs. "Starting in the East is *lakin*, the first *bacab*." She pointed to the same figure on the ceiling before turning back to the camera and scrolling onward.

"Then the story of creation. Then the southern *bacab—nohul—* followed by the story of the Hero Twins." Again she pointed out the equivalent figures on the ceiling.

"You are truly my East, *Lakin*. Hurrying like the beginning of the day, you are! And too busy looking to see! Those machines, they make everyone blind," he scoffed. "And a little stupid, too."

Anya stiffened.

"Yes, it makes you angry, but it is the truth. And you need to be angry to see outside your camera, hmm? Look bigger. See the whole thing."

Anya felt her temper flare then go out. She wanted to know what he saw more than she wanted to be right. "Show me what *you* see," she said irritably.

"From *chik'in*, direction of the sun's setting, begins the story of a ceremony, yes?"

Anya looked. Along the perimeter, from West, through North, and back to East, a grand ceremony had been painted. She fought the temptation to say that it was the same scene she had seen depicted at Dzibanché and Calakmul.

"Yes."

"And are the gods being honoured the same ones everywhere?"

Anya started to look down at her camera and hesitated. Yaxché laughed.

"Yes, you can use the machine."

Anya scrolled.

"At Calakmul, it is *Chac*."

"God of Rain. Good. And at Dzibanché?

Anya flipped through another bunch of pictures.

"It looks like… like *Gukamatz*?"

"The Bat. Good. And who is it here?"

Anya looked up at the ceiling and her jaw dropped. How could she have missed that?

"It is *Hurukan*. The same one named on the *stela* outside"

"God of Wind and Storm. Good. And what about Dzibanché?"

Despite his disdain for the camera, Yaxché watched the screen as Anya flipped through the pictures. Suddenly he grabbed her wrist.

"Stop! What was that?"

The camera skipped through two pictures before Anya took her finger off the scroll button, rolling the display back to the earliest photos in the queue.

"That? That is one of my tourists. Amateur archaeologists. They help me dig in exchange for the experience…" Anya began.

"No, no… after," Yaxché said excitedly, stabbing his finger at the display.

Anya clicked forward to the photos of the map she had sketched in the dust on the temple floor at Calakmul.

"This?"

"Yes! What is this?"

"Just some notes I made at Calakmul. I had no paper so I used the floor to think."

"And what did you think?"

"I'm not sure. It is crazy, really. Not in any of the literature."

"What did you think?" Yaxché insisted.

"That Dzibanché pointed to the date Calakmul should be built, Calakmul pointed to the date this temple should be built, and this points to a date Chich'en Itzá should be built. But then I have the dates mixed up, because the date on the *stela* is a European date, not a Maya one…"

"No, no! Look at the pattern! What do you see?"

"I see the Yucatán. I see cities on a map…"

"*Uay*. Seeing again. Not looking."

"Grouchy," Anya muttered under her breath as she turned back to the camera.

"Ha!" hooted Yaxché. "You are the sky calling water blue! But you are right, I am grouchy. I am the *curandero* and a great thing needs healing. I should know this. But so much was taken from us that I have a broken cup and only a few of the pieces. You hold the other ones, and I want them. I grab for them and when you don't give them, it makes me very grouchy."

"But I don't know them, *Don* Yaxché!" Anya said plaintively.

"You *do*, *mi hija*," he said gently. "You just do not *know* that you know them. Let us try again. I will start by saying what I know, maybe unlocking something *you* know, hmm?"

Anya chuckled ruefully. She was indeed teaching what she needed to learn.

"Now look at your map like a picture instead of a map. What shapes do you see? Like this line, here, that joins Dzibanché, Calakmul, and here at Sian Ka'an?"

Anya shook her head.

"They are the hearth stones, are they not?"

Anya gaped as she finally saw what Yaxché saw. "How incredibly stupid not to have seen that," she said in wonderment.

"The Earth has a pulse. Did you know that?" Yaxché asked, a *non sequitur*.

"What?" Anya asked, now both demoralized and confused.

"Yes. An energy. It flows like blood in the heart of the planet. It is strong and it is weak. Do you follow me?"

Anya nodded. Foremost Mayanists Linda Schele and David Friedel had established that, for the Maya, the Earth was filled with sacred spaces. This matrix of power points was established by the gods and strengthened by human prayer and devotion, principle among which was the construction of pyramids over these sacred sites.

"Like the stars that wheel in the sky, the energy moves beneath the ground, yes?" Yaxché continued.

Anya nodded again. Schele, Friedel, and other Mayanists had discovered that while some power points were fixed, others seemed to shift in space through the course of time: new pyramids were built to strengthen new power points, and old ones were sometimes abandoned when the power was exhausted.

"Yes…" she said slowly. She understood what he was saying, but not what he was driving at.

"And where the energy is strongest is the best place to cross worlds… to speak to the gods above and below, yes?"

"Yes," Anya replied again. Schele was particularly eloquent on this point: kings, channelling the gods from atop their pyramids could, over successive generations, create such a sacred point that the membrane separating the human and Other worlds grew gossamer thin, as easy for a king or shaman to step through as a spider's web.

"So we build and rebuild our temples on those sacred spots for the times when we need to speak with the gods, hmm?"

"That would mean each temple points to a place and time when a special ceremony," she looked up to the ceiling, "… *that* ceremony, must be performed?"

"Exactly, *mi hija*."

"I…I still don't understand…" Anya faltered.

"When was Calakmul built?" Yaxché prompted.

"Almost fifteen hundred years ago."

"And what happened to my people then? *Gukamatz* is a bat. A darkness. Were they beset by something terrible? A sickness, perhaps?

"No…" Anya began slowly, thinking aloud. "No, but there is a school of thought that says there was a terrible darkness and drought about then, a year without summer, everywhere on the whole planet, caused by the dust and ash from a volcano called Krakatoa. It erupted in 535 CE—about the time the *caracol* at Calakmul was built…"

The connection seemed, on one hand, absurdly far-fetched, and yet, on another level, it made a strange kind of sense.

"The ceremony at Calakmul was to appease *Gukamatz* and ask him to bring the sun back?"

"And what happened at the time *this* palace was built? The painting at Calakmul says to honour *Chac*—was there, perhaps, a time without rain?" Yaxché asked. This time he seemed to know the answer; something that belonged to the long oral history he had memorized as a young healer-in-training.

There had indeed been a drought; it had started as early as 900 CE and lasted more than 500 years. The theories for it were myriad: a shift in the Earth's axis; solar flares; aliens. The newest, and most widely accepted, was that the cutting of the forest to burn the limestone to make the lime to paint the pyramids changed the face of the land so much that the rains stopped falling over the Yucatán and the *cenotes* and crops began to dry up. The Maya were actually in decline before the Spanish arrived; many had already left the large cities and gone back to the land. There were those who thought that the Maya might in fact have regained their former glory had the Spanish not arrived.

She told the theory to Yaxché.

"So maybe the Spanish were our punishment for thinking we could take from the land without giving back to her heart?" mused Yaxché.

Anya had advocated the theory that the Maya were pattern-watchers to Stephen a few days—what seemed like an entire lifetime—ago without truly believing it. It had been predicated on reading a date incorrectly; she had discredited herself in the temple at Dzibanché. Now Yaxché was positing the very thing she had argued then dismissed. Even if it was true, how was it possible?

"But how can it be, *Don* Yaxché? How could they know, so far in advance, that these things would happen?"

"You know much, *Lakin*. What do you know of the snake dreams?"

Like many cultures, dreams—their interpretation and their use as a tool for divination—were important to the Maya. In particular, Maya healers like Yaxché practiced lucid dreaming, both observing and interacting with their dreams to gain wisdom from the unconscious. Snake dreams were potent divination dreams, claimed by some to be held in purpose-built chambers like the one in which they now stood, dreams in which the gods imparted to the most senior shamans knowledge of particularly important or dangerous events.

For Anya, it was easy to accept that *curandero*s might tap into a collective unconscious, producing vague signs that, interpreted in context, could yield what appeared to be prophecy. And the Maya did not believe the future was immutable, that prophecies could not be changed. But seeing a volcanic eruption a hundred years before it occurred? Or a global drought?

"You mean vision dreaming?"

"Of course, *mi niña.* Time is round and the future is the past. We dream what has happened and what will happen. The gods tell us when, and then we write our notes, not only on paper, but in our buildings, as they are also written in the sky."

"Please, Yaxché, I am not trying to be stupid, but what are you saying? That a shaman has a serpent vision of a great or terrible thing a hundred—maybe even five hundred—years before it happens?"

"Yes. And then his king builds a *caracol* to commemorate the vision and provide instructions for the next time…"

"Wait, wait," Anya said urgently, trying to grasp what he was saying. "If we use this *caracol* as the example, a shaman had a vision seven hundred years ago to tell the story of a terrible thing that will happen and his king had it painted in the fresco above us?"

"Yes," Yaxché nodded.

"And the date on which the terrible thing will happen—that is the date on which the stars named beside the portals will actually shine *through* the portals?"

Yaxché nodded again.

"And the *place* it will happen is the one named on the bottom of the *stela* outside?"

"Almost right. Not the place where the bad thing will happen, but the place where the *ceremony* painted above us must happen. The ceremony where, like lawyers, we argue with the gods for our deliverance."

Anya had argued for the Maya to have profound predictive abilities but this defied logic. It implied not merely that they could predict the future, but that prayer could alter it.

"How can a ceremony prevent a volcano, or a flood, or…" she looked up at the storm god on the ceiling, "…or a hurricane?"

"Never the words alone, *mi niña*. But change one little thing and the whole world is altered, hmm? Like when a bee visits my corn or does not. If it visits, my corn grows: I eat, do work, heal patients, save a life. But if not? I starve and others die, too.

"It is why we call it the hinge time. Things may go one way or another, depending on the argument we make to the gods. If they believe that we will change our ways, then prosperity will return. But sometimes they are not convinced. Sometimes they punish us for our bad ways. Just because children apologize does not mean they escape discipline, no?"

Anya realized that it wasn't ancient myth: it was modern physics. Chaos theory. The Butterfly Effect and its opposite, the Black Swan Event: the rare, large, completely unexpected event that changed the world. These were the things on which Mayan prophecy was based.

Could it really be that the shaman who had had the vision here in this place so long ago had foreseen the global environmental decline against which Sebastian now battled? Was *Hurukan* a literal storm—a hurricane—that was going to demolish the region?

"*Tun tal cha'ak*?" she asked. "A storm is coming?"

Rather than answering, Yaxché began to recite.

"*Knowledge is lost, of Heaven and Earth and shame. The men of god, their backs to the virgin Earth, will disappear and the pride of the wise men will begin. False leaders will call forward the darkness and the balance will be undone.*"

"*Mein Gott…*" Anya whispered softly. "Chalo was reciting that. He said his grandmother told him…"

"Indeed? It is an old story. His grandmother was a *curandera*, I think."

He paused and then resumed the poem.

"*Life will wither. Those who dip their mug to the bottom, those who stretch everything to the breaking point: they bruise the world. Innocents will die a heartless death, birds and men alike. And so it will come to pass that the Earth will burn.*"

Anya shuddered. It sounded like Sebastian describing myriad environmental ills.

"*The call of Lord Balam, the night cat, will signal the start of the end.*"

Anya thought about Stephen and his meeting on the highway with

Xtabay. He'd heard a jaguar cry. She shook her head at herself, seeing patterns where maybe there were none.

"*The Moon will have white circles of rain; the sky will be soaked and arrowed for the Lord of Heaven is offended. Famine and plagues and disease will come with terrible stride; the leaves of the chili plants will die. Abundance will wane, and bitterness wax, until the night creatures rise; the sky beast and the bat and the owl, carrying the wandering stone and the snake's rattle, within the dark path, the sky bejewelled.*"

Anya looked up at the dome and her knees weakened: the night creatures were there—all of them—each beside its own stellar aperture. Mars the sky beast; Pisces which the Maya called *zotz*, the bat; Taurus 'the owl'; the 'wandering stone' that was Jupiter or Saturn; the Pleiades that the Maya knew as 'the snake's rattles.' And all of them lay on the winter's dark arm of the Milky Way.

"*Don* Yaxché… they're all up there…"

Yaxché nodded and continued.

"*The five eyes will come even as the ocelot eats betana; the Holy Tree will cradle them.*"

The holy tree would be Yaxché himself, but if these were references to individuals, who were the five eyes? Even if they were pairs of eyes, she, Chalo, Stephen, and Rebecca only made four.

"*Then will come the time when the writings on the walls will speak, at last, and at last be understood again. They will tell the one to call the judges and the five will plead for mercy, plead for the evils to be banished again, as the Heroes did before. Then will the spirits come to their city, Hurukan, xekik, and the mysterious Kulkulcan.*"

The figures painted on the north side of the wall seemed to ripple, the ceremony itself come to life. Anya itemized the figures as Yaxché spoke them: the gods as judges; the *bacabs* in their quarters; *Hurukan* presiding; *Kulkulcan* full of wrath; terrifying *Tohil*, mouth bloody as with the disease known as *xekik*. She shuddered again. Probably only a metaphor for death, but *Tohil*, among all gods in the pantheon, was most terrifying. Beside him, unnamed in the poem at least, stood the *Vucub Caquix*—Jade Macaw—the symbol of greed and arrogance. Why him?

Yaxché continued to recite.

"*The Itzás will arrive in the wake of these three. The souls of the dead will groan in the catacombs of the stone city of the Itzás.*"

That would be the ceremony that needed to occur at Chich'en Itzá.

"*Until, at last, time will stop. He will raise their symbol on high, the Tree of Life. Everything will change at once. The change will be manifest to all as the quetzal voice sounds. The successor to the Tree of the Land will appear. And the war will not be lost, here in this land, because the world will be reborn.*"

Yaxché fell silent, the ancient poem complete.

"But Chich'en Itzá is already built…"

"It is the place, *mi hija*, not the building! The pulse of the Earth is strong beneath Chich'en Itzá, and the time to speak to the gods returns there often!" Yaxché chastised. "What matters is when. You are here because you can read the date up there. Read! Do your part so that I may do mine!" Despite his best efforts, Yaxché's exasperation was beginning to show.

Anya took out her iPhone, opened the star-mapping application, advanced the time slider on a hunch, and held it up to the ceiling to compare star fields. They matched.

The date above her was 12.19.19.17.19. The day before 13.0.0.0.0; the new *b'ak'tun*.

"December 20, 2012—3 *Cauac*, Day of Storm," Anya said slowly.

Yaxché tapped his fingers to his thumb in succession.

"*12 Men, 13 Cib, 1 Caban, 2 Etznab, 3 Cauac…*" he muttered before looking up. He sighed with relief, worry lines disappearing.

"We have time. A little only, but it will be enough."

Anya was going to get to see a ceremony—the mother of all ceremonies—after all. She shuddered at the truism, "be careful what you wish for." If Yaxché was right, she was about to be part of a ceremony to determine the future of the world and humanity's place in it.

"Come, now. We go. The drive back is long." Yaxché said perfunctorily as he left the temple.

By the time Anya's eyes had adjusted to the light outside, Yaxché was halfway down the temple. He was remarkably nimble for his age; she watched him with admiration before noticing a thin fog at ground level. It was getting larger despite a mid-morning heat that should burn away all mist—was it something in her eye? Anya blinked but the fog remained, blossomed, took a human shape. Was it *Xtabay*, at last?

The figure looked up at Anya, eyes flashing red, and spoke. Yaxché stopped at the sound, audible only after the spectre's lips had finished moving.

"*Bix tin k'aaba*?" she said, the words delayed, the tone voice challenging.

"*Xtabay*..." Anya said softly.

The red in the ghosts eyes faded to brown. A Cheshire smile crossed her face as she faded away.

Yaxché turned to look up the pyramid and cackled.

"I saw her, *Don* Yaxché. She asked me her name."

"And did you speak it?"

"I... I did. Why did her eyes change?"

"She's a woman! She does not like to be scorned or ignored! But now you name her and are forgiven. Now do you believe, really?"

Anya had believed in part—had wanted to believe but could not, rationally, accept the idea of ghosts. Chalo's friend Stephen didn't believe in ghosts either, but he had been given incontrovertible see-it-with-his-own-eyes evidence and had acquiesced to the existence of *Xtabay*; she had resented him for both his proof and his easy conversion. But now, here was her own undeniable sighting, bright in the light of morning. Something inside Anya snapped, like an elastic stretch too tight finally giving way, a painful relief. If not flesh and blood, *Xtabay* was nevertheless as real as life.

"I do. Really," Anya replied simply. The admission left her humbled and elated in equal amounts.

"Good," Yaxché smiled, "Then we go. You, too, are healed at last."

***

It was near midnight, and Kathy had been watching them on Peter Nguyen's bank of monitors all day: time series of satellite photos, new ones unfolding on the screen in front of her each hour, showing three pinwheeling storms, each spinning counter-clockwise around their own perfect eyes, bands of white cloud against deep blue water. As the day wore on, the vortices closed in upon each other, wobbled as *Tau* and *Upsilon* collided, and collapsed into a single helix. Then there were two storms—*Sigma* and the other—dancing an arc around each other over the face of the sea like lovers, drawing slowly but inexorably towards their inevitable embrace.

She heard Bender's tail thump beside her and knew that Pete was on his way down the hall.

"Like the three faces of God," she said, eyes still on the screen, when Bender rose to demand a pat from the new arrival.

"An interesting analogy for a scientist," Peter replied as he moved to see what his boss was looking at.

"Maybe I don't believe in all the religious claptrap, Pete, but every civilization there ever was has something bigger than us. They can't all be wrong. Did you know that the Maya had three spirits involved in creation, too, and that one of them was Hurricane?"

Peter knew that the word hurricane derived from the Maya word *hurukan*; he hadn't known it was the name of a god.

"The god of wind. A little like the Holy Spirit, actually: it breathed life into the world. To hash my comparison, *Hurukan* is also a little like the Indian god *Shiva*—a creator and a destroyer both. From death comes renewal."

"Now that, to use your own word, is eerie."

"Sure is. Ancient cultures have a better grasp on the unknowable than we do, don't you think?"

"Maybe, but that isn't what's eerie…"

"What is, then?"

"That you know all this stuff."

"Yeah well, my brain is like Velcro for useless facts. They're good for television, though. I'm on with Skandar again in the morning."

"Don't share that little gem," Peter said darkly.

"Why not?"

"Everyone's already in a tizzy over the Maya prediction that the world is going to end next week; you share your factoid and the tabloids will start working overtime!"

"Now that," Kathy hooted, "would be a fine little show, wouldn't it?! Too bad it would probably get me fired!"

"I'd be happy to take your job off your hands…" Nguyen replied with a twinkle in his eye.

"I'm sure you would, Doctor Nguyen. Now scat and write your bulletin, would you?"

"Already on my way," Peter laughed as he started out of her office and down the hall.

Sunday, December 16, 2012 — 12 Men, Day of the Eagle

"See you, Ben!"

The dog woofed once in reply and curled up beside his mistress once more.

***

Almost at his own desk, Peter paused for a moment. *Hurukan*, indeed. He had to admit that the idea of a huge hurricane making landfall on a date the ancient Maya had calculated as the end of the world was, if ridiculous, still a little unsettling. And then the scientist in him wondered what a stormy end of the world might be like.

MONDAY, DECEMBER 17, 2012
13 CIB, DAY OF WAX

CHAPTER 48

"Where'd your cousin go, Kulkulcan?" Travis Rutrauff asked as the rebel leader put his head under a stream of water gushing from the camp's hand-pump. It was midday and unseasonably, oppressively hot; Rutrauff had gone to the pump to try to slake his seemingly unquenchable thirst.

"That is none of your concern, Captain," Kulkulcan replied sharply. "I have sent him on an errand."

The truth was that Kulkulcan did not know where Chalo had gone and it bothered him that he might have miscalculated where the man's loyalty was concerned. Not that Chalo's disappearance would matter; the plan was too far advanced to undo, and now, with the senator as added insurance, not even Rutrauff would attempt to stop the plan. What bothered Kulkulcan more was why he had taken Chalo in in the first place, a question he could not adequately answer. He had told himself that it was because the man's experience could be useful and his obvious self-loathing co-opted, but was that it? Could it have been his own vanity instead—his own self-loathing defeating him at the moment of victory? The man's blood was enviously pure, and his age made him more challenging to co-opt than the young men Kulkulcan had been recruiting but had he wanted to possess Chalo and what he was simply to prove his own superiority?

Chalo's disappearance bothered Rutrauff for an entirely different reason: Kulkulcan's continued ability to pull rabbits from his hat—people appearing and disappearing, their roles shifting with the wind—

gave Rutrauff a pain in the pit of his stomach. If this op went as planned—as the folks back home had planned—it would be a miracle. If he, Rutrauff, lived to see the end of it… He fell back on discipline to avoid thinking about those even worse odds. "What are the next orders then, Boss?"

Kulkulcan smiled with grim satisfaction. So dependable, the Americans. "Walk with me, Captain. We have something to discuss."

Rutrauff felt the cold sweat of danger on the back of his neck.

"My cousin may be gone, but not before he found you out…"

Rutrauff felt his pulse quicken.

"Oh?"

"Let us not play cat and mouse, Captain. I know you were planning on sabotaging all but four of our assassinations. I know about the false information, and I have corrected it."

Rutrauff's heart sank even as his mind began to whirr: God only knew how Kulkulcan had gotten the correct intel, but now that he had it? Now that he had it, Rutrauff needed to identify contingencies. It took him only a split-second to conclude that there weren't any. Until Chalo's arrival, Rutrauff had been the one designated to send the final "go" confirming each target's location to each independent sniper cell—nine that were misdirects. But now it was Kulkulcan himself who would send the go orders. With accurate intel on all thirteen targets. Including Vargas. The American puppet dead with the others, it would be easy for Kulkulcan to take the country. Fuck.

Rutrauff grasped for straws.

"That intel is changing all the time. Maybe your cousin just saw some old information…"

"I admire your spirit, Captain—still trying to salvage the situation—but I have the trump card."

They had made their way to the hut that had housed Anya; Kulkulcan swung the door open and smiled, his eyes narrow with triumph.

Rutrauff looked in, nauseous first with incipient failure, then with horror. Curled in the corner in a foetal position lay an older man, large in both height and girth, his khaki pants and grey Texas A&M sweatshirt rumpled and covered with what looked like dark grease. His fists were cinched together in front of him, the knuckles badly scraped and scabbed. But it was the man's face that made Rutrauff, a hardened soldier, want to vomit: it was swollen almost beyond recognition, the lips split in several places, the nose clearly broken, the eyelids so purple and inflamed that even had the man wanted to open his eyes, it was unlikely that he could. A sniper's work, at least, was quick and clean, not slow and brutal like this.

The man in the corner winced at the sound of Rutrauff's boots as they scuffed the dirt floor. It indicated his fear of more punishment, and intimated that the injuries to the rest of the man's body, invisible beneath his clothes, were probably as bad as those to his face.

"Who is that?" Rutrauff hissed.

"Senator Joseph Wilkes," Kulkulcan said, his voice loud enough for the prisoner to hear. Wilkes recoiled at the sound.

"You're not serious!"

"Deadly, Captain," Kulkulcan said with a sweet smile. "He is my insurance policy. My way of bending you to my will. He is a member of your government—your boss—and if you do not do what I wish, I will kill him."

"You tortured him? Your insurance policy, and you put him on death's door?!"

"Don't worry, Captain Rutrauff," Kulkulcan said as he sauntered with cool pleasure to Wilkes' prone figure.

"I only remind him that the Americans do not rule the world," Kulkulcan said. The guerrilla paused, tensed, and then kicked Wilkes hard in the ribs.

Wilkes grunted; Rutrauff winced in sympathy.

"I know a man's limits; he won't die until I no longer have need of him."

Kulkulcan recoiled to kick again; this time Wilkes, his hands bound together in front of him, reached blindly, catching his tormentor's foot for a moment. He took the opportunity to be heard, his voice dry as gravel, and choked with pain and anger.

"What the hell do you want?! I'm a United States senator with twenty-seven years on the Hill. I can get you anything you want, but you have to tell me what it is!"

Kulkulcan shook his foot free and kicked Wilkes in the head.

"*You* are what I want, you imperialist bastard! You with your thinking you can meddle in my world. You with your plans to use me for your own ends. You with your idea that I am stupid…"

Kulkulcan turned from Wilkes to Rutrauff.

"You, Rutrauff, will proceed with the operation as if nothing has happened or the senator will die," Kulkulcan said, kicking Wilkes in the shoulder for emphasis.

"You will not tell Washington that you have been discovered for the liar you are, or the senator will die," Kulkulcan took two steps and kicked Wilkes in the gut.

"You will not try to stop me in *any way*, or the senator will die." This time the kick was in Wilkes' the groin.

"Don't listen," Wilkes gasped through his pain.

Kulkulcan kicked Wilkes hard in the chest, leaving the prisoner gasping for air.

"And if my threats of his death are not convincing enough, Captain Rutrauff, the senator himself will tell you that you must do as I say…"

"… a crock of shit…" croaked Wilkes.

Kulkulcan kicked Wilkes in the head and continued.

"The senator *himself* will tell you that you must do as I say, because he understands what will happen if you do not…"

"And what is that, you bastard?" Wilkes croaked.

"Your plan has always been to kill a few secretaries least friendly to your country to frighten the Mexican government back to the American fold, like the sheep you think we are. Your plan has been to blame it on me. But if you do not complete the plan as I wish it, I will destroy your country's economy: I will send the Mitnal rig to the bottom of the sea."

"You're an idiot," Wilkes croaked. "You need that oil. You won't destroy the rig."

"Of course I need the oil," Kulkulcan said sweetly. "But that assumes the President and all thirteen secretaries are killed, the country is in panic, and I take power. Then I will need the oil to finance my new kingdom. But if you sabotage my plans, what need have I of the oil? I have a bomber aboard the rig right now and if I die he will send the rig to the bottom of the sea. And with it, the American economy."

Rutrauff blinked. The pieces suddenly fell into place, the picture entirely other than the one he thought he had been looking at. Kulkulcan was a brilliant liar: Rutrauff had believed the complicated story about the

German brother–sister team of terrorists, had believed that Payal would kill the brother once the sister left the camp. But Kulkulcan had just check-mated them all and was going to take the presidency. Shit on a stick.

"Got that sewed up in a neat little bow," Rutrauff said, teeth clenched.

"I do, don't I?" Kulkulcan said, smiling charismatically.

Wilkes, eyes swollen shut and wracked with pain saw the picture Rutrauff had seen, and cursed. Not at fate, but himself. Goddammit if Becky hadn't been right: civil war was coming to Mexico. There would be no cheap Mitnal oil for the hungry US economy—maybe no oil at all. And he'd midwifed the whole thing. The depth of his hubris realized, he felt a pain far greater than his bruised body and broken bones.

"I'm sorry I got you into this mess, son," he whispered, fighting to open one eye and gaze upon Rutrauff. He could have been apologizing to his own dead boy.

Rutrauff clenched his fists, angry and impotent, unable to help the senator and unable to help himself. He was boxed in tight. He nodded to the senator but said nothing. Then he followed Kulkulcan from the hut and into the milky light of the rainy morning. He saw a white figure flit through the forest, out of the corner of his eye and only for a moment.

Xtabay.

How he wished that she had been right, and this was all a dream.

Monday, December 17, 2012 — 13 Cib, Day of Wax

CHAPTER 49

Rebecca, Stephen, and Chalo had been driving for an hour by the time the sight of Joe Wilkes had turned Travis Rutrauff's world upside-down; they were now almost at the parking lot where Chalo and Anya had been kidnapped. They would ditch the car before then to avoid Kulkulcan's pretend police-officer guarding the entrance and walk an hour through the jungle to the camp. A light rain, harbinger of the hurricane, had begun and the windshield wipers thudded rhythmically.

"Explain this to me again," Rebecca said sceptically, her eyes on the road, hands tight on the steering wheel. "We're actually going to walk into the camp and expect that Kulkulcan won't kill us first and ask questions after?"

The plan had seemed like a good one last night after dinner and a few tequilas, but now it seemed ridiculous.

"No, I'm going to walk in," Chalo corrected. "I'm going to tell Kulkulcan I wandered the wilderness searching my soul—partly true—had a vision of *Xtabay*—completely true, though not last night—and decided that being part of his war was the right thing to do…"

"True until you snapped out of it," Stephen interjected.

"And while you're explaining all this to Kulkulcan, Stephen and I are setting the macgyvers. That all makes sense. But why do you think Rutrauff has to be the one to find me?"

"That's Esteban's idea, Rebecca. I only suggested I 'find' you on my way… that you are coming to rescue the Senator…"

"All by myself. I'm either brave or stupid in this plan," Rebecca said acerbically.

"That's just it," Stephen replied. "It's not really believable that you're working on your own—no offense—so we have to provide you with something else plausible. That you've met Rutrauff before is great, actually, because Kulkulcan will think you and Rutrauff are the ones working together, removing suspicion from Chalo. And that will give Chalo free rein in camp to help get the senator out."

Rebecca shook her head. It did make a cock-eyed kind of sense, but it seemed a lot more dangerous now than it had last night.

"Okay, fine. But how do we know Kulkulcan won't shoot me anyway? And Joe along with me?"

"Two American hostages are better than one, Rebecca. Don't worry, I know how to handle Kulkulcan," Chalo said with a smile. "I was a street kid before I was a cop, and reading people kept me alive. You just set the things with Esteban and then meet me behind the barracks. I will take care of everything else," Chalo said. He was actually grinning with delight.

***

Setting the diversions had been more fun than Rebecca had expected: the work had been both painstaking—because each macgyver needed to be laid with precision—and terrifying—because in some instances they had been within feet of Kulkulcan's soldiers. But it had been fascinating to see how odds and ends could be repurposed using nothing but chemistry, ingenuity, and duct tape. Once done, she and Stephen had climbed the back of the pyramid to wait for Chalo's signal—a drink at the pump—and to go over the plan one final time.

Looking down on the semicircular clearing, huts tucked under the vegetation at the clearing's edge, they scanned the scene clockwise. Beyond the ballcourt to the pyramid's immediate left lay the barracks where Rebecca would meet Chalo. Behind this they had set the radio, speaker, and battery, its fuse a cigarette and a piece of string. Behind the next two huts—Rutrauff's and the mess—they had lain a line of Molotov cocktails. The explosives were linked by a narrow braided fuse made of strips of pillowcase and dipped in rubbing alcohol so they would explode in rapid succession. Finally, to their immediate left—between the base of the pyramid it and the enormous *cenote* that had once served its sacred well—Stephen had set his baby-powder bomb: the canister of butane, leaking slowly inside a plastic soda bottle filled with talc hanging beneath a low branch. A single shot would ignite the aerosol gas in the bottle; the canister would explode, and the talc would balloon outward, a giant smoke screen.

Once Rebecca had been "captured," Stephen would light the radio's fuse, followed by the first in the line of Molotov cocktails. That would, in theory, draw attention from the prisoner's hut, allowing Rebecca to free Joe and head to the narrow path between the *cenote* and the pyramid. Stephen and Chalo would meet them there, detonate the smokebomb, and make their escape. Not that it would be an escape, exactly: they were going to hide out in the jungle until dusk, then head for the car, preferring their chances with the night creatures to those with the boys and their guns.

"You sure it's going to work?" Rebecca asked dubiously.

"Well…"

Rebecca shot Stephen a worried look.

"What does that mean?"

"It's going to work, all right, but I'm worried we're going to start a fire. It's the end of the rainy season, but the forest is still tinder dry…"

"Thank you, Smoky the Bear," Rebecca groaned. "Look at me, I'm soaked. I don't think it's going to be a problem…"

"Yeah, and beautiful, too. But you only got wet when we climbed up here; under the canopy, we stayed dry the whole time. The rain isn't strong enough to make it to the ground."

"But still, the rain will get worse. It will put out anything that starts."

"Eventually, you're right. I'm worried about the *cenote*, too…"

Rebecca looked down at the four-hundred-foot wide sinkhole to their right, vines hanging into it, brilliant blue-green water flat and calm fifty feet below the crater's rim. It looked postcard lovely—the epitome of a tropical paradise.

"You worry a lot, you know that? What's wrong with the *cenote*?"

Stephen looked down with the eye of a geologist. The nearest edge of the sinkhole had once been perhaps two hundred feet away from the pyramid, linked ceremonially by a *sacbe*—one of the famed Mayan white roads. Over time, however, the near edge had weakened. Judging by the lush vegetation on the far rim and walls of the well, and its complete absence on this side, he'd guess the near edge had slumped catastrophically fewer than twenty years ago, dragging tons of soft limestone and most of the *sacbe* into the pool. Now only a ragged path less than five feet wide remained between the *cenote* and the pyramid. It would be loose and flaky; it might even give way under their weight.

Stephen looked at the path again and decided not to add yet another wrinkle.

"Nothing, really. It just looks narrow from here."

"Oh, good. I thought you were going to say that it might collapse. Should we go up and over the pyramid instead?"

"No, we'll lose the benefit of the smokescreen. And if Wilkes is pretty banged up, he's not going to be able to climb these steps… we'll be fine."

Rebecca nodded and then inched forward.

"Look, there's Chalo at the pump."

"Be careful, okay?" Stephen said with feeling.

Rebecca smiled and disappeared down the backside of the temple, walking on the diagonal. No one had told her; it just seemed faster that way.

CHAPTER 50

Anya and Yaxché's trip from Sian Ka'an had been long and miserable. Always busy, the roads were now almost stop-and-go congested: tourists clamouring to leave in advance of the expected hurricane; residents transporting lumber and plywood to board up windows; the inevitable accidents that came with roads slicked by the hurricane's advance rains. What should have taken five hours had taken nine. Arriving after midnight, Anya had crept into the extra hammock in Yaxché's hut and fallen asleep even before the healer had finished speaking to Lupita about what he had seen.

Anya woke slowly now, the rain's light patter on thatch soothing, and looked to Yaxché's hammock. Empty. She looked at her watch. Almost noon. Yaxché would be out collecting. In fact, would likely be back soon.

Anya sighed as she rose, her joints sore from so much sitting the previous day, then went outside in search of Lupita; she would know when Yaxché would be back. Anya's stomach grumbled and she hoped Lupita might have some food to share, as well.

The sturdy old woman was on her porch, picking stones from a bowl of dried corn, her brilliantly embroidered blouse and richly woven skirt vivid against the drizzly light. She looked up when she heard Yaxché's door clack shut and smiled, her silver-edged front teeth bright.

"Food for you?" she asked.

"*Si, muchas gracias*," Anya smiled gratefully. "*¿El Mero es en la selva*?"

A gust of wind whipped Anya's hair as she crossed the dirt road; cold and strong, it swept the treetops sideways and brought goosebumps to her arms. A small knot of long-tailed birds rose from the trees and scudded, colour flashing, in search of shelter elsewhere.

"¡*Uay*!" Lupita exclaimed, squinting against a small dust devil. "Cold like death, now. Come in for the food."

Inside, Lupita bustled to restoke the fire and warm some tortillas. One of her chickens crouched in the corner, gabbling softly.

Lupita saw Anya studying the chicken and paused.

"Silly bird, that one. Or maybe smart. She pecks at the other ones in the coop, so I bring her in here. She knows *Hurukan* comes."

"It's going to be a big one, I think. The radio said that it might be bigger than Wilma."

Anya was referring to the Category 4 storm, sister to Katrina, that had battered the Yucatán in 2005.

"Not hurricane. *Hurukan*. You understand?"

The glyph on the temple dome at Sian Ka'an flashed into Anya's mind: a vortex within a stylized square. It still defied reason and yet... here was the storm, right on schedule.

"How is it that *Don* Yaxché knows what is coming, *Señora* Lupita?" Anya asked as Lupita handed her a plate of tortillas.

"No '*Señora*'!" laughed the woman. "Only Lupita. The old stories tell. And old always comes to be new again. But most of us forget. Even the wise ones like *El Mero* not have everything, anymore. Much was lost when your people came."

"I'm sorry," Anya said, almost reflexively.

"Not to be sorry. Time now to fix, instead. The white to help the red, hmm?"

"Will you be part of the ceremony?" Anya asked between mouthfuls.

"The penance? Me? No!" she laughed. "I bring the babies and heal the mamas. It is a different job. He bring the people and heal the land."

"Oh."

"Lucky for us we are always stupid the same way. Make his work easier."

Anya laughed at the idea that all of human frailty boiled down to a single stupidity. "And what is our stupidity, Lupita?" she asked with a smile.

Lupita was kneeling on the floor now, preparing to grind corn with her *mano* and *metate* as she had done with Rebecca. She sat back on her heels and looked carefully at Anya. Then she knit her fingers together, shook them tight, and pulled them apart.

"I not know your word. The gods teach us and we forget. Like forget when weaving not to pull one part too tight or the other will come undone."

"And *Hurukan*?"

"Sometimes when the weaving is very bad, it is too much to fix. It is to be pulled all apart and started again."

"Like the Biblical flood," Anya observed, more to herself than to Lupita.

"Oh no, no. Not flood this time. Flood is ending the Second Creation. We live now in the Fourth." It was a literal explanation for her. But again, how could Anya object when a hurricane was building outside?

"So it would be a hurricane that ends this creation?"

"*¡Si, si!*" Lupita replied delightedly before turning back to her corn.

"But Yaxché will stop it?" Anya asked.

"Maybe he doesn't," Lupita said, looking up once more. She looked disturbingly sanguine. Seeing fear on Anya's face she hurried to qualify her comment.

"You not to worry. Whatever happen is good. An end must happen before a beginning, hmm?"

Anya looked at Lupita with wonder: the old woman's smile was beatific. It chilled Anya to the bone. She went outside to wait for Yaxché, hoping he might say something less "cheerful" when he returned. Something that would offer her more hope.

***

Chalo had been standing with a gun to his head for five minutes before Kulkulcan spoke.

"Where did you go?" Kulkulcan asked at last, his weapon still raised.

"I had to think."

"That was not what I asked. I asked where did you go?"

"Walking. In the jungle. To San Antonio for some tortillas. And I borrowed a car…"

"Walking," Kulkulcan repeated, dubious.

Chalo raised his forearms to show slashes made by the underbrush.

"Walking," Kulkulcan muttered, unconvinced.

"It is what our ancestors did, hmm?" Chalo said nonchalantly. "Your book says we need to regain ourselves. I am a good student, *enchilada*."

"And all you did for two days was think?"

"And walk. It is a big thing to throw away an old life and begin a new one. Christ took forty days. The Maya can be faster, fortunately."

Kulkulcan smiled tightly at the joke and lowered his gun.

"You walked for two days," he said, eyes narrow. "You are a piece of work, Gonzalo. The American thought you were busy betraying us."

"The guilty are always suspicious, no?" Chalo asked. "Perhaps I should go have a word with him?"

Kulkulcan chuckled at the thought.

"And what did you see in the jungle?" he asked.

"*Xtabay*," Chalo lied. He watched Kulkulcan's face carefully as he did so.

Kulkulcan sneered for the briefest of moments—a micro-expression—before his face smoothed into a look of rapture. "Really. So you are lucky then. The lady of the jungle watched over you. Did she speak?"

"'*Keban be*.'" That, at least, was the truth.

"You were wrong? About what?"

About joining you, Chalo thought. "About leaving you, *Ahau*," He said aloud, trying hard not to choke on the honourific.

"I see," said Kulkulcan, nodding slowly. "Very well then, cousin. Like the prodigal son, welcome back."

Chalo heaved a silent sigh of relief: pride was Kulkulcan's weakness and Chalo had used it well.

"So now should I go speak with the American?"

Kulkulcan smiled unkindly and nodded.

"And then come back here. There remains much to do."

Chalo stopped for a long drink at the pump—the signal for Stephen and Rebecca—and then headed for the barracks: Rutrauff was there watching the boys fieldstrip their weapons. This was going to be fun.

"So, *amigo*. You thought I'd betray my cousin?"

Rutrauff looked up and swore.

"The prodigal son returns, hunh?" he said with a sneer.

"Exactly what Kulkulcan called me. Fatted calf and everything. May I speak with you?"

"Sure. Speak."

"In private, I think would be better…"

Rutrauff stood with an irritated sigh, ordered the boys to finish their guns and followed Chalo around to the back of the barracks.

"Okay, so speak," Rutrauff said, crossing his arms. "Where'd you bugger off to?"

"I had a lot to think about, *amigo*. It is not every day a man is asked to become a king's advisor. I would be giving up a lot…"

Rutrauff snorted. "Spare me the melodrama…"

"And then, in the middle of the night, I saw a ravishing woman in the forest…" Chalo said, waxing poetic.

"*Xtabay*, hunh?" he asked, unsurprised

Chalo's jaw dropped; this was unexpected. "You know of her?"

Dammit. There he was again, almost giving away his secret.

"Just…just what I hear from the boys," Rutrauff replied. "They saw her in the forest the other night…"

"So you've never seen her?"

"Seen her? Me? I don't believe in ghosts!"

"Too bad, because there's a woman behind you right now."

Rutrauff turned quickly, his guard up in an instant. Rebecca darted behind a tree.

"Maybe she's real after all, that *Xtabay*…" Chalo mocked.

"That one's wearing pants, not a white dress. I can tell the difference. Now shut up while I try to catch her."

Chalo raised his eyebrows. *A white dress*. Rutrauff *had* seen *Xtabay*.

"Okay, lady, I know you're there," Rutrauff sad to the jungle. Come out with your hands where I can see them."

Rebecca stepped, arms up and wide eyed, from behind her tree.

"Hello, Travis," she said casually, her accent a drawl again.

"You?" Rutrauff asked, lowering his gun in surprise. Behind him, Chalo tried hard not to laugh. Rebecca was very good at this.

"You know this woman?" Chalo demanded.

"Hardly." Sneering at Rebecca he added, "Nice to see you with shoes, by the way."

"Don't play dumb, Travis," Rebecca replied, acting the conspirator.

"He's the only one who knows I'm here. Shoot him now and we can both get away…"

Chalo raised his gun before Rutrauff could.

"Hardly know her? *Hardly*? Sounds like you're on a first-name basis." Chalo said as he disengaged his safety with a click.

"Put your goddamned gun down, man. I met her for the first time in Cancún."

"Jeezuz, Travis!" Rebecca interjected, playing her role well. "You gonna hang me out to dry here? After everything?"

"Listen Becky…" Travis protested.

"So you know her name, too?" Chalo asked, pretending suspicion. Secretly he was as pleased as a cat with a mouse and had to fight not to smile.

"She introduced herself after pouring beer on me. Becky Wilkes, postal worker. Oh shit. *Wilkes*. You're related to him, aren't you?"

"Funny, Travis. Really funny. You know he's my father. You're the one who told me he was here…" Rebecca said petulantly. "You said we had to get him out of here before Kulkulcan killed him!"

"Your father?" Rutrauff was genuinely shocked.

"I've seen enough, Rutrauff," Chalo said, enjoying the game immensely. "Come on. You have some explaining to do to the boss."

"She's making it up!" Rutrauff said to Chalo.

"Sure she is. And I'm a monkey's cousin. Let's go. And you, too, *amiga*," Chalo said, motioning to Rebecca with his gun. "Beside your American friend. Let's march."

Rebecca moved from the forest and fell in step beside Rutrauff.

"You're a piece of work, you know that?" Rutrauff growled.

"You think?" Rebecca smiled.

"I know. You deserve a frickin' Academy Award, you do."

"Me? If you're giving them out, maybe you should give it to him!"

"Chalo? Maybe he's dumb enough to fall for your show but he couldn't act his way out of a paper bag."

"You wound me, Travis!" Chalo said from behind them. "I thought I was doing so well!"

"How exactly is that, *cousin*?"

"You see, that's the first bit of acting. I never met Kulkulcan until three days ago…"

Rutrauff stopped short and, despite the gun he knew to be in Chalo's hand, turned around.

"You're *not* his cousin?"

"Not on your life, *amigo*."

Rebecca was smiling now.

"You two *are* working together," Rutrauff said, his eyes narrowing. With a single sudden movement he grabbed Rebecca by the wrist and twisted her arm behind her back. "Tell me what's going on *cousin*, or I'll hurt your sweet little *amiga*."

Rebecca winced in pain and Chalo's eyes narrowed.

"Alright, alright," Chalo said, raising his gun hand, suddenly worried for Rebecca.

"Now tell me," Rutrauff demanded, tightening his grip on Rebecca for emphasis.

It was Rebecca who answered. Without a southern drawl.

"I work for the State Department. Chalo's working with me. We're here to get Wilkes out of here."

"You're goddamned shitting me…" Rutrauff said, loosening his grip.

"Not a word of a lie," Chalo said earnestly. "It's a long long story, *amigo*, but she is telling the truth. Kulkulcan is a bastard; I'm working with Rebecca; and we're here to get your senator out of here."

"And you thought you'd have a little fun at my expense, while you were at it, hunh?" Rutrauff growled. He released Rebecca with a painful shove and frowned.

"Look, we're sorry about that," Rebecca said, sounding genuinely apologetic. "It was the only way we could think to get you out of camp long enough to listen to us…"

Rutrauff looked at Chalo, then Rebecca, then back to Chalo once more.

"You're really here to get the senator?

Both Chalo and Rebecca nodded.

"Is Wilkes really your father?" Rutrauff asked Rebecca.

"Father-in-law. *Ex*-father in law, actually. And a bastard, but we still need to get him out of here."

Rutrauff sized them both up. If they were lying, they were lying well. But if they were telling the truth?

"What's the rest of your plan?" he asked warily.

"I take Rebecca as a prisoner to the senator's hut and then march you to Kulkulcan, full of accusations. It is a distraction until Rebecca gets the senator out the door. Then you do whatever you need to stop Kulkulcan and we're all home by Christmas, yes?"

"Nice plan, but you've missed the most important part. Like State Department always does," he added, glowering at Rebecca.

"What's that?" Rebecca shot back.

"The whole damn thing is about the oil. Installing a Mexican puppet who would give us the Mitnal oil. If we double-cross him, Kulkulcan is going to destroy the rig. He's got a German ecoterrorist on it even now, ready to blow it up."

"That's why we need you to join our little game, *amigo*. A lie to fool the liar?"

Rutrauff looked to Rebecca, uncomprehending.

"The Maya are good; the foreigners are evil," Rebecca said, mimicking Kulkulcan. "He'd rather believe Chalo than believe you, right?"

Rutrauff nodded, not liking where this was going.

"So Chalo exposes you as a 'traitor,' even as you protest your innocence and accuse him of the same thing. You lock me up with Wilkes and while you two are pleading your cases to Kulkulcan—each of you saying the other is working with me…" she trailed off, not entirely sure how much to share with Rutrauff.

"We have a few things up our coats to get out of the camp…" Chalo took over.

"Sleeves. A few things up our sleeves," Rebecca corrected with a rueful smile. To Rutrauff she said "We'll leave with Joe and you can deal with Kulkulcan."

"You think? He's got us trussed like a pig. If I kill him to stop the assassinations, he'll have the rig destroyed. No, if the oil is the important part of this game, the op has to go ahead."

Rebecca's face grew dark.

"I'm ordering you to stop the op," she said fiercely.

"That's hilarious," Rutrauff snorted. First, I haven't got any *way* to stop it, and second on what authority can you possibly stop it?"

"I'm with State!"

"Yeah? That and three bucks will get you a latte. You didn't order the op; you can't countermand it!"

Rebecca opened her mouth, closed it again, momentarily defeated, and then smiled.

"But Joe can…"

"Joe?"

"Joe Wilkes. Senator Joe Wilkes. Elected official and the one who put the whole black op together. Does *he* have the authority?"

Rutrauff considered, a small smile of hope appearing. It disappeared equally quickly. "What if he won't?"

"He will. Believe me, he will. I can be very persuasive…"

"Yeah, tell me about it. But what if he *won't*?"

"He will," Rebecca said once more.

Rutrauff stood still, undecided.

"Come on, *amigo*," Chalo said impatiently. "This is all we've got and we're wasting time. Let's just get the senator out of the camp and burn the next bridge when we get to it, hmm?"

"Cross the next bridge," Rebecca and Rutrauff said in unison.

"Maybe burning, *amigos*. Maybe burning. Now, if you would be so kind as to be my prisoners, perhaps we could get this party going?"

Rebecca and Rutrauff raised their arms and Chalo raised his gun. They were about to make quite a stir in camp, actors all of them: the stalwart, the traitor, and a girl.

Joe Wilkes lay in his tiny hut, bruises bluing and blood clotted, his eyes woollen shut and his breath ragged.

"Libby?" he croaked, sure he heard his dead wife calling his name. "That you, Libby?"

"No, Joe. It's me, Becky."

"Becky?" Joe asked, opening one swollen eye with effort. "What're you doing here, child?"

"I'm here to rescue you. Now hush."

Joe started to chuckle and then began to cough, a rattle that spoke of fluid in his lungs.

"Don't deserve it," he managed to say.

Rebecca smiled, despite herself.

"Probably not, Joe. But the world works in mysterious ways. How the hell did you get yourself into this mess?"

"Long story. Money. Clayton. Pride… Stupid." He trailed off, lungs rattling. His bottom lip had resplit and he licked the blood seeping from it before trying to resume. Rebecca cut him off.

"I figured as much. We'll deal with your come-uppance later; we've got to get you out of here first."

"No. This first," he grunted, struggling hands bound, to reach for something in his pocket.

"Later, Joe. We've got to be ready to bolt when the sound-and-light show starts…"

"Now," he insisted, vehemence ending in a cough. "From Hayden," he struggled. "Before he killed himself."

Rebecca sat back on her heels, the colour draining from her face.

"Before he what?" she whispered.

"He killed himself, Beck. I covered it up. To save his reputation… my reputation."

"He killed himself?" Rebecca asked softly, carefully, as if the words, if said louder, would cause the world to shatter.

"Read, Becky." Wilkes whispered, infinitely weary.

Rebecca pulled the letter carefully from Joe's pocket and started reading, quickly first and then more and more slowly as tears blurred her vision.

"Yaxché was right. He was hanging around to apologize…" she said to herself.

"Clayton threatened to tell…"

Awakening from her reverie, Rebecca scolded Joe.

"Jeezus Christ, Joe. All this mess for pride?" she asked as she started to untape his wrists.

"Yeah. No. I did it for the oil, too. Pride just got me started…"

"Jeezus Christ," Rebecca swore again.

"So what do we do, Becky?" he asked, one good eye regarding her with infinite sadness.

The sound of loud voices outside, followed by the report of a semi-automatic weapon, made both of them jump.

"It's too late to do anything but keep going, Joe."

"Churchill, hunh?"

"What?" Rebecca asked absent-mindedly, attention on the noises outside.

"*When you're going through Hell, keep going...*"

"Something like that," she said as she helped Wilkes to his feet and slung his unbroken arm over her shoulder. "Except that I think Hell is still up ahead. Come on, it's time to go."

CHAPTER 51

In his hut facing Rutrauff and Chalo, Kulkulcan's face was purple with rage, the vein at his temple pounding.

"You expect me to believe you are not working with her? With all that I already know of your plans? Are you truly that stupid, Rutrauff? Or do you think I am that stupid?"

"I swear to God, Kulkulcan, I've got nothing to do with her! She set me up!"

"A woman from State Department? You expect me to believe this is just coincidence?" Kulkulcan spat, waving Rebecca's diplomatic passport at Rutrauff.

The sound of music outside was followed by the staccato spray of a half a dozen guns. Kulkulcan looked daggers at Rutrauff.

"You told me just a moment ago that she was working alone. If that is so, who is making all that noise outside?" Kulkulcan demanded.

Chalo shook his head and tut-tutted. "I told you he was working with the woman! There are others out there for sure!" he said righteously.

Rutrauff glowered at Chalo, than looked to Kulkulcan, steel in his eyes.

"I'm telling the truth, Boss. Your cousin is lying. Why would I do this? Especially now that you've got the senator! Why would I risk his life? If he dies, I can never go home!"

A series of small explosions sounded outside, followed by shouting.

"¡*El fuego*! ¡*En la selva*!" someone outside shouted, voice panicked. *Fire in the forest.*

"¡*Agua*! ¡*Agua*!" shouted another voice, calling for water to douse the flames.

Kulkulcan looked at both Rutrauff and Chalo, eyes blazing.

"I don't know who to believe right now, but I seem to have bigger problems at the moment," he growled.

"Out!" he said opening the door and motioning both men through it. "We will deal with the present crisis and then I will figure out which one of you to kill."

Chalo looked over his shoulder and swallowed hard. Kulkulcan was swinging a backpack on and hefting the HK-46 connected to it; it was surely the deadly *tohil.*

"You are not going to use that, are you?" he asked, suddenly anxious.

"What the hell is that, anyway?" demanded Rutrauff.

Kulkulcan looked from one man to the other.

"Why should I not? Are you worried about who I might kill out there? Is the Captain right, cousin? Are you my Judas?

"I only worry that you'll hit one of our own boys in the chaos, *cousin,*" Chalo said, derision in his voice even as he feigned umbrage. "If the heat ray is set to kill… well, there is no room for a mistake, is there?"

"Worry about your own aim, cousin. Now go."

"Heat ray?" Rutrauff demanded. "What do you mean, 'heat ray'?"

Rutrauff received no answer: both Chalo and Kulkulcan were already two paces ahead of him on their way to the fire at the edge of camp.

Rutrauff gritted his teeth. A heat ray. Apparently one that could kill. Things were getting worse by the minute.

***

Despite the continued drizzle—Chalo felt it on his face as he ran out into the clearing—the flames, feeding on still-dry tinder and a strengthening wind, were rising. Kulkulcan's men had started a bucket line between the camp's pump and the forest edge but it was barely more than useless.

"No, no!" Chalo shouted as he surged past Kulkulcan. "Make a firebreak!"

The boys watched Chalo as he ran to the pile of empty gun crates beside their barracks, kicked one of them apart, grabbed a liberated plank, and started to scrape the earth bare. Rutrauff and the boys were soon at his side, scraping a trench free of fuel.

"Where's Kulkulcan?" one of the boys asked above the crackle of the fire, the worried follower wanting his leader.

"He headed up the pyramid…" Rutrauff grunted as he dug at the vegetation.

"What? ¡*Chingalo*!"

If Kulkulcan made it to the top of the pyramid, the entire camp would be within the *tohil*'s deadly range.

"Go talk to the senator for your authority!" Chalo yelled as he dropped his plank. "Now, while Kulkulcan is climbing!"

"What are you going to do?"

"Stop him using that gun!"

Rutrauff watched Chalo for a split second before dropping his own plank and turning for the prisoners' hut. The door was already open and the guard who had been posted lay twisting on the ground, clawing at his eyes. Rutrauff swore as a tree behind him, its sap super-heated, exploded. He took off, low and fast, for the now-unguarded prisoners' hut.

"What happened?" he barked when he was near enough to be heard.

"She called me from inside… said the man was having a heart attack. I went in and she sprayed me with something. It hurts!" the young man wailed.

"Which way did they go?"

"I couldn't see! It sounded like that way!" the boy replied, pointing to the south, behind the hut.

"Go wash your eyes at the pump," Rutrauff said as he ran south.

Fifty feet away, skirting the edge of the forest, Rebecca was struggling to lead Joe from the camp. His height and weight, coupled with the severity of his injuries, meant slow progress. Rutrauff ran towards them without any idea what he should do when he got there. Stephen saved him the trouble of figuring it out by stepping from the jungle beside Rebecca and Wilkes, his pistol levelled at Rutrauff's chest.

"Careful, buddy," Stephen said menacingly.

"I'm… I'm on your side," panted Rutrauff, putting his arms up.

"Un hunh," Stephen nodded, his tone dubious. "Stay there anyway."

Rebecca turned at the sound of their voices.

"Stephen! Don't shoot!" she said. "It's okay. He really is on our side."

"Shit," Rutrauff said suddenly. You're the idiot Canadian who asked me for directions to the freakin' bull ring in Cancún. I recognize your hat."

Stephen smiled. "Gotta love the Canucks, eh?" He was enjoying being the one behind the gun this time.

"Who's there, Becky?" Wilkes demanded, his swollen eye toward the forest.

"Stephen Catherwood—he's here with me—and Travis…"

"Who?"

"The marine you stuck in the middle of this shit, Joe," Rebecca said. "You need to give him authority to call the whole thing off."

"Me?"

"You're the closest thing to the US government out here, and higher up the food chain than I am. Your word and he'll stop Kulkulcan before he can gut the Mexican Cabinet or sink Mitnal. Or both."

Joe paused. Politics was a dangerous mistress, her siren call difficult to ignore.

"We need a new government down here, Becky," he said weakly.

"Oh for chrissakes, Joe! This is another country! You've no right! And on top of that, you're half-dead in the middle of a jungle at the mercy of a madman who thinks he is the second-coming of a winged-snake: you aren't exactly the one in control anymore!"

Joe shook his head. "Okay. Okay."

"Now tell Travis to pull the plug."

Joe nodded.

"Son?" he said, turning his good eye towards Rutrauff.

"Sir?"

"Operation Serpent's Nest, right?"

"Sir, yessir."

"I designed it and got your commanders to authorize it, and now we're in the shitcan together. I'm authorizing you to do as Becky says. Do what you need to make that madman think he's still good to go so he won't sink the rig; then stop him any way you can."

"Sir?"

"What is it?"

"He's going to think I let you get away, not that I'm still with him. He'll kill me sure as take me back."

Joe thought a moment, leaning more heavily on Rebecca.

"Tell him he's got my word that I'll recognize him as the new President if he keeps the rig standing."

"No disrespect, sir, but why would he believe me? Your word might be good in Washington, but it's not so great here in the jungle."

"Give him your ring, Joe," Rebecca said suddenly.

"My what?"

"Your football ring. Your name's engraved in it, right? Give it as proof of your word."

Stephen, watching the exchange, smiled. The ring would seal the deal for Rutrauff, but it also meant that Wilkes would have to confess to everything. She was going to see Wilkes brought to justice, after all. Clever.

Joe understood it in an instant.

"Nice work, Becky. Check-mate." To Rutrauff he said "Here, son. Take the ring. It'll frame me and buy back your place with the guerrilla. Then kill him when you're sure the rig's safe and bring the ring back to me in Washington. It's your get-out-of-jail-free card."

"Yes, sir."

"Good. And son?"

"Yes, sir?"

"Good hunting. I'll see you in DC."

"Sir, yessir."

Stephen lowered his gun. "There'll be another explosion on the opposite side of camp when we're clear," he said. "We're heading out past the *cenote*, so anything you can do to send them the other direction would be good…"

Rutrauff nodded and then looked to Rebecca for a moment.

"You really are something else," he said with admiration. "Get the senator out of here, safe and I'll see you stateside."

"See you in DC, Travis," Rebecca replied before starting forward with Joe.

Stephen stepped forward to take Wilkes other arm.

"And hockey-boy?" Rutrauff said to Stephen before turning back to the camp. "You keep *her* safe, you hear?"

"You just worry about yourself," Stephen said, unaccountably jealous. "We'll be just fine from here on in."

Five minutes later Stephen swore at his own confidence. They had emerged from behind the last of the hut around the clearing to see a knot of boys—the few not yet busy with fire-fighting—standing stock-still at the base of the pyramid, staring at something at the top. A glance told Stephen they were not out of the woods at all: Chalo was on the top of the pyramid fighting someone. Probably Kulkulcan.

"Keep going," he said to Rebecca. "I'll meet you at the back of the pyramid. Chalo's in trouble. Again."

***

From the ground, the fight between Chalo and Kulkulcan seemed slow and stylized, a ritual fight against the brooding sky. For the participants, it was brutally real. And Chalo was losing: driven by a messianic fervour, Kulkulcan was now possessed by almost superhuman strength; he had relieved Chalo of his sidearm almost the instant their fight had begun—had sent it bouncing down the eastern stairs—and now, despite Chalo's years of boxing, was gaining the upper hand in direct combat. Chalo was going to have to try another strategy.

"You know you won't win, *enchilada*," Chalo goaded, lunging not for Kulkulcan but for the death ray on its tripod.

"And why is that, *pendejo*?" Kulkulcan asked, easily blocking Chalo's feint.

"Your mistake is that you don't believe in the gods in whose names you fight. It is playing with fire to call on them without faith..." Chalo said. As he did so he dove for the knapsack that held the *tohil*'s fuel cell.

Kulkulcan stepped on the cord to prevent Chalo from pulling the gun and tripod over. Chalo dropped the pack and stepped back, crouching defensively. The power cord that connected the *tohil* to its fuel cell was now lying long and loose on the ground.

"Listen to you, *indio*," Kulkulcan said, using the offensive pejorative. "It hardly matters what I believe if I win, does it? My mistake was believing your conversion. You are a good actor, Gonzalo."

Chalo fumbled with the knapsack, hoping to open it and disconnect the gun from its power supply. Kulkulcan surged forward and kicked Chalo in the chin, knocking him backwards; as Chalo lay dazed Kulkulcan moved in, obsidian blade high.

"The good news is that I always learn from my mistakes…"

"Do you indeed?" Chalo said through gritted teeth. Kulkulcan had inadvertently caught his foot in the cord when stepping forward to kick Chalo; now Chalo grasped the cord and yanked hard, sending Kulkulcan backwards to the ground. On his hands and knees in an instant, Chalo scrabbled for the death ray once more.

Kulkulcan was faster: before Chalo could reach the tripod, Kulkulcan had grabbed Chalo's ankle, flipped him over, dragged him from the weapon, and was raising his obsidian blade once more.

"You should not have come back, *pendejo*. But since you have, let's see if your gods are real. Pray to them for deliverance. I think you will be disappointed. The skies are empty and we get only what we take for ourselves."

Chalo stared up at the warlord above him, feathered serpent tattoo pulsing around his torso, over his shoulder, down his arm, mouth open on the fist that held the obsidian blade and heard his grandmother's voice.

"*—the five will plead for mercy…*"

Could it really hurt to ask for a miracle?

Chalo said a silent prayer and the cold wind driving down the pyramid paused, grew warm and fragrant, and surged towards him.

At the bottom of the pyramid, Stephen had been looking desperately for something—anything—he could use. A V-shaped piece of metal in a wheelbarrow full of garbage destined for the bottom of the *cenote* gave him an idea: maybe he could make a slingshot? He dumped the barrow to look for parts and spotted a hubcap, old, domed, embossed with the letters VW. The reach of the automobile, not to mention the human propensity to litter, was remarkable, he thought fleetingly. But one man's garbage was another's gold, and the hubcap might just do the trick.

Chalo's ribbing aside, the sport of Ultimate required as much skill as billiards and as much stamina as rugby. Stephen had played it for years at the elite level before abandoning it in favour of workaholism. Now, hefting the hubcap, he realized how much he missed the game; how much he hoped throwing would be like riding a bicycle—impossible to forget.

Stephen slipped off his knapsack and hefted the metal disk as he looked up the pyramid. The cap was about 175 grams: almost regulation weight. That would make it easy to throw from body memory alone. But the throw—about twenty-five metres, almost sixty-degrees up and into a downdraft—was a hard one.

Stephen spun the hubcap on his fingertip, not like a circus performer spinning a plate but like a sheriff twirling a pistol, the disc at ninety degrees to the ground as he imagined the throw. Then he made the real thing: two steps, arm curled, shoulder leading as he turned to the right, planted his feet at right angles to the pyramid, and let his arm unfurl, the momentum of his spin transferred from his body to the hubcap. At the last moment, he flicked his wrist, felt the rough aluminum edge leave his hand, heard the sing-song sound of metal sliding through his fingers as he let go. He smiled grimly as he watched the hubcap fly towards the leaden sky: he'd thrown well, but was it well enough?

Another downdraft buffeted the disc; it hovered for an endless moment and Stephen clenched his fists.

"Help, damn you!" Stephen said to the gods as he watched the disc dance on the wind. He thought of Yaxché and changed his tone.

"Please help?"

The wind paused for a pregnant moment as if listening, considering. Then a small current of warm air, heavy with the aroma of burning *copal*, drove upward, carrying the disc with it. Stephen's eyes widened in surprise, then he smiled with relief as the metal disc slammed, edge on, into the middle of Kulkulcan's back.

"Thank you. Thankyouthankyouthankyou," Stephen said reverently as he watched Kulkulcan slump forward. He watched a moment longer to make sure Chalo was alright, then the smile ebbed from his face. Chalo was up, but after glancing at Stephen he had looked towards the centre of the clearing and started yelling. One single word spilled clearly down the pyramid: *run*.

Kulkulcan's soldiers had been watching the fight, too, and when their leader had fallen, they had looked for the source of the flying object and seen Stephen. Now they were running, with murderous intent, straight for him.

CHAPTER 52

At the top of the pyramid, Chalo's eyes widened as Kulkulcan, standing over him with a knife and murderous intent, suddenly crumpled. Chalo scrambled to his feet, looked down on the plaza, and understood what had happened. Down the pyramid he shouted a single word: *Run*. Then he thought fast.

"Okay, *caballero*, I'll never make fun of your stupid game again," Chalo muttered to himself as he opted for the *tohil*: he grabbed it from its tripod, toggled it on, and dropped to his belly to steady himself.

The weapon began to hum; a second later Chalo whistled in surprise as the gun blossomed: some kind of nanotechnology was turning a liquid polymer oozing near the gun's tip into a clear hard disc that would amplify the PSAD's microwave output to deadly effect.

"Son-of-a-bitch," Chalo muttered as he raised the gun's sight and aimed for the first of the young men closing in on Stephen.

Squeezing the trigger yielded the weapon's second surprise, a brief burst of sound, rising from a gut-quivering bass note through to dog-deafening inaudibility in less than a second. And then came dread: he had forgotten to dial the weapon down.

Stephen reached reflexively for his gun when he saw what Chalo had seen: Kulkulcan's soldiers running towards him. Too late he realized that he had given the weapon to Rebecca.

"Oh, shit…"

They were moving fast; he might not be able to outrun them. He reached down for his knapsack, eyes on the sprinters. The lead runner was only fifteen feet distant now; Stephen paused, weighing the odds of running against fighting. And then the lead runner fell to the ground, his young body shuddering. Blood rose to the boy's eyes and a trickle from his nose turned to a torrent; within seconds he appeared to be bleeding from every pore, his skin slicked red. He seized, as if epileptic, for another few seconds before falling still and dead.

The other runners stopped short, their eyes, like Stephen's wide with horror. One crossed himself. A second spat to ward off evil spirits. Then all of them took three steps backwards. Stephen didn't wait to see what would happen next; he turned and ran for the narrow *cenote* path.

He skidded to a stop as soon as he rounded the corner, arms up reflexively in surrender: Rebecca was down on one knee, arms out, pointing his own gun at him. Joe Wilkes lay on the pyramid behind and above her, eyes closed. Chalo was scrambling from the top but had not yet reached his fallen gun.

"What the hell… ?!"

"Detonating the powder bomb!" she yelled, explaining. "Get behind me!"

He hoped she was a good shot. He sped past her and heard his gun fire once, then twice, before he heard the butane canister explode.

Apparently she was. Under Hayden's tutelage she'd become a crack shot with Joe's prize Civil War Parker-Hale Whitworth 451. It wasn't that she had been keen on the gun; it was the fact that using it—and using it well--irritated Joe. In the end, her aim never got as good as Hayden's but it was much better than Joe's.

Rebecca watched the powder bomb explode, beautiful as the talc granules sparked, bright like fireflies. Stephen turned to see her still on one knee and then gasped: the small explosion had been enough to wake a giant. The earth beneath Rebecca was rippling like a liquid, prelude to a cave-in. He tried to shout but could not be heard over the rumble as limestone began shearing into the cenote, sweeping Rebecca with it. He watched helplessly as she scrabbled to climb against the scree sliding past her. Her hands and knees were bloody with the effort of staying at the edge of the precipice; he saw her grab for a gnarled root and his heart leaped. Would it hold? It gave a little and then held firm, Stephen exhaling with relief. A fist-sized rock jounced up and hit her in the head, splitting her eyebrow and Stephen gasped again: the shock of the impact made her lose her footing. Hands still clinging to the root, she was nevertheless swept backwards and out of sight. All Stephen could see was a cloud of limestone powder over the *cenote*'s new edge. And a new fire, the result of the powder bomb, starting twenty feet away .

CHAPTER 53

Chalo, down from the pyramid and still horrified by the blood he had shed, the sight of Rebecca sliding into the *cenote*, and the effects of Kulkulcan's wrath on Wilkes, had been uncharacteristically willing to take direction: he agreed to leave Stephen behind to look after Rebecca while he took Wilkes to the car. It was not that he wanted to leave Stephen; it was that he wanted to leave the camp more.

This assumed Stephen could rescue Rebecca. Chalo had no doubts but for Stephen, it was not a given: it seemed too horrifyingly like Erin's fall. Stephen pushed the outcome of that fall from his mind as he dropped to his stomach and scootched forward to peer over the ragged new edge of the *cenote*, squinting through the thick dust for any sign of life.

Something moved six feet below him and Stephen's pulse thundered hope.

"Rebecca?"

What Stephen had taken for a rock turned to look up at him: Rebecca's hair and face were white with calcium dust. Looking up, her green eyes were bright against the powder on her skin, her gaze preternaturally calm. She had managed to hold on to the root with her left arm—the right one, so recently injured, hung loose and useless at her side—and had jammed her toes into a narrow crevice in the new rock face beneath her.

"Hey," she said, smiling weakly at him. "Could you give a girl a hand?"

"Hang on. Just hang on…" he said, and the echo of memory made his stomach lurch. He inched forward until his breastbone was over the new edge and reached down with one long, limber arm.

"Can you grab hold?"

Rebecca reached up with her injured arm, grimacing as she strained her battered shoulder. Their fingertips met—his warm, hers cold—but he could not get sufficient purchase on her hand. He inched a little farther forward and Rebecca managed to grab his watch strap. It held for a short, welcome moment and then a link gave way; Rebecca's hand slipping back into Stephen's and the heavy steel timepiece fell, splashed, and sank to the bottom of the deep cenote.

Stephen thought quickly, knowing they had only seconds until Rebecca's arm gave out.

"Rebecca?"

"Yeah?"

"I'm going to have to let go. Just for a second…"

"Let go?"

"I have an idea, but I need my hands back for maybe twenty seconds. Can you hold on for that long?"

She paused for a moment and then nodded.

Stephen held steady, unable to force himself to release Rebecca's hand.

"It's okay, Stephen. Let go."

She sounded like Erin. So calm. He held his breath and let go. Her fingertips slipped from his but she held tight to the root with the other hand and did not fall.

A rush of relief galvanized him: he inched back from the edge of the *cenote*, stripped off his t-shirt and tore each side seam open. Then he twisted the t-shirt around itself lengthwise, as if wringing it out.

"Who were you talking to on the phone the other day?" he asked as he tied three quick knots along the length of the fabric to prevent it from unfurling. Then tied a slip-knotted noose into either end. It was the steady patter of the rescue worker, talking to keep the victim calm. Or so he told himself.

"What?" came a confused question from below.

"The sat phone. The other day…"

Love you, too. Rebecca realized she had exchanged endearments with Kathy Howlachuk. Had Stephen seemed sour because he thought he had reason to be jealous?

"That was my godmother!"

"Oh…" Stephen said sheepishly as he put one of the nooses around his wrist, cinched it tight and dropped back to his belly. He flinched as, crawling forward to the cliff edge, the sharp limestone cut into his bare chest. Then he reddened at the pained but amused look on Rebecca's face: it spoke of his jealousy discovered. Stephen felt like a teenager, the crush on a first love outed.

"Put your bad hand in the loop and then pull back against it until it cinches tight," he said gruffly.

Rebecca did as instructed, wincing as she forced her sore shoulder to reef down on the noose.

She looked up and nodded at Stephen when she was done. Stephen pulled up the slack in the umbilicus that now joined them.

"When you're ready, let go of the root and grab the t-shirt with your good hand and I'll pull you up."

"You're not going to let me fall, are you?" She joked.

"Not a chance," Stephen replied seriously.

"Okay, here goes…" Rebecca said. In the next instant she tightened her grip on the tee-shirt that tethered them together, used her good arm on the root to pull herself in to the cliff wall and then, like an acrobat swinging from one trapeze to another, transferred her grip from the root to the tether.

Stephen pulled up on the makeshift rope, arm over arm, and when it was close enough, grabbed for her hand. It was sweaty and the grip bad; Rebecca's hand started slipping from Stephen's. Stephen gripped more tightly but her fingers slipped through his, her wedding ring sliding off in his grip and then falling, loose, into the cenote to join his watch. She was falling now, the only thing holding them together the cotton tether.

"No!" yelled Stephen. "Not this time!"

He yanked hard on the tether and Rebecca cried out with pain as her injured arm took all her weight but she did not slip any further; a moment later, Stephen had pulled her close enough to reach her good hand again. It was cold and clammy; grasping it filled him with a soaring happiness.

Now Stephen pulled her up and backwards, Rebecca clambering up to the lip of the precipice; once she was on flat ground they both collapsed, exhausted, and lay still.

"We've got to get out of here…" Stephen said without moving.

Eyes closed and clutching her shoulder, Rebecca agreed but she did not move either. Stephen looked over at her: the wound he had sewn up was bleeding again—not much, but Stephen was sure it hurt. Blood that had trickled from the cut over her eyebrow had crusted down the side of her cheek like a red tear. Her clothes were torn, her knuckles bloody, her hair white with dust: to Stephen she had never been more beautiful.

She felt his eyes on her and opened her own. Stephen could see the jungle fire behind him reflected in her wide black pupils. He knew they had to go. Now. He kissed her instead. At last. She tasted of limestone dust and sweat and something indefinably sweet, and when she kissed him back, raising her good arm up around him to caress his bare back, he was complete.

"¡*Ko'one'ex*!" commanded a hollow sibilant voice. They looked towards the fire for the source; it was *Xtabay*, her tone both irritated and amused. "¡*Bey'a*!"

The fire was a full blown conflagration now, the kind that Stephen remembered ripping through the interior of British Columbia every summer. The flames sparkled orange through the quick-burning underbrush, crackling and popping as it went, the heady incense of burning tropical brush filling the air. Flames raced up the vines that wreathed the tallest trees. Seeking more fuel, they jumped from the vines to the forest canopy. From there, storm winds whipped them into billowing curtains of fire. Rebecca found herself holding her breath, terrified and exhilarated by the inferno. Stephen watched, too, but mystified: to the right by the *cenote* and the left by the pyramid, the flames should have been roaring into the narrow isthmus on which they lay. Instead, they flared twenty feet away but did not creep towards them. And in the spot beyond which the fire would not budge stood a transparent figure, shimmering like a heat mirage over a desert road in summer.

"*Xtabay*," Stephen whispered.

Rebecca pushed wind-whipped hair from her face and looked closely in the direction Stephen as staring. The ghost woman stood sideways to the fire, back hand up against the flames, holding them at bay.

"¡*Bey'a*!" she said. *Go*!

Now Stephen and Rebecca heard the staccato sound of semi-automatic fire over the roaring flames; they ducked as a shower of limestone chips from the pyramid, dislodged by the gunfire, rained upon them. And now, through the wall of flame, Kulkulcan's soldiers grew visible. They drew closer to the far side of the wall of fire. Then they stopped and lowered their rifles: they were unwilling to shoot through the spectral woman who stood between them and their prey.

Still tethered together, Rebecca and Stephen scrambled to their feet and began to run.

CHAPTER 54

Yaxché had been pacing since treating the last of his patients: into his hut, onto the porch where he paused to look through the thickening rain and darkening light at the empty road, back into his hut.

"They are late," he muttered. "Why are they late?"

At last Anya could take it no longer.

"Stop, *Don* Yaxché. You must be patient."

Yaxché looked daggers at her for a split-second before cackling.

"Teaching me again, hmm? Come, we work instead. You know machetes?"

Anya had grown familiar with them as a graduate student doing fieldwork and nodded.

"Good. Then we chop while we wait."

Yaxché went into his hut and returned with one of the sacks he had filled that morning. Anya looked at the soft steady rain falling over the jungle and the tiny hamlet, turning the road to mud. It filled the air with the scent of ozone and new growth.

"Here. You do this one," Yaxché said with a grin. He held out a large round root the colour and texture of smooth wood. "Peel first, and then make it in small chunks, hmm?"

Anya nodded again.

"What happens when they arrive?" Anya asked at length.

"We prepare for the ritual… since you are being the teacher, tell me something, hmm?"

Anya smiled, humbled. "I'll try…"

"Why is the *Vucub Caquix* on the ceiling this time?"

Vucub Caquix—the god known as Seven Macaw—was prominent among the figures at Sian Ka'an but was not on the other ceilings. Seven Macaw, adorned with jade, his eyes made of gold, who grew so vain he considered himself more powerful than the gods. The Hero Twins had blinded and disgraced him before the world was renewed in the Fourth Creation.

"I don't know, *Don* Yaxché. We are most of us too proud these days, are we not?"

Yaxché paused, machete above his chopping block and inhaled the pungent scent of lemon balm.

"It is true, child. Too true. And still, it means someone. The stories come to life at these times—*the walls will speak... the five eyes will come*—it is a person, not just an idea now."

"If that is so, and you are the Tree of Life that is to hold up the heavens…"

She could hardly believe the temerity of her question; the assumption in it that she was part of an ancient truth.

"… if you are the Tree of Life, then who are we?"

"You don't know yet, child?" Yaxché laughed. The sky is held not only in the midpoint, but in its four corners, *mi niña*. You are *Lakin*, holder of the waking light. Yellow is your colour, like your hair."

Lakin was both the Maya word for East and the name for the sky's eastern pillar. She swallowed at the responsibility, further humbled.

"And the others?"

"*Mi esposa*—she is *Nohul*, the brightness of the South. The tall one is *Xaman*, the wisdom of the North…"

Rebecca smiled at the rightness of the Canadian standing to the north.

"… and the reluctant one…"

"Chalo?"

Yaxché nodded.

"… he is *Chik'in*, the dangerous darkness of West, from which rebirth comes, yes?"

That was appropriate, too, given his flirtation with Kulkulcan, the bringer of death.

"And the judges?"

"Around us, always. But they will stand in the bodies of the nine—

those of us who hold the old secrets."

"The nine?"

"*Tzacol* and *Bitol*. *Gucamatz* and *Tepeu*. *Xpiyacoc*, *Xmucane*, *Alom*, *Qaholom*. *U Qux Cho*. They will all be there when the time comes, in the bodies marked from birth to hold them. They will listen to both sides. They will judge."

Yaxché had named the most powerful gods of the pantheon, creators each of them: the builder and his consort, the one who adds form; the feathered serpent—the true Kulkulcan, not the pretender—and his partner, the conqueror; grandparents and parents both to the Hero Twins who destroyed Seven Macaw; the Spirit of the Lake. It was the board of directors meeting to decide whether to dissolve the enterprise that was humanity.

"Both sides?"

"Of course, *mi niña*. There is always more than one side. If we lose, the Lords of the Underworld get the world back and make it in their image instead, hmm? Bad for us, but good for them, yes?"

That was it: a descent into chaos. The return of lives short, brutish, and nasty. Could it really come down to this one irrational, ineffable thing: a rite as old as time? Anya finished chopping the white root.

"What is this root for, anyway?"

"You don't know it? I am surprised!" Yaxché said with a sly grin. It is *xicamatl*—one of my favourites. The vines and seeds are very poisonous…"

"And the root? What do you use it for?"

It was dark now, their chopping blocks lit only by a small kerosene lamp that Lupita had brought over. Yaxché leaned over to Anya's block, his back creaking, and took one of the *xicamatl* chunks between arthritic thumb and forefinger.

"It is used for eating!" he chuckled as he popped the piece into his mouth. "Try some. You will like it!"

Anya rolled her eyes and laughed.

"Are you ever serious, *Don* Yaxché?"

"Always! Laughter is serious business, *mi niña*—the strongest medicine there is!"

Anya laughed again and took a piece of *xicamatl*. It was crisp, like an Asian pear but sweetly woody.

Monday, December 17, 2012 — 13 Cib, Day of Wax

"It is good!"

Yaxché smiled, eyes twinkling, before looking down the road. Anya followed his gaze and for a moment saw nothing. Then came the sound of a car, and headlights slashing through the rain. A moment later it slid to a stop in front of Yaxché's hut: Rebecca's rental car, with Rebecca, Stephen, Chalo, and a stranger in it. Stephen jumped out even before the car had come to a full stop and was opening the rear passenger door.

"We have Chalo and he's fine, *Don* Yaxché, but the senator needs your help…"

Yaxché was beside the car in an instant, once again surprisingly swift for one of his age. In another instant he had the answer to the question he had asked earlier: the man in the car, his eyes swollen shut, was the fifth, the witness, the blinded Seven Macaw.

TUESDAY, DECEMBER 18, 2012
1 CABAN, DAY OF EARTH

CHAPTER 55

"You look like your granny just died, Pete. Spill it, will you?"

Peter Nguyen had knocked on Kathy's open office door; a politeness he did not generally observe, his face pale and serious. Bender wuffed at the noise and lifted his head from his paws; when Peter remained at the door, the dog cocked its head, confused.

"The first reports are coming in from Jamaica."

"Worse than Puerto Rico?"

"A lot. The eye went through Kingston, Portland, St. Thomas, and St. Andrew Parishes."

"Right through Kingston Town," Kathy replied evenly, a statement more than a question.

Peter nodded.

"How many dead?" Kathy asked, not wanting to know the answer.

"At least four thousand. And way more injured. Two schools being used as community shelters collapsed in Morant Bay and Half Way Tree. There's almost nothing left standing, from what Jamaica Public Service is saying."

Kathy's elbows were up on her desk; she let her head drop to her raised hands and rubbed her forehead for a long moment. Bender wuffed again, this time softly, and then whined.

"S'okay, boy," the woman said, dropping a hand to stroke Bender's head.

"Two days before it hits the Yucatán; another day or so before it is back over warm water. And then it's anybody's guess. My money's on Louisiana," she sighed.

"Why?"

"Nothing's been easy for the Big Easy since Katrina."

"It's going to be worse than Katrina, Kath."

"I know it, son."

"But nobody's leaving!"

"I know that, too. We can only issue the warnings. It isn't a police state, much as I'd like it to be right about now," she replied. Even her sarcasm did not have its usual bite: Kathy Howlachuk merely sounded old and tired.

"But why?"

"Why what? Why aren't they going? Because, Pete, they're too beat up by storms and oil spills to care anymore, poor people. How's the next bulletin coming?"

"We just let 22a out; 23 will be ready to go for 17:00 hours."

"Good. Maybe go down to the lounge and catch some shut-eye if you can… you look tired."

"Yeah, you too."

Kathy suddenly felt lonely, even with Bender there.

"Hey Pete?"

"Yeah?"

"Rebecca's still down there. I don't think there are enough flights left for her to get out in time."

"Jeez, Kathy, I'm so sorry…"

"Yeah, me too."

"She's smart, Kath. And she's your god-daughter: she can't help but know a lot about hurricanes. She'll know how to take care of herself."

"I hope you're right…"

"I know I am."

"Thanks, Pete."

Peter nodded and left wordlessly. He didn't actually believe his pep talk; if *Sigma* had plans for Rebecca, there was no way she would survive.

SENATOR'S ABSENCE DELAYS CLIMATE BILL, OPPONENTS CALL IT "STALL TACTIC"

Washington Evening Post
December 18, 2012—AP

A key vote on carbon emission caps was delayed until after Christmas at the request of the Senate Majority Leader. Supporters of the bill are crying foul, suggesting that this is a last-minute "stall tactic" in an effort to build the support needed to sink the bill. They cite Wilkes' sudden departure for his country retreat in Uncertain, TX, as a calculated risk: in the horse-trading that is Washington, Wilkes's absence might allow the so-called "60/20" to pass but would lead to the defeat of a linked bill on changes to social security that is even dearer to the President's heart.

It makes for good press, perhaps, but insiders aren't convinced: Senator Wilkes is the ranking senator on the Hill, has spent months horse-trading against this bill, and, to the consternation of environmentalists, was rumoured to have six more votes than needed to defeat the bill.

That, in itself, is a testament to the Senator's power: the bill has been hailed internationally as a step forward in the global fight against climate change; environmentalists have painted it as a huge blow to Big Oil; and commentators have called it America's next great leadership moment, opining that it could galvanize American hearts, minds, and the economy the way the race to the Moon did almost fifty years ago. Many fear that failure to grab the opportunity will give the lead to China, allowing that nation to take the lead on—and reap the economic benefits of—green technologies.

Indeed, a recent CNN poll suggests that a slim majority of Americans are already willing to support caps and carbon taxes higher than those proposed in the "60/20" bill put forward by Senators Carolina Schroeder (GOP, NM) and Betsy Denton (DEM, MN); even in Wilkes' home state of Texas, where cattle farms have been stricken by a multi-year drought, support for the bill is rising.

So Senator Wilkes' opposition to the 60/20 bill seems to have him out of step, perhaps for the first time in his life, with the mood of the nation, and everyone is anxious to ask him why. But the senator is conspicuously absent.

So where is he? His office is tight-lipped, saying only that the Senator's position on the Bill hasn't changed. Stranger still, Senator Schroeder, normally to be counted on for a scathing comment, has declined to speak to the media. Some are saying that this is part of another one of his famously byzantine plans to get something for his constituents. Others suggest that he might be ill—a heart attack has been rumoured. And from an unlikely quarter—an insider in the State Department—is a rumour befitting the X-files: that he is the victim of his own politics and that he might be absent from the Hill against his will.

Whatever the reason, the climate bill languishes. And with a super-hurricane approaching the Gulf, the only thing everyone on the Hill can agree is that the storm over Joe Wilkes' absence isn't the biggest one in town.

Tuesday, December 18, 2012 — 1 Caban, Day of Earth

CHAPTER 56

Rebecca woke with a start to the sound of something thumping outside, the remnants of a dark dream clinging like cobwebs. She put her hands to her face to wipe sleep from her eyes and felt herself sway; she was in a hammock. Lupita's hammock. The events of the night before came flooding back.

"He is the last part," Yaxché had said the moment he had seen Joe. "Bring him."

The last part of what, Rebecca wondered.

After they had laid Joe, unconscious and bleeding internally, on Yaxché's examining table, the healer had sent all but Stephen back out of his hut. Chalo and Anya had acquiesced; Rebecca had not been so sanguine. Yaxché had merely pointed to her shoulder—Stephen had rebandaged it on the road—and sent her to Lupita's hut for some much-needed rest.

Another loud noise—a single sound like a gunshot—made Rebecca sit up.

"Lupita?"

"*Uay*, no worries. It is only me now! The wind throws the door closed. You are hungry?"

"Joe—the man we brought—will he be alright?"

"Maybe yes. Yaxché went to collect."

"Where is everyone else?"

"The teacher lady sleeps in her car and the men—*Ka Ili'ik* and the other one—they are in Yaxché's hut. Sleeping, maybe. You are hungry?" she asked again.

She was, and her stomach growled to prove it.

"Yes, please. But can I help?"

"No, you hurt. Wait. Yes. The chickens. Go to get the eggs." She said, pointing to a basket by the door.

Rebecca smiled and headed outside to Lupita's animal pen.

It was raining in earnest now, and gusty. One of the advance cloud bands, Rebecca thought. Kathy was probably having conniptions about the coming storm. And about her still being down here in it. She'd have to call. After the chickens.

The pen was a strange, makeshift affair, more of a barn than a typical pen, made so that if Lupita needed to leave to midwife a baby, she could shoo the animals inside and be certain they had food and water for a while. Rebecca ran through the rain to the squat thatched building and ducked inside, the chickens squabbling in surprise at her arrival. More sanguine, the goats, penned at the far end of the space, merely looked up and then returned to their feed.

Rebecca let her eyes adjust to the muzzy light filtering in through small chinks in the walls, then waited a further moment for the chickens to settle before approaching them. Once they were gabbling softly to themselves, eyes drooping, Rebecca crept forward to take the warm brown eggs from beneath their soft breastfeathers. The wind outside seemed not to trouble the hens: there were nine eggs from thirteen birds.

She could see why: it was nice in here, with the coo and chuckle of hens, the goats' molars grinding, the sow at the very back grunting gently, the shush of rain on the thatch above her head. She sat back on her heels, hands on her knees, and for the first time since arriving in Mexico, realized that it was startlingly close to Christmas. She sighed deeply, inhaling the sweet musk of the barn, and genuinely hoped that Joe was going to make it.

She thought about him, and about Hayden's letter, and about the anger she had nursed all this time. Knowing the truth and seeing Joe so banged up, it didn't seem worth it anymore. Everyone was trying their best. Maybe rather than loathing him, she could cut him some slack.

"He's going to be alright, you know."

Rebecca jumped at the sound of Stephen's voice; she'd been so deep in thought, and he'd come in so quietly, that she hadn't heard him.

"Joe?"

Stephen crept forward to sit beside her and nodded.

"Yaxché is amazing. Really amazing. We wrapped Joe's ribs—at least two were broken—and set his arm—his humerus was broken, too—and I stitched up a gash on his scalp. And then Yaxché mixed up a poultice and a tea that took care of everything else: bleeding, swelling… everything. He'll be asleep until this evening, but you can see him when he wakes up."

"Thank you. Not just for Joe. For everything," Rebecca said solemnly.

"All in a day's work," he smiled.

There was an awkward silence for a moment.

"Is it… is it really that wet out there? You hair is soaked," Rebecca asked.

"No. I stuck my head in the rain barrel to get the top layer of grime off. It is going to be a bad storm, though…"

"Yeah, my aunt said… Hey, you're bleeding!"

"Really, where?" he asked, looking down.

There was a thin line of blood on his t-shirt, over his heart.

"Damn… this is pretty much my last t-shirt, too," he grumbled as he pulled the shirt up to look for the source of the blood.

"Oh my god, how did that happen?" Rebecca said as she saw the angry gash that slashed diagonally across his chest. The bottom of it, almost at his kidney, was bleeding strongly.

"Yesterday when I was pulling you up. A piece of limestone. I must have washed the clot loose," he answered as he finished pulling the shirt off over his head.

Rebecca took the shirt from him without asking, rolled it up, and pressed it against the cut.

"It's stained anyway," she said when he tried to protest. "Where'd you get the tattoo?"

There was a small red maple leaf on the pectoral muscle over his heart, just above the top of the cut.

"What? Oh. Before a competition," he said. "We all got one. We were going to play in Berlin. We thought it would be patriotic."

"It's nice," she said, softly.

"Thanks… ."

"Stephen?"

"Uh hunh?"

"You smell like rain," she said as she leaned in and kissed his cheekbone.

"You smell like the wind," he answered as he ran his fingers through her hair and kissed her ear.

They looked at each other for a long moment, recognizing the same emotions in each other; emotions so long ignored now clamouring for attention. For Rebecca, Stephen's eyes were a beacon, heralding safe haven after a long stretch at sea; for Stephen, Rebecca's touch was like candlelight, and he could see his way, at last, out of the darkness.

They gazed, green eyes on hazel, as if saying grace for a gift bestowed, and then their lips met, kissing gingerly, then deeply, not stopping even as they removed each other's clothes.

Rebecca sank back into the soft sweet hay as Stephen rose onto her, close and closer, long and longer beneath the thatch and rain, until at last they climaxed together and lay, perfected, in each other's arms.

CHAPTER 57

Anya and Chalo had avoided each other all morning as if required to by a restraining order: carefully and always within eyesight but never close enough to speak. When he was on Yaxché's porch, she sat on Lupita's; when she sat in the car to read, he sat beneath the shelter of a tree with his own book. It was Lupita who could take it no longer.

"Foolish! Like *mano* and *metate* fighting. They can only grind corn together," she muttered as she bustled outside, saw the chicken coop, and abandoned hope of using eggs. She needed a new lunch plan.

"You!" she shouted through the rain, finger pointing at Chalo. "Come!"

Chalo dog-eared his page, stood reluctantly, and ran through the rain.

"Get the girl," she ordered. "No eggs. She must to help for lunch."

"I can get the eggs…"

"No. Go to get the girl!"

"I can help, then."

"Not a man! Go! Get!"

Chalo sighed and turned towards the car as if heading towards the gallows.

"Anya?" he asked, tapping on the window.

Anya looked up from her book.

"Lupita says you are to help her make lunch."

Anya rolled down her window.

"What?"

"Lupita wants for you to go help her with lunch."

"Why can't you?" she said petulantly, looking back to her book.

"She won't let me. Because I'm a man. Since we're talking now, I want to say I'm sorry."

Anya's eyes widened.

"For what?" she said suspiciously.

"For everything. I was wrong…"

"Everything?"

"Everything," he replied simply, his tone genuine.

Anya felt herself relent. "Come sit in the car. It is too wet out there."

Chalo jogged to the passenger side and climbed in, spraying water as he came.

"You were right about Kulkulcan, Anya," he blurted. "Everything you said: that he was a madman and a terrorist who didn't know the whole of Maya history and didn't believe what he did know. He is using it for his own ends, and I was a fool to believe in him, to join him."

Anya paused a moment, mastering herself. "Then why did you?" It was a genuine question, asked without accusation.

"At first… at first I did it because I thought it would keep you safe. He threatened to kill you if I didn't join him. I didn't know he had guaranteed your silence with the threat to your brother…"

"You did it for me?" Anya asked, incredulous.

"At first. And then you said things…"

"I said awful things…" she said, ashamed.

"No. I mean yes, some were awful. But true, nevertheless. I just didn't want to hear them. Then I joined him from spite. And maybe because part of me liked his message…"

"But why, Chalo? It is nothing but hate and revenge…"

"*I'm* nothing, Anya. An *indio* kid who became a cop because he could do nothing else. I'm tired of being an orphan. Kulkulcan offers—pretends to offer—something to belong to. A proud history. A proud future. Better than the nothing I am now. But when I watched him delight in his power—frightening his boys, planning murder like it was buying groceries, even killing forest creatures on a pleasurable whim… I knew it was a lie, Anya. I am ashamed of my own stupidity."

The painful honesty of his self-assessment astounded Anya, and whatever anger remained fell away like an iceberg calving from a glacier.

"*Mein Gott*, Chalo, you already belong to something wonderful. Your culture is in your blood. And despite what Kulkulcan is doing with it, it is a wondrous and magical thing. I study it, hoping that it might rub off on me, make me better somehow. But all I end up feeling is like I am the one that is nothing. Or worse: using your culture for my own benefit, just like Kulkulcan."

She looked down at her lap and scowled at herself.

"You? Nothing?!" Chalo exclaimed.

He reached to take her face in his hands and stopped himself. Instead he said, "You have followed a dream, and your own heart, for your whole life. You are so very smart, smarter than I can ever hope to be. You have a business. You write; you teach; you are so very beautiful… How could you possibly be nothing? How I would love to be you, if I could…"

Anya smiled at the bitter irony of their mutual envy.

"I owe you an apology, too, Chalo," she said, looking up into his brown eyes. "I expected you to be the Maya of my imagination, not the Maya that you are… ."

Chalo started to ask a question, but Anya stopped him.

"… and who you are, Chalo, is good. You are a kind, smart, honest man." It broke her heart to say this last thing: she had much vested in hating him as a proxy for her ex-husband.

"You think we might start over again?" Chalo asked.

Anya blushed, despite herself, thinking of the first night they had spent together.

"No! I don't mean that…" Chalo flustered. Anya laughed and he smiled, relieved.

"I have nothing to offer you, Anya," he continued. "Nothing at all. I'm poor and stupid. But I am honest and not too proud to admit it when I make a mistake. And I make delicious *flautas*, if only Lupita would let me…"

"Come," Anya said as she took Chalo's hand. "Let us both help Lupita, and you can show me."

***

Kulkulcan sat in his hut, head still ringing from Chalo's final blow on top of the pyramid, and cursed himself for having been undone by his own prejudices: the Maya had been the turncoat after all. It bothered him to think that the American was the loyal one and so, when he heard

Rutrauff's voice outside the door, he levelled his gun.

Rutrauff knocked, strode in without waiting for permission, and stopped at the sight of the gun levelled at his chest.

"The fire's raging beyond camp; the Senator's gone; there's a bloody corpse on the plaza; the boys tell me your cousin whipped your ass; and you've got your gun pointed at *me*?" Rutrauff demanded as he raised his arms, one fist clenched.

"What's in your hand, American?"

"Something that's going to save your frickin' bacon, Kulkulcan. Now would you put your gun down?"

"Show me first, Captain. I'm not in a trusting mood."

Rutrauff lowered his fist and opened it to reveal Wilkes' heavy football ring.

Kulkulcan's eyes narrowed. "What is it?"

"A football ring. I took it before your cousin—some cousin, by the way—helped him escape. It's engraved with the senator's name. You can use it to make sure he recognizes your goddamned government when the shooting stops. He'll do anything to keep the world from knowing he had anything to do with your little coup."

Kulkulcan lowered his gun, stunned, and then started to chuckle.

"Wheels within wheels. Even I did not see this one coming. Perhaps I owe you an apology, Captain. Perhaps I owe you an apology after all."

He paused and then chuckled again.

"So you didn't really know the girl?" he asked.

"No, sir. She followed the money from Wilkes to me to you, simple as that."

"Indeed. Well, it seems you are on my side, after all," he said, pocketing the ring. "We can proceed as if nothing happened, can't we?"

"Yessir."

"Except that you will be using my security information, yes."

"Yessir," Rutrauff said again, voice neutral.

"Something bothering you, Captain?"

"Besides killing an extra nine politicians?"

"Killing is your business, Captain. Yes, besides that."

"Are we really using those heat rays?"

"Ahh. Squeamish, are you? Yes, we are. They are an important part of my mythology. The gods want blood. I owe it for my power, hmm?"

Rutrauff clenched his jaw and said nothing.

"Anything else, Captain?"

"Yes, sir. You sent Payal off to make sure the German doesn't sink the rig…"

"And he will do as I ordered. He's a smart one, Payal is. He'll do his job."

"Yes, sir. But if he's on the rig, who do I take as the last member of my cell?"

"Ah, yes. You're a man short, aren't you?" Kulkulcan said nonchalantly. "You can take Alvarro. Someone needs to keep an eye on him."

***

Joe had woken by dinner, weak but ambulatory and ravenous: Stephen had helped him to Lupita's hut and dinner—*tortas huevos* made with the eggs Rebecca had collected.

After Rebecca had made introductions—shy ones when it came to Stephen, warm ones for Anya, Chalo and Lupita, deferential ones when it came to Yaxché—Joe tried to say thank you. Yaxché cut him short.

"There will be time after. Now we talk about tomorrow. Anya, this is the Macaw."

Anya looked at Wilkes and her jaw dropped.

"Him?!" she said in disbelief.

"Rich. Greedy. Power he thinks is bigger than god. And look at his eye. Blind. He is Macaw."

Wilkes did not like the characterization.

"Hang on a minute, here…"

Rebecca looked warningly at Wilkes and shook her head; when he opened his mouth anyway she spoke over him.

"Maybe we should catch each other up… and Joe, too, now that we're all here?"

"So much trouble working with sparrowhawks," Yaxché grumbled. "Always needing to be taught. Always knowing so little."

Anya snorted and Yaxché smiled at her and then at Rebecca.

"Of course the *señorinas* are right. Remember that, *mi hijos*, the women are always right."

He winked at Stephen and Chalo; they exchanged glances and

chuckled, amused and embarrassed both.

"It is your thinking, *mi esposa*, so you begin," Yaxché added, serious once more. "Talking now saves problems later, but still we do not have so much time."

"I'm… I'm not sure where to start…" Rebecca hesitated, glancing at Joe. "For me it started with the money you…"

"I stole. You can say it. I'm going to have to pay for it sooner or later so I might as well admit it now. I guess that means I started the whole mess, hunh?"

Yaxché cackled and looked at Anya. "See? The Macaw! Thinks he is the centre of the world!"

Anya laughed and the others smiled as Rebecca resumed.

"I don't actually understand it all…" she said, looking to Yaxché for help.

"*Lakin*. You tell," Yaxché said, turning to Anya. "Starting with your ruins, like a teacher. I will speak after."

Anya took a deep breath and within moments had warmed to her subject. It took almost an hour, but she never once lost her thread or her audience's interest, and by the end—as she described the need for the ancient ceremony at Chich'en Itzá—it all seemed to make an inexplicable kind of sense to those who had lived through so much of it.

Wilkes was far less sanguine.

"Let me get this straight," he said witheringly. "The man I'm buying guns for is part of a prophecy painted on the ceiling of a temple built five hundred years ago in the middle of a swamp. He's taken the name of the Lord—my apologies—the Lords—in vain and they're ticked and are thinking about killing us off. And Yaxché here is the lawyer going to argue our case. Have I got it in a nutshell?"

Yaxché, Stephen, Chalo, Rebecca and Anya nodded. Lupita paused a moment and then nodded vigorously as well.

"Have you all lost your minds?!"

The group shook their heads, Lupita most solemnly.

"Aw, come on, Becky, it's ridiculous!"

"Is it? Aren't you the one that always talks about the power of prayer?"

"That's different!" Wilkes scoffed.

"Because this is the Maya religion, not yours?"

"So chanting inside a pyramid is going to save the world," Wilkes said dubiously.

"Why not, Joe? Why do you think they call you the Bayou Butterfly? You sneeze and all of Washington get the flu."

"That's different, too…" Joe said weakly.

"With respect, Senator," Stephen interjected, "It *isn't* different. If you want logic, it's the physics of chaos theory. Tipping points. Ripple effects. For want of a nail, the horse, the rider, the message, and the kingdom were lost, right? Who knows what Yaxché's ceremony will do? Maybe just being there will change something."

"Like maybe preventing the President's assassination?" Chalo said, avuncular. "Remember he will be at Chich'en Itzá the same day as the ceremony is to take place. To dedicate the Mitnal rig."

Anya thought about Sebastian and said nothing. If he could not change Payal's mind he would be dead, the rig would remain standing—pumping—and the dedication would continue as planned. It was not worth complicating things further with 'what ifs.'

"So the claptrap about tipping-points is true, hunh?" Wilkes asked wearily.

"And not new, either," Anya said, with satisfaction.

"And I'm coming along whether I like it or not, right?"

Yaxché cackled. "You can stay here, instead, if you wish. Lupita is a very good nursemaid. A busybody and worrywart, but a good nurse…"

"Quiet you old goat," Lupita scolded, waving her hand dismissively.

The laughter over Yaxché and Lupita's sparring made Wilkes' irritation worse; he was unused to being boxed into a corner.

"No, I'll come," he said petulantly. "Do we leave now?"

"No no! There will be a little break in the storm tomorrow morning. We go then."

"How do you know *that*?"

"I know much, Macaw. And in ways you refuse to believe. But *that* I heard on the radio. 'The space between rain bands,' they called it," he grinned, his eyes twinkling.

Rebecca snorted at the way Yaxché was teasing Joe.

"Then what do we do tonight?" Wilkes asked, frowning at Rebecca.

"I think night is usually good for sleep," Yaxché cackled. "But you can do whatever you want." He winked at Rebecca and Stephen and both of them blushed.

The others laughed, Yaxché's mirth contagious; after a few moments, Wilkes himself relented, choosing to see the humour in his own predicament: if he was in for a dime, he might as well be in for a dollar.

WEDNESDAY, DECEMBER 19, 2012
2 ETZNAB, DAY OF FLINT

CHAPTER 58

It had been back roads from the outset, Anya and Chalo in Anya's truck following Rebecca, Stephen, Yaxché, and Wilkes in Rebecca's rental: south and then east through Chanchankan, north to Dziuché, northwest through Abal and Tucacab, east through Peto, northeast to Chikindzonot, then north through Chan Chimila, Muchucuxab, Chan-Kom and Chankom to Muchucux, and finally northwest towards Chich'en Itzá. The ruins lay only a few kilometres short of Pisté. Yaxché knew every village and every hamlet, and gave unerring directions despite his failing eyesight.

They had started out once Yaxché had returned from collecting, the sky above them a high overcast free of rain as Yaxché had promised. An hour into the journey the heavens had darkened once more: the clouds dropped, the temperature plummeted, and the rains returned so thick and heavy that talking in both vehicles should have been limited to necessities. In Anya's, it was.

"You are a good driver, Dr. von Eckhardt," Chalo said as Anya negotiated the muddy potholes, truck buffeted by the wind.

"You are a good person, Detective Guerrero," Anya said with feeling, her eyes never leaving Rebecca's car in front of them.

In Rebecca's car, the story was altogether different; Yaxché was bent on teasing something from the senator with whom he shared the back seat.

"Who is the young man, Macaw?" Yaxché demanded.

Rebecca gripped the steering wheel, a small smile on her face. This was going to be interesting.

"What—who?" Wilkes asked, startled; he had been watching the forest slide by with his good eye.

"The one watching you. There is a young man watching you from the other side."

Wilkes craned to look around him with his one good eye and then turned to look at Yaxché.

"I have no idea what you're talking about, Hernando," Wilkes said, a little irritably. He was tired of being cooped up in the tiny car and his ribs hurt when he breathed.

"Never mind. I tell you a story about *Ixtab* instead, yes?"

"Do I have a choice on this one?"

"Listen or not. *Mi esposa* and *Ka Ili'ik* will be interested either way. Right *los niños*?"

Eyes on the road, Rebecca nodded; Stephen swivelled in the passenger seat to better watch the healer. Wilkes snorted. "Democracy in action. Fill your boots, Hernando," he said with a rueful smile.

"So. Who is *Ixtab*?" Yaxché asked, warming to his subject.

"Any relation to *Xtabay*?" Stephen asked.

"No. But a spirit also. Do you believe in spirits, Macaw?"

"Call me Joe, would you? Do you mean do I believe in ghosts? Should I?"

"They are everywhere, even if you do not. What you *should* do is up to you. It is easier to see them if you believe, is all."

"Fine. I believe."

"No you don't. Too bad, but it won't matter. *Ixtab* is the goddess of babies who die while being born, and soldiers who die in battle, and men and women who take their own lives."

Rebecca's thought instantly of Hayden's letter, and her knuckles tightened on the steering wheel. Beside Yaxché, Joe had suddenly grown pale.

"There's a god for suicide?" the senator asked, his voice barely audible above the rain hammering on the roof.

"Of course!" Yaxché said, shaking his head at the things the foreigners didn't know. "We live. We die. We are all equal no matter our way of going. The heartsick leave the world when their souls are too broken to fix in this life; *Ixtab* nurses them in the shade of the world tree until they are strong enough to walk the white road to the sky."

Yaxché fell silent for so long that Wilkes felt the need to prompt him.

"So… ?"

"*Ixtab* is waiting for the boy."

"What boy?!"

"Hayden, right?" Rebecca asked from the front seat as she flicked the headlights on; the heavy sky was growing darker still with the approach of night.

"Yes, *mi esposa*."

"I thought you said he was done with me?" Rebecca asked, blinking away tears. Stephen reached towards her; she took a hand from the steering wheel and gripped his.

"What the hell are you all talking about?" Wilkes demanded.

"The Maya believe the dead are always visiting; those who have unfinished business stay with us," Stephen said brusquely. "Yaxché is saying that your son has some unfinished business; that he's watching you."

"My god," Wilkes said softly. The idea elated him even as it terrified; perhaps he had not lost everything.

"What does he want?" Wilkes whispered, desperate to believe.

"That is between the two of you, Macaw… ¡*Uay*! ¡*Halto*! Rebecca, stop! We are here finally. Now we walk."

Rebecca pulled the car to the side of the road and turned around to look at Yaxché.

"We're walking? In *this*?"

Nature's great destroyers—hurricanes—were nature's great midwifes as well, renewing the natural systems that had evolved to survive them; it was only humanity's hard walls and its passion for permanence that made the storms so dangerous to life and limb. This and more—physical mechanics, seasonality, characteristics, forecasting, tracking, nomenclature, their myriad effects, and their growing intensity over time thanks to climate change—Rebecca had learned as god-daughter to the Senior Scientist at the US NHC.

And still she had not prepared for even *Sigma*'s comparatively tame leading edge. What, she wondered, would its heart—still maybe eighteen hours away—be like, beating destruction?

Before stepping from the car she had thought to try to gage the storm's category by its visible effect—with the trees skewed sideways, she would have guessed a Category 1 already, verging on Category 2. Once outside, she lost her dispassion; she and the others could only concentrate on making it from the roadside—the road a narrow sluice through which the frigid wind and rain tore—to the comparative safety of the jungle's edge a dozen feet away.

In the comparative shelter of the forest, Anya tried to shout over the keening storm, the wind singing the storm's fury in the staccato of each snapping tree and howl of each new squall made her hard to hear. "How far?" she asked three times before Yaxché heard her.

"Not far," Yaxché reassured, somehow taller, stronger, younger in the storm, his eyes flashing bright in the glow of Stephen and Anya's flashlights.

"Hold to each other, by clothes or hands," he ordered. "Be careful of things falling and of the roots beneath your feet. We are ready?"

The group nodded, shivering in the wind.

The paltry light thrown by the two flashlights—Stephen's, second in line behind Yaxché; Anya's in Chalo's hand at the very back of the human chain—only deepened the darkness. Leaves, both green and dead, were visible scudding and tumbling beneath their feet but everything else was left to blind and terrifying imagination: creaking branches might be ready to fall, gusting winds felt like unseen hands tearing at them, the momentary brightness of lightning revealed monsters, bent and grotesque; whether real or imagined it was hard to say.

They had been walking for almost twenty minutes and they were each soaked to the bone: Yaxché, in his old rubber boots, fast and unerring, like a man following an invisible thread; the rest with difficulty, the wet leaf litter grown as slick as marble. More than once Stephen needed to tug on Yaxché's shirttails to force the old man to slow down.

And then Stephen let go of the old man's shirt altogether: Rebecca had stumbled behind Stephen and he had let go of Yaxché to steady her. When Stephen turned back the healer was gone. Stephen shone his light in wide arcs, catching the bright eyes of some small night creature not yet hunkered down, but there was no sign of Yaxché.

"How could you lose him?" Anya shouted when the group had bunched to a stop.

"I… I don't know. He was here and then… gone…"

"What the hell do we do now?" It was Wilkes.

"Look for him? Go back to the car?" Chalo suggested, his voice straining to be heard over the wind.

"Do we even know where the car is anymore?" Rebecca asked. "I say we find shelter."

Stephen was about to agree when he felt something grab his ankle. He fought a powerful urge to kick it away, thinking of the coati he had startled a week and an eternity ago; his heart stopped for a moment when he looked down and he wished he had lashed out when he could; it was a hand that had grabbed him, sticking out from a hole in the ground, and it held him firm.

"Something's got me…" he shouted as he shone his light down.

Chalo and Rebecca reached to pull Stephen from the hands, Anya cursed, anxiety rose in the group. And then Stephen laughed, his flashlight illuminating the depths. Beyond the hand that held him, staring up, was Yaxché's face, grinning slyly. Nor had Yaxché fallen; he was beckoning Stephen and the others to follow him down what was not a hole, but a stairwell leading into the quiet Earth.

The silence in the cave at the bottom of the long rough-hewn stairway was deafening after the noise of the storm, and even a whisper felt like a shout.

"Better, yes?" Yaxché asked, delighted.

It was far better: safe and warm. They might be able to survive even the eyewall winds down here, Rebecca marvelled.

"What is this place?" Anya asked, looking around with a trained eye. The floor of the cave was paved with limestone blocks—a *sacbe*—and the walls had once been washed white with lime.

"It is the way to the ceremony, *mi niña*. Come. The others are waiting."

Tunnels were not unusual in Mayan construction; they connected successive iterations of temples, one built on top of another, and often served as a proxy for the underworld itself in ritual. Anya had even visited a complex cavern system discovered in 2008 that was an eerily literal path—through darkness, water, mud, and a colony of bats—the trials the Hero Twins faced on their journey to the Underworld. But this? An unknown network of tunnels beneath Chich'en Itzá itself, the best-studied temple of them all? How was it possible that it had been kept from the academic eye?

"It goes right to *El Castillo*?"

"It goes many places, *mi niña*. There… the other temples…" he answered as he started walking. "It is the roots of the tree, spreading everywhere. A sacred space and not yours to reveal, hmm?" he warned.

"No, of course not," Anya said—quickly, immediately, regretfully—dismissing thoughts of publication.

At the end of the oval cavern, there were three square doorways giving way into three different tunnels. Yaxché headed unerringly for the left-most portal, the others following him, Anya pausing momentarily to read the glyph—a signpost—over the door's lintel: "*dzonote*." They were going to the sacred *cenote*, the ruins' namesake: the Well of the Water Wizards.

The fivesome followed Yaxché in silent wonder through walls that glistened in the dim flashlights: not wet but crystalline.

"The limestone is laced with quartz…" Stephen wondered, shining his light on the tunnel wall and smiling as it glittered. "Amazing…"

"It's like walking through the night sky…" Rebecca replied softly.

"It is walking through creation, *niños*. Now be quiet, yes?"

They walked on in silence for another ten minutes or so, Yaxché taking one tunnel left and ignoring the next bifurcation; taking two entryways right and one more left, muttering to himself as he went.

It made Chalo think of his grandmother, singing her way to special places to find honey or pick herbs: an auditory map.

Yaxché stopped at last: he was a few feet from an entry on the left side of the tunnel lintelled with ancient *ceiba*, ornately carved. The group smelled wood and *copal* burning; the rippling yellow reflection of firelight danced on the wall opposite the doorway. Someone was already inside.

Yaxché called out, deep and low, a chant that seemed to be meant to reach even the spaces within every living thing. A moment later came the response, a thrumming wordlessness that echoed in each person's chest, the Earth's own heartbeat. The sound died away, and Yaxché opened his eyes; Stephen, Rebecca, Chalo, Anya, and Joe held their breath.

Yaxché looked at them, eyes wide with expectation, and cackled. The sound of laughter spilled from the entryway, with calls of "Yaxché" and "¡*Bienvenidos, El Mero*!"

"We have arrived! Come in and you will meet the judges. Then we eat and sleep, for tomorrow the heart of heaven arrives and the end of the end begins."

THURSDAY, DECEMBER 20, 2012
3 CAUAC, DAY OF STORM

CHAPTER 59

Peter listened to CNN, streaming into the corner of his screen as he pulled down the latest satellite imagery, and shook his head at the reporter's melodrama. Not that hurricane *Sigma* wasn't a dramatic story, but the reporter—a blonde Aussie named Kiley Mathers—conveyed the NHC's most recent bulletin as if presaging doom.

"*—according to the National Hurricane Centre's 8 a.m. advisory,* Sigma, *which earlier swallowed hurricanes* Tao *and* Upsilon, *is now a 'potentially catastrophic' Category Five hurricane; its eye is expected to smash into the Yucatán coast somewhere south of the town of Tulum within the next six hours…*"

Peter looked at the first image through the pipe and nodded: still on track. He pulled the newest wind and pressure data and frowned. Kiley Mathers kept using his 8 a.m. advisory to dramatic effect.

"*—sustained winds nearest the eye are now an unbelievable one hundred and seventy four miles per hour and gusting even higher; barometric pressure—a proxy for storm severity where the lower the number the stronger the storm—are 26.6 millibars of mercury, the lowest ever recorded for an Atlantic hurricane…*"

That was true, Peter observed, and he wouldn't have wanted to be in the Hurricane Hunter—the Lockheed WP-3D aircraft—that had flown the recon to get those data, but scarier by far was the storm surge *Sigma* was pushing towards the coast: twenty-one feet above normal on a high tide. That was higher than the tsunami walls Japan—the nation best prepared for such an assault—had built. The Yucatán would be deluged, and, if *Sigma* kept right on through the Bay of Campeche and into the Gulf, New Orleans would again be awash, even with her new levees.

Now Peter pulled down the Doppler and raised an eyebrow; either the positioning was off, or *Sigma* was veering. He drummed his fingers as he waited for another image and the melodramatic reporter carried on.

"*—The government of Mexico has broadened the hurricane warning to include the entire coastline of the Yucatán Peninsula, including Cancún where I'm now standing, urging that preparations to protect life and property be rushed to completion.*"

Peter wondered fleetingly what CNN paid in the way of misadventure insurance for Kiley Mathers, standing there waiting to report on a Category 5 hurricane; her premiums obviously paid, she spoke on.

"*—at the same time, however, the Mexican President himself has reconfirmed his intention to attend a press conference in the heart of the Yucatán at the ancient Maya city of Chich'en Itzá. The press conference was intended to mark the beginning of Mitnal's commercial production and Chich'en Itzá chosen to represent the height of Mexico's riches, both cultural and economic. With the rig foundering overnight, it is now widely expected that the President will use the press conference to make a commitment to redeveloping the oil field as soon as possible. We'll be bringing you that story this afternoon from Chich'en Itzá itself.*"

Peter looked up at the news reporter's image in surprise; her rain poncho plastered against her, her blonde hair whipped in the wind. It wasn't so much the news that the rig had foundered but the fact of a press conference in Sigma's path that astonished him.

He opened a new browser and searched for news keywords: Mitnal+press conference. Halfway through the article, his next satellite image finished downloading. He glanced at it and stood, swearing.

"Hell. Hell, hell, hell." Then he shouted over his shoulder. "Kathy? You there, Doc? You're going to have to revise the 11:00 bulletin. *Sigma* just made a sharp right…"

No Lessons Learned: History Repeats as Mitnal Rig Sinks

America Today
Thursday, December 20, 2012

Environmentalists today are despairing at the second catastrophic oil platform accident in three years, fearing that populations of marine birds and mammals already hard hit by the Deepwater Horizon *disaster in 2010 will be dealt a fatal blow by last night's sinking of PEMEX's Mitnal platform.*

With no one aboard the platform, ostensibly battened down and evacuated in advance of potentially catastrophic Category Five storm Sigma, *speculation regarding the cause of the rig's demise are rife. That a massive explosion has been reported suggests to some that the shut-down for the hurricane was done improperly. Still others suggest that in fact the storm surge ahead of the hurricane caused some kind of structural failure in the next-generation spar structure, causing the rig to list and eventually sink beneath the high waves.*

A third explanation, as yet unproven, is that this is the latest and most audacious in a series of attacks by ecoterrorists Eden Two. Led by the shadowy figure "Adam," Eden Two has as its stated goal destabilization of global oil production and supply—a kind of tough-love, cold-turkey approach to weaning economies from dependence on petroleum. Eden Two has sabotaged rigs in the North Sea, ruptured pipelines in the republics of the former Soviet Union and South America, and hobbled tankers in the Gulf. The tanker disruption last summer, in particular, created supply woes that briefly drove gasoline prices over the six-

dollar-a-gallon mark.

While Eden Two has not yet claimed responsibility for the disaster, terror experts say that it bears all the hallmarks—particularly that no lives were lost—of the peculiarly compassionate eco-extremist group.

Even if it did not bring the rig down, industry analysts suggest that Eden Two's goal may have been accomplished: the remains of the structure have likely collapsed on the single relatively 'high' point in the abyssal depths that permits access to the Mitnal field; clearing and rebuilding are currently beyond all financial and technical limits. And even if they were not, nations—like the US, which placed a moratorium on offshore drilling after the Deepwater Horizon mess—will now give a further hard look at offshore drilling. All of it spells higher oil prices and further pressure to abandon petroleum as a fuel once and for all.

CHAPTER 60

"What happened, Payal?"

Kulkulcan's favourite warrior, Payal Ek, had returned from the ordeal that was the covert assault on the Mitnal rig an exhausted and changed man.

"I trained with Adam. I learned to set bombs. I learned to climb with ropes in high winds. I rode a tiny submarine. I stole the fuel cells, brought them to shore, and gave them to Alvarro's men for distribution for today's killings. Here, in fact, is the one for the American. And I shot Adam. I did all that you asked, *Ahau*."

Kulkulcan looked first at his watch—they would need to leave for Chich'en Itzá in moments; he should, in fact, be at the airstrip now—and then looked back at Payal. The boy was avoiding eye contact. He was hiding something.

"You shot Adam." He said, sceptically.

"Yes *Ahau*. In the chest."

That much was true: Payal had been the one to pull the trigger, firing the bullet that had ended Adam's life. What Payal did not say was that it had been an accident. That by the end of Adam's gruelling training, Payal had actually respected the ecoterrorist—more even than he respected Kulkulcan. Only fear of what Kulkulcan might do to his young family had made Payal pull the trigger. Not that it had started that way. Payal had committed himself to sabotage with a zeal that would have made Kulkulcan proud: he studied Adam's plan, acquired the needed skills, and worked out his strategy. Eden Two was wealthy, and its members dangerously over-educated; their plan was both brilliant and gadget-rich. To start, four teams in mini-subs, sonically masked and piloted to mimic a pod of whales, would breach the rig's security perimeter. While the climate implications of an oil rig were horrifying, the rigs themselves were quickly colonized by encrusting marine life and were soon lush artificial reefs. Rich with marine life they regularly attracted curious or hungry marine mammals; even this soon after installation the rig's security team would ignore a small pod of whales nosing curiously among the spars.

Once the team had tied up to the spars, they would set explosives on each spar, climb to the rig's underbelly, enter through a maintenance port with security codes provided by a sympathetic insider, disable cameras, steal the battery packs, retrace their steps, rappel to the subs, and detonate the explosives once they were beyond the danger zone. The danger zone was what worried Payal most: the concussive force of the erupting spars, their stored oil ignited by the explosives, would kill any air-breathing mammal that might be underwater when the bombs went off. It was why the team had planned a small pre-explosion blast to startle mammals from the vicinity.

After much consideration, Payal had concluded that his only chance would be to steal the detonator before leaving the rig; then he would not have to worry about the kill zone at all. He would also have to learn to pilot a sub for his plan to work, but how hard could that be?

Not hard, as it turned out, and Adam demanded that everyone know how to pilot them "in case of emergency," so even getting into the cockpit did not arouse suspicion. So after a crash course in climbing, Adam took Payal, José, and Rodrigo out in the four-man submarine.

Payal had been surprised at how patient a teacher Adam had been: as exacting but far more kind than Kulkulcan. Here in the sub, it was no different. Within an hour, José had mastered the basics and returned to shore. An hour and a half later, Rodrigo had returned an adequate pilot. Then it was Payal's turn to take the co-pilot's seat. He had clambered in, watched Adam seal the hatch above them, and then watched through the Plexiglas dome as the vessel thrummed into the crystal sea.

Ten minutes out, the German slowed the craft and turned to his student, his ice-blue eyes preternaturally piercing, as if he looking into Payal's soul.

"Why did you join Kulkulcan, Payal?" he asked earnestly.

"For…" Payal found he could not lie to those eyes. "I do it for my son. That he might have a better future."

"Indeed. Then we work for the same thing."

"You have a son?" Payal asked, astonished. He could not imagine the emaciated man, struggling sometimes to breathe, as a father.

"No, no I don't," he said with remorse. "But my sister—you know Anya, I think—she will one day."

Payal swallowed hard, struggling to digest the information, feeling stupid for not seeing it sooner. The eyes, of course. But also his demeanour: a hard task-master but soft—kind—on the inside. It was why he had felt a kinship with the man from the beginning.

"But I do not understand, Adam…"

"My real name is Sebastian."

"I do not understand, Ada… Sebastian. Why does destroying this rig save your world?"

"My world?"

"The world of the *crillolo*—the foreigner."

"Ah. It is complicated, Payal. In the end, though, it is not unlike the reason Kulkulcan calls for the rig's destruction: the world in which it stays standing will be a hot and terrifying one where drought, disease, disaster, and death mean more struggle than pleasure for the nieces and nephews I will never see."

Payal shifted uncomfortably in his seat at the reference to Kulkulcan. Sebastian saw it and pressed his advantage, carefully, gently.

"And that is what the Lords of *Xibalba* will bring too, is it not? Kulkulcan says they are offended by the hole driven into the heart of their kingdom and threaten the same miseries; it is why Kulkulcan says we must go to it and bring it down, yes?"

Mute, Payal merely nodded.

Sebastian paused and then used what Anya had told him.

"Why then does Kulkulcan wish for you to kill me, that the abomination might stay standing, pumping out the Earth's lifeblood?"

"How do you know?" Payal demanded, surprised.

"Anya told me."

"I… I don't need to kill you. Just make sure you do not destroy the well."

"Look at me, Payal. I'm dying already. You will need to kill me to stop me, since I have nothing left but this. And then what of your gods, if you succeed?"

Payal sat in uncomfortable silence for a long moment, looking into the crystal blue water surrounding the sub, the water darkening as they descended. Rather than prompt him for an answer, Sebastian slowed their craft further and flipped a switch on the console; an instant later, the cabin was filled with the eerie whistling sound of whales vocalizing: the submarine's sonic cloak.

"The voices of the Short-finned Pilot whale," Sebastian said softly. "They are actually oversized members of the dolphin family, growing up to six metres and three tons. Like all the *Delphinidae* they are exceptionally social: they travel in extended family groups of ten to thirty individuals, but sometimes gather in groups of more than two hundred. The Spanish call them *calderón*. They are the most numerous of the protected marine mammals in the Gulf of Mexico."

The song was not what Payal had expected: not just trilling whistles running up and down three octaves, there were clicks and chirps and the occasional raspberry—an underwater fart that made Payal smile despite himself. Nor was the sub's cloak all that he heard: in the distance, more felt than heard, was the heavy thunder of waves, driven by the coming hurricane, pounding the shore. As they passed a small reef, the cabin grew loud with the crackle of shrimp eating algae and the grind of parrotfish grazing on coral.

Payal was about to ask a question when a dark shadow passed over the Plexiglas canopy, forcing him into flinching silence. A heartbeat later the first shadow was joined by a dozen more.

"A family group, curious about us," Sebastian whispered, a smile on his face. "Watch."

Thirteen sleek black whales were swimming beside them now, fascinated by the strange dialect spoken by the robot-whale in their midst. They sang to each other, whistles and clicks that after a time Payal could understand as a conversation. They braided the water, swimming across each other, jockeying for a position beside the sub, bubbles trailing in spirals from their swept-back dorsal fins.

Sebastian slowed the sub and it rose a little in the water column; the pod slowed as well. Sebastian dove a little; the pod kept pace. Sebastian turned off the cloak and hung in the water. A single individual swam forward, turned to face the sub, chirped once and blew a stream of bubbles. A ring, Payal realized, that grew and widened like a smoke ring as it rose until it was the size of a hula hoop. Another squeak, and the whale swam up and through his bubbles. A second whale broke from the pod and swam through the ring, followed by a third. They dove down and blew more rings, swam up through them, squeaked and chirped. They were inviting the sub to play!

"Shall we?" Sebastian mouthed the words so that human voices would not fill the canopy and break the dream. Payal nodded and Sebastian nudged the sub backwards. With a burst of speed he drove the sub up and through the rings, leaving a wash of bubbles behind that the whales dove into, clicking and squeaking, for all the world like joyful children playing in the rain.

And so they frolicked: mini-sub and dolphins, evenly sized and matched, for fifteen minutes, the division between species erased, until the adult whales hanging at the sides whistled an end to the playdate. As one the pod veered off, fading into the opaque distance, all gone in an instant but for a single juvenile, still tubby with baby fat, nose small in the way of all babies, who stayed behind for a final look into the sub's cockpit.

Its white-rimmed eye—black, glossy, curious—spoke mischief and wisdom and timelessness. Payal found himself putting his face close to the glass, his hands on the dome. They stared at each other for a long unblinking moment before a shrill squeak reverberated through the sub and the juvenile, like a lagging child, dashed off after its impatient mother.

The cockpit was suddenly large with cathedral silence, the empty absence of whalesong immensely lonely. What had happened, Payal wondered, as he looked at the whale in that final moment, a god of the deep, his own visage reflected in the creatures bright, inquisitive eye?

"Will the oil that leaks kill them?" Payal asked seriously.

"After the *Deepwater Horizon*, cut-off valves were improved. And if anything does leak, the explosion will scare them away. They will be fine. Better even, when all offshore oil extraction ceases."

"The rig must come down," Payal found himself saying. Then he quailed.

Sebastian could see the boy's worry. "You can say the hurricane destroyed the rig, Payal. He will be angry but you can say it was the will of the gods. He cannot blame you for that, can he?"

So that had been the plan. At least until José had realized what Payal intended and saw an opportunity for his own advancement. The shootout in Mitnal's storage bay had killed both José and Rodrigo and had left Sebastian mortally wounded—more immediately mortally wounded than his cancer. Payal, hand over the gaping hole in Sebastian's chest and listening to the sound of Sebastian labouring for breath, had tried to apologize.

"No, Payal. I was always… going to stay. To detonate. Get the batteries… to Kulkulcan. And after…please look after my sister."

Payal shook away the memory and looked evenly into Kulkulcan's face.

"I shot him in the chest and he died," Payal said, clenching his fist against the sensory memory, warm and wet, on his palm.

"I am sure you did, Payal. But killing him was optional; keeping the rig afloat was your job. So tell me how it is that CNN is reporting that it sank?" Kulkulcan's voice was low and dangerous, the tone that said he would lash out like a snake. The same tone he had used when pressing the muzzle of his gun between Payal's eyes. Payal felt himself shiver with cold fear. He realized fully in that moment that Kulkulcan was a sick and crazed man.

"I… I don't know what you mean, *Ahau*."

"Mitnal sank. It *sank*. It is all over the news. You failed!"

"It… it was standing when I left it, and I felt no detonation. It must be the hurricane that did it." Payal paused a moment and then, unable to help himself, tested Kulkulcan. "Surely it is the work of the Lords of *Xibalba*, *Ahau*?"

"¡*Pendejo*! The gods are dead, and all we have is what we get for ourselves. I needed that oil," Kulkulcan hissed, his lie spilling out, spittle flying from his lips, his face purple with rage.

"Get out of my sight, you stupid boy. And never come back or I will shoot you dead."

Even as he ran from Kulkulcan's hut and then the camp, Payal smiled grimly. He had, at least, made the right choice in throwing his lot in with Sebastian. Beyond the pyramid, Payal circled back and headed for the *sacbe* that was Kulkulcan's airstrip. Now that he knew Kulkulcan for a false prophet, he was going to have to try to stop him.

Thursday, December 20, 2012 — 3 Cauac, Day of Storm

Chapter 61

"*Uay*, Esteban. Wake up. It's tomorrow." Chalo whispered.

Geologist, diplomat, archaeologist, politician, cop—each of them had been captivated by something different in Yaxché's cavern when they had entered it the night before. Stephen had seen the hand of time and the power of water in the great domed space: an underwater river had once pooled here, scouring the limestone until at last the walls had worn away, the water spilling into the *cenote* below. The river long gone, the breach remained as a sheltered window giving into the ancient well below. Rebecca, tuned to political dynamics, had felt the mood, a sacred space that nevertheless held the warmth of family, the mirth of reunion. Anya's trained eye had read the walls, painted with the ceremony she had struggled so long to understand, the people around the fire the avatars of the nine creator gods. Wilkes had seen not the space but its occupants, every one of them a statesman or woman. Even the youngest of them—a girl who could not be more than sixteen—was unconsciously noble, effortlessly modest. Chalo had simply felt as if he had finally come home.

"Food and dry clothes!" Yaxché had grinned, the delighted master of ceremonies. "There is time enough for these before the trial begins!"

At Yaxché's word, two women—one young, one old—had taken Rebecca and Anya into one antechamber; a pair of middle-aged men had led Stephen, Chalo, and Wilkes to another. Twenty minutes later, the group had returned, transformed. Stripped of their modern clothes, the five had been clothed in white cotton pants, sandals, and richly embroidered shirts—egg-yolk yellow thread on a white *huipil* for

Rebecca, blood red thread on black for Anya; white on a white *guayabara* for Stephen, black on black for Chalo, gold and green and red on white for Wilkes. The women's hair had been braided, the braids laced with strands of matching beads; the men gaped at their ceremonial beauty. Stephen and Chalo bore a flash of paint on their right cheekbones; the women gaped at their ceremonial majesty. Yaxché had cackled at their reactions.

"You had no idea what was within, did you, *mis niños*?" They could not be certain if he had meant what lay in the chamber or what grandeur had lain in themselves.

And then Yaxché had called the feast to order: they had eaten richly and with no idea how the feast—pork and tortillas, bean *pozole*, warm vanilla *atole*, spicy chocolate *mole*, hot honeyed tea—had been brought, steaming and delicious, to the cave in the middle of a hurricane. Spiked, the tea had at last borne the four foreigners to a deep and dreamless sleep.

"*Uay*, Esteban. Wake up. It's tomorrow." Chalo whispered again.

Stephen rolled over—and almost out of—a small alcove hewn into the cave's back wall. Made for the Maya, it was short; Stephen tried to stretch himself awake and butted, feet and head, into the ends of the niche.

"Man, that tea packs a punch," he said, wiping the sleep from his eyes. "Is anyone else up?"

"All the *h'men*. We stayed up all night."

"We?" Stephen demanded, sitting up carefully.

"Some things are still only for the Maya, Yaxché said," Chalo replied, proud without gloating.

It seemed more than fair.

"What's next?"

"Waking the others. Breakfast. Getting ready. Saving the world."

Stephen smiled at Chalo's nonchalance. Then he laughed at himself for his own, as if the supernatural were natural and saving the world was all in a day's work.

Then he paused, suddenly struck by the truth beneath the humour. If what Yaxché said was right, saving the world was indeed all in a day's work, each day's actions rippling unendingly outward to interact with myriad other actions, the sum being humanity's fate. Simple and sensible, really, but disturbing and humbling nevertheless, to have the fate of the world always in one's hands.

The fire had burned all night keeping the cavern warm despite the ever-strengthening storm; an overhang kept the wind and rain from driving into the cave itself. Breakfast over, Yaxché gathered the entire group around the fire and spoke.

"We are now at the end of the end, my friends. What happens next brings us back to the start of time; what we deserve, we will get. Let us think on how this all came to be."

He gazed around the circle, making eye contact with each person, offering strength and encouragement; it was going to be harder than any of them could imagine.

"In the beginning, the world was nothing," he began, his voice slow and resonant.

"In the beginning, the world was nothing, and then *Tzacol* and *Bitol*, the maker and the shaper made the world…"

Here Yaxché pointed to two of the nine *h'men*, the oldest man and the youngest woman, their eyes flashing as their patron gods were named. From them, Yaxché glanced through the cave's natural window to the greenish stormlight beyond.

"... and *Hurukan*, the one who breathes form, sighed upon the creation, raising the sky above the land. And they saw that it was good."

Wilkes grunted involuntarily, remembering the same words from Sunday school.

"To hold the sky up they set upon the Earth my namesake, the great *ceiba*—the world tree—and in the four corners they set the *bacabs* to help him."

Now he looked at Anya, Rebecca, Chalo, and Stephen in turn, naming them.

"Yellow *Lakin*, direction of the waking sun. Red *Nohul*, direction of life and warmth. Black *Chik'in*, direction of death and the sun's sleeping. White *Xaman*, direction of wisdom.

"And then the gods, *Tzacol* and *Bitol* and the others…"

Now Yaxché nodded to the remaining *h'men* in turn as he spoke their gods' names.

"… *Gucamatz*, the feathered serpent and *Tepeu* the conqueror, his consort; *Xpiyacoc*, *Xmucane*, *Alom*, and *Qaholom*, grandfather and grandmother, father and mother to the Hero Twins that earned this Creation for us; and *U Qux Cho*, the spirit of the lake—they decided to make people to honour them and admire and care for the creation they had made."

Wilkes knew that most of the world's myths and religions contained a creation story; this was almost like the Genesis he knew, multiple creators aside. He wasn't sure how he felt about that: pleased with the inclusivity or disappointed by being less special. Yaxché ignored Wilkes' discomfited fidgeting and continued.

"All of you… all of you but the Macaw… know the next part of the story. The gods tried three times to make creatures worthy of the gifts made for them: the animals had no voice and so could not praise the lords that made them; the men of mud were weak and washed away; the men of wood were stiff and soulless. The animals were released to the forest; the other men were destroyed, the first by black rain, the next by flood.

"And then the gods made us of maize—the Fourth Creation—and we were worthy of them. They set the stars in motion above us, the story written in the sky to remind us; the story goes around each year tells us of time itself, repeating over and over, and us within it.

"Now that I am old, I see a glimmer of the pattern: people also repeat. They do good and great things and also terrible and evil things, over and over. The good things delight the hearts of the gods; the evils disappoint them and make them sharpen their knives. Most of the time the good and ill are balanced: in people, in things, in the world. So too, is it with groups of people—cities, countries, now the world—good and bad, in balance, repeating.

"But sometimes the balance is lost and the gods must step in. These are the hinge times. In them, like naughty children, we must be called to account. We are asked if we deserve another chance. If we do not make a good argument, the Lords of the Underworld are permitted to walk among us once more, sowing misery and discord, until at last Creation is destroyed again to be made a fifth time, the gods setting a new creature in our place to honour them and care for what is made.

"This is a hinge time, long in coming, and tonight we speak our defence. You will each play a part. It will be very hard. Are there any questions before we begin?"

But for a log slumping in the bonfire and the shriek of wind above the *cenote* walls, the room was silent.

"*They* are ready?" someone asked at last. It was the woman standing for *Tepeu* the conqueror, her round face showing the first signs of middle age, her eyes flashing with distrust.

"The *dzul*— they are ready?" she demanded.

Yaxché did not answer. He turned instead to glance at Stephen, Rebecca, Chalo, and Anya in turn before posing the question.

"*Xaman*, *Nohul*, *Chik'in*, *Lakin*: are you ready?"

They all nodded but Stephen spoke first.

"Yes, *Don* Yaxché, ready to follow you into the darkness and hold the North."

The eldest *h'men* nodded approvingly; Rebecca smiled at the idea of a Canadian holding the North.

"Yes, *Don* Yaxché, and honoured to hold the South," she said, following Stephen's lead.

"Yes, *Don* Yaxché, and humbled to hold the East," Anya added.

"Yes, *Don* Yaxché, and proud to hold the West," Chalo finished, smiling at Anya as he did so.

Yaxché looked at Wilkes.

"And you, Macaw, can you see well enough with one eye to report the truth?"

Wilkes felt like a child before the principal and abandoned all thought of a flippant reply. He had no idea what was coming, and therefore no idea if he was ready, but Yaxché's solemnity left room for but one reply.

"Yes sir, I'm ready."

Yaxché looked at his fellow *h'men*.

"What do you say, then—are they ready?"

All but the custodian from Calakmul nodded.

"Why must it be these foreigners, *Don* Yaxché?" the custodian asked.

"Yes, *Tzacol*, I know you do not believe that white and red shall at last work together, after all that has happened these five hundred years. But I have seen them in my dreams; I know they are the ones. And are we not all part of the puzzle? Do we not all rise and fall on the same tide?"

The custodian nodded reluctantly.

"Good," Yaxché said, standing slowly from his seat by the fire. "The heart of heaven is close now; it is time that we begin."

***

Travis Rutrauff hunkered behind a column belonging to Chich'en Itzá's Temple of Soldiers, wind howling and rain lashing, and reminded himself that the structure had withstood five hundred years' worth of hurricanes: it wasn't likely to come down now. Not that that would be so bad, all things considered: being killed now would save him the headache of stopping the op before Kulkulcan could order the oil rig destroyed. He did not yet know what Payal had done.

The simplest thing would have been to shoot Kulkulcan dead even before leaving camp. Chalo's betrayal, however, had made the guerrilla more cautious than ever: he walked the camp with Alvarro as his bodyguard and slept with his gun drawn and loaded. Killing him in camp would have meant certain death and Rutrauff was still holding out for a Christmas eggnog with the Senator. And maybe with his daughter, if she got tired of the Canadian.

Rutrauff might have killed Kulkulcan on the flight from the camp to the small airstrip near Chich'en Itzá, but flying with two teams of soldiers he had trained himself, that too would have led to his immediate demise. Not that anyone was paying attention to anything more than holding onto his lunch: the nine-seater had flown wild in the advancing hurricane winds, rising and plummeting on draughts, pitching and yawing on shears. It was, in fact, a minor miracle that they had landed at all.

So now, here he was in position, Kulkulcan still alive, and there was no use crying over milk, spilt or otherwise. Rutrauff sighed, hunkered further into his raingear and opened his eyes for a moment to check on his team: ogre-sized Angel—responsible for carrying the *tohil*'s hefty fuel cell—and weedy little Alvarro—responsible for making sure Rutrauff did his job—were each huddled behind their own columns, miserable after an hour in the driving rain.

Suddenly the wind slackened and the rain slowed—the calm between rainbands—and Alvarro hissed at Rutrauff for attention. Rutrauff ignored him. Alvarro kept hissing.

"What is it, Alvarro?" Rutrauff asked at last.

"You asleep on the job, *pendejo*? 'Cuz I'm gonna tell Kulkulcan, if you are…"

"Don't 'dumbass' me, dumbass. *Estoy descansando los ojos. Así puedo hacer mi trabajo cuando llegue el momento*. I'm resting my eyes so that I can do my job. Any other questions?"

Alvarro offered his best sneer unnecessarily; Rutrauff had not even bothered to open his eyes while returning the insult. Offended, Alvarro went on the attack.

"Yah, your job. You don't like killing. I see it in your eyes."

"My eyes are closed, Alvarro." Rutrauff wished the wind would pick up again and drown out the little shit's voice.

"I think you're going to try to screw Kulkulcan at the last minute, American."

"Thanks for the head's up, asshole, but I don't give a flying fuck what you think."

"I think you're going try to screw him and I hope you do, cuz then I get to shoot you. I never killed an American soldier yet; I think it will be fun."

Rutrauff snorted and repositioned his shoulder against the column, letting his rifle arm drop behind it and out of Alvarro's line of sight.

"Shut up, Alvarro. Killing is never fun."

"Sure it is. It gives me a hard-on. It's better than drugs."

Rutrauff saw again the 27 ghosts he had created, recalled again each separate shot, saw again through his scope the close-up surprise, the momentary pain, the life relived in a flash, before each fell dead, half a mile distant. Alvarro was lying: killing was never what anyone expected it to be. It left emptiness in the killer that mirrored the void in the world left by death itself.

"I wouldn't know about that; I've never tried the shit you sell."

"I don't sell it, dumbass, I move it. I'm way up the food chain."

"Sure you are," Rutrauff replied, his tone withering. Then, conversationally to hide the fact that he was powering up the *tohil* behind the column, he asked "How many people have you actually killed, anyway?"

"I lost count after twenty," Alvarro bragged.

Rutrauff frowned, surprised for a moment by the *tohil*: unlike a regular area denial weapon, it was not completely silent. Also unlike a regular area denial weapon it made his arm tingle as, with quick electronic precision, a million million nanoparticles jounced excitedly to assemble the weapon's focusing dish.

Alvarro sat up straight, misinterpreting Rutrauff's frown as one of disbelief. "You think I have not?" he demanded. Water that had collected behind his collar ran a rivulet down his neck and he cursed.

"Oh, I believe you. And now I know what a truly sick fuck you are, Alvarro, because no one should enjoy killing the way you do," Rutrauff said as he glanced behind the column.

The *tohil* was warm now, its silvery dish formed, full like a blown rose. Rutrauff was momentarily awed by the weapon's futuristic beauty: its lines were clean and true; it hummed gently in his hand.

"Which I suppose makes me almost as sick as you right about now," Rutrauff said under his breath as he prepared to turn the *tohil* on Alvarro. From his oblique position two columns away, Angel saw the weapon come to life and wondered what to do. The stolid mind that went with his hulking frame understood that this was not part of the plan and as such, could not be a good thing. But should he stop it? He glanced towards Kulkulcan's position on the Venus Platform; he would be able to see Rutrauff, but not the weapon—not until it was too late. He glanced left towards *El Castillo* and down into the plaza, desperate for someone to tell him what to do, and gasped in surprise: cars and trucks were driving into the heart of the ancient city.

"¡*Uay*!" he hissed. "¡*Uay*! Someone comes!"

In an instant, Rutrauff had toggled off the weapon, signalled Angel to be quiet, and spun in the direction of the great pyramid. It was true: three armoured personnel carriers were rolling into the site—military security for the press conference—and beyond them, advancing like angry insects, came the cube vans with enormous antennae that heralded the arrival of the media.

"You are a lucky son-of-a-bitch," Rutrauff muttered under his breath to Alvarro before swinging his rifle sights onto the plaza below. In a moment the familiar task of observation had settled his mind. The APCs were disgorging their men: too few of them to cover off the perimeter; all of them ill-clad for the weather. And no sniffer dogs because of the storm. He looked through the scope to find the CO. He cursed when he saw that the kid was barely past peach fuzz.

"Put your gun away, you stupid American!" Alvarro hissed. "We don't shoot for another two hours!"

"I know that, you idiot! I'm gathering intelligence… something you're a little short on, it seems. Now shut up."

Alvarro's eyes narrowed but he said nothing.

A few moments later, Rutrauff nodded grimly. The AFI had broken up the makeshift camp at the base of *El Castillo*—the camp that Deb had told Rebecca about, set by about fifty millennial die-hards convinced the world was going to end in a matter of hours—and then sent three pairs of soldiers to walk the perimeter of the grassy plaza. But the walk was perfunctory, the soldiers anxious to get out of the rain: they did not look at the boarded-up Venus Platform, and thus did not discover Kulkulcan's team. They cast only a cursory glance among the columns of Rutrauff's aerie, thus leaving his own team equally secure.

Rutrauff nodded again, then considered the bigger picture and swore softly to himself: nothing, it seemed, was going to keep him from having to kill the President of Mexico. Only once that was done would the oil platform be safe. Only then could he be able to take a shot at Kulkulcan. He'd have to kill both Alvarro and poor dumb Angel to take that shot. And only after all of that could he even think about home. He felt his gut clench before he willed himself to take a deep breath, relax, and fall into the mental killing zone.

Across the plaza, Kulkulcan lay belly to the flat stone surface of the Venus Platform, his soldiers beside him, and tried very hard not to laugh out loud. The myths and legends on which he had built his insurgency had always been convenient; now—concealed and protected within a green womb of scaffolding and netting that shuddered and flapped in the ferocious winds—even he found it hard not to believe that the ancient gods were smiling on his endeavour.

As recently as six weeks earlier Rutrauff had argued vociferously against using the platform as Kulkulcan's aerie: despite providing a perfect position, the low oval plinth was flat and exposed; it offered neither cover nor concealment. And then, on November 1st—another Day of Venus—a fat tourist had walked to the edge of the platform and the entire northern arc had calved away, the tourist breaking his leg in the fall. In truth, the stones had failed because of the acidic rain falling in the area, a rain more and more corrosive as climate change acidified the world's oceans: the bitter rain had weakened the limestone to the point of failure. Kulkulcan had called it a gift from the gods and Rutrauff had not been sure if he was joking or serious.

Following indignant but empty calls for the world to redouble efforts to reduce global greenhouse gas emissions, the secretariat responsible for the World Heritage Site had authorized the platform's immediate restoration. Within weeks the platform had been swaddled in the fretwork and hording of architectural reconstruction. Rutrauff had been forced to agree that now the platform was a perfect assassin's blind.

Kulkulcan scooted forward, peered through binoculars at Rutrauff's position, and the stifled laugh escaped: news of the Mitnal rig's demise had been all over the news, carried on the wings of television and twitter; had Rutrauff known, the jig would be up. But here, too, the gods had smiled on him, allowing him to keep the American in the dark. And so it was that—despite everything—the President and most of his Cabinet would be dead at 5:11 p.m. Twelve hours of civil chaos later, he would emerge, restore order, and then—at the precise moment the world slouched into the new *b'ak'tun*—he would assume the presidency.

CHAPTER 62

Yaxché had positioned everyone around the fire with care: Anya to the east, her back to the cavern's window over the *cenote*; Rebecca to the south; Chalo to the west; Stephen to the north. Over each he said a prayer, touched a forehead, held a wrist before moving on. Circle complete, he took a place beside Anya and gathered a handful of fragrant herbs from a pouch at his waist. Over these he said another prayer before spreading them on the fire. The blue smoke that rose was thick, sweet, and intoxicating; Stephen and the others took a deep breath and felt themselves fortified.

Then, hands raised, palms to the fire, Yaxché began to chant. An ancient singsong in Yucatec, slow at first, that gained in strength and intensity as Yaxché closed his eyes. Chalo could understand a little, Anya a little more, and the other foreigners nothing at all. In a time—how long was anyone's guess—the nine *h'men* stepped forward to complete the circle around the fire. The men had removed their shirts; the women had dropped their shawls: their skin glistened bright in the firelight. Joe Wilkes sat in an alcove at the back of the cavern, the lone witness beyond the circle.

Yaxché spoke again; his cadence held a question. The *h'men* replied as one. Yaxché cast more herbs on the fire and spoke again; the *h'men* replied once more then closed their eyes. Yaxché cast a last handful of herbs on the fire and stood silent. The cavern seemed to hold its breath. Stephen watched carefully, trying to anticipate what might come next but it was no use: he was beyond his culture and beyond his depth. He could only wait. Seconds stretched to minutes and the waiting grew heavy; apprehension replaced with boredom, Stephen began to survey the room and its inhabitants.

The *h'men* were remarkable for their differences: old, young, stocky, bony, the colour of ochre, the colour of latte, a cross section of the Maya gene pool. They shared only the short stature of the ancient people—that and an unconscious grace on the relaxed faces; Stephen felt childish and ungainly among them.

Too bright their beauty, Stephen looked to the ceiling and tried to read the story painted upon it. There were the nine creators; there was Yaxché; there the eastern, southern, and western *bacabs*, bright in the colours Anya, Rebecca, and Chalo now wore. The final *bacab* he could not see; it hung behind him, due north on a compass rose. He felt himself sway like a soldier too long at attention, flexed his calves to keep himself from fainting, and looked at the ceiling again. Barely visible through the branches of the world tree were shadows, some human, some not, ghosts in the leaves. And the brilliant scarlet macaw…

Stephen paused to look at the macaw more carefully. Blinded as in the story Yaxché had told them—like Wilkes who might yet lose his eye. He did not sit off to the side but stood in the circle with the others, between south and west. Why was Wilkes not standing with them? Stephen turned to stare at Yaxché, willing the healer to open his eyes.

"It will come to pass, *Ka Ili'ik*," Yaxché said softly, his eyes still closed. "But you are not in charge. You must let go."

Let go. Again.

Before Stephen had time to groan at the persistent lesson, Yaxché's eyes snapped open, glittering. A split-second later an arrow of blue-white lightning, blindingly bright, streaked into the *cenote* behind him. In its momentary light, shadows reared, the dark figures in the painted tree above them pulling from the ceiling, animating, coming darkly to life.

Outside, over the keening winds, Stephen could hear the hiss of water boiling as the bolt discharged. The ionized air made his skin tingle and the hair on his arms stand on end. In the momentary blindness that followed the flash, the cavern filled with the whispering of a thousand thousand voices and the shriek of an ancient rage.

Stephen blinked, struggling to clear the afterglow from his retina: when he could see once more, the room was not as before. *Balam* was there, the great jaguar, to Yaxché's right, his eyes filled with the grief and joy of ages, his thoughts inscrutable. To his left stood *Xtabay*, her eyes red, a fierce ally. And in the empty spaces around them hung myriad ghosts—some human, some hideous—their spirits taken from the painting, their forms taken from the fire's thick smoke.

The hideous ones Stephen recognized from the ceremony in the forest: they were the Lords of the Underworld, here to prosecute. Teeth bared, tongues out, eyes bulging, they coiled and twisted, weightless in the scented smoke, their movement purposefully aimless, like dogs scenting a new room.

Yaxché was chanting once more. The nine avatars raised their hands at his word and then, as if closing a car trunk, lowered their hands in unison.

Stephen felt a weight descend upon him, as if he were the trunk being slammed downward, and he struggled against the sudden impact. Rebecca, Chalo, Anya, and Yaxché were each bracing against the same weight.

So this was how it was going to be? Stephen wondered. The gods had raised the sky from the Earth and now were going to lower it once more? He readjusted his footing, squared his shoulders, and stood firm. The avatars' hands stopped dropping and Stephen smiled for the barest of moments: *Bacabs* and Yaxché—they could do this.

Or not. A sound like an earthquake—part rumble, part squeal—filled the cavern—the air itself was tearing as the grotesques screamed above them and began to fight back. The avatars lowered their hands again, and the weight on Stephen's shoulders redoubled: he staggered beneath the sudden downward force. Did it have to be such a brute battle? Could they not appeal to the gods' wisdom? Their logic? Was five people against a hoard of demons even a fair fight?

Stephen looked across the fire and saw Rebecca's face, white with pain. They were going to lose after all. It wasn't fair but he wondered why he was surprised: since Erin, he knew the gods never fought fair.

And then came a new noise, like the sound of the crowd in a David Lean film. From within the fire, a new hoard rose to meet the demons. The air grew thick, then thicker with them, cavern filling to claustrophobic overcapacity—who were they? Stephen looked up from his invisible burden, squinted against the guttering firelight, now dancing wildly as the hurricane's dropping pressure outside sucked at it.

Sudden recognition made him gasp: these were the spirits of the world's dead, come to help the living. Stephen looked around in disbelief as each of his friends was joined by their dead: beside Anya a tall wraith, eyes blue even in the grey smoke, must be her brother, newly dead; the stocky old woman beside Chalo had to be his grandmother; the couple flanking Rebecca would be her parents, the athletic blonde beside her would be Hayden. And beside him Rebecca's *mother-in-law*? Jeezuz, she'd lost a lot of people. He was distracted from Rebecca's loss by a sudden lightness, the pressure on his shoulders suddenly and substantially relieved. He could feel, rather than see, the ghost at his side. Erin. *Thanks, love.*

The weight was almost gone now; the battle almost won. He felt the endorphin surge of victory for a split second. Then he was driven to his knees. The wraiths had no interest in giving up so easily: a madness was released in the cave, heavy and deafening, as the battle between light and dark began in earnest, the Lords of the Underworld pressing the sky down more heavily upon them.

Against them still more spirits rose from the fire: a host of unknown shades, the ghosts of long-dead humanity. Here were kings and peasants, friends and foes, ranked together against those that demanded the decline of the human empire. A chill and haunted air, churned by the hurricane winds outside, swirled within the chamber as the apparitions fought, the demons biting and clawing at those that would have the *bacabs* fall, the fire wind-smothered to coals alone. More and more came to help, harrying the darkness. And still Stephen felt himself falter. He struggled to look and saw that the others, too, were weakening. Yaxché alone stood firm in the vortex, an umbilicus between Earth and sky.

The pressure outside was so low that Stephen felt his ears pop. Already on his knees, he was driven down to his hands as well, the weight of the world now on his back. They could not win now without a miracle.

Beyond the fire, Joe Wilkes could see nothing of the supernatural events occurring around him: no *Balam*, no *Xtabay*, no wraiths, no spirits of the dead: all he saw was a fork of lightning stab at the *cenote*, the fire gutter to almost nothing and, in its absence, the bruised light and sheet-like downpour that was the hurricane beyond the cave. Then he saw the children falter and fall. Not children, really, they were adults all of them, but to him they were babies, Rebecca as near to him as his own daughter. All of them, forced to their knees, as if being tortured. He thought of his treatment at Kulkulcan's hands and felt his heart break for their pain.

CHAPTER 63

Joe watched for another helpless moment before a cold pressure between his shoulder blades impelled him toward the circle to help Rebecca from her knees. He struggled against the thick, smoky air, good eye watering, broken arm and ribs aching with the effort, wondering, even as he reached down for Rebecca's elbow, how, so damaged himself, he could lift her. He reached for her elbow anyway and, touching her, was as a blinkered horse suddenly relieved of his blinds; now part of the circle, he could see all to which before had been beyond his sight.

Angels and devils churned around him, the Heaven and Hell of Hieronymus Bosh; the cold pressure was that of Hayden's ghostly hand, the wraith standing beside him was his dead wife; so great was the shock that he grunted as if struck by a baseball bat.

"Hayden? Libby?"

They stood beside him, his beloved ghosts, saying nothing. For a long moment, Joe heard nothing but the keening wind beyond the cave, deep and haunting as it eddied in the deep *cenote* well beyond, saw nothing but the terrifying spirit realm. Then came an image, bright in his mind's eye, and he gasped. The others did, too—Rebecca, her friends, even the old man—as if suddenly sharing memories: they were reliving the darkest moments not only of their own, but of each other's, lives.

Hayden's corpse under the morgue's fluorescent lights, pale against the black body bag. Erin, unnaturally akimbo, at the bottom of the rock face. Rebecca's parents, dead in the front seat of the car, a police light in Rebecca's eyes, the officer's surprise at finding her. Yaxché's wife, taking her last breath, soft hand on Yaxché's cheek. Chalo's parents, set ablaze by the Guatemalan military, his mother telling him not to look even as she died.

Then something came from beyond the group: Sebastian's corpse, blue eyes unseeing, sinking into darkness, water and molten steel around him. There were tears on every face and still the images came, the demons' closing argument: forests stripped bare, the Outback on fire, the Amazon evaporating, the Arctic ice-free, heat waves, wildfires, floods, ice storms, power failures, riots, food shortages—war; pestilence; murder; death.

The group gasped, all labouring in synchrony now, desperate for air in the close, choking space. This then, was life: human folly ending always in destruction, the moments of beauty overwhelmed by the coarse and gross and stupid and demeaning, joy always drowned by fear. What was the point in arguing for themselves? What was the point in speaking for civilization? Was there really any defence in the face of what humans did: poisoners of all they touched, destroyers of all they looked upon, deaf to all the pain they caused, mute before injustice. Humanity was a cancer; one did not let a cancer spread merely because it had not *intended* to harm its host: the solution was to cut it out, throw it away, rid the body of it once and for all. So it should be then with mankind—its individuals swarming the globe, overrunning it, choking it slowly to death—eradicate the mass and leave what remained to heal.

Stephen felt his will to fight ebbing; connected in a shared vision of Hell, he felt Rebecca, Chalo, and Anya giving in, too. He and the others fell from hands and knees into a crouch, the excruciating burden now on their rounded backs; they would have fallen, prostrate, the sky on their shoulders meeting the earth beneath their feet, had it not been for the spirits among them, insubstantial as spindrift, swirling upward against the wraiths' argument and the *h'men*'s inexorable downward press.

The noise—whether the storm outside, the blood thundering in their ears, the shriek of the demons anxious to gain the world—was now nearly deafening. Barely audible above it, Stephen heard Yaxché, voice firm and strong.

"The Lords of the Underworld, *Ka Ili'ik*—they are thieves of the future. You are a policeman. Do not let them steal."

How, Stephen wondered, was he to fight a thief that stole something as insubstantial as fate?

He heard a new sound now—felt it too—deep in his chest, a rumble rising, as with the coming of an earthquake, thrumming in his bones: the jaguar calling for his attention. Stephen looked up from his foetal crouch, searched for the great cat, saw instead Rebecca, looking up from her own struggle, her eyes green, her face beautiful even in the strange cold firelight. His heart sped, as if electrified: the living and the dead felt the jolt.

This was it, then, their defence, the gift at the bottom of Pandora's box: hope, found in the smallest of things. Yaxché had been right: it was the details that changed everything; in each action was the entire world. Stephen struggled to think of a single small thing that would alter everything. He looked on the rain beyond the cavern's window and thought on the heady smell of the first drops of rain on dry summer soil, thick with the sweet tang of ozone. He thought it and everyone knew it; as one, the four corners of the sky inhaled deeply. Yaxché smiled and the *h'men* raised their hands, easing the weight of the sky. The demons screamed, their crowing triumph giving way to shrieking rage.

The others understood and offered their own small miracles, each one tumbling into the shared space: from Rebecca came the sound of her aunt's dog, his tail thumping happily against the floor at the prospect of a pat; Anya shared the dusty contented feeling of brushing warm earth from an artefact; Chalo gave the thick sweet taste of warm chocolate *atole*; Yaxché added the silent, humbling sight of a rain-dappled deer. And something, too, from Joe Wilkes: the weightless feeling of a canoe sliding through the pale mist of a dawn-shimmering bayou.

A hint of a smile crossed Yaxché's face and the demons screamed again, loud as the hurricane winds outside.

Stephen took another breath and pushed himself up to his knees; to south, east, and west the others also rose, the shades rising up with them, buttresses against the wraiths' redoubled efforts to squelch them. A moment, an hour, an eternity, and they all regained their feet.

As one, the nine lords and creators raised their hands above their heads; Stephen lurched with sudden lightness, the pressure he had struggled against suddenly lifted. The demons were confined in a layer above him, battering like flies against glass between the craggy ceiling and the creators' hands. Then, howling, they drew in on themselves, clotting thicker, tighter, smaller, a black singularity. The avatar who was *Gukamatz*, the winged serpent, spoke a single word and the blackness dropped into the cold fire, through it, beneath it to the underworld, extinguishing the strange flame as it went. The cavern, dark only with the bruised light of the hurricane outside, fell quiet but for the teeming rain beyond the natural window. The spirits of the dead had faded; *Xtabay* and the jaguar were gone. What now? They were standing—had they won?

Yaxché broke the silence after a dozen heartbeats, raising his hand as he did so. Something glowed on his open palm.

"The end is ended."

It was the rutilated crystal that Anya had found here at Chich'en Itzá; that Stephen had carried to Yaxché to bring back to its home. Ever so vaguely, Stephen wondered how the stone could glow like that.

Yaxché turned away from the fire, held his palm up and tossed the glowing stone out into the *cenote*. It was returning at last to its rightful place, order being restored. The nine avatars sank, unconscious, to the ground as the stone fell, the hosts abandoned as the gods withdrew to deliberate.

Outside the rain stopped, the winds died away, and the cavern was suffused with a wan watery light more white than yellow: the inscrutable eye of Hurukan—both storm and god—was over them now, watching. The fire rose to an insouciant crackle, burning as though nothing had happened at all.

Yaxché turned back to face Wilkes and the *bacabs*. They strained to hear him in the deafening silence.

"*Then will the spirits come to their city, Hurukan, xekik, and the mysterious Kulkulcan. The Itzás will arrive in the wake of these three. The souls of the dead will groan in the catacombs of the stone city of the Itzás. Until, at last, time will stop. They will raise their symbol on high, the Tree of Life. Everything will change at once. The change will be manifest to all as the quetzal voice sounds...*

Anya checked off the elements in her mind. Everything was accounted for but *xekik*—the bloody death. She shuddered but said nothing.

"The first part is done, *mis niños*," Yaxché said.

"The first part?" Joe asked, incredulous. The others waited patiently for what Yaxché would say next.

"The end ends. Time stops. Everything hangs, waiting. What you do next determines the path we take."

Somewhere outside, carried to them through the twisting subterranean tunnels, came the sound of something like gunfire, the single report sharp and deadly. Everyone except Yaxché flinched.

"Now the children go and do the rest," Yaxché said, his words directed at Wilkes alone. To the others he added, "It is not over until the *quetzal* speaks."

CHAPTER 64

Doctors Kathy Howlachuk and Peter Nguyen watched the computers on Peter's desk with wonder both professional and personal: *Sigma*'s behaviour was unheralded and the press conference in the middle of *Sigma*'s eye insane. Bender lay asleep on the floor, legs kicking gently in a doggy dream.

Peter swivelled his chair to pull up more data from a third computer. and moused the volume up to hear the CNN webcast better.

"*I'm here,*" began the reporter—the blonde Aussie in a yellow rain poncho—"*at the ancient Mayan city of Chich'en Itzá, one of the seven wonders of the ancient world, where in fifteen minutes the President of Mexico will hold a press conference on the ill-fated Mitnal oil rig. It is as if the gods themselves want to hear what the President has to say:* Sigma*'s eye has moved over us, stilling the winds on this final day of the Maya calendar…*"

"It is kind of weird, don't you think?" Peter asked, rolling his eyes at the reporter's melodrama.

"What I think," Kathy replied as she gestured for Peter to mute the reporter, "is that those people should thank God they're on a building that's lasted almost a millennium. As for weird, maybe not. At least not if you believe in an *axis mundi*…" she said.

"What?"

"I told you already that *Hurukan* is one of the Maya gods. That place, right there," she nodded to the temple behind the CNN reporter, "is the centre of the universe at the moment: Mount Olympus, Mount Meru, Mount Fuji, the *bhodi* tree, Jack's damn beanstalk. It's the world's navel we're gazing at."

"That's a little woo-woo, Kath…"

"It's a *lot* woo-woo, Pete. Doesn't mean it's not true. There's more in this world that can be explained by the likes of you and me."

"You don't actually believe the world is going to end today?"

"Maybe it should," she said as she turned to face him. "Maybe we deserve it."

Peter Nguyen's looked at his mentor and boss, the intensity of her stare and the tired honesty of her speech unnerving him. He looked away, unable to bear the deep sadness in her eyes.

"I dunno, Kath. I'd like to believe we can be better than…" he trailed off, distracted by his computer, eyes wide.

Kathy turned from Peter to the monitor.

"What is it, Pete?"

"The captioning… it says shots have been fired at Chich'en Itzá…"

***

In the cavern beneath Chich'en Itzá, the noise still echoing through the tunnels Rebecca was the first to speak.

"The President!"

"Can we get to the pyramid through these tunnels?" Stephen demanded.

Another faint smile crossed Yaxché's face as he stooped to check on the shaman who had harboured *Tzacol*.

"I have taken care of the sky and the darkness. Now it is for you to take care of in between. *Lakin*, are you ready?"

It took Anya a moment to realize that Yaxché was speaking to her. When she did, she nodded, resolute.

"Good. You will read the way for the others. From the door turn *lakin*; after that, go with the white road beneath your feet."

Wilkes turned to Anya, looking worried. "I'm afraid I'm going to slow you down…"

Yaxché spoke before Anya could reply. "You don't go, Macaw," he said with a grin. "What they do is not for old men like us…"

Wilkes scowled, irritated as intended.

"Don't worry, your turn comes soon enough," the healer placated, still grinning.

Stephen could not help but smile as he turned with the others to leave: Yaxché was unbowed by what he had just been through.

"Alright *Lakin*," Stephen said to Anya. "Lead on."

Anya smiled, eyes shining.

"Take your packs, all of you," she said. "We go east."

***

"Turn it back up, Pete…" Kathy said, even as Peter was releasing the mute.

The picture was blurry and bouncing, the cameraman obviously running for cover; the audio was wordless, filled only with shouting and the cameraman's ragged breath. A second later came the sound of drumming, panpipes, cursing, and nervous laughter.

"*Bloody hell*," said the cameraman as he steadied his lens on the dark hurricane eyewall in the distance and then swung it back to the reporter.

"*… Tensions are clearly running high here at Chich'en Itzá*," the reporter said, looking sheepish. "*What we thought was gunfire—a sound that sent us all scurrying for cover—was, in fact, from the site's massive sound system…*"

Peter laughed and muted the feed once more.

"I saw the night-time sound and light show down there once," he said. "I thought it would be a gimmick for tourists, but it was actually pretty good…"

"I saw it too, years ago," Kathy replied. "It was a few months after Queen Elizabeth attended the ceremonial opening. She was there in the dry season, but when the piece of music written to herald the rain god came on, it started pouring…"

"Are you serious?"

"Not a word of a lie. A few years ago a German tourist at the top of the pyramid was struck by lightning coming from a blue sky, too. Some people say the place is still potent. The *axis mundi*."

"Un hunh," Peter said uncomfortably. To change the subject he asked, "Who's writing the next bulletin—you or me?"

***

Wilkes watched the foursome leave and turned to Yaxché.

"So good triumphs over evil?"

Yaxché looked up from the pulse he was taking.

"Triumphs?"

"Wins."

"There is no winning, Macaw. Just balance. Light above, dark below, us in the middle, a bit of each, hmm?"

Shades of grey. Joe nodded slowly.

"So the balance is restored?"

Yaxché checked on the next shaman—the dour custodian from Calakmul—and straightened an arm so that it would not be sore when the man regained consciousness.

"It is a slow thing, Macaw. It took many years and many poor decisions to get to this place; it will take as many years and as many good choices to get back, yes?"

"And what am I supposed to do?"

"Make good choices?" The old man cackled.

"Funny. I meant what should I do right now?"

Yaxché had moved to the plump middle-aged woman who had harboured the spirit of the lake. He *tsked* as he took her pulse and said a prayer before answering Wilkes.

"Come. Sit here. Take her hand."

Wilkes knelt beside the woman who had hosted the spirit of *U Qux Cho* and took her hand. It was icy.

"What's wrong with her?"

"Wrong? Nothing. It is a long journey back. It helps to have a hand in this world to hold on to."

"And she's where? Heaven? Hell?"

"Not either, Macaw. The world is not so simple as you would like it to be. She is in the place beyond this place, with all the others who do not walk the middle world. With your wife and son who were here before, helping."

"Will she see them?" Wilkes asked suddenly.

"Will *U Qux Cho* see your wife and son? Perhaps," Yaxché said, now tending the man who held the spirit of *Gukamatz*, the true feathered serpent.

"Can I…" Wilkes hesitated. "Can I see them?"

"I am sorry Macaw, but after just now? Not again in life. Only when you die. Only those who are called may cross in life. But don't worry, they are always with you. "

Thursday, December 20, 2012 — 3 Cauac, Day of Storm

Joe looked down at the sleeping woman as Yaxché moved off to check on another of the healers. Her face was lined with the first wrinkles of middle age.

"If you see Libby or Hayden wherever you are," he said hesitantly, "… if you see them, say hi for me. Say hi and tell them I miss them."

The woman stirred a little and smiled.

***

"Which way now?" Stephen asked at a fork in the tunnel, shining his flashlight into each of their options.

They had been walking for ten minutes, silent but for the crunch of their boots on the dusty limestone, blind but for Anya and Stephen's flashlights, the still humid air pressing close upon them. Smaller tunnels branched from the main passage every hundred metres or so, each split marked by a red glyph.

Anya stood still, brows furrowed. She walked five metres down the right tunnel, her light playing over the walls, and returned.

"The glyphs are missing…"

"I think we should keep to the right…" Chalo proposed.

"Why?" Anya asked.

"It will keep us in a circle beneath the main plaza, no?"

Anya nodded, considering. It made sense.

"I think we should go left, actually," said Rebecca, crouching down.

Anya turned and shone her light on what Rebecca was looking at; Stephen joined them, adding his light.

"Holy shit! Herkimer diamonds," Stephen exclaimed, flashing his light down the length of the tunnel. Tiny pinpricks of light reflected back at him from the walls and, more thickly, from the tunnel floor.

"The tunnel is filled with them—double-terminated quartz crystals. It's amazing…"

"Yaxché said to follow the white road, right? In all this blackness, that way looks white to me," Rebecca said.

"The Milky Way…" Anya asked, realization dawning.

"A *sacbe*," Chalo confirmed. "Rebecca is right. We go left."

The next fork gave rise to a more serious disagreement, one that divided the group.

"The left one is *Tohil*," Anya said, reading the glyph. "We go right."

"No, I think we should go left," Chalo contradicted. "*Tohil* is the name Kulkulcan gave to his death ray. I bet you that tunnel leads to one of them. We should go and destroy it."

The three of them looked at Chalo sceptically.

"*Uay*, come on! We've been following signs for weeks—why do we suddenly stop now?"

"Maybe, but Yaxché said to follow the white road. There are no crystals that way," Anya replied.

They stood and looked at each other stubbornly.

Rebecca broke the impasse. "We don't have time to argue. You guys go ahead to the President. We'll check this out and then come along after you."

"No way," Chalo replied. "You don't know the *tohil*."

"Any of us can get hurt anywhere, Chalo," Anya said angrily. "Maybe there is someone there with a *tohil*, but Yaxché said to follow the white road. So at least some of us must go on. You are the policemen, so you go. We'll follow once we finish."

"Help me out here, *hermano*," Chalo said. "You've seen what the *tohil* can do."

"I have, but they're right. And you know they can handle themselves…" he added, pulling his gun from the holster at his back and handing it to Rebecca.

"We'll be careful," Rebecca said, smiling at the compliment.

"You better be," Stephen said wryly. "You have to bring that gun back…"

Stephen and Chalo watched the women head into the dark passageway, Anya behind Rebecca, shining the light forward for both of them.

"Esteban?" Chalo said as he turned to follow Stephen down the crystal-studded tunnel.

"Yeah?" Stephen asked over his shoulder, his pace long and loping now.

"If something happens to them, I promise I'll kill you."

"They've been shot at, imprisoned, walked through a hurricane, and Rebecca's actually been almost dead… and here we are. They'll be fine.

As for killing me, you know what?"

"What?"

"If something happens to them, I'll *let* you kill me. Now take the flashlight and tell me which way we go—you're the glyph-reader now."

Chapter 65

"Just keep going, *caballero*; the crystals go straight."

"But that one looked familiar…" Stephen said, distracted even as he pressed forward.

"It *was* a famous one: *Balam*. ¡*Uay*! Why are you stopping?"

"'*Balam*' as in 'jaguar'?"

"*Si*. So what?"

Stephen cocked his head and listened, not to Chalo but as if to a distant sound. Then he nodded and turned back to the tunnel marked "jaguar."

"Esteban! *This* way!"

Stephen shook his head.

"You go on ahead."

"Are you a lunatic, Esteban?"

"You said it yourself: we've been following signs since the beginning. I… I can't explain it, but I need to go this way. It's important."

"Need to?! Have you forgotten that we are to stop someone killing the President? We need to go *this* way! We have one flashlight and gun between us—we *need* to work together!" Chalo said, exasperation in his voice.

"I know, I know. But I have to do this. Go and I'll catch up to you."

"You can't go in the dark, *hermano*!" Chalo protested.

It was too late: Stephen had disappeared.

"*Chingalo*," Chalo cursed as he started forward on the path Yaxché had laid for them. "Alone again. Always alone. And probably going to do something stupid, like I usually do when I'm on my own."

***

Above ground, a sound behind him—gravel ground on gravel—made Travis Rutrauff flinch. The barest of sounds, it seemed enormous against the sudden silence of *Sigma*'s still, cold eye, but neither Alvarro nor Angel, terrified by the sound system malfunction seemed to have noticed it.

Rutrauff turned, slow and nonchalant, to face the sound, and was shocked: a woman, her face level with his own, was staring at him from what he had mistaken for a shallow decorative niche in the low temple wall. Rutrauff had to work hard to feign nonchalance: the woman rising from an unknown warren was Rebecca Holloway.

He nodded calmly just once to acknowledge her and then shook his head—it was unsafe to come out. Then, to maintain her cover, he looked down dispassionately to the great plaza below. It was pretty down there, despite the knot of reporters and the dark AFI trucks: steam rising from the ground as the watery sun warmed the sodden grass like mist on a placid sea.

After a long moment, Travis looked back towards Rebecca: there was another woman with her now, this one with ice-blue eyes. He sighed involuntarily and hid it with a stifled cough: he should have known the German's sister was connected somehow. Rebecca raised a pistol, showing it rather than aiming it.

"How many?" she mouthed.

Rutrauff shifted his weight a little and raised two fingers but shook his head once more: their angle was wrong and Alvarro would have them both dead before she could aim. Anya sank from sight, Rebecca after her, and Rutrauff wished he could tell them to bugger off: he didn't need this to be any more complicated.

Rebecca's face appeared again, another silent question on her lips. Before she could pose it a sound rose from her blind: a single ping, like radar. It came from the satellite phone in Rebecca's knapsack: it had chosen that moment to signal that it's battery had almost run out. Alvarro spotted Rebecca instantly and had his gun on her before she could dive for cover.

Christ almighty, Rutrauff cursed to himself. Now it was definitely more complicated.

***

"*Ladies and gentleman…*" came the sound of the President's voice over the site's now-fixed sound system. "*Ladies and gentlemen of the media, you are brave to be here in the middle of a storm. I speak to you today as one who had good news to tell and has had it snatched away. The Mitnal rig—our birthright and our future wealth—has been destroyed by the cowardly terrorist group that calls itself "Eden Two." But we will rebuild…*"

Rutrauff's vision, eye to his scope, blurred for a moment as the news sank in. Mitnal had gone down? *Mitnal*? Had gone *down*? No rig meant no deal! *Hell yeah—a break at last.* Rutrauff smiled just a little as he switched on the *tohil*, smiled a bit more as the weapon grew warm. The sensation was pleasant after the chill hurricane winds. Alvarro, eyes still on Rebecca, chuckled beside him, anticipating the *tohil*'s gore. Rebecca glanced at Rutrauff for an instant; Alvarro followed her glance and the colour drained from his face: the weapon was aimed not at the President but at his own chest.

"I'd be lying if I said I was sorry, Alvarro," Rutrauff said as he discharged the weapon.

Alvarro's chuckle turned to a gurgle as he began to shudder, drowning in his own skin. In less than a minute he was dead, his blood pooling at the foot of the *chac mo'ol.* Angel fainted, slumping over his gun; Rebecca's eyes widened but she said nothing until blood stopped leaking from Alvarro's boiled body. Then she called softly down into the niche in the wall.

"Anya, you can come up now. It's over."

"Over?" Rutrauff hissed, his disbelief audible over the drone of the president's speech. "Over? Not by a long shot! Kulkulcan is over there on the Venus platform ready to take out the Secretary of Internal Security, and I can't even get a shot at him from here because of the hoarding."

"So we go over *there* and take the shot," Anya said, appearing within the niche and raising Rebecca's hand—still with Stephen's gun in it. "I am sure the tunnels beneath can take us there."

Rebecca tried to speak, but Rutrauff cut her off.

"You're some kind of commando?" he asked, incredulously. "Even if you do kill him, there are eleven other units spread out across the country waiting to take their shots in," he looked at his watch, "in fourteen minutes—how do you plan to stop them?"

"Actually, I am a soldier. And you *can* call them!" Anya retorted. "You're the commander; call it off."

"That's not the way terrorism works, and we're mimicking it—every cell isolated. Your brother was a terrorist, you should know!"

"Don't you even say his name, you swine…"

"Shut up, both of you!" Rebecca hissed, eyes on the President still delivering his grandiose speech about rebuilding Mitnal. "Shut *up*! I didn't mean *over* over. I'm trying to think how to stop the rest of it!"

Anya and Rutrauff fell silent, surprised by the forceful rebuke. A second later, Rebecca spoke again, slithering up an out of the niche as she did so.

"I've got it. You two go deal with Kulkulcan; I know how to stop the other killings."

"How?!" demanded Anya and Rutrauff at the same time.

"It's too complicated and there isn't much time," Rebecca said as she slung her pack from her back. "Just go deal with Kulkulcan and I'll take care of the rest."

Anya and Rutrauff remained still for a moment.

"Go already!" Rebecca exhorted. "Stephen and Chalo are headed for the President; don't let Kulkulcan get them, too!"

Anya disappeared back down the rabbit hole, Rutrauff slithered down after her. A moment later, Rebecca heard the faint sound of two pairs of feet, running.

Rebecca watched to make sure they were gone, glanced at Angel to make sure he was still unconscious, and then hoped that the sat phone had enough battery left for what she needed to do.

"Deb?"

"Rebecca? Is that you? Where are you? The Mitnal rig sank last night…"

"I know…

"… and there's a hurricane smack dab over the Yucatán…"

"I know…"

"… and the Mexican President is on TV in the middle of it right now…"

"I know! Shut up and listen to me will you?! You have to call in every favour you know everywhere in town so that you can get CNN's

Washington bureau chief on the phone. You have to tell him that a terrorist is planning to kill half the Mexican Cabinet in less than fifteen minutes. They're all over the country in offices and at meetings...CNN has to let every news agency in Mexico know and every one of them has to get in touch with their political contacts and warn them. Call Carolina Schroeder's office—she knows the whole damned press corps..."

"*Half* the Cabinet..." Deb began, bewildered. "Which half?"

"It doesn't matter! Tell them all! Get them all under armed guard. You've got just about twelve minutes!"

"But Beck!" Deb protested as the phone went dead.

Rebecca swore, hoping she'd been able to say enough. She jammed the phone back into her knapsack, pulled off her belt and cinched it around Angel's wrists, and took his rifle. Then, trying to ignore Alvarro's wretched corpse, she crouched behind a column, eyes on the plaza, to wait.

CHAPTER 66

Beneath the plaza, Chalo had reached the end of the quartz-studded tunnel and now faced a steep set of stairs leading up to a sliver of dim light. The long, narrow passageway inside *El Castillo*—Chich'en Itzá's famous pyramid—was thick with cobwebs, and Chalo shuddered.

"You just had to put spiders in my path, hmm?" Chalo asked the gods before starting forward, his gun a duster to clear the sticky webbing from his path. It was hard climbing in the still close air, and by the time he had counted his way to the top—91 stairs—he was sweating.

"I win," he muttered grimly at the top as he swiped imaginary arachnids from his hair and wiped cobwebs from his gun.

The source of the dim light was another of the small niches that had permitted the women access to Rutrauff and the Temple of Soldiers; this one looked out into a small dim room fronted by columns. Chalo could see sky beyond the columns; he must be in the temple all the way at the top of *El Castillo*.

Pretty amazing what his ancestors had built, he marvelled, as he considered what to do next. Not many options, really: himself, a gun, his badge. Tackling the President might work, if only to bring him to the ground and make him a smaller target, but it would leave the Secretary of Internal Security exposed for a moment—long enough for Kulkulcan to take a shot. Still, it seemed the best option. Now how many people did he have to get past to get outside?

He peered as far out of his niche as he dared and started counting. Only two that he could see, but each had a *xiuhcoatl* assault rifle that could turn him into Swiss cheese. A third person walked into his line of sight—this one not a soldier but a constable.

Chalo had to stifle a laugh. The gods really did work in mysterious ways: the constable was Rico Mendez, the kid at the resort the day he'd found the heart.

"Psst," Chalo whispered. "Mendez! Psst!"

Rico looked around, on alert.

"You guys hear something?" he asked the soldiers.

"Your nerves are playing tricks on you, kid," one of them chuckled.

"Mendez, down here!"

Mendez crouched down, unwilling to believe the sound was in his mind alone. He nearly fell over backwards when he saw Chalo peering back at him from within the temple wall. Mendez looked from Chalo to the soldiers for an instant; they had turned their backs to him again, alert for threats from outside rather than in.

"Guerrero? Is that you?" Mendez whispered.

"Thank God for you, Mendez. What the hell are you doing here?"

"A sign of cooperation among the police forces. I just think no one wanted to come out in a hurricane. What are *you* doing here?!"

" It is a very long story but it ends this way: someone is going to try to kill the President and the Secretary in just about ten minutes. We have to get them off the pyramid…"

"What? How?!"

"Just make sure those goons don't shoot me while I get out of this hole and I'll take care of the rest, okay?"

"Okay. Oh *mierde…*"

The soldiers were no longer facing outside.

"What the fuck are you doing, *pendejo*?" one of them asked Mendez.

"Someone's going to try to kill the President…"

"You and the goddamned wall? Shut up and let us work, would you?"

"Not the wall, you idiots," Mendez replied with the satisfaction of the bullied getting the better of the bullies as he stepped aside, allowing them to see Chalo's face within the wall.

"Don't shoot," Chalo said, flashing his badge. "The kid is telling the truth. If you let me get out of here we can still stop them."

The soldiers had their guns on Chalo, they stood still and stupefied as Chalo took a risk and pulled himself up and out of the niche.

"Don't move," one of the solders said at last, too little and too late.

Chalo already had his own gun out and on the soldiers; he was motioning Mendez to follow him.

"The sniper is inside the green nets across the plaza," Chalo growled at the soldiers. "Now unless you want to be blamed, aim for the sniper and get out of my way."

***

Naked from the waist up in the close heat within the hoarding around the Venus Platform, Kulkulcan lay, belly down beside his death ray. A quick look at his watch and he toggled the weapon on, watching, delighted as the nanomaterials—as complicated as magic—built the silver dish that focused the weapon's beam to such deadly effect. Five more minutes, and he could pull the trigger. He and the other twelve.

Kulkulcan looked through his scope at the President, still yattering on, dead already and not even knowing it, and smiled with unpleasant satisfaction. He swung his sights to his own target—Secretary Vargas—and scowled: the man had taken up a spot behind his bodyguard. As if he knew. The Americans *had* been grooming him for power.

Kulkulcan pushed the weapon away, grabbed his binoculars, and looked to Rutrauff's position behind the *chac mo'ol.* The President had just announced that the rig was down. Kulkulcan saw blood, Wilkes' daughter, and no Marine: Rutrauff was going to try to stop the assassinations.

"Bastard!" Kulkulcan said as he dropped the binoculars, turned the *tohil* back on the President, and put his eye to the sights: he was going to have to do this now or not at all.

"*Ahau*?"

"Not now, Hector," Kulkulcan snapped at the soldier with him—the peon who had carried the fuel cell.

"Really, *Ahau*—it cannot wait…"

Kulkulcan glanced at Hector and turned back to his gun, then looked back at Hector more carefully.

"You," he said grimly as he swung the barrel of the *tohil* towards Hector. Anya had crept in unnoticed through yet another niche and now had one arm around Hector's thick neck; her other hand held a pistol to his head.

"Dr. von Eckhart. I should have killed you when I had the chance a week ago. I'll have to remedy my error now."

"You would kill him to kill me?" Anya asked, tightening her grip on

Sandro.

"He's very fat; I'm not sure if the beam will be lethal for you through all that flesh," Kulkulcan said nonchalantly. "But it's worth a try…"

"*Ahau*… ?" Hector gaped. "*Ahau*, you can't!"

"Of course I can, Sandro. I *must*. It's the price of victory. I promise I'll tell your mother you died a hero."

"Right, and *that's* a promise you can take to the bank," said a sardonic voice high in the scaffolding. Rutrauff had climbed, stealthy as a cat, up the wooden fretwork while Anya had busied herself with Hector; now Rutrauff was pointing his rifle at Kulkulcan.

"Captain Rutrauff. A traitor, after all. We are at a stalemate, aren't we? I shoot them; you shoot me; the military out there kills you—nobody wins."

"How about I shoot you first? Then the story is that I stopped a madman with a gun. The Mexican government will be so grateful to us that they will rebuild Mitnal and *give* us the oil. I win and the rich get richer. You lose, but what do you care, really? You never actually believed your noble talk about saving the Maya; it was just a convenient way of getting stupid young kids with no hope to follow you straight to the grave. Hector here, for instance. And Payal, what about him? He's dead, too, I suppose?"

"Stupid, perhaps, but not dead yet," came another voice, this one from even higher in the scaffolding. "My gun is on you, as well, *Ahau*. No one shoots anyone."

This time Kulkulcan was stunned. Rutrauff and Anya were equally so.

"Payal?" Kulkulcan asked.

"Yes, me. I hid with the cargo in the plane."

"And just what exactly are you doing here? I told you if I saw you again I would kill you…"

"Before he died, Sebastian asked me to look to Anya for him."

Anya marvelled, for the briefest of moments, at the beautiful symmetry of the whole situation: the hollow green tower standing like the *ceiba* tree at the centre of the Mayan universe, its branches peopled with the wisdom and folly that drove each creation; beyond the tower, like nesting bowls, the same elements above and below—oil, hurricane, stars. And all waiting, as a chemical reaction awaiting its catalyst, to be propelled forward by the very first spark. This was the stillness before creation—the silence before the sound, the singularity before the bang—come again.

And then came the barest breeze, the breath of *Hurukan* returning, the spark. The zephyr tugged at the green cloth swaddling the scaffolding. The soft swish of fabric at his back made Payal flinch and drop his weapon. The clang of the falling weapon against the scaffolding made Rutrauff shoot wide. The rogue bullet tore through Kulkulcan's left bicep, cutting the median nerve that empowered his hand; he watched the useless limb fall away from the trigger of the *tohil*. Young Hector, convinced the shot had been at him, fainted—another one too young to be fighting a war. Hector's bulk, suddenly deadweight, fell backwards, pinning Anya against the rough limestone.

As it had at the hotel when Chalo had seen the heart, time had briefly stilled; now it careened forward to make up for the moments held back.

Anya struggled uselessly. Payal scrabbled, arm outstretched, after the fallen gun, Kulkulcan got it instead with his still working-right arm and aimed at Rutrauff.

Now Rutrauff felt the familiar slash of a bullet, this one burrowing deep into his side, tearing liver, spleen and diaphragm as it went. It would be only minutes before he bled out, he realized grimly. No eggnog in Washington after all. Too bad; he would have liked to get to know Rebecca better. Maybe even have romanced her away from the Canadian. He laughed at that thought, blood sputtering from his lips. Not likely, but still…

He thought about her long lean legs, her bare feet, the flutter of her scarf onto the bed before she'd disappeared. It was a nice thing that she'd been on the right side of the fight, after all.

The sound of another shot tugged at his reverie. He felt nothing and wondered at it: had the bullet hit his spine, too? No, it had hit Payal; the kid had fallen, face down, on the scaffolding above. Rutrauff could see the boy's face. Now there was a waste, he thought, mind wandering as his consciousness faded. No, wait… the kid's eyes were open and searching, feigning death until the shooting stopped. He looked aggrieved by Rutrauff's dying.

Thursday, December 20, 2012 — 3 Cauac, Day of Storm

Rutrauff shook his head, wishing he could tell Payal not to worry. As he did he caught sight of another figure in the rigging, this one above Payal. A woman, dark haired, her figure gauzy.

"The dream is ended," she said in Yucatec, "Now come…"

Her voice sounded like his nanny's calling him in for dinner at the embassy in Mexico City so long ago. So this was death, and it was not the end. That, too, was good.

"I come now," he sighed back in Yucatec, the reluctant child called home.

Payal watched Rutrauff and wished he had more time to think on the man's enigmatic last words but the sound of footsteps on limestone told him that he had none: Kulkulcan was advancing on Anya where she lay, trapped beneath Hector's immense frame. It was time for Payal to honour Sebastian's last request.

"Now, *Doktor* von Eckhardt, what shall we do with you?" Payal heard Kulkulcan say, his voice sweetly conversational.

Anya's eyes glittered with fury as she struggled against Hector's bulk.

"Your friends have caused me more than a little trouble. Perhaps you can fix it for me?" Kulkulcan continued.

"No, but thank you just the same," Anya replied curtly.

"Come now, *Doktor*. The alternative is very bad for your health."

"You don't scare me. I will not collaborate."

"Ah, so very brave, *Doktor*, but you do not have a choice," Kulkulcan said, his voice menacing. Gun in his uninjured arm, Payal watched as Kulkulcan kicked Hector's torso, pushing the man from Anya's legs.

"Get up."

"No."

"Get up!" he said, kicking Anya this time.

"Stop it, *Ahau*," said a steady voice above them. "It's over."

With Kulkulcan's first kick, Payal had let himself down silently from the scaffolding, picked up Rutrauff's gun, and was advancing on Kulkulcan from behind.

"Payal, you have more lives than a cat!" Kulkulcan said, back to the boy, his voice filled with both irritation and delight. Kulkulcan set down his gun and raised his arms.

"Fine. I give up," he said, turning around. "Tell me something, though: why did you side with a foreigner over me?"

"Because, *Ahau*, it is not about skin or blood," Payal said, lowering his gun and his guard. "It is about making the world better than it was when we entered it. It is about what we choose each day."

"Ah, Payal," Kulkulcan said with the weary mockery of a tyrant to an underling. "Ah, Payal, then today you made a very poor choice. And the minutes here that you have wasted will not, I think, make the world a better place…"

In a single motion, fluid as the one he had used to put a pistol to Payal's head a week earlier, Kulkulcan crouched, retrieved his gun, and shot Payal between the eyes.

"Tonalna…" the young man said as he fell, his wife's name offered to the air. He was dead before he fell on the hard limestone platform.

Anya scrambled for Payal's corpse and cradled his head. "I will tell her, Payal, "she said softly, fighting tears. "Go well."

"So melodramatic, *Doktor*," Kulkulcan said, as he dropped the gun, walked to Payal's corpse, grabbed the pistol from the dead man's hand, and pointed it at Anya. "Now get up. It is time to go."

"You do not deserve the blood in your veins," Anya said, eyes and voice hard as she stood.

"Oh?"

"You are not truly Maya. You are just anger."

"And the Maya cannot be angry for all the evil done to us?"

"The Maya have a right to be angry; they deserve far better. But they are not just their anger. Nor just their ancient history. They are a living people with a wisdom that the rest of the world is ready to hear. You cannot win against that. "

"A pretty little speech, *Doktor*. But I have the gun. Now move."

***

Still within the cavern next to the sacred *cenote*, the woman who was *U Qux Cho* opened her eyes and gazed, sphinx-like, at Joe Wilkes. Wilkes called out for Yaxché immediately.

"The boy wishes you peace," the woman said, her voice rich and honeyed, her eyes limpid, ancient, wise beyond time, staring into Joe's own. "And the woman wishes you life."

U Qux Cho's host close her eyes again. When they reopened them, they were gauzy with the confusion of one rudely awoken. She looked from Wilkes to Yaxché.

"It is done?" she asked, her voice now thin and tired.

"Yes, *mi hija*. It is done."

Wilkes considered. Had he just been spoken to by a god? If so, she had delivered a message from his family. And Yaxché had been right: he had never been alone. He had merely been blind to it.

Yaxché touched the woman's forehead gently, said a soft prayer, and uncoupled her hand from Joe's.

"The lake was cold, *mi hija*. Stay by the fire and warm yourself. Tell the others likewise when they wake. We must go."

With that, Yaxché rose, calling on Wilkes to follow him.

"Where are we going?" Wilkes asked, still disoriented by the message, the absolution.

"South."

Joe Wilkes snorted. It was an answer, but one that was not helpful in the slightest.

"South?"

"That is what you asked, is it not? Where are we going? We are going south."

Wilkes felt his temper rising and then considered the situation: in the past forty-eight hours he'd been kidnapped, beaten, rescued, through a hurricane, underground and—if it was possible—to the Underworld, at the mercy of a shaman. He smiled, despite himself. *Going south* was a pretty good description. And all things considered, surrendering to the direction he would be taken felt good.

Wilkes began to chuckle, his growing mirth echoing through the tunnels as if the Earth itself were laughing. Yaxché smiled to himself and led onward.

"And when we get there…" Wilkes said, wiping small tears from the corners of his eyes, "… when we run out of south, what then?"

Yaxché's cackle joined Wilkes laughter. He stopped and turned to face the Senator, his face holding the wisdom of ages, his eyes glittering with amusement.

"The world, like time, is a circle, my friend. We do not run out of direction; we merely change it, yes?"

Wilkes' laugh turned to a thoughtful grunt: how right the old man was.

"And which one will we choose?"

"Not we. You. It is your turn."

"My turn to what?"

"Push."

What?"

"I have told you, Macaw. We are at the tipping point. We go the way you push."

"Why me?"

"Why not you?"

"Why not someone else?"

"Why not everyone else?"

"Fine. Everyone else," Wilkes said irritably.

"Everyone else is already pushing. Now you have to push with us, hmm?"

"And how do I do that?"

"You'll know when it is time," Yaxché replied breezily, turning back towards the tunnel and their destination.

"You're a crazy old buzzard, Hernando," Wilkes sighed, following the old man at an uncomfortably fast pace.

"Not as crazy as you, Macaw. But maybe you'll get better."

Wilkes' had a snappy retort but it died on his lips: a short sound, deepened and distorted by the tunnel system came up from behind them, engulfed them, sped onward.

"That was gunfire, Hernando."

"Yes."

Wilkes heard another shot. "Is Becky alright?"

"I hope," The healer replied, quickening his pace.

His ribs were already aching but Wilkes matched Yaxché's new pace, uncomplaining.

Me too, he thought. *Me too.*

***

The shots rang out from the Venus Platform and Mendez looked at the soldiers who so recently had scorned him.

"Who is the *pendejo* now?!" he jeered as he followed Chalo from the dark temple to the platform outside. Chalo was already on top of the President, pulling him to the ground; Mendez followed suit with the Secretary of Internal Affairs, their bodies shielding the politicians from harm. Chalo, badge still out, was shouting to be heard. Mendez, on top of the Secretary, looked out over the plaza and saw AFI forces surging up toward them from the grassy plaza below.

"Police! Don't shoot! Sniper on the Venus Platform!"

A third shot rang out across the plaza and the media reporting the event cowered even as they turned, like spectators at a tennis match, to find the source of the sound. The cameras, their cyclopean lenses swung from the President, with the dishevelled man in black on top of him, to the green hoarding around the Temple of Venus, and then back again.

In offices and living rooms around the world, in restaurants and on streets, people stopped to watch the news on screens and smartphones, stilled by disbelief. The internet slowed to a crawl as video from a single feed was streamed across the planet.

From his vantage providing cover to the President, Chalo looked into the eyes of a journalist in a yellow rain poncho crouched on the top stair of *El Castillo*—a woman with an Australian accent—shouting excitedly.

"Go tight! On the President. In! In! In!" she urged her cameraman. He was a big bearded guy in a red Hawaiian shirt, he was crouching low beside her, his waist belted heavy with black battery packs each stickered with the CNN logo.

"¡*Uay, hermano*!" Chalo shouted at the cameraman. "Your shirt is a rag to a bull! Get the hell out of..."

Chalo stopped.

A fourth shot had just thundered through the plaza, the sound reverberating within the great space around the ruins.

In the jungle ringing the ancient city, birds, silenced by the hurricane, squawked with sudden fear at this newest noise, harsh, foreign and dangerous, as it rippled outward through the clear cool eye of the storm. And yet none rose to flight: they knew in their featherlight bones that the storm might yet return.

CHAPTER 67

Stephen had been running in the subterranean dark, fingertips skimming the tunnel's limestone wall, and his eyes had gained a feline acuity as he ran. No longer black, the narrow passageway shone, the walls and floor and ceiling crystal-studded once more, glittering like starlight. He was exhausted from the battle in the cavern, panting hard, his breath loud in his ears, and still he went on: a meteor through the heavens, a cat through the night. Why? He had no idea, and yet it didn't matter; all he needed to know that he was supposed to: this had all happened before. It would happen again. It was as it should be.

He loped on. The universe wheeled around him, the sun sinking towards the horizon, first stars in the sky somewhere above him pricking the violet sky above the hurricane's funnel. He was on the right path. The beginning would begin again.

A sound sped towards him, and a second and third, twisted by the tunnels into the snarl of a cat; Stephen followed them as if led by the jaguar lord himself. Then it came again, louder, clearer, not the voice of a cat this time but the report of a gun discharged. Stephen skidded to a halt and blinked hard. Ahead there was light, green like the light beneath the canopy of a willow tree. Stephen had run full circle beneath the ancient city and ahead lay the stairs to the Venus Platform, star of war and peace. He crept forward slowly, fresh cool air thick with the scent of the storm, sinking down the steps to greet him. The sound of gunfire ebbing, a heavy silence enveloped Stephen as he climbed.

There was no niche here; he peered carefully over the lip of the top stair and then inhaled sharply. The white limestone dais was stained with bright arterial blood; on it lay two bodies. Beyond them sat a rifle on a tripod, pointing out not at *El Castillo* but somewhere to the south. Stephen scrambled to the first figure—a handsome Mayan kid barely out of his teens—and felt for a pulse. Nothing. He was warm but dead, and Stephen's stomach tightened.

Not again.

The second figure, face down, looked familiar: Stephen rolled him over with trepidation and swore again.

"Rutrauff! Dammit Rutrauff, wake up!" his whispered.

It was no use, the soldier, too, was dead.

Stephen sat back on his heels, looked around and saw a third figure—one he had missed. This one was only unconscious. Stephen saw that this was young man, a big heavy one. Friend or foe Stephen could not be sure; he relieved the young man of his shoelaces and used them as makeshift handcuffs. Then he went to the rifle and put his hand to the butt and his eye to the sights to try to make sense of what might happen next.

"Oh hell..." he said with quiet horror.

The rifle was hot. And humming. This was the death ray. It was sighted across the plaza, crosshairs on Rebecca where she was, crouched beneath the ancient *chac mo'ol*. Stephen knocked the weapon off aim, grabbed the binoculars beside the weapon, and looked to Rebecca to see if she was alright. She lay on her belly, apparently uninjured, a conventional rifle in her arms, sighting something of her own.

Thank god. But what was she looking at? He turned the binoculars in the direction Rebecca was aiming and relief evaporated: out on the plaza halfway between his own position and *El Castillo* walked a pair of figures, their backs to him. One had to be Kulkulcan, the writhing tattoo on his back a dead give-away. The other was smaller. Blonde. A woman. *Christ almighty*. It was Anya.

Quickly scanning beyond her, Stephen saw cameramen, their enormous telephoto lenses trained on Anya and her captor; above and below them on the pyramid soldiers had their rifles on the same target. And at the very top, security ringed the presidential party.

Had it been an ordinary rifle, Stephen might have taken a shot; having seen the weapon in action he didn't dare: a simple bullet might injure Anya after killing Kulkulcan, but who knew what the death ray could do?

Thursday, December 20, 2012 — 3 Cauac, Day of Storm

He had been so sure, after the ceremony, that it would end well. Now it seemed this would be a pyrrhic victory: save the world; kill his best friend's girlfriend. He slammed the binoculars down, plastic striking loud against the white limestone, glass shattering in the barrels as the casing hit stone. The sound that followed a split-second later, an echo returned from *El Castillo*, stunned him.

What was it that Yaxché had said? *The change will be manifest to all as the quetzal's voice sounds*? That was what he had just heard: the deep one-note caw of the resplendent quetzal. The acoustics of the Great Plaza could transform not merely a handclap but the sound of metal binoculars against ancient stone into the call of the bird sacred to the Mayan gods.

***

Rebecca had been watching the Great Plaza and *El Castillo*, hoping desperately that Deb would get the word out in time. After the first shots from the shrouded Venus Platform, however, she realized that Anya and Rutrauff might be dead and that she might need to do more than watch and hope. She scanned her immediate area: Rutrauff had taken the unconscious boy's gun and she wasn't going to go near the death ray. So what else could she use? She forced herself to look at Alvarro's corpse.

There! Beneath him, barely visible in the muck and blood, she saw the muzzle of a rifle. Steeling herself, she crabbed her way to his side, pushed his body aside, and picked up… an old M-82? Maybe that wasn't so bad; it was not so different from the 451 of Joe's that she'd practiced with. Grimacing at the blood smears, she checked the weapon. All good. And loaded. She crabbed back to her earlier position, sighted Kulkulcan in the weapon's scope, and stopped. She wasn't such good a shot that she'd risk hitting Anya to take Kulkulcan down. She watched them advance towards the base of the pyramid, waiting for an opportunity.

Thirty feet from the bottom step, his gun in Anya's back, propelling her ahead of him, Kulkulcan began to speak

"*I am not a Lee Harvey Oswald...*"

The same acoustics that could turn a handclap into the quetzal's song allowed Kulkulcan's voice to be heard in the farthest and highest reaches of the Great Plaza. Rebecca listened, fascinated.

"*I am not a lone madman who can be silenced with a single bullet. I am a visionary—a Kennedy, a King, a Guevara, a Ghandi—the leaders killed by conspiracy. I am the Quetzalcoatl, winged serpent of the Maya, returned to end five hundred years of oppression and misery brought by the foreigner...*"

Kulkulcan and Anya had reached the bottom step of *El Castillo* now; he pushed her to climb.

"*And the conspiracy? Rich Americans, hungry to have their oil profit, gave me money to assassinate the President up there...*"

Several of the media cameras swung briefly to the top of the pyramid then back to Kulkulcan and his hostage.

"... *They promised me the country that I might return it to the Maya, but all along intended it to give it to their puppet up there, Raul Vargas, in exchange for a promise to give the wealth of Mitnal—it money and its oil—to the United States.*"

The cameras swung back to the top of the pyramid and sought the face of the Secretary of Internal Security. Like the President, he lay on the ground, his body shielded by a policeman's. Vargas' face was twisted with anger. The cameras swung back to Kulkulcan once more. He was climbing now, Anya in front of him. He stopped when he was two thirds up the pyramid.

"*Do not take my word for it. Ask Vargas. Ask the American Senator Joseph Wilkes—I wear his ring. Ask the American oilman Clayton Powell who called me personally. And ask your heart—is this not something at which the Americans excel?*"

Kulkulcan urged Anya another dozen steps upward.

"*You will kill me but I will not die: my legacy will be the discord you deserve: America a pariah and Mexico plunged yet again into civil war.*"

Watching through the scope of her rifle, Rebecca went pale. Kulkulcan was close-enough now to the platform party that he could take a shot. This was everything she had been afraid of: this would start the civil war she had warned of in the subcommittee meeting, what seemed like a million years ago. Kulkulcan would shoot the President, and maybe Vargas, too, and then the soldiers would open fire on him, and both sides would have their martyrs. And in the middle, Anya would be collateral damage, dead for sure.

Shit shit shit shit shit.

Boresighting was something else Hayden had taught her, but with his rifle. It was simple enough in theory: line a big object with the end of the barrel and then adjust the sights to capture the same image. Then the sights alone would give pretty good aim. There was windage and elevation to sort out, too, but she'd never mastered those bits: she was going to have to hope that the wind would remain still, and that gravity would not confound her. Eye to the sights, she considered her shot. It was going to be ugly and dangerous: if she missed, there was a good chance she would kill Anya. Rebecca thought about the ghosts in the cavern and spoke aloud. "I wouldn't say no to a little help, about now, Hayden…" she muttered before taking a long deep breath to slow her heart and steady her hand.

In the split-second between trigger pull and hammer drop Rebecca heard a quetzal call; started by the mournful cry, she shifted her weight—and the rifle's muzzle—a hairsbreadth. The bullet tore away, and she watched as the moment unfolded like a many-petalled flower, impossibly slowly. The tiny slip would ruin everything. Or save it.

***

On the Venus Platform, Stephen heard the shot and grabbed the binoculars. Broken. He exchanged them for the death ray's sights. Though clutching her shoulder in pain, Anya was free of her captor: lithe and fast despite a growing bloodstain on her shirt, she was already half a dozen steps away. Kulkulcan was suddenly completely exposed.

"*Now,*" hissed the air around him, empty but electric. "*Now.*"

Before the army could get permission to shoot, Stephen had pulled the trigger, heard the death whine. Kulkulcan stopped mid-step, his rifle raised half-way.

In front of televisions and computers, notebooks, smartphones, and tablets, people of the world's nations watched as if mesmerized. They gasped and recoiled and cried. And then some retched and some sank to their knees and some few prayed to the sky: alone in all the world only the tattooed man did nothing for a single moment. Telephoto-close on the screens of the world, he stood stock-still, arm to the sky, his angry face frozen. At last his expression melted to confusion, then horror. He began to shiver, as if caught in a sudden gust of frigid air. A heartbeat later he began to convulse and perspire, as if too long in a great heat. Then he began to bleed: a drip from his nostril first. In the next moment his eyes clouded red, brimmed, shed tears of blood. He coughed and bloody sputum stained his lips.

The image widened as if the camera itself were recoiling in disgust and terror but the distance gave no relief: the gunman's chest and shoulders were awash in blood. The source was the man's tattoo itself: the tiny needle wounds that had imprinted him so long ago were open again, the gunman's skin beneath the black ink now porous as a sieve. Glistening scarlet, the feathered serpent was alive and writhing over seizing muscles, its fanged jaw on the man's upraised hand, speaking with heaven.

At last the man could take no more. His knees buckled. The gun fell from his hand and clattered down the pyramid. Kulkulcan was a husk only now, his tissues liquefied. He followed the falling weapon, his limp body leaving a slick red trail as it slid down the steep limestone stairs. His corpse came to rest between the stone snakes' heads at the bottom of the pyramid. Blood soaked into the flat ground and the earth drank gratefully, as if the gods below were bring sated at last.

"*Cut to the top, Derek! Up here! Film the top of the bloody pyramid!*" said a woman's voice, her Australian accent thickened by fear, the gruesome pun unnoticed.

The camera hung a final moment on the corpse and then swivelled to the top of the pyramid. Behind the disentangling security knot that had swarmed the President and Secretary Vargas were two new faces: a middle-aged white man, his face badly beaten, and a little old Mayan man. The white man was US Senator Joe Wilkes.

CHAPTER 68

—Senator Wilkes!

—Senator Wilkes! How did you get here?

—Are you injured?

—Who is the man with you?

—Were you really involved in planning a coup?

—Senator Wilkes, our bureau chief said most of the Mexican Cabinet was about to be killed—is that true?

The terrace at the top of *El Castillo* was pandemonium: cameramen and their reporters were surging forward to cover Wilkes' surprise appearance. Soldiers, their guns out, were holding them back; bodyguards were helping the President to his feet; Rico Mendez was putting handcuffs on Secretary Vargas. Chalo broke through the madness and sprinted down the stairs to Anya, CNN's camera following him.

The sun was at the horizon now, low enough that light shot beneath the hurricane clouds. Spilling slow and warm like honey, the last of the day's radiance was a cinematographer's dream. The cameraman panned to embrace it: the ancient ruins glowed and on its warm steps Chalo tended Anya's wound—a glancing blow more graze than puncture—and Anya smiled at Chalo. The camera moved on, lovingly: a tall dark-haired woman emerged from behind the *chac mo'ol* at the top of the Temple of Soldiers; a tall man emerged from the Venus Platform and walked towards her, his long shadow slipping dark behind him over the rain-glistened grass. At last the camera swung to the sun orange-bright itself, oblivious to the visual magic beneath the cameraman's feet.

Stephen and Rebecca bore witness instead, silent before the ancient wonder, the temple built to transform the solstice light: the staircase shadows merged and became a giant snake slithering down the pyramid as the sun sank. They watched as seven dark triangles thrown long over the limestone mimicked serpentine curves; these joined the immense carved snakeheads, jaws wide, fangs protruding, that lay at the temple's base—the heads between which Kulkulcan's lifeless body lay. Dark and dreadful, the sinuous figure slid downward until at last, like the sun, it disappeared beneath the Earth. The shortest day of the year was over; longer ones were coming now, and with them, renewed life.

Wilkes saw the dark-haired figures standing still across the plaza and knew the woman was Rebecca. He let go the breath held for her safety and turned, relieved, to the newsmen and women on the steps below. Reaching to straighten a tie that was not there, he chuckled at himself and the habit born of the so many previous press conferences. As familiar as it felt this one would be unlike any other: he was about to commit political suicide.

He put his hand up for silence and, waiting, glanced at Yaxché. The sky was dusky now, the sun below the horizon, the thick clouds tinged saffron mauve, the tiny healer bright beside him, his spirit bigger than his body. This, Wilkes marvelled, was what it was to be suffused by something holy, whatever name you wanted to give it.

The old man smiled and nodded; Wilkes smiled and nodded in reply, and the crowd—journalists, cameramen, politicians, security alike—fell silent.

"I know you have questions, but let me ask one first. Has any other politician here in Mexico been killed today?"

The assembled reporters looked blank for a moment, unused to being queried.

"¡*Fueron puestos bajo custodia hace tan solo unos momentos*!" said someone.

"They were just locked-down a few minutes ago!" another repeated in English.

"Good. Keep them that way until my friend down there"—he pointed to Chalo—"gives the police some information on where to find a half dozen or more snipers."

There was a moment of stunned silence before, recovering themselves, the journalists started shouting their questions once more.

Wilkes had to raise his hand for silence once more.

"*Was I trying to avoid a senate vote*? No. Was I kidnapped? Yes. *Am I hurt*? Not irremediably. *Is it true that I was sponsoring a coup*? Yes, and only partly because Clayton Powell blackmailed me into doing so."

Here the questions stilled once more, this time because of the shocking candour.

"*Was it over oil*? Yes. *And the man beside me*? He is called Yaxché and I owe him my life. That's all I've got for now, except to offer my sincerest apology to the President of Mexico, and to tell Carolina Schroeder, if she is watching, that I'll ask the votes I've got to throw themselves behind her bill. The full 60/20, Carolina."

***

In her Washington office, Senator Carolina Schroeder had been standing for half an hour with her staff, eyes glued to the newscast. She sat down, suddenly weak in the knees.

"I'll be damned," she said softly, trying to believe what she had just heard.

"Has he lost his marbles?" someone asked.

"Lost his mind? Found God? Smoked something?" Carolina started laughing. "Fact is, I don't really care—he just said he'd vote for my bill on CNN. Somebody get me his office on the phone and set up a meeting for when he gets back; I don't want to give him any time to renege."

In Joe Wilkes' office, Honey Hampton wiped grateful tears from her eyes, the sight of Joe Wilkes alive both a shock and a relief. Then she shook her head.

"I'll be damned," she said chuckling softly. "After all these years, I didn't think he could surprise me."

She didn't have time to wonder what had changed him so thoroughly; every single one of her phone lines lit up.

In the Latin Americas Branch of the Department of State, Deb Varanides wiped her brow as she watched the news on the computer and then began to smile.

"I'll be damned," she said, astounded by the true reach of the media. Spreading her word, they had stopped a dozen assassinations in under ten minutes.

"It worked. I can't believe it really worked…"

She looked at the expense reports on her desk and then laughed again. To hell with them; today's miracle deserved a nice, long weekend.

In the National Hurricane Centre bunker in Miami, Kathy Howlachuk and Peter Nguyen divided their attention between the news and the incoming hurricane data. Bender lay asleep, head on his paws, by Peter's feet. Kathy caught a glimpse, as the camera panned, of Rebecca, hand-in-hand with a tall man.

"I'll be damned," she said softly.

"What for, this time?" Peter said as he refreshed one of his screens.

Kathy smiled at the jibe.

"Rebecca. She's alive. And right in the middle of my hurricane."

Before Peter could reply, Bender lifted his head, pricked his ears, and started barking. A moment later he stood and, like a puppy fresh from a bath, tore, zagging, around the office. He picked up a pencil, pranced with it, snapped it in two, snorted, and tore in the other direction.

"You think *you'll* be damned?" Peter asked, looking from screen to dog to boss. "Ben's done it *again*. *Sigma* has collapsed."

Kathy turned her attention from dog to screen and gaped. *Sigma*'s windspeed had dropped impossibly suddenly to barely 10 miles per hour, below the threshold of even a tropical depression. Barometric pressure in the eye had jumped by ten millibars in fewer than twenty minutes.

"Yes, I'll be damned. Before you or after you, I don't mind," Kathy said, shaking her head. "Now I really have seen it all. I quit. Job's yours."

"You what?"

"I quit. I was always going to retire after this season, anyway. You can take the interview with Skandar tomorrow," she added with a twinkle in her eye.

"He's going to ask what happened out there!"

"Yup."

"Oh, shit. I *will* be damned. What do I say?"

"Tell them something ugly but comfortable; they want a story with a bow before Christmas."

"Comfortable?"

"You know the old expression 'oil calms troubled waters'?" Tell them the storm stirred up the submarine slicks left over from the *Deepwater Horizon* and that they mixed with the oil spilled when the Mitnal rig went down. In theory, enough cold oil could rob a hurricane of the energy it draws from the sea, collapsing it. It's the silver lining in a pair of disgusting oil spill stories."

Peter looked at Kathy quizzically.

"In theory, sure. But *Sigma* wasn't over the Gulf yet. How is that supposed to work?"

"It doesn't, really. Maybe deep fingers under the Caribbean? It's the best I've got, scientifically speaking."

Peter paused again.

"What do you have, unscientifically speaking, then?"

"Look Pete, how does Ben always know when a storm is done?"

The two scientists turned to look at the dog, rolling on his back, paws in the air, a Snoopy dance on the carpet.

"Just *how* he knows it," Kathy chuckled, "defies explanation—except maybe chaos theory, but we don't know how that works either—and yet we accept it as truth. He just knows."

"So?"

"So maybe somebody bigger was at work."

"God in heaven? You're kidding, right?"

"Am I? Joe Wilkes just said he was going to support Schroeder's climate bill. If that doesn't defy explanation, I don't know what does. But sure as shooting, an American climate bill could stop the worst of climate change. A little thing that changes everything."

"A climate bill stops a hurricane? I can't say that on national television!"

Kathy laughed out loud. "Not if you want the job for more than a single day!"

"What do you believe?" Peter asked, his tone serious.

"Does it matter? Becky's fine. The storm is over. Joe Wilkes is voting for the 60/20 bill. I'm going to sleep well tonight and wake up refreshed and retired to what might just be a brand new world."

Peter said nothing and looked thoughtful.

Kathy waited a beat and then asked "Can I go home now, Boss?"

Peter smiled. "How about you write the last bulletin first? And then when you get home, give Mr. Omniscient a belly rub and a milkbone?"

"It's a deal," she said, turning for her office. Bender flipped from his back to a stand, shook, and trotted after his mistress.

Peter shook his head and smiled ruefully at his mentor's departing back before looking at the newest satellite image, eerily black and cloudless. It really did not make any kind of logical sense.

"I'm not *really* going to start believing in gods and monsters after all this time, am I?" he wondered. He had no satisfactory answer for that, either.

***

A cat's-paw of wind, soft and warm, blew across the plaza from the east, tousling Yaxché's hair. He watched as the journalists turned to their cameramen and spoke to the world. He watched as the President shook himself free of his security guards and walked towards Wilkes, hand outstretched. He watched as Anya and Chalo, on the steps below him, spoke tenderly. He watched as Stephen and Rebecca, hand-in-hand, closed the remaining distance to the pyramid and began to climb. Then he turned to look in the direction of the breeze and smiled. The hurricane's eye wall was breaking up, and through it, low on the horizon he could see the hearthstone stars—Orion's belt—laid in the sky as it had been at the beginning of time.

Looking from the President to Yaxché, Wilkes saw the old healer smile and raised an eyebrow, questioning.

Yaxché looked at Wilkes and nodded, his smile beatific.

"It is done."

Wilkes smiled in return. *Done, indeed.*

Friday, December 21, 2012
4 Ahau, Day of the Lord

Chapter 69

"It is lovely, is it not?" asked Yaxché.

Stephen blinked, startled from his reverie. How long had they been watching the sky?

Long enough that the hours since leaving Chich'en Itzá—hours spent at a hospital, at the US embassy where they had left Wilkes, at the Canadian embassy where he'd been put on the phone with a congratulatory Prime Minister, and finally at Anya's apartment for a hot shower and something amazing and delicious and Mayan from Anya's freezer—had allowed the stars to wheel halfway around the pole.

Orion was high in the sky now; below it he saw Castor and Pollux bright in Gemini; down at the horizon Ursa Major and Ursa Minor were rising. In front of them, bright and strong, ursid meteors streaked across the sky, one shooting star every five or six minutes.

"Beautiful beyond words," Stephen replied at last, his voice husky from disuse. As he spoke, Rebecca murmured in her sleep. Stephen turned to look at her where she lay on a chaise longue beside his own.

"As beautiful, Yaxché, as your lovely *esposa*."

Stephen had meant Rebecca, referring to the nickname the healer always used for her, but for a moment he saw in Yaxché's face the deep hurt of an old loss.

"Oh, God—I'm sorry, Yaxché," Stephen said, ashamed.

No matter, *mi hijo*," he said gently. "It is an old ache and I can bear it. As for that one," the healer nodded to Rebecca, "she is too tall and talks too much. I think she is better for someone else, hmm?

"Thank you, *El Mero*. For everything."

"I am a *curandero*. It is my job and my pleasure, *mi hijo*," the old man replied, self-effacingly. He looked at the sky and inhaled deeply, as if drinking in the stars.

"Do you want to sit, *Don* Yaxché?"

"No, *mi hijo*. I only came out to say good night."

"Does that mean we're in the clear?"

Yaxché smiled. "Tell me what time it is."

"I can't—my watch is at the bottom of a *cenote* near Calakmul…" Stephen chuckled. "An offering to the gods…"

"Ha! They have as little need of it as you do. Look just above the sea…"

Stephen looked out at the horizon. Below the Big and Little Bears in the east, the sky was the flat grey that comes before dawn, a pale smudge promising daylight. The jaguar had again fought the lords of Xibalba; had once again won back the sun. Stephen thought of the yellow eyes, black spots, white muzzle, felt the feline presence again.

"It's tomorrow, isn't it?" Stephen said slowly.

"You *are Ka Ili'ik*, you see?" Yaxché replied softly, his face bright with delight. "Yes, it is tomorrow: 3 *Kankin*, 4 *Ahau*… first day of the fourteenth *b'ak'tun*. The cycle begins anew."

"*B'ak'tun* thirteen," Stephen smiled thoughtfully. "So we have a new lease on life?"

"As always," Yaxché nodded.

"Any chance we'll do a better job this time around?" Stephen laughed, not really expecting an answer.

"For a while," Yaxché replied, his voice serious. "Then we will make our mistakes again and the cycle of death and birth will start once more. It is comforting, don't you think?"

Strangely, it was. Messy and imperfect, life was filled with pain and joy in their own measure, perfect in the round.

Yaxché turned and started inside, his old body moving stiffly.

"Sleep well, *El Mero*," Stephen called as he slid back down into his chair and closed his eyes.

"Without a hammock? Not possible," Yaxché clucked to himself.

Stephen smiled as he listened to the old man go, asleep again before Yaxché had made it through the door.

Friday, December 21, 2012 — 4 Ahau, Day of the Lord

Chapter 70

Almost noon and with everyone else still asleep—Anya on the couch, Yaxché on the floor despite being offered the guest-bed, Stephen and Rebecca asleep on the balcony—Chalo stretched, smiled at the quiet, and turned on the television in Anya's living room, volume muted, to read a closed-captioned version of the headline news.

... in international news yesterday, an attempt was made on the life of Mexican President Ernesto Sabato Fernandez during a press conference at the famous Chich'en Itzá ruin in Mexico's Yucatán province. The President escaped injury, and the gunman, a leader of a violent separatist group, was killed.

... US Senator Joe Wilkes (GOP, TX), also at the press conference, revealed that he and a small group of Americans were behind the assassination attempt that, if successful, would have put Mexican Secretary of Internal Security Vargas in the Presidential Palace. Wilkes—who may escape jail time for revealing the plot and agreeing to testify against his co-conspirators—offered his apologies to the Mexican government and its people; Vargas was arrested for treason in Mexico; American Clayton Powell was charged with the same here in the United States.

... Speaking at the press conference, Wilkes offered an olive branch to longtime senate foe, Carolina Schroeder (DEM, NM), saying that he would support her climate change bill on his return to the US. Schroeder welcomed Wilkes' reversal, saying it would bring profound economic renewal similar to that spawned by the race to the moon in the 1960s.

... Also welcoming the reversal, the EU and China, long opposed to taking action without the US, said that they would match the Schroeder

targets. Experts suggest the twin moves will prevent the worst effects of climate change.

... in business news, oil futures had a rough ride, ending down sharply on news that the Mitnal oil rig had foundered and, for technical reasons, could not immediately rebuild. The impenetrable wreckage will remain a ghostly sentry of the deeps for the foreseeable future. Environmental terrorist group "Eden Two" has taken responsibility for the sinking. Meanwhile, Senator Joe Wilkes' remarkable reversal on the climate bill sent green technology stocks soaring.

... in the weather, the big news was yesterday's startling collapse of hurricane Sigma. *The strongest hurricane ever recorded,* Sigma *had been carving a deadly path across the Caribbean. Shortly after slamming into the Yucatán Peninsula, however, storm winds and rains fell off dramatically; by 8:00 p.m. EST the National Hurricane Centre had declared the storm dead. Atmospheric scientists hypothesize that oil from Mitnal, as well as deep water oil leftover from the* Deepwater Horizon *disaster in 2010, were churned up and slicked the water's surface, depriving the storm of the heat energy it needed to keep spinning.*

... and finally, in other news, yesterday marked the end of the ancient Mayan calendar. New age adherents and psychics had warned that the world would end with the setting sun; today's sunrise proved the fears unfounded. Several groups are now revising their predictions, suggesting that the Mayan calendar, while rolling over yesterday, will not actually end for another thirteen hundred years...

Chalo chuckled as he turned off the television. Thank god for the media: they'd gotten the word out that had saved the Cabinet. But really, now that he knew what he knew? He had been right when he told Stephen, so long ago, that the world was wheels within wheels, the whole picture too big for anyone to see. Nor, perhaps, should anyone see it: the glimpse he'd had was beautiful and terrifying and too much to comprehend all the time. Suffice that it was there, an arbiter when humanity strayed too far from the white road.

Chalo chuckled again and turned to the kitchen. It was time for chocolate *atole*: it was a new day.

Thursday, March 21, 2013
1 Lamat, Day of Venus

Epilogue

In Uncertain, Texas, Joe Wilkes took the first sip of the day's first coffee, creamy and bittersweet, looked out from the open cabin window to the dock at the bottom of the mossy lawn, and sighed contentedly. The warm, damp air was thick with the sulphur of decay, fresh with the sweet tang of new growth. Not unpleasant, the mingled odours promised wetland hatchlings and tadpoles and the summer yip of newly-grown fox kits. Joe smiled as he watched his visitors—Stephen and Rebecca—as they clambered into a canoe. The pair paddled slowly into the bayou and Joe's smile grew: he had a family again, this one made not by blood, but by affection. He felt the air change in the cabin—a breeze from inside, not out—and felt sure it was the rest of his family: Libby and Hayden, beyond the veil, were padding, soft and unseen, around him. In both worlds Joe felt complete.

***

Deep within the Sian Ka'an Biosphere Reserve, Anya von Eckhardt skimmed the morning emails on her iPad, raised her eyebrows, and brushed out through the canvas flaps of the dig tent that she called home. The equinoctial sun outside, already high and bright at ten o'clock in the morning, momentarily blinded her: she stopped to blink her surroundings back into focus. For a moment, scent and sound filled the sensory breach: the air was heady with the fragrances of the rainforest but was falling silent but for the call of cicadas as the morning creatures settled in for the nap that would carry them, drowsing in the shade, through the hottest part of the day. In an hour, all that would remain would be the pressing silence of growing vegetation and the feel of sweat on her back as she made an etching of their newest *stela.*

"Chalo!"

He was crouched over the fallen *stela* that he had stumbled upon what seemed like so long ago, his white t-shirt dappled in the leaf-riven light. Gonzalo Guerrero, former Mexico City detective, decorated and retired, waved and turned back to his work.

"¡*Uay*! Chalo!" Anya called again. "¡*Venido aquí*!"

Chalo shook his head, eyes still on the *stela*.

"¡*Pare sus caballos*! ¡*Encontré algo*!"

"Stubborn as a mule," Anya muttered with a smile as she began to walk towards him. "We've been accepted!" she called out.

Chalo looked up instantly.

"*Cambridge*?" he called, standing, then loping towards her.

Looking down, Anya began to read aloud. "*The Cambridge Archaeological Journal is pleased to provide you with peer-review comments on the paper recently submitted by Drs. Anya von Eckhardt and Gonzalo Guerrero entitled 'Time maps: initial observations on the space-time relationship among Maya temples of the Yucatán Peninsula.' The novel proposition that each city's location relates to shamanistic activity and dictates the location of both future events and shamanistic opportunity has been greeted with favour by your peers and, following appropriate response to peer comments, will appear in Volume 23, Issue 2…*

Chalo whooped, picked Anya up, and spun her around.

"Stop! I haven't finished reading!" Anya laughed with equal delight.

"You know what this means?!" Chalo asked as he put Anya down. He held her at the shoulders to steady them both against the dizziness of his spinning.

"That you received an honourary doctorate degree?" she teased.

"Funny," he said, rolling his eyes. "It means that I have kept my half of our little bargain, Doctor von Eckhardt…"

"Oh, yes, right," Anya said, feigning nonchalance. "Remind me of my half of the bargain? Something about the next solstice, I think?"

"Such a tease," Chalo replied softly. "Kiss me before I call Esteban."

***

"He's a good guy, after all," Stephen said after they'd been paddling for a few minutes, Stephen in the stern, Rebecca at the bow.

"Joe?" Rebecca asked, raising her paddle and turning carefully to face Stephen.

"Yeah, Joe. I'm glad we came down for Easter. A pleasant switch from working at the Embassy."

"He's changed a lot in the past three months. Like Saul on the road to Tarsus."

"Except that it wasn't the face of just one God that changed him," Stephen said wryly.

"Is that what happened?" Rebecca asked earnestly, turning around completely now. They had not talked much about the ceremony in the cave.

"I don't know. Sometimes I think that it was a dream. Or my imagination. That nothing happened at all. Except that because of it—and Yaxché and the ghost and the jaguar—everything has changed. For the better."

He meant being with Rebecca, and she leaned forward over the thwarts, smiling.

Stephen leaned forward to meet her. "Do you know the definition of a Canadian?" he asked softly, lips grazing hers

"No, tell me."

"Someone who can make love in a canoe…"

"You think you could help me get my citizenship?" Rebecca replied softly, pulling Stephen towards her.

"I dunno," he smiled. "You might have to apply more than once…"

"I could do that…"

"Alrighty then," he said, climbing over the thwart. "First we… oh, no way…"

"What's wrong?"

"My phone. It's buzzing. I have to get it. Ottawa is supposed to call."

"I told you that would happen if you decided to take the posting at the Embassy…"

Stephen stuck out his tongue good-naturedly: she knew he'd taken the posting to join her in Washington; she stuck her tongue out in return, smiling: she'd asked him to move in with her the day he had accepted the job.

Thursday, March 21, 2013 — 1 Lamat, Day of Venus

"Catherwood," he said, his voice carefully composed. A moment later he grinned.

"Chalo! Your timing sucks, as usual! *¿Como esta*?"

Rebecca smiled, faced forward once more, and dipped her paddle into the water. Stephen and Chalo would be more than a few moments catching up: time enough to take them out to check on the Spoonbill nest. Her strokes were strong and smooth in the still, tannic water, each pull ending with a small j-stroke that spawned little whorls in the water, a pull that would keep the canoe travelling true. She let Stephen's conversation with his former partner slip into the background, focusing instead on the lick of water playing against the hull, loud inside the canoe's wooden skin.

"Nice to hear your voice too, *caballero*," Chalo replied, his voice gently sarcastic. "What did I interrupt this time?"

"Only my vacation. Again."

"You are not in Washington? And what do you mean 'again'?"

"Nope. Texas, at Joe Wilkes' cabin. An early Easter break. And I never got to Cuernavaca because of you!"

"Maybe we can fix that. But how is the Senator?"

"A changed man, by all accounts. He ate humble pie in front of the entire Washington Press Corps and then named names. Americans like to fry the richest fish they can find, so they roasted Wilkes, forgave him, and then dined on Powell."

"Nice, *caballero*. You are making me hungry! Speaking of which, a little bird told me you're having dinner with young Rico Mendez next week?"

"He's with President Fernandez's delegation, coming for the signing of the Washington Protocol. It's a big wing-ding: Heads of State of all G8 countries plus India, China, Mexico, half the Middle East, most of Latin and South America and a whack of non-aligned states, all signing up to reduce emissions by 60% by 2020 and 80% by 2040. Rebecca and I are sitting at the President's table, thank you very much."

"Listen to you, *caballero*, hanging with the stuffed coats. Is it better than eating donuts and getting shot at and saving the world with me?"

"Stuffed *shirts*, Chalo. Nothing is the same without you, *hermano*, but the company has a better handle on English idioms…"

Thursday, March 21, 2013 — 1 Lamat, Day of Venus

"¡*Uay*! You wound me, *caballero*! So how is the lovely Rebecca?"

"Lovely," Stephen replied, gently, watching Rebecca's back as she paddled, her shoulder healed and flexing strongly.

"Ahh! You are with her, aren't you?"

"As often as possible…"

"Okay, then, *caballero*, I won't keep you. I just wanted to tell you a bit of the news from down here. You have a few more moments?"

"Now that you've interrupted, you're going to hang up? Of course I have a few minutes. Start with Anya?"

"Don't rush me, *caballero*. First, did you hear about Yaxché?"

"No, what? Is he alright?"

The concern in Stephen's voice ruffled Rebecca's calm and she attended to the conversation until Stephen sighed with relief.

"Better than good," Chalo replied, "but grumbling about missing his jungle and his hammock! The President named him, last week, to the head of the Truth and Reconciliation Committee. He will travel the countryside and hear the stories of loss, and build a new partnership among *crillolo* and Maya."

Stephen laughed with pleasure at the thought of it. Yaxché would make it work without descending into the bitter or maudlin.

"Nice irony," he said aloud.

"*¿Qué*?" asked Chalo, his happy patter interrupted.

"Kulkulcan was half South African. The "Truth and Reconciliation" process was born there, after apartheid."

"Is that so?" Chalo asked, pleased with the serendipity. "And did they get you a horse yet?"

"A horse?!"

"How can you be a mounted police—in the United States of all places—without a real living horse?"

Stephen rolled his eyes; Chalo was holding out. "Okay, spill it," he asked at last.

"Spill what, Esteban?" Chalo asked innocently.

"You didn't call just to ask me if I have a horse."

"Fine, fine, *caballero*; you win. I did it…"

"You published?!" Stephen asked excitedly.

Rebecca stopped paddling and turned back to look at Stephen's smiling face, his hazel eyes unfocused as he spoke to the man at the far end of the call.

"The editor of the *Cambridge Archaeological Journal* even called me Dr. Gonzalo Guerrero! Will you come to visit in thirteen weeks?"

Stephen snorted with delight at the "degree" so quickly bestowed on his former partner.

"Congratulations! Why thirteen weeks?"

"We're getting married on the solstice; I need you to be my best man, you idiot!" Chalo laughed.

"You're what?!"

"Anya dared me to publish, saying she would marry me if I did. So we are to be married on the solstice! A good Maya date, don't you think?"

"Chalo, that's fantastic! What should we get you as a present?"

"Don't be crazy, *caballero*. You have already given a gift many times over with your books and your honesty and your very bad sense of humour…"

"It was truly my pleasure, *amigo*. And I owe you a thing or two, too…"

"Pay me back by marrying Rebecca. Can I tell Anya you will come?"

"All in good time, Chalo. It has happened before; it will happen again, right? As for telling Anya, absolutely!"

"Always learning, *caballero*! You'll bring Rebecca, of course?"

"Of course."

"Good. Then I must go. I have the rest of a *stela* to work on before the sun gets too high."

"Say hello to Anya for us."

"And you give Rebecca a kiss for me, hmm?"

"Anything you say, *amigo*." Stephen smiled as he hung up. He looked at the smartphone for a moment and then powered it down.

"What's up?" Rebecca asked.

"Just following orders. Chalo said I should give you a kiss…"

Rebecca turned around once more, the canoe rocking gently as she did so, and stowed her paddle beneath the thwarts. "Mmm. In that case, how about I command you to return to your lesson on how to be a Canadian?"

"With pleasure. But first, will you come to Mexico with me for the summer solstice?"

"Why?" Rebecca asked suspiciously.

"For Anya and Chalo's wedding…"

Rebecca whooped with delight, the canoe rocking dangerously as she did. A moment later she appeared to fall serious.

"Will I get shot at?" she asked.

"This time? Probably not."

"Oh," Rebecca replied, disappointment in her voice. "How about ghosts?"

"What about them?"

"Will we see any?" she asked hopefully.

"Well, I bet Yaxché will be there, so maybe…" Stephen answered with a grin.

"And jaguars?" Rebecca smiled.

"I can't promise that we won't…" Stephen said, eyes bright with amusement.

"In that case, I'm in… . But then, you knew I'd say yes, didn't you, *Ka Ili'ik*?"

"Absolutely. Now come here and let's do something about your citizenship…"

***

On the narrow dirt road in the middle of the Yucatán rainforest, an enormous black Mercedes M-class, incongruous among the few small thatch and cinder houses, stopped to let someone out. Small children and wagging dogs pressed against the side of the car, making it impossible to open the doors.

"¡*El Mero*! ¡*El Mero*!" the children called as the dogs howled.

Lupita came out of the thatch hut on the left, shooing flustered chickens as she came, half-kneaded tortilla in hand. Across the street, a young woman emerged from Yaxché's hut, her blouse richly embroidered, her face long and lean, in her arms a round brown baby, black eyes wide with wonder.

The car's driver, crisp in a black suit, looked into the rear-view mirror at the small old man smiling delightedly in the rear seat and shook his head.

"Here? You live *here*? It is nowhere… nothing here at all!"

"Ha!" cackled the old man. "It is the heart of the world."

"You need your eyes checked, old man," the driver muttered.

"When I have you to do the driving for me, why would I do that?" Yaxché laughed. "As for seeing, come back for me in ten days and I will have finished with my patients for this month. And then I can take care of that pain that you tell no one about, hmm?" he said with a smile as he rolled down the window, waved the children back, and then opened the door to step into the throng. He did not have to turn back to know that the young man was shocked.

"There is more to sight than merely eyes, *mi hijo*," Yaxché cackled as he slammed the door shut.

"Ten days!" he called and the car crept away.

"¡*Uay, El Mero*!" Lupita called. "Look at you! So handsome in your far-away clothes. A little vanilla *atole*, perhaps?"

"They are ridiculous, these clothes, you old hen!" Yaxché laughed as he looked down at his white *guayabera*, navy trousers and leather *huaraches*. "Scratchy. And I am afraid to get them dirty! But yes, *atole*. And food. I have missed your cooking! But one thing, first."

"To the forest, hmm? "

Yaxché nodded.

"Someone to see there, and someone to be seen," he said as he walked, still stiff from the long car ride, to the young mother and child on his porch. She was tall for a Maya, and the old man shrunken with age so that when they met, their eyes were even. The pain in her eyes appeared in his as he recognized it.

"*Hola*, Tonalna," he said softly, when he reached her. "They lie when they say the hurt will go away, don't they, *mi niña*?"

The girl nodded silently, her eyes welling, and she held her breath to prevent the sudden tears from spilling. The baby wriggled, discomfited by his mother's grief.

"I will tell you the truth, *mi niña*, where others do not. The pain will not go away. Not ever. But it will fade, like a scar, until you can touch it. Like old bones, it will hurt only when the weather changes. Like water on a stormy night, it will flash bright only when the Moon peeks between the clouds. And then your Payal will come back to walk with you, will speak to you through every rustling tree, like my Maria. Only then, when the pain is no longer too much to bear, will you be able to see him again when you need him. And then, in time, you will join him in the sky."

The girl nodded and bit her lip as a tear escaped and slid down her cheek.

"Until then, you drink the tea I have made for you, and take the pumpkin seeds, and live here with Lupita as a daughter, hmm? And close by, I can watch over your son."

Yaxché paused for a moment as the girl looked down at her small boy and smiled through her tears. The plump baby looked up at his mother and cooed with pleasure.

"You see! He is a *curandero*, even now... see how he makes your heart light?" Yaxché chuckled.

Tonalna looked up from the baby and smiled more broadly. "Thank you, *Don* Yaxché. I owe you much."

"You owe me nothing, *mi niña*, but you are welcome to all that I have. May I take him now to meet the woods?"

The girl's eyes clouded with worry and then brightened as the baby reached towards the old man of his own accord.

"I will have him back before he gets hungry, *mi niña*. I am too thirsty for Lupita's *atole* to be gone long, myself."

Down the steps and on the trail, baby cradled in his arms, Yaxché walked as he spoke to the little boy.

"Is it not beautiful, Ek Balam?" Yaxché asked, smiling as the infant, naked but for a diaper, clutched at his own toes.

"Smell!" Yaxché said, inhaling deeply. "The spicy smell is *cohonotl*; the sweet is from evening blooming flowers. You will know them all, in time, and what each does for healing mind and heart and broken body..."

Yaxché walked, seemingly aimless, for more than twenty minutes, commenting on everything they passed: brilliant red flowers on vines winding around tall ficus trees, small grey lichens growing on tree trunks, misshapen white and orange mushrooms budding from the foot of rotten stumps, a mot-mot, a family of coatis, a distant howler monkey. To each he gave a name; for each he described a personality, as if introducing members of his family to a new friend.

"And this one? This is a good one and very sweet to those with broken hearts. We will put in your mother's evening tea tonight. Your very first medicine, hmm?" the old man crooned, his expression soft and warm as he regarded the wide-eyed infant in his arms.

Suddenly Yaxché stopped and crowed with delight.

"And look! You call what you need even now," he said as he stooped to break a ruddy twig from a woody shrub.

"Here. Chew this for the pain in your teeth."

The baby took the twig in his fat fist and put it to his mouth, grimaced a moment at the new taste, and then began gumming the gift with zeal.

A moment later Yaxché stumbled in his uncomfortable *huaraches*.

"¡*Uay*! You are alright?" he asked of the child in his arms.

The baby looked at him with wide eyes, sodden twig in his fist, and smiled.

"Ha!" laughed Yaxché. "Of course you are alright. You are young! Me, I'm old and soft from all the sitting I have been busy with in the City…" He paused to catch his breath.

"… maybe we stop here for a moment before we go back to your mama, yes? Here in the roots of the world tree," he said, nodding to an enormous *ceiba* ahead.

Reaching it, he smiled with recognition: this was the tree in which *Xtabay* had first appeared to him.

"Let me tell you a story," Yaxché said to the babe in his arms as he paused among the tree's great buttress roots, curving around like arms.

"A long time ago, Ek Balam, there was no sky and no Earth. And then the gods of creation—*Tepeu* and *Gukamatz*—called for the world to become, and the breath of *Hurukan* spread over the Earth and raised the sky. And then, after many tries, they made man—our ancestors' ancestors—of maize."

The baby began to drowse, eyes drooping.

"And in exchange for life," Yaxché continued, "we honour their creation. That is our job. Mine and yours, Ek Balam, and the job of all *h'men* who follow us. To look after the world and all that is within it…"

A prickling sensation at the back of his neck made Yaxché look up. Half a dozen feet away, gauzy and indistinct, stood *Xtabay*. A moment later, a jaguar slipped through the dappled daylight beside his queen and continued forward to the old man.

"Lord Balam, I present your namesake," Yaxché said softly, holding the infant forward. The great cat sniffed the tiny boy's head, its nosepad leaving a small wet spot of clotted down hair at the baby's crown—a baptism. Then the majestic cat looked into Yaxché's eyes, clear gold meeting cloudy brown. After a long moment, the cat growled, low and soft.

"Yes, Lord Balam. I will teach him. And he will teach the next *h'men* and they the ones after that, until the time comes that the sky must be raised again."

"*Then you have earned your new beginning*," *Xtabay* said to the healer and his tiny charge; her voice arrived after she had evanesced.

The jaguar looked at Yaxché, spoke—more purr than growl this time,--and turned to walk through the bright space where *Xtabay* had been. A moment later, Yaxché and the baby were alone once more.

"Come, *mi niño*. It is time we get you home to your mother. Do you hear the quetzal call to the evening? He is far north of his normal range, here for you. He calls for the stars to rise above us and sing the story of the world once more."

The quetzal called again, and Yaxché smiled, cradling the sleeping baby in the gloaming light, the air rich with the scent of growth and decay. Yaxché listened to the familiar hush of the leaf litter beneath his feet and felt the baby's warm damp head on his shoulder. Soon the sun would begin the last of its descent, swift with desire to exchange places with the underworld. Tonight there would be vanilla *atole* and the comfort of his hammock. Tonight the jaguar would fight the Underworld for the return of the sun. Tonight he would win again. And tomorrow? Tomorrow there would be patients to see. Tomorrow there would be death and life; tomorrow there would be grief and joy. Yaxché smiled at all that tomorrow would bring.

"*Chu'unpahal*," he said to the sky as the baby opened its eyes. "It begins."

Glossary

abuela	grandmother (Spanish)
agua	water (Spanish)
aguardiente	Literally "burning water" (Spanish); a group of home-fermented-and-distilled alcohols with very high alcohol content.
Ahau	Literally "Lord;" one name for the creator god; also an honourific for kings and leaders (Yucatec); pronounced "a-HOW"
Alom	one of the Maya creator gods
Americano	an American (Spanish)
amigo/a	a friend (Spanish)
¡andale!	"let's go!" (Spanish)
aqui	here (Spanish)
atole	A warm corn-based drink, often flavoured with chocolate, vanilla or cinnamon (Nahuatl); pronounced "ah-TOH-leh"
avenida	avenue (Spanish)
axis mundi	Literally "the centre of the world;" a common cosmological theme, the axis mundi is the place where all directions meet and the world is said to have been born. In different cultures the axis mundi is variously a place or geological formation, a plant, tree or garden (e.g. the Garden of Eden), or a temple.

b'ak'tun	A Mayan unit of time equivalent to 20 *katuns* or 144,000 days (394.25 years); calendrically, as significant as a millennium is in the Gregorian calendar (Yucatec); pronounced "b-ahk-toon"
bacab	A group of four deities in the Mayan pantheon responsible holding up the corners of the sky; a loose parallel to the Greek god "Atlas" (Yucatec); pronounced "bah-cab"
Balam; *balam*	Literally "jaguar" (Yucatec); pronounced "bah-lahm;" refers to both the Mayan jaguar god (Chac Balam) and to the great cat, *Panthera onca*
bario	neighborhood, sometimes a derogatory term meaning 'slum" (Spanish)
ben	maize (Yucatec)
betana	a fruit native to the Yucatán peninsula
bienvenidos	welcome (Spanish)
Bitol	one of the Maya creator gods
caballero	Cowboy (Spanish)
caban	earth (Yucatec)
cabrón	Epithet meaning bastard (Spanish)
caracol	Literally "snail" (Spanish); name given by the *conquistadores* to domed Mayan temples used as stellar observatories for spiral staircases inside that, coupled with the domed roof, brought to mind snail shells.
cauac	storm (Yucatec)
ceiba	*Ceiba spp.*; a family of tall, buttress-rooted trees found in the tropics. To the Maya it is called "yaxché" or the "world tree" and represents the centre of the universe responsible for holding the sky separate from the earth. One species, *Ceiba pentandra*, is better known as the kapok tree; fibre from its pods has many applications
cenote	Sinkhole or well (Spanish version of the Yucatec word—see "dzonote"); pronounced "seh-no-tay"
cestrum	A brilliant red tropical flower (*C. fasciculatum*) native to Mexico (Latin)
ch'ulel	The Mayan word for "spirit", "vital force" or "life energy"; similar to the Chinese concept of "chi"

Chac	The Mayan god of rain; also an honourific term for other gods with a rain aspect (Yucatec)
chac mo'ol	Literally "red jaguar" (Yucatec; misnamed by an early explorer). A stylized pre-Columbian sculpture of a reclining figure. Actual purpose unknown; thought to be used as a sacrificial altar (cf: bastardized hotel name, Chacmool)
chicalote	Prickle poppy, *A. mexicana* (Yucatec); pronounced "chih-cah-loh-tay"
Chich'en Itzá	Literally "Mouth of the Well of the Water Wizards"; A ruined post-classical Mayan city designated as one of the UN's ancient wonders of the world. Pronounced "cheech'EN eets-AH"
chicle	The boiled sap of a tropical evergreen (*M. chicle*). Chicle was the original base for chewing gum and the reason "Chicklets" were so named; pronounced "chee-clay" from the Nahuatl word *tziktli* or the Yucatec word *tsicte*
chik'in	"West" (Yucatec); pronounced 'chee-ke-een"
Chilam Balam	A collection of nine manuscripts sacred to the Maya of mixed authorship that contains information about Mayan history, astronomy, herbal remedies, folklore and prophecy. Written in Yucatec using European phonectics, the meaning of the prophetic sections remains heavily debated
chingalo	Literally "fuck;" a commonly used expletive for almost every situation (Spanish)
chiquita	literally "very small;" Often derogatory slang for "sweetheart" or "girl" (Spanish)
chu'unpahal	"It begins" (Yucatec)
chuen	monkey (Yucatec)
cib	wax (Yucatec)
cimi	death (Yucatec)
cohonotl	A medicinal plant native to central America
compadre	loosely equivalent to the friendly term "buddy" (Spanish)
conquistadores	"Conquerors" (Spanish and Portuguese); the name used to describe the Spanish explorers to the Americas in the 15th century. Many conquistadores remain infamous for their brutal treatment of the Aztec and Maya. See also "xekik"

consígala	counselor (Spanish)
copal	"Incense;" (Nahuatl). The resin from trees of the *Copaifera* family; smoky and aromatic when burned, copal or 'pom' (Yucatec) is an important part of many Mayan rituals.
¡corra!	run! (Spanish)
crillolo/a	A person of Spanish descent (Spanish)
curandero/a	A traditional Mayan healer and shaman (Spanish). Called an "*h'men*" in Yucatec
Del Dzonote	"From the Cenote" (Spanish/Yucatec)
demonios	A religious epithet, loosely translated as "devils" or "demons" (Spanish)
Dia de los Muertos	Day of the Dead (Spanish); traditionally held on November 1
Die Milchstraße	The Milky Way (German)
Don	An honorific loosely equivalent to "Sir" (Spanish)
Dos Equis	Literally "2X"; a popular Mexican beer (Spanish)
dumkopf	idiot (German)
dzonote	Sinkhole (Yucatec); pronounced "dzoh-noh-tay"
dzul	Literally "foreigner" (Yucatec). A derogatory term for white people
eb	rain (Yucatec)
El Caracol	Literally "the snail"; a term used to describe the domed stellar observatory at Chichén Itzá (Spanish)
El Mero	"The revered one/the true one" (Spanish)
enchilada	A meat or bean-filled corn tortilla covered in chili sauce. Also a slang term for an important person (similar to the idiom 'the big cheese" in English)
espera	I hope (Spanish)
esposo/esposa	Husband/wife (Spanish)
etznab	flint (Yucatec)
fantasma	ghost (Spanish)
Faros	Literally "lighthouse" (Spanish). A brand of Mexican cigarettes synonymous with the working class

federale	Literally "federal" (Spanish). Derogatory slang for the federal police
flautas	Literally "flute"; a deep fried corn tortilla containing savory meats
fleche d'amour	Literally "love's arrows;" used to describe thin crystal (usually titanium) inclusions in semi-precious gems
fuego	fire (Spanish)
girasol	sunflower (Spanish)
Gott in Himmel	"God in Heaven" (German)
gracias	thank you (Spanish)
gringo/gringa	Usually derogatory term for foreigners (Spanish/Portuguese)
Grundwehr-dienst	Mandatory basic military service in Germany
guayabera	A men's short-sleeved, collared shirt popular throughout Latin America, the guayabera is made of cotton or, more formally, linen. The shirt's distinctive features include two columns of tiny pleats on the front and back of the shirt and front patch pockets with button closures. Traditionally, guayaberas are white or light-coloured; black is also popular in Mexico.
Gukamatz	The Maya name for Quetzalcoatl, the Mesoamerican feathered-serpent god.
h'men	"healer" or "shaman" (Yucatec). Pronounced 'h-mayn'
hacienda	property (Spanish)
hermano	Brother (Spanish)
Herr	mister (German)
hijo/hija	son/daughter (Spanish)
hölle	hell (German)
huaraches	A traditional Mexican leather sandal following a pre-Columbian design
huevos rancheros	Literally "ranch eggs;" fried eggs served on a flour tortilla served with tomatoes, chilies, refried beans and guacamole

huipil	A traditional Mayan dress, ornately embroidered. Stitching colours and patterns vary by region (Yucatec); Pronounced "hwee-peel."
Hunaphu	One of the mythic Mayan "Hero Twins" who defeated evil in the Mayan creation myth; c.f.: Xbalenque
Hurukan	Literally "one-legged" (from the Yucatec "Jun Rakan"); pronounces "hur-oo-kahn;" the Mayan god of wind, storm and fire; one of three creator-destroyer deities
indigeno	An aboriginal person (Spanish); the politically correct term used in Mexico
indio	Extremely derogatory slang for "indigeno" (Spanish)
invidia	"Envy"; one of the four cardinal illnesses of the spirit as defined by Mayan healers. Akin to the western notion of jealousy; it harms both the envious and the envied (Spanish)
Isla Mujeres	Literally "Island of the Women" (Spanish); a small island off Cancún that was sacred to the Ix Chel, Mayan goddess of healing and child-birth. The Spanish named the island for the goddess iconography on the island's ruins
Itzás	"The Itza people" (Yucatec)
Ix Chel	Mayan goddess of healing and childbirth; associated with the moon (Yucatec); pronounced 'eesh-chel"
Ixtab	Mayan goddess thought to be the patron of soldiers who died in battle, women and infants who died in childbirth, members of the priesthood, and those who committed suicide.
javelin	Literally "spear;" Spanish name for the collared peccary (*P. tajacu*), so named for its extremely long tusks. A New World species resembling, but unrelated to, the Old World wild boar.
Ka Ili'ik	"He sees" (Yucatec)
kacke	shit (German)
katun	A Mayan unit of time equivalent to 20 *tuns* or 7,200 days (20 years); because the Mayan numbering system is vigesimal (base-20), a katun is as significant as a decade is in the Gregorian calendar (Yucatec); pronounced "kah-toon."
krake	Literally "octopus;" German slang for cancer

ku	a glyph representing the sound made by the English letter "k"
Kulkulcan	Feathered-serpent god; chief among gods of the meso-American pantheon (Nahuatl). See: Quetzalcoatl
La Jornada	"The Daily" (Spanish); a working-class newspaper
La Odisea	"The Odyssey" (Spanish)
lakin	"east" (Yucatec)
linda	beautiful (Spanish)
lo siento	"I'm sorry" (Spanish)
loco	crazy (Spanish)
Madre del Dio	"Mother of God" (Spanish); an epithet used to express surprise
maledad	evil, often referred to as a force by traditional healers
Mamacita	A slang (usually endearing) term meaning "mom" (Spanish)
mamich	"nana" or "grandma" (Yucatec)
manik	deer (Yucatec)
mano	Literally "hand"; a stone used with a "metate" to grind corn. Similar in function but to a pestle
mein Gott!	"My God!" (German)
men	eagle (Yucatec)
mestizo/mestiza	Mexicans of mixed Spanish and Mayan descent (Spanish)
metate	A large slightly concave rock used to hold corn being ground with a "mano;" similar in function to a mortar.
mierde	Literally, "shit" (Spanish); used as an epithet.
Negra Modelo	Literally "Black Brand" (Spanish); a popular Mexican beer.
mole	A group of different piquant sauces flavoured with chilies, spices, and bitter chocolate (from the Nahuatl 'mulli')
muan	Owl (Yucatec); pronounced "moo-ahn"
nahual	An animal spirit guide. Alternatively, a person who can shape-shift into his/her spirit guide. A force for good or evil, depending on the person. (Nahuatl); pronounced "nah-wahl"
nett	nice (German)

niño/niña	Boy child/girl child (Spanish); used as a term of endearment
nohul	"north" (Yucatec)
oc	dog (Yucatec)
Och-Kan	one of the Mayan creator gods
Pacal	"K'inich Janaab' Pacal" or "Pacal the Great"; Ruler of the Mayan city-state of Palenque from 615-683 CE
pendejo	Literally "dumbass"; slang for someone who is being stupid (Spanish)
pepitas	pumpkin seeds (Spanish)
pesar	"Grief"; one of the four cardinal illnesses of the spirit as defined by Mayan healers. Akin to the western idea of mourning (Spanish/Portuguese)
politico	Slang for a political operative (English)
pozole	a thick meaty stew (Spanish)
pulque	a mild alcohol made from the agave plant (Spanish)
puta	An derogatory term meaning "whore" (Spanish)
Qaholom	one of the Mayan creator gods
quetzal	Literally "sacred". The Respendent Quetzal (*P. mocinno*) is a member of the trogon family, all of which have thick, brightly-coloured feathers; the males also have long tail streamers. The bird has a low repetitive single-not call. Quetzals are associated with the feathered serpent of Maya and Aztec myth; the feathers of the bird are reserved for shamans and nobility.
Quetzalcoatl	Feathered-serpent god; chief among gods of the meso-American pantheon (Nahuatl). See: Kulkulcan
¿quién?	Who? (Spanish)
sacbe	Literally "white way" or "white road." (Yucatec) Straight stone roads paved with white limestone stucco. Many *sacbeob* remain visible in satellite photos
sastun	A sacred stone used by Mayan healers for treatment and divination.
Scheiß-afrikaaner	Literally "shit afrikaaner;" a derogatory term for a person of white South African descent (German)

Schweine-priester	Literally "pig priest;" an extremely derogatory term (German)
Selber schuld	"I should have known" (German)
Señor	Mister (Spanish)
Señor/a/ina	An honorific or extremely polite term for miss/missus (Spanish)
Sheisse/scheiße	shit (German)
Shiva	Hindu goddess
shön	beautiful (German)
si	yes (Spanish)
stela/stelae	A freestanding stone tablet or block inscribed with pictures, words or glyphs
susto	"Fright sickness"; one of the four cardinal illnesses of the spirit as defined by Mayan healers. Akin to the western idea of post-traumatic stress or other anxiety disorder (Portuguese)
tamale	a meat or bean-filled flour tortilla (Spanish)
tamax chi	An omen or portent (Yucatec); pronounced "ta-mash-chee"
taquito	a small fried taco (Spanish)
Tepeu	one of the Mayan creator gods
Tohil	K'iche' Mayan god of war, fire and sustenance. Tohil demands human sacrifice in order to answer prayers. Some scholars suggest Tohil is similar to the Aztec god Quezalcoatl and the Yucatec Mayan god Kulkulcan.
toon	Slang (Yucatec) for penis
tortas huevos	A scrambled egg sandwich on a crusty bun
touché	Literally "touched" (French); often said to acknowledge a point made in a verbal exchange or debate
tristeza	"Sadness"; one of the four cardinal illnesses of the spirit as defined by Mayan healers. Akin to the western notion of depression (Spanish/Portuguese)

tun	A Mayan unit of time equivalent to 360 *k'in* (days) or almost exactly one solar year. To complete the 365 day solar calendar, 5 unnamed days, considered inauspicious, were added to the calendar every *tun* (Yucatec); pronounced "toon"
Tzab'ek	Literally, "the tail of the rattlesnake"; the Yucatec Mayan name for the Pleiades star cluster in Taurus; pronounced "tsab-ek"
Tzacol	one of the Mayan creator gods
Tzolk'in	Literally "division of days" (Yucatec); the name for one of the 260-day Mayan calendar. The calendar is divided into 13 "months" of twenty days each; each day has a particular character used for political, healing, and divination purposes.
U Qux Cho	one of the Mayan creator gods
uay	Common conversational slang, akin to "Hey" or "Eh?" (Yucatec); pronounced "way"
verdammt	dammit (German)
Via de Leche	Literally "The Milk Road" (Spanish); The Milky Way
vohersage	"prediction" or "foresight" (German)
Vucub Caquix	Seven Macaw, the vain demi-god who thought he was greater than the sun; killed by the Hero Twins in order to begin the current Creation
Xaman	"north" (Yucatec)
xaté	*Chamaedorea spp*.; three species of palm which have leaves valued as roofing material (Yucatec); pronounced "shah-tay"
Xbalenque	One of the mythic Mayan "Hero Twins" who defeated evil in the Mayan creation myth; c.f.: Hunaphu
Xibalba	Literally "the place of fear" (Yucatec); pronounced "shee-bahl-bah." The name for the Mayan underworld
xicamatl	Jicama; a juicy crunchy New World root vegetable (Yucatec); pronounced "shee-ca-matle"
Xiuhcoatl	Literally "turquoise lord" or "turquoise serpent" (Nahuatl). The sprit form of the Aztec fire god. Also the name given to the Mexican Army's FX-05 assault rifle.

Xmucane	one of the Mayan creator gods
Xpiyacoc	one of the Mayan creator gods
Xtabay	A female spirit belonging to the Mayan pantheon (Yucatec); pronounced "eesh-tah-bay"
xtabentún	A Mayan liqueur tasting of anise made from honey derived from the *xtabentún* flower. A species of morning glory (*T. corymbosa*), the xtabentún seeds are strongly hallucinogenic.
xekik	Literally "black vomit" (Yucatec); the name given by the Maya to the acute mosquito-borne hemorrhagic disease known as "yellow fever." Probably brought to North America from Africa with the conquistadores, the first north American case of Yellow Fever was recorded in the Yucatán in 1648 and spread throughout north America after that before being eradicated.
Yuum Tunkuruchu	"Lord Owl" (Yucatec); an honourific for the owl-embodiment of a forest spirit
Zapatista	An armed native separatist group in Mexico and/or a member of the group
Zócalo	The town square in Mexico City; a gathering place since the region was inhabited by the Aztec; also the name of Kulkulcan's club in Cancún
zotz	bat (Yucatec)

ABOUT THE AUTHOR

Leslie is a writer and environmental scientist based in Vancouver, Canada. She has an undergraduate degree in biology and a Master's in Political Economy and Environmental Studies.

Leslie's academic writing has appeared in the *Canadian Journal of Physiology and Pharmacology*, the *Oceans Yearbook,* and *Northern Perspectives*; she has also written articles for the popular press that have appeared in *The Globe and Mail*, *the Vancouver Sun*, *Nature Canada* and *Roedale's Scuba Diving*. Leslie's creative writing has appeared in *The Globe and Mail* and has aired on *CBC Radio*. She has also won a number of writing contests, including *The Vancouver Courier*'s prestigious 'Festive Fiction' contest and the *CBC* Sunshine Coast Festival of the Written Arts contest. *The Sum of All Evils* is her first full-length work.

Two weeks after *The Sum of All Evils* was first published, Leslie's short-form work, *Tortfeasor,* placed in the 2011 CBC Radio Literary Awards for creative non-fiction. It appeared in the May 2011 edition of Air Canada's *En Route* magazine.

Leslie lives with her daughter and a nascent ark: two dogs, two terrapins, two leopard geckoes and about fifty crickets, a handful of which seem to live—and sing—under the refrigerator at any given time.